The Cosmos

The Arrivals

by

Professor Gamer

Edge Interactive Publishing
New York

Edge Interactive Publishing Inc.
630 Ninth Avenue #508
New York, NY 10036
212-581-3000

The Cosmos: The Arrivals

This is a work of fiction.

Book designed by Fantasmo.

Created in the United States of America

Library of Congress Control Number: 2014937211

ISBN 978-0615969862

First Edition

To Slaves and their Lovers everywhere

Inspiration

Six Slave Girls & Their Lord: A Tribute

"Thereupon rose the six girls and, kissing the ground before their lord, said to him, 'Do thou justice between us, O our lord!' So he looked at their beauty and loveliness and the contrast of their colors and praised Almighty Allah and glorified Him. Then said he, 'There is none of you but hath learnt the Koran by heart and mastered the musical-art, and is versed in the chronicles of yore and the doings of peoples which have gone before; so it is my desire that each one of you rise, and pointing a finger at her opposite, praise herself and dispraise her co-concubine; that is to say, let the blonde point to the brunette, the plump to the slender, and the yellow to the black girl; after which the rivals, each in her turn, shall do the like with the former; and be this illustrated with citations from Holy Writ and somewhat of anecdotes and verse, so as to show forth your fine breeding and the elegance of your pleading.' And they answered him, 'We hear and we obey!' —And Scheherazade perceived the dawn of day and ceased to say her permitted say." —*The Thousand and One Nights*

Table of Contents

Chant & Dialog

Game Mistress & Cosmos & Slavesex: Chant & Dialog

§ The Cosmos: A Chant

Chant in unison: "Once in the Game one stays in the Game."
Short version: "In the Game stay the Game."

§ Game Mistress (GM) & Slavesex (China Doll): A Dialog

It is the Slavesex whom we first hear speak: "Mistress, the first commitment of a Term at School is to commit to the next Term at School, Mistress."

"You remember that," GM advises her Slavesex. "Recite short form."

"In the Game stay the Game." Simple enough.

GM asks, "But?" She knows her Slavesex wishes to speak.

Slavesex casts her eyes toward the ground. "Mistress, I want to beg you to let me out, Mistress."

GM reacts sharply. "Let you out? Out of the Game? What am I supposed to do, tear out your page?"

"Maybe you could just punch a hole in my page," Slavesex offers, a humble compromise. She adds, "You have already punched holes in my body, Mistress."

Game Mistress ponders this. She speaks. "There is no such thing as 'my' page. And there is no such thing as 'my' anything. We have pierced and tattooed *our* body. You belong to us. You're Slavesex."

"Mistress, your Slavesex understands you, Mistress." This is spoken with more humility and more proper form.

"Maybe if you want to disappear you should beg me to bury you in black ink." GM is not without a sense of symbolism.

"Mistress, please cover your Slavesex in blackness. Make your Slavesex disappear."

"I like that." GM feels proud of this slave.

"Mistress, please let your Slavesex mix lampblack and light oil, rub it into her body, and glisten with the blackness of night!"

GM considers, "You can cloak yourself and just disappear."

"Slavesex will have a low optical index." A titter of laughter.

"You will be like liquid black silk," GM compliments her.

"Your Slavesex will kiss you. I will delight your nipples. I will pleasure you sex. I will tickle your anus."

"I don't think so! No way! You're a pariah! You'll just dirty me up!" GM knows when she's being hosed.

"Tie me spread-eagled and rape me. Make me your toilet. Possess me."

"Get away from me. You're toxic."

They both laugh. A pause.

In the rhythm, it is Game Mistress who speaks next. "Maybe I can arrange for you to practice on a white boy." Oh, wouldn't he be the canvas!

They laugh together, and Slavesex opines, "You're always so thoughtful. And an artist too."

In unison: "I love you."

Plans and Elevations

The Cosmos House and Yard

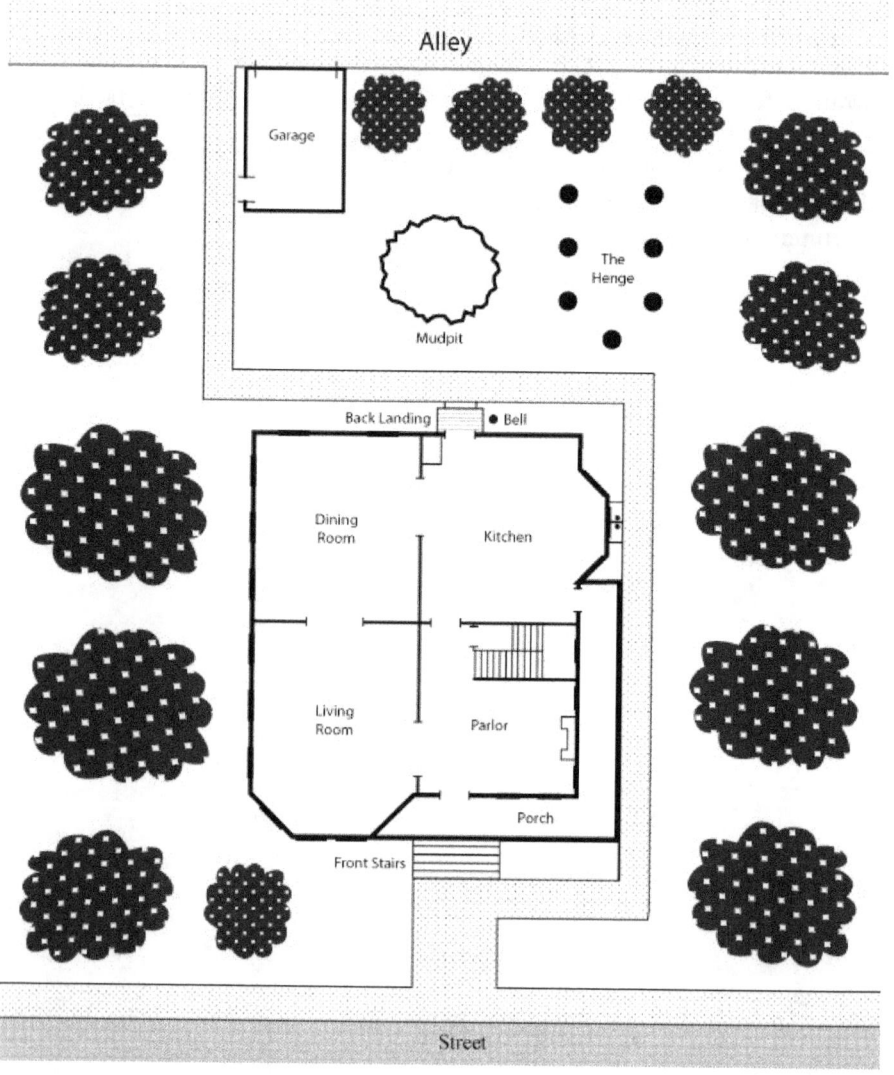

The Cosmos House First Floor Plan

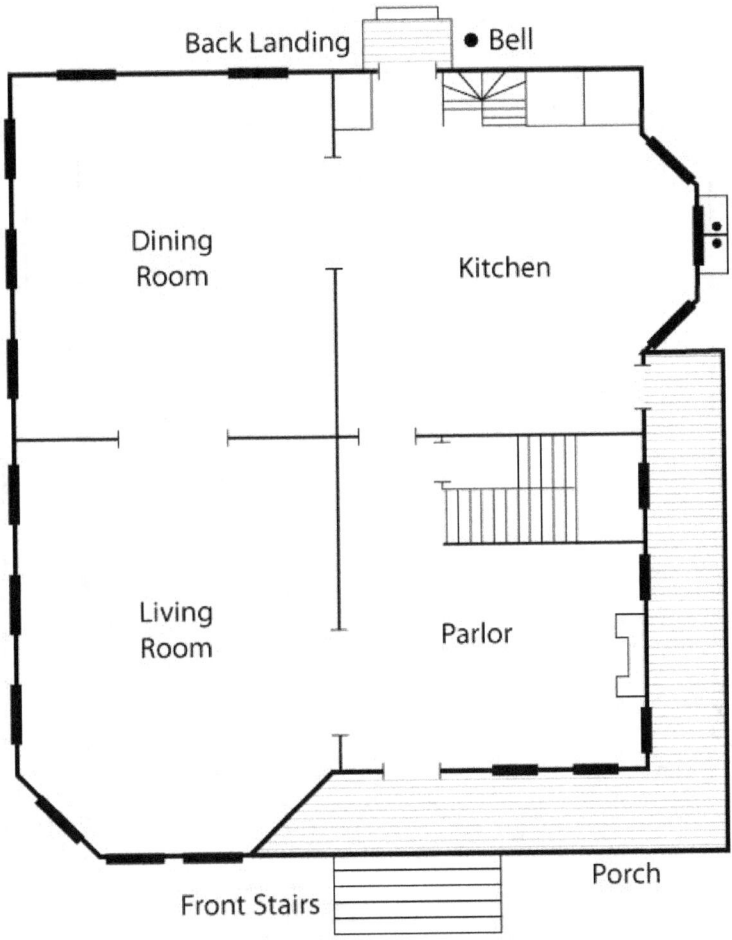

The Cosmos House Second Floor Plan

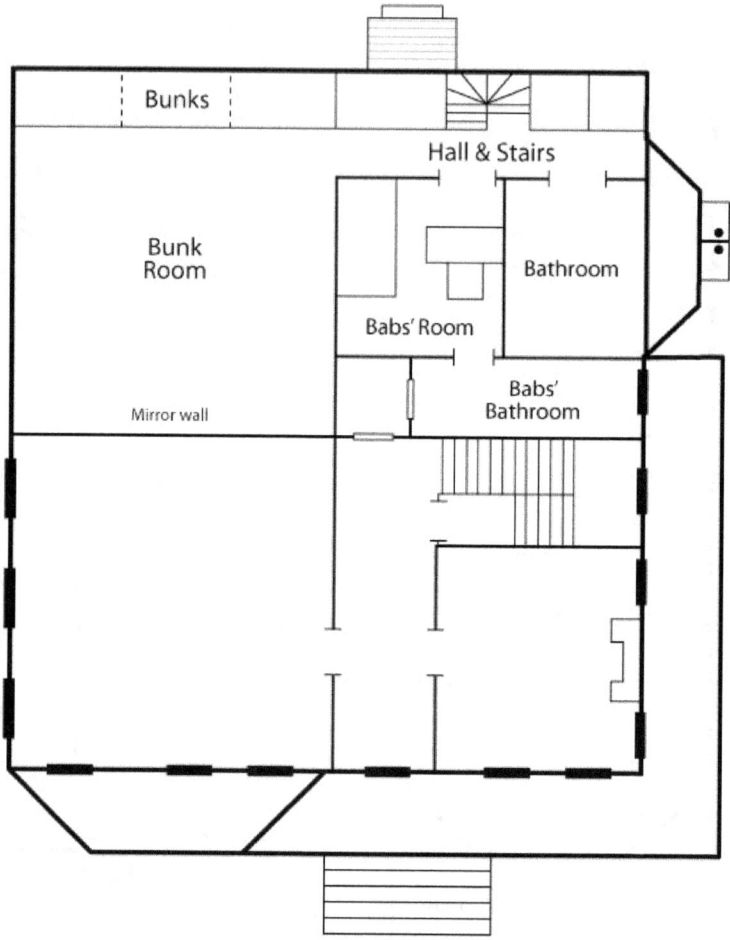

The Plan of the Nugget

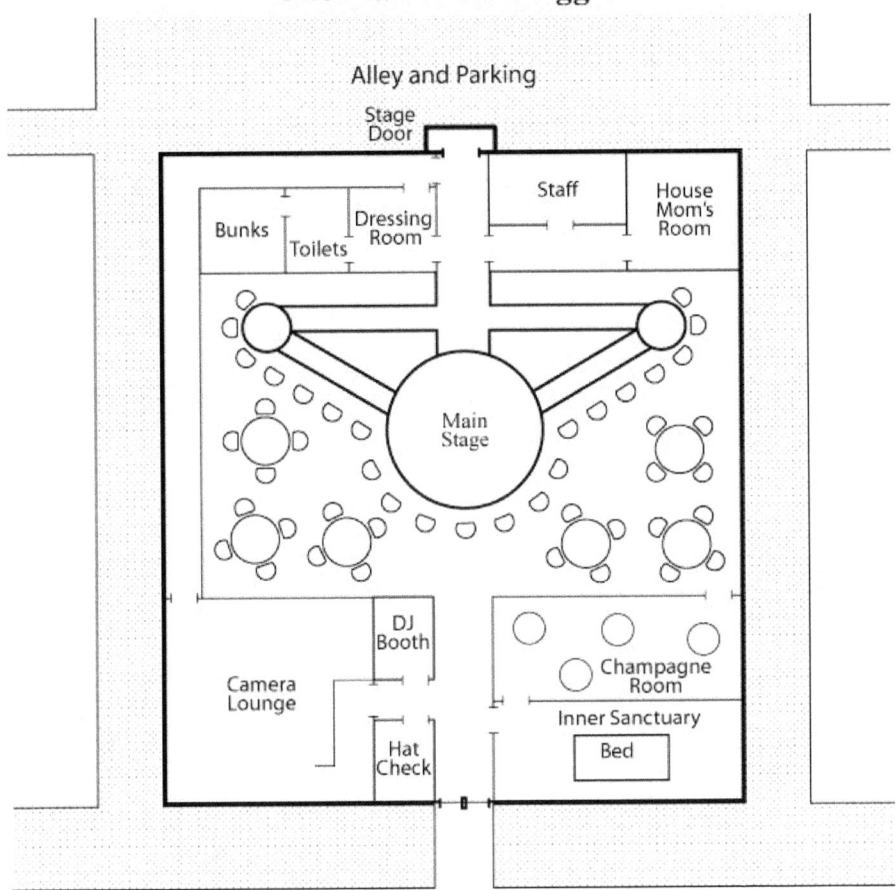

.

The Cosmos

The Arrivals

Babs & Gamers: Cosmos House Convergence

1 Babs: Bikini Babe, now Monitor of the Cosmos House (D01)

§ Monitor Babs: Welcome to the Cosmos House

The Monitor of the Cosmos House is the tall and voluptuous Babs. If you have binoculars and watch from across the street, you might spot her as she approaches the two-story Cosmos House, one of eight boarding houses at School. It is the morning of Day One.

Babs pushes her shoulders back and tightens her stomach. *I feel exposed. I can feel eyes on my bare skin. I know it's important Gamers pay attention to me, but I also need to be in control.*

And no wonder. The statuesque Babs wears a sexy Black Bikini, and nothing else. High cheekbones, smooth olive skin, black pearl eyes, and a big-boned stature reflect possible Mediterranean blood. Cleavage, low waistline, hips.

Despite her outfit, this tree-lined street of set-back houses is definitely not a beach.

Babs accepts her situation. *It is important to be a Cosmos of interest, but being a Cosmos in control is more important.* She tosses long black hair behind one shoulder and stretches her long legs. *I have to be careful where I place my bare feet. Careful about a lot of things.*

Babs feels telephoto paparazzi eyes follow her from across the street and feast upon her statuesque silhouette. *I know I committed to being a "Bikini Babe" in order to become a Monitor this Term.* Babs accepts this and adds out loud, "Bikini Babe. Babs. That's me! BB."

A Cam located on the Front Porch of the Cosmos House spots Babs while she paces down the sidewalk along the side street. It autofocuses and watches her. She turns, climbs up four concrete steps, and leans forward to ascend the slightly-rising concrete walkway that approaches a rambling Victorian structure that has witnessed multiple generations of Cosmos.

Gamers—you included—looking at Babs through the Cam on the Front Porch may explore this exquisite beauty's body in detail… and at their leisure.

Babs pauses halfway up the walkway and acknowledges the Cam. "Okay Gamers, I know you're watching me," she says, casting the Cam an oblique glance. "You know I don't like exposing myself. You know I don't relish running errands around campus, let alone to the Village, wearing only this Bikini." BB ascends two of the six wooden steps, flairs her nostrils, and gives the Cam a look. "But go ahead, look at me. You know I know I can't stop you."

She climbs up two more stairs. The Cam pans and tilts with her. It drinks in her very low-cut bra and low-rise briefs. BB's brassiere enables cleavage so extreme that Gamers can see the S-curve of her under-breast. Her briefs barely contain her lower assets, and her taut horizontal waistline, riding four inches below her belly button, ensures that her very bare belly and navel always stay exposed.

"Don't think I don't know all about the Cosmos House," Bikini Babe tells the Cam. "I know this place. I pledged here last Term. But this Term things are different."

Babs stretches her thighs, climbs the remaining steps, and positions herself upon the Front Porch. She adjusts her waistline and makes sure the leglines gently arch up to cover her butt. All secure. She casts her eyes around the front yard, and realizes that today is the first time she has ever climbed the front steps or even considered entering via the Front Door.

BB senses the Cam vie for her attention and draws in her stomach at the though of persistent voyeurs, the thought of the Gamers out there watching her and judging her performance. Babs considers the Cam and addresses it with a tilted head and firm chin: "Maybe I *do* wear a too-small Bikini, but at least my babambas and bush and bumpkins are covered! And they're going to *stay* covered, too! Better look now while you got the chance, Gamers, because now that I am the Monitor of the Cosmos House, I'm gonna cover up!"

Okay. BB considers the Front Door. *The House should be empty.* Babs opens the Front Door and disappears inside. Inside the Cosmos House. Day One has begun.

§ Babs: Areolage & Blush and the Fear of Self-Reflection

The cooler temperature and darkness and quiet inside calm Babs. The inside of the House is not without Cams, but inside the House it is Babs, the Monitor of the Cosmos House, who controls the Cams. Babs smiles. *I decide whether a Pledge begs to be on cam or not!*

BB's underwire bra barely contains her uplifted breasts, and they ripple when she moves. She leans forward to look at through the front windows while holding her widely-spaced shoulder straps in her fingers to make sure her "babambas" don't spill out. BB scans the wide Porch and front yard with its grass, flowers, bushes, and fine old trees. Nobody visible.

Bikini Babe shakes her shoulders in the dim inner light and cradles her cantilevered breasts in her palms. *It's bright out there,* BB realizes, *and I am fortunate to have shelter here at the Cosmos House.*

Monitor Babs has arrived at the Cosmos House in advance of her seven Pledge. "I am not a Pledge anymore, and I rank above Pledge! I am the Monitor in charge of the House! I am responsible!"

Yes. "Pledge, never Pledges," had been the first thing Babs had learned when she had herself been a Pledge last Term. "Pledge" refers to both individual students as well as the group identity. Seven Pledge will arrive here at the Cosmos House, and each one is a Pledge.

I know I'm having difficulty finding myself in a leadership position. Babs furrows her brow. *Being in charge. It's unreal. I'm not sure I know what to do.*

Babs casts her eyes about quickly but does not entirely digest the previously forbidden room she now stands in. The Parlor, with the Living Room next door, the master stairway.... *This now becomes* my *space to control.* The room seems familiar, but Babs can't place the déjà vu.

She recalls that there might be a Washroom under the stairway. There is.

She ducks inside. She turns on the light to review her face in the mirror, except as she leans forward her gold-dusted black eyes cast downward toward the visage of her breasts and her brassiere, and a blush forms in her face as her boobs almost spill out.

BB clenches herself, then relaxes her arms back so she can give herself a more considered evaluation in the mirror. Yes indeed, BB's bra does enable extreme cleavage. Bikini Babe looks at her red face in the mirror, and it speaks to her: "It is not cleavage that galls you."

"Right," BB affirms to her mirrored self. "What galls me is that my bra is so low-cut that I can't prevent my areolas from exposing themselves!"

Babs transfers her gaze down to her own breasts where the bra doesn't quite cover all of her large maroon disks. She raises her eyes and considers touching her visage in the mirror again. She defends herself, "Well, you're not showing off your *whole* disk, just waxing and waning crescents!"

Right. Babs feels another flush coming on. Even here in the bathroom, all by herself.

"Areolage," the head in the mirror explains to Babs, "that's what it's called."

"I know already," BB retorts back. "Partial exposure of the areola surrounding the nipple. Don't forget, I was a Pledge last Term."

The Babs in the mirror shrugs. "You find the tease humiliating, and you get all red in the face."

Correct. BB's upper chest blushes also. There is a reason Babs avoids mirrors. The confrontation with her humiliation flushes her immediately.

Babs quiets. True. She feels the slivers of her large maroon disks bubble up, watches the crescents of them crinkle up in the Mirror, yet can't retard the revelation of her own arousal. BB speaks to the mirror frankly, "Maybe right now I can't stop myself being compromised, but now that I'm the Monitor of the Cosmos House, I'll find a cure for my overexposure."

She raises both hands, cups her bra under-breast, turns off the light with her elbow, and ducks back into the dusky Parlor.

§ Babs Remembers MomCap: Say Linger Outside for a While

Babs tries the door just past the Washroom that leads into the Kitchen. Locked. She curls back through the Parlor into the Living Room and tries a double door she believes connects into the Dining Room. Also locked.

Babs tosses her hair back, moves toward at the Front Door, and hesitates. Inside looking out. It is the same door Gamers saw Babs enter when we spied on her when she arrived.

A voice in Babs' head interrupts her indecision and tranquility. It is the voice of her Caste superior, House Mom el Capitan, MomCap for short. "Be sure you linger on the Front Porch for a while, Bikini Babe," MomCap had commanded, "so Gamers have time to purview you!"

"MomCap, yes MomCap." Bikini Babe remembers herself acknowledging this order, and confronts the inevitable. *It's dangerous outside. And I know my hasty entrance into the House did not a "linger" constitute.*

"I should know what a 'linger' is," BB admits to herself out loud, surprised at how much the Parlor dampens her voice. "After all, I survived pledging last Term."

§ Babs: Bikini Babe Front Porch Telephoto Purview

Babs exits the Front Door onto the Front Porch with regality. Motion detectors trigger that a Cosmos has come outside, and the Automatron, that vast trove of data and artificial intelligence, goes to work, figures it out, and dispatches an alert far and wide: "Bikini Babe out."

Bikini Babe considers herself. She wraps one arm around one of the upright Porch columns and stretches upward so that her armpit forms a deep cup. She raises her other arm high, opens her fingers out, and deepens her other armpit. She drops a hip. She looks outward and scans to see who might be watching her.

Babs surveys the quiet street of similar houses, all cloistered in lush greenery. The School and campus lie in one direction, the Village in the other. Fresh air, sunshine, vibrant colors, and sounds abound, yet BB sees no watchers. She gathers her arms around herself, and as she steps away from the column she hears the Front Door Cam detach itself from its perch, hover and move toward her, and canvas her body.

Bikini Babe rolls her shoulders back and hoists her chest. She takes a step back and squares off to the Cam. She gives it a stare, holds her position, closes her deep black eyes in disgust, counts two beats, and devastates her voyeurs.

Gamers who know how to remotely operate the Cams collude with the Automatron and direct the eye's movement and focus. BB can only watch as the hovering eye canvasses her Black Bikini in close-up.

Gamers who zoom into her navel see the cratered remains of a center-knot made on her birthday, her initial separation from Mom and her ascent into this phase of life. BB's bare belly button is a Cosmos requirement.

"I know," Bikini Babe states to the Cam as it continues to examine her smooth belly, skin, and navel crater. "All Cosmos must keep their navels bare all of the time. Navelage 24x7."

Babs feels relieved that the Cam hovers around her button and does not dwell on her crescents of areolage. The thought of what the Cam avoids makes her blush again. She raises her fingers to the sides of her bra and tugs upward. Bikini Babe can do that; she knows how to pack herself in. But there is no solution. She crosses her hands across her chest, blocking all views; BB can do this too. She smiles wryly and casts her eyes out across the front yard, the sidewalk, and into the upper story windows of a house across the street. BB imagines the presence of paparazzi who lurk there, senses gyro-stabilized telephotos streaming down her every pore and eyelash. *My "crescents d'areolage" collecting a suntan!*

Bikini Babe addresses her admirers across the front yard, knowing they view her from out of earshot. "Read my lips. I know you're watching me, and I know you're gonna watch me all the time." Bikini Babe smiles, unfolds her arms from across her cleavage, and leans forward ever so slightly in order to shake her uplifted boobs. "But be careful when you spy upon me," she enunciates carefully. "Because after I put on more clothes, I'm liable to get back at you!" Feeling better, Bikini Babe beams a smile. She turns and looks at the hovering Cam. "All of you!"

Bikini Babe straightens and recalls that there was more to MomCap's orders. She shakes her shoulders again, pointlessly hikes her bra, fiddles with her bikini bottoms to make sure she's level, and marches down the stairs. She pauses at the bottom, turns and looks back at the Cam, and twinkles it with her eyes.

She pivots to her left and around the house toward the Backyard. Babs imagines telephotos pulling focus and following her as she paces the old and slightly askew concrete walkway along the side of the House. *No doubt they feast upon the skin of my back and shoulders, the stretchy fabric of my molded bikini bottoms, and the sway of my hips.*

But at least one unseen shadow is not imaginary. This tall and full-figured Gamer, a Monitor from a different House, wears a Bikini that makes BB look conservative. She already knows Babs' height (5' 11"), weight (140 pounds), and measurements (a natural 37D-24-36 silhouette). This watcher doesn't miss Babs' *crescents d'areolage*, and smiles to herself.

BB feels unseen Gamers' eyes follow her past the side of the Porch, past the wooden cellar door, but lose sight of her as she swings left and disappears into the Backyard behind the Cosmos House.

§ Babs: Mudpit Memories in the Backyard

Gamers who know which Cam to link to catch Babs when she emerges around the corner of the House, and a hovering Cam near the Back Door acquires her and tracks with her until she pauses near the Back Door Landing.

Babs surveys the deep grassy Backyard that awaits the arrival of the Cosmos Pledge. Despite being surrounded by a hedge and tall trees, it is hardly sacrosanct; aside from the hovering Back Door Cam, Babs scans across the top of the hedge, observing that nothing prevents paparazzi from spying from adjacent houses or from a car parked in the alley behind the House.

Bikini Babe's *crescents d'areolage* flash through her mind. She flushes. "You paparazzi leech on me," she declares to her surreptitious admirers. "Just because you rogue cammers take down my image doesn't mean you're following the Rules. You might harvest my body, my movements, and my acts. But you distribute them to unofficial channels. You know that."

Whether Bikini Babe is so interesting that Cams alone cannot satisfy the demands of her admirers will remain one of BB's concerns and uncertainties.

BB crisscrosses her arms across her breasts and occults her areolage. She considers how her fortune has improved. *I have more freedom of movement.* Babs carefully steps off the old concrete to wiggle her toes in the scrubby grass and dirt. *I'm allowed to go a lot of places I wasn't before. Except I don't want to go there wearing only this Bikini. Especially this one.*

BB's gaze follows the cracked concrete walkway down the left side of the Backyard until it passes between the Garage and the prickly hedge. Babs wonders if the side door on the Garage is locked and realizes she now plays a new role. *That's terrain that I control now.* BB accepts responsibility. *And if I want to know about locked, I shall let one of my Pledge crawl through the scratchy bushes to find out.* Babs presses her lips together. *But maybe that's too much to ask a Pledge to do.*

Babs runs her eyes around the near side of the Garage, along the alleyway; they come to rest at the far right, at what BB knows is the Post Henge. Seven thick Posts sit in the ground, solid, arranged in two facing rows of three, with a seventh Post at the end. Seven Posts for Seven Pledge. BB resists revisiting memories from last Term. *At least not right now. Because right now the Backyard and the Post Henge lie within my dominion.*

Babs gathers her breath and turns away from the Henge. *I'm not sure I have it in me to train seven Cosmos.*

BB takes a deep breath, shakes her babambas in her clenched arms, and moves toward a patch of bare earth in the middle of the Backyard. Babs moves carefully but breaks into a smile. "I'm not a Pledge anymore! I can walk on the grass. I can walk anywhere I want!"

Well, not anywhere, nobody can do that!

And besides, the Backyard might be secluded, but every sway of flesh in the Bikini demands Bikini Babe's diligence. *I know that Gamers surveilling me quest the faintest provocation: a nipple pop, boob spill, hair leaking out, or butt a-crackin.' The paparazzi would go crazy to catch me.*

BB's eyes narrow on the depression where rainwater has kept the dirt moist. Is this a flowerbed or a garden in the making? No. "I know you why you are not about to be planted with vegetables or flowers," Bikini Babe says to the patch of bare earth. "And I know firsthand why Gamers call you the Mudpit!"

Babs looks at her feet and takes a step closer, into the wet part of the shallows. Toenail polish flashes crimson red into her eyes. BB swallows, then reaches her five manicured toes forward, and depresses them ever so carefully to feel the wetter earth. She leaves a soft footprint behind, but she doesn't mar her toenails. *It is a slippery reminder of what I had to do here in order to obtain my two pieces—my bi-kini—and then promote and Opt Monitor this Term.*

Babs looks at her footprint and reconfigures slightly. *What my Roommate Janet and I had to do. Right here in the Mudpit. What we did, Roommates Together. We mud wrestled two other Cosmos Pledge and dispatched them to the Nugget.*

Correct: to the strip club not far from the Village. The losers, former Cosmos Roommates Penny and Coco, Opted Down Together and shall indeed remain Strippers this Term.

Babs accepts. *It wasn't a nice thing to do.* She looks at her fingernails, matching crimson red. She recalls that her lips are crimson red too. Bikini Babe casts a glance down at how her crescents acquire tan lines. She bites her upper lip and blushes.

Babs turns her back on the Mudpit, uncrosses her arms, lets them swing to her sides, and settles herself. Bikini Babe had beaten her way to Monitor status with a mixture of brawn and brains that had included more good scrap than she had realized at first.

Still, BB considers, *just because Janet and I won doesn't mean we promoted unscathed.* "I mean, look at me!" She glances at the houses around the Backyard and looks toward the alley. She runs her hands through her hair. "I got a very small taste of the alternative last Term. I've been permitted to observe it, and I do not want to go where Penny and Coco went!"

Babs worries more. *Any Mudwrestling vids better have gotten redacted. That's all I have to say.*

BB and Janet had won a commitment to become Bikini Babes and Opt Up and become Monitors this Term, however.

No matter how small the Bikini. Bikini Babe runs her fingers over her crescents of exposed areolas. She touches the widely-spaced shoulder straps of the underwire bra and feels the tightness of the low-rise bikini bottoms. Babs' *culotte* nombril might have wide sides, but its waistline rides her belly low and horizontal below her navel. It barely conceals a very full bush from the prying eyes of Gamers. And from behind? BB knows it just barely contains her perfectly-fleshed buttocks, including the bottom crease of her butt cheeks.

I had thought I would be choosing my own Bikini, BB grits. *Wrong about that one!* Babs looks toward her new home as she approaches the Back Door Landing. *However over-exposed I am, however much Gamers ogle me—and I do remain a Person of Interest—I have Opted Up, and I am the Cosmos House Monitor this Term!*

"I need to be in control of myself," BB asserts, "and if that requires being in control of others, so be it."

Or being looked at.

Babs scratches herself along her lower spine, near where her dimples beg for touch. BB reassures herself that she has adopted a pragmatic view. *So what if my a little too much of my babambas bounce out of my Bikini? Promotion requires compromise.*

Wait and see," BB declares out loud. "The first Pledge who arrives wearing a shirt shall beg me to trade for it!"

BB pads her way back to a pole that suspends a large brass Bell near the Back Door Landing. The Landing is a simple wood affair, two steps up from the ground, not quite centered in the back of the House. A nondescript Watering Can rests nearby. Across the Landing lies the unassuming Back Door.

Babs pauses next to the Bell and considers the clapper and long pull cord hanging down almost to the ground. She frowns as the Cam canvases her cleavage, the expanse of bare belly, and her smooth legs. BB gives the clapper a good pull. And sounds the Bell!

The clear sound of the Bell resonates past the boundary of the Backyard. Bikini Babe rings the Bell whenever she comes or goes because she made a commitment to ring the Bell before she was promoted to a Monitor this Term; Bell ringing is not BB's only commitment but it remains one of them. So too is her belly button exposure. Navelage 24x7.

Babs steps onto the Landing, turns and looks outward with her waist against the railing, and talks to the Cam now intruding in front of her. "Listen, Gamers. I have momentum, and I'm headed in the right direction." BB considers how to form her words as she considers the Term ahead/"I fought hard to Opt Up and become the Cosmos House Monitor this Term. You know I can't stop you from calling me 'Bikini Babe,' but I'm Bikini Babe no more. I'm still Babs, I'm still BB, but I am the Boss Babe now!"

And she brisks into the Cosmos House through the Back Door.

2 Babs & Janet: Tiffany Calendar & Dining Room Pictures (D01)

§ Babs Confronts Tiffany: Calendar Porn Star and Manifest

Babs passes through a short alcove into the Kitchen. "Goodbye, Cams. So long, paparazzi." She returns to the cocoon where she controls the visuals.

To the left across the Kitchen a bay window looks out just behind the side Porch and above the wooden cellar door. A dark Screen hangs on one wall. Babs walks across the Kitchen to check a door opposite the Back Door she entered through. This door leads to the front Parlor, previously locked, where she had caught her breath earlier. She looks down and confirms a Skeleton Key in the lock on this side of the Parlor door.

She turns around. A table and chairs reside in the middle of the Kitchen, surrounded by cupboards, a stove, and a large sink. One of three understated, closed doors incorporated into the back wall opens into a pantry. *I have always wondered where the other two lead,* BB mulls to herself. *Maybe now that I'm the Monitor here, I can find out.*

Later. Babs turns to her right and faces a sliding double door that invites entrance into the Dining Room. But before she can get through this door and face whatever challenges lie therein, she must first confront a large Calendar that hangs on the Kitchen wall just to the left of the doors. This unavoidable color picture vividly depicts a naked woman being triple penetrated via her "tongue, tinderbox, and tailpipe." A title at the top identifies the sexing thumper as "Tiffany Porn Star."

The explicitness of the image stops Babs short. She knows if she canvasses it a second time even more challenging details will emerge. Another glance reveals that "Tiffany" also jerks off a cock in each hand, which spill cum onto this already drenched redhead.

Babs closes her eyes and a wave of fear washes through her body. She squares her shoulders, opens her eyes, and tells the Calendar off, saying, "Well, Tiffany Porn Star, you're quite this month's delight."   Babs worries fear will gain possession of her being.

Somewhere deep inside her, left-brain synapses nag for attention and Babs recalls another "Tiffany."

MomCap, Babs' superior, had demanded BB memorize the Cosmos Manifest—the names of all seven Pledge arriving and their number of Garments. Some will arrive with two costume pieces, like the Bi-kini Babe, and some will wear only a single Garment. *And, yes, I do remember there's a "Tiffany" on the Manifest.*

Boss Babe studies the Calendar. *If "Tiffany Porn Star" is the same as "Pledge Tiffany," then "Tiffany" could present a serious complication—*

with or without a cock in her mouth. Tiffany could be a most exhausting surprise. She's got a lot more experience in the Game of Love than I do. At least here at School.

Babs shakes her head and rationalizes. *No. There is no way a Porn Star—a Whore—could ascend two ranks and Pledge here at the Cosmos House. That just doesn't make sense.*

BB tugs her straps upward. *Maybe Gamers think they can haze me, despite the fact I've been promoted.*

Babs does not turn the pages; the current month sufficently rattles her self-confidence. Tests her. Temps her.

Babs gathers her wits, stretches her body upward. *I will have to do my best to maintain discipline and make sure that when my Pledge sort out who Opts Up and who Opts Down that they don't hurt each other. It's a lot of responsibility, but I feel I can probably handle it.*

BB furrows her brow. *Correction: I must handle it!*

§ Babs: Confronts the Dining Room Picture of Previous Self

Babs turns her attention away from the possibilities of a Porn Star and enters the Dining Room, which occupies the back left of the House. BB turns her head to the right and looks out a row of windows into the Backyard; ahead, two windows look out toward the side of the house and reveal prickly shrubbery. They straddle a large dark Screen that occupies most of the area between them.

A dining table with eight chairs, one for each of the seven Cosmos Pledge plus a head chair for Boss Babe, occupies the center of the room. Beyond that, a wall separates the Dining Room from the Living Room in the front of the House.

Babs walks around the table, ascertaining that this sliding double door that blocked her entrance from the front earlier is locked from this side as well. Another Skeleton Key resides in this lock.

One aspect of the Dining Room disturbs Babs. Four Pictures hang on the interior wall, just to the right of the door that leads back into the Kitchen, and as Babs draws toward them she stops and stares at the Picture at the top, at eye level. The Picture reveals Babs, full figure, standing with her hands on her hips. She stares out into the Dining Room, giving whoever is watching her an evil eye. Babs closes her eyelids and flashes gold dust at her graven image.

I have never seen this before! Babs considers the Picture, then speaks out loud to her own image: "But I know when you got your picture taken!"

Bikini Babe does indeed. The two foot tall framed image was shot at the very end of BB's Pledge days, after she and Janet had defeated Penny and Coco in the Mudpit in the Backyard.

BB casts her eyes around. Janet hangs on the wall below her, and below them the now-Strippers hang side-by-side, at floor level.

Babs feels her face get warm and silently analyzes. *Well, no secrets for me on this wall. I'm wearing the same bra and nombril Bikini I wear today.* "Hello, Bikini Babe in your Black Bikini!"

This is a true statement, but there is a wrinkle. Or, more correctly, a fold of difference.

Yes, BB's exceedingly low-cut underwire brassiere remains unchanged. The Bikini Babe looking at the photo and the Bikini Babe looking out both persistently expose identical maroon-pigmented crescents. Babs feels a flush coming on, but it pales quickly as she casts her eyes down the body of the Bikini Babe on the wall.

Babs' eyes trace the waistline of her past self. That waistline rides considerably lower than her waistline today. *I know.* Babs frowns. *Because I'm the one who had to fold it under. Lower it down.* Babs feels a deeper flush warm her down her neck into her cleavage. She takes a step back, double checks to make sure the waistline and legline of her current Bikini contain her. They do. She looks at herself on the wall. "But you're vulgar!"

The front doorbell rings. BB cocks an ear, turns, and unlocks and allows herself through the sliding double door. She crosses the Living Room, and discovers Janet at the Front Door. Plump Janet, Babs' Roommate last Term.

§ Janet Joins Babs: Admire the Four Dining Room Pictures

"Janet?" Babs exclaims. "What brings you here?"

"I have been assigned to Monitor the Corvette House!" Janet invites herself inside. "You're the first to know. I saw you outside and just wanted to make sure you're settled in." Janet graces BB's shoulders with her fingertips. "Look at you! You are one bodacious Bikini Babe!"

"Be nice. I'm Boss Babe now." Babs cases Janet with narrowed eyes. "And who are you to talk? You should look in the mirror. No secrets for you!"

"No secrets indeed. I'm a whole lot more exposed than you!" Janet preens, "Bigger jugs too!" The rounded, plump, and black-haired fellow Monitor wears an open-mesh Bikini that more or less lets everyone see everything.

Janet bounces. "I got the crochet Spiderweb Bikini. Look at me! My spiderweb halter doesn't really cover my jaboos, and my nipples jut out holes in the middle. Size mini." Janet twists both jutting tips into hardness. And casts Babs askance. My areolas are much bigger around than yours," Janet continues. "Deeper brown, too. You might suntan your purple crescents, but I'm areolage all the way around."

"Officially they are maroon crescents, not purple," Babs corrects. She shifts her chin and eyes down at whatever it is Janet wears around her private parts. Well, not so private actually. "And may I guess that your g-string is also size mini?"

"Correct! Triangular mini-bikini," Janet exudes. "Crochet Spiderweb g-string. It's so small and so open-mesh that it lets my black pussy hair grow wild, not just around, but also through, the string."

"Your wild jungle there," BB provides. "Hairage leaking out everywhere."

Janet tugs the g-string. "Jipijapa jungle growing wild, and a string in between my big fat jaxy hanging out backside!" She slaps herself on her rear end.

"Maybe now that you're a Monitor you can acquire a size small Bikini, or even a medium or a large," BB speculates.

But Janet has none of that. "Maybe a micro. I show off a lot more than you do, Bikini Babe.' Janet wiggles. "And not just my jaboos and my jaxy. Sometimes my g-string sneaks into my jepoot, and when I pull it out it's all crusty."

"You are almost vulgar," Babs admits.

Janet turns and heads into the Living Room, and Babs discovers herself following Janet through the sliding doors into the Dining Room. She catches up full stop beside Janet to admire the four Dining Room Pictures on the wall.

"I came to see if I'm here too," Janet announces as she surveys the wall, and finds her image directly below Babs. "And I am!" Janet considers her fleshy self and turns to Babs. "Correction: I really *am* vulgar!"

BB considers her former Roommate. *Both us former Cosmos Pledge have promoted to Monitors this Term: me here again at the Cosmos, and Janet over at the Corvettes. She and I and six other Monitors reside at our Houses and manage our Pledge. Serious task.*

And yes, Houses can be competitive.

Janet's eyes drift to the two baseboard Pictures, where Penny and Coco lie next to each other as if at the bottom of an inverted T. But Janet doesn't linger; she scans up past herself until she considers Babs' image. At the top. Above hers. As Janet considers this image, she runs her tongue in front of her teeth and inside her lips. She pushes her jaw out, looks at Babs' current waistline, and declares, "You've come up in the world!"

"We both have," Babs sidesteps, qualifying, "We Opted Up, Roommates Together, remember?"

Of course Janet remembers. She taps a finger on the surface of Bikini Babe's image at that spot where BB's areolage shows. "Your crescents are beautiful, and I see that they remain so today."

Babs feels another blush coming on, goosebumps bubble up atop her cleavage, and her areolas pucker up. Enough shows that Janet can see, live, not in the Picture.

Janet glints, returns their attention to BB's image and rubs her forefinger back and forth on the Picture just above BB's waistline. "But look at you: you're hanging your pussy hair atop your Bikini!"

Babs feels the flush in her face descend to her neck and chest. *True, no denying the evidence. The waistline of the Black Bikini that I wear now might makes me decent today, whereas the waistline that confronts me from my Picture cuts so low across my flat stomach that my black pussy hair leaks. Conspicuously leaks over the top of my Bikini bottoms.*

Babs cringes as Janet continues to rub her finger upon the Picture of Bikini Babe's emergent bush. Janet praises, "Hairage or'top. Black bushy hairage. And not like it's getting loose or you had an accident. Hair on display and you didn't put it away!"

"At least my bush is contained now," Boss Babs declares.

"Unlike me," Janet gestures to her own personage on the wall. "I'm hairage everywhere! Then and now."

Boss Babe compares the Janet in person with the Janet on the wall. "I guess we both wear the same Bikinis that we wore at the end of our Pledge days. The end of last Term. Except my waistline has risen."

Janet throws her shoulders back. "Big gal's gotta show off her big jipijapa jungle. I'm committed to crochet Spiderweb Bikini all this Term: areolage and hairage and buttage 24x7. Gotta spin spiderweb over my jugs, leave my jute patch untrimmed, and hang my jaxy out free and clear. Always. Part of my deal. Sort of like you."

"Not sort of like me!" Boss Babe resounds, looks down, and touches her bare belly button, "All I have to do is keep my belly button uncovered. Make sure I'm Navelage 24x7. That's a Cosmos House requirement. Every Cosmos, even your humble Boss Babe. Navelage and ringing the Bell." Babs considers it necessary to say more. "All this other funny business..." BB shrugs. "Well, let me put it to you this way: I'm exchanging tops with the first Pledge who arrives."

"Well, be careful what you wish for," Janet warns. "You first Pledge might arrive topless."

And they laugh together.

§ Babs Tells Janet: The Story of the Dice Game

Janet scratches up and down on Bikini Babe's Picture, again where BB's hair displays above her waistline. "So what happened to you?"

BB startles. "Oh. I got to play Dice, just after we were separated, at the very end of last Term. One die determined how much of the waistline I had to fold under, and the other determined how long I had to keep it that way."

Ah, very sweet," Janet appraises, mulling, "I see you rolled yourself some good dots before you got your picture taken."

"I have no idea where the Dice are anymore. And don't ask me what happened when I rolled doubles."

Janet appraises, "I had an idea something happened. Over at the Corvette House there's a picture of you from behind, cracking your butt."

"Me?" Boss Babe exclaims. *A Picture showing posterior rugage? How? Why?*

Janet graces, "Same as here; four Dining Room Pictures, except only our backsides." Janet ponders Bikini Babe's hairage on the wall. "I'm not sure if it's the same folding as the front here, but you got your Dimples of Venus and Rhombus of Michaelis showing, and then both sides of your bumpkin draw together and dive down into your butt crack."

"I know, I rolled Dice for a while before Midnight," Babs admits, "and Gamers took a lot of pictures. So I made a lot of belly down."

Janet praises, "Bikini Babe, it seems like Gamers got you: hairage and rugage, coming and going."

Bikini Babe—the live one—blushes. "I don't approve of what I did to get to this place. I need to way to stop my Pledge from seeing me on the wall."

Janet takes a step backward and points a toe at the two horizontal Pictures hanging just above the baseboard. "Two naked losers dispatched to the Nugget!" she gloats, bumping her shoulder into BB's.

"Robyn promised all of our clips from the Mudwrestling Contest last Term would be erased, redacted," Babs worries.

Janet again wangles a toe toward the two lowest Pictures. "We squished these 'Baseboard Strippers,' so I don't worry whether clips got left behind or not." Janet scratches herself, "I've never had anything redacted. Don't forget I stripped two Terms ago! Except you never tried to see any of my clips when you were a newbie last Term, did you?"

Babs casts her eyes down. "I'm sorry. You kept reminding me." BB raises her eyes. "Don't worry, I will find an opportunity for my Pledge to beg to see them… and I will watch along."

§ Janet Encourages Babs: Demonize Strippers Penny & Coco

Again Janet points her big toe toward the Baseboard Stripper Pictures. "Gynecology workers," Janet pronounces. "Hello, poot and coot!" She directs Babs, "Take a good look at the down half of the Four Mudwrestling Pledge: Baseboard Strippers Penny and Coco." Janet touches one picture with the bottom of her foot and leaves a grease mark, "Cosmos Pledge Roommates Together last Term." Janet swipes the other Picture with her alternate foot. "Opt Down. Naked Nugget Strippers this Term."

Babs looks down to where two large and explicit 24-inch wide Pictures are centered below her and Janet, floating side-by-side just above the baseboard. She surveys the two naturally big-breasted Pledge—now Strippers—who lie horizontally. BB considers the displays and frames the physics. *The down half of a quartet fission.*

Babs ponders the climatic Mudwrestling Contest in the Backyard that ended the last Term. "I recall you sat on Penny," she says to Janet, "squished her into the mud, and ripped her clothes to shreds."

Janet lifts her crochet halter and lets it drop. "Well, I remember I lost my top somehow. Can't speak for you, but I recall you got Coco in an arm lock and stripped her naked."

Boss Babe clarifies, "Well, actually, Coco stripped *herself* naked."

Janet has none of that. "C'mon, you encouraged her!"

Both Monitors laugh.

"Their pain, our gain!" Janet touts.

Babs purses her lips, "Well, at least I get a Black Bikini out of it. And an Opt Up. You might weigh a lot more than I do and wear a much smaller Bikini, but we both possess two pieces and have risen to the same Caste this Term."

Janet stirs the record. "Perhaps your aversion to spreading your barndoors helped motivate your toughness to Opt Monitor."

Perhaps, although BB knew the alternatives. Babs never stripped, posed, or pinked when she had been a newbie last Term. And neither had Penny and Coco. But the new pictures of the defeated Pledge, now Strippers, capture them on their backs, stark naked, legs spread wide, pulling their pinks open.

Babs curls a lip. "MomCap said they had to streak naked to get to the Nugget," she advances uncertainty. "I never figured about that."

"Sweet!" Janet breezes, and annotates the pair of naked pinkers. "Apparently they got their pussy lips shaved bare and their pubes butched into silly hearts. And then, zip, out the door!"

"Penny and Coco." Babs repeats their names and ventures, "Janet, we have watch out they don't try to get back at us. I mean, we deserve it."

Oh, nonsense," Janet shrugs. "They try and move on us, and by the end of this Term we'll break them to Whores and Porn Stars."

Babs glances at the Pictures again and sees that the defeated and horizontal Penny and Coco both make reluctant eye contact. Babs curls her lips to one side and pushes the Baseboard Strippers away from her mind.

Janet steps back and waves an arm at all four Pictures. "The four Mudwrestling Contestants," she declares.

Boss Babe corrects, "The four Dining Room Pictures."

§ Babs Tells Janet: Anxiety & Opportunity & Torment

Boss Babe focuses the discussion on her own concerns. After all, this is BB's House. Babs acquires boldness, draws up to full height, and points at herself on the wall, careful not to touch or tap her own visage. "There was nothing I could do last Term to contain my areolage."

"Ah, chagrin!" Janet praises her former Roommate. "And still today! With luscious cleavage to boot. Nice babambas, bazoombas, bawagos—whatever you call them!"

Janet tilts a head toward BB's low-waistline Bikini. "And lucky for you. Your *culotte* nombril contains your bush and butt, albeit barely. Elastic around the waistline, and leg holes. Wide sides. Stretchy, but not cut to cameltoe or sneaking its way into your butt crack."

"My posterior rugage," Babs corrects.

"Rugage, crack, bum cleavage; whatever you call it," Janet concedes.

BB stands with her hands on her hips and asserts, "There was nothing I could do last Term, apparently, to avoid playing Dice and containing my hairage, and, per your report, my posterior rugage."

"Oh, double chagrin!" Janet claps. The Dining Room echoes.

Babs opens her mouth and closes it quickly. *After all, Janet could be a rival.* BB grouses, "That's all bad enough. But unless something changes soon, all my Pledge are going to see a Picture of my bushy part."

"Ooh. *Triple* chagrin. And they will delight in what they see!" Janet admires BB's predicament.

"Any Pledge who thinks about my backside might suspect I'm also crackin' my own butt," Babs frets, although not all Pledge think.

"Send them over to visit me at the Corvette House and they can see for themselves," Janet says. "Except I'm the top Picture. You're just beneath, and both Baseboard Strippers hang just above the floor. All of our backsides. I've got a string up my crack just like now, and you can see my lips and rings hanging out. You're cracking butt. And Penny and Coco crawl on their hands and knees and showcase their assholes."

As the words come out of her mouth, Janet realizes that she wants to ask Babs which Pledge might be coming to the Cosmos House this Term.

But Boss Babe gets a question in first: "So who is responsible for hanging this Picture of last Terms Bikini Babe on the wall, and making me out like some kind of bodacious bacchante? Just who is the 'Interior Decorator?' MomCap?"

Janet tilts her head. "Maybe not MomCap. And maybe not Madam Nurse Beautician either. My suspicion is that it is Game Mistress."

"Game Mistress?" Babs echoes. "We have GMs hanging pictures?"

Janet assures, "One GM, with a ring in her clit hood. And a Slavesex on a leash. The most dominate Caste. Be respectful."

"I *am* respectful," Babs defends, "but I doubt the Interior Decorator is Game Mistress." Babs rolls her shoulders. "If not MomCap, then maybe a Madam. But it matters to me."

"Matters?"

"It matters." BB nods at herself on the wall. "Because I'm putting 'remove last Term's Bikini Babe' on my short list."

Janet shrugs. "Good luck. Don't forget that you're also hanging cracked butt at the Corvette House."

Boss Babe glowers. "I'll get rid of all of them. All Four Pictures here and the Four at your House. I don't need poot and coot in my face either!"

Janet breezes, "Now that you're a Monitor you could ask MomCap if they made the streak successfully. And if she gives them anything to dance in. Or just keeps them nude."

Babs frets about Penny and Coco's fate, "Nude like in naked?"

"Bare except for their little hearts, spreading and pulling their pink lips apart, center Stage at the Nugget," Janet relishes.

Babs looks down and shuffles her bare feet

Janet advances another suggestion, "You can ask MomCap to let you visit and have them dance naked and climax for you.

Babs softly draws back.

Janet gives Babs a poke, "Lighten up, you never visited the Nugget when you were a Pledge last Term, but really, you should go watch. It'd be good for you."

Babs firms her body, "I don't want to ever see them again."

Janet extracts her g-string from in between her two thick lips, distending beneath her jepoot. "Well, do what you must, but feel free to leave *me* hanging. But be careful. You didn't hang the Pictures, and you are not the Interior Decorator."

"Trust me," Babs assures her fellow Monitor, "I don't need to know who hazes me to know to leave the Four Pictures alone. I'm here to learn how to overcome obstacles and organize power. That's why I'm in

School. Maybe we won't be able to work together like we did in the past, but I want to stay your friend."

"Gotta go," Janet announces, adding, "You will also need to learn how to let Kundalini loose."

Babs quiets at that as she accompanies Janet to the Front Door. She stays in the Parlor and doesn't walk out onto the Front Porch with her as they say goodbyes. Babs watches Janet retreat and realizes she wanted to show her the Tiffany Porn Star Calendar on the Kitchen wall. *Get a second opinion.* BB considers chasing Janet outside but doesn't. *It's okay; next time.*

As Babs turns her attention to the Parlor, its familiarity deepens, and she casts her eyes from the fireplace next to the window around to the bottom of the grand stairs, with the Washroom underneath. Babs realizes why the Parlor seems familiar. She studies the floor and realizes that the spirit of Game Mistress lingers here, whether GM might be the Interior Decorator... or not.

§ Babs Feels Presence of Game Mistress: Uneasiness

Game Mistress, the highest rank of the Gamers, has purpose in her decorating choices and housewarming presents. A GM, be they Game Mistress or Game Master, often exerts force from a distance. Game Mistress might not be present when Babs arrives to encounter her offerings, but GM pleases herself helping Boss Babe earn her status.

Babs considers Janet's suggestion that the source of the four Dining Room Pictures and the Tiffany Porn Star Calendar might not be their immediate superior, House Mom el Capitan, a.k.a. MomCap. The el Capitan half of MomCap manages House Monitors. *Janet and myself included, and thus, indirectly our Pledge.* The House Mom half of MomCap manages the Strippers who dance at the Nugget. *This means MomCap now choreographs Penny and Coco.* Babs rubs her chin and tables this thought.

Babs follows Janet's alternate hypothesis. *Might the Caste of Gamers superior to MomCap be the source of these unwelcome intrusions into my House?* BB wonders about these Madams and Pimps. *But why would they want to spook me? I'm not even sure who they are, except for Madam Nurse Beautician, and I only know that because I washed feet and painted toenails in her Beauty Salon last Term. Trained me when I first pledged.*

Which returns Babs thoughts to Janet's theory. *Janet thinks Game Mistress is the Interior Decorator. But why are either of us, really, important enough for a GM to bother with?*

And Babs remembers why the Parlor feels familiar. *I was here once before, and it wasn't just earlier today. I saw the boots of Game Mistress in this very Parlor, kissed them actually, when I had pledged allegiance to the Cosmos House*

Babs had never seen the upper part of the Room… or the upper parts of Game Mistress. *I was on my hands and knees and kept my eyes on the floor.*

"Pledge, go prograde yourself!" Game Mistress had blessed her, "and may Kundalini allow your soul to burst with joy and sacrifice."

Babs hadn't been sure what that all meant, but now she scans the room and speaks softly, "And now I need to find out."

Wise Gamers ask permission before lifting their eyes to feast on GM's attire. But Babs knows the legend, "Above the boots Game Mistress is a dark-skinned woman of command and presence who wears a full black bodysuit with deep cleavage and many zippers. Zippers around her nipples, her navel, and straight down to her private parts."

Babs had wisely never even opened her mouth or raised her eyes. She never saw the gloves, or any other of GM's five pieces. BB distrusts legends, envies GM's confidence of power and Caste, and correctly fears her. Legend has it, "Game Mistress owns a Slavesex who maintains her privates and stainless. Shaves her, services her, drinks her piss fresh."

China Doll.

Babs shakes off the image. *That's the part I don't believe. Maybe Cosmos who lose and Opt Down become Strippers. And maybe Strippers who Opt Down get turned into Whores. And maybe Whores who want to sacrifice everything beg to become the Slavesex, that most submissive of Castes in the Game. But if GM really owns a Slavesex—mind, body, and soul—then why would she even remotely care about trying to torment Janet and me with our Pictures?*

Maybe everybody's important.

Babs walks back into the Dining Room and again considers the inverted T of the four Dining Room Pictures. The Ups and Down from a Mudwrestling Contest haunt her; she glances at the slightly more revealed Bikini Babe hanging on the wall above Janet's Spider, pauses, considers, and speaks to Janet's image. "We need to keep our Houses non-confrontational. If that's even possible."

Babs drifts her eyes back down to the twosome she helped turn into Baseboard Strippers. Penny and Coco. She cringes as she looks at how their breasts hang to their sides, how their mouths lolly open. She avoids their eyes, avoids probing to discover what might be seen inside their opened, shaven sex lips.

The four Dining Room Pictures help Babs remember. *Not all Pledge last Term ended up Monitoring while wearing skimpy, revealing bikinis.*

Barely legal plus or minus. So I need to appreciate my success and good fortune; I am in a far better position than Stripping the bump and grind in a titty bar this Term.

One of BB's eyes tick. She retreats from the winners and losers of the Mudwrestling Contest. She turns away, yet concludes, *I must acknowledge that their defeat, coupled with my tease and sacrifice, put me on the only path up. There may be no other way up for me.*

Boss Babe centers herself and marches through the door that leads back into the Kitchen. *Right now I must take charge, no matter how much of my skin and soul I expose.* On a whim, Boss Babe crosses the Kitchen and tries the two doors next to the pantry. They don't open.

She turns, and once again the Tiffany Porn Star Calendar catches her eye. BB gingerly lifts a corner to observe another Tiffany month, this one with Tiffany on her hands and knees, pants pulled down, an eight-inch schlong rammed up her tailpipe.

Madams and Pimps are supposed to manage the Whores, be they Streetwalkers or Porn Stars. They report to the Game Mistresses and Masters. Babs dredges recall memory from her shifts servicing feet at the Beauty Salon. *Madam Nurse Beautician wore four Garments, although mostly all I ever saw of her were her ankle boots. And I never saw any Whores or Porn Stars, male or female, including this one.*

"And I don't want to, either," BB says to the Calendar. "Especially you, Tiffany Porn Star." Boss Babe lifts a chin, yet talks down to the Tiffany servicing five cocks. "I'd heard Whores possess nothing, not even their holes. I guess for you that means all of your holes all the same time."

The Interior Decorator, a.k.a. Game Mistress, hopes that the hangings will affect not just Babs, but "learn" the newbie Cosmos about the stakes of the Game. The Options: Up and Down.

Babs remembers something Game Mistress had uttered while she had worshiped her boots in the Parlor before the start of this Term. "Beware Bikini Babe, because Kundalini won't warn you when the Force reaches across space/time and exerts magic and spells."

Babs now recalls that she had also witnessed a pair of bare feet nearby GM's shinny boots. Bare feet side-by-side with the adjacent big toes tied together. Firmly. That was all she saw: feet. One pair that was shod and she had blessed with kisses, and one pair that was toe-tied. And then Bikini Babe had crawled away, eyes steadily looking down.

3 Babs Anticipates Tiffany, Robyn & Steph: Roommates (D01)

§ Babs: Bedroom Roommate Tiffany • Old Steph & Robyn

A steep and angular stairway adjacent to the Back Door alcove makes two sharp left turns as Babs ascends from the Kitchen to the second floor; it's a counterclockwise upward spiral that is the only way for Cosmos to get to and from their windowless accommodations upstairs. At the top, the stairway terminates in a hallway that runs the width of the back of the Cosmos House.

Directly ahead, across the hallway, Babs walks through a doorway into her assigned Bedroom, a windowless compartment slightly bigger than a Pullman roomette. BB comes into the room delicately—as much as a barefoot Bikini Babe can be delicate. She tamps down residual unease as she crosses the threshold into a chamber she wasn't allowed to enter last Term. Her eyes scan the room, and she silently considers. *This was Steph's room last Term, when she was a Monitor and I was a newbie Pledge.*

BB looks to the bed bunk to her right, and speaks out loud, "Except you're *my* bunk now!"

She leans over, looks at the alcove underneath her bunk bed, and fits her mind around its last occupant. *Steph's Roommate Robyn slept down in there last Term.*

Babs fits her hips into the space between the bunks and a desk that faces the door. *Last Term I might have looked in and seen the desk and bunks, but I've never really been inside the Bedroom before.*

BB passes her body around to the back of the desk and looks back out the doorway. The Bedroom is a tight fit, even for a Bikini Babe. BB looks left and right, out the door, then overcomes her awkwardness, sits on the only chair behind the desk, and digests her new home.

Boss Babe tosses her hair back, straightens her shoulders, waves her hands, and exorcises the spirit of Steph Sorostitute out of the Bedroom. "Be gone, Steph Sorostitute! So much for history. This Bedroom no longer belongs to you. It belongs to...."

BB blinks. *Steph is not entirely gone from the Cosmos House.*

Bikini Babe grabs the front of her bra straps with thumbs and fingers and hikes. She turns and looks at the bunk bed, running the length of the wall to her left, with an open space above.

Boss Babe knows who shall now sleep on the top bunk: "Me!" She casts her eyes downward and looks at the lower alcove. "Last Term Robyn lived there. And it's as long and wide as my bunk on the top, only at floor level, with only a couple feet headroom."

I don't know if Robyn is entirely gone or not. I know I am avoiding the question, but wherever Robyn might be sleeping this Term, she will not be crawling into this luxurious sleeping accommodation. Because I know who will be. Boss Babe stands up, fits her palms into the bare skin above her pubic bone, and considers the lower bunk. *Well. According to the Manifest—and I did memorize it completely—a Pledge Tiffany shall be my Roommate this Term.* BB eyes the lower bunk and concludes the obvious, "So Tiffany will sleep under there!"

Images of Tiffany Porn Star Calendar dance through Babs' head. Just before she came upstairs BB had snuck a look at a different Kitchen Calendar month, and she recoiled at a close-up of Tiffany's face surrounded by cocks, her open mouth overflowing with ejaculate. *I couldn't determine if Tiffany was being degraded or conquering,* Babs analyzes, *but I have to admit, I respect self-discipline.*

Babs sits. She draws her thighs together and squares her jaw and chest. She ruminates, *When I memorized the Manifest it said, "Tiffany, two Garments." And I assumed a broken Monitor arriving.*

Opting Down.

But the Manifest doesn't indicate directionality or if Garments are adding on or wasting away.

"What if Tiffany really is Tiffany Calendar Porn Star? And a Double Opt Up?"

Babs lifts both hands, cups both breasts, and shakes so that her bra fits best. She twitches her head and one eye. She looks out the doorway, across the hallway, and into the top of the stairway. Nothing there. Babs rests her elbows on the desk and her chin on her elbows and munches her thoughts. *Maybe the Manifest and the Calendar are just coincidence? Because why would this Tiffany Porn Star receive a double promotion— from Whore to Stripper to Pledge? That's two ranks—and two pieces of clothing! How could any Whore obtain so much rising momentum?*

BB sits back, crosses her arms in front of her, and worries out loud, "*And* be my Roommate this Term?"

§ Babs: Dice & the Makeup Case

Boss Babe squeezes herself tighter into the chair. Hard to do when it doesn't have any arms, but BB squeezes her arms to her sides, interlaces her fingers, squeezes her thighs together, and crosses her ankles. Aligns her upper and lower teeth. Holds the position and looks around by only moving her head. She observes the desk's only drawer, breaks into a more relaxed posture, and carefully pulls it open.

"Ah, the Makeup Case!" Boss Babe realizes, looks harder and sees, "Dice." Also spoken out loud. And a third item, an Alabaster Flask.

She takes these items out and lays them in front of her on the desk.

"So," Boss Babe declares to these three objects, "Gamers give me three Props!"

May Kundalini be cheered.

BB knows the Case contains makeup of near infinite resource and colors, glitter, adhesives, stains, markers, perfumes, and substances which if misapplied might cause the skin to feel heat or cold or rash up.

Boss Babe accepts the Makeup Case with the passing of pride that accompanies an officer turning over a command in the military. *Except this is the Cosmos House and I am at School. And Steph never "turned over command" to me. She got broken and is a Pledge now. A Cosmos House Pledge. My Pledge. One of seven.*

Babs cradles the Makeup Case and rattles the Dice. Babs has every reason to be proud of her achievements. And she is wise to be mindful of them and the dangers they present. She knows better than to remove the stopper on the Flask.

As for the Makeup Case, Bikini Babe just when through a Term when the Makeup Case got used upon her. Correction, Bikini Babe *begged* for Makeup. Sometimes it got misapplied. Sometimes applied beautifully. Like now.

What happened last Term happened last Term. Babs fidgets. *Yet some of that matters. Momentum lingers.* BB turns to the Case, lays fingers on both side of it, and speaks to it. "All things considered, right now I'm the one holding you!"

She opens it up. The flash of her areolage as the lid's mirror pivots upward startles her. "Whoa!" Bikini Babe steadies herself. She leans forward and carefully frames her face in the mirror. Maintain posture! she says to herself.

Babs studies her makeup. She sees a sturdy face meticulously made up with the regality of a Mediterranean queen. Bright red lips outlined with narrow black lip liner. Rouge provides the subtlest flush. Eyes the color of black pearls sparkle in a cascade of detail: brow-liner perfectly forms the eyebrows; mascara adds finish to already long black eyelashes; deep crimson eyeliner follows the rims of her eyes; and deep red eye-shadow dusted with powdered gold colorizes her lids.

BB closes the Case with an authoritative snap, puts it back into the drawer, and considers the Dice. She considers the Bikini Babe downstairs in the Dining Room hanging hair. BB pats the Dice and puts them in the drawer. "You are mine now," she says to them. "My Game to call."

BB closes the drawer and thinks about what to do next. *Organize my short list? Review the Manifest? Inspect the Bunkroom and Bathroom? Make sure the Screens work?*

§ Babs: Areolage and Blush in the Private Bathroom Mirror

Boss Babe turns around in the chair, looks behind her, and decides to explore the remainder of the small Bedroom. She stands, turns around, and faces a wall that contains two vertical lockers, one with a door and one without, and a closed door to their left.

BB opens the locker with the door and looks inside. One shelf, a hook, and otherwise empty. The other locker also contains a shelf with soap, bubble bath, and shampoo, also a hook, but no door.

Babs opens the closed door to the left and looks into a small private bathroom. She leans in, sees her visage in a mirror above the sink, and again sinks her eyes to her areolage. She looks back into her face and watches herself blush.

Babs balances her weight better and steps in front of the mirror. "Mirrors are one thing when you just have to look at yourself," the Bikini Babe in the mirror says to her.

BB answers back, "But mirrors are different when one must confront oneself overexposed."

BB watches herself in the mirror and witnesses her flush fade. Once again she lifts her hands under her underwire bra cups, hoists, and packs babambas. She reconsiders the mirror. Still areolage. BB shakes her head silently while she considers her situation. *I'm okay with cleavage, bellage, and stretching my legs, but areolage? I guess maybe it is one of the least bad things I could do. I realize it's only a sliver of areolage, but it means I'm in play. I'm playing the Game now. I'm in the gradient somewhere.*

The visage in the mirror talks to her, "Babs, you're a Monitor this Term!"

And BB looks at her face in the mirror and commands herself, "Go do it, Boss Babe!"

§ Babs Considers Steph & Robyn: Threat Potentials

Babs closes the door of her private bathroom and again sits herself in the chair behind the desk, so she faces the door and can see into the hallway and top of the stairs. No one lurking.

BB straightens up, props one elbow on the desk, swishes her hand on the surface before her, and the surface of the desk, the Desktop, glimmers to life with feeds from the two door Cams. No one calling.

Steph knows how to run this. Except I never quite knew what Steph did, and I never saw Desktop from this side.

BB mulls over the implication of her own Pledge out-knowing her, but toughens. *If Steph can operate the Desktop, so can I!* Boss Babe passes her hand through her hair and mulls over the prospect of being out-maneuvered during the Term ahead. She looks at the top bunk again and considers her Game. *Yes, there is a Steph on the Manifest. And yes, it is the same Steph. Yes, all through last Term she was the Monitor Boss of this very Cosmos House, and yes, last Term I was one of her Pledge! Newbie Babs I was.*

BB clenches her teeth together and then talks to the empty upper bunk, "And then one day Steph vanishes. Poof! Gone!"

Last seen wearing a minidress. A cutout minidress buttonholeless. Babs remembers. *Over panties. Two pieces.* BB smiles.

Boss Babe checks to make sure that the back of her nombril hasn't slid down so that she cracks rugage. It hasn't, not that there is anyone here in the Bedroom to look. She wipes a finger under a nostril and considers the bottom bunk alcove.

During the short time from Steph's disappearance until the end of last Term, her Roommate presumed to be in charge, so it was Pledge Robyn who oversaw the final Mudwrestling Contest.

It was Robyn who said that Steph had suffered a reversal of fortunes; she lost her panties, tore her dress, and would Opt Down and Pledge this Term.

BB recalls the Manifest, "Steph, one piece." And projects, *Minidress, no panties.* BB purses her lips. *Just what I need: a role-reversed Pledge sure to have an attitude problem. This is my reward for promoting?*

Apparently so.

"Robyn, one piece," also bespeaks the Manifest, but Babs resists jumping to conclusions. *Could this be the same Robyn? On one hand, it makes sense, Robyn being Steph's Roommate last Term,* Babs weighs. *On the other hand, it makes no sense at all. Because Pledge are required to either Opt Up or Opt Down, Opt Monitor or Opt Strip. Nothing else. No repeating, no pledging again, no do-overs. Just Up or Down.*

BB digs deeper. *So for this to be the same Robyn—last Term and this Term—it means spirit forces enchant the outcome. Maybe Robyn has Charm after all.*

Babs dredges. *The last time I saw Robyn she was wearing a one piece maillot cutout swimsuit; she had gone to great lengths to get her navelage reduced to a small hole around her belly button, but....*

Babs scratches her hair back. She scratches harder. It feels good.

But, BB regains control over her thoughts, *one piece is one piece. And one piece should have Opted Robyn Down to the Strip, and not here to the Cosmos House.*

Babs looks around Bedroom again. At her bunk and the alcove below; at the desk drawer holding Dice and Makeup Case; at the Desktop and Screen; at the lockers and door to the private bathroom.

BB glances down at her body. Bikini Babe. Babs takes a big breath. *Okay. I'm on the Manifest too, two pieces. But why am I here?* BB must think about that answer. But she knows part of the answer, and raises her forefinger into the air, "I'm here to learn about love and power exchange. And discover the force of Kundalini."

§ Babs Reviews Seven Cosmos Pledge Manifest: Full House

Enough daydreaming. Boss Babe stands, takes a deep breath, and refocuses her mind. She inventories potential challengers.

The three other Mudwrestling Contestants: Janet? Penny and Coco? Babs mulls, *Janet could challenge me, but as long as Penny and Coco stay at the Nugget they aren't dangerous. And besides, neither Janet nor the Strippers are Cosmos.*

BB rubs her nostrils and recalls that Robyn supervised the four Mudwrestling Contestants at the end of last Term, after Steph had vanished. *Maybe Robyn will be my Pledge this Term or maybe not, but Steph shall be my Pledge for sure, whether I want her or not.*

Boss Babe addresses both residual spirits out loud, "You two incoming Pledge might know what secrets reside in the morgue from my Pledge days. You come with one Garment each. You had better behave yourselves and keep secrets or you will Mudwrestle and see who ends up with two pieces and who ends up naked."

Boss Babe smiles at this thought and finds her spirits buoyed for a moment.

She escalates, "And no water to hose down with afterwards."

BB smiles, relaxes against the back of the chair, allows air to penetrate in between thighs, and shudders Steph out of her thoughts. Lingers a moment too long at Robyn's last bunk alcove and transfers to its incoming occupant. *Tiffany, as per the Manifest. And no coincidence with the Tiffany Porn Star Calendar on the Kitchen wall. Impossible. That's just some fearless spunked Whore turning all holes out. And grabbing whatever she can get her hands on. Somewhere far beyond vulgar.*

Babs scratches the skin of her back against the back of the chair. She reaches behind and verifies that her three bra hooks are all tidy. They are.

Tiffany, Steph, Robyn, and I account for half of the Cosmos, Boss Babe crunches. The Manifest does include the four other names. *One pair of them each brings two Garments and are newbies. Beka and Elle. The one pair of them each with one Garment, they're Strippers. Kimju and Molly.*

Pledge are the only Caste by which newbies may enter School. *And I don't worry so much about the newbies,* BB circumspects silently as she drums on the Desktop. *I worry about Strippers on the uptick who might challenge me somehow. Like arriving topless. I get tits in my face and Pledge who've got more Terms of School than I do. Even discarding Tiffany, dealing with veterans—Cosmos alumni—isn't something I anticipated I would be dealing with. Although I should have figured it out a long time ago.* BB tallies, *Four Cosmos, me included, will arrive wearing two pieces, and four Cosmos will arrive wearing only a single Garment. Total eight Cosmos, twelve Garments. Full Cosmos House.*

And BB knows the outcomes: the Garments can move between Cosmos, but Cosmos' navels must always stay exposed. Navelage 24x7. As a Cosmos, Babs isn't really required to show off her whole belly, but the bra and nombril Bikini she wears don't provide her any choice in the matter. Babs looks down at her expanse of belly skin and sees the low-rise elastic waistline squeeze out the smallest concave of belly flesh. *But it has no chance of rising up and accidentally covering my button, even sitting down and hunched forward!*

BB knows that bellage can be far more modest, if not more expansive, that her current Game position. It is not even necessary that a Cosmos expose belly all the way around her waist. Navelage 24x7 defines the commitment. *So if a Pledge isn't totally bellage, like me, they'd better arrive with their button displayed somehow, like coy Robyn in her maillot cutout last Term. Just her belly button, but not the rest of her belly.*

Boss Babe also knows that as long as the costume reveals a bare belly button 24x7, these Cosmos stay legal. *This all applies to Steph too.* Boss Babe scowls. *Steph especially better arrive with a hole cutout in her stomach.*

Because Cosmos who cover their button find their Caste broken.

§ Babs: Self-inspection in Bunkroom Mirror

Babs' view out her Bedroom door enables her to see any and all comings and goings up and down the angular stairwell. Should she elect to close her door, a network of surveillance cams, trip beams, and sensors continue to provide her Desktop with total electronic coverage. Any unauthorized Pledge venturing down the stairwell will quickly end up trapped between spring doors that close both the bottom and top of the stairs. That's not a place any Cosmos should aspire to occupy.

Babs exits her room, turns left, and heads into the spacious Bunkroom. The Bunkroom occupies the back left of the Cosmos House and lies above the Dining Room. It has three pairs of bunks stacked along the back wall, whereas the opposite, front wall, is covered with a mirror. *The Mirror, or just, Mirror. And I know, from experience, that Mirror contains latent capabilities.*

Babs approaches the image of herself in this Mirror carefully. It is full size, running from above the top of her head to below her bare toes. She tosses all her black hair back so it rides high on her forehead and falls behind her shoulders, skin taunt over muscle and bones. BB avoids looking at what she knows she must not be obsessed with. She moves closer, pauses, and stands erect with her hands on her hips, and considers her reflection.

The Bikini Babe looking back at her stands pleasantly hour-glassed, not overly muscular, but with good physical stamina. BB's exquisite makeup sparkles her face. Her waist narrows above her pelvic bone, and her nombril hangs on below. Leglines rise only slightly above great legs. Babs dares to look at her bra's generous cleavage. What's not to like?

Babs gives herself a playful grin and relaxes alone with herself. Most know Babs is a beauty, a knockout. But BB treats herself with more modesty. The Bikini Babe in the Mirror shrugs, "I know I'm a looker, I know my babambas stand out, and I know I can tease."

But Boss Babe also has goals, and assures herself in the Mirror, "And I know you can command!" She looks into her black eyes in the Mirror and reflects. Her eyes sparkle.

A chill in the air makes goosebumps on BB's breasts stand up, and she senses the milk glands of her exposed areola crescents pucker with detail. Areolage 24x7! Babs examines herself in the Mirror, breathes deeply, and mutes an oncoming blush. *There's no going back.*

BB catches her irritated eyes in the Mirror and speaks in harmony with her visage, "I don't like things I don't control, and I don't control these exposures." Boss Babe grits. "But I'm about to change that once that my first Pledge arrives." Babs stiffens, cocks her head, and addresses herself in the Mirror, "Somebody gave me this Bikini to wear, somebody resurrects a vulgar picture of me in the Dining Room, and somebody makes sure I get broadcast by Cams and paparazzi outside. Maybe MomCap, maybe Madam Nurse, maybe GM, maybe Gamers outside of School. Maybe Gamers deliberately attempt to rock my boat and unnerve me. But Gamers are not going to get the better of me! Gamers shall not be successful at scrambling my mind, brainwashing me into a new person."

Once again Boss Babe and her visage speak in tandem, "I am not going to succumb. I know what you are trying to do to me. And I'm not even going to let my crescents blush me anymore!"

As if it were as simple as that.

Babs conquers fears and watches herself in the mirror as she slides her shoulder straps off, pushes her bra down, and fetches her breasts into the open. *Yes, this is how I look in the shower; this is what threatens to spill out and get cammed—but right now it's just me watching myself in the*

Mirror. I can do this! It is when I get watched by others that reactions get complicated.

A chill brings BB's nipples to erection, and she cups her firm bosom in her hands and lifts both breasts upward. She traces her fingers across the suntan lines that arc across her areolas and upper breasts. As she follows the lines she dares touch her erect bullets. This is not like her, but it feels good.

Unthinkingly Babs casually drops her hands to her waistband, hooks her thumbs into the top of her bikini briefs, and pushes and wiggles the nombril lower. In the Mirror Babs can see not just her current tan line, but also a fainter tan line lower down, one that bisects her black bush as documented in the Dining Room Picture. The double six Dice roll enabled Bikini Babe to pile tan atop her hairage, and Babs considers the tan line left behind. *It's a vulgar mark, albeit a decoration that will fade eventually.*

BB watches her reflection turn around and shows her how the lower tan line strikes across her butt crack. Cheek-to-cheek posterior rugage. Babs twitches, interrupts herself, and lifts her waistline up to its rightful horizontal position as she rotates around to face Mirror. Boss Babe tilts her head and gives herself a wry smile, watches her reflection move together with her as she lifts her arms up and slides the bra straps up over her shoulders. *At least Mirror conforms to reality.* BB packs her babambas away and blows her visage a kiss.

§ Babs Briefs Seven Cosmos: Roommate Games & Garments

Babs turns away from the Mirror and faces the row of six bunks on the opposite wall. No windows here in the Bunkroom. No windows up here at all.

Babs knows, *I must focus on the now and the future, even if in the days ahead Gamers sleuth the morgue and drudge up further humiliations from my Pledge days.*

"Perverts!"

Bikini Babe knows from last Term that the Bunkroom Mirror can also become one giant Screen or many smaller ones. And that it possesses stimulating touch properties. *Except now it is I who programs the Screens inside the Cosmos House,* BB confirms to herself. *So I have some control over my past, and as long as I remain diligent about my movements and posture my Bikini I will keep my babambas and bush and bumpkins contained.*

In her mind Boss Babe conjures up her seven Pledge side-by-side in front of their bunks. She commands, "Lineup, stand spread surrender position!" And they obey, fingers intertwined behind necks, legs in a wide stance, chests forward, necks high, armpits exposed, mouths ovaled, and eyes looking forward at themselves in the Mirror. BB fills her lungs with air, and prepares to practice an orientation lecture. She retreats, lets the air out of her lungs, considers her Caste and role, and inventories her virtual Lineups: Two newbies, two ex-Strippers, two former Cosmos. And the potential of one ex-Whore/Porn Star.

"You are my Seven Cosmos Pledge Lineup," Boss Babe pans her eyes across this a chorus line holding a uniform static surrender position. "I have arrived with two pieces, my bra and nombril Bikini, and I am on an uptick. Momentum is important in the Game, and I should have enough momentum to retain my Monitor Caste—if not advance costume and Caste and become a MomCap next Term."

Babs considers the practicality of this bold assertion. The Lineup of Pledge can hold surrender position while BB indulges in introspection. *Yes, I did enroll in the School willingly. And yes, I got high marks last Term.*

Babs experiences claustrophobia for a moment. Still, this Term does engender her first promotion. *It is only by a combination of skill and luck that I'm a Monitor this Term.* Babs quietly assesses. *I need to remember that and not over-estimate my good Karma over the vagrancies of Fate. I thought once I promoted I would know more, but that's not turning out to be the case.* Babs twitches a nostril. *Promotion now forces me to assume more responsibility... and face new trials.*

Comes with the territory when one takes charge of Cosmos.

Babs frets what the Lineup might be wearing—or baring. *All navelage, for sure. And lots of cleavage, bellage, leggage, rugage, buttage, and -age in general. Perhaps even topless. Raw tits.*

Babs steadies herself, focuses on her imaginary Lineup, and accepts that two Pledge who present raw tits disturbs her. BB expands her ribcage with air and orders, "Cross your arms over your breasts." And they obey. Babs squares her shoulders. *I know there are three ways to form handbras, and two ways to cross your arms.*

Babs thumbs her waistline and ensures her seam is trim. She considers. *Most of my Pledge have more Terms in the Game than I do. And that could be dangerous. That is dangerous.*

BB furrows her brow at this thought; only the two invisible newbies arrive inexperienced, and so Babs focuses her remarks toward them, saying, "Think of yourselves in a Garment race. It doesn't matter what Garments you arrive in. The clothes you end up with need not be the same, let alone equal in number. However, your costume count determines the outcome of the Game, your Fate." BB speaks as clearly as she knows how. "At the end of this Term, any Cosmos with two or more pieces shall Opt Monitor next Term, and Cosmos with one or no pieces shall Opt Strip next Term. That's the Fate of eight Cosmos and twelve Garments. Fate is very simple."

Except that Fate's not simple at all.

Babs turns her head to the side and looks back toward the hallway, her own Bedroom, and the stairs leading down to the Kitchen. She walks her mind downstairs and outside to review Penny and Coco's naked defeat in the Mudpit, then inside to remind herself about their explicit Dining Room baseboard pictures. Boss Babe returns her eyes to her Seven Cosmos Lineup standing spread arms-crossed position. She hikes her bra, fingers her underwire, and stiffens her frame.

"You will all admire the Baseboard Strippers downstairs spreading their pink," she declares. "I had to defeat them in order to be the Monitor of the Cosmos House."

Babs casts her eyes obliquely. *Maybe Janet helped me crush Penny and Coco last Term when we were all Pledge, but now I have to crush Pledge all by myself. Except maybe I don't really have to do that!*

Babs smiles and gains confidence. "Will I determine which of you Pledge Opt in what direction?" BB addresses this question to her imaginary Lineup holding its position.

Boss Babe answers, "Put it this way. On one hand, all Pledge are equal." BB lets them wait for the next beat. "But some of you are trending one way or another; some of you are acquiring Garments as you arrive, and some are shedding your clothes. There is momentum afoot, and it affects your coverage in the future, even if you keep the same number of Garments."

Boss Babe answers her question about her own limits of power. "I contribute to your Fate," she confesses out loud to her virtual Lineup, "but I don't have to determine which of you Opt Monitor or Opt Strip." Babs finds herself breathing faster but calms her nerves, "So I don't have to pick winners and losers. Because you're the ones who are going to tango with each other to determine your own outcomes!"

BB pauses and claps her hands, leans forward and laughs. "So I don't need to interfere. All I have to do is referee!" She claps again. BB likes the way the room echoes. "I can do that! I will do what is expedient for me. Because you're the ones who are gonna play the Games. Starting right off with Roommate Games.

"You know," BB snides, "sometimes Roommates contest against each other in order to determine who shall Opt Up or Down, and thus be Roommates Apart; sometimes Roommates form alliances and struggle against other pairs of Roommates, and in these struggles the Roommates rise or fall Roommates Together."

Babs falters, casts her eyes to the floor. *Do I have it in me to do this? And not make idle threats?* BB knows the answer. She draws in a chest full of air and rises to her full height to address truth to her standing spread cross-breasted Lineup. Truth to Seven Cosmos Pledge.

"You will play Games with each other whether you want to or not, and you will play to win and lose costumes. I will allow you to practice and compete, make sure you play fair, and when the Clock strikes Midnight at the end of this Term, you Cosmos shall prograde or retrograde," Boss Babe declares, and adds cheerfully, "Just like astronomy. Or physics. Or whatever."

Boss Babe blinks twice and discharges her virtual Lineup. She spins around, squares herself to Mirror, pulls her legs together, and girds her Black Bikini. She strides back to her Bedroom and has no sooner entered when the Front Door Cam trips an alert and forces its image to the top of the Desktop. The doorbell rings.

And BB carefully bites her upper lip.

Pledge Tiffany & Robyn & Steph Arrive

4 Tiffany Transparent: Arrives at Cosmos House (D01 PM)

§ Babs Greets Tiffany: Porn Star Arrives at the Front Door

Evening of the First Day has arrived when Babs answers the Front Door and evaluates a curvy feline that brushes long red hair back in one of those poses that form deep crevices in her armpits. A flirtatious self-confident woman looks Babs in the eye and introduces herself, "Hi! I'm Tiffany!"

Babs' heart skips a beat, and she silently considers what presents itself on the boards of the Porch. Boss Babe instinctively blocks the door with her body, and Tiffany takes a step back. Milk-white skin, darting blue eyes, a flat chest, deep curvy belly, small tush, and tapered legs.

BB breaths deeply, steadies herself. "Hello to you. You are my first Pledge to arrive!" *And you are smaller than I am.*

Yes. Tiffany stands a bit shorter than Babs (5' 10"), weighs less (105 pounds), and last taped in narrower (32A-23-33).

Tiffany straightens. "Ma'am I don't know why I'm here. I'm as surprised as you must be. I Whored last Term so somehow I'm a Double Opt Up."

Babs allows herself to take her time as she stands her ground. But it's hard, because BB has no choice but to accept what she sees, and she nods her head more casually now as she welcomes, "Tiffany, your Calendar precedes you."

"I am a Porn Star!" Tiffany dances, and the door Cam hovers midway down the jam and feeds her framed image to the Prefecture. Mucho bellage. Cameltoe. Translucent, almost see-through sleeveless croptop.

Babs blinks. BB squares herself in the doorframe, gathers her wits, and safely observes, "You're on the Manifest with two pieces."

"Oooh, you noticed!" Tiffany swivels and sweeps a wrist down her torso. "Sleeveless silk croptop and low-rise stretch slacks. Massive bellage. Hairage and rugage. Navelage too."

"Obviously," BB says dryly. "24x7."

Tiffany feels Babs study her shirt. "Ma'am..." Tiffany senses BB's unease and tries to calm her. "Ma'am, I guess we both have two Garments, but I am your Pledge, Ma'am, and I am far more indecent than you are. My croptop stays true to my name. The silk really is translucent, and it reveals my areolage and special titty tip details. My Eraser Heads."

Yes, Babs tries to look at headlights molded in the gossamer of the shirt and not look right through Tiffany's translucent silk at two pert cylinders of erected nipple tissue. Yes, Eraser Heads.

Tiffany tampers, "I might have my Eraser Heads in see-through, but your bling—you've *crescents d'areolage*—are terrific!"

And Babs blushes.

Tiffany turns and stretches her stomach up so the Cam's view is optimized. "My slacks hang so low that my red pussy hair erupts above the waistline. My turf, my thatch, my thicket, and whatever else my fans call it. Gamers love that fire comes up from my twat!"

Babs tries not to wrinkle her nose at Tiffany's overdone costume and makeup.

Tiffany preens in response to Babs' condescending stare. "I'm always hairage!" she declares. She pivots around on bare feet, presents an equally vulgar backside, and preaches posterior assets: "And I'm always showing my tail trough."

"You posterior rugage," Babs utters dryly.

Tiffany boasts, "Ma'am, I bet you don't get to hairage and crack 24x7!"

Babs recalls the top Dining Room Picture and its alleged mate at the Corvette House. She blushes vividly. *Steady! Concentrate on what Tiffany's rugage looks like when Tiffany sits down. Better yet, with Tiffany down on her hands and knees.* The blush recedes.

Tiffany rushes assurance, "Ma'am, I have no secrets. I'm transparent. Some of my Gamer fans even know my blood type."

Babs takes a deep consideration and discounts her first assumption. *Perhaps I not will be taking the first shirt that arrives after all.*

BB offers a dry fact. "The Manifest says you are my Roommate this Term."

Tiffany glances to make sure she retains the Cam's interest, and advances to Boss Babe. "Ma'am, I will sleep whatever you want, look like a Whore, give you all my clothes, climax on cue, and be a Stripper next Term."

And once again Tiffany catches Babs staring at her very erect nipples. Babs wonders, *Do your Eraser Heads ever retract?*

§ Tiffany Offers Babs: To Go Dance for a Longsleeve Shirt

Tiffany lifts her arms up, pushes her hips down, and swivels her belly while she flashes BB her armpits. Tiffany cocks her head a bit and proffers, "Ma'am, my Pimp from last Term said that if I wanted to dance a private show for the Peacocks that they would give me a longsleeve croptop shirt. With buttons down the front." Tiffany gestures her hands down.

BB scowls at this curveball, however enticing.

"Ma'am," Tiffany advances, "My Pimp from Flesh Ranch said you'd have to authorize a live Cam." Tiffany lifts up on bare tiptoes, appreciating Babs' hesitancy. She formalizes, "You know, to make sure I don't break any Rules. After all, I'm a Pledge now, and we're not allowed to suck-fuck-anal. No matter how frustrating that will be."

Boss Babe considers the opportunity, and watches the Cam turn toward her and retreat ever so slightly. Awaiting her answer.

Babs picks words carefully. "Very well, Pledge. I authorize you go to the Peacock House and change into a longsleeve shirt." BB also makes a buttoning gesture. "With buttons down the front." Babs then turns to the hovering Front Door Cam that documents the proceedings. "And I authorize a live Cam to record my Pledge's pleadings," Babs reassures Tiffany. *Maybe a different fabric rubbing against your nipples won't make them stand up so much.*

"Ma'am, I hope you watch Ma'am." Tiffany rolls a fingertip into her exposed navel, a vertical slit set inside a harder, firmer rim, a question mark with a dot at the bottom. Fine body hair graces the fine skin of a vast tract of fine tummy. Tiffany flitters, "Navelage but no piercing, Ma'am." She starts to turn.

BB admonishes, "When you return, present yourself outside the Back Door, ring the Bell, and wait. I'm sure we'll have plenty to talk about."

Tiffany rises up onto her tiptoes. "Ma'am, thank you, Ma'am," and departs with swinging grace down the front stairs. Tiffany knows that the School and Village are filled with voyeurs, if not schemers and rapists. But her biggest danger is herself. And succumbing to temptations.

Tiffany moves quickly down the tree-lined streets. She knows the way to the Peacock House. *Gamers are going to test me and drive me insane with desire.*

§ Tiffany: Her Name and Exposures

Tiffany casts her eyes about as she moves on bare feet. She lifts her chin so that any unseen paparazzi may feast on her gliding body, bare belly, and not indiscrete exposures.

Tiffany isn't her original name; it had been given to her two turns ago when she had been stripping at the Nugget. Back then she still had a last name as well. But then when she opted to Whore her last name was another thing that had been taken away from her, and so the Pledge promoting to the Cosmos still remains Tiffany.

Had she been demoted to Slavesex, Tiffany feared she would have been name-stripped and numbered, if only because Slavesex are owned and possessed completely. Tiffany appreciates that she has sidestepped that potential outcome, yet she remains befuddled to find herself double-jumped to the Cosmos. *All I ever asked for was to Opt from Whore to Stripper this turn. Maybe Strippers can't fuck, but at least they can dance naked and play with themselves. But here? I Double Opt Up and get put into the chaste Cosmos House.*

Tiffany thinks while she walks. *Maybe Pledge aren't allow to have sex, but should a Whore on an up-tick—a Back Door Pledge—get her last name back?*

Tiffany knows her answer. *I can live without it; my last name wasn't even my real last name to begin with. Besides, I like my new self. Tiffany.* Tiffany knows her name "comes from old English and refers to a very thin silk or gauze." Tiffany. Transparent.

People look at her on the street. Double take. Take pictures.

§ Tiffany & William: Porn Star Changes & Pops Peacocks

Tiffany knocks on the Peacock House front door and William, the well-statured House Monitor, opens it. William wears a black t-shirt and pants, trimmed brunette hair. He gestures, and Tiffany follows him inside into a Parlor. A bare-chested, blond and blue-eyed younger man wearing only a jockstrap joins him in the center of the room and conspicuously cams her. Six naked Peacocks, lined up along one side of the Peacock House Parlor, masturbate, all stroking in unison. Tiffany runs a very quick eye down this Lineup. Six erections, some lube swinging down. Some teeth gritting.

"So, why are you here?" William demands.

Tiffany takes a gulp, lowers her chin, and tries to take charge of these admirers. "Hello Peacocks! I am Tiffany Porn Star! Except I'm a Cosmos Pledge this Term. Begging to Strip next Term and then begging to Whore. Until then, you'll just have to look at my tits through this silk gauze."

"And your thatch showing above your twat," the blond Cameraman blurts out.

Tiffany spins and presents rugage in his face. "And my tail trough showing out. What's you name, bare-chested jockstrap Cam boy?" Tiffany extends a hand toward the Cam. "Oh, and your chest is so smooth."

William interrupts the performance. "I'm William, the Monitor of the Peacocks, and this 'jockstrap Cam boy,' as you call my Roommate, we call Rodney."

"Cute." Tiffany sashays. "Pimp Cowboy said if I stopped by you'd let me trade for a longsleeve shirt."

"Seems like you'd have to take off the one you got first," William advises tenuously.

Rodney advances, "On Cam, of course."

Tiffany provides fluidly and talks while she slithers into motion. She runs her fingers around the elastic waistline of her slacks and fluffs her thinnish red hairage upward with the back of her hand, "Can't stop the fire erupting," Tiffany laughs, tossing her red head toward the Lineup. "And it's all natural... all the way down to my twat."

Rodney looks at Tiffany's red hairage spouting above her slacks, looks at her cameltoe, and announces, "You're here to blow me."

Tiffany's body arches backward with the language of rejecting pond scum. "Oooh, sexy, pretty boy. You know you're unworthy of anything like that."

William provides guidance. "This tatterdemalion is here to change shirts... and shake some bare tits in between."

Tiffany advances on prey. She draws her hands upward upon the deep swath of her bare belly. She brags, "I'm belly-up and belly-down. These low-riders float seven inches below my navel, and my shirt rides seven-up!" Tiffany draws her fingers upward across her belly skin until they collide with the hem around the bottom of her translucent croptop. "Oh," she pretends as she grips the crop line across her lower ribs, many inches above her navel. She looks down, then raises her eyes up to the Cam and says, "There is no way this shirt can settle down and cover my birth scar." And draws the shirt upward and over her head.

She smiles to herself.

Tiffany shimmies and extends the shirt out an arms' length away from her body, out on the end of a fingertip. She says, "Hello there from Tiffany, topless Porn Star. Tiny tits and Eraser Heads in full open air."

The masturbating Lineup gasps for air.

Tiffany sways and points to Rodney's jockstrap. "Oh, and look at you! Tiffany topless Porn Star brings you a hard-on!"

There is laugher behind Rodney's back from the Lineup of naked Peacocks. Tiffany suppresses a laugh and covers her mouth. "And look at you!" Tiffany exudes. She steps toward them and gathers both hands to her chest. "You're dangling lube from your swollen erections!"

William interrupts and extends an arm for Tiffany's shirt. "I take that," he says.

Tiffany hands over her silk shirt. She speaks not. *I don't need to. I'll just let them look at me topless.* Eyes run over her body, and Tiffany twists her head so that her long red hair spills down and almost covers her topless titties. Tiffany pirouettes and allows all the Peacocks, inviting, "Take a look at how my tail trough accelerates as it narrows and dives down into my pants." She stretches at the Cam held by jockstrap-swelling Peacock Rodney, and even more red hair erupts above her low-rise waistline.

But then she begs to William, "If you give me my new shirt, I'll show off the rest of my thatch." She crouches down to address the six naked and masturbating Peacock Pledge. "Bet you'd all like to see my tenement house and my tailpipe!"

Rodney interrupts, "I think we'd all like to watch you suck cock."

"Oooh, what a magnificent suggestion," Tiffany exclaims, rubbing both top turrets in the palms of her hands.

William closes one eye. "You're the wannbe Porn Star. Go ahead: pop my Lineup." Tiffany sees that he holds her new shirt in his hand. Longsleeves and buttons.

Tiffany spins on her toes and shawabbles topless down the Lineup of Peacocks. "Oooh, a challenge, and an opportunity for new fans!"

The stroking Peacocks' eyes all graze on her skin and movement. And lines.

Tiffany coos, "I'm a Cosmos Pledge. Button bare all the time. Navelage 24x7. Now, who gets the first prize?"

A first responder pops. The semen almost splatters Tiffany's feet.

"Good Peacock!" Tiffany praises. She advances. "*Everybody* sees my hairage and rugage 24x7! I'm *always* exposed."

A second responder pops. A heavier load.

Tiffany states a question: "But just because you can see my hairage overtop my slacks doesn't mean you can tell if my twat is shaven or not."

Imagination works wonders. A third Peacock pops. This one is oversize, bent, and uncut.

Tiffany spins and walks away from the masturbating Lineup. "My stretch slacks have a seam up the center, and they are so tight on my tush that each butt moves independently when I walk!"

Tiffany turns around and watches a forth Peacock affirm. "Big cock ring, little cock," Tiffany insults.

Tiffany eyes the two remaining masturbating erections. She arches her pelvis up and talks directly to the pulsating dicks in a faux-haunting voice. "The stretch fabric grips my crotch so tightly that the seam parts my sex lips. Has Monitor William taught you to recognize cameltoe?"

One more Peacock, this one matted in body hair, ejaculates. This one cascades across Tiffany's bare foot.

Tiffany adjusts her stance wide in front of the holdout. She touches her fingertips to her waistband, tugs it, and snuggles the crease in the fabric up even deeper into her parted lips. Tiffany permits, 'I'm not allowed to have sex anymore, but when I get excited I stain this cameltoe with tasty tapioca." Tiffany gives a beat. "Now, you pop for me. Because I need to collect my new shirt."

And the last Peacock pops. Shaven genitals.

Tiffany bows to a startled William and an open-mouthed Rodney. They did not anticipate a "Porn Star."

William looks at Tiffany's new shirt, which he holds in his hand, then looks at the red hairage spouting above her slacks and bluntly inquires, "Are you going to blow me?"

Tiffany's body clicks into motion again. "Oooh, sexy, pretty boy. You know I'd love to *charge* you to fuck me, but this Porn Star has been furloughed this Term! So you're just gonna have to jerk off to my pictures and sex vids. Vote for me for Stripper next Term, and in the Term after that, I'll come to wherever you are and blow everybody!"

And with this Tiffany reaches out and takes her new long-sleeve croptop from William's hand.

It is a croptop made out of vinyl, clear vinyl in fact, and she glides first one arm then the other into the long sleeves, buttons up, and shakes her tits toward Rodney's hard-on. "Before: translucent silk gauze. Now my Eraser Heads rub totally transparent clear vinyl. This is going to keep me *very* aroused." She casts a broader look and bows to the Lineup. "Thank you, Peacocks!" She takes a step backward, closer to the door.

But Rodney isn't quite ready to let go. "Maybe you should clean up after yourself."

Tiffany raises eyes, and William gestures to six paintings of cum on the floor. "Maybe tittering a see-through shirt and butt-cracking too-low tight pants doesn't quite qualify a you as a Porn Star."

Tiffany raises her chin. "Monitor William, if you please. I've done group sex in front of documentary Cam crews at music festivals, worked in token joints, done gangbang, snowballing, bukkake, gokkun. I've made Gamers cum so hard that they empty their piss in my face! I'm hot money."

Tiffany turns to Pledge Rodney. "You just cammed me topless talkin' your Peacocks to pop. But if you want a Lollydor, I've heard that Stripper Lee got promoted to Pledge this Term at the Corvette House. Beg them to send Pledge Lee over. Lee Lollydor. She's the lick-up specialist." Tiffany twists her neck ever so slightly. "Or do it yourself."

Mission accomplished. "Guess I'll be goin' now." Tiffany backs toward the door.

Rodney wags inside his jockstrap and unleashes a nasty, "Go tell the Boss Bitch to cam you peeing all over yourself. Go pee in your own mouth. You can still be Porn Star."

Such a statement might unnerve some Cosmos, but Tiffany has the self-confidence to parley, "I'll beg Babs to Pledge naked and cum be a Stripper next Term. And I'll tell her you made a big mess in your jockstrap." And she's gone. William looks, and yes, a pleased yet embarrassed Rodney has provided pop seven.

Rodney shrugs and queries his Monitor William, "So, do you think Tiffany still twists?"

And William purses his lips. "Let me say to you: she's a Cosmos to watch. Whether or not she's still a Porn Star."

§ Babs & Janet: Talk about Tiffany Porn Star & Pledge

Babs returns to the Kitchen to discover Janet looking at the Tiffany Porn Star Calendar. "I came back to see who all's on your Manifest this Term," Janet advances.

"Well, my first Pledge arrived." BB gestures to the Kitchen Calendar. "And that's her!"

Janet raises her eyebrows. "Wow, Tiffany Porn Star. What's she doing here?"

Babs takes in a deep breath and silently exhales. "She says she's a Double-Opt Up Whore. Ex-Whore. She still looks like a Whore. She's going to crimp my authority."

Janet scratches her bare jaxy. "Don't overreact. Tiffany was a Whore last Term. And a Double-Opt Up is not supposed to happen." Janet casts her eyes about. "Where is she?"

Babs sits at the Kitchen table and rests her chin in one hand. "I sent her over to the Peacocks to get a shirt change. Sleeveless translucent silk for something more respectable: long sleeves, buttons down the front."

"Two Garments," Janet twinkles. "Sounds like something you can change into and cover your crescents d'areolage. You are the Monitor Boss after all."

"You know her?" BB guesses.

Janet turns a chair around so she can squeeze her jugs into the back of the chair and flush her jipijapa between spread legs. She carefully extracts two heavy sex lips, each with three rings, and lays them to each side of the string that advances from the bottom of the Spiderweb toward her jaxy crack. "Double triplets, one piece," Janet says.

Babs presses, "Com'on. You danced the Nugget. Two Terms ago. I bet you knew her before we became Cosmos Pledge."

"Yeah, okay," Janet bemuses. "She was my Roommate when I Stripped the Nugget."

"You never told me about her!" BB accuses her former Roommate. *And you're my friend?*

"You never asked," Janet retorts, "and why would you? Tiffany and I were Stripper Roommates two Terms ago; I Opted Up to Pledge, and Tiffany Opted to Whore. It never mattered before. It doesn't matter now. What *does* matter is that you need to find out what this former cum receptacle did to deserve two Garments and a Double Opt-Up."

Babs wrinkles her nose. "I don't get her. And the way she's dressed—with her tamtart-face and silky top and vulgar slacks—why she's *still dressed* like a Whore. She shows off in public like this! She *wants* this public persona! Hello, paparazzi!"

"Once a Porn Star, always a Porn Star," Janet recites an old Gamer Saying, then advances complications: "Don't be surprised if Tiffany already knows any incoming Pledge promoting from Stripper this Term."

Babs frowns a question.

Janet advances, "It's because Whores frequently Feature Dance at the Nugget...." Janet tucks a cheek into her neck and smiles. "During their visits they can turn tricks in the Champagne Room. And act like Porn Stars in the Inner Sanctuary."

Janet smiles and centers her nipples in the Spiderweb halter. "Dancing and turning tricks are two different Castes," she clarifies. "We had a bunch of Feature Dancers pass through when I Stripped, and they all sucked dick in the Champagne Room. Ate pussy too. And of course they all fucked. But work Rules forbid Strippers to cross this line. Strippers dance 8x5; Whores trick 12x7."

"Tiffany will freak out any newbies," Babs frets.

"Tiffany Porn Star will freak out any promoting Strippers even more," Janet raises. "They won't know what to make of her turning up in your Cosmos House. It's very out-of-School."

"Yeah, okay, so Tiffany is going to ferment unease in my Pledge. If they peel away her history and discover her infamy, that is," Babs confesses. "Unease with me too. This Porn Star and former Whore is gonna mind-fuck all of us!"

Janet pauses to make sure she is correct in her assessment. "Tiffany can dance as well as any Stripper can. She knows all the steps, six ways to pull pink, and how to make her naked twat squeak the pole. And she also knows all the tricks!"

BB understands. "She doesn't need to intimidate to intimidate."

"So who decided this ex-Whore should go from being naked with dicks in her holes to wearing two pieces of clothes at *my* Cosmos House?" BB demands.

Janet hems and haws. "Well, not you or me. We didn't decide who would be a Cosmos this Term. Get real! We were both Pledge last Term. We were in no position to make any decisions."

Babs gives pause. "It's one thing Tiffany 'bin ho,' but she's also *my* Roommate. Why is that? Who assigned her to occupy that little cubicle underneath *my* bunk?"

Janet raises her hands.

BB continues, "Maybe she's got power alliances, a sponsor, some latent factor driving her advancement."

Janet understands. "Maybe you worry more than you need to, because maybe she really does crave being a Porn Star. She's hip to the Game, she's already 'tainted' by porn, and I bet all she wants to do is Opt Down and Strip. The last thing Tiffany wants is an Opt Up next Term. I know her. Stripping gets her halfway back to Whoring out at Flesh Ranch."

Babs seems unconvinced. "I can't believe anybody would want that. Maybe Gamers want to mix it up a bit and see how the Cosmos chill."

Janet nods. "Maybe." Janet works a finger in through her Spiderweb and wiggles a jaboo. She laughs, "Or maybe Gamers just want to drive Tiffany—and her fans—crazy with desire."

Babs seeks assurance: "So maybe Tiffany won't challenge me for dominance after all?"

Janet circumspects, "Not unless you want to be a bigger Porn Star!"

They laugh together at this ridiculous idea.

Janet raps, "You have to remember: you're the Monitor now. The Boss Babe!" Janet assures Babs, "And the hardest thing for Tiffany to do is achieve the will to hold back. When we were Strippers she was kept wet all the time and had to climax at least once a day."

"In front of the Crowd?" Babs wonders cautiously.

"Right on Stage at the Nugget!" Janet brags. "Although occasionally during a lapdance. Except Tiffany always wanted more than getting her twat felt up. Her wickedness is that you can't threaten her with Stripping or Whoring; Tiffany just loves to strip naked and fuck for real. She loves to perform, and she's proud of her performances."

Babs begrudges, "Right. She's already offered to find her suck and fuck clips, play them on the House Screens, and then strip naked, pull pink, make wet, and cum on cue for the House Cams."

Janet waves her arm toward the Kitchen Calendar. "Feast your eyes on Tiffany's titties and twat, every month, every hole cocked. Unmentionables in your face! Always."

"Every Cosmos' face." Boss Babe sees more to the Game. "My Pledge will sense she can out-twist them if need be. And that will certainly intimidate them, even though they should know that sex is forbidden for Pledge."

Janet appraises, "Right, sex is not something any other Cosmos will want to challenge Tiffany on. Even you are leery of her; that's because she possesses the power of knowledge. She doesn't need force or encouragement to fuck. Her discipline requires you maximize, yet contain, her frustration."

"That doesn't sound easy," BB hedges.

Janet plays with her chin with the fingers of one hand. "Before today she's been able to endlessly play with herself and have sex. I guess it's now up to you if she still plays with herself, but the very fact that she's a

Cosmos means sex is a no-no. Hopefully she won't try to sneak sex, no matter how horny she gets. Because if she tries and gets caught, it could be really bad for you, too."

Babs seems to not hear and wrings her hands. "Maybe you'll tell me why her nipples are always erect?"

"Ah, the Eraser Heads." Janet rolls her own protruding nipples in her fingertips. "She got them when she begged Stripper and was my Roommate at the Nugget, two Terms ago. I do know they are in lieu of a piercing, but I don't know how they work. Aroused from rubbing up against her shirt all the time? Super sensitivity caused by wireless implants or pharmaceuticals? I do know they are tattooed with ultraviolet ink, so they glow when she dances in blacklight."

Babs bemuses in disbelief, "Glow in blacklight? Maybe Tiffany likes her Eraser Heads, but they will terrify everyone else."

"Makes her even more powerful," Janet hearties. Then hurries, "Listen. You must be firm and stay in charge. She isn't allowed to have sex. Period. You must help her channel her Kundalini."

Boss Babe advances, "I'll make her use the Bathroom with all the other Pledge!"

"Right on!" Janet teases. "No sharing your private bathroom! I bet she begs you to put her on the Pee-Cam! I beg she claims she's already qualified."

"Stop it!" Babs decries and raises her right hand.

"Careful," Janet warns, "because she will love you for letting her!"

Babs relents, and they both laugh.

They hear the Bell ring. The clapper resonates through the neighborhood, advertising to all that a Cosmos begs admission. Janet tilts shoulders to Babs, and the two Monitors and former Roommates tiptoe barefoot into the Dining Room. They look out adjacent windows into the Backyard and observe Pledge Tiffany standing next to the Bell. Tiffany now wears a transparent long-sleeve front-button croptop. And slacks erupting hairage.

"That's her!" Janet affirms. "And it looks like she brought you back long sleeves and buttons."

And BB clenches her eyes shut for a moment.

§ Babs & Janet: Penny & Coco Threats & Acquisitions

BB opens her eyes and steps back from the windows. She can still see the Backyard outside: the Garage and alley, the Post Henge, the Mudpit. She hesistates, "You know Janet, I feel bad about what I did in the Mudpit."

Janet shimmies. "Hey, the Mudpit holds legacy for both of us." She gestures toward the Baseboard Strippers. "We stripped them naked and dispatched them to the Nugget!"

BB hedges, "Whatever happened in the Mudpit better stay in the Mudpit."

"Maybe you don't like the process, but you're fine with the outcome," Janet teases a friend.

Babs sighs, "Monitoring is going to be a real challenge. Except that the alternative, what happened to Penny and Coco, is even more of a burden."

Janet spins on a heel—barefoot—and points toes at the two bottom brunettes on the Dining Room wall. "Baseboard Strippers. Penny Prancer and Coco Cachachas."

"You're making that up," Babs laughs. "But not the Strippers part. That's real." Babs saddens. "They're not just losing the privilege of wearing clothes; they're losing any and all privacy of their own bodies… and bodily functions!"

Janet throws her shoulders back and waggles hands in the air. "Hello, Prefecture!" Janet speaks to both bare spread and naked Baseboard Strippers. "May your contributions to sex media grow and prosper, and may your cream and cum attract Gamer fans."

Babs feels even worse for the defeated Penny and Coco and details more of their woes: "Opt Downs to Strippers, earn one tattoo and one piercing each; that's not going to make them very happy."

Janet breezes, "In a Game where pairs count as one piece this means *both* of them can get *both* of their nipples pierced!"

Babs feels a cringe coming on.

And Janet caps, "And may their tattoos be big, bold, and conspicuous!"

"And they shall blame us for doing this to them," Babs tightens.

"Blame us?" Janet exclaims. "We're all playing the Game. We're not here to lose after all. Except some Gamers can't get to the bottom fast enough."

Babs feels reluctant to study the Pictures for early traces of ink or steel, and she trails Janet through the Living Room almost to the Front Door when a lost thought bolts through her mind. "Tiffany! She's still standing by the Bell outside the Back Door! Waiting."

Janet waves a dismissive hand. "Oh, she'll wait for you. Wait for us, as if that should make a difference."

"No," BB hurries, then shakes her shoulders. "Yes. Right. She can stand there indefinitely. Hours."

And they almost laugh together.

§ Janet Probes Babs: Steph on the Manifest? Also Robyn!

Janet opens the Front Door partway before she parlays, "By the way…" Janet touches Babs on her bare shoulder. "You got Steph on your Manifest?"

"One and the same," BB affirms, "and a Robyn too."

Janet blinks. Pushes her lips out. "Okay. I understand how Steph Pledges the House, but Robyn? Pledge aren't allowed to Repeat Terms, to Hover. You know that. Us Monitors can Hover, but for Pledge it's either an Up or a Down."

"So maybe she's a different Robyn," Babs shrugs. "Or maybe she really does have Charm."

"It's something else not supposed to happen," Janet declares. She considers, "Maybe if it really is them you can find a way for them to Mudwrestle!"

They both laugh. Janet slips out toward the Front Door. And BB ponders, *If Janet knows Tiffany, then why did she elect to not greet her?*

She turns, strides back though the Living and Dining Room, ignoring the Pictures on the wall, and returns to the Kitchen. Shoulders straight, babambas uplifted, belly narrowed. Crescents; no blush. Boss Babe scans the Kitchen perimeter, frowns at the Calendar, yet acquires the confidence of patience. *There is no rush. The time belongs to me first. I set the pace, not a waiting Pledge. Tiffany can wait until I am ready to deal with her. And not the other way around.*

Pledge Tiffany waits. *No problem.*

§ Tiffany: Teases the Cosmos House Back Door Cam

Tiffany returns from her shirt-changing errand via the back alley; she detours around the near impenetrable concrete walkway between the Garage and the prickly hedge, crosses the Backyard, muddies her bare feet by accidentally walking through the earthen Mudpit, and comes to rest by the Bell near the Landing and Back Door. She gives the clapper a sharp pull, and the intensity of the sound makes her ears ring.

She puts her hands over her ears as the Back Door Cam buzzes off its perch to surveil her. She catches its eye and recites to it, "Hello, Gamers. I'm Tiffany Porn Star! Reporting to the Cosmos House!" Tiffany bats her eyes. "I've done everything explicit, all holes, all sexes!"

Tiffany breaks off eye contact, cases the Back Door, and ruminates about her current assignment. *Who decided I'm a Double Opt-Up and sent me to this House?*

Tiffany studies the Backyard. Most certainly Tiffany had been a Pledge her first Term in the Game, but it had not been at the Cosmos

House. She had earned a slot at the Nugget and Stripped her second Term, and then Whored all last Term. *Now my fourth Term begins.* Tiffany shuffles her bare feet. *Here at this House. In a Game all about tradeoffs. I might look like a Whore but I am not one anymore; I am a Cosmos Pledge with two Garments. I'm not supposed to put out, although I sure do know how to!*

Tiffany runs her palms over her belly while she stands and waits outside. Once again she seeks out the Cam. She sways in place, waves her hands down her body, and talks to Gamers and fans. "Do you like what you see? I'm a bellage temptress. Go ahead. Look at my tits through transparent see-through. I can't stop you. I don't care. I like it when you look."

The Back Door Cam hovers downward, and as Tiffany wiggles her belly even more hairage flashes in and out of her slacks. "Go ahead, cam my thatch," Tiffany taunts. "You know I can't hide it." She turns around to the Cam, pleased she stays ahead of its intentions. "Go ahead and cam my tail trough." Tiffany dances a long finger across her waistline, lingers at the exposed crack of her ass, and snaps the elastic waistband. Some Gamers melt.

She spins back, faces the Cam again, and tightens her slacks up into her partition. "Detail my cameltoe!" Tiffany commands Cam.

She steps back and positions more of her body into the frame; she waves a dismissive hand up and away from her body. "Eraser Heads in see-through; hairage, rugage, and button bare all the time. I am a Porn Star. And I have arrived at the Cosmos House!"

Once again Tiffany shakes off Cam contact. Even Tiffany is not completely sure why she is here. *Denying me sex seems like too easy an answer. And ringing the Bell and Navelage 24x7 seems like too easy commitments. At least I can still cream and climax. And show off for my fans.*

Tiffany crouches and locates the Cam. "This Cosmos Pledge starts the Term with two pieces, my croptop and slacks, which means that I hold a ticket to a Monitor slot next Term." Tiffany laughs and tosses her head back, yet retains eye contact. "But Gamers, you know I don't want to hold on to two pieces. You know I want to strip naked for you and show you my treasures." Tiffany looks deep into the eye and confesses, "You might have chastised my sex. But I am still Tiffany Porn Star. Please let me burn my clothes, collect the ash, and wear the ash on my body. Please let me Pledge naked and cum be a Stripper next Term."

Tiffany strikes a time out sign in front of the Cam. "That's enough for you," Tiffany patricians. "Why don't you stop hovering and go charge yourself up? Vote for me. And after I make Stripper next Term, trust me, I will beg to Whore. I am Tiffany Porn Star."

And thank goodness I'm not Slavesex!

§ Babs Greets Tiffany: Shirt Disappointment & Proclivities

The alcove between the Back Door and the Kitchen functions like an airlock, and Boss Babe halts Tiffany in this space to examine her and her shirt change.

Tiffany announces, "Ma'am, just as promised, long sleeves and front buttons. Still a croptop. And no more translucent silk. Totally transparent clear vinyl. Ma'am."

Boss Babe smolders but remains outwardly facile. *If indeed Tiffany Porn Star thinks that a trick has been pulled on me, I am not going to show it.*

Babs' silence and careful pace make Tiffany uneasy, and she feels Babs stare at her nipples. Eraser Heads. Tiffany's nips talk to Babs through the transparent clear vinyl shirt; there is now nothing to stop anyone from assaying how Tiffany's round carnation-colored areolas and nipples are constructed. Babs want to linger her eyes but doesn't allow herself.

Except BB cannot resist indulging. Tiffany's areolas are small, featureless, darker round circles no bigger than quarters, which contrast sharply with her pale skin. Carnation-colored nipples sprout upward in the center of this disc. They are half that diameter and form equally tall cylinders when erected. Like now.

Like always. "Eraser Heads 24x7," Tiffany offers. Tiffany shimmies her shirt and shares truth with Boss Babe. "Some people think it's because my titties are constantly aroused by rubbing against the fabric, but there's more to it. That's why if you let me go topless, they will still stay erect."

Babs discovers herself with her lips pursed together and her teeth biting her tongue inside her mouth, which Tiffany can't see.

Tiffany watches Babs' eyes tick and attempts to console her. "Hey, it's not like I'm telling you any secrets about me everybody doesn't already know. Okay, maybe some of my videos reside in private collections, but plenty of me lies out there... in the, the Prefecture!"

BB seeks to confirm truth: "You were a Whore last Term."

"You got it! I am a Porn Star!" Tiffany acknowledges. "I'm committed. Last Term I sexed for real, and whoring enabled me to become famous."

Tiffany rattles on, "Ma'am, you don't need to trade me for my clothes; you can take them. Please let me Pledge naked and cum be a Stripper next Term. I mean it. Just please let me strut my stuff, and I'll show off for the Cosmos House! Ma'am."

Babs seeks to confirm what Janet had suggested. "You *want* to Strip next Term!"

Tiffany does. "I'm still a Porn Star, of course, since all my pictures and videos are still out there. Everywhere! All of me." Tiffany beams.

"I see," Babs accepts reluctantly. "I guess you've got fans."

"Ma'am, I can devour a two-inch diameter, eight-inch long cock down my throat, up my tailpipe, or into my twat!" Tiffany declares. "I've done everything explicit, all holes, all sexes."

Boss Babe tucks an eyelid inward. "Except, Pledge, that Gamers have cut you off. Haven't they?"

"Cut me off?" Tiffany teeters; she knows the answer. "Ma'am, yes Ma'am. No sex. No BJs, no twatarooney, no tube tunneling, Ma'am."

Afterthought: "They could have let me Strip, and that would have cut me off also, but no, they sent me to here. Pledgeland. Double Opt Up."

BB affords herself modest enjoyment. "Hey, maybe there weren't any empty bunks at the Nugget, so you got bumped to Pledge Caste."

"Ma'am!" Tiffany emphasizes, "just please let me get pink, wet, and ready and cum be a Stripper next Term. I'll shave bare. I'll shave bald. I'll ride the Double Dong. I'll fuck a dildo, a buttplug, or take on both at once. Double Penetration. I'll do anything legal, private shows, naked in public, Cams anytime anywhere."

Babs raises her hand to silence this Pledge. "Maybe you need to slow down."

"Ma'am, once I get to the Nugget then I can beg to Whore again. And after I make Whore I can start making new sex vids. I've done everything explicit. All holes. All sexes. Maybe Pledge aren't allowed sex, but I am still a Porn Star!"

Boss Babe listens.

"Ma'am, I'll do anything to help you send me to the Nugget next Term. I'm hip to what's happening to me: Gamers are gonna get me crazy frustrated for cock!"

BB speaks. "Maybe they're turning a 'bin-ho' into a scarce commodity."

"Ma'am," Tiffany declares, "you go ahead and Hover or Opt MomCap. I'll sleep under your bed. I'll give you everything I've got, if you just let me Opt Strip next Term.

Babs sighs, "Thank you. I don't make deals. But your wish to sleep under my bed shall be granted."

§ Babs & Tiffany: Calendar Pride then Bedroom Dynamics

Babs expects Tiffany to register embarrassment upon seeing herself on her own Calendar. Wrong! Instead, vivacious Tiffany praises the product the moment her eyes set upon it when she enters the Kitchen.

"Ma'am, that's me with the cocks!" Tiffany brings her hands to her mouth. "Each month I do something different."

Babs opens her mouth, but not in time.

"I do girls, too. You'll find a month with me eating really sloppy taco while I'm getting fucked with a strapon. I am not just the Porn Star of the Month, Ma'am. I got my own Calendar for the whole year!"

Babs does not need to hear this. "Enough. Upstairs." Babs herds her up the steep, curving back stairs, rugage and Spandex tush in her face, and guides her into their Bedroom. "You're my Roommate this Term. Wasn't, isn't my decision. Maybe your seniority procures you this coveted Monitor's Roommate position, or maybe you've played the Game longer, come from a lower status, or a host of other reasons. You might share the room with me, but your portion of the space is that sleeping alcove underneath my bunk. I'd offer you a chair, except there is only one, and I'm about to sit on it. So that's about the only space in the room for you to occupy." Boss Babe shrugs, points with a knee, and orders, "You can crawl in right now."

Tiffany crawls in, rolls onto her side and elbow, and looks out; she is beneath Babs in Caste and position. "Ma'am," she teases, "you can dress me up like your French maid. I'll run errands for you. I'll shave your legs for you. I am a Porn Star. I'll tell you all about myself."

Babs sits at the desk and frowns. "You can put things in the open locker behind me. It's more than you need because you have nothing to put. You're equal to all the other Pledge, who will occupy the stacked bunks in the Bunkroom."

"Ma'am, thank you, Ma'am," Tiffany responds. "Perhaps if you permit me to go naked I might hang my shirt and slacks there." She breaks formality and chortles, "That will give me something to put."

Well, perhaps. Babs considers that rooming with Tiffany might provide her with benefits... but also liabilities. Indeed, multiple dynamics between the two Cosmos are bound to emerge: one is newer to the Game and rising, the other has more experience, and is rising even faster. Smart Gamers are keeping an eye on Tiffany, and not just gazing at her navel.

§ Tiffany: Begs to Strip Naked & Volunteers for the Pee-Cam

Babs finds herself disturbed by Tiffany's determination to be a Porn Star, and in the beginning it blinds her to the benefit of Tiffany's experience, her willingness to share information freely, and her outgoing soul and even big heart.

Babs has little practice with discipline, yet she still wants to ensure that the more experienced, yet lower Caste Tiffany, understands who is in charge.

Tiffany looks at the back wall, with its two lockers and unmarked door, and provides opportunity for correction. "So is that the door to our private bathroom?" she inquires.

Boss Babe corrects, "There is no 'our private bathroom.' Yes, that door opens into *my* private bath. Instead of sharing my private shower, with its basin and toilet, you may share the Bathroom at the end of the hall with all the other Pledge."

Tiffany questions Babs to make sure she heard correctly. "I am to share the Bathroom with all the other Pledges?"

And Boss Babe responds cheerfully, "All the other *Pledge,* singular and plural. Pledge aren't worth individual identity. But even more importantly, Pledge are not to question their Monitors. You should know that."

Tiffany realizes Babs is right and demonstrates proper form to her: "Ma'am, you are correct, Ma'am. Pledge are not to question their Monitors. Ma'am. Singular or plural."

But it is not over. Gamers observe that Tiffany now makes a second faux pas.

BB smiles. "Perhaps you've had it too easy sucking cocks for too long, and you've forgotten Pledge Rules. Your first offense was to ask a question. Your second offense is a failure to beg correction for your first offense."

Tiffany ameliorates the problem. "Ah, Ma'am. Ma'am, I'll volunteer to use the Bathroom while naked."

Tiffany watches BB contemplate this offer. She raises, "Every time, Ma'am." Tiffany offers, "Always. No exceptions. Ma'am."

Boss Babe considers. "You're quite a tatterdemalion. You're begging to get naked before you go into the Bathroom?" It is a fine point, but a significant detail.

"Naked entry," Tiffany affirms, "I can do that. I will strip naked and hang my clothes in my locker." Tiffany points with a gesture of her body. She is correct on this one. "And, may it please you to keep me naked all the time, I will leave my clothes in my locker all the time."

"I see," Babs frets. *I can't let Tiffany get too far out ahead of me.*

"Ma'am!" Tiffany blasts. "I long ago vowed to submit myself to prying eyes whatever the chance, no matter what my Caste. I am a Porn Star! My fans desire me and desire to frustrate me. They want to watch me get horny. You can cam me 24x7, as many Cams as you want. Multiple views. Front Door, Back Door, any Cams in the House you control."

"Perhaps you need to let the Cams follow you around," Boss Babe suggests sardonically.

"Ma'am especially." Tiffany digs a deeper trench. "Please let me light up the Cams whenever I go into the Bathroom. Please let me be a Pee-Cam Pledge. Your first! Please let Gamers watch me shower and wash naked, apply makeup, and use the toilet. Live, clips, replays. I'll always pee on cam. I'll Pee-Cam on the Back Landing; I'll Pee-Cam the Front Porch. No privacy for me."

Babs tries to gather her breath at this onslaught. *Slow the Game down, Boss Babe,* BB says to herself and slowly gathers reins in. "I suspect if you can handle making the Porn Calendar you can handle the Cosmos House Cams," Babs compliments.

Tiffany looks up from the floor as BB absorbs her lobbying efforts. Tiffany nudges, "Ma'am I'll pee in the Bathroom… or anywhere you say. Anytime you say. Inside, outside, in front of anybody."

Babs doesn't need to hear more of this pleading. "Listen. How about you either pee in your own mouth or you close it and keep it closed." Babs snaps, startled at her own bite. She softens. "No offense, but go ahead, strip naked, use your clothes for a pillow, and go to sleep. I've had a long day."

Tiffany wants to help BB remember to make sure her clips get saved for posterity. She closes her eyes for a moment in the dimmer light inside her shallow alcove. Tables her inquiry. She opens her eyes and blinks once, then obeys her Roommate and Monitor.

Babs' head spins. *Tiffany begged the Bathroom naked and then exploited her second mistake and begged the Pee-Cam—before I could put punishment into play myself. Now she is a naked Pee-Camer. She's fast.*

BB considers quietly, *Slow it down Bikini Babe; you're Boss Babe now. It's important that Pledge wait for me to get around to disciplining them. It's the only way I can be in control of them, in control of the Cosmos House, and in control of myself.*

5 Babs & Tiffany: Dining Room, Backyard Scratch, Bath (D02)

§ Babs Indulges Tiffany: Observe Penny & Coco's Pictures

Morning has come on Day Two, and Babs discovers Tiffany downstairs in the Dining Room admiring the four Dining Room Pictures. Babs blushes.

Tiffany deflects BB's attention downward, asking, "So who are the two horizontal pinkers lying naked on the baseboard?"

Babs goes along with the question. "That would appear to be Penny and Coco, the Baseboard Strippers, currently dancing the Nugget."

"Where they may blossom their flowers," Tiffany compliments, pointing with a foot that is bare below her shrouded calf. "I like how they both make secretions!"

Babs looks more carefully. *Somehow I overlooked that.*

"Perhaps you had a hand in contributing to their promotion?" Tiffany perks.

Babs blinks. Boss Babe carefully takes charge. "I assisted in their Option fulfillment."

Tiffany volunteers, "Ma'am, I'll strip naked, part my twat, secrete tang for you, and be your Baseboard Stripper next Term!" Tiffany cheerleads, "You can visit the Nugget with me and watch me dance naked. You'll see my Eraser Heads light up in blacklight."

Babs fails to be convinced. "You hardly need to revisit the Nugget."

Tiffany expands vision. "You could also watch Penny and Coco, and see one of them part her poontang and the other open her clam." Tiffany gallops, "I mean, if you were to add a Garment and Opt MomCap, wouldn't you be running the joint? If not the Nugget, another like it?"

"I don't think I'm ready for that," Babs carefully answers.

Tiffany ploughs forward, "Which is the one with the keloid near her asshole?"

Tiffany points. Once again BB must orient herself to a detail to which she has been oblivious. She tracks her eyes from the anus to the face and eyes connected to it. "That would be Coco," she states simply. "She kept that hidden all last Term; maybe it embarrasses her."

Tiffany twists her shoulders as she turns her bare belly toward Babs. "Betcha were I to put the tip of my tongue on it she'd cream immediately... even if she resisted it."

Babs envisions this. "She'd probably need to be strapped down."

"I know her type," Tiffany asserts, "and then it won't take but a tongue-wiggle to take her up to full steam and let her sing out full throttle for a while."

"Too bad Strippers aren't allowed to play contact sports," Babs narrows to Tiffany. "Or play with you either."

"I know all about Stripping," Tiffany assures Babs. "I Stripped the Term before I made Whore. I stayed wet all the time." Tiffany draws calm. "Ma'am, you can try to order me to not stain my slacks, but parts of my body run on autopilot."

"Perhaps you need a collection device," BB suggests. "Less obvious."

"Ma'am, I'll take my pants off and transude tapioca," Tiffany offers. And clarifies, "Anytime, anywhere, any situation!"

§ Babs Indulges Tiffany: Observe Janet's Picture

Babs feels like she has been entrusted to tame a wild horse. *A bucking bronco. No, that's not right either. Tiffany presents—*

And Tiffany leads, "So did you break Penny and Coco all by yourself? What happened to the person in the Picture just below you?"

Two questions, Babs registers. *And should not Tiffany know who this is?*

"She and I defeated Penny and Coco in a Mudwrestling Contest, so now we each Monitor our own House," Babs provides.

"Interesting." Tiffany rubs her nostrils with the back of a finger. "Crochet Spiderweb Bikini. Halter and g-string with nipples pokin' out. And hairage aghast." Tiffany touches her own red hairage. "I'll show it all too."

BB huffs, "Excuse me, but that g-string runs right up the crack of her big fat jaxy, except you can't see it hanging out behind in this Picture."

Tiffany glides, "She's pretty committed to areolage, hairage, and buttage. 24x7. She's pretty vulgar."

Tiffany refocuses, "You know, before I Stripped I was a newbie Pledge. Just like you were last Term."

"And after you Stripped you Whored," Boss Babe reverses temporal direction, "And now you Double Opted Up here to the Cosmos House."

"Right." Tiffany looks Babs in the eye.

Babs tips her head toward the Picture directly underneath hers on the wall. "So do you think she wears any stainless?"

"Ma'am, how would I know that?" Tiffany postures.

"You mean you don't recognize your Roommate from two Terms ago?" BB recriminates.

Tiffany flusters, "Oh. Yeah. Well. Yes. Well, of course. Janet. Janet here." Tiffany tosses her hair. "But I'm not sure if she's got rings in her right now. In this Picture. Maybe when we both stripped at the Nugget. Maybe then."

Tiffany puzzles her eyes. "Ah, Ma'am, how do you know about Janet's rings?" Tiffany inquires. It's an inappropriate question, of course, just like all questions are.

"Janet was my Roommate last Term," Babs explains, "here at the Cosmos House. And together we defeated Penny and Coco. This Term Janet is the Monitor of the Corvettes, and I Monitor here."

Tiffany hustles, "Ma'am, I really didn't know what had become of her. And I don't know what you will allow me to reveal to you!"

"Reveal to me?" Boss Babe *does* know. "Everything: Mind, body, and soul. Understand me?"

"Ma'am, yes, Ma'am," Tiffany retorts. And uptakes: "Janet saw my Calendar? Ma'am."

"She did," BB confirms, again ignoring to discipline Tiffany for asking another question. Babs provides, "We watched you stand by the Bell and wait."

Tiffany shrugs, "Janet Jintoe. Did she tell you how she got her last name?"

Babs closes her eyes momentarily, considers lying, but slowly admits, "I guess I didn't know Janet had a last name...."

Tiffany scratches an ear. "Yeah, probably there's a lot I can tell you about Janet."

BB frowns.

Tiffany accelerates, "Did she tell you she modeled pictures detailing how her g-string bisects her asshole?"

"What?" Babs startles. "I mean, I know she's pretty vulgar, like with rings in her thick lips and all, but she was a good Roommate for me last Term."

"Did she ever show you her Stripper vids collecting juice?" Tiffany wonders.

"I ah," Babs stammers, "I never thought it was appropriate to impose my eyes to view past transgressions of my Roommate. It never mattered to me. Still doesn't." Curiosity overtakes Babs. "But tell me: she did this on Stage at the Nugget? In front of a Crowd?"

Tiffany touches Janet's Picture and rubs a finger over her hairy crotch. "Janet kept a spoon and collection jar in her jepoot." Tiffany dips a finger into the front of her slacks. "That pretty much describes Janet."

"Well, get this straight," Babs retorts. "Janet is different than I am!" Babs points at Janet's unashamed eyes, which look out at her from the wall. "Maybe Janet doesn't care if Gamers shoot pictures of her g-string inside her juicy jepoot. She could have said 'no,' but she willfully obliged them! Whereas I would never stand for that. I have some self-dignity."

§ Babs Indulges Tiffany: Observe Her Own Picture

Babs' eyes drift up to the top Picture, the one of herself. Bikini Babe in Black Bikini. She squares herself, hands on hips. *Let's see what Tiffany sees. I can handle it. I am in control now.*

Tiffany wags a finger at Babs' Picture and praises the image, "I love the way you dish out the cleavage. You still do. And I love that you hang your bling on the wall. Guess you still bling!"

"They are my *crescents d'areolage,*" BB corrects, her cheeks reddening.

Tiffany charges forward. "And I love the way you blush at any thought, any reminder, that you bling all the time!"

Babs bling crinkles, but she stands her ground. "I'm trying to get over being embarrassed, but maybe I'll never not be ashamed. But mark my words: my bling will be contained soon."

"Bling and Blush!" Tiffany teases BB.

"What about you? How did you get over it?" BB demands.

"Me?" Tiffany inclines. "I was born this way."

Babs pouts, "I only 'bling' because I'm forced to."

Tiffany squirms, "Well, okay, being forced to do something helps to overcome shame." Tiffany shrugs, "Me, I'm a Porn Star."

Tiffany scrutinizes Babs' nombril and compares it to the one in her Picture.

Babs advances, "It's not like I haven't made progress. I have contained my bush, as you can tell!"

"And perhaps also your butt crack," Tiffany lightens.

Babs' rubescence glows around her waistline, and BB feels that skin grow warmer. Tiffany can't quite perceive infrared in Babs' olive skin, but the warm blood still courses where the tight elastic waistline grips her belly. *As posterior rugage, I suspect it shows at the Corvette House. Get over it.* She runs her fingers around the top of her waistline and inventories her situation. She purses her lips. "Most importantly, I Opted Monitor this Term." Boss Babe casts Caste clearly. "As for my nombril, it's barely legal, and I know if I become inattentive and let it droop I risk becoming vulgar front and back. It's effort for me to keep the briefs in the sweet spot, so no bush leaks out, no butt crack shows at the top, and no bum hangs out the bottom."

"All Castes come with liabilities." Tiffany waves, shifts, and asks outright, "So were you topless or nude while you Pledged?"

Babs stalls. "Err, ah, no. And I'm not like you either."

Babs touches her bikini bottoms. "And this is how I intend to maintain my coverage. Until I put on something that covers me more."

Tiffany nods a chin toward the Bikini Babe on the wall and tacks, "So who let you beg to fold your Bikini down?"

Babs feels the blush coming on. She draws her hands up across both breasts and tightens her folded arms.

"Put it this way, I got to roll Dice at the end of last Term," Babs informs. "Before they took this Picture. Only now, I've got the Dice. And the Makeup Case. They are my sole possessions, along with my Black Bikini."

"Ah, Dice and the Makeup Case!" Tiffany warms. "I played Dice once to determine how many Gamers would put lipstick on me. I was made a mess, let me tell you. I didn't mind teasing my tits or twat, but my face was humiliation. It made me know I was being sold for money." Tiffany humors, "If you let me roll Dice I will stay naked for that many days."

"Don't be silly," Babs retorts.

"And, Ma'am, since you have a Makeup Case," Tiffany advances, "please allow me to take on the burden of applying your makeup."

"You'd do that for me?" BB confirms, unsure.

"Ma'am! I completed Madam Nurse Beautician's Makeup Course with high marks! Look at you! You wear the face of Cleopatra. You deserve excellence."

Babs opens her mouth to share the fact that she too knows Madam Nurse Beautician. BB closes her mouth. *Tiffany doesn't need to know that Beautician trained me in pedicure at the Beauty Salon.*

Tiffany gestures to her own face. "Ma'am, I'll do makeup for you and all the Cosmos. Me too. Any way you want. I will make us up like Cleopatra's Strippers, or, if you want, Clowns, Drag Kings, or disgusting, strung-out, diseased Whores."

Babs hesitates. *Free assistance frequently has a price.*

Tiffany misreads BB's hesitancy and pushes forward. "Furthermore, because you got Dice, anytime you want to complement your bling you can just roll Dice and fold your nombril belly-down."

Tiffany points to Bikini Babe's hairage on the wall. And casuals to Babs. "Show me where that tan line hits on you."

BB stiffens.

"Hey, there's nobody here: no Cams, just us. Right? I mean, look at me. I'm way belly-down. So down I'm *always* hairage. So go ahead, let me see."

And so Babs gathers her thumbs into her waistband, pushes downward, and shows Tiffany not just her current, but also her lower, faded tan line, from where the folded-down nombril had crossed hairage. Enough demonstration. Babs pivots around on bare feet, and, still using her thumbs, shows Tiffany the tan line from when the folded-down nombril had cracked her rugage.

Boss Babe restores dignity as she rotates to face Tiffany and firm control. "Enough of what you want. Upstairs. Bunkroom. Go kiss Mirror until it knows you. Put your palms on it to the sides, rub your Eraser Heads firmly through your vinyl, and pump your bare belly. Keep it up until I need you for something. You're not supposed to ask questions, issue orders, or try to get me to expose myself!"

Tiffany stiffens, considers, recites, "Ma'am, yes, Ma'am," and exits toward the upstairs.

Boss Babe looks at Bikini Babe on the wall, and conquers fear. Not all of it, certainly. *Some.*

§ Tiffany Meets Mirror: Another Automatron Appendage

Tiffany was a Pledge once upon a time, but she has never Pledged in the Cosmos House, until now. So she must learn about the Mirror, or simply Mirror, which attests to its personality. As a Prop, Mirror can reflect or change into a wall-sized Screen, but it is Mirror's electro-stimulating touch screen that captivates Tiffany almost from the instant she presses her body up against it and starts kissing and rubbing against it.

For the Screen kisses and rubs back. Tiffany, insulated by her clear vinyl croptop and slacks, presses harder, and she feels the tickle back. *I can't tell what I'm feeling—vibration, electricity, thought waves?* Tiffany feels her nipples stimulated: she feels her bare belly make contact with bare skin; her lips want more, and she wettens them with her tongue and carefully lays her lips on the reflective surface, kisses Mirror more passionately. *It's alive.* Tiffany freshens and spots cameltoe. *It doesn't matter how it works. Kiss me. Feel my tips. Smell my tapioca.*

Tiffany tries to climax but fears putting her fingers into play upon her tender button. She touches noses with herself and senses something in Mirror restraining her when she tries to race for the top.

When Babs eventually rescues her, who-know-how-long later, Tiffany's skin is covered with sweat. Babs doesn't ask her about the experience, and Tiffany decides not to volunteer.

§ Babs & Tiffany: No Costume Trade for a Wannabe Porn Star

And so it comes to pass, ironically, that BB's lack of leverage, coupled with Tiffany's experience, contribute to an uneasy alliance between the Roommates. Together they combine the designated Cosmos Leadership with the most experienced Cosmos. Thus far. Boss Babe understands and values this power structure. They both do, and it is by a freak of the

Game that Tiffany isn't actually prey for her Roommate, with Babs simply swapping her smallish Black Bikini for Tiffany's shirt and slacks. Or taking one or the other. Or both.

Tiffany knows. *Boss Babe has the power to do what is expedient. She may choose to collect from me, let me cut my Garments to dust, or let me twist while she figures out what suits her best. I'll make it work.*

Babs suspects Tiffany did not volunteer chastisement to earn her Double Opt Up to Pledge. *And it certainly wasn't fucking a porn star, because she did that over and over and over again!*

It is later in the day, and Babs and Tiffany relax at ease in the Kitchen. The four Dining Room Pictures remind both of them that costumes between Roommates can be shared, exchanged, traded, even fought over.

Tiffany projects calm. "Thank you for letting me make out with myself in the Mirror. I was almost able to climax, but it wouldn't let me."

Babs shrugs. "Maybe next time."

Tiffany compliments, "I like that you shared with me your tan line from where you folded your nombril down last Term. You're very curvy. You should be proud you're hanging hairage on the Dining Room wall.

BB asserts, "I have to pay attention to keep my bikini bottoms properly suspended and tugged into their sweet spot. It's not easy." Babs details, "If I hike up the backside I wisp hairage or'top the front, and if I tug up the front I'm liable to crack my behind."

"Especially when you sit down." Tiffany dares, "And, Ma'am, were you to trade for my slacks you'd be able to crack butt for sure. Just like I do. Tail trough all the time. Hairage, too." Tiffany pesters, "Ma'am, if you trade your nombril for my slacks, you could cover your legs!"

"Cover my legs?" Babs appears taken aback. "Pledge, if I want to cover my legs I'll just take your slacks and wear them overtop my nombril. Don't insult my legs. I like my legs." Boss Babe statures, "And Gamers and Cams like my legs, too. Even paparazzi. You can keep your slacks."

"Ma'am, my waistline hangs lower on me than your Bikini does in your Picture," Tiffany boasts.

BB scans her eyes across Tiffany's waistline and fingers the elastic in the waistband of her own. "Excellent. Let's keep it that way. You just keep showing your fiery thatch and your tail trough. Standing, sitting. And you can start begging me to keep you on your hands and knees, too."

"Ma'am, thank you, Ma'am," Tiffany retorts. "I'll pull my pants down and show you my tail-pipe. I'll pull my treasure chest open for any Cam."

"You'll stop begging to expose yourself," Babs decrees, "that's what you'll do."

Tiffany pauses for air, ignores the aggression, pushes gently, and adds courtesy, "Ma'am." She teases, "Does you know you can trade your

Bling Bra for my vinyl croptop, and the croptop would cover *all* of your breasts?"

Boss Babe gives Tiffany soft twinkle smile. "It is so kind of you to make such a generous offering. But I am not about to exchange my 'Bling Bra' for your shirt so I flop my bazoombas around inside a completely transparent clear vinyl."

And they both laugh.

And the Roommates intermingle a line: "No matter how long the sleeves," says one. "Or how many buttons," adds the other.

And laugh again.

Babs pushes a chest full of air out of her body. "I hated it at the end of last Term when I had to go outside, run errands, and parade in this Black Bikini. And I still hate flouting my *crescents d'areolage* this Term, like walking over here, paparazzi and Cams. No matter how good I am at carrying myself. Or becoming popular with the Prefecture."

Tiffany sympathizes, "You're laying a tan line across your areolas so deep your original color will never come back. You're gonna bling forever."

Babs carelessly touches her tanned crescents and wonders the truth.

"I'll go out with you the next time you need to," Tiffany offers.

"Right," BB rushes. "Your even more overexposed body will attract them like flies." Babs wishes she hadn't spoken the thought and considers this idea seriously.

Tiffany tries a different tack. "Let's be frank: you already have two pieces, but you still need a third piece if you wish to ensure yourself a promotion. Right?"

"Well, okay," Babs agrees warily. *Yes, an Opt Up to House Mom el Capitan does require three pieces,* if *I want to become a MomCap next Term. But mostly I want to cover my* crescents d'areolage. *Now. This Term.*

"So take my shirt," Tiffany breezes. "That would give you have three pieces and solve your problem. Yes?" Tiffany senses Babs' hesitation. "You don't even need to trade with me. You can take a third piece from any Pledge. You can take my croptop, Ma'am, please."

Yes, well, but not quite. Babs visualizes and advances Tiffany's benefits. "So that you would be totally topless! And with just one piece! That suits you fine! But it still leaves me showing my bling."

"Except through a layer of transparent vinyl," Tiffany asserts, prepared for the objection. "You'd have a layer of separation overtop your bling."

Babs paces herself. "Very true," BB circumspects. *Oh, it's so hard not to be in a hurry!* She grasps her bra and bazoombas in both hands and pushes inward and upward. *I must wait and see what other, more advantageous costume choices arrive to trade for. I must stand firm.*

Tiffany crosses the palms of her hands over her Eraser Heads and rubs them through her transparent clear vinyl croptop. "Hey, Open Up Cover Up," Tiffany shrugs. "Exposing body parts is one of the least 'bad' things a Cosmos can do."

Babs concedes agreement. She worries, "What's really bad is what Janet and I did to Penny and Coco. We really messed them up. First the mud all over their bodies. Then we send them off to the Nugget. They had to streak to get there."

"Ouch!" Tiffany makes a face. "I hope they made it. Risky business running around out there naked. Sometimes streakers end up in suspended animation."

Babs bursts a question: "So do you know if Janet ever streaked?"

Tiffany waves a dismissive hand. "You consider your exposures embarrassing, but it's your lack of control to change them that raises your ire. You're BB, Bling Blush! Bling Bra! Bling Beauty! Yet you are the most beautiful Bikini Babe in the Game. You rule."

BB pouts, "I am Boss Babe, thank you. And I agree, we won't be trading any Garments." BB lets Tiffany wait while she considers, then speaks. "So where does that leave us? If we have nothing to swap, do we stalemate each other?" Babs gathers her bra straps in her fingers and hikes.

Tiffany gives this a quick analysis. "We might both have two Garments, but we're not equal. You don't need to engage me in any Roommate Games, like Flip-Flop or Winner-Takes-All, because here in the Cosmos House, you're the Monitor Boss. You rule. You don't need to play Games, least of all with 'Tiffany Porn Star.' You want it, you take it from me."

Tiffany checks that her cameltoe contours her treasury. "You know what I need. I need you to strip me naked. I'll roll my pants down, open my trap doors, freshen and twiddle my twat until I cream and climax. You don't even need to wait until the end of the Term for me to turn on and cum on the Cams. I am a Porn Star!"

Boss Babe feels anger rise up. The precipitate forms and falls out of solution. *Enough Whore! Just who are you to constantly remind me about your sexual prowess—inside my House?!*

"Enough." BB smiles and carefully challenges Tiffany on her claim. "Maybe once upon a time you were a Whore and a Porn Star—I understand you don't want to leave that behind—but now you have become a Cosmos Pledge."

Tiffany interrupts with protest. "Ma'am, I was a Whore and a Porn Star, but I am *still* a Porn Star! Once a Porn Star, always a Porn Star! And okay, I know I'm not allowed sex here at the Cosmos, but I still have my fans. You can find pictures and vids of me eating pussies and doin' cocks. I've got a long tail. I've done everything explicit! All holes! All sexes! Fame doesn't leave one just because one isn't on Stage. I mean, look at me; I'm a titter, taphole, and tailpipe in one, Ma'am. Gamers desire me."

Babs stands tall and erect, breasts uplifted, belly curved in. She points her finger at the floor and drolls, "Hands and knees, Pledge."

Tiffany moves with measured grace. Lots of tail trough, but not quite tailpipe.

"Maybe you're a has-been wannabe Porn Star," BB advises. "You might be ex-Whore, but you are a Cosmos Pledge right now. And I'm sure your Gamer fans will take whatever they get." Boss Babe constructs, "If indeed you get cammed at all!"

"Ma'am, I am any kind of Porn Star you want me to be, Ma'am." Tiffany grits her teeth and squares her position up. Hand and knees on the floor. Clear plastic shirt hanging down and away from Eraser Heads. Lots of bare back and a deepened tail trough.

Tiffany chants, "Please let me Pledge naked and cum be a Stripper next Term."

Babs distrusts the hubris and makes a noncommittal, "Right. Show me. Crawl your way out to the Garage and see if the side door in the brambles is unlocked. Count the number of Posts in the Henge. Then rub your face in the Mudpit so I can evaluate just how wet it might be. After you ring the Bell to beg reentry, stand spread surrender and wait for me."

Boss Babe points a painted big toenail toward the Back Door. And Tiffany scoots, or as best one can who moves on all fours.

And yes, her tail trough works lower. BB sighs and turns her attention elsewhere. *Tiffany's tail trough needs to be the least of my priorities. I must make sure she behaves herself, because the consequence for me could be terrible.*

BB hears the Bell ring the first time and realizes that now she knows why the clapper pull hangs almost down to the ground.

§ Tiffany Tells Babs: The Life of a Whore

Babs feels badly that she may have overexerted herself when she hears Tiffany ring the Bell a second time and present herself nearby the Back Door Landing.

The Cam surveys her muddy face and broad expanse of scratched belly and back. And hands and feet. Because Tiffany's deep flat belly and lower back really are the only parts of Tiffany's body not covered. Her only skin exposed to the air. Tiffany stretches her arms up in a little dance; the shirt bottom rides up and exposes even more of her ribcage, expanding her belly-up.

Babs appears on the Landing, and gasps as she considers Tiffany's muddy face and scratched belly and back. The protection afforded by Tiffany's clear vinyl shirt and stretch slacks make BB believe, somehow, that maybe these Garments are useful after all. And so she demands them immediately and unthinkingly, almost on impulse. "Strip naked, Pledge. Hand over what you got."

BB stands and watches awkwardly as Tiffany breaks surrender position and strips. She realizes, *Duh. This is dumb of me. All I am doing is advancing Tiffany's nudity for the Cam, Automatron, and the Prefecture.*

A naked Tiffany ascends the step to the Landing and extends the transparent top and stretch slacks to her Monitor Boss. "Ma'am, the Garage door is unlocked, and there is van inside. There are seven Posts. And you can see mud on my face."

Babs blinks, and a wave of guilt engulfs her. "You run upstairs and draw yourself a deep bath. Enjoy it. You deserve it. You'll find soap and shampoo and bubble bath."

Tiffany feels like scratching her tummy and comparing her scratched and muddy parts with the rest of her body. She resists this temptation and darts inside the Back Door.

Gamers know that walking naked from the Bell to the Back Door doesn't count as a streak, nor does romping anywhere in the Backyard.

Babs feels awkward holding the two Garments, so she drapes them over her forearm and lets air out of her lungs as she discovers the Cam canvassing her own bikini-clad body. She discovers herself pushing her lower lip forward with her tongue, and with apparent leisure follows Tiffany inside. No blush this time.

Monitor Babs hurries upstairs lest Tiffany steal an opportunity to play with herself. She hangs Tiffany's croptop and slacks in the Bedroom locker, and curls into the Bathroom to join the Bathroom Cam as a naked Tiffany descends into the bubbles, her long red hair up in a knot so it doesn't get wet in the tub.

Tiffany lounges into the warmth and watches BB sit off to the side as the Bathroom Cam shoots at Tiffany from over BB's shoulder. Before it settles to rest, the Cam manages to capture Babs' beautiful back and spine. Three hooks on her bra back. Collar and shoulder blades. And yes, her dimples and rhombus.

Tiffany will tell any Gamer her life story, but she talks to the lingering Cam as much as she does to BB. She absorbs Babs' discipline of her for pretending to not recognize Janet—the warm water does soothe her scratches—but also relishes the opportunity to languish for the Cam.

Babs' curiosity overtakes politeness, and BB queries, "So, what was it like being a Whore?"

Tiffany lets water stream off her shoulders. "I want you to know I was a very classy Whore. I escorted, fucked hotel pickups, and when I was not on the set of a porno movie or visiting the Nugget as a Feature Dancer, I was stationed at the 'notorious' Flesh Ranch. It was the most stable of 'my' environs—although nothing was actually mine, of course. It's strange not having your own place. I found security in the work, and I enjoyed the camaraderie with the other Whores and the simplistic business relationships with the Patrons. Line up, get picked out, and get fucked. And I'm a workhorse!"

Impulse drives Babs to ask another question. "So are Whores real or an act?"

Tiffany laughs, "I wish I knew. Yes, Whoring involves the creation of fantasy. Gamers can think of me as a wife, a girlfriend, a Porn Star, a dirty low-class tatterdemalion. It doesn't matter. I'm here to find love and share love and experience. With anybody. With you."

Babs startles; she finds Tiffany's enlightenment scary. BB gathers her thoughts, inventories her own senses, and audits her costume. All accounted for.

Tiffany lifts her body up so that her Eraser Heads bob in the bubbles. "I know I'm not allowed to turn tricks here, no sex even. I was a Pledge once, a long time ago, and back then about the only thing I wanted to do was get laid. I guess I still do."

This is almost more than Babs wants to know, and she discovers herself hunching over and drawing her arms close around her. She shakes her shoulders, straightens in her sitting position, and attempts to steer the conversation. "So that left you 12x7 to sleep, eat, and go out. Shopping. Clubs. Whatever."

Tiffany corrects BB, "Well, a Whore has nothing, not even her holes. So unless one get perks, a Whore ends up naked off duty. Makes it hard to go out. Harder. You'd have to streak."

"Nothing to wear out," Babs repeats, and deepens her curiosity. "Okay. But what was the worst of it?"

Tiffany jumps on this one. "Well, the Madams and Pimps wasted no time breaking me in! What I hated most were the Bachelor Parties, where I got gangbanged and roughhoused. The creeps though it was very funny to get me piss, puke drunk and throat me. Or puke all over me and force the groom to fuck me. But in general, taking cocks in all my holes one after another, sometimes all at once with guys spunking all over me. Wears you out after a while."

"That is not sexy!" Babs reacts. "That is inappropriate behavior!"

"No kidding!" Tiffany beams. "And the videos when I climax are unbelievable!"

Babs tries to steer straight. "And what did you like most? When you weren't shooting porn or getting gang-banged."

Tiffany splashes the water. "Oh, that's easy! The bookings as a nude figure-drawing model. I can still do that of course, may it please you, Ma'am. And I'm also cool with any photoshoots; I've got great skin, I'll pull my lips wide apart, lay a vibrator on my trigger, squeeze fresh tapioca out my taco, let go, and trill. All legal for your Pledge Tiffany!"

"You'll climax in the Mudpit in the Backyard?" Babs suggests.

"Oh, absolutely!" Tiffany waves her arms. "I'll roll Dice and wallow for hours. I'll roll Dice and rub-a-dub as many Posts as there are dots."

Right. Babs considers Tiffany's body, slippery with soap and bubble bath. A nude torso with knees above bubbly water. *You not only want to get yourself on each and every Cosmos Cam—like the one here in the Bathroom—you want to position yourself where paparazzi harvest you. You're shameless.*

Babs discovers that, while crossing her arms in front of herself, she has slid her fingers inside the cups of her bra.

Tiffany interprets BB's measured consideration and advances her data dump. "Ma'am, you gotta check out a series called *Titty Flat Fuckers.* I am a Porn Star. I masturbate, insert toys, ride a fucking machine, pee, suck cock, swallow bukkake, and get fucked solo and gangbanged by roughhouse rowdies."

Babs feels disgusted with herself when she asks, "So did you have relations with females as well?"

"Aaah…" Tiffany makes a rolling motion with her body; bubbles of water grace her face, and she speaks in the third person. "In the beginning Tiffany was resistant to lesbian sex, but, as they say, 'Whores must be learned to kiss girls and love the smell and taste of fresh pussy!'" Tiffany switches voices. "Pimp Cowboy at Flesh Ranch trained me. I had to shoot videos kissing and making out with girls, eating out girls, and enjoy all the variations of the strapon. I worked with first-timers and seasoned Whores. And I'll pee on anyone."

Tiffany instants, "So have you watched me on the Pee-Cam already? You're the one with the Desktop."

Babs has not. *And it's not like I don't know that I can. Live, or on the replays.*

Tiffany interrupts BB's silence. "Ma'am, please let my Pee-Cams play on all the House Screens! Please let Automatron service the Prefecture."

§ Tiffany Confesses to Babs: Piss Mouth Obeisance

Enough! What is it that jars Babs' sensitivities, probes her forward, and causes her to react viscerally? "You're pretty willing to pee on other people, how about getting peed on? You like that too?"

Tiffany wrinkles her nose and cringes. "Well I never got peed on... at least, not by somebody else."

"You never volunteered as a Piss Mouth?" BB asks jokingly.

"I didn't say that," Tiffany backpedals. Suddenly befuddled: "Hey, there was a reason I volunteered. Any Slavesex is a Piss Mouth, obviously, but any other Gamer may volunteer. It's, like, not forbidden, you know?"

"You volunteered Piss Mouth to avoid Slavesex," Boss Babe projects.

"Something like that," Tiffany admits.

"Once a Piss Mouth, always a Piss Mouth?" Babs asks.

"Something like that," Tiffany admits. "Except. It was my own pee that got on me. So it probably doesn't count."

"Poor you," Boss Babe teases. "And now you have the opportunity to make your fans desire you? Piss Mouth for life."

"Ma'am, oh, Ma'am. That's very harsh." Tiffany splashes.

"Maybe you don't really mean 'anything legal?'" BB teases.

Tiffany stammers, not expecting this. "Ma'am, yes. Absolutely. I am a Pee-Camer and a Piss Mouth. You can pee on me anytime. Please position me in front of any Cam and in my mouth. Ma'am, please let me Pledge naked and cum be a Stripper next Term!"

Babs blinks.

Tiffany consoles, "I'll even clean up, Ma'am."

"Any other Obeisance you want to tell me about?" BB raises a chin.

Tiffany straightens, and soapy water streams off the ends of her Eraser Heads. "Ma'am, I've got ultraviolet ink tattooed into my Eraser Heads. So they glow when I dance with blacklight in the Nugget. And I'll show you my—"

"I know all about your invisible ink," Babs interrupts, avoiding the remainder. She advances, "So why are you here?"

Tiffany squares shoulders. "Ma'am. Look. I am a Porn Star. Okay, I'm a Wannabe Porn Star. Gamers don't want me shooting porn right now, so they've promoted me. But instead of Opting me Up to Stripper, where I could dance naked and show my stuff, they've decided to Double me Up and send me to this place."

"The Cosmos House," Babs affirms.

Tiffany elaborates, "Furthermore, Gamers double dress me so that, left undone, I'm a Monitor next Term. Three hops from a Porn Star."

"So now you're a sexually frustrated Cosmos Pledge." Babs toys with her Pledge. "Is that how it works? Instead of being demoted and cast into the Dungeon. How come you never begged for the chains? You could be a sexually frustrated Slavesex. Yes?"

Tiffany splashes water. "No!" She draws her arms upward, forgetting that her hair is up in a bundle, and touches it with wet hands. Armpits flashing, Eraser Heads cresting waterline. Magnificent.

"You're still restrained," Babs reminds her wet and naked Pledge. "Pledge are forbidden to sex, or to play with themselves."

Tiffany sighs. "What can I say? I love being a Porn Star! I love being a Whore because it's a great thing to fuck and climax, and ever better when others watch. I love to make love. I love to fuck, and I love to be fucked. I love hugging and kissing, rubbing my body with passion, and sharing experience. Hey, it's very simple." Tiffany draws back and sits up straight in the tub. "Look. I'm cool turning tricks, but I *do not* want to be tied up and torqued. Restrained, caged, beaten, screwed, gagged and force-fed. I don't mind twisting and losing it with a guy—on or off camera. But it's something different when you're restrained from cumming. Or when you can't stop."

"Listen," Tiffany advances. "There are two kinds of Slavesex: prudes and exhibitionists. For the prudes, the worse is to get tied up and fucked. Anally, vaginally, in the mouth. For the exhibitionists, the worse is to get tied up and frustrated. Capisce?"

"Ah, the perils of Slavesex," Boss Babe mindfully loudmouths, then ventures, "You're pretty chastised here at the Cosmos House."

"Right," Tiffany agrees, "I might be chastised here, but a chastised Slavesex is worse fun. Restrained and unable to masturbate. Getting forced to cum. Totally restrained: sensory deprivation, breath controlled, put into a trance, and then getting one's stomach and tail pumped while being brought to climax, and then unable to stop cumming? Slavesex isn't like being a Porn Star or Whoring, where you can climax on your own. Slavesex get Zoned."

Babs jiggles her boobs. "Well, at least here you are safe."

Tiffany tosses up hands. "I will try my best, Ma'am; I will do whatever is required to stay away from that place. Now you know my secret, so now you can control me, even though I hate being sexually chastised here at the Cosmos House. But I'll do for you. I'll play with myself against Mirror. I'll masturbate to myself on the Cams."

"I'll entertain your begging me to masturbate," Babs decrees.

"Ma'am, yes, of course," Tiffany acknowledges, and rubs wet Eraser Heads with the butts of her palms. "Ma'am, I've pledged before. And don't forget I was a Stripper, with Janet, two Terms ago."

"Perhaps you'll beg me to climax and Pee-Cam at the same time?" Boss Babe suggests.

"Ma'am, yes, of course," Tiffany rushes. "I'll Pee-Cam my Piss Mouth and climax naked in the Mudpit in broad daylight. Ma'am." Babs appears not to notice that Tiffany's hands extend far under the bubbles in front of herself.

Tiffany reads Babs hesitancy at causing her a demotion. "It's okay, Ma'am. I know you don't make deals, but this Pledge will do whatever you say. Anything legal. Just please let me Pledge naked and cum be a Stripper next Term!"

§ Tiffany Describes Janet to Babs: Strippers Two Terms Ago

Tiffany rushes to qualify, "The difference between me and Janet is that when Janet and I were Strippers at the Nugget we both got our tits and twats fondled a lot. But when I was a Whore last Term and Feature Danced, let me assure you that when Patrons fondled me they popped corks in the Champagne Room."

"You blew them." Babs speaks very matter-of-factly.

"Hands and knees! Or I took their dick out and slipped it inside me as I sat on their lap. I had a big advantage: I'd dance on Stage and get tips, I'd lapdance, and then I'd take them to the private room. The Strippers aren't allowed to Whore. Too bad, 'cause they can't all become Whores."

"I guess the Patrons don't have a chance." BB recounts. Now she takes charge: "But you didn't just screw in the Champagne Room. Judging from your Calendar, you're also a public fuck."

"Anywhere, anytime, anybody. Check out Automatron. I shot pornos at the Inner Sanctuary at the Nugget. I've done everything explicit. All holes. All sexes. When I was a Whore I got to decide Up or Down. I knew that if I begged Slavesex they would force-masturbate me, possibly even stroke me on real cock, but frustrate my release. It would be very intense, I'm sure. And very dangerous for me, because I would beg *anything* for release. And I do mean *anything*."

"You'll have to negotiate any and all cumming here at the Cosmos House just as well," Babs reminds Tiffany. "Not just pussy and cock. Touching yourself, too."

"I know Ma'am," Tiffany's hands slide up her chest, out of the bubbles, and Babs realizes that her own hands are still crisscrossed, with her fingers inside her bra. She can feel that her bullets are hard, and as she backs her hands out, she sneaks a peek at bubbled areolage. It is not by accident that the Cam stays by BB's side and focused on Tiffany.

Tiffany wiggles Eraser Heads up into view and rolls them in her fingers, not making them any harder, impossible, of course. She offers Babs, "You can touch them." Tiffany brushes water off of her shoulders. "You can touch me whenever you want, anywhere, anytime you want.

I'm number one Pee-Cam and Piss Mouth. I know I have to please you. No, I don't need to be tied up to be sexually frustrated. Listen, my current state of chastisement defines my value. Gamers will pay the Cosmos House to watch me release myself."

Babs takes a deep breath. *That's not quite what I have in mind, but....* BB breezes, "Pledge Tiffany, I shall remember you said that!"

§ Babs & Tiffany: Guilt, and Not Remembering Janet

Once again Babs lets curiosity about her former Roommate and contemporaneous Monitor avail her of an opportunity to probe Tiffany. "So when you and Janet stripped together, did you two let the Patrons have sex with you? When you were both Strippers two Terms ago. Before you Whored."

Tiffany runs her fingers around a body buried in bubbles. "Well, you knows Cosmos Kimju & Molly know, nobody comes into the Game as a Whore. And let me tell you that the Nugget is one of those strip joints where nobody stops the lapdance patrons from fondling the talent. But MomCap warned us if we let any lapdance customer take his dick out of his pants that we would for sure Opt Whore. Well, as soon as I let some guy do this, the next thing I know I am sitting on it. Right there in the Club. And the next thing I know I'm Opted to Whore. It wasn't hard, but I was surprised with the speed at which I was turned over."

"And Janet?" Babs questions carefully.

"Janet? Well, maybe Janet let the Nugget Patrons fondle and finger her, but otherwise she behaved herself. And stayed naked. So we both got what we wanted: Janet got to Opt Up and Pledge, I gather with you last Term, and I got to go turn tricks. I'm a lot better Whore than Janet would ever have made, and besides, becoming a sex-for-money type enabled me to become a famous Porn Star."

"You are a Pledge and a wannabe Porn Star," Boss Babe reminds.

Tiffany redirects, "Listen, Ma'am. I don't know which ex-Strippers might be heading here from the Nugget, but whoever it is, I probably already know them."

"Perhaps it might be Kimju and Molly?" BB hazards her best guess.

"Ah, bingo." Tiffany brushes her forehead with wet hands and rinses her face. "If you treat me right I can tell you a thing or two about them that you won't see on their Camera Lounge videos or Pink Pages."

"You will tell me no matter what," Boss Babe reminds Tiffany.

"Ma'am, of course. I will tell you everything I know," Tiffany insists. "So by deduction I figure Janet will be getting ex-Strippers Ginny and Lee. Lee's a Lollydor, a lick up lezzy, and Ginny is not just an ex-

Stripper, not just an ex-Whore; Ginny's a guzzle grinding Whore-for-Life!"

Tiffany lifts and waves a finger over her head as soapy water streams off her elbow and down her armpit. It is as if she points up to her Calendar. "There should be a month where Ginny and I mouth the opposite sides of a humongous black erection with a streamer coming out the front. We shot porn together in the Inner Sanctuary."

Babs casts dryly, "Maybe the ex-Strippers will remember your Feature Dancing and Champagne Room exploits. Maybe Janet will have a story or two about you from your time Stripping together."

Tiffany senses unease at the possibility of Janet's participation, and her body makes waves in the tub. "Ma'am," she advances, "Ma'am, I'll perform on the Pee-Cam with Janet. I'll match anything she does. And I'll beg to Pledge naked and cum be a Stripper next Term."

"You were not forthcoming with me about knowing Janet, earlier, in the Dining Room. You mislead me," Boss Babe recriminates, forgetting that Tiffany's warm bath represents compensation for crawling through prickly bushes.

Tiffany reconsiders this admonition and tries to think a way out of her predicament. None obvious. "Ma'am, I was confused, Ma'am," she stumbles. "You did the right thing to make me scratch myself up in the Backyard. I deserved it. It's important that you affirm that actions have consequences."

Like a warm bubble bath?

Tiffany promises, "Ma'am, it won't happen again, Ma'am."

Boss Babe tosses her hair, rises, and leaves Tiffany alone with the Bathroom Cam.

6 Robyn: Thin Maillot • Small Hole • Lost Memory (D03-D04)

§ Robyn & Front Door Cam: Pledge in Maillot Cutout

Robyn makes her appearance at the Cosmos House the following day, the Day Three in the Term. Gamers know the type: the young woman who wears seductive clothes to lure men into giving her responsibility and then threatens them when they attempt to correct her for substandard performance.

Paparazzi spot the medium-build, self-confident, green-eyed blonde with big, streaked hair gliding down the sidewalk. If they want to query Automatron they may superimpose her stats: 5' 6", 108 pounds, and a knockout 34C-25-34 figure poured into a strapless maillot cutout.

Robyn walks tall and with a stride, swinging her arms at her sides. She considers herself. *I know my golden skin tans easily, and I'm proud of my four tan lines. Two of them surround my smooth shaven legs, and one of them molds itself around my rigamarole. And the smallest surrounds my buttonhole. My navel commands Gamers!*

Robyn casts eyes about, searching out the more brazen paparazzi, but she finds them not. *My stretchy one-piece maillot cutout swimsuit molds to me like a second skin. And I've got the smallest navel cutout of anybody. So I know Gamers have to watch me, illicit or not.*

She tosses her magnificent flowing hair so instead of hiding one eye it hides the other. She runs a hand through this power accessory and flashes a concave, shaven armpit. She double checks gold-painted fingernails. *My value demands Gamers' surveillance.*

If you don't ask, Robyn will inform you, "My heritage is central European royalty." Robyn has no use for men and no understanding of women. The exception is the very rich male, and she has yet to find a prince sufficiently worthy to embrace, yet alone bear children for. She has no comprehension that women frequently hold positions of responsibility and power.

Robyn turns from the sidewalk onto the walkway to the Cosmos House. Her strapless maillot crosses her back, wraps around her sides below her armpits, and stretches across the top of her rig; it leaves her armpits and shoulders bare. The stretch fabric does indeed contour Robyn's shapely torso, but it also allows the left and right sides of Robyn's rah-rahs to bounce independently, a freedom of movement savored by Gamers in high-speed video replays.

Robyn has forgotten that the maillot is but a single Garment. One piece.

Robyn catches the eye of the Front Door Cam upon her as she approaches the House. The Cam comes off its perch, hovers down the wooden stairs, stops, and tracks her motion until Robyn stops in front of it. They both take a step backward, so to speak.

Robyn considers her admirer, currently blocking the front stairs, Front Porch, and Front Door. A flick of the nose would be invisible were it not for the power of the lens. "You would be wise to stay out of my way," Robyn declares to the Cam, "whether you're being controlled by Gamers or by Automatron."

The Cam retreats a few feet and rises a few inches.

"Go ahead, admire my beauty." Robyn raises her chin in defiance. "My attire is more appropriate for the gym or the beach, but if I have to walk in daylight to get to the Cosmos House, I'll consider it."

The Cam whirs, as if to convey empathy to Robyn. That Robyn doesn't have a choice in the matter is lost on her.

Robyn takes a big breath and addresses the Cam. "I'm sure my coverage will be among the most modest of any Cosmos trekking to the Cosmos House. I'm not molestable, but everybody wants to molest me. I know. Gamers ogle my bare shoulders and legs. My little bit of cleavage. My beautiful face and radiant personality."

The hover Cam pulls back and circumnavigates her in a loose spiral. Robyn's way is no longer blocked, so she approaches the steps. The Cam collects swinging long blonde hair, her eyes and nose, her lips and dimples. It collects bare feet with golden toenails. It follows her articulated thighs as she climbs up the wooden steps. The front steps of the Cosmos House.

Once on the Porch Robyn discovers the Cam hovering; it settles itself midway between herself and the Front Door and collects her button in the shadowed daylight.

"You Gamers never miss the hole for my button!" Robyn exclaims, double-checking herself. True. The front and center round hole is two inches in diameter and encircles a belly button that Gamers call an "outie," which was formed by how her birth cord was tied once her lungs turned on. It's not all that big of a buttonhole, but it's big enough to ensure this is a maillot cutout.

Robyn sasses the Cam. "There's a reason why the cutout hole in my maillot is the diameter it is! And the smallest of all!" Robyn takes a step forward and the Cam backs up. "So Front Door Cam, stay out of my way!"

Robyn takes another step forward, and the Cam retreats to an oblique sideways position. Robyn puts her hand on the Front Door handle, pivots to the Cam, and issues an ultimatum. "You'd better watch out, Gamers, inside and out. I like it when you look at me, because I know you can't touch. I control you."

Robyn considers the Cam drinking in her birthmark. "Enough of you," she exclaims. She waves her hand in front of herself and darts through the Door.

§ Robyn: Arrives via the Front Door… with Memory Issues?

The Front Door Cam catches only a fleeting blur as Robyn sashays through the doorway. She doesn't ring the chime, and she makes sure the Cam doesn't follow her in. *Might there exist any prohibitions against using the Front Door, or if the front Parlor and Living Room are off-limits to Pledge, there is no reason for me to know about them. I am a newbie Pledge, after all.*

Gamers wince.

Has Robyn been here before? Is she familiar with this place? Is this the same Robyn who was a Cosmos Pledge last Term, who was Roommates with Steph? Certainly Babs will be able to make a positive identification, even though Robyn might not.

If a returning Robyn had memory she would find the Parlor inside the Front Door familiar. Two windows look out over the Front Porch, two more windows straddle a fireplace and look out onto the side of the Porch, and a massive staircase ascends upward to the second floor. There is a door underneath the stairway that Robyn might remember as a small Washroom with only a toilet, a sink, and a mirror. A short hallway heads from the Parlor past the Washroom toward the door into the Kitchen; Robyn doesn't advance to test if it opens.

Robyn takes a parting glance up the main staircase; any Pledge who dares sneak up would encounter a landing with locked doors leading to places about which most Pledge know little or nothing. Something about looking up and away from the stairs makes Robyn imagine the rooms upstairs. *Except I've never been her before. And even if I had been, it doesn't count.*

Perhaps this Robyn has no memories of any secret passage connecting the upstairs landing to the Monitor's private bathroom, which would (should it actually exist and if Babs even knows about it) enable a Monitor to pass messages, secretly entertain visitors, or exit and enter unnoticed.

An assumption leaks from Robyn's black hole back into the present. I shall be the Monitor's Roommate this Term! I don't know why, but that's the most important place here! For a Pledge, anyway.

Robyn moves to her left and passes easily into the Living Room, which occupies the left front of the House, as seen from the street. She looks out the bay window across the Front Door and Porch, down the front steps, across the yard and toward the sidewalk, the street, and the Houses beyond, on the other side of the street.

Robyn backs into the center of the room and gives herself a final check. The stretch fabric maillot is taut; her leglines aren't riding up, and it isn't cheeking her rump, wiggling into her crack, or cameltoeing her intimate parts. Robyn checks to make sure her buttonhole is spot on, and she thumbs the maillot's elastic around the top of her rig so the strapless neckline holds firm. She exposes just the tiniest bit of cleavage.

I Pledge the Cosmos with a strong opening position. And I'm convinced that my promotion to Monitor next Term is ensured. I am here to be carried upward. Robyn takes a deep breath, strides toward the sliding double doors at the back of the Living Room, and pushes them apart so she can prance into the Dining Room.

§ Robyn: Studies Four Dining Room Pictures

No one there. Robyn scans quickly. A table and eight chairs, windows and a dark Screen to her left, and windows at the opposite end which provide a glimpse of the Backyard, with its Mudpit and Bell outside. She does not compute that the Kitchen lies through the next door, or that the Bunkroom sits directly above.

The four Dining Room Pictures immediately attract Robyn's attention. The confident one breaks her pace and draws up tall in front of them to examine the former Cosmos Pledge hanging on the Dining Room wall.

I recognize them. Robyn tosses her hair back off her shoulder. *But I'm not sure I've ever met them before.*

Nametags identify all four Pictures. Robyn looks bemused at Babs' Black Bikini: navelage 24x7, areolage and hairage to boot. Robyn chortles at Janet's crochet open-mesh, pretty much see-it-all Spiderweb Bikini, but it is Penny and Coco who garner her attention. She bends over to survey the humiliations of the two naked and spread Baseboard Strippers. Robyn licks her lips and more closely considers the two pairs of pussy lips uplifted toward her face.

"Oooh," she disses the Pictures out loud. "Shaven slits, each with a little patch of butched pussy hair trimmed into a heart shape. How banal." Penny pulls wings to open a pool of pudding; Coco's tongue hangs out of her mouth, and one finger caresses her clit with fresh curdle. *Good riddance.* Robyn forms her nose like she smells bad things. She pronounces, "Whoever you are, Penny and Coco, you deserve to be Strippers. And maybe next Term you two cock teasers will make Whores."

Robyn scans the images of Babs and Janet again and augments her thoughts. "And maybe one of you still needs to dance and Strip."

But enough of the memory joggle; Robyn swings into the Kitchen.

§ Robyn Encounters Babs & Tiffany: A Kitchen Surprise

And comes face-to-face with Babs. And the rear end of Tiffany.

Boss Babe confirms Robyn is Robyn from last Term. *I know you!* BB sits at the Kitchen table in her Black Bikini, facing the door. She heard Robyn coming, and, even absent a face, Babs recognizes the footsteps and the voice. BB heard Robyn pause before the four Dining Room Pictures and heard herself called out. She steels herself for this moment.

Tiffany, facing the opposite direction and on her hands and knees, hears Robyn enter, but she continues to mop the Kitchen floor with the long red hair on her head. A Watering Can containing soapy water sits on the floor nearby.

Robyn breaks to a stop. *Occupied!* Babs looks at her silently.

Robyn matches Babs, who looks at her silently from the chair, with the Bikini Babe at the top of the four Dining Room Pictures. Robyn's eyes canvas Babs' cleavage and detail her *crescents d'areolage*. Crescents confirmed. Robyn casts her eyes downward, and although the table blocks her view, it doesn't block Robyn from assuming that Babs' bush flows out the top of her nombril, just like the Bikini Babe in the Dining Room. Anther conclusion: *Cosmos Pledge.*

Robyn casts her eyes about. A tush presents itself to her; the body attached to it faces away from her, supporting itself on hands and knees and apparently scrubbing the floor. The buttocks and back above the gouging waistline look badly scratched.

Yard work.

Robyn casts her eyes behind her and to the right of the door she entered, where she encounters a big Calendar hanging on the wall. The Calendar contains a vulgar picture of a gangbanger whose face, small tits, and tinderbox appear to be drenched in splooge. There are more erect cocks above the face in the Calendar than Robyn can count in a glance.

Robyn looks back at the Pledge washing the floor, but there is no reason she should connect the Tiffany Porn Star Calendar with the floor mop, so she doesn't.

Robyn glances at Babs for an instant, but Babs doesn't offer any introduction; BB waits for Robyn's attention. Robyn darts her eyes back toward the washerwoman: long pants and long tail trough. Posterior rugage headed toward tailpipe. Robyn scans back to Babs' full cleavage, then up to Babs' deep black eyes, still silently appraising her. Babs continues to await recognition.

Robyn tosses her head so her hair covers one eye and opens the conversation.

"I saw your Picture and read your tag." Robyn gestures to the Dining Room behind her. "You're the Bikini Babe. Bra and *culotte* nombril." She plunges forward. "I'm Robyn! I've arrived. I'm new to the Game. I've never been here before." She gestures toward the curving stairs that lead upward. "I need to go upstairs and find the Bedroom. I'm rooming with the Monitor, you know."

Ah, such hubris. BB gathers her chin in her palm and furrows her brow. *Yes, Last Term you shared the Bedroom with Steph, then Monitor of the Cosmos House. You are not a newbie Pledge; you can't fool me. So why might you pretend to be returning to Pledge? You can't Pledge again. That's contrary to the Rules.* Boss Babe narrows her beautifully made eyebrows. *Except here you are.* BB exchanges air with her environment. *Robyn returning has always been a possibility, ever since I saw her name on the Manifest. Now she's for sure.* Babs folds her fingers in front of her and rests her hands on the table. *What's going on here?*

Babs has upheld Robyn's momentum with body language. Now Babs speaks: "You don't know me?"

"Know you?" Robyn retorts. "No, I don't know you. Should I have seen you before, except for your Picture in the next Room? Hey, keep your bazoombas and bawdy beard and belly button far out. You can see that I'm a lot more covered up than you, Bikini Babe." Robyn tosses a thumb over her shoulder in the direction of the Dining Room. "I read your name tag."

BB touches the center of her back to ensure her own nombril shows no rugage. And all three hooks are engaged. *Very well, have it your way.* Babs knows from last Term that Robyn doesn't necessarily remember the same things the same way twice, if she remembers them at all. *But this is more than that: Robyn should not be here. Pledge can't Hover, and I know she is no newbie. We were both Cosmos last Term.*

Babs' eyes canvas Robyn's torso. Strapless maillot cutout; small buttonhole, same as the end of last Term. BB studies Robyn's eyes. *So do you really have amnesia and have forgotten you were a Pledge last Term? Or are you pretending?*

Facts intrude. *After all, Robyn stands in front of me, and she appears on the Manifest. And if she has been erased or redacted, did she do it to herself, or did Gamers decide she should return to start all over again? Repeat the Term as a Pledge? "Pledge Again," or whatever Gamers want to call it?*

Babs scowls. More facts. *This is bigger than just Robyn. If Robyn has been brain wiped, erased, rewound, then why?*

BB consolidates her own recollections. *The last time I saw Robyn she wore this same one-piece maillot cutout. She should be stripping at the Nugget this Term, except here she is again. Something happened that made the last Term never exist for Robyn; that way she really isn't Pledging again. She's Robyn Redacted. And she doesn't even know it.*

Robyn moves toward the back stairs. She sends another question to Babs. "So are you also a newbie Pledge, or were you a Stripper last Term?"

Boss Babe raises a finger. "It's like this, Pledge. I was a Pledge last Term. I Opted Up. I am a Monitor this Term. In fact, I am the Monitor of this Cosmos House."

"Monitor Babs?" Robyn sounds incredulous. "I thought—"

"You thought incorrectly, I might add." Babs stands up and lets fly. "As if thinking was ever much in your mind."

"I—"

Shut up." Babs means it. Robyn closes her mouth. Boss Babe gathers her wits. "Kneel and spread you knees; hands behind head."

"Monitor Babs—"

"Don't make me repeat myself!" Boss Babe hisses. "Kneel spread surrender. Oval mouth."

And Robyn acquiesces; apparently this much resides in her knowledge base.

BB spins on her heels. *Should my correction start with Robyn's first transgression, the proper doorway to use? Or with Robyn's improper form of address? Or her presumption of rooming with me?* Babs gathers her thumbs along the top of her nombril and rolls a fingertip inside her belly button. She considers. *Perhaps Robyn doesn't remember the Mudwrestling Contest, the one* she *refereed. Perhaps she won't remember Steph. Perhaps Robyn doesn't remember a lot of things.* A small bead of sweat pops out on Babs' brow. *But I have first-hand knowledge when we were both Cosmos last Term. I remember.*

Tiffany silently dips her hair in the soapy wash water again. Tiffany's pants have ridden so far down her tail trough that her tailpipe almost sneaks into view. She listens but doesn't talk.

BB studies the kneeling yet unrepentant Robyn and sees her looking up at her. Boss Babe fills her lungs and points to the washerwoman, still wiping the floor with her soapy wet hair. Robyn's eyes follow the finger point. Robyn can see the soap bubbles running as the cracker wrings her hair out. Robyn's seen rugage before, but she curls her lip at what she considers vulgar excess.

Babs tilts her chin toward Tiffany. "Know who that is?"

Good test question for Robyn.

Robyn casts her eyes across Tiffany's raised tush and then back to Babs. She tosses her head back. "Well it's certainly not Janet," she ventures. "I saw her Picture too. She's a big jelly bag. So hair mop here could be either of the two spreaders hanging down on the baseboard, Penny or Coco. Turn her over; I can tell from the tits." Robyn laughs.

Boss Babe waves a hand in the direction of the butt cracker and says drolly, "That's a former Whore who has pledged the Cosmos House. And Gamers have assigned *her* to bunk with me."

Robyn breaks her hands from behind her neck, runs them through her hair, and opens her mouth to correct what must be an obvious mistake. Babs points a finger toward Robyn, and Robyn unhurriedly returns her hands behind her head. Sweat beads pop out in both exposed armpits. Robyn suddenly worries her maillot might slip down.

Babs provides, "You'll sleep in the Bunkroom upstairs; you get first pick of which bunk to sleep in. Pick any: top or bottom."

"But, but, but..." Robyn stammers now, no longer able to restrain herself. She breaks position to check her strapless neckline, returns her hands behind her head and rotates, first one elbow down and then the other. "It's bad enough having to bunk underneath the Monitor—real second-class—but having to sleep in the Bunkroom is unacceptable."

Tiffany, listening to every word, wonders how Boss Babe will treat this argumentative arrival. Tiffany would never interject herself at this point, nor would most other Pledge, but Robyn grasps for an injection.

She comes up with a line. "I mean, I'll need to use the private bathroom!" Robyn means Babs' private bathroom, obviously.

Babs considers. *Maybe Robyn has memories after all.*

"There is no 'private bathroom,'" Babs corrects, "at least not for you, nor for any other Cosmos Pledge." Robyn prepares to reply, but BB pounces. "I said 'oval mouth!'" She adds detailed instructions. "You shall use the Bathroom at the end of the hallway, just like everyone else."

Robyn looks from Babs to Tiffany, and Tiffany's crusty red scratches stare up at her. Scratches across her back, dimples, and rugage. Robyn flinches.

Tiffany holds her position. She might be eager to give Robyn a blast of Eraser Heads in see-through, but she remains respectful and professional enough to let Boss Babe direct the show.

Robyn dips an elbow toward Tiffany. "I don't need an ex-Whore sleeping in *my* bed! Or using the private bathroom...." Robyn's defense crumbles, becoming interspersed with voids between logic and memory of Rules. As if it matters whether Robyn talks sense or not.

Babs tightens control. "You are not my Roommate." Babs pauses for emphasis before adding, "Besides, my Roommate already begs to share the Bathroom along with the rest of you Pledge! And if you're so into sharing the Bathroom with my Roommate, why not let her tell you its perks?"

Babs pauses, and calls to the Pledge on the floor, "Tiffany! Turn around. Meet Robyn."

Tiffany lifts and pivots her body so she sits on the floor with her legs wide. She braces her body up by putting her hands on the floor behind her back. She studies Pledge Robyn. Tiffany has been listening and paying attention to the exchange and wonders why Babs appears to exert lax discipline on this newcomer. Tiffany knows BB can lash out; she also knows to perform when BB demands it. Like now.

Tiffany looks Robyn in the face and nods. "Hello," she says. "I am Tiffany Porn Star. Ma'am only allows me to use the Bathroom if I'm naked and all the Cams are on." Tiffany pauses and gropes for a punch line for this precocious princess. "I'll help make you a Stripper next Term, but if you want to be like me, you need to beg to become a naked Pee-Cam Pledge. Then we can Pee-Cam together!"

Babs tilts her head back, squints; BB smiles at her Roommate's contribution, but still keeps her eyes on Robyn.

Tiffany's recitation unnerves Robyn, as does kneeling on the floor and thus being closer to Tiffany, who is now sitting before her. Robyn does a double take; she suddenly sees Tiffany's bare tits and distended Eraser Heads clearly through the vinyl front-button longsleeve croptop. Robyn eyes acres of scratched and welted bellage with a belly button front and center. Robyn scans down to consider that Tiffany's slacks stretch so tight that they cameltoe and so low that lots of red hair fluffs above the waistband.

Robyn curls one lip and speaks to Tiffany, "Hello, Tiffany Transparent." Robyn lifts a nostril. "You're a hairage Whore!" Robyn leans forward without thinking and talks across to Tiffany. "I'm Robyn. And you're in my bunk!"

"Stop it!" BB interrupts. "Be nice. Tiffany has two Garments and wants rid of some. Let's be friends here." Boss Babe firms control. "Your sleeping arrangements have been decided: you shall sleep in the first bottom bunk in the Bunkroom. Furthermore—"

A badly mannered Robyn interrupts her, crying, "Wait! I thought you said I could pick any bunk, because I was here first."

Boss Babe draws in a chest full of air. *Silly Pledge. You're thinking now? When did this begin?* "If you want to argue about where you rest your head, then I will make decisions for you," BB announces. "And I just did."

Robyn blinks.

Tiffany brings a hand around to her front, fingers her cameltoe, and returns her hand behind her body to help balance her weight. She spots herself.

§ Robyn Challenges Babs: So Tiffany Will Make Up Robyn

Robyn pouts, smoothes her tight maillot, and considers her setbacks: no private bath, no privileged position, and physically farther away from the center of power. She launches a new foray and blurts, "So where is stuff for me? What's with my locker?"

Tiffany glances toward Babs, and they trades eyes. Tiffany brings her other hand around, touches her wet spot, moves her fingers to her mouth, and touches her tongue. Tiffany has learned that asking question gains one a naked Pee-Cam, that pretending to not know Janet earned a reward of scratches and mud, and that too much coaxing Babs to reveal her tan lines resulted in making out with herself in the Mirror.

Tiffany teases Babs. "Ma'am, she's so full of questions, Ma'am."

Babs nods a "thank you," feels the top of her molars with the tip of her tongue, and elects to set her own pace. BB restrains her tendency to compensate for Tiffany's deeper experience in the Game with more rigid discipline. *Easy does it. My handling of the vacuous Robyn must consider why this Pledge was allowed to restart. Start over. Repeat the Term. But here she is.*

Some even say Robyn has Charm.

BB gathers her thumbs in her waistline and reads law to Robyn. "Listen to me, Pledge. There is no 'your locker.' There is a Cosmos locker I am allowing you to hang your maillot in, may you choose to go naked."

Robyn rushes words. "But what about lipstick and hairspray for me? Foundation and rouge? Eyeliner and eyelash brush?" Robyn pauses, trying to remember. "And... and everything else I need?"

Babs agrees, "But of course. Another reason to be nice to Tiffany. She will do your hair and make you up."

"Tiffany?" Robyn looks with disgust at the wet-haired washerwoman sitting spread legged on the floor before her.

Tiffany nods back. "I'll make you sexy."

"I don't need you to do my makeup," Robyn insults.

Babs corrects, "I'm sorry, Robyn, but *I* decide what you need. And Tiffany has volunteered to maintain the Makeup Case."

"I make up Babs with the regality of Cleopatra," Tiffany twinkles. "And I'll make you up like one of Cleopatra's Strippers."

Robyn snaps, "You'll probably make me look like a Whore, having been one and all."

Tiffany smiles at what she considers an excellent suggestion.

"You'll beg me to have you made up anyway I want you to look!" Babs snaps in irritation. "And it's 'please, Ma'am.'"

Robyn stammers at this; Gamers appreciate her reversal.

"Get it right the first time!" Boss Babe steels her command. Robyn's eyes scan Tiffany; reality check; no give there. "Now!"

And so Robyn speaks from a kneeling spread surrender position, and she speaks correctly, albeit with a bit of a singsong. "Please, Ma'am, order Tiffany to use the Makeup Case and make me beautiful!"

Tiffany looks at Robyn's streaked blonde hair and green eyes. Then she glances at Babs and squints ever so faintly. Babs smiles. *Yes, Tiffany will give this ditz plenty of makeup.*

BB considers ordering Robyn to repeat the "Ma'am" mantra for an hour or two, but she savors that holding pattern for another time. *Best I pace myself; this one is going to need a lot of correction, although as far as I'm concerned, Robyn's Fate at the end of the Term is decided.*

Tiffany delights that Babs unleashes the Makeup Case into the Cosmos House. *Such momentum so early in the Game! I don't know what dynamics Babs and the Cosmos might provide, but at Flesh Ranch some very special makeup and even perfumes were frequently applied to a Whore's body.*

Babs looks at Tiffany and makes the smallest lift of her jaw, which Tiffany correctly interprets as an order to terminate her floor scrubbing. She bundles her wet hair carefully to one side, returns to her hands and knees position, kisses her Monitor's bare feet, and pushes the Watering Can toward the Back Door.

Perhaps Tiffany will be able to make it to the Mudpit, spill the bucket of water, and slip and wallow in wet mud amidst a gaggle of invisible paparazzi before BB comes to her rescue?

"Hands and knees to the stairway," Boss Babe orders Robyn, "then on your feet up the stairs. Then install yourself in your bunk."

Robyn scampers.

§ Robyn: Heads Upstairs to the Bunkroom

It is déjà vu for Robyn as she stomps up the angular stairway. *The servants' stairs.* At the top of the stairs to her left lies the common Bathroom; to her right lies the Bunkroom with its cascade of stacked bunks. Across from the top of the stairs Robyn looks into the Bedroom that tickles her deneuralized relationship with her former Roommate and Monitor Steph. *A Bedroom that I should be sharing!* "But no," she mutters, "Boss Bitch now shares it with Tiffany."

Robyn turns right and enters the spacious Bunkroom. The three successive pairs of over-and-under bunks built into the back wall are long enough to lie down in and almost tall enough to sit up on. Robyn curls her lip at the accommodations. Less space than a cell, but much more space than a cage. But no mattress, no pillow, and no linen to hide under while sleeping?

Hey, Pledge must have some goals to aspire to!

Open lockers, set into the wall adjacent to each pair of bunks, form an alternating rhythm down the back wall. Each locker consists of a shelf near the top with a hook beneath to hang clothes... might one have clothes to hang. No doors, no privacy, and no hiding anything. Robyn smolders. *I will just have to sleep in my strapless maillot cutout. No way I'm going to swing my Garment from the locker hook and be naked with anyone else here.*

Robyn looks at her full-figured reflection on the mirrored wall 15 feet or so opposite the bunks. She admires her curvaceous figure, clad in the stretchy strapless maillot with its minimalist cutout. "Navelage 24x7," she says to herself in the Mirror. "I got the smallest buttonhole of all."

Yes, the Mirror that covers the entire wall is tactile, and yes, Tiffany did feel herself kiss herself when she made out with herself yesterday. And were one to ask, Tiffany might admit she still feels the buzz and wants more of it. But Mirror reveals none of these aspects of itself to Robyn. Robyn might have no memories of Mirror, but it doesn't mean Mirror doesn't remember her.

Robyn pirouettes in the center of the Room. "Big enough," she says out loud, filling the Bunkroom with her voice. "I shall show Boss Bitch how to lay her Pledge on the floor spread-eagled. They can lie on their bellies and kiss the floor, or lie on their back and imagine they float above the ceiling."

Robyn studies the windowless, plastered, and smooth wall at the far end of the Bunkroom and curls her lip in a snarl. "Maybe it will please Boss Bitch to have her Pledge paint the wall and practice rubbing their bodies against the wet paint."

Perhaps it will please Boss Babe to order her Pledge up against the Mirror and have them practice kissing and rubbing themselves. *Should I let Mirror take on some load, then I could take on more time for thinking.*

§ Robyn: Visits the Cosmos House Bathroom

But enough speculation. Robyn returns down the short hallway and enters the Bathroom. Were Robyn to consider her spatial position she would deduce the Bathroom is located above the Kitchen. It could have a window looking out just past the side of the Porch, but it has no windows at all. Nor does the Bathroom possess any door or protective barrier, and its lack of privacy creeps Robyn. Robyn curls her bare toes to feel the tile underfoot. Tile also covers all the walls except for one wall, which is mirrored, and another wall with two stools facing a makeup table with a different mirror behind it surrounded by lights.

Robyn inventories a washbasin, urinal, bidet, toilet, standup shower, and a large deep bathing tub, all to facilitate cleaning and disposal of waste. There is running water throughout, a floor drain, and an overstep at the entrance to ensure water doesn't flow into the hallway.

Robyn needs to pee. No one else occupies the upstairs. *Tiffany has already warned me that the moment she enters the Bathroom the Pee-Cam starts rolling. That's disgusting, so I really don't need Tiffany barging in.*

Robyn hurriedly elects to pee in the bidet, keeping an ear tuned to the old wooden stairs. She squats over it, pulls the gusset of her maillot to the side, revealing a trimmed blonde bush that no one ever sees, and releases a light yellow stream until her bladder drains empty. She shakes herself off and makes sure not to stain her maillot.

Robyn restores her maillot to its proper decorum, navel encircled by the taut hole, and carefully places the strapless neckline across her cleavage. She washes her hands, and in the process of drying them manages to wetten the fabric covering her shapely breasts. When she glances at herself in the mirror she can tell that her nipples have erected beneath. *Headlights,* Robyn admires to herself in the mirror. *But only I know my rosettes are rose-colored.*

Robyn turns, retreats to the Bunkroom, and installs herself in her bunk. *I know. I'm pretty important.*

§ Robyn Tells Tiffany: About Her Maillots Last Term (D04)

Robyn and Tiffany clash the next morning, Day Four, after Babs orders Tiffany to prepare Robyn's makeup. Robyn, still wearing her maillot of course, finds herself confronting a naked Tiffany in front of the Bathroom makeup table and mirror. Nothing hides Tiffany's Eraser Heads and thinnish red bush, and Robyn does not compute that Tiffany's fading and now darker red scratch marks relate only to that part of her body above the tan line left behind by her stretch slacks, and below the protection afforded by her longsleeve croptop; in other words, her bellage and lower back.

"I know you always have to be naked in here," Robyn derides, "and with the Cam on. You're a Whore and a Pee-Cam Pledge! I saw your Calendar downstairs. And your not just a Pee-Camer, you're also a Piss Mouth. You can't fool me."

True, the picture of Tiffany in the Calendar captures her lying on her back with her legs raised above her, her hands pulling her tossaroon wide, and a stream of pee arching downward into her mouth. It does fully qualify the lithe redhead as a Piss Mouth.

"Don't forget that I am a Porn Star," Tiffany emphasizes. It requires a pro to make an accurate self-assessment. "I'm proud to have been a Whore, and, I might add, a mighty good one. I didn't just work Flesh Ranch; I've worked the streets, peep-booths, and shot porn. I've jerked off cocks stuck through glory holes. Blew them. I've done everything explicit. All holes. All sexes. So don't start thinking you're my equal!"

"Your equal?" Robyn is shocked. "I'm here to make sure you cam yourself peeing and then lick up after yourself."

A chill goes through the Bathroom and the fine hairs on Tiffany's naked body stand up. She soothes gently, "Ah, so ambitious. And you're just a newbie this Term!"

"Well, perhaps," Robyn confesses. Sometimes her amnesia wears thin. "But I'm better than that. I've got a really small buttonhole."

"Oh?" Tiffany rolls her eyes and squints. "You might have the smallest buttonhole, but your maillot only counts as one Garment." She tosses one shoulder back. "You plan on Stripping next Term?"

Robyn snaps back, "Look, you thatch hatch, there's a lot you don't know. Lotsa Pledge arrive in one piece; some even pledge totally naked."

Tiffany tosses a softball. "So tell me about the Picture underneath Babs in the Dining Room Pictures. The Gamer with the humongous jugs and jumbo jute patch in the Spiderweb Bikini."

Robyn curls a nose. "Janet. I could *smell* her Picture. It's like she smeared her juice all over it. I'd bet she's another Stripper who wallowed around in the Mudpit and jacked off in her g-string. I bet she pinked just like the two on the bottom."

"The Baseboard Strippers, Penny and Coco," Tiffany claims. "Last seen streaking to the Nugget."

"Good riddance, I'm sure," Robyn confirms. She helps herself to the razor from the Makeup Case, then soaps and shaves her armpits and legs. Robyn makes sure the Cam captures that first long stroke down each thigh, where the razor makes a pathway of skin through the lather.

Once finished shaving Robyn finds herself uncertain what to do with the razor. But Tiffany fills the void: she reacquires this asset, which belongs inside the Makeup Case, and places the Makeup Case out of reach of the "newbie."

Tiffany takes Robyn's face in her hands and begins to rub moisturizer into it. "So do you know if Janet has any rings?" she probes.

Robyn sits on a stool and examines her own "perfect" figure in the makeup mirror. She contemplates the ex-Cosmos in the Dining Room Picture, now adorned with the Spiderweb Bikini. "Rings? Well, not in her nipples," Robyn laughs. "The way they stick out the center of that spiderweb! Although studs might be better."

Tiffany applies a primer gel to Robyn's face. She listens.

Robyn continues, "As for between her legs, I don't know if they show or not, but Janet's probably the kind of juju who would spread her legs wide in a crowded Strip joint, thread a cord through some rings, and pull the cord to divaricate her jam pot wide open."

Tiffany frames another query. "So what about Monitor Babs? Areolage and hairage on the wall, but did Babs ever take any ink and steel?"

Robyn looks back at Tiffany in the mirror and forgets that the presence of Tiffany lights up the Bathroom Cam, picture and sound. "Boss Bitch?" Robyn snarls. "She's never even been to the Nugget."

Tiffany again touches her fingers to Robyn's cheeks to carefully blend foundation into her skin, followed by loose powder.

Tiffany thinks ahead but speaks in the present as she brushes Robyn's hair back. "Do you intend to take a second Garment from your Roommate and Opt Up next Term?"

Robyn observes Tiffany, naked as always here in the Bathroom, and snorts, "Well, obviously you don't have anything to offer me." She apparently forgets that Tiffany possesses a shirt and slacks, currently hanging in her locker inside the Bedroom. They have been there since bedtime last night.

Tiffany works rouge onto Robyn's cheeks; Robyn will get her first touch of the harlot today.

Robyn volunteers, "Furthermore, you're not even my Roommate. My Roommate hasn't arrived yet."

"Hold still," Tiffany instructs.

She darkens Robyn's upper eyelids and under the eyebrow. She finesses eyebrows and eyelashes. And she computes. *Let's assume the two newbies will arrive as Roommates. That means that Robyn's Roommate could be Steph, but more likely it will be one of the Nugget Strippers Opting Up to Pledge here at the Cosmos House. Probably with just one Garment each. Sweet.*

"Quiet now," Tiffany orders. She adds heavy and wide bright red lipstick onto and around Robyn's lips.

Robyn examines her figure in the makeup mirror and aggrandizes herself. "It wasn't easy to finagle this maillot. It's the smallest buttonhole possible, only two inches across. It really frames my navel, and because I have reduced my exposures to men, I have made myself even more precious and attractive to them." Robyn thinks and adds, "But...."

"But what?" Tiffany prods.

"Well, somehow, this maillot altogether lacks straps or a lining, and it uses really thin stretch fabric." True, Robyn's strapless maillot possesses no foundation; a gusset sewn into the crotch and hems up the two sides contour the Garment. The advanced Gamer tracks such things.

Tiffany sprays light yellow glitter onto Robyn's bare shoulders.

Robyn reminisces, "I thought I'd be getting not only my smaller cutout hole, but also shoulder straps. I need the straps because they hold the maillot up more securely... and increase my number of edges."

Tiffany can't resist a wicked assist, and she tops Robyn's makeup up to hottie status. "Oh, don't worry. You look gorgeous! And if you move carefully you can maintain your modesty, even without your straps. And besides," Tiffany confides in her ear, "you have steel eyes in your neckline hem, so your straps must be somewhere. Maybe you should tell Babs to assign them to you." Tiffany leans back. "But you didn't hear this from me."

Robyn nods. "Of course not. I'm entitled to them. I'll make sure BB understands that."

Making the cutout hole smaller had involved exchanges, but Robyn no longer remembers what they were. It doesn't matter. *I'm ahead of the Game. I can feel my maillot grip me about my rigamarole; I know the elastic will keep the swimsuit up, and I know that the stretchy fabric contours my rig and rear end and flatters all of me.* Robyn looks in the mirror, admires her outie in its tightly controlled buttonhole, and accepts her makeup.

Robyn fails to thank Tiffany, instead leaving her and the Makeup Case behind in the Bathroom. *I know I possess a superior costume starting out this Term, and I have just become an even better man magnet!*

Might men prostrate themselves before Robyn, Robyn will certainly walk all over them.

Yet Robyn has no idea of what tricks her new maillot might play.

§ Babs & Tiffany: Discuss Robyn & Anticipate Steph (D04)

Tiffany stays naked as she walks from the Bathroom to the Bedroom, and she elects to remain naked once she discovers Babs sitting on the chair behind the Desktop.

Babs points a toenail at the cubicle on the floor beneath her bunk, and Tiffany crawls into the alcove, leaving her clear vinyl croptop and low-rise slacks to continue to hang in her locker behind Babs. No Cam here; still, Tiffany will attempt to stay naked as much as possible, and to shed Garments for good.

Babs leans forward and talks down to Tiffany. "Tell me what you learned about Robyn."

Tiffany stumbles. "Ma'am, I touched her up like one of Cleopatra's Strippers, Ma'am. She's very proud of her small buttonhole. And she thinks she needs shoulder straps."

Babs firms her jaw. "Robyn may have amnesia from last Term, but just because her histories appear erased and she wasn't 'officially' a Cosmo Pledge doesn't mean *I* don't remember!"

Tiffany reclines on her side and draws a single finger through her triangle of love, aligning it with her reclining position. "I don't know enough about what went on here last Term to know if Robyn has any memories or not, but if you didn't watch us live on the Cam, you can always watch the replay."

Tiffany shuffles, and the side of her belly that's all scratched up stings when the scratches contact the wood. She exhales. *A small price to pay to entertain my fans.*

Babs rests an elbow on her desk and avoids looking at Tiffany's scratched bellage. "I remember Robyn," she advances, "but Robyn doesn't seem to remember me. Maybe I must accept that." BB draws a finger to her cheek. "But precisely why she's pledging again remains a mystery to me, since Pledge are supposed to either Opt Up or Opt Down."

"Selective amnesia, huh?" Tiffany says. "Maybe Robyn assumes she is exempt from Rules. I'm sure she has conveniently forgotten whatever factors annulled her last Term and enable her to repeat Pledging. Or maybe she was brainwashed, or administered nepenthe."

"She Redacted herself or got Redacted," BB concludes.

"Robyn Redacted," Tiffany sings. "I like that!"

"And you're not uneasy with the uncertainty?" grouses Boss Babe.

"Maybe I should be, but what's the story with her maillot?" Tiffany scratches a shallow scab on the front of her belly.

Babs knows. "Well, last Term was actually the first Term for both of us, or at least it was purported to be. Robyn had pledged at the very last minute, and the only available slot required that she pledge with only one Garment. So she enrolled wearing a bulky tank maillot, a swimsuit with straps that buttoned over her shoulders; it was fully lined, had lots of elastic and seams, and uplifted her rack. It showed cleavage, but the straps always allowed her to contain herself and preserve her freedom of movement. Retro, yet very becoming. She does have a great pair of rah-rahs, I'll admit. Her legline arched up very gently from her receptaculum, and it made her legs look great. The bottom never crawled up her rump; it had a hem up the back, which separated her rear end into two halves."

"Sounds tasty," Tiffany considers.

Babs rolls her nose. "Robyn never knows when she's got it good. She complained that the maillot contained this huge cutout hole in the middle.

Which it did, like eight or ten inches across. So it opened a whole lot more real estate than was necessary for exposing her belly button." Babs laughs.

Tiffany resettles her naked body inside the lower alcove. *Ouch. I can feel the wood, and the scratches sting. My Karma. I failed to divulge that I knew Janet, but my fans got to watch me crawl through the prickly bushes. And they got to see me bathe, use the toilet, and make up Robyn. But after the scratches heal, then what?*

BB continues the story. "Steph was the Monitor last Term—you'll meet her soon enough, I suspect—and somehow Steph convinced Robyn that the size of her cutout hole presented her with an exposure problem. A big negative. The fact of the matter was that the very bottom of the cutout hole almost kissed her the top of her pussy hair. Her roughage. Almost, but never. Steph laughed at her about her navelage, and Robyn soon wanted to reduce its diameter."

"Silly Pledge," Tiffany concurs. Her back itches. She reaches behind to scratch her tail trough.

BB augments, "Robyn should have realized the positives about her swimsuit: its stiff foundation kept the buttonhole from moving around, and it contained and molded her figure. But no, Robyn assessed her condition differently. And it wasn't all Steph, either; Robyn reduced herself."

"So what happened?" Tiffany probes, curious now.

Babs brushes her long hair back. "I'm not quite sure how, but she used her wiles and steadfastly reduced the cutout hole diameter. Her first success came when she traded the tank for a tighter and more streamlined maillot. It had halter straps, and it was slightly thinner, unlined, had a rising legline, and a deeper but more notched cleavage. But the biggest improvement was that the cutout hole only spanned four inches!"

"And now she's got an even smaller and thinner maillot with an even smaller buttonhole," Tiffany observes. "So she can get even more looks and control even more men."

The Roommates laugh together.

Tiffany inquires, "So, how do you figure her handicapped memory plays into the Game?"

"I distrust anyone with selective memories, no memory, or who just makes stuff up." Babs speaks emphatically.

Tiffany attempts to give Robyn a gentle cast. "I think her brain blurs, biases, and consolidates observations. She told me you're wearing the exact same Bikini as last Term. Sort of true, even though, and pardon me, Ma'am, your Dining Room Picture shows your waistline folded down. You don't show hairage any more, or cleave your butt."

"Robyn's a poor observer with a bad memory," BB agrees. "But that's just her good side. She's malicious, pure and simple. She'll do anything to advance herself. She'd never consider it cheating, of course, because in her mind, Rules and honesty only apply for other Pledge."

"Last Term Steph was the Cosmos Monitor and Robyn was her Roommate?" Tiffany double checks.

BB confirms, "Right, and Steph used Robyn as her henchman, her enforcer. Robyn was an all-too-willing accomplice; she still doesn't care who she steps on. She's forgotten all that, but many of those Gamers still play the Game, remain irritated, and do not suffer from amnesia!"

"Like yourself," Tiffany suggests.

"Not just me. Janet also harbors grievances. And not just about the Mudwrestling Contest." Babs tucks her nombril up.

Tiffany stretches. "Well, it seems like you both came out on the side you wanted to. You're both Monitors this Term. What's not to like? And besides, Robyn thinks you are her ally. She thinks she befriended you in the past and that you owe her. And that Janet is a Stripper somehow."

Babs expresses irritation, "I suspect Janet will enjoy straightening her out on that one."

"So did you ever audition at the Nugget when you were a Pledge last Term?" Tiffany gentles. Tiffany knows how the Game works.

Babs adjusts, "Er, ah, no. And I never ever ran around topless, outside the House or inside. Once, before I enrolled in School, I visited a beach where some of the women were topless, but I would never take my top off. Last Term I became the Bikini Babe, and even that was a stretch for me. At least now I'm the Boss Babe. Sooner rather than later I will take whatever Garment the next Cosmos arrives in and cover my bling. Sorry that your clear vinyl longsleeve front-button croptop doesn't meet my requirements, but I will cover up just as soon as it pleases me."

Sounds easy.

Tiffany probes for snags. "Maybe Janet danced the Nugget on your behalf last Term?"

"No way. I know better." BB gathers her arguments. "Maybe I never asked her much about her Stripper past two Terms ago—and you were there—but if she had ever danced at the Nugget *last* Term I'd know it."

Tiffany suggests, "Maybe the Nugget Crowd was tired of her act by the time she became your Roommate last Term."

Babs spouts off, "Janet really did arrive naked and really did have to live in the Mudpit for a days before Steph let her hose off and ring the Bell. Janet stayed naked for most of the Term, even inside. Steph got her to volunteer to thread her rings and jigger herself to climax in the Backyard in front of any Cosmos who wanted to watch. I'm sure not only the Back Door Cam, but the paparazzi too, took it all in, but at least I didn't have to watch. She didn't get even get her Spiderweb Bikini until just before the Mudwrestling Contest at the end of the Term." Babs catches her breath. "I guess if Janet doesn't mind then I shouldn't. Janet actually likes people watching her jack off and blowing her top. But she also likes power."

"So she never Pee-Cammed last Term?" Tiffany sidles casually.

"Maybe she Pee-Cammed when she was a Stripper with you two Terms ago, but there is no way Janet Pee-Cammed last Term when we were Pledge. That's because there wasn't any Pee-Cam at the Cosmos House. Listen, none of your Obeisances are a result of my hand. You brought the Pee-Cam to the Cosmos House with you. You arrived with your Eraser Heads and tats. None of that's my Karma."

"Maybe bringing the Pee-Cam to the Cosmos House balances my Double Opt Up?" Tiffany theorizes. "But fact: I'm a Pee-Camer because it brings value to the Game. *I* collect views. And the sooner you take away one or both of my Garments, the happier I'll be, and the more Gamers will love you. I *want* to Opt Down and become a Stripper next Term. Helps me head toward Flesh Ranch. Ma'am. I'll do whatever you need. I'll masturbate in the Mudpit."

"You'll move into the Mudpit if I have to keep listening to you," Babs admonishes. "I doubt that Robyn even considers that one of your Garments would assure her an Opt Up."

Tiffany surprises, "Ma'am, surely you don't mean that Robyn's that oblivious to Fate?" Tiffany reads the response in Babs' eyes, reconsiders, and inches forward. "And respectfully, Ma'am, I can't help but notice that you don't correct Robyn for any misdeeds."

"No one corrected her for her misdeeds last Term either, especially Steph," Babs responds, slightly testy. "And you're right: she thinks I will be taking care of her and assuring her of a promotion. She thinks I will take another piece from some other Cosmos, bestow it upon her, and that next Term she will be a Monitor, where her many talents will be highly valued."

Tiffany understands. "You intend to allow her to continue her self-deception and become over-confident." Tiffany watches Babs start to object and rushes, "Hey, no problem! Maybe she doesn't need to. I am a Porn Star; I'm above her judgmental deprecations of me and her aggrandizement of herself. Today she looks like one of Cleopatra's Strippers, Ma'am. She and I both, Ma'am!"

Babs concedes, "I shall inspect her, and I have every confidence she will be as stunning as you are!"

"Ma'am, thank you Ma'am." Tiffany scrunches forward in her alcove and chaffs skin and scabs.

"We shall see how long it takes the other Cosmos to react to Robyn's apparent privilege," Babs muses.

"How long will it take them to figure out you have a hand in the Game?" Tiffany parks her tongue in her cheek.

"Listen." Babs clenches her teeth. "Robyn is not worth the effort for me to crush. I don't know any of the Pledge who are arriving except Steph, but I do know this: Steph will endeavor to devour her."

"Devour her?"

"Devour her!"

Tiffany licks a forefinger, reaches, and touches it to her clit. "Don't forget, you are the Monitor Boss, so if you don't want Steph to go hog wild, then don't let her."

"I get you." Boss Babe straightens her shoulders up and pushes her chest forward. "Maybe I can arrange for them to devour each other."

7 Steph Encounters Babs & Janet & Robyn, also Tiffany (D04)

§ Steph: Costume & Body Semi-intimate Details

Steph approaches the Cosmos House with confidence. It is the day after Robyn arrived, Day Four, and dusk settles over the Village and the Cosmos House. Steph will be the third Pledge (and fourth Cosmos) to arrive at the Cosmos House, following Babs and Tiffany and Robyn.

Steph walks on the sidewalk, aware she is overexposed. *Paparazzi desire to collect titter from inside my hacked cutout minidress. Inside my gaping armholes. Possibly also hairage, from inside the huge, hacked-out belly hole, if not from the minidress being too short.* She tries to move quickly. *I know the destination ahead. I was the Cosmos House Monitor last Term! I know a lot.*

Steph is correct about her paparazzi value. Steph's more intimate lady parts have remained a prize that paparazzi have long craved... and have been denied access to. Steph tightly controlled her own exposures when she Monitored last Term, and whatever happened during her initial newbie Pledge Term (two Terms ago) seems to be absent in Automatron's memory.

Maybe things will change this Term.

Or maybe not.

The fact of the matter is that I shouldn't be headed to the Cosmos House this Term! Steph pauses to look at her reflection in a window: a slender white woman with determined blue eyes and thin lips, a smile with sparkling white teeth. *I look pretty darn good. For someone being treated unfairly.*

Steph kicks into motion again, hair flowing, and legs stretching as she paces atop the sidewalk. She tries to balance her pace with the enveloping dusk of the evening. *The darker it is, the even more challenging for paparazzi to stalk me. I can't stand those illicit perverts. Last Term they wanted to collect my panties upskirt. Now they just want to me to trip and fall so they can harvest any titter or upskirt when I get back up. Put me on the black market.*

Only now any upskirt won't present panties. Steph squares her shoulders and keeps her arms close to her sides. She casts her eyes at building she passes. Upper stories. Rooftops. She snarls and speaks out loud, "You paparazzi and you Gamers you can't get enough of me through official channels, so you resort to extremes. I'll show you."

Maybe, and maybe for not very long.

It's hard to learn that playing the Game torments Fate. *In the Game, stay the Game. I know that.* The paparazzi are wildcats to Automatron, but Automatron can still clarify Steph's identification, and stores any shared streams in its memories. In return, Automatron caches forward basic Steph stats: the slim 5' 5" tiny-titter weighs 105 pounds and last taped in at 32A-23-32. Never nude. Never topless. Never vagflash.

Steph tosses her figure and smoothes her minidress. She walks carefully, placing one bare foot in front of the other, looking ahead to where best put her feet down, how to balance and pace. She looks up. Around. Behind her! She steps on a stone and must pay attention to her feet again. *I can't stop paparazzi from collecting my bellage from my sternum almost to the top of my short and wavy hairs. And I can only move so fast. So they can take their time with me.*

Steph squares up her posture again. *I* know Gamers can look at my nice legs almost all the way up to my crotch. I know this minidress presents challenges, and the faster I move the quicker the Garment looses its ability to cover me up. I know that Gamers can be careless and inconsiderate of my exposures; some have never even lifted a finger to help, and some have worked against me. But there is no way paparazzi are going to collect any shrubbery while I'm on my way to the Cosmos House!

Last term Steph wore panties through her crotch. Not anymore.

Last Term Steph kept herself covered in a shortsleeve minidress with either panties or heels. One or the other, but always two pieces. Not anymore.

Last Term auspicious Gamers had figured Steph didn't own a bra and coveted Steph's flat but perky chest, hidden just below her scooped neckline. They hunted for sideboob. And Steph slayed them whenever she crossed her long legs and pretended to not flash her panties. She was very blasé about that.

Even when Steph had worn the minidress sanpan with heels, *Gamers never got to see crotch. Never scruff, nor shrubbery, nor short hairs, nor shag, nor sugar bush. Nada.* Steph had pressed her legs together when she sat, crossed them the most carefully, and rose into a vertical position without the hemline riding up.

Today Steph still wears her minidress, but her panties are gone. Gone also are any heels; the minidress is Steph's single Garment. Or what's left of it. The sleeves are missing, and it is way too easy for Gamers to look into the where the armholes were cut back. The hacked minidress has a huge hole ripped out of the midsection that reveals not just a small puckered navel, but also an acre of creamy skin with fine hairs around it.

She keeps walking, headed in direction of the Cosmos House. Steph knows the way. Spent last Term there.

§ Babs & Robyn visit Janet: Corvette House Examination

Babs anticipates Steph's arrival with dread. On the morning of the fourth day, not knowing Steph heads for the Cosmos House, she sends Tiffany on an errand and gathers Robyn to visit Janet at the Corvette House. Babs intends that Janet not only examine Robyn's memory but also provide backstory about Tiffany and advice about handling Steph.

Once past the Back Door and the Bell, Babs leads Robyn through the Backyard into a maze of alleyways and street crossings. Babs' public exposure haunts her, and she directs her eyes downward at her own areolage. Bling blush. But then recovery, as a more steely part of her brain interrupts and lifts her chin up. *I shall take careful steps, keep my babambas contained, and rob paparazzi of any payday. I'll pick my own path. And Robyn shall stay with me.*

Babs delivers Robyn to the front door of the Corvette House. Janet smiles as she collects Robyn inside; Babs sits on the porch behind the railing. It provides protection from paparazzi, but not from any Corvette House Cam. Babs can't stop a blush from coming on. She takes a deep breath. *Maybe I can't control areolage—yet—but I do have a plan to make sure my babambas stay contained, using something I found in the Makeup Case.*

Babs crosses her arms in front of her. She keeps her arms crossed and her areolage sequestered. She waits while Janet appraises Robyn inside. *Trade offs. I get to know what Janet thinks about Robyn, but I have to expose myself. I am the Bikini Babe. I not only still have to walk back, but everyone now knows I'm here.*

Babs wonders what conclusions Janet will come to about Robyn. *What if Robyn's amnesia isn't fake? What if the Gamers really did some kind of reset? Robyn Redacted. And if they can do that to Robyn, what about me? Is it something one can even see coming? Know if it has even happened to you?*

BB evaluates her Game status. *Last Term I was one of Steph's Pledge, and yes, this Term Steph shall be one of my Pledge.*

What don't I understand about that?

Babs clarifies a thought and practices in her mind what she might say to a virtual Steph standing spread surrender before her. *Last Term you made me wash your entire foot with my tongue. Suck the toes one by one. Lick clean in between them. Wetten the soles of your feet with spittle, so as to wash, but not tickle.*

You and Madam Nurse Beautician conspired to foot train me. Mouth practice. Maybe sometimes Beautician made me wash feet before I licked them, but she never made me lick soap off of them. But you, Steph Sorostitute, you made me clean soap off every Cosmos foot.

Last Term Steph had acquired the behind-her-back nickname, Steph Sorostitute, a term for that mythical seductive and spoiled sorority princess.

You, Steph Sorostitute, are one aptly-named Gamer. Maybe you made me lick soapy feet, maybe you confined me to my bunk with a chamber pot, and maybe you put me in the Mudwrestling Contest. But whatever happened to you to at the end last Term didn't happen as a result of anything I did. I am not responsible for any role reversal between you and myself.

Of course not.

A barefoot Janet barges out the Corvette House front door with Robyn in tow. Janet's walked barefoot ever since her very first Term in the Game, and she navigates the wood and then concrete underfoot with ease.

"Come on," Janet says, jingle-jangling her spiderweb jaboos at Babs. "I told Robyn we'd show her around. She recognized me from my Dining Room Picture, but no other memories seem to gel." Janet centers the ends of her nipples in the center of her crochet Spiderweb halter and shakes her head. "I'm afraid she doesn't even know any Positions or Hand Signs, and she's probably forgotten she just talked to me."

Robyn perks up. "Don't be rude. I'm not the one flashing my areolage and bush. Or lotsa bellage; I'm the one with the smallest buttonhole. And besides, you two, since you say Steph was your Monitor last Term, maybe Steph remembers Positions and Hand Signs. After all, didn't she give the both of you lessons?"

Janet fiddles her sex lips back inside her g-string. She raises her eyebrows toward Babs, but BB chooses not to make this a teaching moment. Babs straightens her head and shoulders, draws her belly taut, and matches pace with the other two. *Janet jaboos and jipijapa and jaxy. Better for Janet to let it all hang out.*

BB considers herself. *And yes, I learned Hand Signs last Term.* She shifts to a lateral thought. *And if Robyn really did bring Steph down, then how? And how do I stay out of any snapback?*

Boss Babe considers Robyn in her thin strapless maillot cutout. *Littlest hole around!*

§ Steph Considers Babs… and Commits Robyn: Takedown

Steph pauses where she must turn from the sidewalk and considers the walkway up toward the Cosmos House. Just because the current dynamics occurred through no action of Babs, the sexually self-confident and exploitative Steph still considers Babs an impediment to her progress. Be it real or symbolic, the role-reversal adds insult to loss.

Am I hostile to the Bikini Babe? Do I hold her responsible for embarrassing me in public today? We'll see.

Steph speaks out loud as walks, "Bikini Babe, all you need to do is stay out of my way! Because I'm going to promote to Monitor next Term. If not sooner! So you'd better not disrespect me!"

Yes, Gamers understand that Steph was the Cosmos Monitor last Term, and for reasons Steph considers "most unwarranted and unfair," Steph returns to the Cosmos House, only as a Cosmos Pledge this turn. Demoted. Monitor Opted-Down to Pledge.

The root cause of Steph's demotion lies deeper than Babs. *An unplanned, unfortunate, and unfair set of circumstances conspired to stall* (more correctly, reverse) *my upward progression.*

"Hello Robyn, wherever you are, I'm coming to get you!"

Steph raises her chin. The huge, hacked armholes ensure titter. The huge, hacked buttonhole opens the stomach all the way down to her scruff. But Steph remains determined. *I shall transcend my current transitory diminution to Pledge status, so that next Term (if not sooner!) I shall return to my rightful Monitor Caste. Actually, I need to Double Opt Up and make it to House Mom el Capitan. MomCap! That's where I belong.*

And Babs better facilitate my advancement!

Steph forms Babs in her mind. *Well, perhaps Babs will not facilitate, but she will not dare get in my way. I won't be asking, I don't need to; I'll just take what I need. This is my third Term, and I do know how to play the Game.*

Steph has always been a creature of privilege. She assumes truth accommodates her needs, and knows: "I am a pure-breed!"

§ Steph: Arrives Front Door into an Empty Cosmos House

Steph turns from the sidewalk and strides up the walkway towards the Front Door of the Cosmos House. *I anticipate that I will leave the paparazzi behind me.*

Steph pauses and balances on her delicate bare feet at the bottom of the front steps where the walkway branches off around the Porch toward the Back Door. Steph does know the Rules.

So? I have never done Babs any wrong. Or Janet. I need to find out where Janet ended up. And I do need to establish my own privilege, right away.

Steph's long legs mount the front steps. She ignores the Front Door Cam, which officially collects her dirty, unkempt, overexposed, and bedraggled appearance in the deepening dusk. Steph turns a shoulder, knowing that it's too dark for the Front Door Cam to collect color details.

"Too bad, Automatron," Steph mocks. She doesn't ring the chime and disappears inside.

Steph breezes through the dusky Parlor and heads down the hallway toward the Kitchen. She sidetracks into the small Washroom under the front stairs, easily slides the remains of her minidress up, and lowers her sitter and bare thighs onto the toilet seat. She watches her urine release, dabs herself dry, flushes, and looks at herself in the mirror as she washes her face. *I'm back home... although with one complication....*

The door from the Parlor to the Kitchen is locked, so Steph retreats, swings back around into the Living Room, and sidles through the sliding door into the Dining Room. She stops short in front of the four Dining Room Photos.

"My, my." Steph admires the Bikini Babe and the Spiderweb. "So. You two won your Bikinis after all. And it's so great to see you stuck on the wall. You're both revealing more areolage and hairage than when I last saw you."

But it's the naked and wet-holed Penny and Coco who present the most delight for Steph Sorostitute. Steph doesn't need nametags to address the two naked pinkers, who were also her Pledge last Term. "Congratulations, Baseboard Strippers, maybe I'll be visiting to watch you pee and pink at the Nugget!"

Pledge should be careful what they wish for.

Steph takes a step back and continues to talk down to the Strippers. "It wasn't my hand that Opted you Down. You know who did it to you: the two on the top, Babs and Janet. So talk to them about it. I wasn't there."

Besides, I have my own beef. With the same Pledge whom I think refereed what should have been my call.

Robyn. A dispute no doubt stemming from something that happened near the end of last Term and contributed to Steph's demotion... and her missing the Mudwrestling Contest.

Steph assails the Kitchen. It's empty.

She heads upstairs, fully knowing her way. She appropriates the Makeup Case in what is now Babs' Bedroom, extracts the razor, showers in the Bathroom, and shaves her underarms and legs, including the insides of her thighs. She borrows a towel she finds in Babs' Bedroom to dry off, combs her long blonde hair, puts her soiled and hacked minidress back on, adds lipstick and rouge and mascara, and returns the Makeup Case to the drawer in BB's desk. She touches the Desktop, but it fails to light up for her.

Steph retraces her steps downstairs to the Kitchen. She finds a bottle of wine chilling in the refrigerator, opens it, and pours herself a glass. The Calendar on the wall is a new addition, and although she recognizes

"Tiffany Porn Star," she fails to anticipate that the naked, gangbanging Whore is now one of her Pledge sisters.

A glance out the Back Door reveals that the Backyard is empty. The Bell pull chain still hangs down almost to the ground, the Mudpit looks damp, the seven Posts stalwart the Henge, and the bushes down the side of the Backyard reach out prickly branches all the way down to the alley and fill in next to the Garage.

I made Pledge run circles around the Garage last Term. I made them hug Posts. I made them wallow in mud. Now I'm a Pledge, just like I was in my first Term. I should be a MomCap already.

The door from the Kitchen to the front hallway has a Skeleton Key in the lock, so Steph turns it, and, carrying her glass and the bottle, passes through the door, closing it behind her but leaving it unlocked. For a second time this evening she ducks into the Washroom underneath the front stairs and checks her face in the mirror. Much better now. She moves into the Parlor, sits in a big easy chair, crosses her legs, sips the wine, and contemplates her future.

My next goal is to demand a clean and less-revealing minidress, and after that to acquire panties... if not also heels! Steph furrows her brow. *The panties will rightfully advance me to Monitor rank, and the further addition of heels will give me a total of three pieces and accelerate me to a House Mom el Capitan rank. And catch me up to where I should be. MomCap. I know my entitlements!*

§ Babs & Janet & Robyn Greet Steph: Role Reversals

Babs arrives. She comes in the Front Door, accompanied by fellow Monitor Janet and trailed by Robyn, who allows the Front Door Cam to hover in beside her.

Steph knows Babs and Janet, even Robyn, from last Term—all were *her* Pledge—and Robyn in particular was her Roommate. Steph has been briefed that Babs is now Monitor, and she deduces from the four Dining Room Pictures that Janet has also Opted Upward, albeit at a different House. Steph curls her lip. *I saw Janet disgrace herself at the Alumni Reprise at the Nugget last Term! I know some things BB doesn't know about.*

Okay. But why is Robyn here?

Steph does not know that Janet has just finished inventorying Pledge Robyn's memories, found déjà vu but little else, and confirmed Babs' suspicions that, yes indeed, Robyn has been Redacted, whatever the method, whomever is responsible.

But Steph does not know this, at least not yet, and Robyn's presence inflames her. It is hard for Steph to control her reactions. *Monitors Babs and Janet I can understand; they are, after all, the top two Dining Room Pictures and apparent victors in the Mudwrestling Contest. But Robyn? Robyn betrayed me last Term. Has she also been promoted to a Monitor?* Steph studies Robyn. *But. Maillot cutout, maybe smaller buttonhole, but only one Garment. What's going on here?*

Steph returns her consideration to Babs and Janet. She squeezes her thighs tighter, points a finger, and barely suppresses laughter at Babs and Janet's Bikinis, Janet's especially.

"Spider Janet." Steph draws a hand to her mouth. "And Bikini Babe." Steph doesn't even bother to stand up.

Babs and Janet look at each other, and Janet responds, "Well, if an ill wind didn't blow in Steph Sorostitute. You look like you walked into a fan, Pledge."

Makeup doesn't disguise the fact Steph's minidress has been hacked. Steph keeps her arms tight to her sides and surveys plump Janet from her sitting position.

"Well, congratulations to you, too," she says. "You haven't changed. Jaboos and jepoot, with your jaxy hanging out backside."

Janet almost snarls and inventories her own body. "Take a good look, Pledge, 'cause my jewels poke out the center holes of my Spiderweb, and my dark jipijapa grows out around and through my open-mesh g-string."

Steph curls a lip. "You never did exhibit much restraint."

"You put me into this Bikini last Term, remember?" Janet prods.

"I did!" Steph claims credit. "I said the Spider belonged in her web." Steph waves an arm in the air in the direction of the Dining Room, revealing a luscious concave armpit for the lingering Cam. "Congratulations for hanging this very same Bikini on the wall."

Janet presses, "I recall you told me it was 'not really barely legal,' but 'I had to wear it outside anyway.'" Janet pauses. "'And keep wearing it.' Yes?"

Steph shrugs. "Obviously. Maybe now that you're a Monitor you can put your jugs away. And hide your jipijapa and jaxy." Steph wrinkles her nose, "Except you like being an exhibitionist!"

"Maybe you'd like me to pull my lips apart, so you can masturbate while you whiff my scent," Janet threatens.

Steph takes a sip of the wine, smoothes her dress, and turns her attentions to Babs.

"Hello Babs," Steph ventures, with a glance to Babs' waistline. "I saw your Dining Room Picture. It looks like you've come up in the world."

Boss Babe tightens her lips and represses touching her waistline to ensure her hairage remains covered.

Steph sips again, leans back, and presses on in her analysis. "And Babs, I love your cleavage, and it's super that you retain your crescent moons. At least you're still barely legal."

Bling. BB opens her mouth; that Steph would taunt her to her face takes her back. And so she carefully speaks her first words to Steph.

"Good evening, Steph. Welcome to the Cosmos House. I recall I have you to thank for my areolage. Pledge."

"I'm the one who ensured you promoted," Steph asserts, then broadens her focus. "Both of you. Don't you ever forget that."

Janet presses back, "You made me piss in the Mudpit and masturbate to climax in front of the Back Door Cam. For paparazzi, too."

"I'm the one who ensured both of you promoted," Steph repeats, "whatever it took. Don't you ever forget that."

And Babs begins to gather her wits.

§ Steph Reacquaints with Robyn: Do I Know You?

Besides knowing her two former Pledge, Steph also knows Robyn, even if her former Pledge and Roommate from last Term doesn't remember her. Steph hates Robyn and directly blames her for her own misfortune, even more so than she might blame Babs and Janet.

Robyn remains uncertain as to just what memories possess her, and that includes any amnesia about a queenly Steph Sorostitute sitting in the chair drinking wine. Robyn fails to read the lethality of Steph's body language, with her arms coiled tight before her and her legs crossed.

Robyn perks up, borrows Janet's salutation, and introduces herself. "Hello, Steph Sorostitute. Pleased to make your acquaintance. I'm Robyn!"

Steph turns, partly closes one eye, and tries not to hiss when she replies, "Really? So now you don't know me?"

"Know you? Monitor Babs has told me all about you," Robyn counters. "How could I have ever met you before? I'm a newbie Cosmos Pledge this Term!"

Steph scowls. On the final day of her tenure as Monitor last Term Steph never learned what Robyn's outcome had been. *Only earlier today did I discover that Babs and Janet Opted Monitor this Term, and I thought for a moment Robyn had Opted likewise. Apparently not. I had Robyn positioned to Opt Strip, and then she did what she did to me. Could that be why she's Pledging again? Rewarded?*

Steph cocks her head and inquires, "So, Pledge Robyn, why aren't you dancing at the Nugget right now?"

Robyn shimmies bare shoulders in her sleek one-piece strapless maillot cutout and talks down to the sitting one. "Don't try to fool me.

I'm more important than you are. I'm a first-time Pledge, and Janet told me you're a broken Monitor."

"Okay, so you don't know me." Steph makes a promise: "You *will* know me before the end of this Term!"

Steph, like Babs, has full memories of Robyn. Steph realizes, *Once upon a time last Term my Pledge Robyn suggested I could also wear just the panties and heels—still two pieces—but of course Robyn knew I would never do this. And then everybody present would laugh at stupid Robyn. That's when I decided she wouldn't be getting a second Garment, no Opt Up. I told her 'Happy Opt Strip, Robyn,' and after that I never saw her again.*

Steph uncrosses her legs and crosses them in the opposite orientation. She trades eyes with the nearly naked and full-figured Monitor Janet and finds a twinkle there. Knowledge about the past cuts more ways than one and enters into the momentum of the present. Robyn may be forgetful about last Term, but Steph remembers all the ex-Cosmos, especially Robyn.

"Tell me about the four Dining Room Pictures," Steph probes Robyn. She watches out of the corner of her eye as Babs and Janet trade looks.

"Well, what's to tell?" Robyn shrugs, gesturing to BB and Janet. "See for yourself. Bikini Babe and Janet Jepoot. Same on the Dining Room Pictures. Bling and bush or'top the nombril, and jumboblats and jipajalala overflowing the Spiderweb." Robyn laughs.

"Do you know how they got their Bikinis?" Steph asks Robyn while watching Janet out of the side of her eye.

"Hey, stop asking me stupid questions." Robyn rises onto her toes. "You're the one who should know this. You were their Monitor last Term."

Steph turns her eyes to look at Babs gently and at Janet more full on. *Well, maybe Babs looks me over carefully, but Janet has evil intent.* Steph looks at Robyn again.

"Robyn Redacted," BB speaks, as if to accelerate process.

Steph squints. "Robyn Redacted?"

"Robyn Redacted," Janet repeats, and Steph's fuse burns shorter. *Could it be that this creature not only pretends she doesn't know me, but she has been completely expunged of what she did to me?*

Steph looks to Babs and Janet again. "Robyn Redacted," Steph says slowly.

Steph considers Robyn. *Blame it on amnesia or not, but Robyn has never paid attention to anything that wasn't centered on Robyn.*

Handicaps take many forms.

Robyn plumbs depths. "Let me tell you about the bottom two Dining Room Pictures. The naked, pink, wet, and ready poot and coot. The

Baseboard Strippers. That's Penny and Coco. You should know. Didn't you referee their Mudwrestling Contest last Term? The Strippers lost. I guess they got their pictures taken before they streaked naked to the Nugget."

Steph scratches an ear; she knows she did not referee the Mudwrestling Contest last Term. And she can tell from their wry smiles that Babs and Janet know this also.

She doesn't argue. "Well, Robyn," she says, "that's some memory you've got!" Steph looks up toward BB and Janet, makes an ever so slight movement with her head, and speaks to them as if they are equals. "I certainly know a lot of Robyn's traits, especially the bad ones. Let me know if you want me to help train her."

Robyn might not remember Steph, but she feels compelled to contain her. "My swimsuit has a smaller buttonhole than your minidress!"

Steph sweeps her eyes up and appraises the Redacted one. "My button hole got hacked."

Allusions to history seems lost upon Robyn. She advances, "Fact. I am the most covered of all four of us, and not just you in your titty-tattered minidress. I'm even more covered up than Babs' *deux-pièce* Bikini and a whole lot more than Janet's Spiderweb."

Steph narrows her eyes. "Your one-piece maillot qualifies you for a ticket to the Strip, Cosmos Pledge. And ultimately public denudement."

Robyn brushes the challenge aside. "Don't be stupid, Steph Sorostitute. I'm royalty! You're the broken Monitor with only one Garment, and you're gonna be flashing your tits."

Perhaps. Steph tightens her arms against her body lest the hovering Cam, which Robyn so graciously let into the Parlor, collects any careless arm movement. Steph carefully moistens her lips and shifts gears, saying, "Robyn, please help yourself to my wine glass. Drink a toast to a Term that has only begun."

But Robyn can't decide how to react. She tries to figure out if she remembers this person and why she acts like she know her. She wets her lip and squints at the offered glass.

Robyn should be wondering why Babs and Janet have not been offered the glass first.

But before Robyn can think this through Steph redirects her attention up from the easy chair toward Babs and Janet; enough with the casual. "Well, here I am!" Steph presents herself. "I've arrived. I've showered and cleaned up." Steph gives it a beat, crosses her legs once again in the opposite direction, draws her hands up tight before her, and advances to Babs, "Gamers say you have a new dress for me."

§ Babs & Janet Award Steph: Minidress Vagflash 24x7

Oooh. Babs and Janet look at each other again. Babs has no choice in the matter.

"I do have a new minidress for you." Boss Babe states fact. "And you shall beg me for it."

"Uncross your legs, Pledge." Janet's interruption cuts like a knife.

Steph looks to BB, observes concurrence, and uncrosses her legs and holds them together, with her thighs touching.

"Ask me nicely to keep your legs apart," Boss Babe commands.

Steph stumbles, but gets it good enough. "Please let me sit so my thighs aren't touching."

"Show me," Boss Babe demands.

"Ah, yes," Steph deliberates casually. She is not about to readily give ground to her former Pledge. She sneaks a quick look at Janet and opens her legs just enough so that her thighs are not touching. Shadows inside.

"Looks like the Cam collects the first Steph vagflash!" Robyn claps her hands. "You're the Cosmos vagcam Pledge!"

Steph tries to think as she opens her mouth. She opens and closes her mouth several times at the humiliation of exposing herself.

And if there is any doubt Steph might clamp her thighs shut, well, Janet's presence adds weight. The presence of Janet unnerves Steph. *I feel unfairly outnumbered.*

Silly Pledge; she's also outranked.

Janet admires Steph. "I like your costume. Upskirt all the way up to your snatch. Everyone always wondered what your snapper looks like."

Babs solidifies her demand. "Pay attention to me. That's how you shall keep your legs from now on. Thighs *never* touching. Legs apart, 24x7."

Steph gives Babs a cold look. The look of an animal prepared to lash out.

That's right," Babs announces. "Everyone can see up your minidress. And the Cam feeds the Prefecture."

Steph feels it necessary to object and opens her mouth, but Janet takes charge. "Don't complain. You'll get your chance to spread your legs really wide soon enough."

Babs presses, "Stand up. Hands behind your head. Stand spread surrender."

Steph rises carefully, thankful to terminate her shadowy upskirt. The dress she wears really is in tatters, but standing does allow the minidress to settle down to her thighs, although it still allows a tiny bit of Step's stern to show a crease. Steph stretches herself into surrender position as the Cam caresses her silky armpits. But armpits are the least of Steph's problems. Indeed, the hacked minidress is sufficently loose, and the armholes sufficently big, that it is not even necessary for Steph to lean forward for the Cam to survey inside her armholes, to see Steph's sand dollars and stalks, indeed her entire chest, and feed her first titter out to the Prefecture. Maybe last Term Steph hid her breasts and nipples, but not any more.

Steph knows. She feels her milk spouts grow hard. Maybe there is a way to put a stop to this.

Maybe not.

Ask me nicely." Babs also knows protocol.

"Ah," Steph stammers, uncertain about what to ask, but then she remembers her number one goal. She'll play along. She frames her request. "Ah, yes, Ma'am, I understand you're supposed to give me a new minidress."

"And?"

"And I'm supposed to sit with my thighs apart." *That should qualify as asking nicely.*

But Babs knows the time has come to subject Steph to some twist. "From now on you'll wear whatever I give you to wear." Babs raises the stakes.

Steph doesn't like the sound of this Game, but she responds with reluctance, "Ah, okay."

Janet interjects a correction. "Pledge," Janet firmly addresses Steph, "it's 'Ma'am, yes, Ma'am,' 'Ma'am, no, Ma'am,' or 'Ma'am, I don't understand, Ma'am.' These are valid answers. Do you understand me, Pledge?"

Steph does. "Ma'am, yes, Ma'am."

Steph opens her mouth, but Boss Babe leads with a suggestion, "Maybe you'd like to trade clothes with your Roommate?"

Steph stammers uncertainly, "Trade? With Robyn here? Robyn, my Roommate from—"

Robyn interrupts, "You're not my Roommate. Not now. Not ever."

Steph frowns. *Really?* Steph recalls Babs' comment from moment ago. *Robyn Redacted! Maybe she really doesn't know what she did to me, so as some kind of reward she has been redacted and starts afresh? Except I don't believe she has Charm.*

Babs instructs, "You know, Pledge should not be asking questions, so don't. But let me set you straight: Robyn is not your Roommate. Your bunk is right next to hers. Middle bottom. Your Roommate hasn't arrived yet."

"She's due in from the Nugget," Janet augments casually. "Not sure she'll be wearing anything at all." Janet touches her crown jewels, protruding from the center holes of her Spiderweb halter. "But don't worry, I'll help BB make sure you get the best correctional training!"

Steph decides silence is best for this one. She shuffles her spread feet, keeps her hands behind her head, and squares her shoulders. She considers Robyn, who now holds the wine glass. The Cam has retreated into a dark recess somewhere in the Parlor.

Steph thinks, *I know Janet arrived naked from the Nugget last Term; after all, I was the Monitor then. And I tried to humiliate her with her past... without luck. Janet was not to be shamed by pulling pink, making wet, and climaxing. Or by wearing the Spiderweb outside, making an Alumni Reprise appearance at the Nugget last Term, or other stuff.* Steph bounces her eyes back and forth between the two Monitors. *I don't fear Babs. But I do fear Janet.*

"Who told you to open a bottle of wine?" Babs sounds curious.

"I thought..." Steph begins... but thinking is not such a good lead.

Robyn senses trouble ahead, hurriedly puts the glass down and interjects. "I'm going upstairs."

Babs spins to her. "Fine. Sit yourself down on the Bathroom floor, spread your legs wide, and put your hands behind your head surrender position." BB keeps looking at Robyn and wiggles a finger toward Steph. Boss Babe instructs, "Take her with you. Same position, both of you. Beat it. Now."

Steph knows a good offer when she hears one. "Ma'am, yes, Ma'am," she responds smartly, with an indistinguishable tinge of sass. She breaks out of her surrender position and takes two steps toward the Kitchen.

Boss Babe cuts her off before step three. "Don't." BB points to the Front Door. "You don't belong in this part of the house. Out. Back door, Pledge."

And Steph flees, with Robyn holding the Front Door open and scooting out after her. The last thing Steph hears is "No talking!" She realizes that handling Babs may not be so easy after all.

The Cam sneaks out with them. It watches them head down the steps and around the side of the house before returning to its perch.

"Don't worry," Robyn whispers as they pass the Porch, the cellar door, and around to the Back Landing. "I've got the Boss Bitch under control. Now ring the Bell: once for yourself, and once for me too. And in we go."

§ Babs & Janet: Discuss Robyn & Steph

Babs and Janet trade looks and adjust their bikini tops, or what they possess of them anyway. *Crescents d'areolage* and areolage with nipples jutting out. The two Monitors laugh and relax. Babs nods her head in the direction of the glass and bottle of wine, and the two sit down in adjacent easy chairs. They will share the glass and finish the bottle.

It is the first opportunity since Tiffany arrived that they've had an opportunity to compare notes. Notes on Tiffany, but also notes on the more immediate arrivals, Robyn and Steph.

"Steph does know a lot of our secrets," Babs advances carefully.

"Secrets? I don't have any secrets," Janet responds. "I pinked the first Term I Pledged. And then I was a Stripper two Terms ago, remember? Last Term you were my Cosmos Roommate. I've already stuffed the big toys. Jerked myself off, like, for real, on Stage and off. You're the one who's a prude."

"That's harsh," Babs replies. "But Steph better keep her mouth shut if she knows what's good for her."

"You've got the tools to keep her in line," Janet bops.

And BB scowls.

Janet computes, "The way I figure, Tiffany's transparent croptop isn't worth you taking or trading for. And Robyn's maillot won't cover you enough to make a difference. But Steph's minidress provides all the coverage you need."

"And leaves her stark naked," BB concludes. "That would be very humiliating for her."

"You could promote to MomCap," Janet confirms. "Or, hey: strip both her and Robyn naked, and you'd have four Garments and could Double Opt Up and become a Madam."

Babs suspects Janet may be joking. She responds, "I doubt if I'm able to do that. Besides, four pieces might send a wrong signal to MomCap. After all, she's only got three pieces. And besides, running Whores—or even Strippers—might not be for me. I think I already know what I'm going to do. I'm going to Hover next Term. I know what's good for me."

BB queries her former Roommate and fellow Monitor, "What about you? You gonna Hover or Op Up MomCap? 'Cause I know you'll never Opt Down and Pledge again."

"Like Steph," Janet laughs. "Jeez, BB, if I told you my plans I'd need some collateral to hold."

"Like maybe Steph," Babs jokes, and they both laugh.

Janet offers, "I listened to Robyn earlier. And I think you're right that she really is void." Janet rustles her substantial body.

"More brainless than ever before," Babs agrees. "But what if whatever happened to her happens to one of us? Like me."

"She said you're the only one in the four Dining Room Pictures who hasn't done a stretch at the Nugget," Janet spins. "I don't know if she knew that, figured it out, or if someone told her."

"Tell her disinformation and she won't know the difference," Babs grumbles. "You're right. She's a bigger black hole now."

Janet tweaks, "She probably doesn't remember that she promised your Mudwrestling videos would stay confidential."

Babs pours the last of the wine into their glasses.

Janet advances, "Let me suggest you convince MomCap to let Penny and Coco do a Mudpit reprise. They could both piss in the mud and wallow. They can win and lose whatever piercing and tattoo credits you're so worried they've accrued."

Babs' eyes narrow at this idea, but she restrains herself. "That wouldn't be fair, and MomCap would never do that to them."

"Of course she wouldn't," Janet agrees. "More likely it will be Penny and Coco themselves who will beg, so instead of one ink and steel each, one of them gets doubles and the other gets off unmarked."

Babs finds the logic compelling but not motivating. "Okay, Janet," she says. "Sound fair and balanced."

Janet shifts gears. "But you don't need MomCap's approval for Steph and Robyn to Mudwrestle. They've each got one piece. They each think they need two pieces. So let them duke it out."

Babs retreats. "Yeah, and what if Steph wins?"

Janet must fall silent on this. "Yeah, okay, you're right. And what if Robyn wins? That's pretty awful too."

"Maybe they both need to lose. Besides, they're not Roommates," Babs exasperates. "MomCap has made it clear to me that Roommates get first dibs on any Games."

"Have it your way," Janet flips. "But remember, I expect you to trade me Steph for one of my Corvettes."

"Stop it!" Boss Babe drains her glass and puts it down on the table with impact. "I'm not doing anything until after all my Cosmos arrive. I'm still expecting two ex-Strippers and two newbies. I've got my hands full."

§ Babs Queries Janet: About Stripping with Tiffany

Boss Babe fingers her bra straps and probes Janet carefully. "So Tiffany told me a lot about when you two Stripped together. She says that you let lapdance patrons wallow in your jaboobies."

Janet pouts, "Tiffany says a lot of things. I mean, we both lapdanced naked. I mean, I was never *not* naked the entire time I was a Stripper."

"Never?" Babs exclaims. "Not even—"

Janet cuts her off. "I mean *never*. I was still naked when I pledged and become your Roommate, remember?"

"I guess you're not alone. I'm worried MomCap will make Penny and Coco commit to stay naked all this Term," Babs frets. "Assuming they made it to the Nugget."

Janet praises, "Nice, huh? We don't just send them off with no clothes; they will get no bathroom privacy. No privacy at all. I mean, know, I danced there. I had to masturbate and pee center Stage."

Babs blocks the answer, yet forwards another question. "You and Tiffany both peed on Cam?"

Janet blazes a trail. "All Strippers do. It's not like here, where Tiffany has volunteered to Pee-Cam. The toilets are made of clear glass, and there are Cams everywhere. And if you don't use the house toilet the Nugget Cams still follow you. Have to pee sooner or later."

"Follow you?" Babs double checks.

Janet nods. "The Nugget Cams can follow Strippers anywhere. Especially on Stage. Did Tiffany say if she ever peed on herself?"

"Well, she claims she's not technically a Piss Mouth."

"Not a Piss Mouth!" Even Janet expresses surprise. "My, my!"

"Apparently there is a month in her Porn Star Calendar—" Babs begins.

"Get real." Janet pushes down a little too gleefully. "I've seen Tiffany down shots center Stage at the Nugget!" Janet pauses, then continues, "And besides—"

BB cuts her off and takes the initiative. "Tiffany says you let lapdance Patrons finger-fuck you."

Janet shrugs off Babs' initiative, "Whatever that means."

"Like, put their middle finger into your vagina and wiggle it around," BB presses, "or rub it on your clit."

Janet draws in air. "Babs, listen, Strippers either Opt Up and become Pledge, or they Opt Down and Whore. Here's how I am different than Tiffany. When we were Stripper Roommates two Terms ago, Tiffany and I both let the Patrons fondle and finger-fuck us, but Tiffany let them take their dicks out. She wanted to go there, but I didn't. Don't. So afterwards I pledged the Cosmos House, and Tiffany shipped out to Flesh Ranch. We both got what we wanted, and that's a very good thing whenever it can happen."

Babs comprehends. *Yes, Janet's Opt Pledge had been a good thing, but I remain unconvinced that Tiffany's Opt Whore was equally uplifting.*

BB renders another question for consideration to her former Roommate. "Tiffany said your full name is Janet Jintoe and that I should ask you what Jintoe means. And how you acquired the nomen?"

Janet considers, "You know, sometimes Tiffany is too innocent for her own good, so be careful, because that helps make her the most dangerous of all."

Babs agrees, "You were right before: Tiffany really isn't malicious. And she's probably a great Stripper."

Janet takes offense. "Hey. I'm a great Stripper, too. I did a whole Term of pink work. Last Term, I pinked on your behalf."

"Whoa, Janet!" BB protests.

"I had to climax naked on the Back Door Landing. You never even took your clothes off inside," Janet attests. "It's okay. I don't mind. I'm your buddy. I mean, even now, look at us. You: little crescents, bra and nombril, Black Bikini. Me: Crochet Spiderweb. I took on a whole lot more areolage and hairage and buttage than you!"

Babs looks back at her, flushes, and sighs. "I'm sorry. I'm trying to get beyond blushing every time I'm reminded of my areolage."

"You bling." Janet nods her head. "And it also seems like Tiffany and Robyn and Steph have all seen your hairage in the Dining Room Picture."

Babs casts her eyes down.

Janet buttresses, "Don't worry. After bling doesn't make you blush anymore, the Gamers will let you cover it up. Okay, neither Tiffany nor Robyn has a Garment you want, but maybe Steph?"

Babs shakes Steph out of her mind and shifts her thoughts to Tiffany's nipples, standing up behind clear vinyl.

"Tiffany said her Eraser Heads light up in blacklight," Babs recites correctly. "But do you know what keeps them constantly aroused?"

"Ask her," Janet quips, then slows down. "Ask her about her latest ultraviolet ink tattoo."

"Her latest tattoo, from when she became a Whore?" Babs verifies.

Janet reminisces, "Well, you don't know this, but I had to make an Alumni Reprise visit to the Nugget last Term. That's how I know about her latest ultraviolet ink tattoo. We were both naked. I had to lick down her tail trough. And then they turned on the blacklight, and I could see that in addition to her Eraser Heads she's also got a tramp stamp down her tail trough that lights up."

"You licked her asshole," BB states.

"Something like that," Janet admits.

Babs scowls. "And she saw *you* dance, no doubt." BB lifts her nose up.

"Tiffany saw me pull pink and masturbate naked on the center Stage pole," Janet offers.

"Anything else?"

"Well, I did have to pee. On Stage. In front of the Crowd."

Babs advances cautiously. "So you know Tiffany not just from Stripping with her? You had to dance naked in front of her and the Crowd at the Nugget, last Term at this secret Alumni Reprise?" Babs shakes her head. "You must feel horrible; you must really resent Tiffany."

"No! Not at all. We've always been friends."

Janet collects a thought. "Listen, I'm not sure if she has a third tattoo or how many piercings the Eraser Heads count for, but if you take her over to the Nugget, put her down on her hands and knees with her face on the floor, yank her slacks down. and order her to pull her tail mounds apart, you will see that the ultraviolet inks become visible around her tailpipe."

Babs considers less ultraviolet ink and more Janet. "Any other Cosmos accompany you to the Nugget last Term?"

Janet jerks. "No, not really. Except Steph came along."

"Steph?" BB exclaims. "I can't believe Steph danced at the Nugget!"

"No, no, Steph didn't dance at the Nugget. Nobody even knew she was there; she was my 'chaperone.' She went in stealthy and cased the place from a private box. She wanted to see what the Strippers had to do. And she did."

"So she got to watch you and Tiffany dance!" BB rushes to a conclusion. "How come you never told me before?"

"You never asked." Janet brushes her hair back. "It was not a Roommates thing. It really was an Alumni Reprise. Most any Pledge who promotes from Stripper—any Alumni—is expected to Reprise."

"You squatted and peed right up on Stage?" BB is still incredulous about this.

"Not quite. I packed a shot glass into my jepoot, then took it out and poured shots. There's a lot you blocked out. I told you to check out my vids," Janet defends. "But you never bothered. Face it: what you've let yourself see has been pretty controlled."

BB confesses, "Sometimes it seems impossible to determine who's in control."

"Maybe nobody's in control," Janet muses. "That's also possible."

§ Babs Worries to Janet: Kimju & Molly are Ex-Strippers

BB shares a new worry with Janet: "Tiffany confirms that I'm getting two Strippers who were Nuggets last Term, Kimju and Molly. That's also an unexpected surprise."

Janet needles, "You're surprised that some former Strippers might be rising and become some of your Pledge this Term? Tisk tisk, you know better than that. I was a Stripper before I was your Roommate last Term."

The Manifest said one piece each," Babs tells. "Do you know them?"

"Maybe they danced the night I visited the Nugget last Term. But I can't connect any names and faces. Maybe we can locate their videos?

But if they arrive wearing only one piece I suspect they'll pledge topless."

"Topless?" Babs feels her intuition confirmed.

"Hey, I ought to know: Strippers promote with one piece or naked. And you ought to know too, because when I pledged to the Cosmos House last Term I didn't exactly promote topless, I promoted nude. Nude as in stark naked. All I had was the hair on my head and jepoot." Janet shrugs, "You were there."

"Maybe they'll wear a maillot or minidress like Robyn and Steph," Babs proposes hopefully.

"Unlikely," Janet sings. "Maybe they will wear slacks, shorts, bikini bottoms, panties, but I'd say a g-string or loincloth is more likely. But who knows? Maybe all they'll wear are strings tied around their little toes."

"Bare boobs and nothing for me to trade for," Babs grouses, "or even take."

"I know my toplessness last Term always embarrassed you," Janet spares. "You can always order them to cover their boobs with their hands. Handbras. After all, you are the Boss Babe."

Babs accepts, "I certainly shall. But whether they wear clothes that cover them completely or dress like sluts and begin the Term nearly naked, they both must make sure they keep their umbilicus uncovered. Navelage 24x7."

Janet leans in. "By the way, does Tiffany know if any Nuggets are expected at my Corvette House?"

Babs tries to remember. "Let me see. A Lee Lollydor and a Ginny."

"Okay," Janet affirms, "that matches my Manifest. A lick up specialist! I like that. Maybe you'll trade Steph for Lee Lollydor," Janet teases.

"And Ginny is a Whore-for-Life." Babs adds.

Janet leans back. "Whoa? A Whore-for-Life? Really now? Tiffany said that?"

"Tiffany. She ought to know." Babs startles herself with her own analysis. "She might have been a Flesh Ranch Whore last Term, but apparently she did a lot more Feature Dancing at the Nugget than your Alumni Reprise. There's a month in the Kitchen Calendar where Ginny and Tiffany suck cock together."

Janet rises and detaches herself from a chair that wants to stick to her bare jaxy. "Good luck," she salutes. "I'll be checking the feeds for Steph's titter and upskirt. Don't disappoint me." They both laugh, and Janet departs from the Parlor out the Front Door.

§ Babs: Secures the Cosmos House

Babs heads down the short hallway from the Parlor to return the glass and empty bottle back to the Kitchen, but she discovers that the door is locked—obviously Steph tidied up after herself when she and Robyn returned through the Kitchen en route from the Back Door to the upstairs.

Babs detours via the Living Room into the Dining Room, closes the sliding door behind her, turns its key in the lock, and tucks the key into a pocket inside the top of her bikini briefs. She dares a look at Bikini Babe's bling and hairage on the Dining Room wall, blushes, and wonders if she should be ashamed of herself.

No!

Back in the Kitchen, BB gathers the Skeleton Key from the door to the front hall and Parlor and adds this second Skeleton Key to her nombril pocket collection. The Bikini's wide sides and taut elastic ensure the weight doesn't show.

Certainly Cosmos tradition dictates that these doors stay closed. Babs jiggles on her bare feet so she can hear the two keys jingle. *But I think keeping them locked and controlling their access will facilitate Monitoring. So far I've accumulated nothing but wildcards and wannabe Porn Stars.*

Indeed, most of the Cosmos Pledge will traverse only some of the House much of the time… and the rest of it not at all.

BB clarifies in her mind. *I ought to know about controlling access. I Pledged here last Term. I remember one stretch when I stayed in my bunk, and Janet brought me food and a chamber pot. And then Janet vice versa. So it's not like we didn't get hazed.*

Thank you, Steph.

§ Robyn & Steph: Sit Spread Surrender in Bathroom

Robyn and Steph sit themselves down side-by-side in the upstairs Bathroom. They rest their backs against the side of the bathtub and face the mirrored wall before them. Robyn impishly draws herself into a sitting spread surrender position: smooth armpits deepened, legs apart, knees wide and up, and navel on clear view. "You too," Robyn says to her fellow Pledge. "Obey me."

"Obey you?" Steph considers. Obey Babs and Janet? Perhaps. Steph carefully adjusts her hands behind her head and slowly opens her knees.

"Obey me," Robyn affirms, taking charge. "Open you legs wide. This isn't just sitting with your thighs barely apart. This is legs spread. Wide open. Trust me. I've been here longer than you have. You're to obey me."

Steph reluctantly surveys herself in the mirror on the wall facing them. It is not the hands behind her head or the cupped armpits that dismay her. She encounters Robyn surveying her visage in the mirror as well, sees Robyn observe the obvious, and laugh at her, "You shrubbery doesn't quite hide your slot machine."

Steph closes her eyes. Doesn't hide it at all. Not Steph's shrubbery, not her creamy inner thighs, or even the concave curves where her pelvis joins her legs. Anger rises.

"Pardon me," Steph informs. "I am quite able to see my secret parts, you dumb ragazze."

Robyn considers; she isn't sure she understands what Steph says. "Ragazze?" Robyn asks.

Steph has been plotting what to do when an opportunity might present itself to needle her nemesis, such as now. "A 'ragazze' comes after a 'ragamuffin' and before a 'ragho.' Got it?"

Robyn doesn't get it at all. But she digs in, "Be nice to me, because I really am royalty, but I never tell anyone." She tilts her head. "And I'll call your 'secrets parts' anything I want. Janet calls them your snatch. Maybe BB will make you call it your snapper, your satchel, your snizzaroo, your smoo. Because you're gonna be a sizzle splurt skank before this Term is over!" Robyn laughs, but holds surrender position.

Steph grapples with holding onto the power. She turns her eyes toward the reflection of Robyn's crotch, covered with the maillot. Steph seeks the initiative. "Nature used a semi-cubical parabola to form my most perfect sanctum," Steph asserts. "My figure has always been very prized but never revealed. My breasts are like fine sinusoidal curves with flowing slopes. My buttocks resemble perfect spheroids, but curve like beautiful splines. My walk defines a serpentine curve. Go figure it out. I'm studied."

"Yeah." Robyn wiggles her body. "But my buttonhole is the smallest." Robyn resists Steph aggrandizing her body. "Hey, you might have been a Monitor before, but right now you're a sitting spread surrender Cosmos Pledge staring at your snizz in the mirror."

And Steph stares. *Nothing blocks my view of my wavy thin blonde hairs, two negative depressions where my crotch joins my thighs, and a shadow of my slit down the middle. Unacceptable. And especially unacceptable for Robyn to look.*

Robyn doesn't just look, she forecasts. "You don't know this, but Tiffany has also begged a Cam here in the Bathroom," Robyn alerts Steph. "The Pee-Cam. But it's not on right now. Only if Tiffany comes into the Bathroom does it turn on. That's because she's a Pee-Cam Pledge."

"Tiffany?" Steph inquires, and glances at her exposed shrubbery in the mirror.

"Tiffany Porn Star, like on the Calendar downstairs," Robyn elaborates. "You know, some ex-Whore who is now Babs' Roommate. Instead of me."

Steph digests. *Tiffany. I have never met Tiffany. But I did get to secretly watch her Feature Dance with Janet at the Alumni Reprise at the Nugget last Term.* Steph puts a question to Robyn: "So if Tiffany was a Whore last Term, why on Earth is she here at the Cosmos House? That would require a Double Opt Up."

Robyn knows all. "Obviously she wasn't a Whore last Term. You can't Double Opt Up any more than a Pledge can repeat a Term. That means that her Calendar has to be older, that's all. I might be a newbie, but at least I know all about the Game."

Perhaps. Perhaps not. Steph considers the Pledge sitting spread surrender next to her, whom she remembers to be her Roommate last Term. She observes out loud, "They erased you."

Robyn reacts. "Huh? Nobody erased me. I remember everything I need to."

"You really don't know me," Steph double checks.

"I know all about you," Robyn exaggerates. "Janet and BB told me everything. You were their Monitor last Term. They hate you: Janet especially, Boss Bitch not so much. But they said they didn't know why you got Opted Down."

Steph checks to see what else Babs and Janet might have told Robyn. "So what happened at the Mudwrestling Contest at the end of last Term?" *You were there after all, even if you forgot. I wasn't there at all.*

"Well," Robyn pouts, wiggling her knees and twisting her body toward Steph while still holding her hands behind her head, "I get the idea from Janet that Penny and Coco ripped BB's Bikini top off and flopped her bazoombas in the Mudpit."

Steph perks. "Now that would be a feast for the eyes."

Robyn says, "I'm sure it all got cammed. Filthy mud slippery everywhere."

Steph bemuses, "Maybe you can convince Bikini Babe to screen all the action, especially the part when she falls out. But just so you know, it is I who secured BB's promotion. She'd better treat me right."

Robyn suggests, "Maybe Janet also lost her top in the Mudpit. I hear she arrived naked last Term, moved into the Mudpit first stop, and that you made her masturbate to climax before you let her get out and get her Bikini."

Steph snorts, "Janet didn't win her Spiderweb until she and Babs mudwrestled with Penny and Coco. I missed that. Although it is also I who got Janet her promotion!"

Steph caps, "And you better be careful with me, because I'm full of equations."

§ Tiffany's Cams Robyn & Steph: 1st Spread-Leg Vagcam

Babs had not needed to tell Robyn and Steph to stay put, and their forbidden conversation hushes as they hear footsteps climb the stairs. They do not actually see Tiffany until she enters the Bathroom, totally naked, as she always is when she enters.

Steph recognizes Tiffany immediately and reacts by drawing her legs together. *I know who you are. You're a Whore. I saw Janet lick your tailpipe during the Alumni Reprise at the Nugget! I saw the two of you climax on the Double Dong together!*

Steph quickly corrects her reaction and stabilizes her position. She double checks herself in the mirror: legs spread, knees bent upward, low cut neckline, big armholes enabling side views of her sweet-glands inside, a huge hacked out buttonhole, *and my thin blonde scruff far too clearly on view.*

The Bathroom is not dimly-lit like the Parlor. Steph pulls her hands against her head tightly and assesses that Robyn remembers at least one new thing correctly. *Tiffany's naked entrance brings to life the Bathroom Cam. As it always does. Only now I share the illumination. Well, so does Robyn. Except Robyn has a gusset through her crotch, and I have nothing. I'm sanpan, upskirt without panties; this isn't even vagflashing, I'm about to give the Cam full up.*

Hummm.

Steph holds her position but adjust her eyes in the mirror to evaluate the reaction of Robyn, who sits next to her. Robyn has already turned her head and seems uncertain about keeping her hands behind her head. Steph evaluates. *Tiffany and Robyn know each other since yesterday. And I'd know if Robyn knew Tiffany before.*

Tiffany pauses in front of the side-by-side, sitting spread surrender pair of Cosmos Pledge and surveys their armpits, navels, and crotches. Their adjacent, widely-spaced knees touch. One has cloth in between her legs; one does not.

"I'm Tiffany," the redhead announces to the one without cloth. "And you're...?"

Steph looks at her and says, "I'm Steph."

"We've never met?" Tiffany seeks to confirm.

Steph affirms, "I've never seen you before."

Robyn breaks in, "She's Steph Sorostitute! Babs and Janet told me her full name."

Tiffany bows to Robyn and gestures, and Robyn tightens her hands behind her head. She and Steph sit stiffly with their backs against the vertical tub side, their butts and feet on the floor, and their hands behind their heads. Yes, they are both Pledge, and yes, there is certainly a Cam about somewhere.

Tiffany bows to Steph and proclaims, "We've been expecting you." She waggles a finger. "Don't get any big ideas! I am a Porn Star and the first Cosmos Pee-Cam Pledge."

Steph stares. *Maybe you don't know I've seen you dance.*

Tiffany steps back and appraises Steph. "Surely you passed by my Calendar on your way through the Kitchen. Did you like it?"

Steph doesn't care about Tiffany's Calendar. Her head spins, and she tries to calm wild thoughts. *I don't care that the Cam that went live when Tiffany entered the Bathroom. I don't care that it scrutinizes Tiffany naked. I don't care that it scrutinizes Robyn's thin strapless maillot with a puffy gusset through her crotch, hiding a rug with a full pile. I do care that the Cam scrutinizes my unencumbered upskirt bonanza of light blonde short hairs. And my slit, threatening to part.*

Tiffany brushes imaginary dust off her Eraser Heads and leans over. "Congratulations to a fallen Monitor on making her vagcam debut!"

Robyn tattles, "She got vagcammed legs apart downstairs."

Steph squirms but hold her hands behind her head and keeps her knees wide. Tiffany praises, "Now she gets vagcammed legs spread." The hovering Cam has placed itself to Tiffany's side between Steph and the mirror, down low, a full-bore view up Steph's minidress.

Tiffany squats in front of Steph. "And I love the way your clitty tries to poke out. What do you call yours? Some kind of curve?"

And Steph replies, "I call it my strophoid!"

Robyn interjects, "I'd call it your stamen, from the way it stands up." She turns her head from the view in the mirror to the real deal.

Steph expresses reserve to Tiffany. "My strophoid curve passes back through itself and allows me to auto-stimulate. Some us who are more advanced in the Game know how to bring Kundalini out."

"Oh! I'm looking forward to a demonstration!" Tiffany catches the Cam's eye and touches her own tender button.

Once again Robyn almost moves her hands off her head. "BB ordered Steph to keep her thighs apart. No touching. Snatch 24x7."

Steph opens her mouth, but Tiffany speaks first. "Listen up, Pledge. Maybe you get keep your snizzle spread all the time, and maybe you're gonna splurt. But remember: I am a Porn Star, and I'm the one who makes the Cam come alive here! I fully intend to Pledge naked and cum be a Stripper next Term. I've done everything explicit, all holes, all sexes. So don't try to upstage me!"

And with this Tiffany parts her thin pale red bush, opens her pale burgundy trap door, squares off facing the Pee-Cam, and urinates onto the tile floor. Robyn and Steph, and the Cam ahead of them, get a totally intimate view of the yellow stream as it exits her divided pink sex lips.

"Congratulations, you two," Tiffany praises as she rises and shakes off the last droplets. "You're the first Cosmos to see me tinkle."

Steph snarls, "Right, 'cause Boss Bitch is too goody-two-shoes to lower herself to watching you."

Robyn augments, "Yeah! You're not even worth her watching on the Cam feeds. And hey, aren't you going to clean up?"

Tiffany pushes an upper lip forward and curls her eyebrows down to Robyn. "You want it cleaned up? *You* lick it up," she says, and exits.

Steph observes that a tan line crosses Tiffany's posterior rugage. She watches the Cam turn off.

Robyn hesitates, then draws her hands forward and stands up. She addresses Steph. "Maybe last Term you had privacy and possessions. But not anymore. Too bad the Cam got turned off. You stay put, sitting on the floor here. Keep an eye on your snizzle in the mirror and wait for your feet to get wet. Maybe Bikini Babe will lick them up for you. I've heard you trained her good at that."

Steph stays put. "Last Term Babs worshiped every Cosmos foot," Steph snaps.

Robyn leans over to her. "This Term is different."

8 Babs Dresses Steph: Robyn Cams Her Titter & Upskirt (D05)

§ Babs Dresses Steph: Titter & Vagflash & Navelage 24x7

Day Five begins. And with it will come challenges both for Babs, Monitor of the Cosmos House, and for Steph, last Term's Monitor of the Cosmos House. They have much to say to each other, but they must also speak carefully.

Babs has risen for the day, cleansed herself in her private bathroom, and sits in her requite Black Bikini behind her Desktop. Tiffany lies on her back on the floor, partly contained inside in her lower alcove and partly into the room, arms and legs spread in a broad X. From the moment Boss Babe confirmed to Steph, "You shall wear whatever one-piece minidress I choose for you any particular day," BB has hung firm to her impulsive bite, and has begun to relish her role as Steph's costumer. *I remember there exist hair and eyelash scissors in the Makeup Case. Finger and toenail clippers also. A brush. And, I have soap and shampoo on my shelf!*

Overnight Steph's mind had imagined a rack of minidresses of all shapes and proportions; she simmers at the thought of Babs modulating her access to this treasure trove, yet still presents herself before Babs' Bedroom Desktop the following morning. She allows her eyes to linger upon BB's cleavage and crescents, and she grazes her eyes across a naked and X-spread Tiffany lying on the floor. Steph absorbs that Tiffany's transparent croptop and low-rise slacks hang on the hook in a locker, behind Babs' back.

Steph returns to look Babs face-to-face; she forces a smile, smoothes her hacked cutout minidress, and tries a coy angle. "Good morning, Ma'am. I understand I'm trading this in."

Babs considers her former Monitor, tilts her head, and mocks, "Or perhaps not." But then she relents, "Just kidding," and extends a hand. "Okay. Gimme."

Steph blinks. She does what she did not anticipate: she pulls what is left of the minidress over her head. She tries to stand casually as BB takes the hacked-up minidress in her hands and leaves Steph embarrassingly naked. The air feels cold; goosebumps form, the hair on her arms stands up, and her nipples erect, stalks centered in sand dollars atop a pair of sinewave peaks.

Steph covers herself with her hands, one hand and an elbow across the sinusoidals, the other hand defending the scrub.

It is fine for Babs; she doesn't have to see. She nods her head in the direction of the Bathroom and says, "Come back for a new minidress." A naked Steph scurries toward toilet business, a possible shower, and back here before Tiffany gets loose. *Tiffany is already naked. I know the moment she comes into the Bathroom the Cam lights up.*

Steph hurries to the shower first, blending her pee with the shower water in the process, and hurries back to BB's Bedroom while still damp and naked, obviously, to see what choices Bikini Babe might offer. *And make sure Tiffany stays out of my private life.*

Steph draws her naked body up and queries, "Yes, Ma'am. So now I'm ready to see what you have for me and how well they fit." Steph puts a bare foot down. "It better provide sufficient coverage so I can walk to class in daylight, go to the practice field, or, for that matter, run any errands you assign me into the nearby Village." Steph shimmies with her hands at her sides. She knows her nakedness shames Babs.

Babs absorbs the attack without flinching. "Your minidress will always provide sufficient coverage!" BB sounds hearty. "Can't let Tiffany catch all the rays."

Steph glances across Tiffany's Garments hanging on a hook on the back wall. *Tiffany lies on her back X-spread, tits and twat hair on the up.* Steph feels the hair on her arms rise again. *I made it to and from the Bathroom, but I'm still naked.*

"And as for 'sufficient coverage,'" Babs says as she rises from her chair behind the Desktop, "you shall wear whatever I provide you. If I provide you with nothing, you shall wear nothing. Are we clear on this?"

Steph stumbles. She stands minidress-less at the moment, and again her sand dollars percolate. "Ma'am, er, ah, yes, Ma'am. You are the Monitor of the Cosmos House."

Babs crosses her arms across her chest, blocking all bling and much cleavage, and produces Steph's next minidress over a finger. "No matter what color or style, no matter what sleeves, straps, armholes, cleavages—your birthmark must always speak out through your costume, no matter how the rest of the minidress fits. Or doesn't. Capisce?"

"Ma'am, yes, Ma'am." Steph fidgets and covets a neck and legline. She crosses her hands in front of herself, matching the position of Babs' arms. She glances at Tiffany and observes that Tiffany has her eyes closed and bites her tongue in her teeth. Steph accepts, *I'm move covered than Tiffany. I'm a handbra bottomless, and Tiffany's nude.*

"Tell me why you were demoted to Pledge," BB demands of the hostile one. "Robyn told me it was because you covered you button last Term, although I don't know how she'd know that."

Babs knows Steph covered her button, but she seeks confirmation that this triggered Steph's demotion. Steph gathers both her sweater-dandies into one forearm and hand and lowers her other hand to cover her shrubbery. She twists a shoulder. "Ma'am, Robyn betrayed me last Term, and her memory got wiped so she doesn't remember. But I do."

BB rationalizes, "It wasn't Robyn who covered your cutout last Term; it wasn't me either."

"You're not even my minidress seamstress," Steph asserts.

"You're right about that one," Babs replies.

"You're just the enforcer," Steph snides.

"You're the one who must be attentive that your cutout always hovers about your belly button." BB smiles. "Go ahead. Get caught with it covered. You'll be stripped naked so fast you won't have time to get shaved first. And instead of being halfway to being a Stripper, you'll be totally there."

"Maybe I'll take you with me," Steph slithers.

Babs isn't amused. "You. Stand spread surrender. Now."

Steph tries to hold eyes with Babs over this but can't. Situational facts express themselves. Steph puts her hands behind her head and positions her feet wide. A flush overtakes her naked body, and both spigots harden. Steph curls her lips and holds her position.

§ Babs Reminds Steph: Not Equals & Better Keep Secrets

Boss Babe lets Steph stand and busies herself with the Desktop. When she returns attention to Steph she carefully aggresses, "Don't you think we are equals. Listen to me. Should *any* leakage about my past emerge, no matter what the source, you may expect to promptly find yourself 'bare, bald, and naked' and begging to Strip next Term."

Steph twists her body but holds position. "Wait a minute. I'm not the only one who knows about your last Term. What if Janet tells on you? She wasn't very nice to me when I arrived downstairs yesterday. She's nobody's friend. Don't forget that she was a Stripper before she became your Roommate last Term. She's into showing herself off."

Babs squares her jaw. "Then you had better hope Janet keeps secrets, because I'll hold you responsible anyway if the wrong secrets come out."

Steph opens her mouth, but Babs speaks first. "I'm surprised Janet never begged an Alumni Reprise at the Nugget last Term."

Steph blinks...and advances a partial truth. "You never know about Janet. She can be pretty sneaky sometimes. And you never quite know about what comes out of her mouth." Steph isn't prepared to abandon the accountability trap, and she advances her case. "Penny and Coco will talk about you, too. They'll make up stuff. And who knows if Robyn's Redaction is perfect."

Babs squints at her Pledge, who stands naked before her. "Janet has offered to trade one of her Corvettes for you," she threatens. "She said that once she gets her hands on you, you won't just be tittering or showing your snapper to the Cams."

Steph feels a chill go down through her naked, standing body. Goosebumps form across her belly. Her bare feet feel warm. Steph exerts discretion with her previous Pledge. "Ma'am, don't misunderstand me; I don't hold you or Janet responsible for my demotion. I know who's responsible. Robyn did this to me. So, Ma'am, you and I might be role-reversed, but we are on the same side. You need to please hand me my new minidress, and let me take Robyn's maillot. As far as I'm concerned she can spend all the rest of this Term naked, and she deserves to be a naked Stripper next turn! Even you know that."

Babs studies her former Monitor. "Roommate Games require you deal with whoever arrives as your Roommate," she humors. "At least initially. You'll have to save Robyn for later."

"Ma'am, thank you, Ma'am." Steph bows, assuming she's getting a green light.

Babs smiles and hikes her nombril up. *Shall Steph wear a minidress sleeveless, or with straps?* BB knows the answer. *Steph shall forgo all secrets about her strawberries and scruff and shall keep them in the public domain. Along with her belly button.*

Babs hands today's minidress to her anxious Pledge; Steph breaks out of position and eagerly takes the Garment into her hands. *Enough!* She turns and exits the Bedroom, failing to even say "thank you."

Once in the Bunkroom, Steph watches herself put the minidress on in the Mirror. She smoothes the dress as she looks in the Mirror to inspect what she wears. This morning's minidress is a particularly risky concoction with oversize armholes. Steph straightens her posture in the Mirror. *It is going to be a challenge to keep Gamers from looking in and seeing my stalks and sand dollars. Maybe Boss Bitch has it in for me, however unjustifiably, or maybe she's just a pawn. Janet's more revengeful, and, given the chance, she would reduce my minidress to only its cutout hole. I'm lucky that she's not the Monitor here. All I need to do is maintain a low profile and not cross BB. I can do this; I really don't need Babs in order to collect a second piece and Opt Up. Or collect two more pieces and Double Opt Up.*

Steph furrows her brow. However! If there is an opportunity to be gained, especially a Double Opt Up, I will consider trampling upon Boss Bitch so fast she'll never know what hit her.

§ Babs Orders Steph: Titter & Upskirt on Library Steps

Babs sends Tiffany after Steph to the Bunkroom. "Powder her face and lipstick her lips." Babs enters the Bunkroom just as Tiffany finishes these tasks, and commands Steph, "Stand spread surrender. Face yourself in the Mirror."

Steph obeys. She expects Tiffany to advance her makeup, but instead Babs and Tiffany return to the Bedroom. Steph waits. She studies her armpits in their oversize armholes. *I know how this dress works. I'm not stupid.*

When Babs returns she bears good tidings. "I hope you like your minidress," she advances. "You will not just keep your button exposed at all times; Gamers want to collect your titter and vagflash getting in and out of vehicles, sitting on park benches, and perched on bar stools. Time for you to be a Cosmos House show-off. Out in the real world!"

Steph squares herself and looks deeper into herself in the Mirror. *My makeup remains unfinished. My cutout hole is adequately large, but the dress is too short.*

Babs crosses her arms. "Enough of your self-admiration. Head over to the Library, sit atop of the Library steps, and be sure the sunlight illuminates your upskirt. Don't forget to keep your thighs apart, and I do mean 24x7."

Steph wants to react, but Babs lifts a finger. "Might upon occasion strangers catch your act, make sure you keep upskirting your snizzle for them also."

Boss Babe spins on her heels and returns to her Bedroom.

And so Steph walks to the Quad and sits on the top Library step so that everyone who climbs up gets to peek at her shrubbery. Correction: everyone gets to slit scan a slice of Steph's snapper as they climb the stairs.

If Steph becomes mindless and careless she may also titter. Correction: her oversize armholes make it impossible for Steph not to titter. Steph chaffs but can do nothing to block total views of her brown nipple stalks, centered on beige sand dollars atop two gentle sinusoidals. All not quite hiding inside, and the moving fabric rubbing constant arousal to the fruit bursting forth.

Steph Sorostitute might fume, but she can't stop her personal, yet very public, revelations. *I can't believe this all comes from Boss Bitch; she's too weak to do this. I bet Janet's behind this. I need BB to back her off!*

Gamers love the way Steph must compromise herself to keep her button shining. Gamers who collect navel details observe a round, negative crater with flesh hanging over not just at the top, but all around. And a round, hard bulb in the middle, not unlike a solidified dabble of white chocolate. An outie.

Steph raises her eyes to cast about and see who might be watching. She imagines she spots paparazzi and grits, *I bet that Boss Bitch tipped them off!*

Steph fidgets and pretends she don't know that she gets photographed. She moves her body and hands, turn her head, twist her torso, and wiggles her toes. But it's really very simple: *All I must do is keep my legs barely apart and not block the free view. I hate this, although it's hard to imagine anything worse could happen to me.*

§ Robyn Cams Steph: Library Armhole Titter & Upskirt

And then Robyn appears. She has walked from the Cosmos House carrying the Back Door Cam, and now, once arrived, lets it loose to hover about. The haughty one lays it out. "Boss Bitch sent me over to cam your vagflash and titter. And to make sure your button shows out. Document your compliance. Smile for the Cam, lean forward so your smurfs are in full view, and keep your legs apart so your thighs aren't touching." Robyn laughs.

Steph seethes but holds her legs-apart position. Mission accomplished, Robyn let the Cam roll on its own. "Listen to me, you sulfurous skeeze skank. You might have a cutout buttonhole, but I've got the smallest buttonhole. And I'm gonna make sure you beg button-for-life."

"Button-for-life? Says who?" Steph challenges.

"It is a beg you're gonna make," Robyn strengthens her affirmation.

"Fat chance," Steph dismisses. "I'm going to Opt Monitor next Term. Maybe even Double Opt up to MomCap. Like I deserve. When the time comes for me to grab another Garment, BB won't be able to stop me. You can't stop me either. You're a nobody. So watch out, Robyn Redacted, because if you redact again, I shall be your Monitor next Term! And you'll be following my Hand Signs."

"I'm a nobody who can never remember the Hand Signs!" Robyn asserts. "Thank goodness none of them apply to *moi!*" Robyn snorts. "Somebody told me to make this Sign to you and for you to obey." Robyn extends a hand and opens two fingers apart and signs Steph to open her legs. Not spread and full wide, but halfway there, enough to eliminate shadows.

Steph, uncertain of the authority of the order but cognoscente that the Cam witnesses her every move, chooses to interpret the Hand Sign as "legs open," not just legs apart, not spread just as wide as possible. *Midway.* Steph bites her lip and complies.

And what a magnificent, expanded view!

Steph's cutout minidress is suffcently short that even Steph can see for herself that her exposed and open crotch has parted just enough so that her scruff begins to divide itself into two halves, one to each side of an emerging slit no longer hidden beneath the short hairs or shadowed by thighs. Steph constructs her vagina. *I'm almost modest. Correction: I'm not modest at all. I can't let this happen.*

Steph struggles to keep the pose. She looks again and can see the depressions, the concave dimples where the sides of her crotch connect to her angled-out legs. Once again Robyn directs the Cam. *But it is not Robyn ragazze who ensures I keep my legs apart. And it is not even Boss Babe. It's Janet. Janet's the one.*

"You're letting everyone see your cheap assets," Robyn proclaims. "I am a Royal Princess, and my reliquary stays covered." Robyn rolls her hand. "My rigamarole too. And mark my words, you're gonna beg to 'Pledge naked and cum be a Stripper next Term.'"

Ouch! Not what Steph wants to hear. *Robyn appears to have forgotten she was my Pledge last Term.* Steph tightens the muscles inside her thighs and cups the dimples deeper.

Robyn wrinkles her nose. "I'm heading back the Cosmos House. See if you can make sure your swizzle stick pops out of your stinky socket box," she cackles. "Count 1000 seconds, gather the Cam, and bring it back to the Cosmos House. Don't forget: accuracy matters!"

Robyn give a final look-see before she departs. "And never forget," she mocks, "Navelage 24x7."

§ Babs & Tiffany: Remember Steph & Janet • Soap Mouth

Babs reclines on her bunk in the Bedroom that evening while a naked Tiffany sits on the chair behind BB's Desktop. Tiffany has spread her legs and casually cleans out crust from her tinderbox. Babs pretends to ignore Tiffany grooming herself.

"Your newest arrival seems reluctant to expose herself," Tiffany probes, offering, "She only got one piece. With proper training, Steph Sorostitute could make a great Stripper. It's good you remain firm with her. I guess you really don't have any choice."

BB appreciates the sympathy and shares history, saying, "As a Monitor last Term Steph tightly controlled her own exposures. Wickedly so, I might add. She controlled the length of her hemline, and she pressed her thighs together or crossed her legs when she sat."

Tiffany shrugs. "Monitors do what they want; they are in charge. You ought to know that."

"Yes, but listen. Steph also wore panties last Term," BB argues. "She even picked them out. Expensive lingerie."

"So? I guess last Term she could tease, hold back, and make Gamers drip for her. Compel them to speculate if she sported a full bush, was trimmed, or maybe shaven." Tiffany laughs. "And now she's sanpan! Like I said, she's a natural born Stripper. And so hostile, too!"

BB breaks a smile. "She anticipates that each minidress I assign will have a different cutout hole. She hates that."

"Isn't she right?" Tiffany appraises. "Today she had to wiggle up the hemline to ensure she showed her outie in a tight buttonhole. It seems like whatever minidress you select for her will be either short or very short, but always short enough that when Steph sits, any mystery about her shrubbery resolves."

Babs nods her head. "Blonde."

Tiffany rubs her chest. "Everyone wants to know when you intend to sign her pink and wet?"

Babs chokes.

Tiffany advances, "Hey! Momentum matters in the Game, and the momentum of last Term plays into this one! And Steph isn't moving in the direction she wants. How about you let *me* teach her to Strip?"

"Steph can't recall that she ever did anything evil to me when she was my Monitor," Babs reports.

"Yeah," Tiffany retorts, "except she probably badly shamed and humiliated you."

BB acknowledges Tiffany with a look.

"Do you know Janet's take on her?" Tiffany queries.

"I do." Babs firms her mouth. "Janet thinks she's a deceitful opportunist. Janet wants me to keep her legs spread."

Tiffany scratches her bare midriff. The prickly scratches above her tan line have mostly faded away. She offers another gambit. "Steph fears that behind your calm, low-key manner you could be planning payback, which is what she would be doing. But luckily for Steph, you resist vengeance. I can tell that about you. But she doesn't know that."

Babs pivots into a sitting position and swings her legs over the side of the bunk. She lets air out of her lungs. "My fundamental issue is Steph's rebellious attitude, her assumed privilege, and her challenging of authority," BB explains. "I've observed her sitting with her thighs pressed together and pretended I didn't see. I can't let that kind of behavior continue. I have to promote home rule."

"Maybe Janet wants to trade for her," Tiffany suggests. "I can talk to her about it."

BB smiles. "Thank you very much, Tiffany Transparent. Janet has already inquired! And she and I are quite capable of conversation."

Tiffany gets one word in edgewise, "Ma'am—"

Babs continues, "I'm sure that if and when Janet wishes to talk to you she will offer something of value. She knows you're here, after all."

Tiffany accepts, but antes, "Did Janet tell you that we shot Pee-Cam clips together when we were Stripper Roommates, two Terms ago? She had the Pee-Cam, and I acquired it from her. I took it with me to Flesh Ranch last Term. And this Term I bring it with me here to the Cosmos! Ta da!"

Babs tries not to glower. "I hear Janet visited the Nugget last Term…and you dancing together?" Babs spins. "One of those times when you were a visiting Feature Dancer and not sucking dicks at Flesh Ranch."

"Ah," Tiffany remembers more clearly now, "Janet's Alumni Reprise. She wrapped her jaboos around the pole and masturbated up a slick spot. How come she never told you? You were her Roommate, after all."

"You seem to have neglected to tell me about this Alumni Reprise," BB states.

Tiffany stiffens. "Ma'am, I though you wished to be shielded from Janet's indiscretions, Ma'am. I mean, it's her story to tell, not mine. She outranks me."

Boss Babe takes charge. "Excuse me, Pledge. You deceived me by pretending you didn't recognize Janet in the Dining Room Picture."

"Ma'am, yes, and you punished me. The prickly bush scratches hurt me. You know that, Ma'am." Tiffany shifts her position in the chair. Squeezes her thighs together.

"I let you soak in the bathtub," Babs parlays. "You promised me you would tell me everything you know."

"Ma'am," Tiffany falters, then regains, "I told you about Kimju and Molly. I told you I sucked cock with Ginny and about Lee Lollydor. You've seen my Calendar. I've told you about Pee-Camming with Janet. I told you her last name." Tiffany rubs her Eraser Heads in the palms of both hands. "Ma'am, there's a lot to tell, Ma'am. It's hard to get it all out."

Babs takes a very deep breath and squares her bra on her breasts. "Finding out about you from third parties instead of from you puts me at a disadvantage."

"Ma'am, I'll run around the Garage naked and get really scratched up. I'll collect all my pee in the Watering Can. I'll pour it all into the Mudpit and wallow in broad daylight. You can issue an advisory via your Desktop. You can control the Back Door Cam, so you control the media."

"I don't control paparazzi from shooting over the fence," Babs dignifies. "You just want more exposure. You don't deserve exposure."

Once again Tiffany gets a word in edgewise, "Ma'am—"

"You've also forgotten to tell me about all your tattoos," Babs develops. "Get off my chair. Hands and knees on the floor."

Tiffany scrambles. "Ma'am, please take me to the Nugget! Let me dance naked, pull my butt cheeks apart, and show my tramp stamp in blacklight. It becomes visible around my tailpipe. I'll show you right now."

"You'll do nothing of the sort!" Boss Babe commands.

"Ma'am, perhaps you'll let me show you my other hidden tattoo," Tiffany begs.

"Silence!" BB commands. "Perhaps I was too kind to you last time, awarding you a nice warm bath after you got scratched up. You seemed to forget the message."

"Ma'am, I didn't deserve the bath, Ma'am," Tiffany agrees, looking up from her hands and knees on the floor.

"But we can't redact the bath, can we? So what do I need to do, Pledge?"

Tiffany knows the answer. "You need to repeat your graciousness, Ma'am, only make it painful."

Babs considers this response. "Any suggestions? Hey, you avoided Slavesex; what would a Slavesex beg?"

Tiffany shivers. "Ma'am. It could be anything. I'll move into the bathtub. Ma'am, I failed to use my mouth properly; Slavesex get fed soap if they fail to use their mouths properly."

BB considers. "Very well then. Crawl yourself into the Bathroom and draw yourself another nice warm bubble bath. Dunk your hair in the bathwater."

"Ma'am, thank you, Ma'am. I'll wash that Janet right outta my hair."

"Use lots of shampoo. Only before you put any shampoo on your head, pour the shampoo into your mouth. Then dispense it back into your hands and then onto your head. Think you can handle that?"

"Oh, Ma'am," Tiffany responds.

"You don't have to earn a soapy mouth by not being forthcoming with me," Babs informs her charter. "You can beg anytime."

"Ma'am, thank you, Ma'am." Tiffany bows. "I'll wash my hair twice."

9 Babs & Tiffany & Robyn Sign Steph: Vagcam Excess (D06)

§ Tiffany Makes Up Steph: Navel Restraint & Opt Strategies

It is the morning of Day Six. Steph makes sure to be the first to wake up. She had surrendered yesterday's maillot to Boss Babe last night, slept naked, and had found, as promised, a new cutout minidress folded and waiting on the shelf of her locker.

Santa Claus.

She hurries to shower, hopeful that Tiffany has not arisen. She pees first, showers, and looks at her naked self in the makeup mirror as she struggles her head through a high-collared minidress. She considers, *Well, I was going to demand BB give me something more decent, and I guess this is her idea of an improvement.* Steph examines the minidress more carefully. Small armholes, a hemline partway down the thigh, and, yes, a big buttonhole. No need to worry about navelage 24x7!

Steph considers the length of the tight minidress in the makeup table mirror. *Yes, I will have to work to keep my thighs apart, but no one will see much upskirt.* Steph wiggles her stomach. Fine hairs and a navel, and at the very bottom of the oversize buttonhole, the smallest tad of hairage. Steph shakes her head. *If I move carelessly even more hair will squeak out, but otherwise no one will notice.* Steph looks at her visage one more time. *Headlights.* Steph sticks her tongue out. *No titter for Gamers today!*

Tiffany steps into the Bathroom, and the Cam goes live. It gravitates toward Tiffany first. Fair enough; Tiffany does deserve the respect of the instigator.

"Sit," Tiffany commands. "I'll do your makeup."

Steph sits. Tiffany "Porn Star" works naked, of course, with the fine grain of her skin divided by a single tan line that circumvents her body seven inches below her navel. Her clear vinyl croptop leaves not a trace, but the tan line of her slacks crosses through her pubic hair and below the top of her tush.

Steph shimmies her stern back and onto the stool in front of the makeup table and mirror. She checks in the mirror to check on her upskirt. She grits her teeth. No secrets: the lights around the mirror illuminate Steph's upskirt all the way to the short hairs covering her snapper.

Steph looks away from herself in the mirror to discover that the live Bathroom Cam has also discovered her. It hovers and collects full purview.

Tiffany kisses Steph's cheek and considers the Cam also. "I shall turn you into another of Cleopatra's Wannabe Strippers today." Tiffany steps back, and the Cams also backs away. "Gamers want to see the look on your face while the Cam takes down your upskirt," she consoles. She gazes in the mirror at Steph's hairage, then moves in front of her, places fingers on Steph's cheek, and commands, "Hold still."

Tiffany applies foundation.

Steph seizes upon her first opportunity to question Tiffany. She doesn't wiggle around, but she says, "Okay, so you whored at Flesh Ranch last Term and occasionally 'Feature Danced' at the Nugget; your reputation precedes you. But you have no knowledge of Babs' Pledge days?"

"True," Tiffany accepts. "I was a Whore, not a Cosmos Pledge. I met Babs the day I arrived at the Cosmos House." *Although I do know Janet, as well as the two ex-Nuggets expected to arrive soon.*

"Well, I know all about Babs!" Steph advances. Tiffany cocks her head to listen. "She was my Pledge last Term!" Steph speaks quietly now, cognizant that the live Cam might also capture sound. "I am the one Cosmos who witnessed Babs from a Caste above, and I know where all the dirt is."

Tiffany rouges Steph's cheeks, overworks her eyes, and applies over-thick mascara. She compliments, "I like your cutout minidress today. Good choice. The high collar and small armholes require Gamers to glorify your buttonhole. Short hemline, too. Lots of belly; lots of leg."

Steph rustles herself on the stool but makes sure her thighs don't touch.

Tiffany frowns. "So far you're getting more vagcam time than I am."

Steph advances, "That's because you haven't gotten any. I'm the one getting flashed. Doing the flashing. Whatever."

Tiffany shudders. "You've seen me Pee-Cam. So when you're ready to join me, and not just spread your sanpan snatch to the Cam, then you'll be as qualified as I am to Opt Stripper next Term."

Steph doesn't appreciate the encouragement, but she does observe that the Bathroom Cam—the Pee-Cam—continues to focus on herself. *Especially my upskirt. I'm more important than Tiffany right now, even though Tiffany is naked and can pee anytime. Pee-Cam later for sure.*

Steph volunteers fresh data. "I'll tell you something you don't know. I know how Babs got her nickname."

"BB?" Tiffany follows along.

"Bikini Babe." Steph snides, "She begged it. She begged it from me." Steph tries to adjust the minidress to minimize surveillance of the very bottom of the oversize buttonhole. "And not just Bikini Babe. How about 'Bodacious Baudetrot'? Or 'BooBs,' with two capital Bs."

Steph laughs, "How about 'Bling Bra'? That's one of yours!"

They laugh politely together.

"How about 'Boss Babe'?" Tiffany inquires.

Steph raises her eyebrows and caps, "How about 'Boss Bitch'?"

Naked Tiffany quiets Steph's mouth while she carefully applies over-wide lipstick, and probes Steph's demise. "So, from what I hear, you broke some Game Rule, but now you want to repent? You *did* Opt Down."

"I was *Opted* Down. I got dissed by Robyn. Robyn Redacted," Steph asserts. "I'm here because of her duplicity."

Naked Tiffany draws two moles, one to the side of Steph's lip and one on the other side of her neck. "You look like a Stripper. Splay your snatch like a Stripper. I'm so sorry you can't titter today. BB thinks everyone's gonna stay Roommates Together, so she thinks both you and Robyn will both beg to Strip sooner or later." Tiffany rubs one tit then the other with the palm of one hand. "Of course you will, so my job is to train you as best I can."

Steph raises both hands and brushes her hair back. "You just think everyone wants to be like you."

Tiffany agrees, "I'm the best. Maybe you overplayed your hand last turn for a reason. Sometimes when a Cosmos gets too coy, it's a signal that the Cosmos *wants* to be put down."

Steph snaps back, "Speak for yourself, trollop; that's certainly not a theory that I would subscribe to. There's a lot about me you don't know. I was the Monitor of the Cosmos House last Term. Right here. Maybe I didn't witness the knockdown, boob-spilling Mudwrestling Contest that pitched Babs and Janet against Penny and Coco, but I saw everything else up until then. That's where the real story is."

"And somehow Robyn doesn't remember she refereed?" Tiffany probes.

"Robyn got jealous of me and set me up!" Steph clarifies, almost falling off the stool. She puts one bare foot on the floor, then regains her balance on the stool, double checks that her upskirt carries all the way, and grouses to Tiffany, "Robyn knowingly contributed to my demise last Term. And now she chooses to forget about that. Don't worry; I'm going to deal with that rattlebrain no matter what Gamers did to her. She could have AIs inside her for all I know."

Tiffany smiles. "Seems like she got to you."

"Listen, I'm confident my Pledging is a transient low point in my Game, because I *deserve* to bounce right back up to Monitor Caste. More correctly speaking, I deserve to be a MomCap this Term."

Tiffany smiles. "Robyn claims the smallest buttonhole and the biggest Gamer attention. She is dangerously strapless, prone to shine headlights, and has the capacity to cameltoe, if not get cheeky or buttage."

Steph doesn't follow. "That won't happen. So?"

Tiffany closes, "So. Robyn's desirous of attention but doesn't want to show off for it, and she becomes instantly jealous whenever *you* titter. And of course your vagflashing makes her go mad."

"We can trade Garments anytime," Steph growls. "My titter and vagflash are just a temporary phase." Steph pokes Tiffany in her belly. "You should talk. You probably not only know *how* to flash, but to flash *dance*. You're the Porn Star and wannabe Whore. You're the one with a clit like trisectrix, folding you into yourself so you take pleasure with no shame."

Tiffany squeees her lips before she speaks. "You got me."

Steph considers Tiffany's Eraser Heads, now presented close to her face, no clear vinyl overtop. *I saw you climax on the Dong with Janet at the Alumni Reprise, but you don't know I know that.* "Tiffany Transparent," Steph appraises. "Good luck on Opting to Strip. You really do deserve to get back to Fuck Ranch, or whatever it's called."

"Flesh Ranch." Tiffany preens, "And may Kundalini be praised. Kundalini formed me well, and not just my tits, tummy, and twat. Also my tush, what you call my trisectrix, and even my tongue." Tiffany wrinkles a lip. "Kundalini taught me how to give pleasure as well as receive it." She brightens. "Maybe Babs will let us go visit the Nugget and audition on Stage together."

"Maybe not!" Steph responds sharply, then qualifies, "Besides, you're not my Roommate, and neither is Robyn, for whatever that's worth. You said my Roommate would be a topless ex-Nugget. Right?"

"Right," Tiffany agrees. "Either you or Robyn will get Kimju, and the other will get Molly. They're great gals; gonna be arriving wearing minimums from the Nugget. One piece each." Tiffany pauses with a makeup applicator in hand and asks Steph, "Did you see the Calendar month where I make out with another woman while sharing a Double Dong in out twats?"

Steph reluctantly admits that she has thumbed through the Calendar and examined all the months.

Tiffany deepens Steph's eye sockets to the point where Steph sees Cleopatra's Stripper looking back at her in the mirror. She blinks. *I don't need to look like this target.* Steph welcomes Tiffany's next probe. "I understand that when Robyn ratted you out last Term she only had one Garment. So why is it that Robyn Redacted pledges again? Do you think she got rewarded somehow?"

Steph doesn't contradict Tiffany's proposition, but she also really doesn't know what happened at the end of the Term. She calculates, "Listen, I might have been chloroformed before Gamers demoted me to Pledge. But according to the Rules there is no way a Pledge can repeat a Term."

"She's Redacted." Tiffany waves an arm. "After all, you and Babs and Janet all saw Robyn here last Term. She was your Pledge. And Pledge aren't allowed to Hover or repeat a Term. You know that. Pledge must Opt Up or Opt Down."

"So the only way she can be here is if she never had a Term before."

"So she was never here before," Steph grumbles. She presses forward, "Lookit. Right now Robyn and I each possess only one piece, although Robyn certainly does not comprehend the implications of this. Make no mistake: she put me down last Term, and I'm going for a reversal, whether she knows it or not."

Tiffany accommodates, "Babs says some Gamers think Robyn has Charm. Whatever that is."

Steph up-ticks, "Charm is nothing, that's what it is. I don't believe it. Never did, never will."

Steph trades mirror eyes with the naked Pledge standing next to her. *Tiffany Transparent, the Pee-Cam Pledge.* She looks at what she has become in the mirror: Cleopatra's Stripper looks out at Steph from the mirror. Proclamation aside, Steph remains suspicious of Charm, after all. *Because Robyn is a Pledge here at the Cosmos House this Term. Like magic. Like Redaction. So could Redaction be the price of Charm?*

Steph turns, looks at Tiffany directly, and hardens her tone when she says, "Listen, I'm going to make sure that ragazze gets broken. Opts Stripper next Term. Show all her holes. Masturbates. Climaxes a dildo. She's gonna pay."

"How are you going to do that?" Tiffany asks while she fusses with an eyelash.

"Humph." Steph tugs her minidress down enough so she can sit on it, though just barely. Her navel beams clearly. The Cam collects more scrag; might Steph reach a tiptoe to the floor? Steph feels caught short, but tries. "Why should I tell you my Robyn plans? I have a lot riding on this."

"I trust I'll be joining you every time you want to take a Bathroom break," Tiffany muses.

"Don't be obnoxious," Steph counters, appalled at this suggestion. For a moment she slides her palms inside her knees, then relaxes. "Okay, it's very simple. Both of us, Robyn and I, must first Game with our Roommates."

"Right," Tiffany agrees. "If Molly is your Roommate she'll be happy to give you whatever she wears, but if it's Kimju, she'll try to take your minidress away."

Steph wants to ask more about them. But Tiffany maintains initiative, querying, "So after the Roommate Games, then what?"

Steph brags, "Well even before, whenever I get the chance, I intend to convince Robyn to lockstep her moves to mine. Her thinking too, what little there is of it. She won't even perceive she's synchronizing to me. And then, when the time comes, it will be nothing to take her maillot away and Opt Monitor Caste!"

Then a more pragmatic Steph speaks. "Face it: left loose and unattended, Robyn has the stupidity to crush me. To Opt me Down again, so I'd end up Stripping next Term. That's unacceptable and needs to be prevented. She could do it to you, too, so you need to help me neutralize her completely."

Steph might think it is Robyn Redacted who seeks to crush her, but Gamers know it is all of us.

Still, it is unlikely Steph will forget to keep her belly button always exposed. The bare navel remains a Cosmos identifier, and Steph will not make that mistake twice. Navelage 24x7. No exceptions.

Tiffany tops off Steph's makeup and claps her hands. "I have transmogrified you into a sassy sorostitute!"

"Sorostitute?" Steph considers her mirror image. "You've made me look like a Stripper!"

"Listen Pledge," Tiffany affirms, "many aspire, but only a few qualify for Stripper work. But you are fortunate to be made up by the best!" Tiffany assesses her handiwork. "When they Cam you, they Cam me also. I'm metadata; that's me on your face!"

Steph isn't sure how to take a complement. "Listen, Tiffany Transparent, be a wannabe Whore. Please, go Pledge naked and cum be a Stripper next Term. But don't try to sell me on the prospects of Stripping. It's not necessary. I intend to be a Monitor next Term and, if possible, Double Opt Up."

And with this Steph stands, bows to Tiffany, and announces, "Now that my makeup is finished, I want to leave before my feet get peed on." She exits the Bathroom.

Tiffany sighs. *I do need to put Stripping into the realm of possibilities in Steph's imagination,* she ponders. *And convince my Roommate Babs to Opt Up and take at least one of my Garments. Then Steph and I can both make the Nugget, and Babs and Robyn can Opt Up.*

Tiffany develops a wrinkle. *Maybe Steph doesn't want to Strip quite yet. No problem; Steph will want to Strip more in the future.*

§ Babs Signs Steph: Sit Stay Legs Apart Kitchen Upskirt

During their last conversation Janet had suggested to Babs that enabling Hand Signs might provide BB a tool to help channel Steph.

Janet had rubbed her hands together with facetious delight. "She'll love that."

And so BB prepares to implement this discipline. She locates Steph sitting in the Kitchen and commands her to back her chair away from the table.

Steph obeys, carefully making sure her legs stay apart. The high collar and small armholes ensure Steph doesn't titter, and her buttonhole is plenty large, but her upskirt is total. Steph finds herself awkwardly sitting the middle of the room.

"It dawned on me you know all the Hand Signs," Boss Babe spins.

"Me?" Steph appears flustered. "Who says?"

"Janet reminded me," Babs admits. "She recommended that I put you on a Cam feed to the Nugget. She says the Crowd there deserves a preview of next Term." BB admires Steph's makeup. "Tiffany certainly prepared you for the role."

"Maybe you don't know where I am headed," Steph barters for time. "Janet's an ex-Stripper. Maybe you should preview her."

Babs doesn't wait. The fact that Steph has declined to reveal that she secretly watched Janet and Tiffany dance at the Nugget last Term galls her. *Patience.* "Remind me about some Hand Signs," Boss Babe commands.

Steph might be skilled at issuing Hand Signs, but she appears reticent to remember them. "Well, perhaps I know some of them."

Babs smiles. "I'm sure you do. Remind me."

It is an order, of course, and Steph feels her vagina constrict. But she keeps her thighs not touching. It's dark down inside the minidress, but sanpan still. Steph knows not to err. *I've run Pledge through prickly bushes for that. Seen them put into the Cravat.*

Steph raises a wrist, extends a hand, and crosses her first two fingers. "Do you know how to issue this command?" She inquires.

Babs does, and Steph crosses her legs.

They share a rare laugh. Both know they play a dangerous Game of power flows. Both fail to observe Kundalini lurking inside.

BB exerts initiative. "I'll try to forget that one. Show me another."

Steph holds two fingers together and mocks her Monitor, "Oh, Ma'am, please sign me this, Ma'am."

So BB signs Steph "legs together," and Steph uncrosses her legs and presses them together on the chair. Steph double checks her navelage, smoothes the minidress across her smarties, and smiles at Babs.

Babs smiles back. "In the unlikely event I need your legs together I'll try to remember that one. Please elucidate me on something more practical for your requirements."

Steph stops smiling. She extends her hand, opens two fingers wide enough apart so they aren't touching, and carefully adjusts her legs so her thighs aren't touching. "Maybe you learned this last Term."

Maybe Babs did, but maybe she always wore cloth in her crotch.

BB parts her two fingers into a "V." Steph opens her legs wider, forcing her minidress to ride high all the way up her thighs.

She seethes. And feels her slit part ever so slightly.

§ Babs Lets Robyn: Sign & Cam Steph's Titter & Vagflash

Robyn breezes into the Kitchen…with the Back Door Cam trailing her inside. She stops short and appraises Steph's situation. "What do you know. Another opportunity for the former Cosmos Monitor to broadcast vagflash to the Prefecture!"

Steph extends her disgust past Babs and toward Robyn. "Hello, Robyn Redacted," she greets. "Nice buttonhole."

The Cam avoids Babs and zeros in on Steph's open sashay.

Robyn directs a highfalutin' attitude toward Babs. "Turn on the Screen so this skeeze can watch herself!"

Babs slowly closes then opens her eyes, takes a step back, and snaps her fingers. Steph's graven image from the Cam appears on the Kitchen Screen.

"Look at you!" Robyn taunts. "You can admire your upskirted sex cavity on your own feed. Nice."

Constant humiliation. Everyone at the Nugget can watch, too. Live audition.

Babs watches. But if part of her considers intervention, part of her considers intervention unnecessary.

Steph's legs are already akimbo. "Arms surrender," Robyn orders, and Steph folds her hands behind her head, sitting legs apart surrender. On Cam.

"Admire yourself on the Screen, you skuddy squim slot," Robyn rants. And cackles with laugher.

Steph's eyes roam past a Babs who seems oblivious and come to rest upon the Screen and her own head-and-shoulders, hands-behind-her-head image. The minidress she wears today might have a high collar and small armholes, but it is sleeveless. Headlights, but no titter. Steph squares and cups her armpits, firms her stern on the chair, and makes sure her spread feet are toe-and-heels touching the ground. She simmers.

Robyn curries Babs' favor. "Did Monitor Babs teach you this Sign?" Robyn asks. She points a hand toward Steph and wiggles two fingers as she holds them in a wide V.

Steph understands the Sign. So does Babs, even if Robyn might not. Steph's mind races. *But the question is not an interpretation of the Sign; it is one of command and control. Like yesterday, when Robyn signed my legs open on the Library steps.* Steph hesistates.

Boss Babe answers the unspoken objection, commanding, "Obey Robyn's Hand Signs!"

Steph obeys the twitching fingers and opens her legs wide. Robyn's wiggling, stretched fingers command them wider still. The minidress rides past the top of Steph's thighs until Steph's legs can't spread any wider. *This isn't open halfway, like yesterday; this is full spread. I might be inside, but this Cam takes my image to Screens inside and out.* Steph looks at Robyn and shoots daggers with her eyes. *I will get you for this. I swear.*

Robyn laughs and points at Steph's spread slash. "You might have worn panties last Term, but you wear panties no more. You might have crossed your legs when you were a Monitor, but now, Pledge, you keep your legs spread."

Steph quivers with anger. *You betrayed me. You're the reason I'm here.*

"Look at yourself in the Screen," Robyn orders. "Don't take your eyes off yourself! What you see is what you are, you skeezy shag skank."

Steph seethes, but she yields to the power of Babs and the Cam's presence. She affixes her eyes to the Screen. Robyn touches the hovering Cam and issues controls, and Steph watches the image canvas her own face, armpits, what appear to be headlights, a navel in cutout, and her exposed lady parts. Nothing covers Steph, from her thinnish, natural blonde scruff to her legs, bare feet, and painted toenails.

Steph watches the Cam return to canvas the insides of her opened thighs, study her single line slit, and observe her clit trying to sneak out.

Robyn taunts, "Tell the Prefecture what you call your stamen there."

Steph grimaces and tries to connect to Babs, talking to her although the Cam watching her, "Ma'am, that's my strophoid, Ma'am." Then, harder: "Ma'am, I'm a very curvy Cosmos. And if you'd like me to trade costumes with Robyn I will. Ma'am."

Robyn steps back—Gamers can see the jerk in the feed—but the Cam twists and turns as Robyn insults, "Be nice to me, Steph Sorostitute, and I'll keep your snizz and shrubbery in focus! Gamers don't want to miss out once your inner lips start leaking satchel slop!" Robyn laughs. "Maybe if you fingerball your strophoid you can stir up some splurt in your snizzaroo, you Stripper wannabe!"

Steph opens her mouth to speak, and Babs retakes control. "Pay attention to Robyn, and from now on always follow her Hand Signs."

Steph grits her teeth, but before she can bite, Babs squeezes harder. "It's important you master how to take directions instead of giving them… especially for where you are headed."

Steph opens her mouth to retort but closes it. *I've played the Game before, and I know when to hold,* Steph grits to herself. *Still, it is I spreading shrubbery, and not my former sidekick, Robyn Redacted.*

And I still only have one Garment.

"Come upstairs with me," Boss Babe orders Robyn, who abandons the hovering Cam surveiling Steph and follows BB.

"We'll keep an eye on you on the Screens upstairs," Robyn promises as she ducks up the narrow, angular back stairway. "Because you're going to pop your stamen out, discharge some slippery slop out your snook, and then you can beg to Pledge bare, bald, and naked, and cum be a Stripper next Term!"

And Robyn is gone.

Steph tightens her face around its centerline and considers how to play Robyn Redacted. *Twice now that ragabash ragazze dares to expose me!* Steph silently grits as she makes eyes with the Cam, then looks at the Screen. The hovering Cam surveilling Steph has zeroed in on an upskirt that totally reveals everything between her creamy thighs. Indeed, Steph can see in the Screen that her strophoid has indeed made an appearance. And not just Steph: all Gamers can see.

That ragho thinks she can make me reveal my intimate secrets? Wait 'til I get my hands on her. And Boss Bitch doesn't fool me either. Maybe BB thinks she's gonna let Robyn force me to masturbate, ooze out some sloppy slush, and climax. No way. As for BB, I'm going to butch that blowser and turn her into a bang box!

Steph looks down at her crotch. Her minidress has ridden so far up she can view herself with impunity. *I hate Boss Bitch for letting Robyn cam me! Or for leaving me under surveillance. But I don't hate her as much as I hate Robyn.*

Steph quivers her thighs, but she doesn't close them. She waits. She knows the alternative, and it's called the Cravat. Nobody closes legs in that iron contraption. Monitors can demand Pledge get disciplined in the Cravat, I ought to know, after all, it was I who arranged for Janet's secret sitting. But that was last Term.

§ Tiffany Warns Steph: Don't be a Better Stripper than Me

Tiffany, returning from errands, observes Steph immediately upon entering from the Back Door into the Kitchen. They trade eyes. Steph evaluates Tiffany. *Still clad in her see-through front-button, longsleeve, transparent, clear vinyl croptop and low-rise, cameltoeing, tush-*

separating, skin-tight stretch sacks. Tiffany concludes, *Steph continues to wear today's high-collared big cuout minidress. And what is the delta?*

Tiffany knows. *Steph sits spread surrender on chair in the middle of the Kitchen. Upskirt sanpan vagcam.* Steph returns her eyes to her visage on the Screen and pretends to be oblivious to Tiffany's arrival. The Cam doesn't take its eye off of her, and looks up her pantyless spread legs from the front.

"Oh!" Tiffany exclaims. "What are you up to?"

"I'm looking at my snickerdoodle on the Screen," Steph flips, knowing that now is not the time to test limits, even with fellow Pledge.

Tiffany observes that the Back Door Cam, let inside by Robyn and normalized to Steph's body, fails to turn its attention to her, so she walks across the Kitchen, positions herself behind the fallen Monitor, and verifies via the Screen that the Cam now includes her in its vision. *Better.*

Steph watches herself again and can see that her stamen has wormed even further into the open. Two lines now descend from this bulb, augment her center slit, and define her inner lips. Steph catches herself. *I must not let my smoo come apart any more. And I must not get wet.*

Tiffany doesn't miss Steph's revelations. "Oooh, you have potential after all. You got your strophoid and inner lips out. I'll help you slippery your slot. And I'll show you how to use your sex sauce to lubricate your short hairs so you can shave them all off. I'll make a Stripper out of you."

Steph decides the best policy is to sit still.

Tiffany draws her hands around both sides of Steph's body and tidies her minidress. Steph's minidress might have a high collar and armholes too small to titter, but it does have a large buttonhole that Tiffany explores with her fingers. Steph squirms like she's ticklish. She considers moving her hands from behind her head but reconsiders and holds position, also keeping her knees wide and allowing her minidress to continue to upskirt her short blondies.

Tiffany lifts her hands upward and cups Steph's breasts through the tight minidress. Steph whimpers, and Tiffany whispers into her ear, but loud enough so the Cam hears, "And just because my fans love my titter in see-through doesn't mean your fans won't love you too. Don't worry; your makeup makes you look tremendous, and I'll make a Stripper outta you before you know it. See me next time you've got your scones loose, and I'll lipstick your nipples."

Steph blinks, and the Cam resigns itself to gathering the headlights that Tiffany popped up.

Tiffany wiggles around to Steph's side, making sure she remains in Cam view. She gathers the sides of her own slacks in her thumbs, pushes them down all the way below her crotch, and exposes all her thinnish red thatch. She looks at Steph look at her in the Screen, smiles, opens her trap door, and reveals a burgundy-color vagina within.

"I'm not to be upstaged," Tiffany warns. "Although you shouldn't think I have a monopoly on making pink shots."

Tiffany draws her slacks up and steps behind Steph, leans over the back of Steph's chair, and rubs her Eraser Heads (through the clear vinyl of the croptop) against the back of Steph's head. "Be nice to me and I'll let you lick the tattoo around my tailpipe," Tiffany preens.

A flummoxed Steph tries to articulate, "Tiffany Transparent, you are a Cosmos begging to Pledge naked and cum be a Stripper next Term."

"I am a Porn Star," Tiffany affirms, then pushes harder, "and you're a Wannabe Stripper."

Steph challenges, "You're a Wannabe Whore!"

Tiffany gives Steph a peck kiss on the top of her head. "When you get tired of sitting in the chair, move and make yourself comfortable in the corner. Just make sure you keep your legs spread and your eyes on the Screen. You won't be able to hold your arms up indefinitely, so relax with them at the side. Just be sure not to use them to block the view. This could be a long day."

Tiffany has been unbuttoning her clear vinyl croptop while she speaks, and now she leans deeper into the Cam shot and flashes unfettered Eraser Heads to the Cam. Photons direct. She spins, cracks deeper tail trough using both thumbs, and heads upstairs.

§ Robyn & Tiffany: Remembering Steph & The Button Rule

Tiffany discovers Robyn alone in the Bunkroom, and rather than exploring Babs in the Bedroom or stripping and checking out the Bathroom, she sits down next to Robyn on her lower bunk.

You really showed up that slut." Robyn points to what is normally the Mirrored wall, but which has transmogrified into a room-wide, life-sized Screen displaying the Cam's view downstairs in the Kitchen. "Steph Sorostitute sitting spread surrender and practicing Hand Signs." Robyn chortles. "I'm sure Babs feeds the Cam out to the Nugget Crowd, if not the entire Prefecture."

Tiffany realizes that Robyn, who rejected she was a Cosmo Pledge last Term, might still retain trace memories of whatever happened back then, including some knowledge about the now role-reversed Babs and Steph. *Also Janet may be relevant, and ditto Penny and Coco.*

Perhaps Robyn's selective amnesia weakens when she perceives she can do damage to others or build supplicants. Besides, Robyn wants to make sure Tiffany never accidentally lights up the Bathroom Cam while she's naked in the shower or "using the facilities." And so Robyn shall share secrets, might she remember any.

Tiffany opens, "So I hear that Steph was the Cosmos Monitor last Term, but somehow she got Opted back Down to a Pledge. Like where she started from her very first Term."

"She Pledged in two Garments, I warrant," Robyn presumes. "That's how she promoted to Monitor last Term. Now she's got one piece and falling momentum."

"I heard that what happened was that Steph ignored the bare button Rule?" Tiffany inflects the question subtly.

Robyn explains casually, hiding one eye with her hair, "It wasn't even like she was careless or anything like that. She traded for a very sleek and sexy minidress that let her tease her legs and fancy panty lingerie, but it *did not* have a cutout in it and *did not* expose her navel at all!"

"And just for that the Gamers broke her?" Tiffany wants to make sure she gets the whole story correct. Tiffany assesses that Robyn's belly button currently sits in a tidy hole in her strapless maillot cutout. *My own centers on a vast expanse of belly flesh floating above my low-rise slacks and below my transparent croptop. Even Babs stays well revealed. Navelage 24x7.*

Robyn draws Tiffany's eyes away from the Screen and back to the story. "Steph covered her button near the end of the Term," she elaborates. "She came to think she was above the Rules." Robyn pauses to think about it, then continues, "I mean, like, her minidress didn't just make it hard to see her button or even flash it. It simply covered it up. Cutout minidress buttonholeless!" Robyn laughs, then adds nervously, "But nobody did anything about it, until somebody signed an affidavit...." She thinks again, then shrugs her bare shoulders. "Steph had opportunities to reverse herself; she received hints, she got told. But she simply believed that she was above navelage 24x7. She was always demanding and in charge. She did herself in. At least that's what I've heard," she qualifies.

Tiffany prods, "So what happened?"

"Er, ah, well... nothing." Robyn purses her lips. "Except until the last day of the Term." Robyn pauses to gather attention and deliver the punch. "And then Gamers descended upon her, took her panties away, cut a big hole in her minidress, and suggested to her that she beg to Pledge."

Tiffany considers. *Makes sense.*

"So here she is at the Cosmos House," Robyn proclaims.

Now a part of the Mirror/Screen changes, and a clip plays showing Steph shadowy vaging in the Parlor the day of her arrival.

Tiffany studies the footage. She had missed the Steph's arrival with Babs and Janet in the Parlor.

"I cammed that," Robyn announces proudly.

"And you've seen this before," Robyn informs as the video cuts.

Tiffany studies this footage. *Actually I* haven't *seen this before, but I am in the picture. It's from when I came into the Bathroom, enlivened the Cam, and it collected Robyn and Steph sitting spread surrender. Except the Cam collected Steph's spread satchel in its full glory.*

Robyn, also in the shot but with her crotch covered, runs her mouth with details as if Tiffany doesn't know. "You can see what they did to her. They hacked a cutout hole in her minidress so huge that it reveals her scruff at the bottom and the bottoms of her 32A specials at the top. The sleeves have been cut away so that her sand dollars and stalks can't hide inside her armholes, and Gamers hacked her skirt so short that the bottom of her round stern shows below the hemline."

Tiffany watches the video as she draws up in front of the Cam, parts her temple and tinkles in front of the twosome.

Robyn suggest, "Next time you should pee all over her, not just next to her foot."

The video cuts to a third scene, this one from the Library steps. Tiffany had seen this live, but Robyn continues to prattle. "This is me camming more of her shaggy socket box." Robyn laughs into her hand. "More titter, too. I cammed her titter in the Parlor, in the Bathroom, and on the Library steps."

Tiffany takes exception to Robyn's claim of credits but worries a different spin. "I guess today will mark Steph's fourth vagcam. Perhaps she will be gaining fans in the Prefecture."

"The Prefecture?" Robyn acclaims. "I'm going to turn her into a slippery slush slut and make her pull pink at the Nugget. And not via a Cam either. Live." Robyn recounts, "From what I heard Steph thinks that being forced to Opt Down was really unfair. She keeps complaining that somebody ended up with her panties who didn't deserve them. Who cares? Last Term she crossed her legs and flashed her panties to her advantage. This Term BB has appointed me to uncross her legs and flash her vag to *my* advantage."

"You were there last Term?" Tiffany asks Robyn a loaded question.

And Robyn replies, dodging, "Well, no. Not officially, that's for sure." She deflects, "But that doesn't matter. You and Steph are both the same: two Cosmos headed for the Strip next Term."

Tiffany takes umbrage at this comparison. "Excuse me, Robyn, but I am not the same, and Steph is not my equal. I am a Porn Star!"

§ Babs & Tiffany: Strategies to Humiliate & Arouse Steph

Tiffany finds Babs in her Bedroom, the Bikini Babe in her Bling Bra, lounging in her bunk and watching Steph on a tilted Desktop Screen. Tiffany knows the scene. *Steph sits in the Kitchen downstairs and struggles to keep her thighs spread wide apart.* She flicks a head toward the Screen and says to Babs, "Ma'am, she's struggling, Ma'am. It's something that's hard to keep doing after a while; there are so many reasons to close the legs."

Babs waves to Tiffany to sit in the desk chair. BB seems to have forgotten that only yesterday she confronted Tiffany for failing to recount the Alumni Reprise, and Tiffany ended up washing her hair and using her mouth as a shampoo dispenser. And of course the Bathroom Cam took it all down. And it collected toilet later, as the Pee-Cam always does.

Babs and Tiffany remain unaware of Steph's primary motivation to not close her legs. But Steph knows one very good reason. *Babs and Tiffany don't know about the Cravat. But Janet does, and if Janet catches me, she won't be as nice to me as I was to her, when she sat locked in the Cravat naked for days. Well, a day perhaps. Maybe not even.*

Tiffany transfers her eyes from Steph on the Screen and considers her flesh-and-blood Roommate lounging in the bunk. *One broken Monitor, now Pledge, looks like a Stripper and sits spread surrender, auditioning for the Nugget. And a current Monitor, whose self-image fails to include the possibility of her following Steph's footsteps, Opting Down and Pledging again, maybe with only half of her Black Bikini.*

BB gives Tiffany a compliment. "You put a nice face upon Steph."

"Ma'am, thank you for letting me handle the Makeup Case, Ma'am," Tiffany appreciates. "I'm doing my best to cast Steph as a slutty Stripper for next Term."

Babs looks at Steph on the Screen. Cutout minidress. Vagcam.

Tiffany helps, "Ma'am, you're tormenting Steph with her haughty need to command attention with her looks and personality, yet affording her simple humiliations, like having me make her up like a Stripper and letting Robyn spread and Cam her. You will get her to topple soon, and it worries me that she will become as willing to pink as I am."

Babs seems oblivious to Tiffany's worries. "Steph Sorostitute must learn to beg to Pledge naked and cum be a Stripper next Term." BB casts down a marker. "Like you do all the time."

Tiffany adjusts her weight in the chair. "Did you like it when I pinked on her?" she asks.

"You never want anyone to get ahead of you," Babs laughs. "You're bad sometimes. On one hand you want to get to the Nugget, and on the other you want to help Steph achieve her most distant goal."

Ma'am," Tiffany offers, "I admit I've said before that she'd make a great Nugget. But do you intend for make her pull pink?"

Babs hesistates. "Robyn seems intent on making Steph cream. Make her pink wet and ready! Seems like a good next step. Especially if she gets used to exposing herself." Babs stops short, startled by her own vengeance.

Tiffany slips her hands inside her croptop so she can rub her Eraser Heads with her fingertips. She pitches, "But however, Ma'am, if it's her or me who has to go to the Nugget wearing only one piece or nothing at all, please make sure I get to go! You know I'll strip naked and cum for you anytime, anywhere, in front of anybody."

BB tickles Tiffany's fancy. "I should make you climax right here, where there aren't any Cams. And all by yourself."

Tiffany pretends to pout at the insult. "No one to watch? Ma'am, I will dildo and dong for you, eat pussy, kiss girls. I'll massage your body; I'll do your hair and makeup."

"You begged to drink my pee and lick my bunghole," Babs recalls.

"Ma'am, may it please you," Tiffany cries.

"It pleases me not," Babs settles. And they laugh together.

Tiffany brushes that part of her thatch that rides above her waistline with the back of her hand and descends a palm into her slacks. "Ma'am, let me tell you a secret: I'm convinced that all of Steph's titter and vagflash arouse her. She should be scared of herself, instead of being scared of you or me!"

"True," BB agrees. "Steph's worries are just beginning. She will get more unnerved when the ex-Strippers, Kimju and Molly, arrive, because one of them will be her Roommate and will be, according to you, arriving topless."

"Well, with one piece, according to your Manifest," Tiffany hedges. "Don't forget that both Robyn and Steph have only one piece, and they're not topless."

"Fair enough. And then of course there is Janet. Yes, it's true Steph made Janet live in the Mudpit after she arrived, but Janet's vengeance is deeper than that. Deeper than eating soap and a chamber pot." Babs considers, "She's hostile, but even more hostile than those things."

Tiffany considers this also. "Steph hates Robyn, and it's not just that you let Robyn sign her. It's some of whatever Robyn did to her last Term, but it is also that Robyn keeps acting like a princess."

"I'm only marginally responsible," Babs agrees. "Mostly Robyn acts."

Downstairs in the Kitchen, Steph awaits. *I wait for whatever might happen next.* Steph closes her eyes. *I can't take a chance; I have to stay safe for the moment. I definitely, positively must make sure my thighs never close. No matter who looks or for how long.* Steph opens her eyes and sees her sitting spread surrender self on the Screen before her. Armpits. Face. Bellage. Legs spread. Vag. *Hard, hard, hard to maintain this pose, but it sure beats sitting Cravat. Because I know Janet watches me now. If she isn't watching live then she has someone watching for her, or Automatron running motion detection on me and isolating out any faux pas. Maybe Janet never got sexed in the Cravat, but she did get fondled and pinked, which is what she probably wanted in the first place.*

No, thank you. Steph closes her eyes, realizes that's against orders, and opens them again upon the Screen. She examines her short, wavy blonde hairs and the shadowed line of slit beneath. Details? *Yes, my strophoid stands out. But one thing I am firm about: no way I will make slippery! Not for Babs or Janet. Not for Robyn. Not for Gamers like you!*

Kimju & Molly Arrive: And the Games Begin

10 Kimju & Molly: Strippers Promote to Topless Pledge (D06)

§ Kimju & Molly Beg Switch: To Pledge Topless

A Switch had interviewed Kimju and Molly while both were still Strippers at the Nugget last Term, after they'd applying to pledge the Cosmos House. The Switch—a Gamer who relishes both the Slavesex and the uppermost Game Mistress Castes but whose current Caste was unidentified—had announced to both of them, "I've done the Gay Pride Parade wearing just a collar and a g-string."

Kimju, a.k.a. Kim, had twitched her neck at that one; she realized she had actually seen this on television, in the newspapers, and in the vast Prefecture. The Switch had continued, "You'd do that to get to the Cosmos House?"

Molly had squinted her eyes in thought. Both Nuggets had already done all the nudie things: danced topless, danced fully nude and pulled pink in a juice bar, shot naked photo sets, and stuffed big toys for the Cams. And of course every Stripper makes the Pee-Cam. Nonetheless, parading Fifth Avenue topless in a g-string would present a much bigger social space, a much bigger audience, one that would be more alive, and so a much higher risk. Would they do this?

Kimju and Molly had traded looks and answered together, "Yes." And took the only upward path offered.

And so the Switch let them Pledge topless. Kimju wears an orange stretch-fabric tanga, a.k.a. a thong, a T-back; Molly sort of fits into faded red, washed-many-times cotton panties. Gamers shall observe them more shortly, but unless you have sufficient Gamer privileges to view Automatron's Archives, you must wait for them to arrive at the Cosmos House and plead their next stations in real time.

Kimju and Molly both know their alternative, of course: Whores, the fate of Strippers who retrograde one Caste. Now, it is true that before they ever joined the Game, however many Terms ago, Kimju and Molly notched many guys. Both enjoy picking partners and circumstance, although at the Nugget neither got to have sex in any way whatsoever. But neither is keen on Whoring, or, as Kimju puts it to Molly once, "It's one thing having the House make you dance naked and cum on the pole. It's quite another thing having the House decide what dicks get put into you."

Molly agreed, "Right. Stripping is the easiest thing to do, but when and where and how you get banged? No thank you."

§ Babs & Tiffany: Anticipate Kimju & Molly • Janet Physics

Babs and Tiffany continue their dialog in the Bedroom. Babs fingers her shoulder straps, covers her bling with her palms, and squeezes her bra. She confesses to Tiffany, "I worry because Kimju and Molly have more Terms in the Game than I do. Yet I am their anointed Monitor Boss. Higher Caste. So how do you know them? You weren't a Nugget last Term."

Tiffany smoothes the low-rise stretch slacks on her legs. "I met them because Flesh Ranch sent me out to Feature Dance there... and trick the Champagne Room. And I know they've both played the Game for a while. Hey, lots of us have Gamed Up and Down the Caste scale! I believe they met at the Nugget and were Stripper Roommates all through last Term."

"Do you think they will remember Pledge Rules?" Babs wants to make sure they will arrive knowing them.

Tiffany tucks a hand into her stretch pants, tugs her cameltoe, feels the exposed part of her tail trough, and touches fiery hairage erupting above the elastic waistline. Eraser Heads in see-through, bellage N-7. She says, "All of us Cosmos, except the two newbies still to arrive, have Pledged before, at least once, if only for our first, newbie Term. When we begged admittance to School."

"Right," Babs agrees. "You know *I* was a Pledge last Term."

"From what I hear you were very determined to Opt Up and Monitor this Term," Tiffany says politely, then adds, "Ma'am."

BB feels better. "I know Pledge Rules. You and Steph know Pledge Rules. So Kimju and Molly will know Pledge Rules as well."

"A slight refresher, perhaps, might be good for all!" Tiffany endorses. "But be forewarned. Kimju and Molly, they also know Stripper Rules."

Babs blinks.

Tiffany advances, "I know Stripper Rules, too! And I also know Whore Rules!"

BB tries to forgive Tiffany's enthusiasm. "They danced naked, then?"

Tiffany studies Babs, "Put it this way. Last Term at the Nugget Kimju and Molly pinked and peed on Stage and lapdanced naked. Kimju likes being looked at, but didn't like getting her knockers fondled, whereas Molly was just fine getting her clit fingered."

Babs isn't so sure, "Well, maybe last Term Kimju liked being looked at more than she does now." She frames carefully, "So did Kimju and Molly witness Janet's Alumni Reprise?"

"Perhaps. A lot happened that night. Look, you already scratched me up for not recognizing Janet's Picture, then made me eat shampoo for not telling you about her Alumni Reprise."

"You can do worse than that for your fans," BB breezes. "Any other Cosmos ever visit?"

"What do I know?" Tiffany answers quickly. "I was only there sometimes, and I only saw Janet. It was a big sensation: she arrived naked. I already told you she slicked the pole with her jam and peed center Stage. You want to know how Janet knows I got a tramp-stamp tailpipe tattoo? She had to lick my asshole; that's how she found out."

"Perhaps you will get an opportunity soon to lick her ass back," BB opines.

"Don't be a silly," Tiffany brightens. "We had to lick each other's assholes. MomCap said that it contaminated our tongues, so ergo we couldn't eat each other out. All it did was make us both really horny and wet."

Babs seeks boundaries. "I didn't think Strippers—Nuggets, in this case—were allowed to engage in lesbian behaviors. You know: kissing, sixty-nining, riding Double Dong."

Tiffany explains, "That's correct, Ma'am, but neither Janet nor I were Strippers last Term. I was a Whore. And Janet was a Pledge. You ought to know. You were her Roommate, Ma'am."

"Well," Babs pouts, grateful for the gossip about Janet, "maybe you won't need to wash Janet out of your hair again."

§ Kimju & Molly and Ginny & Lee: Motives and Streaks

It is a busy night at the Nugget, and Kim and Molly hobnob in the Dressing Room with another pair of Roommates, Ginny and Lee, who will also ship out tonight.

"We never insisted we pledge topless," Kimju explains. Her brown eyes have fire in them. Her curvy topless figure and firm knockers are major attractions, treasured by many a patron.

A picture of Kimju adorning the Nugget lobby matches the topless thong she wears here in the Dressing Room. On the lobby card Kimju's beige, silver dollar-sized areolas pucker, her knob-like nipples crinkle up, and she spreads her legs wide apart. The thong bares all of Kim's keister, narrows the most where it crosses what the patrons call Kim's kawazoo, and widens to hide her deeply pigmented inner lips and rosy kypsey, the Crowd's term of endearment for Kimju's vagina, also known as her koot.

Both on the lobby card and here in the Dressing Room Gamers can see that Kimju's pussy hair has been butched and shaved *just outside* the legline of her tanga, which rises in front along her inguinal. This enables Kimju to outline her thong with stiff brunette stubble. Kimju accepts the highlight. *It makes Gamers wonder if my kohlrabi, hidden inside, has been butched also. I know all their names for it: my kale, kava, kelp, kerf, kohlrabi. Hopefully Gamers have seen it all for the last time.*

The shorter, Rubenesque Molly confides to the other pair of Roommates, "We would have pledged nude... in a finger-snap. Anything to Opt Up."

Molly, equally topless, has a reputation around the Nugget for letting patrons grab her huge floppy mammaries, droopy, natural moombabas sagging with large, splotchy areolas. She lets patrons grab them with both hands.

At the moment, the only Garment adorning Molly's body is a pair of thin panties, with a waistline beneath an overhanging belly and a deep navel depression. Gamers will soon see that Molly's panties actually don't ride as low as Babs' nombril, but Molly's muff is significantly bigger, and her ratty, low-cut panties just barely contain her puffy black outgrowth. Backside, the panties more or less cover her gluteus maximus.

And there's more to Molly's hair beside the long black hair on her head or the fluffy muff barely hiding. Unlike Kimju, who keeps her legs and armpits shaven, Molly retains *all* her body hair. Molly sports thick, unshaven legs, hairy arms, copious hair in both armpits, and a centerline of fur that rises from her muff all the way up to her navel. Molly doesn't know yet that she will be the only totally unshaven Cosmos, but it's a good guess. *I will stay this way, or Gamers will shave me; however it pleases them.*

Ginny and Lee, the other pair of Strippers, are more pragmatic. "We begged to pledge naked. We got our wish, and we're scheduled to move into the Corvette House. So it looks like we're going to be in rival Houses. But we never committed to parade topless."

Kim and Molly nod their heads politely. *Subtleties matter.*

They do. The waistline of Kim's solid orange Spandex swimsuit thong rides an inch below her navel, and her birthmark forms a vertical oval with a custard swirl inside. Kimju needs that for where she is going. Navelage 24x7 rules at the Cosmos House.

Kimju and Molly have gotten along well during the past Term. Neither is shy about exhibiting their body, be it on stage, in a studio, or lying next to a bubbling brook *au natural*. The freedom of being nude. But their conceptions and goals are different, however topless both might be at this moment.

Kimju likes to get looks, and her lobby card fully details her showgirl stats: stacked 35C-24-35, 5' 8" and 117 pounds, with not quite shoulder-length brunette hair and a tad of melanin in her skin, probably a polyglot South or Latin American. Some Spanish, but also some Chinese or Japanese, a touch of African, and a dash indigenous Indian. Not unlike the modern skins Gamers might see in a nightclub in New York or Rio or Caracas.

Molly is happy to open herself up so that a looker can stare. Being topless right now is actually a step away from total nudity and not a motivating factor. Molly's lobby card isn't out tonight, but the last of her Pink Pages are available for the asking from the Hat Check Girl out front.

Every Stripper has a Pink Page, even through pink comes in many shades and flavors. Molly's Pink Pages includes all her stats: her astrological sign, blood type, favorite color (red), and a glossy gynecological shot of her pulled-wide-open, deep brown vagina, a.k.a. her muliebre, her mooe, and a lot of other names. No secrets: shorter squatter Molly (5' 3" tall, 140 pounds) is an Irish-Spanish cross with long black hair and a square face with gray eyes. And a fleshier 38DD-30-37 physique.

But Molly will not be seeing her pile of Pink Pages, and Kimju will not see her lobby card tonight. The expiring Strippers expect to leave by the Stage Door and not exit through to the Club and the Crowd out front.

"You two are Pledging because that gets you all that much further away from the Whores," Lee observes, rotating her naked torso.

Lee's right. Kimju and Molly's motivations include avoidance. Strippers are one Term away from the Whores, and Pledge are two turns disconnected.

"And you." Ginny stretches her naked body in an easy way and address Kimju. "You are considering the possibility of a further promotion. You're already thinking about adding a second Garment so you can become a Monitor. And create still more separation."

"Fair enough," Kimju acknowledges. "I don't care to Whore. Degrees of separation matter to some of us."

Ginny bites her tongue. All four expiring Strippers know that "degrees of separation" don't matter for Ginny. Naked Ginny might be a Stripper promoting to Pledge, but two Terms ago Ginny volunteered and will always be a Whore-For-Life.

Ginny shrugs. "Okay, so I Strip and I work the Champagne Room. You know I shot porn in the Inner Sanctuary. So I guess I'll be turning tricks for Janet. She should like that, especially since she's never had to put out."

Lee asks a question. "We're going to have to make a run for the Corvette House—you know, like, naked of course. So does that count streaking or not? Like, maybe it's in between Terms?"

Kimju shrugs off Lee's worry. "It's not like you have any choice." Kim runs her hands over her own near-naked body. *Topless tanga outdoor. That's next for me.*

"Assume it counts as streaking," Molly says, surrendering to judgment.

Ginny grimaces and retorts, "Maybe topless is too good for the both of you. May the both of you streak before the Term is out! May you both pull pink in public, cream yourselves, and climax."

Lee augments, "I bet both of you beg the Pee-Cam."

Kimju holds firm. "I said I'd parade in public wearing only a g-string." But she flinches. *Might I take up more explicit behaviors? Ongoing Pee-Cam?* She bites her front teeth together and continues, "But I am not a cock garage. And I am not a Lollydor!" Kimju directs a pointed comment to Lee: "I no licky spent cum off the floor."

Lee shrugs, "Lolly becomes me."

Ginny intercedes to smooth things over. "Listen, all Whores lolly, but only one Pledge per House is allowed to Lollydor. Maybe Lee's allowed to lick up sex drip, but don't forget that I'm a full service Whore."

Kimju evaluates the two naked but promoting Corvettes. *Ginny and Lee. No hair on either's lips; all they have are little racing strips up above their pudenda. That's it. I can match that. I can swallow a fat dildo into my kypsey, pump out white kloop, and koekjedoodle any day. But I'm not into Whoring or cleaning up, either before, during, or afterward. I intend to get a second Garment and Opt Up.*

Lee's pushes again. "You two got off easy. And besides, I bet volunteering to parade topless isn't the only reason you made Pledge."

Kimju says nothing.

Molly has remained largely silent throughout this exchange. She casts her eyes around the Dressing Room. *I am going to miss this place.* Unlike Kimju, Molly is less motivated by the possibilities of the more senior Caste of the Opt Up. Molly is more sanguine. *My interpretation is that the Game performs its own manipulations. Not much I can do about it. Unlike Kimju, I don't assume that further upward mobility will be happening for me. My advancement to Pledge is one of chance and convenience.* She scratches her belly and swings a mam to the side. *I like pulling pink for the Crowd. Masturbating. Anytime, anywhere, in front of anybody.* She accepts Ginny looking at her. *Ginny understands. I'm comfortable with the ease of the lifestyle, and even if the guys get frisky sometimes, I know they appreciate me.*

"And what about you?" It is Lee who engages the quieter of the pair and brings Molly out of her thoughts.

Molly pinches a roll of fat around her belly. "I don't care so much if I Pledge or Strip," she says. "But I am glad I'm going with Kimju. And I'm gonna miss the Nugget, but I expect I'll return next Term. Either just like I am, wearing soiled panties, or fully naked." Then she says clearly to Ginny, "But I'm not going to miss the prospect of becoming a Whore. Sorry, but not all of us want fucked."

§ Kimju & Molly: Present Themselves Topless at Front Door

The topless Kimju and Molly and the nude Ginny and Lee leave the Nugget under the cover of darkness.

The last thing they see are two naked and disoriented arrivals—Penny and Coco, in fact—get vacuumed in the Stage Door, swept onto center Stage, and get their two pussy hair hearts depilated. But there is no communication. The ex-Nuggets exit the Stage Door while the raucous Crowd still beats in time with naked arrivals pulling pink, masturbating, and trying to climax. Hello, goodbye Nugget. Time for Penny and Coco to learn about staying naked, keep pink wet and ready all the time, and fending off frisky hands during a lapdance.

The topless duo begins their furtive journey toward the Cosmos House, while the nudies streak toward their new home, the Corvette House. Gamers know that darting to the Cosmos House topless does not count as streaking, but running naked does. Both are risky, but streakers who get caught sometimes get screwed. Or get discovered in stocks on the Quad after their Clock starts running again.

Molly puts the four other Strippers out of her mind, those who have been demoted to Whores and must transport themselves to Flesh Ranch or the Fancy House. Molly had braced herself for that possibility, and she considers herself fortunate to pledge the Cosmos. She doesn't want to think about what might happen to those defeated, but the image of a cock being forced down a throat and gagging phlegm keeps returning to her mind. Never mind where else the cock might have been, or where it goes next.

Kimju and Molly both know they are fortunate to wear anything at all; but then, Ginny and Lee are equally grateful to be nude. They all know that Pledging presents an opportunity, nothing more. Kimju and Molly have been Pledge before, have been allowed to become Strippers, and shall now Pledge again.

Not knowing better, they arrive via the Porch at the Front Door of the Cosmos House, but both aspirant Cosmos know better than to walk in, and both are smart enough to know they trip a Cam on. Kimju finds it first and trades eyes as it collects her infrared. She clenches her firm knock-knocks in an improvised handbra. *My knockers, my knock-knocks, my kajoobies. And a lot of other things the Crowd at the Nugget named them. More mine now than before, but not yet mine completely.*

Molly mostly tries to hold up her mammary glands so they don't impede her movement, and vacillates between topless and a handbra. She's the one who pulls the chain connected to a chime on the inside.

Robyn comes around from the side of the Porch to greet them. Robyn assumes she does this task because Babs favors her; she does not consider that she may actually be Low Girl. Her yellow strapless maillot cutout really is her only piece. Tiffany has given the big-haired blonde a touch too much black and gold eyeliner, gold lips lined in black, and a big black mole on the side of her chin, but Robyn doesn't know she looks like Cleopatra's Wannabe Stripper disguised as a slutty baby doll.

Robyn contemplates the arrivals with scorn. "You're Back Door Pledge." Robyn shoos the pair off the Porch and thinks her humor is original. "Ring the Bell, and be prepared to wait a *long* time."

Kim and Molly trade a silent look. They backtrack their topless, barelegged bodies down the front stairs and scramble around the side of the house past the Porch and cellar door. They turn to find the brass Bell with its long pull rope at the foot of the Landing and Back Door. They stop, look at each other, and pull the clapper together as a symbol of good luck.

The ring sounds much too loudly. Kimju looks at Molly and speaks. "We have gone from dancing naked but inside the Nugget to waiting nearly naked outside a Back Door. So this is progress?" She shifts her weight and covers her knockers with two palms. *All through last Term, up until this very moment, I never cared who saw me topless or nude, and Molly still doesn't care. Last Term I did what I had to in order to Opt Up. But this Term I shall make my own decisions. And if that requires that I learn how to make decisions for other people, so be it. That is a process School teaches. It teaches mastering Gamers, and that's not necessarily a bad thing.*

Kimju shifts on her bare feet, antsy. Kimju opens her fingers just enough so that one knobs shows out, then closes her fingers again. *I still present the bare skin of my keister to the Cosmos House Backyard, whereas Molly's maximus stays covered. On the other hand, my waistline rides higher than Molly's. As if that matters at all.*

Of course it does. Everything matters.

§ Robyn Disses Steph: Collects Cam & Exits Kitchen

Steph took Tiffany's advice hours ago. She has moved from the chair to a corner of the Kitchen and stayed there all day. For hours. She had gathered up the uncomfortable hem of the short cutout minidress so that it no longer creased across her rounded stern, relaxed her arms to her side, and let her opposing legs rest against the two walls that join in the corner, allowing her snatch to be fully displayed without having to think about it. The ever-relentless Cam had moved with her, and now it continues to hover in front of her spread offering.

Steph resigns, *At least my collared miniskirt ensures that there exists no way the Cam can collect titter.* Steph quaints a nostril, resists touching herself or blocking the view, and drifts in and out of sleep.

It is late in the day when Robyn appears and makes a prediction. "Your Roommate arrives tonight... and she wears panties. Maybe you can give her your dress so that you can go naked." Robyn laughs at her own brilliance, signals the Cam to follow her, and disappears out the Back Door with the Cam trailing behind.

Steph, numbed by hours of spreading her legs for the Cam, feels relief, yet she remains uncertain if she should close her legs or not. *I can barely keep myself together, or, to put it another way, keep myself apart. And it's not just Robyn who mistreats me; Boss Bitch lets it go on. Why doesn't she step in and defend me?*

Patience. Tiffany will rescue Steph soon enough.

§ Robyn Greets Kimju & Molly: Backyard Arrogance

Kimju and Molly have resigned themselves to waiting when Robyn bounces out the Back Door with what is actually the Back Door Cam trailing her outside. She directs the Cam and moves with a cocky attitude. Kimju and Molly exchange glances with quizzical eyebrows. Robyn speaks down to them from the Landing.

"From now on your tits and ass belong to the Cosmo House. Now stand spread surrender while *I* shoot five views: your full figure, head-shot, and close-ups of your boobies, bellies, and butts."

Robyn descends and sounds the Bell. The Cam follows her as if perched above her shoulder like a hummingbird.

Kimju dislikes this arrogance. "So who are you?" she challenges while Robyn collects the close-ups.

Robyn raises her chin and heightens her body at this challenge. "*I* am Robyn, and Babs, your Monitor Boss, has sent *me* to cam you!" Robyn detects Molly swiveling her eyes toward Kimju.

"You're a Pledge!" Kimju laughs at her.

"*I* am Babs' assistant, and she is watching you this very minute!" Robyn stamps her feet. "The Cam follows me and feeds the Prefecture!"

Molly accepts the potential for truth in this statement, as well the consequences. She knows all about Cams. She stands topless, hands behind her head, thick legs wide apart. Bare feet on cold concrete. She holds her position.

Kimju forms concave armpits. Her 35C kajoobies stand out. She feels goosebumps form on her bare behind. She's humiliated.

"Now shut up, both of you!" Robyn never considers that her actions might exceed her authority. "Monitor Babs values my judgment. My command. My control!"

"I shall now water the garden," Robyn announces firmly, already in motion. She picks a hose up nearby and sprays the Mudpit in the middle of the Backyard, several yards away from the Bell. The dry dirt garden plot becomes moist. She preens, "Now both of you Cosmos wannabes sit your sorry asses down in the Mudpit. Get those thighs apart, keep your hands behind your heads surrender position, and loll your tongues out. You're lucky to be here at all!"

The shorter and heavier Molly moves quickly. She must grip her mams as she moves and sits down, but not before Robyn laughs at her. "Pledge, you'd better swing those heavy majonkers around carefully. You could knock yourself out!" she cackles.

Kimju hesitates before she follows and sits herself down adjacent to Molly, getting mud on one hand before she puts it behind her head, inadvertently transferring mud to her hair. Both have mud on their heels. Molly's panties provide some protection from the bare earth on her hindquarters, but Kim's thong provides no such protection. She winces as the moist dirt muddies up the skin of her firm keister. She glowers.

Robyn presses her luck. "You both look really stupid." She brings her chest forward and her head upright and laughs at them. "You're messin' up your panties and g-string!"

Enough. Kimju knows how to dance naked and climax herself outdoors at a bike feast. She snaps back at her fellow Pledge, "You're the one who's stupid. I'm wearing a tanga, a thong; it's not a g-string, not a fio-dental." She pauses and catches an open-mouth Molly watching her.

Robyn snaps back, "You don't know what you're talking about."

Now Molly interjects, easy-going and laughing as she tells Robyn, "You're silly. Both a tanga and g-string bare one's ass, but a tanga has some material on the sides and center back, whereas a g-string is just a patch, a string, and a knot."

"I'm knockers with a kunny kover," Kimju suggests. "Except I'm still wearing one piece, just like you."

Curious Gamers following the live action in the Backyard seize control of the Cam and pan to gather Robyn's reaction. She's speechless and flummoxed. Then she pulls the lever on the spray nozzle and lets both former Nuggets enjoy a blast of cold water. Night chill envelopes the Backyard. The water knurls up Kim's knobs atop her firm knockers, and Molly's splotchy mauve areola shrivel into a moonscape. Goosebumps everywhere. Mud splatters all over their bodies.

Robyn cackles. She points to Molly's midsection; Molly's minge shows right through her soaking-wet, now see-through panties. For once Robyn acts smart. "You two have just become more balanced. You both show your tits 24x7." Robyn points to Kimju. "You show off your cute keister." Then she focuses on Molly: "And you show off your full minge, albeit in see-through-when-wet! So you'll just have to *keep* yourself soaking wet!"

This time Kimju raises a chin and snaps, "You need to lay off of Molly."

Robyn takes a step backward, pouts, and blasts Kimju with still more water. She spits to both ex-Strippers, sitting in the wettened Mudpit, "Be nice to me and do what I say. I'm Monitor Babs' assistant. I'm a newbie this Term, not some knockers and thong kitty, or some majonkers and panty maladroit churning in the Game. Betcha you two Strippers had to spread naked last Term. Tell me now."

Molly confesses, "We both spread naked, pulled pink, and dripped cream."

"Oooh," Robyn coos, then inquires of Kimju, "So did you masturbate and climax for the Cams?"

Kimju again finds herself overextended. She must admit the truth: "Yes."

"Excellent. You'll do whatever is necessary to ensure they get screened."

Kimju blinks. *I did not think that I would be bringing any of my old media with me.*

Robyn accelerates, "Both of you are gonna go Strip again next Term. So just stay like you are; it's a done deal."

§ Robyn introduces Tiffany & Steph to Kimju & Molly

Kimju has her mouth open, but rescue comes suddenly. All heads turn as Tiffany precedes Steph out the Back Door and off the Landing. The Bell rings twice. The ex-Strippers recognize Tiffany but stay silent.

Robyn falters but recovers quickly. Kimju and Molly dart eyes and hold their hands behind their heads, armpits deeply concave or hairy. Both keep their knees wide apart, feet muddy now, with mud splattered onto their torsos and faces. Kimju's bare keister becomes even more slippery. *Wet dirt.* Molly's panties have snuck into the crack between her moons as well as her sex meat, so now her fat gluteus maximus also rests on bare earth. *Mud.* Water runs off both of their bodies. They're soaked.

Robyn turns to face Tiffany and Steph and feigns grace. She jerks a thumb over her shoulder toward the two increasingly muddy topless, bare-assed arrivals. "Apparently that's Kimju and Molly. They're Strippers," Robyn laughs.

Tiffany takes in the scene and narrows her eyes. "They *used* to be Strippers. They're Cosmos now."

Robyn stops laughing, wrinkles her nose, considers, and forges ahead. She sweeps a hand from the two Pledge in the Mudpit toward Tiffany. "Meet Tiffany." Robyn stretches her arm out and bends as she points. "Tiffany Transparent. She Whored last Term, fucked herself into a Double Opt Up, and rooms with Babs, your Monitor Boss. Tiffany's the Porn Star on the Calendar inside."

The introduction ignores Steph, who raises her chin and furrows her brow. *Good job, Robyn! But be careful what you say about me.*

Tiffany holds the stage and nods her head politely; she's prepared herself in anticipation of this meeting, and she carefully trades eyes with Kimju and Molly. *I Feature Danced while you two were Strippers last Term.* Tiffany smiles, "Hello Cosmos Pledge." Then she warns, "Watch out when you use the Bathroom, because whenever I visit I always turn the Cam on."

Robyn rushes in. "Tiffany can't get enough of the Pee-Cam. And it'll be running when she does your makeup each morning. Maybe she'll even let you eat soap with her."

Tiffany elongates her body upward onto tiptoes. "I shall prepare you both to rival Cleopatra's most magnificent Strippers." And then, turning to Robyn, she says, "Shampoo, not soap."

And Robyn replies, "You'll drink laxative if it gets you some Cam shot."

Kimju and Molly wince. Might Robyn have acquired knowledge of what happened at the Nugget last Term? Maybe not, for she evidences no consideration that Kimju and Molly might have performed onstage with Tiffany.

Tiffany remains quiet. She stands erect and tidy in her stunning makeup, Cleopatra's Stripper incarnate. The Cam dwells on her, and she delicately tests her lipstick with the tip of her tongue.

Robyn finds the silence awkward, so she details, "See Tiffany's long, cylindrical tit-tips that peer through her clear vinyl shirt? I call them her Eraser Heads. That's what you call them, too."

Tiffany tops, "With ultraviolet ink. They glow in blacklight." She shimmies as if Kimju and Molly don't know this. The hovering Cam hesitates, then descends down Tiffany's figure so Gamers may collect red hairage rising above skin-tight, purple, low-rise stretch slacks. The Cam retreats, and Tiffany gives it that "has she or is she about to" look. Then she projects herself to the ex-Strippers spreading in the Mudpit before her, announcing, "I sport bellage galore. My low-riders hairage and cameltoe." Tiffany twinkles, "And sometimes come with a wet spot."

Kimju nods her head and trades a look with Molly. *We know. We saw you dance in blacklight. We know you got a tramp stamp that descends to your tailpipe. And that when you get down on your hands and knees and pull your tush apart that the ink around your tailpipe doesn't need blacklight.*

Molly follows Kimju lead and remains silent. She looks down. *We watched Janet lick your tailpipe during the Alumni Reprise. And not only that; we've had to watch you suck cock. Fuck, too.*

No thank you.

Kimju also remembers, *I watched you lick Janet's jet tunnel. She was a Cosmos then, so I wonder where she might be at the moment. Molly and I never crossed paths with Janet after she played the Nugget that one night, and we never had any opportunity to find out what Penny and Coco might have told us.* Kimju shuffles her body and works more mud up her keister and feet.

Tiffany silently smiles as she considers Robyn. *It is not required that I correct Robyn's misunderstandings. As for Kimju and Molly? I have seen the both of them lapdance buff naked, watched Patrons take liberties they shouldn't, and I appreciate that Kimju and Molly respect that I coordinate when any disclosures get made. We shall talk later.*

Kimju uses a moment when Robyn diverts her attention to Tiffany to shift her hands from her head to her sides. *Mistake!* Her palms instantly acquire mud. Water still trickles off her into the wet dirt. Molly rotates her head to look at Kimju for guidance, sees that Kim keeps looking straight ahead, and turns her head back and reclines also, except that Molly rests herself on her elbows and forearms; another mistake.

Steph chaffs at Tiffany's attention and seizes upon Kimju and Molly's nervous movements to advance herself. "Pledge Robyn seems to have forgotten to introduce me. I'm Steph. I was the Monitor here last Term. Pledge Robyn should be disciplining the both of you for breaking position. Maybe if you ask nicely she will let you both wallow in mud."

Robyn rushes to regain control as Kimju and Molly realign themselves, getting even more mud in their hair and on their bodies. Robyn pivots toward Steph, bows, and sweeps out an arm, declaring, "Meet Steph Sorostitute!" She smirks. "She Opted Down to Pledge this Term. Here she is! She's wearing whatever cutout minidress Monitor Babs gives. One piece. Sanpan."

Steph nods her head at this truism and appraises the newcomers with steely blue eyes, thin lips, and a face with hawkish Egyptian makeup. Like Tiffany, Steph already knows who Kimju and Molly are, although neither ex-Nugget recognizes the slender blonde currently wearing the small, high collared, sleeveless minidress with a huge cutout hole centered around her outie bulb and birth crater. It is so short that Steph's shaven legs seem endless.

Neither former Nugget knows that Steph has spent today in the Kitchen with her legs spread and her scruff on display. Robyn educates them, "Steph keeps her legs apart 24x7, except when I sign them open or spread. Like all day today."

Kimju and Molly watch Steph squirm. Kimju at least appreciates Steph's stress, and she watches as Steph tugs and smoothes the tight stretch fabric to try keep the minidress level below her crotch. Kimju thinks she sees a few short and curlies at the bottom of the buttonhole, but she reserves judgment. *After all, I am not even looking downward.*

Steph does look downward, though, and gazes upon the two ex-Strippers sitting in the Mudpit. *Kimju and Molly don't recognize me at all. Furthermore, both ex-Nuggets and Tiffany act like they don't know each other either. However, I know they do, because I saw Kimju and Molly dance the night of Janet's Alumni Reprise. Kimju and Molly were naked then, lapdancing, and the Patrons were sucking their knockers and mams. So for sure they saw Janet and Tiffany climax together on the Double Dong! I suspect Janet never told Tiffany I secretly saw the two of them together. Certainly Tiffany has had plenty of opportunity to tell me today, but she hasn't. She's dangerous.*

Steph has never before considered if what she had seen might be legal. She glances down to see if her buttonhole leaks hairage. *I guess, given that a Pledge is allowed to Double Dong, and a Whore can do "all holes, all sexes," then maybe Janet and Tiffany could do what Strippers aren't allowed to do and share the Double Dong.*

Still, analysis aside, the arrival of the two former Strippers surprises and disquiets Steph. *Why are they here and not routed off to Flesh Ranch or some other Whorehouse?* But then an insight: *One of them is my Roommate and currently wears my second Garment.* Steph considers the muddy tanga and panties. She grimaces, but accepts. *Molly has the panties; she'll do.*

Tiffany addresses the two topless Pledge sitting in the Mudpit without any accent of past histories. "Nice of you to bring your kajoobies and mazoomas." The slim redhead slides her fingers along the bottom of her croptop shirt. "And if either of you want this croptop, it's yours. I was supposed to be a Stripper this Term, so my next best thing is to Pledge naked and cum be a Stripper *next* Term."

Molly reacts, "Ma'am, please, I want to stay topless."

Kimju adjusts herself in the Mud. She considers the vinyl croptop, no matter how transparent. "I'll take it," she says. "Please."

Tiffany acknowledges neither ex-Nugget. "Anything goes. Just don't forget: I am a Porn Star!"

Steph frowns at this possible complication.

And Robyn watches, irritated. *How dare Tiffany interfere with my Roommate!*

The newbies haven't arrived yet, but Kimju and Molly don't know that. Once again the former Strippers trade eyes with the former Feature Dancing Whore, and they communicate comfort with each other. Even though Kimju and Molly are startled to find Tiffany here—a Pledge with two pieces—they resign to whatever power this communicates. Tiffany makes the slightest curl with her head, turns, pulls the Bell, and disappears inside the Back Door.

§ Robyn & Steph Brief Kimju & Molly: Roommates Aligned

Robyn twists her upper lip in the direction of the Back Door and addresses Kimju and Molly. "You needn't concern yourself with Tiffany Transparent, she's just a misplaced Whore." Robyn nods her head toward Steph, who continues to stand and watch silently. "Or with Steph. She does what I sign her. You'll see. You two concern yourself with me. I'm important."

She directs her next vocalization to a muddy Molly. "You will be bunking underneath Steph; you are her Roommate." Molly moves an arm, brushes her forearm against the side of her belly, and leaves a mud streak behind. Oops. Steph smiles. *At least Molly is eager enough.*

Robyn mock-bows to the slippery, near-naked Kimju and decrees, "And you are bunking above me, so you're mine!"

Kimju and Molly trade looks. They had roomed together at the Nugget, but that was last Term; they are Roommates no more. Right now they are just Cosmos Pledge. One of their goals has been achieved; Gamers have spoken; yet one of the ex-Strippers' bonds disengages. The topless, muddy, wet duo isn't sure how to interpret this, but it does mean they won't be scraping with each other over a tanga and panties. No Roommate Games, at least not for now.

Kimju drills into Robyn and computes a fresh appraisal. *My Roommate's yellow maillot or 'top my thong could be my ticket to Opt Up!*

Molly and Steph trade eyes; Molly wonders if Steph wears panties under her tight cutout minidress. *I hope not.*

Steph sees blubber. Fat blubber with melons hanging down to the waist, hairy armpits and legs, gluteus maximus, and yes, panties. Dirty panties, perhaps, but Steph sizes up Molly fast, and Molly senses the over-made-up eyes of the hawk canvass her. Unspoken, but both understand that Steph intends that the panties shall pass from Molly to her. Steph feels her inner sanctum swell and her stamen grow out; Cleopatra's Wannabe Stripper makes a pearl-drop of wetness. Can't see it, but it's there.

And does Robyn calculate her prospects with Kimju? Has she figured out that all the Pledge who wear but one piece have now arrived at the Cosmos House? Robyn's memory might be handicapped, but notwithstanding, Robyn doesn't think about things she doesn't think about.

Robyn, oblivious to the dynamics, orders Kimju, "Okay Roommate, on your hands and knees. Crawl to the Bell. You're about to learn your place."

Kimju observes the Cam following her. *It's been looking all this time.*

Robyn appreciates Kimju's realization, leans, and whispers into the ex-Nugget's ear, "Don't worry, Boss Bitch has been watching you ever since I came out. You're on all the Screens; they're probably all watching you back at the Nugget."

Robyn lifts the hose up, points, and sprays Kim directly in the face. Then she hoses the mud off the rest of her body, soaking the thong and reaching underside to blast her knocks. Goosebumps everywhere. Water runs down Kimju's arms and legs, and streamlets drip from her knobs and nose tip.

"Monitor Babs doesn't want you tracking outside inside," Robyn chortles. "Now stand up."

Kimju feels strangely complacent. *I know I'm being hazed. But now is not the moment to explore Gaming with Robyn. If this is as tough as it gets then I can handle this place—despite my dripping hair, soaked thong, and knurled knips. And being cammed.* There are no towels; Kim rises on her knees, wipes droplets of water off her buttage using her hands, and tries to accelerate her air-dry. It's cool, and as she rises to full height her areolas stay bubbled and her knobs remain erect. Kimju discovers the Cam looking at her in the eye and blinks.

See the Bell cord hanging down there?" Robyn commands, "You already rang it for yourself; now ring it for me."

Kimju finds herself annoyed at performing this task. But she yanks hard, and the Bell rings itself twice.

Robyn studies her Roommate. "I'll remember you're the type of Pledge who wants to do everything twice. Now get inside."

Molly, still leaning back on her hands with her legs spread, watches from the Mudpit as Robyn shoos Kimju up the steps. Kimju disappears through the Back Door, trailing water behind. Molly pines, *I need to help Kimju.* But then Molly sees Robyn turn around and focus her attention upon the Mudpit. *Anybody can clean up water on the floor, and if not it will dry. And I need Kimju's help about now.*

§ Robyn Wallows Molly & Presents Steph: Dirty Roommate

Molly considers her new Roommate.

Steph adjusts her minidress. *My cutout hole might be a whole lot bigger than Robyn's, but I'm not strapless and in danger of popping my spouts out. Unfortunately my minidress demands constant attention, while her maillot requires much less care.*

Steph waits. *Robyn can go inside now.*

Robyn pauses, knowing she should follow Kimju inside and take charge of her Roommate, but instead she advances back to the Mudpit and points a comment to Molly about Steph. "Just because your Roommate here only shows headlights doesn't mean Steph Sorostitute doesn't show her sprouts nearly every day. If you look at the right angle you'll see short hairage at the bottom of her big buttonhole, and if you look upskirt you won't see any panties there."

Steph coils her body up. Controls herself. *Wait.*

Robyn gives Molly a final looking over. A compartment of Robyn's brain leaks imprints of all of her lackey work last Term.

You learned from me well, Steph appraises. *You relished all the discipline work. You still do. But I'm going to get you, you rancid raghole, and turn you into a rimjob rum doxy redliner.*

Of course any learning is an over-thought for Robyn, because last Term shouldn't exist for her.

Robyn spins her hand in a rotary motion and instructs Molly, "Roll over. Get on your hands and knees, too." Molly scrambles her position, and now the Cam follows Robyn's advance. "Well, look at you: fat hairy muddy mambo meatlocker. Molly Mudpit!"

Molly casts panicked eyes about; the only eyes she can find are Steph's. *Last Term's Cosmos House Monitor is my Roommate this Term? Something bad must have happened.*

Steph stares at her with an expression of appraisal. And once again Molly apologizes with her body that her panties are available to Steph.

Robyn escalates and snaps Molly and Steph's eye contact. "You got the world watching you, Molly Mudpit, so let's see you grovel. Show Gamers you wanna be a Cosmos Pledge!" Molly opens her mouth, but she hesitates to put a word in edgewise. "On your belly, you flesh moll!" Robyn demands, louder. "Do it. Take those massive milk sacks and mop mud!" Robyn laughs at her own brilliance.

Molly lowers her belly and mammaries into the mud and feels the rush of wet earth.

Robyn spits at her, "Shove your mammies all the way into the mud. Feels the mud flow in between your legs. And grovel, you massive mottob mammoth."

Molly reluctantly obeys. *I am not at all sure I should be taking orders from another Pledge. I wish Kimju were still here. And shouldn't Steph look out for me?* Molly pauses.

"I didn't tell you to stop, you mud-humper half-breed," Robyn's voice declares from above her.

Right. Now is not the time to question Robyn's authority. Molly grovels harder into the mud.

"Rub your face in the mud; grind your belly. Spread your legs, you fat mumping maladroit mandragorite. Scoop mud up with your hands and smear it all over those maximus moonatonentot mounds you carry around behind you. Qualify to be a Cosmos Pledge, maggot! Show Gamers you want it."

The spray hits Molly's body before she hears it. She jumps as more water drench her backside. The slick mud thickens. The Mudpit encourages ugly business.

Molly feels the spray stop and turns her head to the side, keeping one eye closed and one cheek in the Mud. She sees that off to the side Robyn has accidentally gotten her feet muddy. From her ground-level view Molly watches Robyn use the hose to wash her feet off. Molly turns the other cheek, hearing the water stop.

Then she hears Robyn sass Steph, "I guess Molly Mudpit is about what a scruffy satchel skag like you deserves for a Roommate." Molly hears Robyn pace to the Landing, then hears the Back Door slam.

Molly doesn't see the snarl on Steph's face or hear the Bell ring. Robyn doesn't remember to ring the Bell, and she has forgotten that Kimju already rang for her.

§ Steph Introduces Molly: To the Watering Can

Molly endures the filth by herself. Underneath the coating of mud her skin still shrivels with goosebumps, and her areolas pucker up around her hardened minarets. Mud streaks down her long hair and accumulates in her hairy armpits and on her hairy legs. Her pink cotton panties have wormed their way into her butt crack and muliebre, and sticky, soft earth now covers the mounds of flesh she sits upon, thickening into her hairaged minge. Molly slows her groveling and becomes conscious that Steph approaches her.

"You can stop now." Steph's voice sounds very matter of fact. "Robyn's gone inside to haze her new Roommate. We shall deal with her later."

Molly makes a squishing sound as she rolls onto her side. Steph holds the hose in her hand. From her low vantage point, Molly can see up Steph's dress.

Steph reads her look. "You're right. There's nothing there." Steph squats a few feet away, makes sure she keeps her thighs wide, and points her slash directly toward Molly. "But I didn't come over here to get my feet dirty or to vagflash."

Molly can see Steph's clit poking out above a moist swamp, and a bead of splurt start to transude out her satchel. Molly blinks, and Steph eggs her on. "Tell me why I came over here, Roommate."

It's Molly's turn to talk. "You came to take my panties away."

"Close." Steph stands up. "I came for you to give them to me."

Molly panics. "You can have them right now. I'll strip naked. I'll go back to the Nugget. I just don't want to suck cock."

"I'll collect them later," Steph oozes confidently. "But first we need to get you cleaned up enough to go inside. The Boss Bitch wants to meet you. On your feet. Over by the Bell. Hold still."

Mud squishes as Molly lifts herself up and positions herself near the Bell. She pulls her feet together, crosses her hands behind her back, and resigns herself into a well-understood position. Her mind goes blank in a second, and she holds herself at ease, resting as Steph sprays the mud off her body and out of her long hair.

The blonde hawk treats her deliberately, professionally, and dominantly. Molly yields to her cleansing and vows to serve her new Roommate. At the Nugget Kimju usually provided the guidance, but now that allegiance transfers to Steph.

The hose-down stops, but water continues to run down Molly's plump and hairy body. Water streams off the big sagging milk bags, down her chest; it saturates her very full, unshaven black muff and keeps her panties see-through. The water evaporating from her skin sustains her goosebumps and crinkled areola.

Steph allows a more friendly tone. "You're a mess."

Molly considers straightening her panties out. They bifurcate her mooe and bury so deep that virtually all her big mop lies to one side or the other. And both moons shine. "I guess I'm putting on quite a show," Molly admits, aware that the Cam collects her.

Steph provides calmness. "That's why you're here. BB will use you and Kimju to assuage the newbies. You've already rung the Bell; now ring it for me. It's really just a request to enter."

Molly pulls the cord, albeit quietly, and feels free to talk. "That Robyn, is she sadistic or just Monitor Babs' henchman?"

Steph cocks an eyebrow. "Robyn's Redacted. She was here last Term but apparently doesn't know it."

Redacted?" Molly sounds concerned. "That doesn't sound right."

"Don't trust Robyn Redacted. I'm here because of her," Steph says firmly. "She might not remember anything, but everyone else does. She's capable of holding herself accountable, but I guess you don't need to when your past doesn't exist and your Karma is tilted somehow."

Molly accepts, "I guess if Monitor Babs wants to send her lackey out to hose down and dirty up her new Pledge, then Kimju and I will grin and bear it." Then Molly asks innocently, "And is it true you were the Cosmos Monitor last Term?"

Steph considers her Roommate. "Be nice to me and you will get panty-stripped. You should be grateful to be here. Consider the alternative."

Molly must agree. "Right. It sure beats throating cocks in my mouth, stretching my rectum, and banging my moneybox. Or eating out gals."

Molly volunteers a tidbit: "I've seen Tiffany do all of that. That's nice. She was a guest Whore at the Nugget last Term. Feature Dancer."

Molly wipes water off her hanging mams with the edges of her hands. She wipes water off her torso, her belly and butt, and her legs. "You might not know this, but Tiffany actually danced and donged with one of the Cosmos last Term. Big gal, taller, but not as big as me. Janet. Maybe she's here?"

"Really now?" Steph gives pause, then provides, "Janet's the Monitor of the Corvette House." In a steely voice she adds, "Don't think we'll see much of her around here." Steph adds icing: "Although I'm sure Tiffany will do anything legal to get her clips played here on the Cosmos House Screens."

Molly queries, "Is Tiffany still a Whore? Why is she here?"

"Sounds like you know her better than I do," Steph replies candidly, then answers, "She's a Pledge, just like you. Ask her how she got two pieces and a Double Opt Up. We're all dying to know." Steph teases, "At least you don't have to worry about Tiffany taking your panties away."

Molly humors her Roommate. "Right, 'cause I'm gonna be giving them to you." Molly uses the opportunity and collects her panties into her finger tips and readapts them over her muff and moons. As if it matters, Molly's saturated minge remains completely visible through her soaking-wet panties.

"You're gonna keep your panties for now," Steph regrets. "Gamers have designs for them before you give them to me."

"Designs for my panties?" Molly asks cautiously. Rivulets of muddy water still run down her bare flesh. She has goosebumps all over, and a chill starts to set in. The cold air keeps Molly's medallions bubbled up. Molly is very health conscious. Wetness worries her.

"See that Watering Can?" Steph points toward the Back Door Landing, and Molly's eyes follow. "That's right. The thing with the handle and spout? For watering plants?"

Molly looks at the Watering Can. It appears to be steel, painted with a flower on the outside, and might hold a gallon or two of water. A wide waterspout on one side has many small holes. Steph hands Molly the end of the hose. "Fill 'er up!" she commands.

Molly asks, "Am I taking this inside?"

And Steph responds in a schoolmarmish tone, "You will keep the Watering Can with you always so you can keep your panties wet all the time." Sometimes Steph relishes dishing it out, even if it isn't hers to dish.

Keep my panties wet all the time?" Molly shivers. She is not sure she hears this correctly. "Who wants me to do this?"

"I wouldn't ask questions if I were you," Steph kindly advises.

"Right." Molly picks up the nozzle and examines her fellow Pledge; now that the nozzle is in her hand she considers giving Steph a soaking. *No, my Roommate would not appreciate such playful camaraderie.* And so Molly passes on the opportunity, sticks the nozzle into the can, and squeezes.

A full blast of water hits the bottom of the can and explodes in a torrent, splashing back up and directly into her face. She recoils. Another dousing, this time at her own hand.

Steph laughs, but in a friendly fashion. She offers free advice: "You're supposed to fill up the Can, not spray your face, dumb-dumb!"

Molly, dripping from the face now, looks at Steph directly and reconsiders. She says,, "I should spray you."

Steph winces. She takes a step backward and draws her hands up. "You should fill up the Can, just like I told you," Steph sounds out. "The Cam illuminates us with infrared light, so Monitor Babs might watch your every move on night vision. Gamers also. Obey me."

Molly abandons the thought of soaking Steph's thin dress to the skin. Even dry the dress can't hide Steph's chilled-up headlights. And instead of looking at Steph's short and wavies up her minidress, Molly looks into Steph's cutout hole and sees a wisp of scruff at the bottom.

Molly values caution and deference. She has yet to meet her Monitor, and so she rather carefully returns the nozzle into the Can, squeezes it gently, and fills the Watering Can most of the way up. Not enough to slosh out. *And I'm really going to be taking the Can inside with me?*

Yes indeed.

"There you go." Steph compliments Molly as if she speaks to a child.

Molly's movement has raised her body energy and driven the goosebumps away, and she realizes that the running water has made her want to go to the bathroom. *I need to pee. But most importantly, I really do need to make Steph understand that I need to stay healthy.*

"If my panties are wet all the time I'm likely to get—" Molly advances her concern to her new Roommate.

"You'll have to talk to Boss Bitch about that one," Steph advises truthfully. "Maybe you can beg her to let you wear your panties over your head."

"Right." Molly again considers soaking Steph with the spray, but she puts the hose down instead.

Again Steph augments, "I suspect your panties are gonna stay soaking wet 'cause the Gamers wants to look at your big, shaggy minge. But the sooner you beg Babs to give me your panties, the sooner I can Opt Up." Steph expresses a wry humor with this statement.

Molly shrugs. *Okay, the only way out of wet panties is maybe no panties at all. So it's better that way.*

11 Kimju & Molly: Tiffany Prepares for Babs' Inspection (D07)

§ Tiffany Makes Up Kimju & Molly: Intelligence Gathering

It is not until the next morning, the morning of Day Seven, that Kimju and Molly get an opportunity to renew their relationship with Tiffany.

Tiffany spends the night in the Bedroom, beneath Babs.

Kimju and Molly spend the night in their bunks, grit and all. Kimju sleeps above Robyn; Steph reclines above Molly. Steph again sleeps naked with the expectation that Babs will provide her with a new minidress in the morning. The Watering Can on the Bunkroom floor nearby remains filled with Molly water. Two empty bunks at the far end await two Newbies, but they will not be arriving today, nor tomorrow, nor the day after.

Neither of the former Strippers has any idea of the landscape of the Cosmos House. They are not of its pedigree, and their inhabitation and isolation at the Nugget last Term assured that they were not privy to Cosmos House Games.

Except for Janet's Alumni Reprise at the Nugget last Term. Kimju and Molly do remember that Janet, who danced with Tiffany, had descended from the Cosmos House. Kimju recollects, *Janet danced naked, pulled her ringed flaps wide, and rubbed juice on the pole. Solo, before she danced with Tiffany. So where is Janet? And why is Tiffany here, Double Opted Up?*

This means that probably Babs and Steph, but apparently not Robyn, know Janet, because they were here last Term. Former Cosmos somehow Caste reshuffled.

Kimju and Molly never spoke to Janet that fateful night, Kimju recalls. *But we both know Janet did indeed watch us perform; she watched us both not just dance naked and pink on Stage... but also lapdance.*

And yes, we both saw Janet pour shots for Tiffany, masturbate the pole, and finally climax with Tiffany on the Double Dong. We even talked about it afterwards with Tiffany back then. But our understanding was never complete, not only because we never had an opportunity to meet Janet, but also because our conversation with Tiffany threatened to venture into behaviors that even Molly and I found scary. Tiffany's abject Whore professionalism. Her joy of sex. Time for another conversation.

This morning Kimju and Molly tiptoe into the Bathroom ahead of any Tiffany turning on any Pee-Cam. Not that being naked on Cam would be new to either of them; after all, the glass toilets of the Nugget were always cammed. Molly might not care, but Kimju seeks the opportunities that her new Pledge Caste might confer upon her that her last Caste did not. *Maybe Molly wants to Opt Strip next Term, but I don't. Maybe Molly will beg a Pee-Cam. I won't.*

Perhaps. Kimju reconsiders the ex-Strippers' prospects inside the Cosmos House. *The presence of ex-Whore Tiffany suggests a much higher level of risk. This I know. Molly and I have both watched Tiffany twist. And now she's a fellow Cosmos Pledge? Yikes.*

Tiffany enters the Bathroom just as Kimju washes off soap from the shower and before Molly steps out of the spray. Tiffany has just completed Monitor Babs in the Bedroom and carries the Makeup Case in her naked hand.

"Hello both of you. You get to share some of my Cam time. I'm here to make you up. Babs wants you looking your best. Cleopatra's Wannabe Strippers, both of you."

Stark naked Tiffany dominates the live Cam, of course, but it does manage to catch both Kimju and Molly as they scramble into one thong and one pair of wet panties. The Cam gets around to inventorying both topless, collects Kimju's bare butt and butched hairage outlining her thong, and collects Molly's hairage and moons in wet see-through.

Naked Tiffany teases the two topless ones getting Cam time. "Don't make me jealous."

Kimju smiles and glances at the Cam out of the corner of her eye. *Molly and I are both used to living with Cams. Living with them while perpetually naked. Like all last Term.* Kimju crosses her arms in front of herself: handbra. *But that's not me anymore,* Kimju confirms, *no matter how much Molly doesn't care. I need to cover up and acquire another Garment.*

"Don't forget I am a Porn Star," Tiffany reminds them as she looks at herself in the makeup mirror and applies stunning purple lipstick and eyeliner. The top half of the redhead's body has a slight suntan; the lower half, where her low-rise slacks would otherwise cling to her, remains a paler white. The tan line bisects her thatch and posterior rugage; it hangs just below the crests of her ilium, where her curves go negative.

There is no reason for Kimju not to tumble a question out. "Hey, Tiffany, I never expected to see you here. Are you really a Cosmos House Pledge?"

Tiffany concentrates on painting purple stain into her pink Eraser Heads. "I am," she confirms. "Gamers pledge me to make me grow horns. I am now two Terms away from Whoring again. I should be Stripping right now."

Tiffany's reply sounds honest enough.

Kimju sympathizes, "I see how you need to make Whore Caste to rekindle your Porn Star career. Maybe Gamers want to build up some steam in you."

Molly volunteers, "You can make me up like a Stripper, Tiffany. I want to go back."

Tiffany controls her itch. She sits the two former Nuggets on two stools facing the Bathroom makeup table, with its mirror with light bulbs around. They sits with their arms at their sides, legs akimbo. Kimju feels the stool on her buttocks' flesh; she crosses her legs.

Tiffany demands, "Now hold still. Babs grants your wish. She wants all Cosmos to be made up like Cleopatra's Wannabe Strippers." Tiffany turns to Kimju. "That's harder for you than for Molly, right?"

Kimju counter-queries, "What about Babs?"

"Ah!" Tiffany preens. "I make up Monitor Babs. She's Cleopatra."

This is not the spin Kimju seeks to access.

Molly blurts, "Tiffany, how come you arrived with two pieces, but Kim and I only got one?"

Tiffany smiles playfully. "Don't complain, or I'll thicken your look toward Whore."

"Please, Tiffany, make me look like I belong in the Nugget," Molly begs. "I'll be Cleopatra's Stripper anytime. I just don't want to Whore. No disrespect."

"Trust me," Tiffany asserts to Molly, "I am a Porn Star. I've done everything explicit. All holes, all sexes. So take a complement from a pro. Because I saw you lapdance at the Nugget last Term, and nobody can grind a lap better than you can. And I've seen your photoshoots, magazine layouts, Pink Pages, and, well, those really explicit masturbation videos where you let go completely. You're a natural."

All true. But Kimju rises to defend her friend and former Roommate. "Wait a minute Tiffany, Molly might not mind pinking naked center Stage in the Nugget, but we've seen your videos on Screen there. You've made videos with cocks in all of your holes at the same time. It's not the same."

"Right!" Tiffany beams. "I am a Porn Star. And it is BB who demands I declare myself a *wannabe* Whore. I'm clearly begging to 'Pledge naked and cum be a Stripper next Term.' Have been since Day One." Tiffany gathers air and spills words out to Molly. "You are a Rubenesque goddess, and Gamers love you. You and I both desire to Opt Down next turn. I need to get rid of at least one piece, and you don't want any more."

Molly agrees, "I guess so, Tiffany. But what I really want is to get rid of these wet panties. I could get infected."

Kimju looks at Tiffany via the mirror in front of the makeup table. She probes Tiffany again. "So what about Babs? Does she know you're carrying ultraviolet ink tattoos? What was she last Term? What's she like?"

Tiffany brings the topless duo up to a Stripper look up but not quite as Whorish as her own face. *Unlikely BB will notice the difference, but overall I stand out.*

Tiffany shares, "I've known Babs since I arrived, one week ago, and that's it. Don't call her BB, but she was Bikini Babe and a Newbie last Term. She roomed with Janet, it turns out. Now she the Boss Babe, Monitor Babs, or 'Ma'am' to you."

Kimju trolls, "Same Janet whom you climaxed on the Double Dong at the Nugget with? Poured shots? Watched us lapdance at the Alumni Reprise?"

"Same Janet," Tiffany curts.

"Where's Janet now?" Kimju demands.

Tiffany puts a dab of purple on the question mark dot in her navel pit. "Ah, Janet is the Monitor of the Corvette House. She and Babs still talk. They're peers."

Tiffany organizes a thought. "Maybe you two will get to do your own Alumni Reprise at the Nugget and bury the Double Dong in *your* vaginas. The Dong can climax you just like it did Janet and me."

Kimju curls a sullen lip. "Maybe if I have to, but I don't want to go back. I want to promote to Monitor. I can take down my Roommate, Robyn; she seems like a ditz. Next Term I'm a Monitor, and the Term after that I become a House Mom el Capitan. Trust me, Tiffany, because with what I know about Stripping, I'd be a House Mom who'd make the best of them."

Molly has a different worldview. "Tiffany, I just want to get back to the Nugget. Maybe Steph and I can go there, and I can give my panties to her there. I don't want to streak nude to get there."

Kimju details, "We saw two streakers arrive from the Cosmos House, and that was pretty scary."

Molly tilts her head up and down quickly. "They were swept up on Stage, shaved bare, creamed, and climaxed."

Tiffany asks a rare question. "That would have been Penny and Coco. Do you know what happened to Ginny and Lee?"

Kimju provides, "Last seen streaking naked to the Corvette House."

"Maybe Babs can ask Janet if they arrived," Tiffany mulls.

Molly interjects, "Tiffany, I don't need to wait to get back to the Nugget to get naked." She surrenders, "I'll pink and masturbate and cum anytime. Even here on your live Bathroom Cam."

Kimju seeks a grounded position. "Molly, slow down. Hold on." She shifts focus to Tiffany. "Okay, isn't it true that Pledge aren't allowed sex? So what about you?"

"Pledge aren't allowed sex, and I'm a Pledge this Term. Gamers intend to make me crazy horny. If I cheat and get caught sexing I'm instant Slavesex. If I do nothing I'm going to lose control of myself in denial." Tiffany catches her thought and considers if she should say what she says next. "Well, not only that. BB has forbidden me masturbation, and I'm not allowed to touch my thighs together. I'm trying hard, but I don't know how long I can hold out."

"What about us?" Molly wonders.

"Ask her." Naked Tiffany drops a hand to her treasure chest, opens her trapdoor, and checks for tapioca.

"I feel confident I'm able to control myself," Kimju declares.

Molly saddles, "No wonder Robyn and Steph call her the Boss Bitch!"

"Don't be so harsh. I don't think it's BB's decision." Tiffany shakes her head and smells a finger. "It doesn't matter. Yes, I'd rather be Stripping this Term. It's one less Term away from Flesh Ranch. And at least at the Nugget I could get my twat fingered. You sure did."

Kimju counters that assertion, saying, "You know you're not supposed to, Tiffany. If you're a Stripper, you're not supposed to let the Patrons touch you."

Molly pooh-poohs this conclusion. "I don't care who feels me up. It's not for me to control their hands."

Some Strippers have to drift into climax before the loss of self becomes real, but Molly is always selfless.

Kimju argues on behalf of herself and Molly. "We only let Patrons fondle because we didn't want to go Whore. I'd rub my knockers on their faces, but I never let them feel up my kooch."

Molly exchanges a questioning look with Kimju via the mirror, and then Kimju looks at herself in the mirror: handbra and tanga, legs crossed, kaboose sticking to stool. She flinches at what she sees. *This is Cleopatra's Wannabe Stripper? Molly and I both look more like Cleopatra's Concubines, with lipstick way to wide and too bright. The rouge on our cheeks puts price tags on our bodies, like Tiffany puts onto her own face.*

Tiffany smiles, reaches, and gives one of Kimju's knobs a twist. "Silly you. The fact that you want to Opt Up will only make Gamers want to reduce you all the more. So don't think you're special. You'll strip, you'll dance, you'll pull wide. Gamers want to assure you that your advancement is in name of Caste only. You're gonna climax for the Cam whether you want to or not. I can't help that and if it makes it any easier for you I'll cream and climax with you. The bottom line is you quest two Garments. But it doesn't need to be Robyn's maillot: how about you take my shirt?"

Kimju nods. "Yes. Please, even if it is see-through and the Gamers can still see my knocks move around. I'll help you reduce; you help me acquire."

Molly nods too. "Tiffany, I don't need wet panties to get back to the Strip. Please help me get naked. I've done it all before. Nude beach, the nudist colony, a strip-down and dildos at a biker rally; I've even exhibited my insides outside at Nudes-a-Poppin', totally public, anybody could shoot, white meringue and all. Gamers posted me full Prefecture, and Automatron permissioned Creative Commons, so anybody could use me."

Kimju reviews the past Term. *Molly's last round as a Stripper was her first time on Stage. Center or side Stage, little dais or a lapdance, Molly always remained completely lackadaisical about nudity. I might have pinked because I had to, but Molly is totally indifferent to spreading her merrymaker and getting white meringue to flow. Her powerful musk could permeate the entire Club.*

My bet is that Gamers let Molly return to the Strip, sooner rather than later; she is hardly management material.

Tiffany watches Kimju calculate and adapts her own strategy. "Don't worry, Kimju, Molly's gonna give her panties to her Roommate, Steph. Aren't ya, Molly?"

And Molly meekly answers, "Yes, I already promised them to her."

Kimju looks down. *Supplicants can slip away from you in an instant.* Maybe Steph has already put talons into Molly's soul; nonetheless Kimju actually retains affection for her fellow ex-Stripper... and the feelings remains mutual. *Friends for now.*

Molly remembers something Steph told her last night. "Robyn says she's a newbie Pledge, but Steph says she Redacted. What does Babs say? Like, she was here, right?"

Tiffany tosses her hair back. "Right. Babs finds Robyn's forgetfulness unnatural. And Steph was the Monitor here last Term, and she also attests to Robyn's presence. Something happened between Robyn and Steph. Somehow Steph Opted Down to Pledge, and Robyn got Redacted and Pledges again. That's about all I know." Tiffany holds a brush with thick, colored fluid and signals them both to stand up. "Nipples. Stand spread surrender."

Kimju's heart sinks as she watches in the mirror as one topless tanga over-the-top ex-Stripper surrenders knocks and knobs to the Bathroom Cam. Kimju bits her tongue as the Cam feeds her topless posture out to the Prefecture.

Kimju wilts. *Must Tiffany color my nipples my first morning out?* Tiffany must. She outlines the edge of Kimju's compact beige areola before she paints color, gilding the nipple at the conclusion. *Orange knobs and an orange Spandex thong. That's me today for the Cosmos House. More Kimju for the Prefecture.*

Molly doesn't mind at all. Molly's broad areolas receive a narrow black outline with rose-gold mammilla. The brush and makeup arouses them, and moonscapes bubble up.

Kimju understands that she aspires to a Fate opposite the outcome desired by Tiffany and Molly. Opposite Castes. But that does not rule out the possibility of conflicts, of being pitted against each other. *And I know Tiffany. If I must I can certainly match her blow-by-blow in the pink and masturbation departments, but what happens if toys and dicks come into play?* Kimju wrinkles her brow in thought for a moment. *Well, maybe a toy like the Double Dong is easy to decide, especially if Babs wants the newbies to watch Tiffany or Molly or I vibe ourselves into climax. But if Monitor Babs decides to put dicks into play, that's a harder dilemma, because Tiffany loves dicks, and dicks are forbidden to Pledge. All Pledge. Just like Strippers are forbidden to let lapdance Patrons fondle them.* Kimju grimaces. *Sometimes Rules matter, and sometimes breaking them is necessary.*

"You're done!" Tiffany announces with a splash of perfume on their necks, shoulders, and displayed armpits. "Keeps your hands behind your heads, go into the Bunkroom, stand should-to-shoulder in spread surrender position. Face the Mirror and look at yourselves why you wait." Tiffany makes a flourish and shoos them out of the Bathroom.

Kimju glances into Babs' Bedroom as the twosome go off-Cam and down the hallway. Tiffany's transparent vinyl croptop and slacks hanging on a hook on the back wall, catch her eye. *When Tiffany gets dressed everyone can see her tits through transparent vinyl. However Gamers don't see my tits through transparent vinyl; Gamers see my knockers all the time. Still, Tiffany's see-through croptop will fit me just fine, so I will beg for her Garment and to Opt Up next Term. See-through or not.*

§ Robyn & Steph: Head for Morning Makeup

Robyn and Steph, still in the Bunkroom, are the first to hear Babs' chair scrape in her Bedroom, and they seize the opportunity to dash to the Bathroom. Once again Steph discovers that Boss Babe has left her a fresh minidress on the shelf in her locker, one she is able to step into quickly, lift upward, and halter tie behind her neck. Short? *Yes.* Buttonhole? *Big.* Titter? *For sure in a loose floppy fit.* Robyn and Steph pass by Kimju and Molly in the hallway, and Steph wonders why the two ex-Strippers hold their hands behind their heads.

Steph falters, knowing that sitting in the makeup chair with her legs apart shall be her next Cam performance. *Getting made into one of Cleopatra's Wannabe Strippers.* She closes her eyes and shakes her head. Opens to see Robyn turn into the Bathroom, and follows her in, more apprehensive now. *Haven't I already shared my stuff with the vagcam enough already? When I arrived in the Parlor, no thanks to Robyn, and then this very Bathroom that very first evening, no thanks to Tiffany. And then my first morning here Tiffany makes me up like a slut, and Robyn signs my legs open on the Library steps and cams me. And not just Robyn, either. Anybody. And then yesterday? Tiffany makes me up, Babs sits me down in the Kitchen, and Robyn brings the Back Door Cam in and signs my legs spread. I looked at Babs, but she wouldn't look back at me. I had to watch myself on the Screen. I know I was wet inside, showing my lines, but I kept my slippery inside me.*

And then after Kimju and Molly arrived Robyn made me vagflash Molly.

Steph looks over her shoulder as Kimju and Molly position themselves before, but not against, the Mirror. *I know Boss Bitch channels Robyn, so if Robyn signs and cams me I have to obey. Maybe BB won't do anything if I cross my legs or ignore Robyn, but Janet is laying for me, and Janet will make me sit Cravat.*

And so Steph follows Robyn into the Bathroom. *I don't have a choice; Robyn is Boss Bitch's Pledge, so whatever Robyn does, BB really is responsible. So if I acquire morning makeup every day, then Tiffany's Bathroom Can will collect me every day.* Steph grimaces.

Just before they go into the bathroom Robyn whispers to Steph, "Be nice to Tiffany and maybe both of you can pee together!" Robyn flees inside, and Steph considers, *Maybe spreading will be the easy part.*

§ Babs Greets Kimju & Molly: And Molly Begs Panty Doff

But Babs, rustling in her Bedroom, does not follow Robyn and Steph into the Bathroom. Instead she turns and walks into the Bunkroom, where she must greet—and deal with—her two newest Pledge, Kimju and Molly. *Maybe Robyn hosed them down and slopped them in the Mudpit last night, but this is my first encounter.*

The two ex-Strippers continue to stand spread surrender, sufficiently experienced to not take their eyes off their own visage in the Mirror, colored nipples and all. They see Babs enter behind them, but they must leave her a blur and focus their eyes upon their own bodies. Babs' footsteps adequately audio-locate where she moves behind them.

Both have settled themselves into a posture they may sustain for a while, and, as BB examines them, both sneak looks at Babs' reflection when she is not looking. They see a tall, voluptuous, olive-skinned woman with a flat belly, two full breasts, and a bra that almost contains them.

Babs walks around them, blocking their views of themselves in the Mirror, and checks their hair and faces, armpits (one overgrown with black hair), bare breasts, and button clearances above one panties and one thong. *Plenty of inches.* Babs returns behind them and inspects one buff kabedis uncompromised by a thong, and one panties with a moonshadow via wet see-through.

"Welcome to the Cosmos House, Pledge," Boss Babe begins. "I am Monitor Babs, Ma'am to you, so please make it easy for me. You already have your hands full with your Roommates, Robyn and Steph, so you don't need to test me. You need to conduct yourself properly at all times, and stay on my side. Do you understand?"

And Kimju and Molly reply in unison, "Ma'am, yes, Ma'am."

"I don't know why you have arrived topless," BB admits, "that's not my beg. But now that you're here...." Babs trails off. *I know why you arrived topless. Gamers sent you here topless to haze me. Because they know I didn't like being surrounded by topless—even nude—Pledge last Term. Even Tiffany gets to me.*

Babs provides a stiff upper lip. "Now that you're here: no bra, no halter, no bandeau, no vests, no... not even pasties. Don't expect any such thing this Term! Word is you've arrived topless, you're going to stay topless, and you're going to leave topless. And if Gamers want you to expose your most intimate recesses, you'll do that too."

BB leans over and assures herself that the Watering Can does indeed contain water and that Molly's panties are indeed wet. Molly makes the mistake of straying her eyes to Babs' uplifted bosom, BB's deep cleavage, and her maroon *crescents d'areolage.* Boss Babe doesn't miss anything and steps forward.

"Do you wish to admire your Monitor or to admire yourself in the Mirror?" BB asks. Babs enjoys the confidence that comes because she has made her bra more secure than it was when she arrived.

Ma'am," Molly advances, unsure of herself, her eyes already returned to stare into herself. "I wish to obey your commands. Ma'am."

Boss Babe gathers one of Molly's mamazulons into her hand and squeezes. "I bet you're Molly, the hairy fat Stripper from last Term."

"Ma'am, yes, Ma'am," Molly replies.

"Were you admiring my bra because you want your own?" BB inquires.

"Ma'am..." Molly stumbles, "oh, no. Ma'am, I forfeited my bra two turns ago!"

BB snorts, "If anybody should be wearing a bra it is you. No doubt Gamers want to see you pack in those majonkers and heave 'em forward in some underwired, cantilever-engineering marvel. Two pieces. You could Opt Up?"

Molly finds the introduction confusing. She tries, "Ma'am, after I forfeited my bra I begged my panties off so I could be sure to go Strip, and during last Term I stayed naked. Always. 24x7. So these are new panties I'm wearing. Used panties, but new for me. You can take them, and I'll Pledge naked. I *want* to be a Stripper next Term."

Babs steps forward and cradles Molly's breasts, one across each palm. "I'd say you're a bit bigger and more saggy than any other Cosmos here. And your own splotchy areolas are demonstratively the biggest around. Welcome to the Cosmos House, Pledge."

Molly watches her areolas bubble up in the Mirror. And she keeps her eyes ahead as Boss Babe moves to one side and slides the palm of her hand under Molly's breast and allows it to be trapped between where it hangs down and where it would normally touch her chest.

BB shuffles her palm up and down. "Tiffany says one of your acts at the Nugget involved dancing with these droopy mamazulons holding up rods underneath."

"Ah, Ma'am, yes, Ma'am," Molly stumbles. "Holding up all kinds of stuff. But rods especially." Molly calibrates, "Rods of different weights and diameters."

Babs' palm retreats, and Molly gathers focus. "Ma'am, I will dance topless, strip naked, and beg to Strip again next Term. I'll stay topless 24x7." Molly nods to Kimju. "Just like Kimju."

§ Babs Allows Kimju & Molly: To Beg… Learns a Secret

Kimju processes the proceedings while holding her position taut. She does not appreciate her former Roommate making commitments about her goals. Kimju's 35C knocks don't sag like Molly's 38DDs; Kim's armpits concave, her ribs stands out, and her waist ticks in. The only cloth covering her body is the thong that stretches tight across a butched and trimmed kava patch. The brown stubble that sits just outside the legline embarrasses Kimju because she can't control this indignity. *I don't really care that my knockers and kabedis hang free. And I wouldn't even mind showing all of my kohlrabi. But splitting hairs so I can outline my thong with hairage only calls rude attention to me.*

Kimju wonders, *Maybe the Mirror ahead of me might be one way. Maybe Gamers stand in darkness on the other side and watch me. Study my made-up nipples. My outline of hairage. My buttage, were I to turn around.* Kimju tries to look through the Mirror and see if she can see eyeballs hiding beyond. *Gamers who snuck in the Front Door, came up the grand stairway, and watch from a hallway or perhaps even individual darkened peep booths.*

Enough! Kimju adjusts her eyes to her own image in the Mirror. *Sometimes imagination is too much of a good thing. It doesn't matter who's on the other side of the Mirror. I need to gain another Garment and Opt Up!* Kimju adjusts her gaze in the Mirror to again study BB during a moment when BB isn't looking; Kim doesn't have to turn her head, only move her eyes. *Maybe I don't like it, but it sounds like Molly and I are gonna be showing our knockers 24x7,* Kimju assesses. *But the statuesque Babs will be showing her breasts not at all.*

What are the odds Kimju is right about that one? Even as BB seeks to reduce the risk of spilling boobage out her underwire.

Babs turns upon Kimju and extends a fingertip toward the crease under one of Kimju's knock-knocks. She closes her eyes at the last moment but opens them again when her finger makes contact. BB acquires courage. *It's important I take charge. Let these two ex-Strippers know that they have nothing off-limits to me.* Boss Babe draws her finger upward into the crease, and Kimju's knock bounces. Bounce, but nowhere as mopey as Molly's mazoomas.

"So you're Kimju?" BB inquires as her finger graces a contour up the side of the breast toward Kimju's armpit. Babs almost tickles with the back of her finger. 'You're quite conical, so tell us your cup."

Kimju acknowledges, "Ma'am, yes, I'm Kimju. C-cups. Ma'am. 35C, 24x7."

"So did you also dance like Molly?" BB inquires. "Holding rods under your kajoobies?"

Kimju clears her throat. "Ma'am, not every dancer has lift, Ma'am." Kimju licks her lips. "Ma'am, but you can put suction cups on my knockers for sure. And I've even had to dance wearing chopsticks and rubber bands."

Boss Babe doesn't like what she hears, but she nods in approval. She surveys Kim's cupped armpits and buff kaboose. "Tiffany says we must all watch your masturbation and cum videos." Babs casts her eyes upward. "She suggests I put them up on the Screens and let her use them as examples to train the Newbies. You like that idea?"

Kimju squirms. "Ah, Ma'am, surely Tiffany has plenty of her own clips she could use, Ma'am."

BB ignores Kimju's foray.

"Robyn suggested you two masturbate in synch with your clips. You'll do that for the Cosmos House?"

"Ma'am, yes, Ma'am." Kimju fidgets and provides a harmonious answer. *I don't like this idea.*

"Ma'am, we'll cum naked on a live Cam feed. For the entire Prefecture," Molly volunteers. "Just like you said, in sync with our Nugget videos… and each other."

Kimju clenches her teeth and quivers. *Maybe it's good Molly has Steph for a Roommate, so she can volunteer performances with Steph and not with me.*

Babs pinches both cheeks. "You're darlings. Both of you. You shall so freak out the newbies!" BB clasps her hands together. "Perhaps you can give them dancing lessons!"

It's not a question, really. Molly, who has been seeking an opportunity to raise the subject of her see-through-when-wet panties, decides to venture an opening. "Ma'am, I will give the newbies the Watering Can, Ma'am. They can learn that dancing soaking wet is even more lascivious than being nude."

Kimju and Molly watch in the Mirror as BB walks behind them and compares Molly's covered moons to Kimju's smaller double-keeled and totally buff kabedis. Both equally topless, of course.

Molly gets the connection and blurts, "I'll yank my panties into my crack so that both my moons hang out. So I'm as exposed as Kimju. We'll both be like 'topless tanga Pledge.'"

Boss Babe catches Molly looking into her eyes via the Mirror. BB appraises, "You'll beg me to yank the front of your panties into your muliebre. You both will."

Kimju flinches at this suggestion, but Molly pivots eyeballs, looks into her own visage in the Mirror, and surges, "Ma'am, please, Ma'am. Anything to please you. To please Gamers. Get me back to the Nugget next Term. I'll bury my panties so deep in my mooe that you'll see all of my muff."

Boss Babe smiles; she waits. She saw the feed from the Back Door Cam last night. She knows about Molly's weakness.

Molly feels her wet panties on her body. They are uncomfortable; worse, they are *unhealthy.*

Molly begs, "I'll even doff my panties completely. I'll wear my panties over my head, may it please you."

Babs jokes, "If you beg for them in your mouth maybe you won't have to beg so much."

Molly suddenly remembers. "Ma'am, I've already promised to forfeit my panties to Steph. I'll stay hairy and naked. One piece or zero, please let me head back to the Strip next Term!"

Boss Babe nods quietly. "Maybe you're in too much of a hurry to get back to the Nugget! Just because you want to Opt Down doesn't mean the Gamers want to make it easy."

Boss Babe turns her attentions to Kimju. "And just because you want to Opt Up doesn't mean Gamers don't want to reduce you."

Kimju finds herself startled. "Ma'am, I'm nearly naked already. I'm prepared to Game with Robyn or anyone else, and to incur your goodwill as I try to acquire a second Garment, Ma'am."

Boss Babe nods, "May the both of you beg to be the most underdressed and most exposed Cosmos." Of course they will. "You shall wear whatever this House wants you to, or wear nothing at all. Navelage 24x7 is your only mandatory exposure requirement. All the rest is volunteering!"

Kimju still holds optimism for a different Fate. *Yes, Molly and I will volunteer a lot. But the bottom line? I have to acquire a second piece and Opt Up next Term.*

Boss Babe focuses her attentions upon Kimju again. "Maybe you should beg to trade with Janet. Didn't you see her dance an Alumni Reprise at the Nugget last Term? She's got a size mini crochet Spiderweb g-string so small it shows hairage everywhere."

Kimju stumbles, "Ma'am, Janet danced naked. She had to streak to get to the Nugget."

Babs remains unfazed. "So check out her Dining Room Picture as soon as you get a chance."

Kimju acquiesces, "Ma'am, yes, of course, Ma'am." Then Kimju hurries, "Anything I can wear that is smaller before I cover up suits me fine."

Not fine. But if that's what Gamers want I will consider it... for a while. I'm not a Stripper anymore; I don't want to go back. If the Gamers want tease, I will have to tack with it until I can find my own tangle. But I still need two Garments.

Kimju advances, "Ma'am, Tiffany already offered me her croptop."

"So you know Tiffany from when danced at the Nugget last Term?" Babs asks casually.

"Oh, yes, Ma'am. She visited to Feature Dance sometimes. She wasn't actually a Nugget. A Stripper."

"So do you know if Penny and Coco arrived? Have you seen their Pictures in the Dining Room yet?"

Kimju and Molly answer simultaneously, "Yes. | No."

Kimju elaborates, "We confirmed them with Tiffany. They arrived as we were leaving. They had to run up onto Stage naked and holding their lady parts open and finger-balling their clits. They came pretty quick."

"They'll do fine," Molly augments. "Also, Tiffany said you'll want to ask Janet if Ginny and Lee ever made it to the Corvette House. I guess Kimju and I care too, them being fellow ex-Nuggets."

Kimju adds logic: "I think Tiffany's worried that Janet will use her as a Piss Mouth again."

Babs recoils. "What!?" BB's eyes widen. She steps back. Then turns toward Molly and narrows her gaze. Advances.

Molly leans backward and confirms, "Ma'am, it's the truth, Ma'am! We both saw Janet masturbate the pole. Naked jelly bag. Then she took a shot glass outta her jepoot, poured a shot, and Tiffany drank her pee. Tiffany made herself a Piss Mouth; nobody forced her."

"And then they climbed on the Dong together, and Tiffany climaxed Janet."

Kimju rushes balance, "Ma'am, I'd say that they climaxed each other."

§ Babs Orders: Robyn & Kimju to Kitchen • Molly to Mirror

Robyn, discharged from the Bathroom by Tiffany and dazed by fresh makeup, returns to the Bunkroom and discovers herself face-to-face with Babs. Babs, punched twice now, turns to face a Pledge Robyn who didn't hear Kimju and Molly's revelation about the Alumni Reprise. *Robyn isn't aware of just how flustered I am at this moment!* BB turns, realizing, *Robyn is not a part of this problem.* BB stoops and praises Robyn's makeup, "Gotta love Cleopatra's Strippers." BB reaches out with her fingertips and fingers the neckline of Robyn's elastic maillot cutout. BB points out, "Smallest buttonhole!"

She gathers her reserves together. Her babambas sway but, thanks to gum arabic, stay contained without her thinking about them. She presses her shoulders back—a widely-spaced shoulder strap is all that covers them—and addresses her two ex-Strippers: "Listen to me, both you. I don't want to have to look at your painted nipples any more.

"You," Boss Babe commands Molly, "press your mazoomas up against the Mirror and kiss and make out with yourself."

Molly moves quickly. She snuggles her mams together so her colored areola press tightly into the Mirror, and adores Mirror with lipstick and surplus nipple paint.

"And you," Boss Babe commands Kimju, "cross your kajoobies with your hands. Keep them that way. Just make sure I don't have to see them anymore. You like that?"

Kimju does, and she trades eyes with BB as she carefully and deliberately crosses her hands and arms in front of herself. She notices Molly seems indifferent to her; she seems drawn into Mirror.

"You," Boss Babe commands Robyn, "take your Roommate down to the Kitchen. Sit her down in a chair, and brief her on the on the significance of Tiffany's Porn Star Calendar."

"Brief Kimju?" Robyn echoes.

"Don't tell her anything you've forgotten," Babs mocks.

Babs tilts her head to the now clenching Kimju. "You keep a hold of your handbra, observe Tiffany's Porn Star Calendar, pullaside, and arouse yourself."

Kimju knows she can do this. "Ma'am, yes, Ma'am!" She tries to catch Molly's eye, but Molly seems engaged in kissing the Mirror. Kimju scrams down the angular stairs. The masturbation question has been answered.

Robyn looks at Molly; Robyn's heard about Mirror.

Boss Babe snaps, "Move!"

And Robyn skedaddles.

Babs watches the Bikini Babe in the Mirror hike her bra with both hands. Bling 24x7. She watches her finger the nombril's waistline and tidy it along its tan line. Babs turns and looks at Molly slowly kissing herself and feels guilty. *Maybe I overreacted?*

Babs blinks, pinches her lips together, and marches herself toward the Bathroom.

12 Babs Trains Tiffany & Steph: Piss Mouth & Mirror (D07)

§ Babs Orders Steph Join Molly: Roommates Game Mirror

Steph and Babs collide just as the Bunkroom narrow into the Hallway. It is after Robyn and Kimju have headed downstairs and while naked Tiffany, still in the Bathroom, works on her own makeup.

Visions of climaxing Dongs dance in Babs' head. Babs outreaches a finger toward Steph. "You!"

Steph takes a step backwards. "Ma'am, I'm sorry, Ma'am."

Might Steph assume BB takes umbrage at their collision, Steph's assumptions are misplaced.

Yet convenient. BB slows her pulse down. *Am I embarrassed that Steph has known all along what I just found out?* Babs glowers, and Steph takes another step backward. *I don't like that Steph Sorostitute keeps a secret from me.* BB glances past Steph, down the hallway toward the Bathroom entrance. Reconsiders Steph.

Steph curtsies. "Ma'am, Tiffany said I should ask you to approve my makeup, Ma'am. I think she wants compliments."

Boss Babe considers Steph's makeup and loose-fitting haltered minidress. Adequate belly hole. Short. Four edges between fabric and skin. *I've known all along that you secretly attended the Alumni Reprise. You've always known the full Janet and Tiffany details, which I only now just discover! You're playing me!*

But BB's face and posture reveals not a clue that she knows Steph keeps secrets. In fact, she bows to her Pledge and former Monitor. "Good morning, Pledge." Now BB steps back. "I see another of Cleopatra's Wannabe Strippers steps forth to audition and Game!"

"I need you to let Molly give me her wet panties." Steph looks past Babs into the Bunkroom and the marmalade affixed to Mirror. "She's phobic."

"I need you to thank me for letting you wear that minidress today." Boss Babe inches one side of her chin up.

Steph shuffles and smoothes her Garment. Feels that her button is holed. *No problem.* "Ma'am, thank you for letting me wear—"

"So did you titter for Cam?" BB nods in the direction of the Bathroom.

Steph squirms but retains her footing. *Bare footing.* "Ma'am, Tiffany made sure I leaned over. I contributed not only a titter but sat legs apart and contributed upskirt." Steph puts on a smile and swivels her hips. "Don't worry, Ma'am, some Cam or another collects my spouts and short wavies every day. So do my exposures make you happy? Ma'am."

"Anything else to tell me?" BB inquires.

"Er, ah...." Steph racks her brain, unsuspecting. "Well, yes. Two things. Tiffany told me I'm supposed to beg her to make up my nipples. Like whatever she did to Kimju and Molly perhaps. Can she do that? She's just another Pledge, after all."

Bikini Babe touches her bling. "My *crescents d'areolage* will carry permanent suntans because of you. Be adaptive; that's my free advice if I were you. You put yourself where you are. Nobody did it to you. So deep down inside, you want to be here."

"You're crazy." Steph should not speak like this to her Monitor.

Babs ignores the insult.

And Steph fills potential vacuum. This time she tilts her own head backward toward the Bathroom door. "And, like, I don't get Tiffany. Tiffany always wants to train me to Strip, but at the same time she always lets me know she's ahead. So she peed in from of me again today, and once again the Cam watched both of us at the same time. Ma'am, it's fine with me that Tiffany wants to be a better Stripper than me; I don't want to be a Stripper at all. And I don't need Pee-Cam fans." Steph blinks, then adds, "May it please you, Ma'am."

BB takes another step backward and sweeps a path forward so that Steph can pass easily into the Bunkroom. Again Boss Babe points a finger. "You, Pledge: position yourself next to your Roommate, Molly there, and make out with the Mirror. Palms on the Mirror. Kiss it, and rub your bare stomach and legs against it, too. Move! Now!"

Steph moves. If she titters moving quickly there are no Cams here in the Bunkroom to share it. She looks back, and Babs has vanished. She quiets, positions herself next to topless Molly, but she can't seem to draw Molly out of a kissing and rubbing passion with Mirror. *Okay.*

Steph touches the Mirror with her hands, imagines she is up against a wall being arrested, looks at herself, and draws her smallish buttonhole forward toward the Mirror... and into contact. Sensation cruises through Steph's body, and she tilts her thighs forward until the skin of her legs contacts Mirror. She presses her chest and feels Mirror stimulate through the thin fabric and instantly stand up her sweet tips. She looks again at her now-Roommate and wonders why Molly doesn't interrupt kissing and rubbing against Mirror to acknowledge her. Molly's smell fills the Bunkroom. A thought flashes through Steph's mind: *Maybe Babs' sharp reaction wasn't all colliding with her. Maybe Kimju and Molly said something and Tiffany's gonna get it again.*

But it is Steph's last thought for a while; Mirror makes sure she doesn't wonder very long. Mirror draws her in; Steph presses her body harder again the electro-stimulating reflecting service, kisses herself, and commences to grind.

Babs watches. *I know you saw the Nugget Alumni Reprise. Even today's illicit details. And you deliberately handicap me with ignorance. Bye.*

Babs catches a fleeting glimpse of Bikini Babe looking out from the Mirror. BB tries to hike the straps of her bra. Bling! *Bling? No problem!* Babs touches the waistline of her nombril and considers the naked Pledge inside the Bathroom. *Tiffany Transparent. Here I come!*

§ Babs & Tiffany: Bathroom Piss Punishment

Boss Babe sweeps into the Bathroom. Tiffany, working naked of course, has just finished making up the last of Cleopatra's Strippers, herself. She reacts viserally at the force of BB's charge into the room.

"You, Pledge," Boss Babe commands, "stand spread surrender."

Tiffany obeys and wonders what's coming.

"You were not forthcoming with me," Boss Babe begins. "Once again. About Janet."

Tiffany pivots her naked body around her narrow waist but keeps her hands behind her head and her armpits displayed. "Wait a minute, Ma'am. I told you about Janet letting me have the Pee-Cam."

"That's when you were Strippers. Two terms ago." BB snaps her elastic waistband. Checks to make sure her legholes lie on her tan lines. "That's not what we are talking about."

"Ma'am, you scratched me up for that, and then you washed my mouth out with soapy shampoo because I hadn't yet told you that Janet visited the Nugget and masturbated the pole. During her Alumni Reprise last Term."

Boss Babe presses, "You told me she peed, but you didn't tell me she poured shots, or that you became a Piss Mouth!"

Tiffany pleads, "Ma'am, please. I only dashed one shot, and I only did it once. I had a good reason."

"So it was incorrect when you claimed earlier that only you had pissed into your *own* mouth?" Babs challenges. "As seen on your famous Porn Star Calendar?"

Tiffany adjusts her naked posture. "Ma'am, apparently that is correct, Ma'am."

"So your claim that you only Piss Mouthed once isn't correct either?" BB inquires.

"Apparently not," Tiffany grants.

BB quickens, "And you got what you wanted, didn't you?"

Tiffany confesses, "Okay. I avoided Slavesex."

"But you acquired Piss Mouth, yes?"

"Ma'am, yes, Ma'am. And you've been good to me, Ma'am. You can pee in my mouth and Cam me at the same time. I'll kiss you anywhere on your body for as long as you want. I'll lick your asshole. You can climax if you want to. You're allowed. I'll spin your wheels anyway you want."

Babs rebels at her Pledge's casualness, her freshness, and her indifference to the fact that both of them are indeed females.

BB looks away to gather her thoughts; Tiffany steels a glance and looks the Cam in the eye.

BB remembers to what to do next. "So have you also forgotten that you and Janet climaxed on the Double Dong together?"

Tiffany swallows hard. "Uh, ah, Ma'am, I did so many things, Ma'am. Like, I am a Porn Star. *Was* a Porn Star at the Nugget... and, well, Janet was like just another Pledge dancing an audition." A small bead of sweat forms in one of Tiffany's armpits. "Look, Ma'am, I know Janet was your Roommate last Term. How come she never told you? Maybe you never cared what she did. I bet you even let her pink and cream and climax on your behalf."

Tiffany watches Babs as BB slowly recites, "Maybe I owe Janet some favors, but twisting a Dong is not one of them. And show some respect: Janet's the Corvette Monitor now."

Tiffany quests an opening, "Ma'am, Pledge are allowed to dong with each other, and Whores can dong with anyone, so Janet and I didn't break any Rules. It's only Strippers who aren't allowed to dong together. Or do lesbo stuff."

Babs stomps a bare foot. "Enough. This Term you shall get your very own Alumni Reprise and Double Dong on Stage at the Nugget once again."

Tiffany accepts the challenge. "Ma'am, yes, please, Ma'am! I'll Double Dong with any Cosmos—anyone, anywhere, anytime. I'll join Molly and Steph and make out with myself in the Mirror. I'll—"

BB glowers and holds a hand up. "You stay right here in the Bathroom." The Cam stirs. Babs points to the tile floor and signs Tiffany onto her knees. "Apparently soap in your mouth for forgetting to tell me Janet made a Nugget Alumni Reprise wasn't a sufficient inducement to remember all the details."

"Ma'am—" Tiffany begins, but does descend to a kneeling position, still keeping her hands behind her head.

Boss Babe lifts Tiffany's chin with a finger and gently guides, "Once a Piss Mouth, always a Piss Mouth?"

"Ah, Ma'am, yes, Ma'am. But I am inexperienced. Only twice."

"You lied to me, Pledge," Babs states, very matter-of-factly.

"Ma'am, I apologize, Ma'am. Lies deserve Piss Mouth also, Ma'am. So if you want to piss in my mouth I'll try to learn how to consume a stream."

Babs fills her diaphragm with fresh air. "You wish. But maybe Janet will contribute again. Or some other Pledge. But here's what you can do right now, Ms. Tiffany Totally Transparent. Roll onto your back, lift your legs up, and practice Pee-Camming into your own Piss Mouth. Right here. Right now."

Tiffany hesitates for only an instant; then, a sudden worry and she moves onto her back. "Ma'am, are you gonna make Janet a Piss Mouth as well? She didn't tell you either." Tiffany positions herself not far from the mirrored wall, draws her knees up, and grabs her ankles so she can roll onto her back and lift her pelvis above her head, using the mirror to brace against as necessary. The Cam follows her in.

Not drawing an answer, Tiffany advances, "Ma'am, I'll piss all over with Janet. Ma'am. I took Pee-Cam away from her a turn ago, but I never thought I'd have to taste her."

"You had to swallow?" Sometimes Babs really does want to know.

"Yeah, center Stage at the Nugget." Tiffany looks up at Babs. "Ask your Roommate; she was there."

BB refines her response. "Pardon me, but Janet is no longer my Roommate. So you have to just piss all over yourself. Piss in your mouth. Roll around and rub your tits and body and face around in piss on the floor. And if you see Janet sometime, may you beg her to piss all over you! Think your fans will like that?"

"Ma'am, thank you, Ma'am," Tiffany says.

"You're welcome." Babs shakes her head: several small, fast rotary twists.

"Ma'am, I think sometimes my fans want me bound, beaten, and banged." Tiffany laughs and connects her feet with the mirror, behind her raised tail-splines. She catches the Cam's eye. "I'm Tiffany Transparent, one of Cleopatra's Wannabe Strippers, and I'm about to show you how I piss into my own mouth."

Babs takes a step backwards, in the direction of the door into the Bathroom.

Tiffany transfers eyes to her. "Ma'am, don't worry, Ma'am. I can do it. I'm pretty lithe; on a good day I can eat my own tacamahac."

And again BB feels the anger. At Tiffany. *And yes, Janet. Neither one told me they climaxed together on the Double Dong. I have to find out the long way. And such a wannabe Whore she's scary.*

And anger at Steph. *Steph Sorostitute has yet to even reveal to me she was there; she's gambling I don't know. She's not stupid; she assumes nobody knows she was there except Janet. She thinks there's more air between Janet and I than there is. Wrong.*

Steph can wait.

Here in the Bathroom it is a naked Tiffany who lies on her back, holds her ankles in her hands, and braces her feet on the mirrored wall.

Babs feels the Cam turn on her, but she steps forward anyway. "If you're going to keep your naked feet on the mirror at least spread yourself wide. Push your back up against it so you have you don't have to arch so far to reach your target."

Tiffany tightens her position, and the Cam returns from BB's bling to Tiffany's spread crotch. "Ma'am, I've never done this before. I'm going to get pee all over myself and all over the floor, Ma'am." Tiffany rests much of her weight on her shoulders; her Eraser Heads point gently upward. All her crotch turf lies completely wide open.

Boss Babe scratches her nose and runs her fingers inside the waistband of her nombril bikini bottoms. "Perhaps you like the attention of getting scratched up, eating soap, and from now on drinking piss. But you really do need to tell your Monitor *everything*. And I will *still* let you get scratched up and eat soap and drink piss on Cam every day if you insist."

Tiffany agrees, "Ma'am, thank you, Ma'am. It won't happen again. I am your Pee-Cam Piss Mouth. Please let me Pledge naked and cum be a Stripper next Term. Ma'am, please let me keep drinking water, pull pink, and pee all over myself. I'll spend the night here, I'll sleep in my pee on the floor, I'll clean up after myself. I am a Porn Star."

Tiffany catches Babs' frown.

"I'm a wannabe Porn Star," Tiffany hedges.

Tiffany catches the Bathroom Pee-Cam out of the corner of her eye. *This will be tough, but all my fans are going to watch and love me.*

Babs closes her eyes, shakes her head, and heads out the doorway. What next?

§ Robyn orders Kimju: Masturbate to Tiffany Porn Calendar

Kimju had scrambled down the angular stairs in her bare feet while clenching her knockers in both hands. Once in the Kitchen she approached the large, colorful Calendar and turned the months with modest trepidation. *Tiffany all right. No hole is left unsatisfied, no sexual act fails to be documented. I do not need, nor do I want, my own Calendar.* Kimju returns to one particular image of Tiffany, in which Tiffany sits as the centerpiece of a banquet table, naked and covered head to toe in honey and food. Her eyes return to the colorful food mess image a second, then a third time.

Kimju hears Robyn's footsteps enter the stairway. She sits her bare kabedis on a Kitchen chair, adjusts so she contains her knockers with one arm, opens her legs, and slides her tanga to the side with her other hand. The hand that stretches the thong away from her koot can both hide her privates as well as finger herself. *I was brought inside last night before Robyn made Molly totally immerse herself in the Mudpit... and Molly isn't even Robyn's Roommate. I am. And now Robyn going to haze me. So am I ready to take my Roommate on?*

Kimju catches her breath. *No rush. I can play this Game! But I don't underestimate Babs; she retains a sly countenance, even at a distance. She knows I clenched myself before she met me. She made me stand spread surrender topless. And now I have to display my kava patch and diddle my kypsey.*

Robyn descends into the Kitchen. The higher-strung, ever-confident, and Cleopatric Robyn feels the comfort of a Cosmos who has been here before, yet acts with the innocence of a newbie. Robyn presumes superiority to her topless and bare-assed Roommate, and she talks to Kimju as she approaches her chair.

"Look at you! Kimju, clenching her knockers and finger-fucking her koot. You couldn't wait for me to come down and command you."

"I'm following Babs' orders," Kimju retorts, "not yours." She casts her eyes about the Kitchen, looking for hidden cams. Finds none. Double-checks that her hidden finger really can reach her clit.

Robyn aggresses, "You're a kootch dancer through and through. You no longer belong to Molly; you belong to *me* now. Your number one goal while you're here as Cosmos Pledge will be showing me you've got what it takes to make it back to the shake shack next Term. Tell me, Pledge, what's the name of the dive?"

Kimju puts a strong face on her near-nakedness and decides to not challenge now. "It's called the Nugget."

Kimju knows how to not tip her hand; she probes Robyn, "So if Steph was the Monitor last Term, why is she here again? And did it have anything to do with Tiffany?"

Robyn snorts and points her chin at Tiffany's Calendar. "With Tiffany? Tiffany thinks she is a Porn Star. And Steph? I might be a newbie, but everybody knows Steph was the Cosmos Monitor last Term and got broken, and there is a lot of talk about what happened. You watch: Steph's gonna beg to Pledge naked and dance at the Nugget next Term. Just like you are. Mark my words."

Kimju removes her fingers from what has become an erect keystone and carefully recovers her kohlrabi. The butched hair continues to outline her tanga.

"Done masturbating? You should check out the Dining Room Pictures." Robyn tosses her long hair over one eye in the direction of the Dining Room. "Not only does Babs show the world her bling *and* bush, but maybe you'll recognize Janet and the two Baseboard Strippers, Penny and Coco. Miss poot 'n' coot, last seen streaking to the Nugget, end of last Term."

Kimju hold pat. *Molly and I saw Janet dance the Alumni Reprise with Tiffany, but we've never met Janet. We never met Penny and Coco either, although we saw them lose the last of their pussy hair, pull 'poot 'n' coot' wide open, and climax center Stage, just before we left the Nugget to come here.*

Kimju reaches out. "Perhaps you'll be allowed to visit the Nugget and watch Penny and Coco perform. Or we can visit together."

Robyn dismisses, "The Nugget is not a place I need to know about." Robyn shimmies in her strapless maillot cutout. "Besides, it's already decided. I shall Opt Up!"

Kimju explores her new alignment. "So it seems like we will both need to acquire one extra Garment and Opt Up Roommates Together. Yes?"

Robyn fast-talks her Roommate. "Listen, I don't know if Gamers will be giving your tanga to me, or give me a Garment from somebody else. It doesn't matter, really; they will provide." Robyn curls a lip. "As for you, one piece or zero you're still back to the Nugget. And if for some reason they want to dress you up and promote you, that's up to them."

Kimju twists in her chair. *It does matter. Robyn doesn't listen. My Roommate looks down on me because my 35C kajoobies always stand out and my taut keister always trails behind.*

Actually, Kimju should not feel so special; Robyn looks down on everyone. Robyn escalates, "You should have Opted Down and become a Whore this Term. Everyone knows you made explicit vids squeezing your knockers. You simulated arousal. You pulled your kleave wide open, raised your karat, and dripped knittel. You reached around behind you, pulled your twin-keels to the side, and displayed your kawazoo for vulgar close-ups. You played kazoo outta your knot; don't try to fool me."

Kimju grids and corrects her Roommate, "Excuse me, Robyn, I did not just simulated arousal, I came on camera for real! Kundalini loose inside me."

Kimju adjusts her posture and crosses her arms across her opposing breasts. *My hands like the feel of my kajoobies, and my kajoobies like the feel of my palms. I'll obey Monitor Babs and keep my knobs covered. Handbra.*

Robyn observes, "I heard Boss Bitch tell you to arouse yourself looking at Tiffany's Calendar. You're supposed to keep your thong pulled to the side, your kunny spread wide, and finger your kootch. Obey me or I will get the Back Door Cam and report you!"

Kimju hesitates, then taunts Robyn, "So did you turn Steph in last Term?"

"Listen, you Whore wannabe," Robyn insists. "Boss Bitch is sending you a message. You really are in the wrong place. You should be fucking at Flesh Ranch."

Kimju considers Robyn's button inside the smallest buttonhole. *I am not at all sure what I am dealing with here... here with my Roommate Robyn.* She adjusts her position again, tucks an elbow across both knock-knocks, and dips her free hand into the tanga to test for wetness.

She extracts her fingers, offers the fingertips out toward Robyn, and inquires, "Perhaps you'd like to taste kloop, as you call it?"

Robyn backs off. Kimju looks at her fingertips, brings them close to her nose, breathes in, touches the fingertips to the tip of her tongue, tilts her head, and sucks her fingertips clean.

The tease irritates Robyn. "Masturbate, you koekjedoodle," she demands.

Kimju reluctantly obeys. She again pulls her tanga to side, exposes her trimmed brunette bush, opens her deeply pigmented inner lips surrounding a rosy pink vagina, and arouses herself. Kimju's clithood sparkles, but Robyn doesn't see it. She's too busy giving instructions. Kimju feels still more wetness inside and cringes. *I may not be able to control myself.*

Robyn advances, "You and Molly are gonna beg Babs to screen your best Nugget clips from last Term. Be nice to me and I'll help BB pick your most vulgar carnage. I'll practice you to cream and cum in sync with them, and then cam both of you."

Robyn runs her mouth again. "Don't get me wrong, Pledge. No matter what you stuck in your kunny and kawazoo at the Nugget last Term, none of your media will have any effect on me. And you did more than just cream and climax. You for sure peed on Cam last Term; you gonna bring a Pee-Cam with you? Like Tiffany?"

Kimju steadies herself. "My understanding is that Tiffany acquired the Pee-Cam from Janet two Terms ago. She brought it with her. She's the one who begged Babs to let her always use the Bathroom naked and with the Cam on."

Robyn shrugs at technicalities. "Boss Bitch will require you to beg your own indecencies!" she snarls. "You won't have a choice in the matter. You're gonna beg to climax and Pee-Cam at the same time!"

Kimju considers, *I wonder if Robyn is insane? What if Babs withholds a second Garment after I exhibit myself more than necessary? I'm going to need more than one pathway Up.*

Kimju recalls that her and Molly's revelations not long ago in the Bunkroom about Janet and Tiffany climaxing on the Double Dong seem to have startled Babs. Rattle her. So Kimju explores, "Do you think Molly and I got Tiffany in trouble?"

Robyn shrugs, "How could you do that? You're a koekjedoodle keekelay who needs knockwurst rammed up your koot. Tiffany's a tawdry temptress tail peddler who keeps getting herself into trouble. First, Boss Bitch made her run circles around the Garage while naked so she got her body all scratched up. And that was only because Tiffany pretended she didn't recognize Janet from the Dining Room Picture. I know; I saw Tiffany's body afterward. Next, BB discovered that Tiffany failed to reveal that she and Janet danced an Alumni Reprise at the Nugget last Term. Babs made Tiffany chew up and eat an entire bar of soap for that one."

"We told Babs that they climaxed the Dong together," Kimju hedges.

"Oooh, that would do it!" And Robyn stretches her arms up almost to the point of popping her rack out the top of her strapless maillot. She tidies herself back up. "Boss Bitch said that if there was ever a next time she would confine Tiffany to the Bathroom, fill her up with water, and make her pee into her mouth. On the Pee-Cam, obviously. Just like in her Calendar." Robyn squares up her strapless maillot cutout neckline.

"I gather that should build some Gamer audience," Kimju offers. "On the feeds, that is."

Robyn snorts, " BB's so stupid that she doesn't know she's giving Tiffany exactly what Tiffany wants. Tiffany's a media Whore, and when Babs dirties her up, all BB does is make Tiffany even more famous."

"Babs put Tiffany in the Mudpit?" Kimju asks.

"Not yet," Robyn assumes. "Soon."

Robyn gestures to where Kimju cups her knockers in her palms. "Tiffany did a nice job of topping off your knock-knocks. I saw your painted knobs and sand dollars before Boss Bitch made you cover up. Too bad Tiffany won't see what happens to you next." Robyn laughs, a hearty laugh, all by herself.

Kimju suppresses her irritation. She still covers her knockers with the forearm of one hand, still pulls the tanga to one side with the other, and still carefully slides one finger up and down and just inside her sex lips. Kimju can feel the klammy, but she is able to control herself to make sure no knittle hangs out. *Now is not the moment to lose oneself in climax.*

"So that's your favorite Calendar Month?" Kimju throws out. "Tiffany pissing into her own mouth?"

Robyn hasn't anticipated this question. "Listen," she says, "Tiffany's Calendar doesn't faze me. I've seen the month with the cucumber jammed in her twat, so whatever pink and toy humiliations you and Molly might foist upon the Cosmos House, I am immune! Your solo girl actions aren't gonna faze me. Cucumbers or honey and cake. I know what you are. I know where you are going. I know where you should be! I know it all."

Kimju plays it cool. "May you pleasure yourself. And I'll cherish how my graven images might enrich your Cosmos House experience."

Robyn sits. It has taken her time to stop pacing and waving her arms.

Kimju considers Robyn's bare shoulders and exposed neck. *Robyn elects to remain oblivious that I, like herself, bear but a single costume. We're Roommates, and we both wear one-piece bathing suits.*

Might Robyn consider if my topless tanga obscures a piercing or a tattoo, me having been a Stripper last Term? I doubt it.

Robyn catches Kimju studying her and blurts, "My maillot covers me and makes me decent; I can go anywhere without getting arrested! What about you, Pledge?"

Kimju play-acts, "You mean that I can't wear my tanga to class? Even clenching myself in my hands? I know you're much more decent, but I've already promised to parade topless. The Mermaid Parade. Gay Pride. Fantasy Feast."

Robyn fails to appreciate the sarcasm and addresses Kimju as if speaking to her inferior. "Listen, kippersnapper, we are not equals!" Robyn details, "So we both wear a costume with a gusset between our legs, but that is the end of the similarities. Your tanga is little more than a swatch of cloth across your smelly kunny and dirty kawazoo. It doesn't cover your keister at all. And it definitely doesn't cover your knockers."

This is all true. Robyn wants to make sure Kimju understands. "Listen, you silly knockabout," Robyn insults, "you're a 'knockers and kunny kover,' that's what you are!" Then Robyn declares, "I'm a maillot with a mighty-small cutout hole!"

§ Babs Strips Steph next to Molly: Mirror Kiss & Embrace

Babs leaves Tiffany behind in the Bathroom so she may piss all over herself on the live Pee-Cam. She glides into the Bunkroom and watches an enthusiastic and topless Molly and an awkward and minidress-clad Steph kiss themselves and rub on the Mirror. BB smiles. She can tell that Mirror's heuristic circuits have already ensnared the sensitive Molly. And that Steph remains a loose fit. *May Mirror improve.*

Boss Babe walks behind Steph, grasps the end of the knot behind her neck that connect the two sides of the halter together, and pulls. The knot unravels, and both sides of the no-longer haltered minidress fall forward and down onto Steph's chest, now less certainly grinding the mirror. BB pokes opposing sides of Steph's waist with her fingertips, and the tickle tension enables Steph to release her grip upon Mirror, arch away for just long enough to allow the minidress to fall past her spigots, catch on her waist, and come to rest midway across her hips. Steph gasps and reaffixes her bare spigots onto Mirror.

Bikini Babe compliments, "I guess now it's your turn to volunteer a bare back... and posterior rugage. Too bad Tiffany hogs the Cam in the Bathroom, 'cause you know she loves the Mirror."

Molly, standing next to Steph, remains oblivious, lost in her trance with Mirror.

"You're joining your Roommate, whether you think you will or your won't," BB provides. "It doesn't make any difference what you think. You should know that; you were the Monitor once." BB steps backward. "Maybe your sinusoidals will improve Mirror's sensitivity, but be sure to keep your milk spouts pressed up against the Mirror so you don't titter. Like Molly. Yes. I know this is hard for you to understand. But do you understand me?"

Steph thinks so. *The Mirror feels powerful, engaging, enticing.* Before, with the overly short minidress, the only bare skin Steph could rub on the Mirror was her legs and her buttonhole. And face and cheeks and hands and arms. Now Steph presses her stovepipes and snatch directly on Mirror. *The stimulation it puts into my spigots arouses me.* Steph feels Babs' presence behind her. *Don't give in right now.*

Steph flashes that Molly's painted nipples have already greased the Mirror, transferred color there. She begs, "Ma'am, please let Tiffany color my nipples." Parting words for the moment.

Steph hears Babs speak, but BB's words seem to come out of a haze now. She looks into the Mirror and sees herself. *No, I see Mirror looking into me.* She hears BB give her permission: "Pledge, you just keep on dancing with Mirror. Sooner or later your suspended minidress will slide over your pelvis and spheroids and makes its way to the floor. That way you can not only keep your spuds, but also scruff, tight up against Mirror."

Steph goes with the flow, rubs her stovepipes against Mirror, and settles into the flow. *What's not to like?*

BB takes a deep breath and twitches her pelvis bone. *Easy does it. I must control my anger at Steph's secret visit to the Nugget last Term. And yes, Steph might be hard to tame and remain totally untrustworthy, but she's not necessarily in* my *way.*

Boss Babe steps back from the two Roommates now slowly grinding topless bodies against Mirror. *An ex-Nugget and my former Monitor. I'll bet that Molly—and Kimju—don't know that Steph saw them pink and lapdance the night of Janet's Alumni Reprise,* BB calculates. *Steph assumes only Janet knows she was there and that Janet has kept this secret. This is another reason why Steph fears Janet.*

Steph wants to worry about multiple ways Up and plan contingencies. Instead she looks at herself, sees Mirror lean forward to kiss her, and connects lips.

Babs looks at the Mirror into her own eyes. Considers her cleavage and *crescents d'areolage.* Her belly button. Her legs. *Be careful about getting looked at by looking at yourself.* BB breaks off the gaze and heads toward the stairway, wagging a finger behind her as she walks away.

13 Robyn & Kimju and Kimju & Molly: Hazing & Game (D07)

§ Babs & Robyn & Kimju: BB Orders Robyn Practice Kimju

Boss Babe's sudden appearance in the Kitchen startles Robyn, and it ferrets unease into Kimju. Kimju had heard the footsteps and uses the moment to dig a finger, collect fresh kloop, and lubricate her keyway and keystone. Kimju worries, *I don't really know what BB has in mind, but this should satisfy any requirements.*

BB looks sharp but not overdone; she modulates the Roommates' dynamic. "As you know," she informs Kimju with a detached demeanor that appears indifferent to the keystone and keyway presented, "Robyn is studying to be a Monitor next Term. Maybe even a House Mom."

Kimju stiffens. *I do not like where Babs heads!* She lets the tanga cover her kava partway but keeps her clit fingered. And one arm covering both knocks.

Babs further advises Kimju, "And if Robyn is to MomCap next Term she'll need to know all about Strippers. You've pole danced before. Robyn shall escort you out into the Backyard, and you can demonstrate pole dancing for her. At the Post Henge."

Kimju accepts the invitation to speak. "Ma'am, they are not the same! The pole at the Nugget is small around and shiny metal. What is in the Backyard isn't a pole. It's a Post. A wooden Post. And bigger around."

Robyn interjects, "Listen, Pledge, it's good enough for you to show me all the moves. 'Cause you're gonna need them all for your audition, Kimju kookamungins!" Robyn laughs, all by herself.

Boss Babe answers an appeal from Kimju's eyes and raises her hands, palms out. She advises, "Robyn will tell you what she wants you to demonstrate. You obey her. And makes sure she learns some good moves."

Kimju blinks.

"And don't get splinters in your kajoobies!" Babs twinkles, then vanishes out one of the doors.

§ Robyn Cams Kimju: Post Henge Titty Tease, & Paparazzi?

What could be a benign lesson is not. Among the Cosmos Roommates Robyn and Kimju share the least homogeneous view of the world. Robyn assumes promotion; Kimju develops strategies for promotion. The Post Henge presents an opportunity for one of them to learn about the other, and for the other to forget about what happens.

Robyn orders her Roommate, "You heard the Boss Bitch. Go. Wrap your knockers around a Post in the Henge. And make sure paparazzi don't harvest your brightly-colored knobs! Think you can do that, Stripper wannabe?"

Kimju tidies her tanga across her kohlrabi, gathers her hands across her chest, and silently launches herself into motion. Handbra and tanga. She trips the silent Back Door alarm, dings the Bell while crisscrossing her arms, and walks toward the Post Henge.

The two rows of three Posts each sit far enough apart so that no Cosmos could touch two at once. A seventh Post at the end forms an equilateral triangle at the apex; it is this Post that Kimju grabs, kneels before, sidles her arms around up around, and affixes herself to. No nippage and no titter here. Just cleavage.

Kimju presses against the Post and tests its solidness in the ground. Won't rock. Kimju looks around. Seven Posts for seven Pledge; there is no eighth post, no post for the Monitor Boss. *I get it. Each pair of Posts is for a pair of Cosmos Roommates, and this seventh Post—the one I'm holding on to at this moment—is for Babs' Roommate.*

Kimju contemplates moving Posts when she hears the Back Door slam and the Bell ring in rapid succession, and she knows she has chosen this Post to clench today. Robyn finds her with her arms wrapped around the firm wooden Post, but the haughty one overlooks Post position as she lords over Kimju. Once again Robyn seems to have invited the Back Door Cam into the fray.

Kimju goes with the flow. The Post is wooden but smooth, taller than she is, and about nine inches in diameter. Robyn digs sharp fingernails into Kimju's keister and forces her to stand up.

"Wrap those bare knocks around the pole," Robyn commands, "and keep your knobs outta sight! Now squeeze your koot tight," Robyn continues, "and fuck the Post up and down like the Whore you oughta be."

Kimju obeys, and the Cam watches her as she silently thinks, *I know how to do this. You cross a line when you call me a "Knockers and Kunny Kover," but I know how to rub on a pole. I've done this inside the Nugget, stark naked, on a brass pole. Only now I'm in the big outside and rubbing on a wooden Post. What I need to do is collect another Garment.*

Kimju searches her eyes toward windows in houses that overlook the Backyard. *Certainly I've gone naked in public before. And masturbated naked inside the Nugget. But I've never masturbated in bright sunlight, outside, where anyone can watch.* Kimju grits her teeth and scans the adjacent hedge and houses beyond for signs of figures and lenses. *I can do this. If I have to masturbate in front of people, inside or out, I can do this. But I don't need this ragazze lording over me. Exhibiting me. I resent that.*

"Paparazzi getting you?" Robyn taunts.

Kimju shakes a bare keister and considers, *I should be embarrassed, but I'm not embarrassed at people looking at me nearly naked. What really irks me is Robyn. Gamers watching me let myself be humiliated by Robyn. And BB just lets her get away with it! Maybe BB's allowed to humiliate me, but not this way.*

"Kiss the Post, you worthless hootchy-kootchy dancer," Robyn commands. And again Kim obeys her. "This is your Post, Kimju Koekjedoodle, and you need to love it!"

Kimju decides to get a word in edgewise. "There's a Post here for you too, Robyn."

Kimju jerks upward as sharp fingernails pinch her inner thighs.

"Maybe you have to obey me, but I don't have to obey you," Robyn asserts. Then raises, "Or BB, or anyone else!"

Kimju decides not to argue, knowing at least the first part of Robyn's claim remains operant. *Babs did indeed order me to obey Robyn.*

Robyn reaches a hand in between the Post and Kimju's pelvis, grabs the opposite side of the front of Kimju's thong in her fingers and thumb, pulls it narrow, and jerks upward. Kimju feels pain as the cloth buries itself between unshaven sex lips. *Unnecessarily hard if Robyn's goal is to expose all my kohlrabi. Butched and natural brunette, all can see now.*

Robyn advances, "Maybe before you hairaged an outline of your brunette fuzz exposed around the sides of the thong in the past. Which I'm sure you thought was very inappropriate. What you think doesn't matter." Robyn grabs the front and back of the thong with opposite hands, lifts upward, and rocks the fabric. It hurts Kimju, who lifts her onto her tiptoes, but still clenches her knock-knocks tightly.

"Thank me for making sure that now *all* of your hairage lies exposed," Robyn demands. "Kava left and kava right. Kimju Knock-Knock Kava-Kava, that's you."

"Ma'am, thank you, Ma'am," Kimju recites.

Robyn walks around the Post to look at Kimju front the front. "Titter for the Cam," she commands.

So Kimju rubs her nipples on the Post and then flashes her oranged knobs. She gasps as she recovers them again. *I don't just titter for the Cam, I titter for paparazzi too... may they exist and be watching. And what if Babs watches, or sees this clip?*

"Tell your Post you love it," Robyn commands.

And Kimju responds, "I love you, Post," and kisses it.

"Now rub yourself on the Post and work up a slick spot."

Kimju carefully draws her hairy pubes against the wooden Pole.

"Let's see you practice, kunny-bunny," Robyn instructs. "Love your Post, kiss your Post, rub your Post, titter the Cam."

Kimju take the hit but keeps her grip on the Post. "I love you, Post." She kisses the Post, masturbates her yank-tanga crotch, and titters the Cam.

Robyn interrupts, "Slick, but no cumming. I'll be saving making you koekjedoodle for a later date."

Robyn leans forward and spits into Kimju's face.

Kimju takes it. She keeps her arms covering her knocks, pressed against the Post. And carefully tests to see if she can rub her keystone through the bundled thong fabric. *Yes. This may not be where I want to be, but it is where I am now.*

Robyn explains, "Stand here long enough and you shall become the next Cosmos Pee-Camer." Kimju blinks as Robyn continues, "And the next time you insult me by suggesting I'm your equal you'll take on Piss Mouth!"

Robyn spins on her bare heel and marches toward the Back Door.

The Cam hesistates, uncertain if it should follow Robyn, and decides to linger on Kimju embracing the Post. It watches as Kimju recites "I love you, Post," kisses and copulates with the post, titters, and starts all over again. "I love you Post."

Kimju tries to think. *Hard to do and not lose track of assignment. I have done nothing to BB or any Gamer to deserve this. Maybe Robyn really does have power beyond her status and costume. Charm? A way to walk away from bad Karma? Or is Babs really letting her walk the plank?*

Kimju almost breaks her rhythm; she eyes the hovering Cam romancing her and focuses on her own task. "I love you, Post," she declares. She kisses it, squeezes her kunny around it, and clenches her boobage, yet titters one knob or the other. "I love you, Post."

§ Robyn Hazes Kimju: Shoulder Straps vs. Knockers & Dirt

It is not until the afternoon that Robyn's voice behind Kimju's ear breaks her out of her trance. Kimju's orange tanga cuts deep through her kypsey and publicly displays her butched pubic hair. *My kale, my kelp, my kohlrabi, my kava-kava. I've heard all the words. I danced the Nugget last Term.*

Robyn delights in augmenting detail. "Oh my, Kimju, you've slobbered the Post and soaked your tanga as well. Kloop everywhere. And you got some dried kloopings ground into your butched kava." Robyn repeats the jerking motion that sunk the tanga into Kimju's kypsey earlier today. "Kava left and kava right. Kava-kava."

Robyn laughs. And Kimju holds onto her Post.

Robyn puts it succinctly: "Kimju knockers and kava-kava."

Kimju wonders, *Just who plays me? Robyn? Babs? Maybe even a Janet I've never met? Or MomCap. I need to Opt Up, but right now I must exhibit myself shamelessly. Babs will Opt me however it's convenient for her. I need to be convenient for her to Opt Up; I don't need her fearing I'm going to go rogue. But I also need alternate Option paths, even if I must sacrifice all self-respect. Still, Robyn is my Roommate, so I must navigate her first, even if she's got Charm.*

Robyn struts purposefully; Kimju observes that Robyn's maillot cutout has acquired shoulder straps! Robyn smiles at Kimju's cognition. "I control my situation," she appraises her masturbating Roommate. "I don't need to pay attention to Boss Bitch. I do what I want. I used to have four tan lines. Now I have six. You've got three. I'd say you're headed for zero. I might have to put up with you as my Roommate, but I know I am Babs'—and the Gamers'—favorite Cosmos. The Game Masters want me to Opt Monitor because I'm so exceptional! At least Opt Monitor, maybe even Opt MomCap next Term! I'm blessed!"

Kimju has no choice but to listen to Robyn brag. But she does quietly consider her status. *For most Pledge, pretending to not understand Babs' directions would invite immediate correctional training, but Babs makes no attempt to discipline Robyn's poor learning abilities. BB disciplines everyone else sternly, but she overlooks Robyn.* Kimju wonders why. *Am I being used to help Robyn become ever more confident, or am I indeed Robyn's practice dummy? Or does Robyn have Charm?*

Robyn commands, "Back down on your knees."

Kimju obeys. She keeps her knockers clenched tight to the Post.

Robyn commands, "Back your knees up and spread them apart."

Kimju hesistates. *This will ensure that my knockers, with the bright nipple makeup, suddenly become totally visible, not just a titter. For the Cam and paparazzi alike. And contrary to Babs' orders.*

Robyn clarifies, "Babs told you to obey me. Now obey me!"

Okay. Surrogate overrides; I obey, Cam documents. Kimju modifies her position; she keeps her arms hugging around the Post, but as she backs her knees up both knockers spring free of her grip and swing free. They hang down and away from her chest. *So, for the first time today at the Post Henge, I fully expose my kajoobies, colored knobs and all. Babs tests me from afar.*

Robyn uses a foot to stabelize Kimju's face as it reaches the dirt. Kimju still stretches her hands before her head around the Post; she clasps her fingers together, presses one cheek into dirt, and holds tight. The spit on her face dried to crust a while ago. Now one side of her cheek acquires dust from the earth, the other from Robyn's foot bottom. Kimju appreciates Robyn's toenails.

Robyn eggs her on. "Now lift your bare keister up in the air. Rotate it around. Act like you want to get fucked up your asshole, you cheap wannabe knockabout."

Kimju swings her bare knockers in the air and rotates her twin keel. *I know this pose. But I don't like having to perform for Robyn. Or let paparazzi document my colored knobs.*

Robyn escalates her aggression. "I'm sure a keekelay like you *wants* to show off your rosy pink down inside your kypsey lips. And stick a thermometer up your kawazoo and show how hot you are." Kimju hears the sound of Robyn snapping her spaghetti shoulder straps. Robin invites a question, "Steph's already flashing her scraggy snatch. You gonna match her? And not just pullaside and pink in the Kitchen. Display your klammy kuder to the Prefecture."

Kimju breaks into a Chant without even thinking, "Please let me pullaside, pink, and finger my holes."

Made no mistake; Kimju is a superb Stripper. And she's so good at it that she thinks she can run the Nugget.

Kimju still hugs the Post. She studies its surface, but it is too close to focus. No problem. Kim knows how to shake her hanging 34C knockers in the clear air. She adjusts her posture, armpits and legs freshly shaven this morning, hairage spilling out from a tanga buried in her kypsey, knobs hardened at the thought of this explicit public exposure. Kimju chaffs at Robyn, yet calculates quietly, *This is easy. I know how to kiss a Post with a dildo buzzing up my kawazoo. Buried in my kypsey. Or both at the same time. Double Penetration.*

Kimju glances at Robyn. *I'm going to crush you.* Kimju rotates her keister in a figure-eight pattern. And chants, "Please let me pullaside, pink, and finger my holes."

But Kimju is disturbed at how easily the mantra comes out.

Robyn presses into Kimju's knockers with a row of painted toenails and then mashes her foot upward into first one knock and then the other, feeling and observing them. Mauling them.

Kimju knows. *Exhibiting me like chattel. Handling me like an animal.*

Robyn commands, "Flatten yourself on your belly, you knock-knock kava-kava kickshaw." Robyn laughs. "Keep your hands around the Post, rub your face in the dirt, and spread your legs wide apart. Make sure you keep your knockers ground into the dirt, because BB's gonna visit, and you know she doesn't want to see knobs."

Kimju obeys. *Robyn just provided the Prefecture with a possibly unauthorized view of my kajoobies and painted knobs. And I'm lying in dirt.*

Robyn places one foot atop Kimju's back and then steps with both feet onto Kimju's prone form. "So, Pledge, did you notice anything different about me this afternoon?" Robyn invites Kimju to talk.

Kim doesn't need to address Robyn as "Ma'am," and she flares her nostrils and speaks to the dirt, overcoming resistance to talk by the body standing on top of her. "I'm wondering what trick you performed to get those sexy string spaghetti shoulder straps!"

Robyn considers if this is an insult or not. Robyn flaunts mighty haughty with her maillot; it rides horizontal across her bosom and hints a most modest scoop of cleavage.

Robyn's answer comes to her. "No trick to the shoulder straps." Robyn feels Kimju's back with her toes and runs her lines. "I simply told Boss Bitch I wanted them."

Kimju feigns empathy. "You get everything."

"I'm special. The straps provide insurance should I need to move quickly."

"You're smart!" Any mocking tone from Kimju's lips goes unnoticed.

"I'm important." Robyn steps off of Kimju's back, wiggles a bare foot in between Kimju's spread thighs, and kicks dirt forward. "I know my rigamarole is much nicer than yours... except I don't share my knockers with the cheap seats. With anyone. No lookie, no touchie."

"You've got the smallest belly buttonhole in the House." Kimju pushes a Robyn button.

Robyn brightens. "Steph and I are the only Cosmos with buttonholes. And mine measures far smaller than hers. It's all Gamers get to see. I concentrate my navelage, and everybody pays attention to me and my button. I radiate!"

"You are like the eye of Kundalini speaking out to them!" Kimju exclaims.

"I command! Pledge obey!" Robyn exalts. She rubs the bottom of a dusty bare foot upon Kimju's upwardly exposed kabedis, curls her toenails downward, and digs into curvy flesh. "Grovel for 1000 seconds, then handbra yourself, ring the Bell, and come in the Back Door. Don't forget: accuracy matters." Robyn spins on her heels and marches away.

Kimju hears the Bell and the Back Door. But she maintains the Cam's attention. And of course, paparazzi. *Thanks to Robyn they all briefly collected some free colored knobs. But I am not at all sure Babs approves of what Robyn did to me.*

Kimju grovels. *One. Two. Three....*

§ Robyn Hazes Molly & Steph: Mirror Romance

Steph never does get a fresh minidress for the evening. She had kissed the Mirror for what seemed like forever—hours most certainly—and at some point Robyn seemed to drift into the Bunkroom. Steph hears Robyn coo, "Oooh, Pledge, you've dropped your dress to the floor. Nice spheroids. You gonna pull them apart and show everyone your septic pipe?"

Mirror engages Steph with a kiss and tickles her stems, and Steph pushes her short and wavy hairs tighter against Mirror. Mirror looks into her eyes, and Steph gathers her presence and tempers a return. *I must keep my surge under control. Wet inside perhaps, but never leak out. And I'll deal with Robyn eventually. After I take Molly's panties away.*

"Gamers love how your struggle," Robyn mocks. "Too bad Tiffany hogs the Pee-Cam. Still, you're still naked and able to drench your minidress with pee. That way you could show Gamers how much you wants to wear a minidress again."

Mirror attracts harder, and Steph stops listening. She never hears Robyn try and be unable to detach Molly from Mirror, nor does she process the Watering Can being using on Molly's topless body by Robyn, who remains unaware of Molly's fear of germs.

Molly comes out of her trace just enough to hear Robyn whisper, "I've got more lines than you do. It's six to three, you mangy maladroit moerskont. I know you're begging your panties into your mouth, but what you need to do is soak them with pee first." Mirror electro-stimulates Molly across a broad swath of breast and belly and leg, and Molly presses against splotches on the Mirror where her makeup has rubbed off. Wet panties hang lower, crack her moonshadow now.

Robyn puts in a last word before she exits. "Trust me, you're both gonna beg Nudie Cam! And not just titters and upskirt." But this promise falls upon inattentive ears.

Needless to say, Molly's Watering Can is not the reason Steph's minidress will acquire dampness and scent later today. Somewhat later, when Steph discovers the minidress that tangles her bare feet on the floor, she steps out of it delicately and kicks it away. Steph may be naked now, but she doesn't think about it.

Later still—Steph had no idea of when—Boss Babe lets the Mirror fade away, and Steph does finds herself dress-less and naked, alone in the Bunkroom with Molly. She covers both smurfs with one arm and her satchel with the other hand and scuttles to her bunk. Steph will sleep naked, clenched, and anxious tonight.

Molly, also discharged, forms a handbra above her wet panties. Molly will sleep topless and worry about germs, but Molly isn't ready to sleep or hide yet. She ventures downstairs.

§ Tiffany & Robyn: Pee-Cam Piss Mouth Feed Prefecture

Robyn heads down the hallway. She looks into the Bedroom and sees that the Desktop shows Tiffany live and that Tiffany's two Garments hang on a back hook. She proceeds down the hallway to the entrance into the Bathroom.

There are no hiding places inside the Bathroom. Robyn rolls her toes on the raised curb that separates the Bathroom from the hall and prevents any slosh. Tiffany remains sequestered in the Bathroom. She rises to her feet, and Robyn looks in and ambles toward the entrance.

"You're welcome to step in," Tiffany offers.

Robyn takes a step back and looks Tiffany over. "You smell. What happened to you?"

What happened to me? I'm punished for not remembering everything I know. I've had to run through scratchy bushes and eat soap, and now I have to piss on myself." It's hard not to fess up to, since the smell is indicative and the tile floor has puddles.

"Piss in your Mouth," Robyn clarifies. "I know your type. Media whore. Anything for attention. You got scratched up because you pretended you didn't know Janet. And you ate soap because you didn't tell BB about the Alumni Reprise. What this time?"

Tiffany bats her eyes. "Apparently Kimju and Molly recollect that Janet and I climaxed the Double Dong. And this makes Babs jealous."

"Poor Boss Bitch when a Dong needs a buff bodacious banshee astride," Robyn mocks, then projects, "I bet you and Janet made Piss Mouth together at the Nugget last Term."

"Not quite," Tiffany clarifies. "Janet poured the shots; I tossed them. Apparently Janet apparently told Babs only a part of the story."

Robyn snorts, "Too bad. I'm sure the Bitch probably owes Janet, and she'd better hope Steph keeps her mouth shut."

Tiffany advises, "You should speak respectfully of Boss Babe."

Robyn curls her nose. "Boss Bitch perhaps. Look at me. What do you see that's new? Shoulder straps. You told me my eyelets entitled me to them, so today I demanded BB give them to me, and she fessed right up."

Tiffany charms, "You're courageous!"

Robyn agrees, "Listen, Boss Bitch still has more tan lines than I do, but only one more. She used to lead me seven to four, counting my buttonhole. Now that I've got shoulder straps it's seven to six. I'm gaining! And besides, I'm not making... what do you call it?"

Tiffany smiles. "Bling."

"I like that." Robyn smiles. "You're okay sometimes. And it's not like I didn't know you were up here. You're on the Screen in the Dining Room and on Babs' Desktop, to say the least. I saw you to pull your tail trough wide apart and showcase the tattoo surrounding your tailpipe. You really are a tawdry triple torque."

Naked Tiffany dances lightly on bare, albeit damp, feet. "Robyn my dear, the Cam stays on me all the time. It takes me from every angle."

Tiffany turns to face the Cam, hovering behind her and transmitting the proceedings… or not. Tiffany speaks to the Cam as if she addresses Monitor Babs. "Ma'am, thank you for letting me perform on the Pee-Cam, Ma'am." Tiffany wipes her mouth and crotch with opposite fists. "Ma'am, please watch me, Ma'am. Please push my feeds out, and not just to the Dining Room, Kitchen, Bunkroom, and your Desktop. Please broadcast my piss-soaked body out to the all the Houses at School. To the Nugget, the Spunk Pit, Flesh Ranch. To the entire Prefecture."

Tiffany turns back to Robyn. "How about that, Pledge? Care to join me? I'm bringing Prefecture traffic to the Cosmos House. I'll teach you how."

Robyn angles her eyes. "You don't have anything worth getting my feet wet for. Let alone tracking your pee into the Bunkroom. Tell me, Pledge, how come you don't wash yourself?"

Tiffany raises an eyebrow. "I did at first, and I drank a whole lot of water. But then, no more running water. But I am cleaning up after myself, if you know what I mean."

Robyn doesn't quite know what Tiffany means. Robyn scans the Bathroom interior: a shower with no stall, a toilet, a bidet, a bathtub, and a floor drain. Robyn offers condolences. "Maybe Molly can visit and bring the Watering Can. Or maybe you can beg that all the drains get turned off."

"You're welcome to come in and use the facilities," Tiffany says.

"I'm welcome to come in and piss in your mouth," Robyn asserts.

"Ma'am, may it please you, Ma'am," Tiffany uptakes.

Robyn licks her lips. "No, thank you. You'll just have to piss in your own mouth. Maybe now. Maybe forever."

Tiffany retreats from the doorway. *Who needs Robyn anyway?*

Robyn hurls an insult. "You need to get back to Whoring, but until then Gamers shall still condition you to *desire* Slavesex, so you can get bondage fucked and force climaxed. Full 24x7, not just during a daily Whore shift."

Tiffany smiles. "Really? Robyn, never underestimate the power of ignorance. Sometimes what people don't know allows Karma to ground."

Robyn finds this statement confusing and stabs, "And sometimes it doesn't. You're still a cock-sucking, cunt-cocking, anal Whore. Except you're not allowed sex here at the Cosmos House! You're as chastised here as you would be in a Slavesex Dungeon somewhere."

Tiffany sits back against one of the makeup stools, opens her tamtart, and points her peehole directly in Robyn's direction. "Here's what I am allowed to do. I'm allowed to lick your asshole. Suck your ridottos and rotor button, lap your runnel, and kiss you. Use my tongue even." And she shoots a squirt of pee out. Short enough so the arc of it hangs in the air, all by itself.

Robyn recoils and backs away from the door. "Stay away from me. You're a tamtart tinderbox thumper."

And Robyn hears Tiffany laugh and call after her as she retreats down the hallway, "Right you are!"

§ Kimju & Molly: Dining Room Huddle re Tiffany & Steph

Molly is thumbing through Tiffany's Porn Star Calendar when she hears the Bell and looks to see Kimju arrive into the Kitchen via the Backdoor. It is evening of the Seventh Day.

They trade eyes. Both keep their breasts covered with handbras. This is the ex-Strippers' first contact since morning, and both have had a long day of kissing and rub-a-dub, be it Mirror or Post, and their makeup and painted nipples are worn. Kimju tips her head toward the door into the Dining Room. Molly gathers her Watering Can, and they slip in.

They are confronted with a large Screen live feed view of Tiffany in the Bathroom upstairs. The large screen sits between the two windows that look out into brambles at the side of the House, which have become shadowy. The two ex-Nuggets look at each other, and then, as if on cue, Tiffany rolls onto her back and sprays pee down onto herself. Kimju and Molly both cringe. Pee gets on Tiffany's tits, on her face and hair, and yes, a little bit of pee makes it into the opened mouth that tries to chase her stream.

Kimju and Molly look at each other and sit themselves down at the table next to each other so the Screen is behind them. "Practice," states Kimju, "will improve Tiffany's coordination."

Behind them Tiffany grovels in pee on the tile floor, but the ex-Roommates don't see it. Tiffany knows, *My fans harvest the clips; only my most devoted fans spend the hours necessary to be with me all my time on the Cam.* Kimju and Molly try to not care. Time to catch up.

"I think we said something to Babs about the Alumni Reprise that made her go after Tiffany," Molly explores.

"Climaxing the Double Dong," Kimju isolates.

"I feel bad about what we did to Tiffany," Molly says.

"We spoke truth to power." Kimju shakes her head. "It's not our Karma how Babs and Tiffany and Janet sort out facts. After all, Janet was Babs' Roommate, but maybe not forthcoming."

The full color, high resolution Screen behind them depicts a hands-and-knees Tiffany licking herself up off the tile floor. The Pee-Cam chooses to also document her tailpipe tattoo from above and behind, so Tiffany reaches back with a hand to part her lips and pink for the Cam. *Maybe I need to extrude some tapioca in order to get ahead of the pack.*

Kimju fumes, "I don't like it that Tiffany's here. She's way deeper than either of us; she was a Whore when we were Strippers. That was all right last Term. But now we are *all* Pledge. That's not right. Now Tiffany's live Cam collects anyone who wants to pee. I understand I begged to Pledge this Term, but I thought Pee-Camming stayed at the Nugget."

"Maybe we need to explain to Babs it's now impossible to use the Bathroom," Molly suggests. "I mean, it's not like I care about Pee-Camming. That's nothing, Kimju; we both Pee-Cammed all last Term. The real problem is that if you go in the Bathroom you get Tiffany's pee all over your feet. And track it out. That's even worse."

Kimju isn't sure she agrees with Molly on this. She takes a large breath, pivots around to scan Tiffany on the Screen behind her, and sees naked Tiffany drenched in her own pee. She looks back at Molly. "Tiffany will do anything to get Gamers to watch her; she just wants to get back to the Nugget, and once there she can get back to Flesh Ranch and advance her Porn Star career. But I am not a Pee-Camer."

Molly shrugs. "Like I said, I don't care about Pee-Camming, but I am not a Piss Mouth, despite Robyn's suggestion I pee on my panties and stuff my mouth. All I want is my panties off."

Molly hugs herself; like Kimju she also holds her breasts in both hands, even though no Cam monitors the Dining Room at this moment. Molly predicts, "I know you. You want another piece. You will bide your time before deciding what Garment to impound. And from whom."

Kimju confesses, "You're right. Tiffany would be all right, like, her shirt would do me. I'll take it even though it's clear vinyl."

"If she puts it back on she's liable to get pee all inside it," Molly worries.

"No problem," Kimju declares easily. "You can wash it off using the Watering Can."

They laugh together.

"You can have the Watering Can!" Molly proposes. "And you know you can have my panties too. Anytime. With or without the Watering Can."

"I know." Kimju rubs her knobs with the palms of both hands. "I appreciate your affection and understand our histories spin on different axes this Term." Kimju tries humor. "We aren't allowed to Game, at least not right now." She teases, "Who wants a pair of wet panties anyway?"

"Steph wants them," Molly enunciates. "You know she made me beg to give them to her. She'll take them wet. They would put a stop to her vagflashing."

Kimju stops rubbing her nipples. *Except that leaves Steph having two Garments and in a stronger Opt Up position than me. I guess I don't care if Molly keeps one piece or gets totally naked. But more fun would be for Molly and Steph to Flip-Flop. I kinda dig that Steph would get to go topless for a change and not just titter. And besides....* Kimju drifts deeper into thought. *My Plan A is to take Robyn's maillot away from her in a Winner-Takes-All; that gives me two Garments and an Opt Up. However, if Robyn doesn't have Charm, Gamers might want her topless tanga for a while, and so there is a chance we might Flip-Flop, in which case I'd end up with just her maillot. And still need a second Garment.*

Either way I'm better off if Molly Flip-Flops with Steph for the minidress.

Molly taps Kimju out of analysis. "You're gonna wait until after the newbies arrive before you make a move." Molly again proscribes Kimju behavior. "I know you."

"You do. Beka and Elle, that's what their names are," Kimju admits. "And then the whole House will be here."

Kimju advances he fingertips to her nipples and twists her knobs. "Newbies are always prospects, and, yes, I shall wait until they arrive to see what I might want to divest them of."

Kimju turns to Molly again. "Maybe you're a willing Pee-Camer, but I'm not. I want to keep my 'Kunny Kover' over my kava. And get a top. My goal is to Opt Up next Term."

§ Kimju & Molly: Assess the Four Dining Room Pictures

Kimju gestures Molly's eyes toward the four Dining Room Pictures, hanging on the wall opposite them. Four large, framed images. Two verticals and lower, on the baseboard, two side-by-side horizontals. Kimju runs her fingers inside her thong to feel her own stubble. *I might have had to vagflash Robyn and Babs, but I didn't vagflash a Cam.* Kimju nods her head toward Babs' minimalist Bikini atop the four Dining Room Pictures. "Bling blush bush. That's what Robyn says. End of last Term."

Molly shrugs. "Well, I guess Babs took care of the bush. And I don't see her blushing much." Molly points to the Spiderweb Bikini who hangs on the wall directly beneath Babs. "Same Janet we saw dance with Tiffany." Molly acknowledges as she digests the images. "Tiffany told us they had been Stripper Roommates a couple of Terms back. But how come they were allowed to climax the Double Dong during the Alumni Reprise, when Strippers were not?"

"Here's how that worked," Kimju explains. "Pledge are allowed to Double Dong, whereas Strippers are not. Janet was a Pledge when she donged with Tiffany at the Alumni Reprise. And Tiffany was a Whore, a visiting Feature Dancer."

"Outreach from Flesh Ranch," Molly confirms. "Now she's here."

"I don't want to be a Whore, Kimju," Molly confesses. "Whores suck and fuck anything, any hole, any time. Dildos, Dongs, real pussies and cocks, even kissing and spit."

Kimju studies the two horizontal Pictures. The Baseboard Strippers. Kimju reads the naked pinkers' nametags. "Penny and Coco. Tiffany and especially Babs wanted to know they'd arrived at the Nugget."

"They were scary!" Molly sputters at the creamy poot and coot spread out before her on the Baseboard. "The moment they came in the Stage Door, they got swept naked on Stage, pinked, shaved, creamed, and climaxed. I've never seen it happen so fast. We were kept weeks before House Mom let us cum."

Kimju closes her eyes, tilts the spin. "I guess they had to streak over."

Molly worries, "Speaking of streaking, I hope Ginny and Lee made it to the Corvette House all right. Maybe Babs will ask Janet. They don't deserve to get captured, chloroformed, and cage fucked."

"They had to really want to become naked Corvettes," Kimju perks.

Molly double-checks that her own panties are indeed wet; they are somewhat wrung out and gathered into her moonshadow so she doesn't get the chair wet.

An equally bare-assed Kimju studies Penny and Coco's explicit poses. *Congratulations, both of you, on a successful streak. And may you stay naked all Term. I did.*

"Look at them." Molly studies the pink-wet-and-ready Penny and Coco Pictures. "That's where I want to be next Term. Back at the Nugget, naked and spreading pink. And it would be sweet for you to come too."

Kimju squeezes her breasts together with her elbows and draws both hands to her chin.

Molly continues, "They're not only showing their clits and hoods; you can also see their pee holes."

Kimju nods. *Yes, and I can also see that their insides are wet.*

"Betcha Penny and Coco get to pull pink and pee at the same time," Molly proscribes. "We did."

Kimju nods. *And maybe that's something I won't be doing any more.*

§ Kimju & Molly: Assess Robyn & Discuss Prey

"I asked Robyn what she knew about this Mudwrestling Contest that transpired at the end of last Term," Kimju says, shifting the conversation slightly. "And Robyn said that it settled the Fate between Babs and Janet and Penny and Coco." Kimju gestures to the four Dining Room Pictures. "But Robyn says she wasn't there…."

Molly helps. "I heard she refereed the Mudwrestling Contest but has forgotten. And Steph says she wasn't there either. Babs knows the truth. Steph said something bad happened due to Robyn, and this is why Robyn's Redacted. But Steph doesn't think this is because Robyn's got Charm."

"Pledge aren't allowed to hover and repeat a Term." Kimju focuses her thoughts toward her Roommate. "But here she is. Robyn Repeating, Robyn Redacted."

"Well, she's your Roommate!" Molly explains the obvious. "You get first dibs on her in the Roommate Games."

Kimju twists her knobs at the thought of this; she feels them knurl up in her fingers, and then pinches them hard, so pain shoots through them.

Kimju agrees, "Yes. And the Game I want to play is Roommates Apart, Winner-Takes-All. So I can add her maillot cutout overtop my tanga, and cover up my kajoobies and kabedis."

Molly hefts her mams. "You'd get to Opt Up and Monitor but Robyn will be a naked Pledge. Naked Stripper next Term."

Kimju ponders, "I like that. She went out of her way to humiliate me today. It wasn't necessary to despoil me in dirt next to the Post. Make me titter and then offer me topless to any paparazzi shooting from a second story nearby."

"She made me wallow in the Mudpit," Molly reminds he fellow ex-Nugget. "Despite a hose down last night and an afternoon making out with myself in the Mirror, I still feel grit on my body. In my hair, and you know I got hair everywhere. Grit in my panties too, and even inside my mooe. And then Robyn tells me to beg to pee on my panties and stuff my mouth."

"Well, it would put a stop to your begging," Kimju observes. "And you won't have to worry about vaginal infections anymore, you know, whole colonies of germs."

Molly hefts weight toward Kimju. "You can take her, Kimju. You're much more savvy, and besides, she's the Cosmos most adjacent to you."

Kimju accepts, "My Roommate, and such a convenient target. And so attractive! What a delectable meal!"

"She's malicious," Molly says.

Kimju shakes imaginary dust off her bare back. "Okay, so she's a nasty raccoon. But Babs already knows this, and probably Steph does too. What I don't appreciate is Babs letting Robyn use me as a foil."

Molly takes life in stride. "Maybe Babs is just letting Robyn game with you. Don't forget, you're the one who gets to play a Roommate Game with Robyn. We get to spook all the 'newbies,' and 'newbie' Robyn gets to spook us!"

Kimju claws at her knockers. "Well, I'm not going to just sit and wait and see how Babs dials her in."

Molly shakes Kimju off and nervously touches her wet panties. "I'm the one you should feel sorry for, Kimju. I'm the one who's gonna get germs." Molly manipulates her panties until they are gathered as tightly into the front of her mooe as they are between her buttocks. "Steph knows all she has to do is initiate a Winner-Takes-All contest, and I'll pick a Game I'm sure to lose."

Kimju twitches. *Once Steph gets Molly's panties, it will be hard to take the minidress away from her, whereas if Molly can Flip-Flop for the minidress she will happily give it to me. Depending upon how it fits or reveals me, it could provide me a superior second Garment.*

Kimju narrows her eyes. "Robyn reminded me that Pledge can volunteer to do things that we Strippers weren't allowed to do at the Nugget! Besides Double Dong. Hetro-sex is forbidden both Castes. Same-sex is forbidden for Strippers, but it's permitted for Pledge. You would think it would be the other way around."

Molly rubs the bundled-up panties against her clit. "It's very simple. Strippers have to expose themselves completely but stay totally chastised. And a Stripper can Opt either way; they can Opt Pledge like us and play with gals, or Opt Whore and play with the guys."

"Play with guys and gals," Kimju corrects.

Silence falls over the two ex-Strippers. Kimju speaks, "Lookit, neither of us can end up a Whore next Term. I want to Opt Up, and you want to Opt Down. That puts your Fate one Caste closer to Whore, but I guess that's your decision."

Molly stretches her body and lets her mams flop around. "It's okay, Kimju. If I tried to Monitor I'd fail at it immediately, and the Gamers would cast me down horribly. I'd be lucky to fuck. I'm better off at the Nugget. I like it there, and then maybe I can Pledge again. Off in the future."

Kimju shuffles her posture. She again considers Babs' bling, blush, and bush in the Picture ahead.

Molly relaxes her hands so that her mammaries hang free. She pokes Kimju in the waist. "I know you," Molly starts as she turn to her friend.

"You have already assuaged yourself of any guilt should you decide to take away Robyn's maillot. What's your plan, anyhow?"

"Wait, I shouldn't answer that question!" Kimju stalls, jesting. She considers, then speaks her mind. "Okay, lookit, no secret." Kimju gestures toward the explicit pink-wet-and-ready Baseboard Strippers. "You and I have been there, done that. Lots of it. Even climaxing the pole. You find it easy to go back to. I want to try the upside. That's all." Kimju blinks. "Yeah, sure, I don't need to trade costumes with Robyn, doing a Flip-Flop; I need a Winner-Takes-All Roommate Game."

"I'll keep it a secret, Kimju, really I will." Molly scratches her hairy body and protests, "But I think everyone's gonna figure this out. Like, one of you gets all the clothes and one of you ends up... well, naked."

Molly tightens her damp panties up into her mooe, rolling, practically speaking anyway, all her minge outside the taunt cotton. *If a Cam inhabits the Room, I will draw the bundle to the side and lift my clit into view. Clit and peehole, actually, just like Penny and Coco, except with a pullaside. Like Kimju in the Kitchen, apparently.*

Kimju muses to Molly, "This last Term was the first time in the Game that I ever advanced myself, and it was largely due to a new determination."

Molly provides comfort. "You just didn't want to go Whore. That's what motivated you. Me too, I guess."

Kimju ruminates, "Sometimes when Nugget Patrons fondle your body they can be sweet to you. Like during a lapdance. But sometimes Gamers can be inconsiderate, inept, even hurt."

Molly nods. "Robyn accused me of me of being a pocket jobber."

Kimju shrugs, "Well, weren't you? I mean, well, sometimes, anyway?"

"Maybe here at the Cosmos House there will be less touching."

"No touching by men certainly." Kimju wipes her nose.

"I don't care when I lapdance if they handle me nice." Molly fondles her large areolas. "And I'm okay if they pop in their pants. I feel like I collect compliments."

Kimju distinguishes, "You may help me Opt Up to Monitor, Molly, so I get to pick what hands touch me, if any at all."

"And touch any Pledge that pleases you," Molly teases. "Maybe Babs isn't just playing Robyn against you. Maybe Babs ratchets up your aggression toward Robyn," Molly observes. "Except it's not just you; Babs lets Robyn cam Steph's titter, spread her, and cam her sanpan upskirt. More than once. Even though Steph blames Robyn for Opting Down and Pledging this Term."

Kimju crosses her hands back across her body again. "Well, I got to pull pink today, but the Cam wasn't there. And yes, Robyn's maillot or'top my thong provides me the two Garments necessary to Opt Up."

"So how are you gonna take it from her?" Molly asks.

Kimju considers before she speaks. "Well, Robyn has certainly not tried to win me as a friend during my short stay so far." Kimju cocks her head back. "Win you, either! First thing she makes you do is wallow in the Mudpit! And you're not even her Roommate!"

"Steph's not her Roommate either," Molly augments. "You are."

"Maybe some of this is Babs' doing," Kimju defends, "but Robyn relishes dishing out suffering." She scowls, "She's naturally sadistic."

Unpleasant impressions trigger Molly's firmer response. "You should go strip Robyn Redacted stark naked and then ship the reptile off to the Nugget." Molly catches herself amidst this outburst, rationalizes, "Because that's where she's headed anyway, with her one piece. It's where she belongs. Maybe she really is masochistic and asking for it."

Kimju straightens her chair; it is unusual to hear Molly speak ill of anybody, and she impulsively tells Molly her thoughts. "I hate how she treated me too. She forced me to titter on the Post even though Babs told me not to. I could get in trouble for that."

Molly continues to grind. "Robyn doesn't need any maillot, won't need it next turn, so take it away from her!"

"Okay, okay!" Kimju slowly lets her body relax and breaks her hands free of her breasts. She scratches herself all over her body. "Listen, there's no rush for you to give your panties to Steph." Kimju snaps her own waistband. "My problem is I'm not sure where the power resides. I don't know if Robyn's got something on Babs, got Charm, or if BB just keeps letting Robyn build false self-confidence. Or if BB's playing me, albeit indirectly, although she has no reason to."

Molly shrugs, "Gotta love Gamers. Gotta love BB if she just might be letting Robyn spin out a lot of rope."

Kimju rotates both knobs in her fingertips. Vertical lines form all around the outside. "I'm not sure I know how to take Robyn's maillot away when there's an opportunity for the rope to jerk." Kimju tightens her jaw.

Molly supports a friend. "Ah. You'll figure it out. When Robyn stops moving, her maillot will continue without her."

And they laugh together.

Kimju ruminates, *But it's not funny. I'm concerned about the timing, finding the right moment. Because if BB protects Robyn somehow, it could get really tricky to cross BB.*

Molly breaks into the silence, "You're the one who is Robyn's Roommate, so everyone is watching you and her now, more so that her and Tiffany or her and Steph." Molly puts a hand on Kimju's leg. "You're the one. You get first dibs on any dust-up." A pause. "And if Robyn throws the gauntlet down, you get to pick the Roommate Game!"

Kimju runs opposing fingers up the narrow backside of her tanga and ensures the narrow fabric sits flat across her kawazoo and between the two sides of her buff keister.

Kimju gathers her wits together. *There is one Cosmos who really hasn't figured out that Robyn is overextended; there is one Cosmos who really doesn't know where Robyn is headed. And that Cosmos is Robyn.*

Unless Robyn has Charm.

14 Molly & Steph: The Drawing Class & Medical Exam (D08)

§ Tiffany & Molly & Steph: Bathroom Beautification

Roommates Molly and Steph, opposites though they may be, quickly settle into a comfortable relationship: Molly offers to forfeit her panties to Steph from right now, the morning of Day Eight, through the end of the Term.

The Roommates are different in physical type and temperament, and they come from different classes and backgrounds.

Slovenly Molly, with her "droopy milk udders" (to quote Robyn), wet panties, and Watering Can, is the perfect Pledge for Boss Babe to dispatch to rescue Tiffany this morning and clean up her pee from the Bathroom tile floor.

Boss Babe is short of patience with her: "You want to be a Stripper next Term? So clean up."

Molly recoils. "Excuse me, Ma'am, but I am not a Piss Mouth."

"Use your long hair and the Watering Can. You want to make it to Strip? Then convince me. You should aspire to be everything you can be!"

Molly tries to clean her body and rinse her hair out with her Watering Can water, but then running water returns to the Bathroom and Tiffany showers. Afterwards Tiffany drenches Molly with perfume in an attempt to mask the scent of urine, and Molly tiptoes out of the Bathroom, still carrying the Watering Can and still feeling grit from the Mudpit.

Molly frets, *I'm not sure if I'm better off with my panties spread wide across my pussy and butt or yanked tight into my muliebre and moonshadow.* No one else is sure either. "Beg Babs to let you wear them around your ankles," Steph suggests. "No germs that way!" Steph lacks sensitivity at reading Molly's phobia completely, but she does detect that the attractive force between the wet panties and Molly is weak.

Steph, who spent yesterday pressing her naked body into the Mirror after Babs pulled the string on her haltered minidress, and who slept naked overnight, exhibits relief when Babs silently hands her a different cutout minidress. Steph hurries it on before any Cam might invade the Bunkroom. Today's minidress is a scoop neck that invites downblouse, titters, and, of course, a legline suffciently short to invite upskirt and vagflash.

Steph scowls, yet considers, *It's a good thing I got a minidress back. Babs certainly pushes my limit. It's not that I can't take being naked overnight; it's that she might not understand my importance.*

In the Bathroom Steph insists that Tiffany groom her fair skin pristinely and brush her long blonde hair. But she can't stop the

Bathroom Cam from savoring her shrubbery. Nor can she stop Tiffany from putting an edge on her that suggests merchandise and from dousing her with cheap perfume.

Robyn and Kimju visit Tiffany in the Bathroom. Kimju showers; Robyn doesn't even give that to the Cam. Neither pees. Tiffany decorates another pair of Cleopatra's Wannabe Strippers, neither of whom are wannabes.

Tiffany trails them back to the Bunkroom, not bothering to duck into the Bedroom to recover her transparent croptop and slacks after putting on everyone's makeup. Naked suits Tiffany just fine.

§ Babs & Molly & Steph: Roommate Stress Test

Boss Babe enters the Bunkroom and institutes a morning ritual, Reveille.

Without thinking, Babs orders her five Cosmos into a Lineup. "Stand spread surrender! Face the Mirror. All of you!" Babs directs this comment toward Robyn, who hesitates before she falls into position in her maillot cutout next to her Roommate, the ever topless and increasingly frustrated Kimju.

Babs finds herself confronting three pairs of bare breasts, one pussy facing forward, and two bare asses facing backwards. Babs blinks at Tiffany's Eraser Heads, Kimju's shapely knick-knacks, and Molly's saggy mammary glands. *Time to overcome my topless phobia... at least for the other Cosmos.*

Babs resists an urge to try to hike her own bra up. She sets her teeth. *I might still bling, but I no longer blush!*

Babs relaxes her breath, focuses her attention upon Molly and Steph, and expounds to Steph, "Well. Now that Molly's arrived I guess you have a titter companion. Congratulations, my titter and vagflashing girls."

Well, sort of, but no Cosmos Pledge is about to correct Boss Babe. A topless Molly can't really titter because her mams aren't flashing. Nothing to titter, mams all the time; ergo, topless.

Babs rectifies Molly, "Handbra." And Molly folds her arms across her chest and cups her mammaries in her hands. Now she can titter.

But Molly never really vagflashes, although by using the Watering Can to keep her panties soaking wet, Molly's black minge and muliebre don't really hide inside the worn, see-through-when-wet, pink cotton panties.

BB considers Steph's scoop neck minidress and Molly's wet panties without comment. She has a decision to announce to these Roommates. "Gamers have decided to 'stress test' you two."

And what does that mean, to stress test? It means for Gamers to exercise the Cosmos a bit, work them, put pressure on them, and put them into play. Let them play! Molly might be eager to give her panties away and Steph might be ready to conquer, but the Gamers encourage more moxie than lazily surrendering oneself.

Boss Babe steps back so she can observe the Lineup via the Mirror, but she continues to address Molly and Steph. "Today you shall model for a Figure Drawing Class in a city nearby." BB adds a nod to Molly. "And since you are so concerned about germs, afterwards you shall get a quick Medical Exam."

Molly twitches and sways her mammies but keeps her medallions cupped in her hands.

Babs accelerates, "A minivan awaits you in the back alley. Why are you still standing here? Go; move it!"

Molly and Steph corkscrew down the stairs to the Kitchen and out the Back Door, bumping into each other as they stumble off the Landing, ring the Bell, and detour around the Mudpit and Post Henge toward a minivan parked in the alley. The driver appears shrouded in dark glass. Steph considers climbing in the front seat, but Molly quickly crawls in the back, still topless and still with her Watering Can. Steph joins her on the floor. The door closes from the outside.

At first neither Pledge talks as the van bumps into motion. Steph bears it, but the longer the ride goes on the more fearful Molly becomes and the more she waters her panties with the Watering Can. A passing bus casts shadows and reflections across one body topless and wet and one body barelegged and spreading upskirt.

Steph waggles a finger at Molly. "Don't get the impression that we are equals in the exposures department!" Steph pokes at Molly. "Me flashing my smarties is less exposed than your hanging mams!"

Molly understands. "No problem, Steph. I'll stay topless. I'll cover myself with my hands. I'll bubble up my medallions and elevate my minarets. I'll do whatever you want."

Steph gives pause. "You'll finger fuck yourself until the meringue pours out. And you'll mambo and scream."

Molly finds it easy to agree. "Sure. You name it, it's me."

Steph sighs. *Nothing like a Stripper for a Roommate.*

Molly clenches her panties tight into her mooe and wrings water out. "Kimju told me that Robyn made her titter on the Post Henge. And that the Cam took it down, with her painted knobs all knurled up."

Steph shrugs. "Maybe Kimju worries too much."

Molly nods her head in agreement and offers, "Steph, if you want me to cover my mams with my hands and, you know, let a little bit of nipple out every now and then, I'll do that for you. That qualifies as titter. I had to do that at the Nugget, sometimes even for multiple shifts. And even before last Term, after I surrendered my bra and stayed topless 24x7."

Steph probes, "Does Kimju know that everyone who saw her Cam feed from the Kitchen saw her beg Robyn to vagflash? What's that about?"

"Oh, that's just a Stripper Chant," Molly swallows. "A beg, 'Please let me pullaside, pink, and finger my holes.'"

"You mean that?" Steph inquires.

"Well, uh, ah, sure. It's a Stripper Chant, but there's nothing about being a Pledge that prohibits begging like that. Kimju her tanga, me my panties."

Molly wants to cover all tracks. "You can keep both of us can pink, wet, and ready, and we'll cum on cue."

Nothing prohibits, indeed. Steph dangles a morsel: "Since Kimju's already begging, perhaps it will be Robyn who takes Kimju's tanga away. And not the other way around, as you and Kimju seem to believe?"

"We've both creamed and climaxed stark naked. On Stage," Molly boasts, "but Kimju doesn't want to go back to the Nugget. She wants to Opt Up. Like you."

Steph curls a lip. "Maybe Gamers want Kimju back at the Nugget. She already knows the Caste. Doesn't she already have fans?"

"Yeah..." Molly drifts. "I guess I would like for that to happen. Both of us Opt Stripping together next Term. We both have fans."

§ Molly & Steph: The Figure Drawing Class

Eventually the van backs up to a loading dock inside a multi-story office building. The doors opens, and the Roommates scurry down a walkway into a small office. One walks tall and proud; the other hunches over and clenches herself.

The Drawing Class Matron greets them inside the office. She wears a uniform with a jacket and a mid-calf skirt, and she addresses them with efficiency.

"One of you may model for the Figure Drawing Class, many floors upstairs. It is a fully nude assignment. The other will escort and hold onto whatever clothing the chosen nude model takes off."

The two Roommates look at each other.

Steph speaks first. "You can do it," she tells Molly, then follows with the rationale, "Since you're mostly naked already."

Molly doesn't wonder what Caste the Matron might be. *It is true that I am mostly naked already.* Molly stops clenching herself. She says nothing out loud. *It doesn't matter if my majonkers are covered or not.* Molly hooks thumbs to the sides of her waistband, rolls her panties down, steps out of them, hands them to Steph, and sighs with relief. She considers her body. *I am naked now. Not just mams, but also minge in full view. But no wet panties!*

The Matron hands Molly a towel to wipe her body free of dirt and makeup and dry herself. She also loans Molly a brush and comb.

Steph smirks at Molly's willingness to extract herself from her wet panties. She also must consider what to do with the wet panties just presented to her by Molly. They are suffciently wrung out that they don't even drip water.

The Matron tucks in her chin and gives Steph a hint, "May I suggest you unroll them before you put them on."

Steph untwists the panties in her hand until she can distinguish the front and backside. Damp, thin, faded, pink cotton panties. Previously worn.

Steph looks the Matron in the eye, and the Matron points toward a trash can. "Well, if you don't want them, throw them away."

Steph clears her throat and clarifies, "Ma'am, yes I want them!"

Matron simplifies, "Then put them on."

Steph does so at once.

Steph hadn't considered this possibility, the possibility of acquisition being this easy but also this consequential. Steph makes a mess pulling what were only moments ago Molly's panties up and on under today's scoop neck minidress. *This Matron should give me new panties. And not Molly's cootie underwear. Probably she is not as smart as I am.*

A freight elevator nearby crawls upward slowly, climbing many stories to deliver the nude figure drawing model and her escort to the drawing studio floor.

The elevator clunks to a stop, and the steel accordion door opens into the drawing room. Both Cosmos feel the eyes of the class upon them.

Steph catches a glimpse of herself in the mirror opposite and immediately flushes with embarrassment. The wetness from the panties has soaked into the minidress, and a stain around her hips and below her buttonhole has begun to grow.

Steph finds a corner in the drawing room and leans her shoulders back. *No way I am sitting down!*

Steph watches Molly make her way to a small posing dais in the middle of the room. Molly acquires confidence. *I can do this! I've modeled for drawing classes before! Heck, I've even modeled with my mooe pulled open and a toy sticking out.*

Steph marvels at how Molly seems able to hold poses for long periods of time. She possesses no embarrassment, even though some of the poses splay her hairy legs apart and let some of the sketchers skewer her muliebre. The class surrounds her on all sides and transcribes her face and body, mammaries, mammilla, navel, gluteus maximus, thick hairy armpits, and pubic muff. All onto paper.

Steph wonders if the art students come from the School she now attends. *Perhaps not. They are outsiders somehow. They could be like Gamers, but probably most of aren't even aware of the Game.*

Steph's eyes canvas the drawing studio, looking for hidden Cams. *With zoom lenses to harvest that meaty molliwog.* Steph brushes her hand down the cutout minidress atop the front of her body, careful to neither titter nor upskirt. *Molly should be grateful to go naked here... it isn't like she hasn't made hundreds, probably thousands, of spread wide open pussy shots.*

Molly doesn't give much thought to whether Gamers might furtively collect her nudity. *It really doesn't matter. All that matters is that I strike my best poses here and now for these students.* Molly might be lethargic and indifferent to being looked at, but that doesn't mean she doesn't take pride. *I know I am worth the model fee, whoever is paying it and whoever is receiving it. For it is certainly not me, and maybe not even the Cosmos House.*

Steph is not sure if Molly earns status by posing or loses status because she is relegated to nude work.

Steph ponders, and again the panties feel clammy and cold on her skin. She confirms that the scoop neck minidress shows an even bigger ring around her waist, a wet spot that almost intersects the cutout hole.

Molly stays silent during the long ride down the freight elevator. The office appears empty, and the van is parked at the loading dock with its back door open. Molly, stark naked, scrambles for the cover of its inside. Steph, turning around to look around the loading dock, follows, and she delivers an upskirt to a curious security cam as she unthinkingly climbs inside. But it's not a vagflash, because Steph now wears panties over her snooch.

The van door closes behind them. The Roommates feel the motor start and adjust their bodies on the grimy metal floor as the van bumps into motion.

§ Molly & Steph: Roommate Competition | Cooperation

The van travels along a new route. Steph again sits on the metal floor, except with panties worn through her crotch. And Molly sits totally naked, legs also apart. More apart than during the Figure Drawing class.

Molly might be most naked, but Steph complains first. "I hate it when Gamers get to look for free," she contemplates, "or get to download my titter and vagflash shots without shelling out for them."

"You resent being conditioned so that your titter and upskirt exposures arouses you," Molly consoles. "And that now Babs determines your pace of arousal..."

A series of bumps make Molly's mams flop around.

Steph waggles her finger at Molly. "Listen, you fat hairy maduro. We might both be Cosmos Pledge at the moment, but don't you think we're equals! Because flashing my smoo is less exposed than showing off your slimy mutton all the time. And now that I have panties, I'm not even flashing my smoo anymore. Besides," Steph threatens the former Stripper, "I know that you already know how to open up that meatlocker of yours, bury your finger, dig out your muscovado, and eat yourself."

Molly shrugs, unable to argue with a true statement. "Yeah. Well. Okay Steph, I'll do whatever you want, Steph, anything to ensure your promotion."

"And your demise!" Steph snaps, as the van crosses railroad tracks and the bumps bruise both behinds.

Molly curts her head. "Sure. Yes. Just let me stay naked now."

Steph collects the given authority. "I've seen you perform. I've seen your videos. I've watched you play with yourself. C'mon, you mollisher, chant for me!"

And Molly obliges, "Please let me pullaside, pink, and finger my holes. Titty titty. Clitty clitty. Hole mouth."

Steph pokes a finger toward Molly. "You are a displaced undesirable. You've accidentally risen from the bowels of the Game, and await...." *Await what?* Steph knows. "Await a 'return to sender.' So do it. Beg to Pledge naked and go Strip next Term!"

Molly clasps her hands to her head and begs her Roommate, "I'm trying, Steph! I kept begging Babs to let me give you my panties. And now you got them."

Steph blinks. She appreciates that she wears Molly's panties. She casts her eyes around the inside of the van. No Watering Can.

Molly insists, "Steph, I don't need panties to go back to the Nugget; I can go back naked. Please keep them. It doesn't matter to me whether you keep them or give them back to me."

"It should matter to you that it matters to me," Steph asserts. "I need them to Opt Monitor next Term."

Molly nods her head and continues to beg. "Steph, I know all the Hand Signs, and if you want to sign me to pink, cream, and diddle my mooe I will obey you. For anybody anywhere anytime."

Steph finds Molly's over-assertions annoying but comforting. "Maybe Boss Bitch doesn't know all the Hand Signs you do. You're a lot more down and dirty than she is. You're practiced in all the Stripper lore. You probably know the Sign to pull your mooe apart."

Molly veers, "Maybe revealing intimate secrets hidden deep in my minge will really intimidate the newbies. I mean, I'll make pink, wet, and ready anytime."

Steph snaps her eyes to the side. She doesn't speak, but she wonders to herself, *Might Molly have ink or steel inside? She was a Stripper after all. Her and Kimju both.*

Molly persists, "Listen, Steph, I've danced on the Strip. I've been there, done that, and I presume I will get to go back next Term. One piece or naked. I'll do whatever it takes to get there."

Steph closes her eyes.

Molly considers, then continues to plead to her Roommate, "I know you want a promotion and a return to Monitor status. Whether you deserve it or not."

Molly's conditional rankles Steph, but Steph doesn't let it show. "You will enable me," Steph explains, "to Monitor again, where my vibrancy and glamour shall be even more valued. You will do whatever I need you to do. And that may extend beyond just giving me panties."

"I'll do anything not against the Rules, Steph. Just please keep the panties." Molly fears, "I don't need germs."

§ Molly & Steph: The Medical Exam

Molly and Steph finally feel the van come to a halt. Daylight streams as their anonymous driver opens the van door and shepherds the two Roommates out onto the gravel and broken asphalt of an industrial park parking lot. Molly clenches her mams in her arms; she fears the consequences of streaking, even if it is only from the van to a doorway across the parking lot.

She takes a step, and her foot hurts. The sharp stones also hurt Steph's bare feet, but with her minidress (and panties) Steph has the luxury of placing her feet carefully and taking her time.

Molly does not. Okay, maybe running from the Bell to the back alley earlier today doesn't count. The loading dock earlier wasn't very far. This is longer... and far more exposed. She casts her eyes about for danger.

Molly clenches her mammaries in her arms and heavy-foots her way toward the door. Molly tries to be as inconspicuous as possible, but Molly knows unequivocally, *This is a streak. Even if I move slowly.*

Molly doesn't set any long-distance streaking records here, but she acquires practice. Molly fears streaking. *You get caught streaking by certain Gamers, and there is a good chance you might not be returned to your House. The streaker who gets caught and is lucky ends up dipped in molasses, rolled in feathers, and left chained around the flagpole on the*

Quad, to be discovered the next day. The unfortunate streaker ends up in Jail.

Okay.

A surveillance Cam outside has alerted the inside to the Roommates' pending arrival, and they are greeted inside a small lobby by a Nurse wearing a white rubber dress with a red cross and red trim, white rubber hose, red boots, and white rubber gloves.

Nurse says, "Which of you is here for the Medical Examination? Something about germs?"

Steph defers to Molly. "Sounds like you're the one."

Only this time Molly responds, "Wait a minute, I'm not wearing damp panties anymore."

Nurse is not interested in excuses. She tilts her head toward a door to the Medical Room, which has an examination chair in the middle. Nurse orders Molly, "Sit, feet up and in the stirrups, and let's get you spread wide."

Molly moves slowly but settles in: naked, mammaries hanging to each side, feet fully spread, minge no longer hiding her insides. Molly appraises that she is not only bathed in flat medical light but embraced by multiple Cams as well. *No secrets here!* Molly's eyes look at the ceiling. *Is Steph keeping an eye on me?*

"Open!" Nurse instructs, and Molly finds an oral spreader presented to her mouth and clicked wide. No more closing the mouth. "Hold still!" And Molly's body tightens as she feels the end of a greased speculum penetrate her muliebre, descend into her womb, rotate, and spread her wide, wider, until the deep brown vagina opens widest. Big gape.

"One more," Nurse declares, and Molly feels a long, thick anoscope penetrate her mawk port. The probe keeps traveling and traveling until Molly draws her body tight, and when she relaxes it travels more, then settles to a stop.

"Time to record some measurements," Nurse briefs her patient.

Molly has her hands free, so she could free herself of all devices, but she knows not to. She feels a prick and knows that her blood just got typed. Nurse efficaciously records all the settings, and a hovering Cam dutifully collects views down her throat and inside her lit vagina.

Steph watches Molly's face out of the corner of her eye. She can see in Molly's expression the pent-up desire to worry out loud; difficult with the spreader holding her mouth open. Steph curls a lip. *Who cares what Molly wants?*

"Does she get to pee in a cup?" Steph inquires of the Nurse.

Nurse laughs off this idea. "More likely she'll beg for a cath!"

Molly gurgles, forgetting for a moment that the oral spreader keeps her mouth held wide. She sighs and closes her eyes. *Can't beg right now.*

Nurse dutifully pronounces, "You're healthy!" She quickly relieves Molly of all the stainless and gestures her naked body out of the chair.

Molly stands, expecting Steph to follow her in the chair, but that doesn't happen. *No problem. It isn't necessary to be fair and balanced.*

Nurse points to the door and utters a single word: "Van."

And Molly finds herself streaking again. She doesn't know that the Cam watches her depart safely.

§ Molly & Steph: The Ride Back to the Cosmos House

During the ride naked Molly doesn't ask for the panties back and Steph doesn't offer them. The Watering Can, no longer with them, remains unmentioned.

Steph calculates, *I didn't take the panties from Molly. The Drawing Class Matron ordered her to give them to me. And afterwards nobody told me to give them back. Seems like I got my two Garments and my way to Opt Up!*

When the van drops them off at the back alley anonymous hands once again open the door to let them out and drive the van away. Naked Molly hurries through the Backyard; she gets to the Bell first and gives the clapper a jerk, waking up the Back Door Cam.

Steph refuses to run. She strolls briskly, casting a furtive look left and right in search of paparazzi. She worries, *They don't necessarily know I've acquired panties.*

Steph draws herself up next to the waiting Molly and pulls the clapper herself. The twosome look at each other, and Molly looks down at her naked body and bare feet. Steph crosses her arms. They wait together in silence, one of them with the two Garments needed to Opt Up and Monitor, and the other vectored to Opt Down and Strip.

After a while Molly sits down on the Landing, but Steph continues to stand. She is determined, *No titter and no upskirt for this Cam. Even if I am wearing panties.*

A hand extends out the Back Door and beckons Steph inside. Steph licks her lips and gives Molly a look just before the last of her vanishes inside the Back Door. "Masturbate, you fat muffin," she orders. "Finger-fuck your musky manhole. But *no* cumming! Obey me."

And so Molly curls up, with her naked body nestled into a corner against the railing, and makes herself "comfortable." She parts her muff to the sides, peels lips back, and is about to ready a fingertip when she remembers the Watering Can. The Cam watching her sees her body jerk but it can't read her mind. *The Watering Can! My Watering Can? I know the Watering Can didn't get back into the van with us when we left the*

Figure Drawing Class. It must have gotten misplaced after I gave my panties to Steph.

The Cam registers Molly furrow her brow and draw her eyes together. *Maybe I'm not responsible. At least not totally responsible. Besides, I don't need the Watering Can anymore; I have no panties to wet. I'm naked now.*

Molly works a finger deep into her mooe and swivels it around. The memory of the speculum seems retained in her nerve cells. Molly relaxes, feels her muscovado gush, leans back, and pleasures herself. Steady flow, but Molly doesn't cum. *I guess I'll pretty much do whatever it takes to stay naked from now on. And if Steph wants to save up my climax, it's hers.*

15 Molly & Steph: The Bachelor Party (D09)

§ Babs Tells Molly & Steph: Entertain a Bachelor Party

Then there is the Bachelor Party.

Day Nine begins with Tiffany making up Babs like a queen in their shared Bedroom. Tiffany knows that Kimju and Molly and Steph all need to be turned into Cleopatra's finest Strippers.

Steph, who sacrificed her minidress last night for a trade-in this morning but still retains what were Molly's panties, uses the Bathroom while Tiffany finishes Babs next door. *Tiffany knows better than to enter the Bathroom before I'm showered and dressed,* Steph affirms to herself.

Tiffany comes in anyway, and with her license to enliven the Cam.

Steph, wearing only her panties, crisscrosses her hands over her breasts and carefully sits on a stool facing the makeup table mirror: handbra and panties, legs apart. *Talk about trade offs. Maybe I don't get my shag cammed, but for my handbra I am topless. If I complain to Babs about toplessness, then tomorrow she'll take my dress and panties away, and Tiffany will make me up nude. And always with my legs apart.*

Steph fumes as Tiffany tips her makeup slightly toward that of a Whore. *Boss Bitch hopes that the Bathroom Cam collects me totally topless. What I hope is that her bazoombas spill out.*

Kimju, always topless and wearing only her tanga, discovers herself with the face of a clown: circles around her eyes, a wide red mouth, and a bright red nose. Once again Kimju's knobs are brightly colored, only today concentric circles circumnavigate both knocks, both sides of her kabedis, and around her belly button. Kimju feels humiliated by the treatment, and it doesn't help when Tiffany gently tugs on her thong and observes, "You've spotted yourself."

Molly, still naked following the donation of her panties to Steph at the Figure Drawing Class yesterday, doesn't get to shower today, and the crust in her thick pubic hair documents yesterday's evening of meringuing on the Back Door Landing. For Molly, Tiffany's makeup, applied overtop the crust, only accentuates a Whorish look. Molly takes it. *At least I don't have wet panties anymore!*

Once again Boss Babe summons her Cosmos to a morning Reveille in the Bunkroom. "Lineup. Face the Mirror. Stand spread surrender."

Steph hustles to Babs' Bedroom before Tiffany seizes upon any opportunity to pee on her. She acquires today's cutout minidress and finds time to steady herself. She studies herself in the Mirror. Today's delight is a slippery-strapped minidress with spaghetti string straps, a big belly hole with loose fabric around it to give it some swing, and of course adequately short.

Steph secretly gloats as she stands in the Lineup. *Big surprise for the Bathroom Cam: Gamers thought they were gonna collect my tits and vag while Tiffany made me up. Wrong. Maybe I always sit with my thighs apart, but I'm wearing what were once Molly's panties under my minidress!*

Now, as Steph stands in the Lineup and examines herself in the Mirror, she makes a small shimmy. *Yes, this minidress will titter, and yes, if I shimmy wrong Gamers can look down my buttonhole and get to see my panties there! Don't worry, Gamers; I'm gonna shimmy right!* Now that her spuds hide inside the minidress, Steph tests that she can cup her armpits and suspects that no matter how high she might try to reach her navel will always remain in its buttonhole.

Steph examines Molly, reflected in the Mirror next to her. Molly, naked because naked defines Molly's steady state, still has all of her full body hair: head, puffy underarms, pubes, legs. Steph observes dust and dirt accumulated in Molly's body hair, as well as water-spots and the vaginal crust. Steph curls her nose. *This hairy, mud-humping, cum-moll Roommate of mine hasn't bathed since she arrived three days ago. She stinks!*

Steph also stinks, only it is from the cheap perfume that Tiffany sprayed all over her neck, arms, and inner thighs.

Tiffany, by design or convenience, positions herself in the Lineup wearing only her hanging-waistline stretch slacks, hairage and rugage of course, and holds her hands behind her head while topless. Topless tanga defines Kimju's state of dress. She also stinks of cheap perfume.

Robyn appears exempt from Reveille, so takes the opportunity to use the Bathroom and cleanse herself absent Tiffany's Cam. Besides applying the most glamorous makeup to her face, touching up her finger and toenails, and brushing any kinks from her long blonde hair, Robyn again affords herself the opportunity to shave her armpits and legs. She gloats at her recent addition of shoulder straps to her maillot cutout.

Boss Babe appears unfazed by the three pairs of breasts, two pairs of bare buttocks, and one full bush that confronts her in the Lineup. She once again addresses Roommates Molly and Steph, "Your Drawing Class and Medical Exams were so successful that you two have been selected to entertain at a Bachelor Party!"

Molly tilts her eyeballs toward BB and holds her position, indifferent to her own nakedness. Steph shuffles her bare feet, and a bead of sweat forms in one armpit.

"Some poor Groom is about to get married," BB pines.

Molly listens more carefully than Steph to BB's description of the destination and a possible route. It's a hike. "No van today! You Cosmos must walk!"

That's no problem for Steph. Steph's panties, under her minidress, have long since dried out since she acquired them at the Figure Drawing Class yesterday, and although Steph remains forbidden to touch her thighs together, she does understand physics. *Maybe my new panties can't stop the upskirt, but they do prevent vagflash!* Steph twitches her nose. *Now I'm just like I was last Term!*

Steph also assesses today's looser minidress with its narrow shoulder straps. *Control is power. This enables me to lean over and titter, but it does not compel me to do so. Unlike some of my earlier minidresses, where I couldn't control access at all.* Steph tests making a face in the Mirror while Babs looks in a different direction. *It's a good thing that Babs and the Gamers realize I need to have a choice to titter or not. Especially now that my snatch is no longer showing when I sit down.*

Steph wonders how her naked and hairy Roommate is going to make it to their destination. She can see in the Mirror that Molly focuses on BB. *Not my problem.*

"Any questions?" Babs invites.

Steph thinks about what she might ask, but Molly rushes first, "I have to make a run for it? You're gonna make me streak?"

"You do have to make a run for it," Babs affirms, addressing the question as if it has been a sentence. "But only *you* can commit to streak. I can't make you."

Molly resists an urge to move her hands from behind her head and draw her legs together. *I feel my mams flop. I can feel air between my opened thighs.*

Steph observes Molly in the Mirror and tightens her face down the middle, pulling the skin center forward, unaware that she forms the expression. *If Molly has to streak to get to this Party, then who knows just what will be expected of her once we arrive?*

Steph's panties might be dry underneath the miniskirt, but now, down inside her panties, her stamen erects amidst a field of thin blonde hair. And now, for a reason quite different than the Watering Can, a spot in the panties become damp.

"Move it! Now!" Boss Babe commands, and they both scramble downstairs and shoot out the Back Door. Steph gathers her wits, pulls the Bell with confidence, swivels and follows the sidewalk around to the front of the House so she can stroll down the streets. And why not? *I'm perfectly decent. I'm in control.*

Naked Molly hesitates as she steps down from the Back Landing and feels the concrete, grass, and dirt on her feet. She pulls the Bell but not loudly, just enough so the BB and the Cams can hear it, and roughs out her route.

§ Molly: Streaks to the Bachelor Party

This will not be easy, Molly says to herself as she pads her way across the Backyard. She avoids the Mudpit and threads her way through the Post Henge. *I've already given my panties to Steph. But if streaking is what Gamers want from me then I'll either get to the Party or I'll get fucked in the process. And I will beg to Pledge naked and cum be a Stripper next Term. First chance I get.*

Molly pauses at the edge of the alley. She knows. *Once I step into the alley I'm no longer just naked in the Backyard.*

Molly glances up and down the alley, shudders, and acknowledges, *I have to seriously streak now. This is not like walking across a loading dock at the Figure Drawing Class or hobbling from the van across an industrial parking lot to and from my so-called Medical Exam. This is a long run. I am out here without anyone to help.*

Molly steps carefully forward, moves along one side of alley, and quickly discovers herself bruising her feet. "Ouch!"

She controls her utterances; she finds she must move carefully. She chooses grass and sidewalks for ease on her feet in exchange for concealment. Unless she must move and gain cover quickly, in which case bruising her feet is her only option.

A car crosses ahead of her, and Molly forces her naked body into the bushes. Scratchy mamazulons, briars in the muff, and thorns marking her rearward-facing Hottentot mounds of flesh.

Molly considers the bright sunlight and full shadows. *I pulled my mooe wide open and masturbated on a beach in bright sunlight last Term. For a video shoot.* She shrivels. *But streaking is different. I'm outside by myself, naked, unauthorized, and no crew. If I get caught I won't be masturbating myself to climax; I'll be gang-banged. Strapons, cocks, fucking machines.*

Molly keeps moving, even if it is hard on the feet. She picks out steps carefully. *I wonder if paparazzi have been clued in and stalk me.* She darts through a park, moving quickly, but observes nothing suspicious. She runs across the gravel along the edge of a small parking lot when two guys in a truck, turning in with a delivery, spot her, and she must crawl under a chain link fence to escape.

I can't take any chances. Molly checks her swinging milk sacks and hanging belly and confirms that they are getting scratched up by now. *Streaker getting spotted doesn't necessarily mean streaker getting caught, but streaker caught means streaker jailed. And Jail is a place for violation.*

Molly assesses her situation as she darts and runs in fits and starts. *I have to assume Gamers have my movement under control,* Molly breathes to herself, *because I am way over-extended out here right now. The Cosmos House and the Party and are my only safe havens, and I'm somewhere in between them.*

If I wanted to escape there would be no place to run to.

Molly gets down on her belly to crawl in the dirt under a hedge. The dirt streaks down her body and feels like worms. *I sure hope Babs knows what she's doing, forcing me to volunteer to streak. Because I was taught long ago that "Babs ordered me" is no defense. I'm the one who put myself here. I "volunteered" to streak, so I'm the one who invites a capture. It's not like I was kidnapped and freed naked on a country road somewhere after my ransom got paid.*

Molly clenches her majonkers in one hand, keeps her head down, and runs the length of a hedge. Once again she fits herself into the hedge so she can see out. She discovers that she is closer to her goal than she realized.

My last bit of streak, but the most dangerous. Molly brushes thorns off her gluteus maximus. *Yes, I know about streakers who have made it. Like Penny and Coco, who made it to the Nugget. And Ginny and Lee streaked... although I don't really know if they made it at all. But to each her own. I saw a streaker captive, handcuffed to the flagpole, get fed their handcuff key and await its return so they could unlock themselves and return to their House.*

Molly's hairy arms and legs reduce the scratchiness of the hedge she hides inside. Still, she shivers, and once again she confirms the number on the building across the street. There is a sign on the front with the name of a restaurant, but the neon is off and the windows are curtained. Cars have been parked behind. Molly distinguishes the side door to the building, halfway between the front and the parking lot. "Through that door is my destination," she affirms.

Molly considers her own body and the final dash, a traverse of high risk. *Gamers know when I left, and they know I have to pass through this space before I can pass through that door. Once I pass through the door I am no longer streaking. And I'll be safe.*

Getting caught streaking isn't as severe as trying to escape, but it's not a scene I wish to step into!

Molly discovers that her nipples have erected. *My mammae, my minarets,* she inventories. *And could it just be the cold air?* She watches the building for signs of movement. She observes the arrival of whom she suspects to be the Groom and Best Man. Patience has virtues.

Molly tries to rub dirt off her chest with her hands; she brushes her melons and combs her hair with her fingers. *I don't know how long I can go without a shower. But if I sneak a shower Babs and Gamers will know instantly.* Molly closes her eyes for a long second. *Why oh why do I keep doing this?* Then she ponders, *Doing what? Jeopardizing my health? Or playing the Game? OK, so what's not to love about dancing nude in the Nugget? I love the guys looking at me. I like feeling their hardons during a lapdance. Letting them smell my muscovado. I can shower and eat as much as I want. I'm free, and anyone is free to watch me. Life couldn't be better. But being dirty and naked outside like this? In order to get back to that?*

Molly drops down onto her knees to rest for the final sprint. She maps out a pathway. On an impulse she touches her mooe and draws her finger to her nose. *I'm wet already.* She touches herself again and worms her finger until she hits her g-spot and salves her maraschino. *Gotta love the Game!*

Perhaps being outside nude is even more revealing, more exhilarating, than being naked inside the Nugget. *What if streaking gets into one's blood?* No maybes; Molly launches herself into the final, lumbering dash.

§ Steph Meets William: On Her Way to the Bachelor Party

Steph takes a less-than-direct way to the Bachelor Party, a little reconnaissance to see what might be happening this Term. On the way she intersects someone she already knows, William, a fellow Monitor last Term, today wearing a t-shirt and pants. They make eyes; Steph lets a strap slide off her shoulder, puts it back, and leans forward just enough to give William a titter as they converse. She still wears panties.

"I'm a Hover and still the Monitor of the Peacock House," William offers, pretending to ignore Steph's revelation. "And we all know how you've ended up."

Steph frowns.

William cants, "What's it like having a Stripper for a Roommate?"

Steph throws bare shoulders back. "Well, I've already taken her panties away. And today? Molly's streaking fully nude!"

William lifts a chin. "Not to be redundant, but isn't all streaking fully nude?"

Steph honors William, and they laugh together at Molly's commitment to risk.

"Fact is," Steph observes, "Molly's been naked every time she's been outside the Cosmos House since she arrived. Today's her longest streak so far. She thinks she signed up for a topless parade."

They laugh again, and Steph plays another titter. No mercy for men.

William expresses curiosity. "I saw Molly's shots from her Medical Exam. They got posted almost instantly, especially the shots where everyone can see her deep purple insides held open by the speculum. So are you the one playing her, or are Madam Nurse and BB making her spread her merrymaker wide open?"

Steph shakes her head and rolls her shoulders up. "I keep Molly totally naked. 24x7. No showers. Although so far Tiffany's hasn't barged in to light the Cam up when Molly wants to make toilet."

"Can't wait," William drolls.

"Hey, don't be facetious," Steph snorts. "The entire Prefecture watched this Nurse spread Molly's vag wide open and measure her manhole."

"Maybe she'll be the first Cosmos to provide climax," William predicts. "Won't be the last."

Steph provides silence.

"I've seen some clips and shots of you, too," William slips in a word.

Steph squares her body upright. "If you say so." She adds, "You're lucky you'll able to see me in the flesh right now."

William nods.

"Let's get together and hook up sometime," one of them suggests.

"Okay," says the other, and they split.

§ Molly: The First Cosmos Masturbates to Climax

Molly flies through the side door of the restaurant into a party room. A party room on the backside of a restaurant that appears closed for the evening.

The partygoers, already boisterous, instantly quiet when an already naked Molly barges into the room. Then cheering erupts. A small dais materializes, music suddenly plays, and Molly finds herself dancing on the small round platform. The Groom, Best Man, and other Revelers clap.

Nude a go-go? Molly asks herself, then affirms, *I can do it! Think I'm fat? You're gonna love me fat.*

Steph slips in via the same entrance but garners little attention away from naked frug dancer flopping mazoomas. Steph postures as if she is a Monitor responsible for protecting Molly from the creeps—not an unreasonable proposition given Molly's naked vulnerability.

At the end of a number Molly affords herself an opportunity to halo her Roommate with her just due. "This is my Roommate, Steph. I do whatever she wants. She wears my panties and commits to Opt Monitor next Term. And I'm a naked Pledge begging to Opt Strip."

Steph fiddles both spaghetti shoulder straps into place, shakes so the minidress falls clearly around her open cutout hole, and bows sufficently shallowly that no titter occurs. She raises her chin. "It will please Molly to pull her mutton wide open, freshen up some mung, and mambo in front of you until she runs out of breath!"

The produces applause, but it also causes some Revelers to study Steph with more attention.

Steph retreats into a position with her back to a wall and finds herself offered a stool. She moves it behind her, leans back against it, and finds herself helped to sit upon it. She smiles, adjusts her legs to make sure that her thighs don't touch, and lets everyone at the Party consider her panties upskirt. Cam them. *I hate this, but I don't dare close my legs.*

Molly rescues her Roommate; she squats, spreads her legs wide, pans her muff left and right to the Revelers, and nods to as many Cams as she can. Molly works her fingers deep into her thick minge until she is able to roll her thick lips to two sides and open her mooe wide to reveal her maraschino budding out at the top. "Don't let Steph steal the show upskirting her panties," Molly declares. "Look here, and you can see all the way into my power magazine."

Indeed Molly's inner lips and canal are brown inside. With a patch of purple way down deep inside. The crowd hushes. Molly can see that many Cams have come out. "Go ahead, all of you," she proclaims shamelessly. "I'll hold my mooe open until you're tired taking shots."

And then Molly fingers the sparkling, stainless steel ring through her clithood and teases it into clear view. She says easily, "This was one of my rewards for becoming a Stripper last Term. It hurt a lot, but I've learned to love it."

Steph gives the clithood ring a double take. She blinks. *Well, yes, Strippers do get pierced, and well, yes, Molly was a Stripper last Term.* Steph feels increasingly uncomfortable with the balance of power and wonders again if Molly might also harbor a hidden tattoo.

But there's no stopping Molly. "I love the way my ring rubs against my maraschino and keeps it engorged. Like now. And when I pull open my merrymaker I get excited and my muscovado flows out. Like now."

Applause builds. Steph knows Molly speaks truth. Not only does the white cream flow out between Molly's legs, but Steph can smell it. The whole room catches the scent; no stopping it, no looking away. Primal evidence.

Molly masturbates harder. White magma sloshes and spills, and Molly smears it onto her breasts and face. The whole room seems to swell larger.

And then she climaxes: a noisy, wild, willful abandonment to the pleasures of Kundalini! Steph appreciates that the mambo looks real. It *is* real, and the Groom, Best Man, and other Revelers applaud and appreciate Molly's intimate sharing of total sexual surrender.

And so Molly becomes the first Cosmos to cross a fine line and cum for Gamer fans.

Molly stands and takes a blow. "Thank you!" she pants out of breath, leaning forward and swinging her heavy mamazulons about. "Thank you for letting me share cumming with you!" Molly appreciates their applause and tastes herself for a laugh. "It's very simple really," she admits. "I've been a Stripper before; I've done it all. I'll stay naked. I just wanna be a Stripper again next Term."

§ Molly: Begs a Pee-Cam & Acquires a Piss Mouth

As the applause fades Steph interjects, "Any time a bunch of guys or gals need a naked dancer to show off how a gal cums, just order Molly!"

This time the laughter turns dirty; too many in the room share affection for Molly and resent Steph's lack of civility.

Steph, disgusted at Molly's lewd dancing, ups the ante. "Get on your hands and knees, your hairy moll. Stick your gluteus really maximus up in the air and show everybody your furry mawk portal."

The Revelers hush, and Molly obeys. She pivots her body and pulls her mounds of flesh to each side so that every single Reveler at the Party gets a full and unobstructed view of her hairy asshole.

A quieter appreciation ripples through the room, and Steph wrinkles her nose, yet at the same time feels dominant. She raises again, "Maybe Molly would like to pee in a glass for you."

There is a collective "Oooh" in the room. Then scattered applause from the Revelers. And then a hush.

Molly, back on her feet now, cups her mammies in her hands, bows, and makes a professional, respectful request. "Please let me be on the Pee-Cam." Applause. Molly wonders if she has just signed up to join Tiffany. She knows that many Cams have been rolling since her arrival, and they most certainly document her commitment. She looks toward Steph, makes eye contact, and encounters the hardened face of Steph Sorostitute.

Still, Molly knows she owns the dais; she climbs onto the bar top, collects a stein glass, squats, and announces, "I'll pour a draft for you!"

A steady clapping starts once she establishes a yellow flow, which builds throughout the many seconds of stream, then turns to silence as the flow reduces to a dribble. Stops. A huge roar of applause. Molly grins and raises the filled stein.

Steph brazens a claim: "Maybe now Molly just qualified to Pee-Cam!"

Applause endorses Steph's assertion, and Steph, irritated that Molly commands all the attention, escalates, "You are such a pink wet and ready wannabe Whore. You got sent here by mistake. You should be getting three-hole fucked at Flesh Ranch. Splattered."

This hurts. "Jeez, Steph," Molly begs, "You know I'll stay naked and play with myself for you anyplace anywhere anytime. I masturbated myself on the Landing outside the Back Door, just like you told me to. I just creamed and came for you. For everybody here. And beyond. And I peed, too."

Molly adjusts her position to her knees and sets the stein between her spread knees on the bar top. A ripple of appreciation flows in her direction. Molly eyes the Groom, Best Man, and Revelers and says, "I did not get sent to the Cosmos House by mistake. And I am not a wannabe Whore." Molly drifts her eyes to Steph. "I might be a wannbe Stripper next Term, but nobody has flashed titter and vag more than you."

Heads turn to watch Steph takes offense. "You should beg dirty panties in your mouth for saying something like that. Robyn's got you pegged; you are a mumping mandragorite."

A murmur ripples through the assembled. An evil uncertainty. Indeed, has not Boss Babe provided two Cosmos to play and perform? Roommates! Stress Test!

Molly senses the bar top is no longer necessarily a power spot, but she has nowhere to go.

Indeed, the power of the stage has flowed out from her. Out from Steph, wearing her spaghetti strapped cutout minidress and upskirting panties underneath.

Yes. The Groom, Best Man, and all the other Revelers know where some panties are! Pandemonium erupts.

The Best Man is the first to cry out to Steph, "Off!"

Molly knows she is helpless to intercede, and Steph knows she is surrounded.

"Off! Off! Off!" the Revelers chant in unison, building their determination. Steph processes quickly, watches a kneeling Molly stir uncomfortably. She draws air in through tilted nostrils. Almost a snort. A first tinge of fear, uncertainty, strikes her. *I'm trapped. I've been set up. Double crossed. Now is not the time to argue.*

Steph lifts her hands to gain the forum to speak. She slides off the stool, pretty much showcasing all of her panties in the process. The Revelers quiet, wondering what will follow.

Steph Sorostitute smoothes her cutout minidress. Makes sure it does cover her panties. She carefully reaches under her minidress, hooks her thumbs in the waistband of the panties beneath, then rolls them down and relinquishes a pause to the many Cams in the crowd for a picture holding the panties apart with her thighs, somewhere below the lower hem of the dress and her knees. And then out of the freeze position, down to the ankles, and stepped out of, one bare foot at a time.

The Revelers hoot and politely applaud, and Steph does a great job making sure none of the flash cameras or vids catch her scruff. But she realizes as she straightens up that she has delighted all those present (and their Cams) with a full titter down the front of her loosely fitting minidress. *Perverts!* Steph thinks to herself. *Not fair trapping me like this.* Steph scowls as she holds her warm and worn panties in hand and shimmies to shawabble both spaghetti shoulder straps toward her neck and away from falling off her shoulders.

The Revelers hush. Again Steph smoothes her minidress, showcasing her bellage and button. She takes a step forward, and the throng parts. She extends the panties away from her body, and, as if they are a magic wand, a path parts in front of her.

Quiet applause becomes polite as Revelers understand. Steph walks to the bar, where Molly kneels with a stein of her piss in front of her. And stops. *Wait. I do not want to give panties away.* Steph turns to her left. She turns to her right. Revelers crowd around behind her. She can feel them now. *This is not about one or two Garments. This is about whether I am going to carry out my threat.*

Steph holds the panties directly about the stein and lets go. "You want a Stress Test? Try this one, you fat flesh moll! Borrow these in your mouth for a while."

The Revelers stir. They are not at all sure they agree this is a fun Game.

Steph lifts a chin, pivots, and returns to her position in front of the stool. Perfect makeup; striking navelage. No more titter.

The room quiets. The panties float in the stein and sink as they soak up the urine. There emits a soft murmuring and "oooooh" sounds from the chests of the Revelers. But there is also an "uuuggh" growl in the room. The Revelers don't entirely approve of Steph's treatment of Molly, but despite any disgust and disapproval, their curiosity perks.

An uneasy hush falls over the Party.

Molly wishes someone would put a big ugly hickey on Steph's neck but closes her mouth. In one sweeping movement she dips her fingers into the stein, pinches the panties, and swoops them out, cascading a yellow spray across the room that peppers Steph, starting at the bottom of her white minidress and, as Molly's hand rises, up past her neck, across her face and hair, and up to the ceiling. Big yellow splotches. Ouch!

The eyes in the room track the hits but pan to Molly's face in unison as she gathers the waistband in her teeth. And then, with the panties streaming yellow onto her saggy mammies and down to her muff, Molly slowly stuffs the soaked panties into her mouth until they push her cheeks out. Chipmunk cheeks and rising applause. Does she have tears in her eyes? The Revelers appreciate that this is no easy feat and applaud wildly.

Molly bows at the top of the applause, squeezes the panties to compact them in her mouth, pushes them forward with her tongue against the back of her teeth, and discharges a stream of urine out of her mouth that sends the Groom and Best Man hot-footing it out of the way as the piss splatters onto the floor, amidst much merriment and sustained applause.

Steph scowls.

And a new rhythm picks up; the Revelers chant, "Kiss! Kiss! Kiss!"

Steph blocks this. But it isn't her.

Molly understands. She sees the dawn in the Groom's eyes, extracts her panties, wraps her arms around the Groom, and kisses him on the mouth. The Groom kisses back, and the kiss swells Molly with pride. She kisses the Best Man on the cheek, garnering more approval and new fans.

Molly sees in the Groom's eyes that he has regained his senses and has discovered that the taste of piss on his palette does not wash out easily. Molly offers a welcoming smile.

"I've tasted pee before. And pee is sterile. You'll live!" she adds, and the room laughs.

"Me Pee-Camer Piss Mouth now," Molly declares to a room slightly out of control. She cringes as she steps into the panties. *Mistake?*

Molly trade eyes with Steph and says to her, "I'll wear these panties back to the Cosmos House for you!" *And I won't be streaking anymore.* Molly makes a little wave and bolts out the door. Gone.

Molly hears howls and applause behind her as the door closes. She orients. Feels panties wet with her own urine. She pushes her lower teeth forward and bites her upper lip. *Gamers gonna wring me out before they let me go back to the Nugget, but at least right now I'm not streaking anymore. And that may be my first lucky break this Term. I can give the panties back to Steph at the Bell.*

And sure, Boss Babe will force me to beg more Pee-Cam. No problem.

Perhaps Molly will even get to beg Piss Mouth.

§ Steph: Exits the Bachelor Party

Steph, suddenly abandoned at the Bachelor Party, finds the full attention of the Revelers upon her. She folds her palms forward to the sides of her hips and declares, "That hairy maduro splattered piss on my bare feet!"

The guests laugh uneasily. The Revelers are well aware that Steph has been splattered with piss, and they don't care to make an issue out of the insult.

"And she ruined my dress!" She looks up and juts her chin out. "But I don't have to worry, because BB gives me a new minidress every single day."

Well so far, anyway. Different cutout minidresses; different titters and upskirts. Something for Revelers to seek out from the Prefecture.

Steph struggles to regain control. "And you may rest assured that Molly will wash herself out of my panties before she gives them back to me."

There are murmurs of approval, and Steph finds herself surrounded and helped to again sit on the round bar stool. She opens her thighs as per orders handed down via BB and discovers the Revelers camming her natural parts. She manages to recover her composure only after discovering a shoulder strap has fallen down to her elbow, leaving one entire breast totally exposed. As she rescues her spud, she feels the hem of her minidress press between her stern and the barstool, and her entire uncovered crotch come into view.

"This is so inappropriate." Steph touches a palm to her face. *And my legs are open way too wide.* She laughs delicately. "I'm displaying my finer lines." She wiggles as she descends from the barstool.

"I am so sorry, but Molly and I must leave together!" Steph continues her announcement. "We're Roommates!"

Steph routes her escape, takes charge. She walks backwards toward the door. She bows briefly, another quick titter to much of the Party, and she smoothes the minidress, rounding her cutout around her buttonhole. She assesses her splattered minidress a second time and decides further complaints can only provide a reason to take it away from her.

Gamers look at her flowing legs and short hemline. Bare feet. Neck. Navel cutout. Steph stops and throws back her shoulders. She makes a shimmy, shows armpits, and the Revelers acquiesce. "We've really had a such *great* time, and Molly is *so* grateful, but I *must* go..." Steph falters off, makes a little wave, pivots, and flees out the door.

Steph runs to get out of sight should any fans follow her out the door, bruising her bare soles in the process. But then she slows down. *Maybe Molly's got some panties on and doesn't qualify to streak, but she still must move with stealth.* Steph walks back to the Cosmos House comfortably, even without panties.

But I am so disgusted! Steph realizes. *Disgusted at Molly for putting piss-soaked panties in her mouth and then fleeing out the door with them. I know it's so she needn't streak. As if I care. I just need the panties back. And Molly can retain a Piss Mouth.*

But I am also disgusted at whoever is behind all of this. The Groom and the Best Man? The Revelers inside? They're pond scum; they wouldn't know a Gamer if they met one. Maybe Boss Bitch put them up to this.

Steph got rattled inside, and some of it sticks with her. The trickle of fear about an increasingly unsettled future grips her chest for a second time this evening, and she pauses to look at her reflection in a store window.

Very hard to not conclude that I'm beautiful. Self-confidence returns to Steph. *Very hard to not conclude that I'm smart. I really am a favored one; it's the only thing that makes sense.*

And the practical. *If I must flash my shimmies and snizzle—and I certainly have been—it is because this device empowers me to control a situation. It enables me to gather fans while running an errand, or entice somebody to gossip who isn't supposed to... like William.*

Steph stays to streets where possibly normal people do double takes. She fumes. *But I resent having to baby-sit Molly. Getting splattered with piss. And getting my snatch cammed by amateur Bachelor Party types.*

Steph spots a paparazzo recording her and snarls at what just happens to be a female. *Another paparazzo seek to record my exposures! They all want my sand dollars and stalks, my snatch and strophoid, my semi-globes out back. I am the most popular Cosmos!*

The steeliness of Molly's clithood ring reminds Steph of the stakes, yet her confidence deepens. *I'll have to ask Molly if she gets pierced a second time when she Opts Down, or if her existing piercing gets stretched bigger.*

Steph pulls the Bell clapper by the Back Door Landing and waits; there is no Molly. She waits about 15 minutes before she resigns, sits on the steps of the Landing so her parted inner thighs lie in shadow, and tempts the Cam to harvest her upskirted sanpan. *Too dark for any details.*

Robyn bops out the back door. "You know Molly just can't wait to give you your panties back!" Robyn wiggles her fingers and signs Steph to spread her legs.

Steph doesn't know what to say, and she traverses her eyes from Robyn to the Cam surveilling her. *If I open my legs my smoo won't be hiding in shadows anymore.*

Robyn bemuses herself. "Take your time. But until you spread your legs just as wide as you can and beg the Back Door Cam to let you inside you'll be sitting here for a long time. And however much time you take, Boss Bitch is gonna take it, too." And Robyn disappears inside the Back Door.

Steph can tell that the Cam awaits her compliance. It doesn't take long. Steph relents and lets her minidress ride up to her hips as she spreads her thighs wide and displays her blonde shrubbery. She leans back and confronts the hovering Cam, as her vertical slit comes into view beneath her wavy blonde pubic hairs and her stamen rises. She clenches her jaw and resists touching herself. *I will not give Gamers who watch me any satisfaction. They drive me to manipulate myself. Show them my nice rosy pink inside. Or collect me slippery.*

Steph scowls and confronts the hovering Cam. "Ma'am, please let me in, Ma'am. I'm spreading for you."

§ Molly: Second Pee-Cam Volunteer But Must Wait

Tiffany and Kimju have spent the day admiring themselves in the Mirror; Tiffany relishes another opportunity to rub her body against the surface, this time topless, and for equally topless Kimju the Mirror provides a gripping experience. Both have creamed themselves long before Robyn rescues them and escorts them downstairs to join Babs and Molly to watch the Screen in the Kitchen as Steph begs the Back Door Cam, but it is Robyn who takes full credit for Steph's exposure. "This is not Steph's first display of her shrubbery, nor the first time her swizzle stick has stood out, nor the first time her snizz has parted. But it's about time she spilled her satchel slop for the Cams."

Kimju, Robyn's actual Roommate, watches carefully. *Robyn already made me finger my koot in the Kitchen and then smear kloop on the Post.*

Robyn escalates, "I'm going back outside to make that skuddy splurt skank grab her lips and pull her screwhole so far open we can see all the way—"

Babs shuts Robyn up. She points to Steph's Roommate Molly and issues the simple command, "Go. Fetch."

Molly had found herself in the dark outside after the Bachelor Party and had moved swiftly. The aftertaste of piss mingled with spit flooded her mouth, and once in the Backyard she had tried to use the hose to wash her mouth and panties out, but no water came out. *The one time I need the Watering Can it's missing.* Molly had shrugged, rung the Bell, and had been waved inside.

Molly brings Steph into the Kitchen, and all six Cosmos relax as they listen to her recounting of the Bachelor Party, verifying the story Molly had told upon her arrival. Steph makes sure to especially detail Molly peeing into the stein and squeezing her panties out in her mouth.

"The more urine I could squeeze out, the less there was to swallow!" Molly recounts as Cosmos' eyes swing in her direction. Everybody laughs except Steph. All the Cosmos can tell Molly has her panties back, but Molly understands she must mollify any pride of their reacquisition and divest them to Steph as soon as possible.

Steph conveniently omits recounting her own titter and vagflash at the end of the Bachelor Party. Molly had already left and wasn't a witness.

Steph vacillates between considering herself lucky to get out with her minidress still on her body vs. her ability to command a roomful of Revelers. *And yes, I am aware that I no longer possess the two pieces necessary to Opt Up. I'm not stupid.*

"I would say that Molly volunteered to be a Pee-Camer… and a Piss Mouth," Steph tattles, then turns to Tiffany. "So now you can micturate together!"

Molly accepts this accusation and trades a fearful look with the friendly ex-Whore whom she mopped up after yesterday, albeit using her long hair and not her mouth.

"Wait a minute." Molly fearfully scans the assembled Cosmos. "Okay, at the Nugget last Term all the toilets had Cams. All the showers too. Absolutely no privacy; no hidden spots." Molly seeks out Kimju's eyes. "Right?"

Kimju dodges, "Well, if Molly wants to carry on the Pee-Cam tradition here at the Cosmos House, is sure seems like she's qualified." *We both are.*

Molly offers to Steph, "I'll join in on the Pee-Cam if you take your panties back."

Tiffany objects, "Wait a minute! It is I who is the official Cosmos Pee-Cam Pledge!"

Babs raises a hand to intercede and addresses Molly. "If you choose to beg the Pee-Cam you may not attempt to impose conditions."

"Ma'am—" Molly attempts to orient.

"Quiet." Babs speaks firmly. "All of you. Upstairs. Bunkroom."

And five Cosmos Pledge scramble.

Molly is the last of them to ascend the angular servant stairs. Molly realizes that any sacrifice she makes—forfeiting panties, volunteering for the Pee-Cam, even begging the horrific Piss Mouth—is illusionary. *We Pledge might beg or volunteer, but some Gamers will always just take what they want.*

Molly fingers the waistband of the pink panties and worries. They still remain wet with her urine. *I can handle this; I know that urine is sterile and will dry quickly. But if Steph doesn't take these away soon, should I ask BB about the Watering Can?* Molly grits her teeth. *I generally believe that making suggestions contributes to staying even in the Game. But I know that there is no formula for "getting ahead."*

Beka & Elle are the Last Cosmos to Arrive

16 Beka & Elle: Newbies Arrive & Titter Robyn's Cam (D10)

§ Beka & Elle: Newbie Friends Arrive at the Cosmos House

The last two Cosmos to arrive, Beka and Elle, knew each other before they enrolled in School and pledged the Cosmos House. They are best friends, yet competitive, especially when attracting the attention of guys. They are similar in age, slightly different in build, and shall be Roommates this Term.

Gamers lust to know where they came from and how they found out about the School. Are they wayward gals, clubbers, or in it for the thrill? Yes; all of the above and more.

Why is it that they arrive after all the others? Today is Day Ten, so are they late? No, it has just come time for their arrival. Newbie spice into the Game.

The two newbies arrive at the Back Door wearing their own clothes—two Garments each—clothes they have actually worn in the real world. They fidget. Beka sports a sleeveless, open-armhole croptop and miniskirt; Elle arrives armed in a loose-fitting, front-button halter and ripped jeans shorts. Both show navelage, an obvious admission requirement. Despite their different outfits, both sport six tan lines.

They do not arrive totally ignorant. They have had to pass rigorous physical and mental examinations, submit detailed personal information and sometimes humiliating documentation, and have been interviewed and surveilled... often without their knowledge.

Beka and Elle have always decided where to go, what to wear, and how to show off their bodies. Both do very good jobs on their own makeup, and each optimizes her behavior as each see fit. Whatever past dynamic brought them here may well be revealed, if not warped, in the days ahead.

Newbies!

Beka and Elle laugh as they decide who shall first pull the clapper on the brass Bell.

"You do it," Beka cajoles Elle. But Elle hesitates.

"It's okay," Elle concedes. "This was your idea. We've come this far already."

Both newbies have. Both have studied the Game Rules before begging admittance to School, although Elle studied longer and harder. Both passed the entrance exam, and they both know their final step to beg admittance is to ring the Bell. And wait to be granted entry.

"This is a cinch, Elle," Beka says, embracing the situation. "We already got our two pieces comin' into the Game! We're gonna keep 'em and Opt Monitor next Term!"

Elle hesitates. "Well, I hope so. But it's important we stay together and make sure things don't get complicated."

Beka waves a hand. "Listen, if they didn't want to play with us they wouldn't have invited us, let alone let us pick our own clothes. We're like famous club kids."

Elle frowns.

Beka advances, "Elle, don't be a nigmenog. I'll ring the Bell first!"

"Hang on," Elle commands. "We'll ring the Bell together. We'll both grab the rope and pull twice."

And so they do.

§ Beka & Elle: Newbies Get Detailed

Beka and Elle don't presuppose and ergo don't detect a stealthy Back Door Cam feed their live presence into the Cosmos House... if not beyond. The Game attracts them with its promise of excitement, and it shall take a while for them to discover that the Game's excitement transcends anything they can imagine. Delivery matters.

The friends and emerging Roommates use the wait time to double check each other. Make sure they na-na and bedazzle. To whatever extent Elle studied harder, Beka influenced their makeup and costumes more. Although they both know how to put on the face, put on the salacious clothes, and put on the attitude.

Beka licks her lipstick, tosses long brunette hair over her shoulder, and looks at Elle with brown eyes. Eye color is one of the few attributes both newbies share. "I'm excited." Beka bounces on bare feet. "We're going to have a lot of fun!" Beka mixes blood from Hong Kong, stands 5' 7", weighs 105 pounds, and tapes a modest 33B-25-33 frame.

Elle scans the Backyard with darting eyes. There is a garden plot in need of a plant, some poles in the ground, a garage and alley out back, and prickly bush hedge on both sides. An old sidewalk around to the side of the house. They had not come that way; they arrived via the back alley.

Elle also bears a petite frame, 5' 10" and 115 pounds, with curly brunette hair and a 34B-24-34 figure. Beka knows that Elle contains a blend of Middle East blood and religion.

Automatron spools Back Door Cam; Automatron already stashes Beka and Elle's stats from their applications, right down to their blood types. Automatron's archives span all formats: text and pictures, test scores and questionnaires, written answers, video clips, hedges, secret recordings.

Elle considers Beka's outfit. The twosome had not conferred about what to wear, although, like many times in the past, they each picked an outfit that promises seduction and rivals the other. Beka's sleeveless croptop flies her lower ribs inches above her navel. Beka's croptop encourages, but doesn't mandate, that Beka flash the berries inside her oversize armholes. Beka has always welcomed looks.

Elle discovers that the Cam has hovered to a position to collect Beka's open armhole, and she warns her friend, "You're about to provide your first titter to the Cosmos House Cam."

Inside the armhole Beka provides a shallow conical boob supporting a beige areola with a rising nipple berry centered on top. Full booby. She adjusts her posture to correct her exposure.

Beka looks at her friend. "Don't show off; maybe you know more words than I do, but I'm qualified too. I'm not stupid. You're as able to 'titter' as I am!"

Elle must admit, *Beka sometimes makes sense; it's her carefree extravagance that disconcerts.* Elle squares her shoulders back. "You're sort of correct. I can make sure that no one sees my nips while I still move freely." Elle firms her jaw. "But I am not at all sure you can avoid flashing your boobies, whether you want to or not."

"So?" Beka bounces back. "I really don't care who looks." Beka shrugs and scratches her bare ribs somewhere below the croptop hem. "Okay, Elle, so you have more control over your titter. So what?"

Elle snorts at her Roommate, "Maybe you don't care about flashing your nips to anybody, but I care about you. We can't be indiscriminate. You need smaller armholes, if not sleeves." Elle runs her hands around her torso. Like Beka, Elle bares her arms and belly; unlike Beka she also bares her shoulders and the space between the two halter triangles, above the front button. Elle checks behind her neck to make sure she stays secure there too. *I'm better prepared than my Roommate and have a lot more control over myself.*

As part of her application Elle had been asked to write a description of her areola and nipple, and she had submitted that they "resemble a weathered volcano with crevices that run from the tip of the nipple down to the very edge of my coffee-colored pigment." This thought flashes through Elle's mind as she watches the Cam pan to distinguish her from her Roommate. She assesses this admirer. *No coffee for you.*

Beka and Elle wait by the Bell. They have more to discuss that the politics of titter.

"Maybe we should sit down," Beka suggests, and gestures toward the Back Door Landing.

"Maybe not," Elle worries.

"We can sit on the sidewalk or grass," Beka suggests.

"We can do that," Elle agrees, but she makes no effort to do so.

Beka scratches her huge swath of bellage. "Elle, I can't stand the waiting. It's worse than waiting in line at a club. Even the VIP line."

"Listen, calm down." Elle advances, "This whole adventure is your idea. And you're way overexposed."

Beka brushes her hair back with one hand. "*I'm* way overexposed? How about you? Don't forget I was with you the day you bought your halter way back. I know you wore this to not just nightclubs and bars. The fit was always sufficiently imperfect that you could let it fall away from your noogies just enough to let a roving eye look down at your puckered nips." Beka stretches a silent Elle: "Don't act so innocent, because you actually wore this outfit to your bookkeeper job!"

Elle gives in. "Okay, I give up. You're right. My boss didn't have a chance."

Beka adds a detail. "And we both fucked him."

Elle laughs. "I remember. Me first, then you later."

They both laugh.

Elle takes a deep breath, then gets serious again. "Yeah, okay, Beka, but this is different now. We have to be careful here. Overexposing is a fine line."

"Elle, relax. This is gonna be fine." Beka shakes her head and fiddles with her miniskirt. "Get real. This is no different than clubbing, only more advanced. Back then sometimes you and I went after the same guys. Sometimes one of us nailed, and sometimes the other spiked. Sometimes we scored together. This is the same. We'll take whatever we want. And if you have to flash your noogies once in a while, stop worrying about it. You've done it before."

"Stop it!" Elle reacts. She adds, "We must maintain decorum. And it's not like your open-armhole croptop is your only problem; it's also your low-hanging miniskirt."

Beka fingers the miniskirt's waistline; Gamers know two Garments imply no panties underneath. She defends her sanpan. "So? I mean, look at you, Elle. And I don't just mean your loose-fitting halter. Look at your little cut-off jeans shorts. All you've got between your legs is a half-inch wide ragged inseam, and your legholes are torn off so high your short hairs and butt cheeks hang out. Creases. You gotta know that."

Elle blinks. *I'm not just cheeking my butt; if I'm not carefully my nappy leaks out.*

Welcome more hairage to the Cosmos House.

Elle wiggles in her shorts. *I know Beka pegs me, yet this is not the first time we've both dared to lure men. Except Beka never cared how much people look. I do.*

Elle checks that her waistline is level with her navel. The shorts lack the snap just above the front zipper, and Gamers find Elle's belly button framed in this inverted triangle; a horizontal oval centered in the V-notch displayed at the bottom of her midriff exposure.

Beka is jealous of Elle's concentrated navelage. But it's still navelage, 24x7. Beka jests, "You'll have to tell everyone how the overhang on the top of your button is ripe for a piercing."

"And you'll need to beg a really big tattoo to cover all of your bare belly," Elle taunts back.

They laugh together.

And wait.

Beka's navelage sits amidst a vast tract of bellage. This bare patch of skin traverses from the bottom of Beka's croptop far above her navel, then down and across her belly until it finds the waistline of her miniskirt, freely suspended six inches below her belly button.

The navel in the middle of this belly-up belly-down bellage expresses itself as a long and narrow vertical oval with a lightning bolt scar jagging down inside.

Elle watches Beka adjust the waistline of her miniskirt. *It rides is so low on Beka's hips that it kisses her hairage and rugage. A thumb tug away from showing.* Elle observes where the miniskirt crosses Beka's thigh... below her crotch certainly, but high above her kneecap. *It's short enough to allow her to flash her trimmed boneroo if she sits. I ought to know; we've clubbed together before. But then we wore panties. Well, usually. Sometimes. But not any more.*

"Elle, I want to stick with you, 100 percent." Beka slides a hand into her croptop from the bottom and rotates her berries. "Okay, so we both picked our own costume from our own closets, and okay, I agree, we're not identical. We never were. We've picked powerful combinations of Garments, man-killers in our past life. These other Cosmos Pledge, they don't have a chance. We're comin' in wearing our *exit tickets,* and we won't titter or vagflash unless it suits us. It's very simple."

"Yeah," Elle says. "Although the consequences of failure remain a trip to the Strip next Term. That's very simple." Again Elle looks around. "Maybe this isn't the right House and we should leave while we still have a chance."

"Will you calm down!" Beka doesn't understand why her Roommate gets herself so worked up sometimes. "Stop it. We rang the Bell. We rang it together!"

Elle brushes her hair with her fingertips. "Strippers get pierced and tattooed you know."

Beka waves a hand in front of her face. "Game to Elle: failing will never happen to us. It can't, because we are too good, and we would never Opt Down and go Strip anyway. Stripping is for players who want to tease men for a career but never fuck them. Forty-hour workweek. That's not us. And if I wanted a tattoo or piercing, I'd have gotten one a long time ago."

Elle settles the matter. "Good. I don't want to be the Pledge getting pierced and tattooed on her way to the Strip. I'm determined to Opt Up next Term."

Beka agrees, "Yeah. Me too, Elle. We wanna stay together in this."

§ Beka & Elle: Fret about Costumes Outside the Back Door

Babs and the other Cosmos hang out in the Kitchen and watch the Screen showing the feed from the Back Door Cam.

Beka and Elle fidget and wait. The longer Beka and Elle wait the less confidence they have in their outfits.

Elle blurts first, "It's you fault I'm wearing this!"

And Beka retorts, "Nonsense, you picked knowing you could control your exposures. And we're both covered enough to go anywhere. You know Gamers hardly ever let Pledge pick their own costumes. We're special!"

Elle accepts, "I understand. We've worn trash like this to bars, out shopping—"

"—and even to work. We're sexy hot!" Beka rationalizes. But then she interprets Elle's doubt. "You just think we're being too manipulative."

Elle loses more confidence. "Too manipulative? We're too overexposed."

The newbies lapse into silence. It demonstrates bad caste for them to complain about their own teases and tastes. Beka and Elle have anticipated that Pledging might be a challenge, and although they both enter the Game willingly and as equals, the longer they fidget the more anxiety they exude.

Elle worries, "These Gamers are going to subject us to all kinds of pressures."

Beka waves off her friend. "We're going to be 'Roommates Together' and stay Roommates Together all through the Term. And Opt Up and Monitor next Term. You already promised me no 'Roommates Apart.'"

Elle takes a big sigh. "Yes, Roommates Together, not Roommates Apart." *Cause if we're Apart, that means one of us ends up a Monitor and the other hustles off to Strip naked. And I have no intention of Stripping. Not next Term. Not any Term.*

Beka is too curious sometimes. "I can't imagine what a strip club looks like, but I'd like to see the Nugget some time."

"You can go without me," Elle suggests.

"I mean go see from the Crowd," Beka replies. "Hey, as long as we stay together we'll persevere and acquire promotions. All we have to do is 'lean into the blast.' I'm confident of that."

Elle nods her head. Waiting rattles her confidence. *I know that abstractions are in reality not.*

§ Robyn Greets Beka & Elle: Haze and False Assumptions

Robyn emerges from the back door. "You rang?" She trades looks with the newbies, who look up at her on the Landing. Robyn wears her golden stretch maillot, strapless but for two recently acquired spaghetti straps, with a legline that showcases her shaven legs but hides all inguinal and rump. Once piece, with a belly button cutout.

Elle calculates, *Smallest buttonhole possible and still stay navelage 24x7. Not even an inch of skin all around her outie.* Elle studied the Rules. *Navelage 24x7 is only requirement, and I know my V-notch ensures this.*

Subtlety matters.

Robyn studies the newbies from the Landing's raised position. She knows the Back Door Cam covers her. She tightens her arms to her sides and ripples her spine. Like when she greeted Kimju and Molly, Robyn again flaunts her self-importance. *BB sent me out to welcome these newbies because I'm the best. I'm the best looking, and deep down inside she knows that I'm really the one in charge. Everybody watches me. I look hot. I am hot. I control my containment. I demanded straps, and Bikini Babe turns them over to me.*

Inside in Kitchen, Pledge cluster around Babs and watch the Cam feed. Kimju holds herself handbra and rests a bare keister on one of the chairs. She studies Robyn carefully, intent on digesting how her Roommate handles this situation, and she is pleased that the Cam shares her fascination with the tormenter as well as the tormentees. *I remember how Robyn treated Molly and I when we arrived four days ago.* Kimju can see that the excitement of hazing the two newbies has hardened Robyn's nipples—headlights atop a firm rig inside thin stretch fabric.

Robyn remains unaware of her own presentation; she's too absorbed evaluating the newbies.

Beka and Elle evaluate a blonde with a gold streak that follows the contour of her hair, with gold dust arches on her high cheek, eyelids, and eyelashes. Goldened lips, outlined with fine black, match Robyn's golden maillot cutout. Golden finger and toe nails. A dab of gold inside her outie. Robyn acknowledges Beka and Elle looking at her and proclaims, "I'm dusted with real gold power! I'm royalty! You shall obey me."

Beka and Elle look at each other. However long they have been waiting doesn't matter. Never did.

Robyn descends the Landing and approaches the newbies as they linger near the Bell. She stands herself directly before them, one knee slightly bent, hands at her side. She imagines she holds a long cigarette holder between the fingers of one hand. With red-hot coals on the end.

Robyn's imagination getting away from her is shattered when Beka speaks and provides an inappropriate introduction. "You must be Babs. I'm Beka. And—"

Elle completes, "—I'm Elle."

Robyn lets this sink in. Pity the Pledge who speaks without being spoken to. The Back Door Cam peers forward as Babs watches on a Screen inside with amusement and a twisted brow. Tiffany, who has somehow managed to stay naked ever since doing makeup and Pee-Cam, casually extracts her trinket from her treasure chest; no shame. The topless Kimju and Molly observe silently and consider if Robyn's got Charm. Molly's Roommate Steph, still wearing yesterday's flowing strapped cutout minidress (but no longer with panties underneath) puts a hand over her mouth. Kundalini stirs, Steph squeezes her snooch, but no one can see if slush leaks out.

Robyn adopts the script; she doesn't offer corrections. She takes a big breath and speaks again. "So, Beka and Elle. That's who you are, but why are you here?"

"We ah—" Beka begins.

And Elle finishes, "—are begging to Pledge at the Cosmos House. Ma'am." Elle does remember her manners.

"We're newbie Pledge," Beka assures her.

Robyn assesses this, then responds, "Really? Perhaps admission standards have been lowered recently?"

"Ma'am, we're here to learn ways to label, understand, and relate to the world, Ma'am," Elle panders. "We're begging to be permitted to join in the Game."

"You should be expecting us," Beka augments, then offers, "We'll do what you want."

"What I want?" Robyn questions herself. "What I want is for you two unworthy ingrates to Pledge naked and become Strippers next Term!"

"But, but—" Beka and Elle sing chorus.

"Oh, shut up. Both of you." Robyn speaks sternly. There is a further agenda. "Did you learn how to stand spread surrender?"

Elle tries to cover for both of them. "We both passed the test in Positions. And we assume—"

"Shut up. You should not make assumptions about anything. Now move it, Pledge," Robyn commands.

Beka and Elle fall in side-by-side, almost touching elbows and spread feet, hands-behind-heads. It's a good start. But then they look at each other.

"Eyes straight ahead. Oval your mouths. No talking. Close your eyes," Robyn details, then recites liturgy: "You now belong to the Cosmos House. Mind, body, and soul."

Elle finds herself gasping, but gets control of herself. She snorts but keeps her eyes shut. Tries to control panic. *I can't even assess where Babs might be right now! I'd sneak a glance at Beka to make sure she's all right, except that's exactly playing into their hands.* Elle discovers something. *I can hear Beka breathing! She stands right next to me!*

"And what we got here?" Robyn romances. Beka feels a breeze in her armhole and between her legs, but she keeps her eyes tight. "A titter and vagflash specialist to give Pledge Steph some company. Too bad you're not Roommates."

Inside the Kitchen, the laughter around the Screen isn't polite. And Steph steels herself to deal with a nemesis. *Crush Robyn.*

Beka feels uncomfortable not being able to see. She hears Robyn direct Elle, "You, Pledge, come over here." She hears Elle move away and opens her eyes to observe.

And be observed by Robyn: Beka with her eyes wide open, her head turned, and her hands over her mouth.

Beka catches herself before Robyn can utter a word and reverts to form, but the mistake has been made. Elle still has her eyes clenched. Robyn pushes a bare foot against the back of Elle's knee. "On your hands and knees, Pledge."

Elle obeys. *In this position my halter offers little protection.*

Robyn spins to Beka. "You want to open your eyes, so open your eyes. You want to turn your head, so turn your head and look at your Roommate. Look at her, Pledge! Look at her on her hands and knees!"

"Ma'am, I'm sorry, Ma'am," Beka pleads.

"Of course you are," Robyn flaunts, then turns to Elle again. "And you, Pledge, open your eyes, tell the Cam your name, and beg to titter the on behalf the Cosmos House. What have you brought us, Pledge?"

Elle knows. *Full noogie show.* She opens her eyes and discovers herself staring into the Back Door Cam. She instinctively looks down to confirm that her loose-fitting halter has indeed fallen away from her body. Elle doesn't comprehend that paparazzi also collect her first titter, although she does understand, *Now I must titter the Cam.* She remembers to say hello. "Ma'am, I'm Elle, begging to be a Cosmos Pledge."

Again Beka tries, "Ma'am, I'm sorry I opened my eyes. I didn't—"

"Shut up." Robyn whirls back to Beka. "Stay shut up. You shall remember your sorry-ness because your Roommate shall be punished in your stead!"

Robyn spins and points at Elle. "You, Pledge." Robyn pivots her finger and points to a doorway in the latticework beneath the Back Door Landing. "Get in there."

Elle looks up at Robyn in disbelief.

"Crawl," Robyn commands. "Stay on your hands and knees."

Beka watches Elle crawl with forlorn eyes. The doorway ahead of Elle is wood, less than two feet tall, with flaking paint, rusty hinges, and a latch on its right side. The Cosmos watching on the Kitchen Screen are quiet.

The apparent commander commands, "Your Roommate needs to learn to obey me. So *you* can spend the night in the Doghouse. I'll be back for you tomorrow."

"Tomorrow?" Elle finds herself drifting through this as she opens the door and looks into the earthen space underneath the Landing.

"I'm hearing echoes," Robyn frowns. "Thank me!"

Elle backs herself into the opening and tries to make eye contact with Beka. She spins, "Ma'am, thank you, Ma'am, for letting me into the Cosmos House. Letting me Pledge, Ma'am." She backs all the way into the space underneath the Back Landing. Elle trades one anguished look with Beka before Robyn's bare, manicured foot pushes the door closed.

Elle finds herself in a small, narrow space with a dirt floor. She can't stand up, can't sit up, and she has no choice but to lie down. The inside slopes down a bit and into a muddy low spot. Uuuggh. "Disgusting," Elle tells herself. "This is all very juvenile."

Elle doesn't see what happens next. Robyn draws her saliva together and spits in Beka's face. Beka, too astounded to react, watches Robyn waggle her finger toward the Back Door. "And you, Pledge, go wait inside!" Beka doesn't wipe the spit off her face and cautiously climbs the Landing. Elle hears her footsteps pass overhead, followed in a minute by the more deliberate footprints of Robyn.

Elle feels very alone.

§ Babs Greets Beka: 1st Encounter 1st Discipline 1st Beg

Babs scrambles her brood upstairs so that as Beka arrives in the Kitchen from the Back Door she confronts a tall, statuesque woman with long black hair wearing a revealing Black Bikini.

Beka runs a fast once-over, reads the cleavage uplifted in the widely-spaced shoulder straps bra, the *crescents d'areolage,* the swell of belly above a low waistline that almost hairages, and the long legs.

Once again Beka volunteers a first impression. "Hi. I'm Beka. Babs sent me in. Is she a Bitch or what? So what's your name? You're wearing less and showing more than I am."

For once Babs is speechless. For once Robyn rescues her. Robyn queens in from the back door, and BB signs her to halt and stand at attention.

Robyn obeys.

BB directs the question to Beka. "So did this person tell you she's Monitor Babs?" Boss Babe knows the answer; she been watching the Cam feed.

Beka stammers, "I'm not sure. But she looks golden. Regal, I mean. I assumed—"

Babs slaps Beka across the face. Beka staggers, and BB spins her and wraps her long brunette hair into her fist. Walks her backwards. Beka's ear rings. "You drew your own wrong conclusion." Babs grips with discipline, not anger. "I watched you."

Babs bends Beka backward, and Beka sees the Kitchen ceiling. From across the Kitchen Robyn watches Beka's belly stretch taut, tan skin with fine hairs.

Beka raises her hands to where BB wraps her hair. "You don't need to do that," Beka complains. "We're all Pledge here."

Not. BB pulls downward with Beka's hair wrapped in her fist, and Beka finds herself on her knees with her head twisted around and looking at the Cosmos in the golden maillot with the smallest buttonhole.

"Who might you be?" Boss Babe queries Robyn.

Robyn clicks her heels and sings out, "Ma'am, I'm Cosmos Pledge Robyn, Ma'am!"

Beka's whole body twitches. She turns her head up to the woman who wraps her hair in her fist and innocently inquires, "And who are you?"

"Babs. I am your Monitor here."

Beka lowers her eyes. "I was afraid you were gonna say that."

BB slaps her a second time. Harder. And this time the imprint of Babs' hand forms an instant red glow on Beka's cheek.

"I'm 'Ma'am', Pledge." Boss Babe pauses for a heartbeat or two for this to sink in, and then pulls Beka's hair harder still so that Beka finds herself looking at Tiffany's Calendar. "If I ever hear you say 'Bitch' again you will not just be washing your mouth out with soap. You will be on a soap diet."

Beka kind of gets this; she feels disoriented and mutters, "Ma'am, soap, please!"

"You are here to answer and obey, not ask questions. Do you understand me?"

"Ma'am, yes, Ma'am!" Beka squeaks.

"Don't speak unless you are spoken to. Do you understand me?"

Panic, then a glimmer of remembrance in Beka's mind about manners. She flashes on how adept Elle is at manners. "Ma'am, yes, Ma'am. I obey you. Ma'am."

Beka gathers her swirling thoughts together; the hazing comes at her faster than she can process. Part of her remains uncertain which Babs is real—the one holding her hair or the one standing attention.

Still?

Beka's thoughts grapple with reality. "I'm sorry I opened my eyes and looked at Elle. Maybe it's okay she has to lean over and titter. But she doesn't deserve any Doghouse. I'll join her there. I deserve it."

"Maybe you can beg to trade places," Boss Babe advises. "Right now, lie on the floor on your belly. You should feel bad about what you did to your Roommate. Actions have consequences."

Beka looks up from the floor and watches Babs makes a signal Beka can't decipher. The golden Pledge Robyn bows. Robyn smarms toward Beka, "You got dirt on your cheek. You should be worried now." She disappears into the spiraling stairs leading upstairs.

That leaves just the two of them. Except for the Cam, which seems to have snuck in with Robyn and hovers with them.

Beka still can't believe she saw Elle crawl into the Doghouse. *We are supposed to be Roommates and hang together.* Beka wants to ask, "Has Elle been let out of the Doghouse yet?" but yields to the haze; its strands threaten to overwhelm her logic circuits. *I know I can't win, but I didn't think giving in would happen this fast! And where's Elle when I need her?*

Beka's confidence is sufficently rattled that Babs speaks to her in a tone of confidence. Babs helps her up onto her knees. "Let me give you a tip." Now, with arm and hair, the tall Monitor guides Beka to her feet and relaxes her grip on the brunette as she drapes an arm around her shoulders. "Did you notice what Goldilocks was wearing?"

Beka wonders if her nose is bleeding. It isn't. She feels the tall, curvy Cosmos squeeze against her so that BB's babambas almost fall out of her Bikini. Sharp fingernails suddenly penetrate her booty; Beka jumps and BB purrs, "Answer me!"

Beka responds, "Ma'am, Robyn was wearing a maillot, Ma'am. Barefoot." She casts her eyes down. "One piece."

Babs extends her playtime. "So, are you stupid?"

"Ma'am, yes, I'm stupid, Ma'am." Beka demonstrates: "Robyn can't be a Monitor; she has one piece. You have two pieces! But I have two pieces, too!"

Boss Babe clarifies, "True, but of the two of us, only you shall beg to strip naked." She looks Beka in the eye.

Beka startles.

Boss Babe adds for emphasis, "Now."

Beka considers the haze. She isn't sure what to make of it. She acquiesces, "Ah, yes, Ma'am, I'll beg to strip naked for you. Ma'am." Beka doesn't mean it, of course. *This is silly. I know this is not real.*

Beka doesn't know that her love box goes wet and that her brodeas seeps out.

Beka augments her commitment, offering, "Elle will strip naked too."

And Babs points to the angular stairs. "Upstairs. Bunkroom. Fit yourself into the far bottom bunk. Stay."

§ Beka Meets Cosmos: Learns about Titter & Vagflash

Beka meets the other Cosmos upstairs in the Bunkroom. Robyn and Kimju, and Molly and Steph, stand or sit on the floor around her as she sequesters herself inside her bunk bed. The bunk above her, Elle's bunk, remains empty. Beka's face stings, and her bruised lip smarts; the croptop and miniskirt cover her, sort of. Beka's miniskirt slides far enough up one booty that BB's nail marks become personal. Beka collects herself.

Robyn laughs and points at Beka. "You were such a stupid blubber mouth! And you put your Roommate in the Doghouse. What's next for you?"

"You let me deceive myself," Beka charges. "And Babs really cut into me."

Tiffany emerges from the Bedroom. She had slipped into her clear vinyl croptop and poured herself into tight low-rise stretch slacks after coming upstairs. She has grabbed the Makeup Kit, and now she advances toward Beka. She soothes, "Don't mind Babs; that's just the way she is. She lashes out at you like that and then feels guilty afterwards. School needs to teach her to slow her rise and assuage her guilt."

Robyn advances, "Boss Bitch needs to be staked out in the Mudpit and given a good fucking."

Tiffany applies salve from the Makeup Case to Beka's tender lip and powers over BB's paw print on her face. "Don't worry," Tiffany comforts, and preaches virtues: "I'll show you all the tricks of the Strip. Just don't get in my way getting there."

Beka appreciates the salve and powder, but, being new to School, her preconceptions may not match the Game actually being played amongst her fellow Cosmos. The fact that two of her fellow Pledge are topless and a third is topless-in-see-through annoys her. *Some are more advanced than I am. Some have fewer Garments.*

Beka pays insufficient attention to Steph, who already envisions Beka as an easy relief valve to take off titter and vagcam pressure. Steph scans the Room. *Kimju wants Opt Up*, she thinks. *Molly wears my panties. I just need to time taking them. And an opportunity to crush Robyn.* Steph does have a score to settle. *After all, she's the reason I'm here and not a MomCap.*

Robyn Redacted leads again. She touches her own chest and identifies herself to Beka, saying, "I am like you. This is my first Term."

Robyn takes it upon herself to introduce the other Pledge. "Tiffany Transparent was a Whore and is a Double Opt Up. She likes Whoring better than Stripping and Stripping better than Pledging."

Tiffany smiles. "I like being out there."

Beka seeks safety in Tiffany's outfit. "You wear that outside?" Beka really wants to know.

Tiffany forms curves and caresses her fiery red hairage. "I sure do. I am a Porn Star, except I'm not allowed to have sex while I'm here pledging the Cosmos House. The Gamers are frustrating my fans."

"Frustrating Tiffany as well," Robyn politely chuckles.

Robyn gestures to Kimju and Molly. "Kimju and Molly were Strippers last Term and have pledged topless."

Molly grasps her mams in one arm, touches her panties with the other, and tries to offer consolation to Beka. "I've been outside like this, you know, topless and panties. But mostly I've had to streak."

"Naked?" Beka wants to know. She has a hard time accepting Molly's coat of body hair.

"Right," Molly affirms. "You only streak naked. Stark naked."

"And now clothes arrive," Kimju provides, trading eyes with Molly. She crosses her arms in front of herself and blocks her knockers for the moment.

Beka doesn't understand why the Pledge all seem to find this funny.

Despite her predatory posture, Kimju has held back in order to watch Robyn. *I want to discover Robyn's envelope. I want to see if she treats newbie Beka as nastily as she treated Molly and me. I need another piece; any piece will do, but the first Game I play must be with Roommate Robyn. Robyn Redacted somehow.*

Beka offers a consolation prize to the two ex-Strippers. "Well, I guess it's fair to say that you still look like Strippers."

Robyn generalizes, "Tiffany makes them up like Wannabe Strippers because they're mostly begging to Strip. Be nice to Tiffany and she'll make you up like a Stripper too."

Tiffany shimmies and explains to the newbie, "Babs' orders. Cleopatra's Wannabe Strippers. Don't worry. I'll make you beautiful too."

Beka observes that Tiffany's nipples look like pencil erasers and wonders, *Do they every retract?*

Tiffany takes pride that one of her feature attractions gets recognition. "Eraser Heads," she perks. "They're up all the time. 24x7."

Beka feels a flash of anxiety and rotates her chin in her fist. She hasn't anticipated the complexity of momentum, and although Beka might not be one to verbalize impressions, she certainly does feels them on her body.

Robyn gestures to Steph, standing tall at the outer rim of the cluster. Beka shifts her eyes to the blonde in a short, spaghetti-strapped minidress with a big cutout hole. Robyn advances, "Steph Sorostitute was the Cosmos Monitor *last* Term. And Babs, the real Boss Bitch whom you met downstairs in the Kitchen, was one of Steph's Pledge. This Term Babs is the Monitor and Steph Opted Down so she could be Babs' Pledge. Neat, huh?"

Beka shifts her eyes between Robyn and Steph and wonders if she should believe Robyn. Babs is not to be seen, but Steph's eyes sparkle with hostility toward Robyn.

"You got broken?" Beka asks Steph a rude, brutal truth.

Steph narrows her eyes. Standing properly, her minidress appears "decent," and newbie Beka don't consider that Steph wears nothing underneath. Only one Garment.

Robyn says, "All the Pledge beg Tiffany to make up their nipples. Kimju and Molly begged three days ago and Steph begged and tittered her colors this morning. You gonna beg too?"

Beka looks for evidence. No makeup on Molly's large areola and nipples. Kimju crosses her arms, and Steph wears a minidress, loose fitting, with spaghetti straps that barely keep it on her body. Beka remembers the question. "Sure, I already tittered downstairs. Elle and I both. You can make both our nipples up. We'll titter as much as you want."

Robyn informs, "Steph expects that her red spots are going to rub off inside her minidress."

"So what?" Beka doesn't care.

"Tomorrow," Tiffany interjects, "Steph will beg Babs to wear her minidress inside out. That way Gamers will see red spots where the lipstick rubbed off."

Tiffany watches Beka absorb this concept, then augments, "It will imprint Gamer brains, so that when Steph finally does dance topless she'll be worth more. Pent up anticipation."

Steph rises onto her tiptoes, slightly horrified that Tiffany suggests such a humiliation. *That I might drift downward in Caste!* She snippets to Tiffany, "All you think about is money and valuation."

And they laugh together uneasily. It is a laugh that Beka doesn't understand.

Steph turns to Beka. "Left to her devices Tiffany kinda makes me up like how she wants. But now I've got her doing it the way I want. Tiffany will do anything get to the Strip."

Robyn shoulders forward. "Steph's already on her way to the Strip." She orders, "Show her, you scraggly sex sanpan."

Steph, uncertain if she should honor Robyn's suggestion, nevertheless walks over to Beka's bunk, places a bare foot up on the bunk next to her, and vagflashes an open-legged upskirted socket box in Beka's face. Steph smiles daggers and focuses her aggression upon the newbie. "Take a good look; this is you next!"

Beka flinches when she sees soft scruff over a slit.

"Don't let her spook you," topless Molly intercedes. "Just because Steph considers how she might swap costumes with you doesn't mean she's going to. She's my Roommate!"

Mild confusion ensues. Beka clenches herself and draws her legs together. Steph rocks her foot on the bunk and keeps her slit pointed toward Beka's eyes. Beka's eyes seek explanation, and Steph speaks to them from a position of power. "My Roommate Molly keeps begging me to take her panties. So please don't make her jealous and beg me to trade for *your* croptop and miniskirt instead."

Very funny. Beka thinks she understands and squeezes her tights tightly together. "Ah, yes. You're taking Molly's panties. And Opting Up. Elle and have I two pieces, so, er, ah, I guess we're Opting Up too!"

"Elle's in the Doghouse," Robyn affirms, "and your Options may lie in contesting with Steph. You are a perfectly matched pair. Both of you titters and upskirts."

Steph glowers at Robyn, who in turn flashes her a Hand Sign for "legs spread." Beka certainly has no sense of Cosmos history, but every Pledge in the Bunkroom knows BB has ordered Robyn to "sign Steph's legs apart and cam her." Steph considers a technicality: *Given the absence of any Cam in the room, this order may well be specious.* She yields anyway and obliges the request. Wider means Steph must ride the minidress up to her hips and present her snatch so it is fully accessible.

Beka reads the irritation in Steph's face, but because Beka doesn't understand the hand of Boss Babe enabling Robyn's domination, Beka assumes Robyn holds power.

Robyn watches as Beka catches a whiff of scent. She cackles to Beka, "You just gotta love how Steph's thin blonde scruff doesn't quite cover her stamen."

"Her stamen?" Beka registers uncertainty about fun laughter in the Bunkroom. Another sniff.

"My stamen," Steph takes over the conversation, looking down at Beka sitting in her lower bunk, "is what you might call my clit, my strophoid. And my scruff covers my smoo, which defines the entrance into my sex cavity. So what do you call your clit, newbie Pledge? Your bead? Your beanie? Your bolus?"

Beka squirms. *I wish Elle were here.* Once again Beka shifts her weight around, and once again Steph's open legs follow her.

Steph articulates, "You're gonna beg the Boss Bitch to keep *your* thighs apart! Instead of me."

Beka squeezes her thighs harder and darts her eyes over Steph's blonde shrubbery lying across her slit. They linger on Steph's stamen again.

Robyn confirms reality to Beka. "Don't worry, Pledge, you'll learn to open up. Before you arrived Steph was the only Cosmos empty in-between. Vagflashing raw snatch. Now she's got you to keep her company. Maybe your briar patch will divert the paparazzi away from her upskirted snapper," Robyn laughs.

Beka's eyes dart around the Bunkroom. Kimju's thong and Tiffany's slacks both hairage, as do Molly's panties, narrowed upward into her mooe. But all of them put cloth through their crotches; Robyn too.

Steph pretends joviality as she lectures the new arrival, "After I put Molly's panties back on, you shall command all the vagflashing attention." And they all laugh, except Beka, who doesn't know that Steph already wore panties once and already gave them back once. And yes, vagflashed too much to count, although she has managed to not share any slush with the Cams.

Steph breaks her posture, and as she moves away Beka smells her scent fade and her own scent whiff upwards. Beka worries, *Where might Elle be?*

§ Elle: Spends a Scary Night in the Doghouse

Elle does not expect to spend the night in the Doghouse. She has certainly not done anything to demand this level of sacrifice, and some Gamers object to this hazing. Some argue the Doghouse should be a place reserved for Pledge who have arrived late, failed to ring the Bell, or some other act worthy of atonement. And it is not fair to demand that a newbie free spirit be disciplined for the oversights of her Roommate.

But fair or not, Elle understands. *Beka is the one being disciplined, and I'm just the vessel. So I must submit to this ordeal. I can crawl out, but if I do I will have failed. And abandoned Beka.*

Elle has enough space to lie down, sleep on her side even, and almost crawl, but she must squirm around on her belly. She can just barely roll over onto her back. The dirt floor is hollowed down under the Back Landing, some of it muddy, and it smells of animals and piss inside. Elle worries about her allergies and regrets checking "none" on the Application.

And so as the evening progresses to night Elle becomes more afraid as the darkness outside renders the darker inside even darker. Soon Elle discovers she can no longer see her own hands and body, nor the dirt floor, ceiling, and four walls of the Doghouse. She resists the urge to scream and allows her intellect to prevail.

I can do this, Elle resigns herself with determination. *I don't need to panic. This is all very under control. I am spending the night here. It's warm enough. The dirt and mud on my face and bare belly and legs... well, I'm going to get dirty for a little while. It's cramped, it's scratchy, but since it's all part of the Game, it's fine.*

Elle rolls over again. *Actually, it's not fine; it's miserable. And I guess this is what the Gamers call hazing.* Elle tries to forget about spiders and snakes and eventually drifts into sleep.

Sometime after dawn, but before anyone has arisen, Elle pulls the hem of her shorts to the side of her crotch (just below the zipper) and augments the smell of the box with her own urine.

And as the light comes up in the morning Elle can smell as well as see that she lies in her own piss-mud.

17 Babs Greets Beka & Elle: Backyard Reveille (D11)

§ Beka & Elle: Cosmos Morning Lineup & Reveille

Elle is rousted out from the Doghouse beneath the Back Door Landing early on the morning of Day Eleven; she sees the Cosmos in their morning Lineup. Reveille, only today in the Backyard.

This is Elle's second encounter with Robyn, whom Elle still misconstrues as Monitor Babs. Robyn opens the door of the smelly box and hisses, "Don't mess with me. I know why your lady-parts are all n-words. Now squirm on your belly toward the Lineup." The dirty, bedraggled Pledge scratches herself on concrete, gravel, and grass.

Elle titters as Robyn stands her up and positions herself at one end of the Cosmos Lineup. Elle finds herself next to a looking-straight-ahead-and-ignoring-her Beka. *My friend and Roommate.* Elle strains her neck and watches Robyn fall into formation toward the far end of the Lineup.

This last action worries Elle. In a glance she had detected that two Pledge stand topless, one presents wearing a see-through croptop, one sports a minidress with a very large button hole and spaghetti straps, and that the Pledge Elle thinks is Babs wears a swimsuit with a tiny buttonhole.

Elle feels dazed, and she again needs to pee. Mud streaks across her face, belly, arms, legs, and back. Across all of her chest too, except where her halter covers, although the halter, like her jeans shorts, is also covered with grime.

Elle wonders about Beka, standing next to her but obediently face-forward and ignoring her. *Did Beka also suffered a horrific sleep-fitful night?*

No Pledge has fresh makeup and no Pledge has showered, but none rival Elle's muddy face, dirty hair, streaked stomach, and muddy hands and feet. And none rival her vapor.

A tall, statuesque, olive-skin beauty clad in a Black Bikini emerges from the Back Door. Underwire bra and low-rise nombril. Bling!

Monitor Babs orders, "Stand straight. Hands behind back, wrists crossed, feet planted wide, eyes straight ahead, and lips touching!"

These new directions startle Elle. Beka, standing next to her and drilled in the position last night, adjusts promptly. Elle follows.

Stand spread crossed. Eyes forward. No eye contact; Elle feels very alone, even though all the Pledge seem to know the position.

The arrival of the two newbies completes the Lineup for the first time, and it's fitting that Boss Babe brings the Lineup out into the fresh air. If paparazzi might inhabit any house on either side or lurk in the alley, they will collect seven Cosmos Pledge this morning: Tiffany, Robyn and Kimju, Molly and Steph, and Beka and Elle.

The Bikini Babe walks down the front of the Lineup and settles herself in front of Elle and Beka. "Keep your legs wide enough apart so that someone can lay their palm in your crotch," she informs them.

Being touched is not on Elle's short list, and she releases a droplet of pee; luckily the jeans' hem through her crotch absorbs this indiscretion.

"When I say something, remember it," Babs admonishes. "I do not expect to repeat myself."

Elle scrunches her brow. *I fear who this person might be.*

Monitor Babs speaks directly into Elle's face. "Who are you?"

Elle's turn to talk. "Ma'am, I'm Elle, Ma'am."

"And why are you here?"

Elle ponders; she actually knows the answer. "I'm here, Ma'am...." Elle needs to start over and nails the formalities. "Ma'am, I'm here to beg to become a Cosmo Pledge." There. Done. Well, almost. "Ma'am!"

Boss Babe considers this newbie Pledge. She purses her lips and speaks. "You're here to beg me to Pledge naked and cum be a Stripper next Term."

Oooh. Harsh. No gentling into it.

Who is this? Elle wonders. *Maybe this is Babs? Certainly not someone to mess with.* Elle considers how to say this right. Her mind turns quickly, accepts that hazing need not be playful, and retorts, "Ma'am, please let me Pledge naked and become a Stripper next Term." Pretty good, and almost forgetting, "Ma'am."

Babs probes at her. "You can remember that?"

And Elle runs it in her mind. *Yes I can.* "Ma'am, yes, Ma'am." *I can do this.*

"So if I invite you to talk, what do you say?" Babs expresses an affected, situational curiosity.

"Ma'am, please let me Pledge naked and become a Stripper next Term."

"You won't forget?"

"No, Ma'am." Elle gets a little less formal. Babs squints and pats her cheek.

"I'm Babs, your Monitor Boss. Don't be stupid like your Roommate and confuse me with someone else. You newbies need practice, but before the Term runs out we Gamers will make a Cosmos out of you."

Or, as Tiffany puts it much later, "You must prepare to meet Kundalini, the power of sex."

§ Beka & Elle Beg Babs: Pledge Naked & Strip Next Term

Babs shifts attention to Elle's Roommate Beka, standing next to her, eyes forward, legs apart, wrists crossed behind her back midriff. Lower ribs, dimples, almost the bottom of the Rhombus of Michaelis.

Boss Babe speaks like a cat. "Soooo," BB purrs, "This is your own outfit? You wore this outside *before* you pledged to School?"

Beka's eyes dance. She wiggles her fingers behind her and unavoidably titters her open armhole. Beka displays a huge swath of bellage, and her low-riding miniskirt downstairs barely covers her crotch.

Babs senses Beka's nervousness. Beka wants to tell Elle so many things but realizes she must answer Babs' question. "Yes, Ma'am. I wore it before." It's a slightly hurried response.

"You flashed your tits to men on the outside," BB accuses, spinning the line somewhere between a statement and a question.

"That's possible, Ma'am," Beka hedges.

"Women as well," Babs adds.

"I'm not so sure, Ma'am." Beka appears confused; she questions herself.

"So did you flash men deliberately" BB curves, "or just let them look?"

Beka feels worried that she titters at this very moment, but she dares not turn her head. "I'm not sure," she admits.

Boss Babe presses, "Get sure."

And Beka's mind whirls. *What would Elle tell me to say?* She tightens up and augments her answer. "Possibly. Probably. Sometimes anybody could look."

"Your broom closet, too." Babs draws it out, matter of fact, but again midway between a period and a question mark.

"Ah, yes." Beka doesn't quite know what to say.

BB helps out. "Robyn says that you're a tittering bimbo who wants to open her legs apart." Beka hears Babs turn, walk around Elle, and come behind the Lineup. Then she feels a palm lift up into her crotch. "Well, well," BB announces. "No panties on this newbie, and not much briar patch either."

Beka blurts, "I'm shaven bare except for a racing stripe. I've got smooth lips with a landing patch of bristles above."

The Back Door Cam has detached itself from its perch, and now Beka can hear it hovering somewhere in front of her but below her straight-ahead eyesight. Beka wonders just how low the Cam flies. *Does it collect impartial evidence about my breach?* Out in the Prefecture, Gamers debate if BB lifts Beka's miniskirt enough to reveal her broom or bare brim.

But the touch stimulates Beka to hint at the future. "I'm begging you to let me Pledge the Cosmos House. And I guess if you need to me go topless like the others I'll take my shirt off for you," Beka volunteers.

"You will spread your legs apart and open your broom closet," Boss Babe pronounces.

And Beka agrees, "Yes, absolutely, no problem. I'll show everyone. Ma'am, please. Just like Steph Sorostitute!"

Steph bristles at hearing this reference, and the comparison fails to wins her affection. She's not wearing panties anymore. The huge buttonhole will hairage, and the inside out minidress does have two round spots where yesterday's nipple makeup rubbed off.

Babs squints an eye and paces down behind her Lineup. She pauses behind Molly and jerks the back of Molly's panties up into the crack of her ass. Now two Cosmos effectively tanga.

BB walks around Tiffany at the far end, and then back down, in front of the entire Cosmos Lineup. BB is pleased with herself. She turns and faces Beka directly.

"You want to beg to get in the Doghouse with your Roommate? You want to be with her? How about you beg me to get naked and cum be a Stripper next Term?" BB speaks flippantly, almost teasing, but Beka isn't so sure. Her face still stings from the slap last night.

"Ma'am, yes, Ma'am." Now Beka is thinking, and the words come out slowly. "Please let me Pledge naked." Beka doesn't argue now; she's too green for that. She finishes, "And become a Stripper next turn."

Elle twitches. *Technically speaking both of us newbie Cosmos have now begged to Opt Strip.* And hearing Beka recite only reinforces Elle's uneasy commitment.

Boss Babe purses her lips. "Very well," she intones, then addresses both newbies. "May you learn to chant in unison. And may Gamers make your wishes come true!"

Elle realizes she clasps her wrists together very tightly and that Babs speaks to her directly. "Go inside the Back Door, then left and up the stairs. Shower or bathe in the Bathroom, then find the furthest upper bunk and put yourself in it. You're rooming above Beka."

"Ma'am, yes, Ma'am. I know that." Elle tries to be helpful.

BB scowls at her but speaks kindly. "You know that now that I've told you." Elle opens her mouth, but Babs raises her hand and her chin. "And next time, thank me for letting you sleep in the Doghouse."

These are stern words, and they hit Elle's brain at an oblique angle. Elle will remember. *Even if I consider the recitations a Game, the Game demands attention if I am to preserve and get ahead. So I'll play along. I don't need miracles; I can learn the formalities necessary for promotion.*

Memory training at School. And the perseverance of a dog.

Once again Elle opens her mouth, and again Babs raises her posture and speaks dismissively. "Go. Always ring the Bell on your way in or out. But you don't need to ring again, because you rang hours ago."

And so Elle doesn't hesitate. She doesn't run; she just turns, walks through the Back Door, and enters the Kitchen. She breaks her pace as the Calendar on the wall startles her, but she fails to connect it with the redhead with her see-through popup nipples at the end of the Lineup.

§ Beka & Elle: Bunkroom Assessment Cosmos' Game Status

And so Elle becomes the last Cosmos to arrive and be welcomed to the Cosmos House. Do Gamers want to know why she is here? It doesn't matter. Gamers do not need to know why she enrolls, only that Elle begs to play the Game and has been allowed to. *And now that I have arrived I am no longer sure why I am here either,* Elle recollects. *Except Beka says she wants to discover how Kundalini works. And I'm afraid to let her do it alone.*

The twosome find a moment in the Bunkroom as Elle figures out who's who among her fellow Cosmos. *Rule One is navelage 24x7.* So Elle inventories all of their buttons: Robyn and Steph in their cutout holes, herself in her notched V, Kimju and Molly just above their respective tanga and panties, even Babs above her even lower bikini nombril.

Roommate Beka's button sits far above her very low-riding miniskirt, lower than Babs' waistline, but Tiffany's button lies the most far away from still lower-waistlined stretch slacks. So low that Tiffany spills her thicket out in front and displays the trough between her two rounded tailstocks out back.

All navels accounted for!

Elle carefully breathes in and out and assesses her status. *Did I compromise my own exposures as part of the deal I negotiated in order to play the Game?* Elle rotates her shoulders. *Hardly. I actually chose to wear this halter and ripped shorts; it is one of my costumes from the outside, just like Beka's outfit. So get a grip. I've done this before.*

Okay.

Elle compares her own nipple exposures to those of her Roommate. Beka sits on the bunk next to her. Elle tucks her halter strap and makes sure her nippies remains safe. She admits, "I guess Robyn made us both titter yesterday. Me downblouse and you sideboob."

Beka reconciles, "Yeah, okay, but so what? We're both titters. And besides, our boobies are more covered than most other Pledge. Steph had a strap fall off during the Lineup and had one of her smurfs hanging out;

Tiffany's teats are always in see-through; and Kim and Molly are always topless—knockers and mammies."

Elle details, "Except when Babs is around Kimju reverts to handbra." Elle draws the conclusion, "Only Robyn always stays covered. And Babs, although Babs blings, and I don't know how she keeps from spilling herself out."

"I told Babs we'd both go topless," Beka says casually.

Elle exasperates, "Listen, I'm not just concerned about flashing our nips. I got hair leaking out, and you..." Elle catches her thoughts. "You're the one inviting upskirt," Elle scolds. "BB's gonna vagflash you."

"I know, Elle," Beka confesses. "Last night Robyn made Steph open her legs in my face. I didn't quite know what was going on. She said I was next. I think Steph expects me to flash my bush instead of flashing hers."

Elle grits her teeth. *And maybe not just Beka flashing. Gamers won't be satisfied with just a little bit of hairage; they're going to want to see nookie.* Perhaps in the past Elle skillfully controlled her revelations, but now, here at the Cosmos House, it is she who will be skillfully controlled. Taught the language of Strip. Lots more.

Elle realizes, *This groove might be deeper than I anticipated. I'm starting to worry I won't be able to control my own exposures.* Starting to worry? *Already worrying; after all, Robyn made both of us titter for the Back Door Cam. So that's pretty serious. She didn't ask; she just did it.*

Standing, Elle's shorts tend to protect both her hairage and buttage, but when she sits down her nest flushes out both sides. Not shaven, this notch.

Having inventoried navelage and titter, Elle now quickly inventories her fellow Cosmos' hairage vs. her own ragged inseam: *Tiffany can't hide her red turf spilling out above her waistline. Kimju and Babs practice containment, although Kimju outlines her thong with a stubble of hairage, and Molly's panties only barely contain her muff. And then there's me.*

Elle doesn't know Molly's minge could become fully visible again if the Watering Can is recovered and her panties become see-through-when-wet.

There is a lot for Elle to learn, and it is to her credit that she continues her analysis. *Babs and Robyn don't leak any hairage, but Steph must keep her legs apart and show off her snizz. I suspect it won't be long before my Roommate, Beka, likewise exercises her potential to upskirt her miniskirt and showcase her bristly stripe. Open her breach is more like her.*

Elle blinks.

Gamers do covet the details.

Gamers assume that both newbies will soon learn to follow Hand Signs, beg more fervently to expose themselves, and discover that coyness is the property of the Cosmos House.

18 Beka & Elle: Flash & Observe Ginny Corvette (D11)

§ Tiffany Pee-Cams for Beka & Elle: Bathroom Consultation

Morning has turned to afternoon, and Beka and Elle huddle in the Bathroom. Boss Babe enjoys putting the slow squeeze on her newbies. She makes sure to ferment the presence of the two topless ex-Strippers Kimju and Molly, going so far as to ignore enforcing any handbra dictums.

BB also intimidates the newbies with the presence of ex-Whore Tiffany, whom she sits with in the Bedroom at this moment. "Go into the Bathroom and see if my newbies need make up," Babs orders. "Make sure you demonstrate the Pee-Cam."

"Ma'am, yes, Ma'am!" Tiffany smiles, promptly strips naked, and curls around into the Bathroom, interrupting the two newbies. "When you hang out in the Bathroom and I come around know that I enter naked and turn the Cam on," Tiffany advances.

Beka and Elle trade a look; they knew already, and they were dressed and presentable before Tiffany lit in.

"Watch me now," Tiffany commands, as she carefully cups her hand in between her crotch, and carefully drains less than a teaspoon of fluid into her palm. "I am a Pee-Camer," she details, "and I can teach you everything you want to know about Strippers and piss."

Beka blurts, "So are you really a Piss Mouth?"

"Ah, such a candid sweetheart you are." Tiffany raises her palm to her mouth and appears to pass piss into opened lips.

Elle startles. *Perhaps Tiffany knows slight of hand!* But she also bursts out a question, "So are you really a Whore and a Porn Star?"

Tiffany blows Elle piss breath and applies gentle correction. "I was a Whore last Term, but I am still a Porn Star. Once a Porn Star, always a Porn Star!"

Beka scolds, "Except you're not making Porn anymore. You're reduced to licking your pee to get attention."

Tiffany wettens both lips. Urine does tend to dry out the mouth.

Elle observes more carefully, "You did Double Opt Up."

"Listen, newbies," Tiffany deflects, "you must study my Tiffany Porn Star Calendar in the Kitchen; it provides proof *and* persistence to my claim." Tiffany stretches her naked body upward. "I've done everything explicit. All holes, all sexes." She rubs her Eraser Heads directly. "I need to lose one piece and go Strip next Term so I can get back to live cocks the Term after that. But don't worry; I'll help you both come to the Strip with me. You two and Molly, the four of us."

Elle scratches her exposed rib cage, checks that her belly button sits in its triangle above the jean shorts' zipper, and keeps her legs together. *Why does Tiffany assume that our begging means anything? After all, Beka and I both have two pieces.*

Whereas Tiffany's aggressive nakedness and past Caste intimidates Elle, Beka relaxes toward it and leads the curiosity. "So does Babs decide which Cosmos go topless?"

Tiffany brushes her long hair. "Does Babs decide topless? You're the ones already begging to Pledge naked and Strip next Term. So nobody's making you do anything." Tiffany plays with them. "Besides, once you get topless you wouldn't be titters anymore."

Elle closes her eyes for a moment. She thinks she gets it. *Kimju and Molly aren't titters; they're simply topless all the time. I don't need to be topless, except I'm already begging to get naked. That's crazy.*

Tiffany speaks the obvious. "The only Roommate Game that makes any sense for you two is Flip-Flop, since you each have two pieces and nothing to lose or gain." She examines both faces carefully. "Once Roommate Games conclude you can beg topless and trade Garments with Robyn and Kimju. Two for one; whoever gets the maillot can roll it down and into their rugage like the tanga, so you can both go topless and buttage, 24x7. Molly gives her panties to Steph, and I need rid of at least one Garment. Then we four can Opt Down. What's not to like?"

Elle's head spins. *Things could get out of control really fast here.* Elle considers asking out loud, but for the moment she channels inside. *Maybe Babs is a change agent, and maybe she has accomplices, superior officers, Gamers even. But somehow or other Beka and I are begging to get naked... even if I don't buy crazy.*

"Don't worry," Tiffany confirms, "I'll make sure the both of you learn how to Strip! Learn to pullaside, pink, cream, and climax. And not just climax your hole; climax your whole body."

Elle recalls, *My pleading involves more than just begging to Pledge naked. I'm begging to become a Stripper next Term.*

§ Babs Orders Beka & Elle Visit Janet: Obedience Training

Boss Babe strides into the Bathroom before Elle can correct impressions. By now both newbies have heard the double-B allusions to Babs: *BB. Bikini Babe. Black Bikini. BooBs. Bling Bra. Boss Babe. Boss Bitch.* Beka and Elle know to keep silent.

Other Cosmos trail in after BB. Robyn sports her maillot cutout. Steph still wears her loose-fitting strapped cutout minidress with its big button hole. Still inside out with colored spots defining where her spiggots lay inside, begging to titter the Cam. Kimju and Molly hang topless and fully buttaged, Kimju because her tanga provides no other alternative, and Molly because BB pulled the rear of her panties into her moonshadow at the Lineup this morning and Molly knows to not undo BB's handiwork. Except now the front of Molly's panties are pulled in tight too. Muff spilling everywhere, but no explanation offered.

"Listen up." BB points to Beka and Elle. "Monitor Janet wants to meet you. So you're gonna take a hike over to the Corvette House."

The Room stirs. BB augments, "But first Tiffany will do your makeup." Babs spins on the balls of bare feet and retreats to her Bedroom.

§ Tiffany Makes Up Beka & Elle: The Cosmos Tell on Janet

Tiffany sits Beka and Elle on adjacent chairs facing the makeup table and mirror. Robyn and Kimju and Molly and Steph cluster behind, and Beka and Elle look at them reflected in the mirror standing behind them. Two topless Pledge, two spaghetti strapped Pledge; all seven Cosmos Pledge barelegged, all navelage 24x7. And Tiffany not merely navelage, barelegged, and topless; here in the Bathroom she is naked of course— tits, thatch, and tush—and the Cam is very much alive. Lively, even.

Molly wonders. *Given what happened at the Bachelor Party, I may also qualify as a naked Pee-Camer.*

The Cosmos clustering around educate the newbies about the momentum of history... although mostly they educate Elle. They tell her that Babs and Janet were Roommates last Term, Monitors this Term. "Bikini Babes," Robyn provides. "They lost their tops Mudwrestling last Term but gained Opt Ups... and sent Penny and Coco Opt Stripping."

Kimju adds an event, saying, "We found out that Babs didn't know Janet had climaxed the Double Dong with Tiffany at an Alumni Reprise at the Nugget last Term. BB jumped when she heard."

Molly augments, "Janet saw Kimju and I lapdance that night." She gestures toward Tiffany. "Tiffany knows. She was there that night. That's when she became a Piss Mouth."

Tiffany casts her eye away from the Makeup Case to the Cosmos standing behind Beka and Elle.

"Boss Bitch hasn't begun to forgive Janet Jintoe for not telling her she climaxed the Dong with Tiffany," Robyn bloviates. "So I don't know why BB would let her play with the two of you."

"Boss Bitch owes Janet big time," Steph says, forgetting that the Cam is present. "Janet's the one who danced the Nugget, and Janet's the one who paid when Bikini Babe crossed her legs." She leans forward and titters unknowingly. "Be sure to remind Janet she 'jaculated when she

Pledged for me, and to show you the vids of her juice dripping off her labial rings."

Steph looks at herself in the mirror. *Nobody knows I saw the Alumni Reunion except Janet, whom I took over that night. And Janet hasn't told Babs anything; she didn't know about the Dong and pee until Kimju and Molly arrived and spilled the beans on Janet.*

Steph watches Beka and Elle squeeze their thighs together while Tiffany applies makeup. She makes a mental note of their modesty.

Beka and Elle watch themselves in the mirror. Tiffany assures them, "You're being loaned to someone Babs considers important, so I am making you beautiful!"

Tiffany finishes just as BB again sweeps into the Bathroom, gives Beka and Elle an approving look, and orders them, "Hands and knees. On the floor."

Beka and Elle scramble, and all the other Cosmos fall back.

Boss Babe stands so her bare feet are in clear view of two Cosmos' faces. She address them both. "You want to move into the Doghouse? So prove you're worthy to be dogs. Stay on your hands and knees and scurry over to the Corvette House. Present yourselves at the front door and bark until somebody tells you to stop. You think you're Cosmos Pledge? You're barking dogs begging to be let in. Don't fail to make me consider you worthy!"

Elle leads the answer, "Ma'am, yes, Ma'am!" and Beka gets in a "Ruff!"

Elle looks up at BB from her position on all fours.

Boss Babe advances, "You shall obey Corvette Monitor Janet no matter what she tells you to do, just as you shall obey me at all times. Now tell me, are you prepared to accomplish this mission?"

The answer is a jumble of Beka and Elle's voices, with some of the words twice. "Ma'am, please, bark, obey Janet." And then together on a final, "Ma'am."

"Scram," BB instructs, and they end up sliding down the angular staircase on their bellies, swinging the Back Door, and yanking the long Bell cord. Twice.

§ Beka & Elle: Transit to Corvette House

Beka and Elle talk as they glide out around to the front of the Cosmos House. "You know that BB's ex-Roommate is gonna make us both titter," Elle complains. "Babs owes Janet somehow."

Beka gyrates to the side and doses Elle with an armhole titter. "Relax, Elle, this will be a blast." Beka dances her arms up into the air, unaware that paparazzi, may they exist, might collect her armpits and expanded ribcage as well as her titter. Beka knows a good time. "Besides, Elle, didn't everyone see *you* lean over and titter yesterday? Downblouse, down-halter, on your way to the Doghouse."

Elle checks the neck strap of her halter to make sure it remains fastened properly. If it is a bow tie it must be tied only once; if it is buttons or snaps they must fit through the holes. Duh.

Beka turns onto the sidewalk. "Don't put me on, Elle. I've seen you flash noogies lots of times before we joined the Game."

"Well, maybe once or twice when we were clubbing perhaps," Elle confesses. "And more than one boss." They laugh together and steady their paces side-by-side. *But I have most certainly not tittered since we rang the Bell on our way out. And I don't intend to here outside.* Elle fingers her halter so she can look down inside. She sees a breast hanging with proper sag and a nimbus and nip coming up. "Let's not talk about it, okay?" Elle requests.

No problem. Paparazzi, might they exist, already collect Elle leaking hairage and the crease of her butt cheek outside her ripped jeans shorts. They await a Beka sit-down.

Monitor Babs estimates Elle will travel safely today. She, like Beka, is "dressed enough." Elle is too timid, too new, and too cautious of the Game to try any funny business like reconnoitering a candy store, detouring one block out of the way, or being pressed into carrying a note or comment.

Elle finds herself attempting to shrink into her costume. *I know I get looks, and I know that sometimes people stare at me. But I can handle it.*

Elle toughens her resolve as she walks, careful about where she places her bare feet. *I wore this outfit with confidence before I pledged, so I should maintain my confidence here, because this is an even freer environment than the office.* Elle pauses to question the veracity of her assertion. *Let's say this is a more charged environment, and leave it at that.* But then, once again Elle questions her choice of costume. *Beka influenced me to pick a too sexually suggestive getup.* Elle considers if she's being watched or not. *It doesn't matter. Here out on the street I can still control my own exposures, but I am reluctant to advance my teases in the Game environment.* Elle knows she is Pledging. *And one of my goals is to learn what is necessary so I may Opt Up, manage, and control others.*

But first Elle must learn to be controlled herself.

Beka doesn't want to let got of titter. She senses Elle's unease and seeks to reassure her Roommate. "Hey Elle, don't worry. I really can control my own titter, just like you can. But why bother? We're gonna be tittering all the time."

Elle snaps, "Titter and hairage are the least of our worries." She quickens her pace. "We just begged to pledge naked and become Strippers next Term," she affirms. "We need to walk that back."

Beka waves her idea off. "You're always too literal. Relax. We can titter or tease or even go topless. We've done that before."

Elle finds a pace that balances putting feet down on sidewalk and forward momentum. "Right. Topless beaches. Nude skinny-dipping. All of that. But teasing here to garner attention is different. Higher risk."

Beka shrugs. "You know, sometimes I'm not sure if I'm playing the Game or being played by Gamers."

Elle agrees, "I don't like the uncertainty."

Beka nods. "It could pretty scary and pretty exciting."

Elle cautions, "You're a croptop and miniskirt sanpan with the bristle and bare boneroo."

Beka understands. "I know Elle. I'm gonna drip broda outta my box."

§ Beka & Elle Visit Janet: With Ginny locked into Cravat

Three strong images will stick in Beka and Elle's brains after the newbies complete their mission and return to the Cosmos House:

The first is Janet herself, greeting them at the door: Big, bold, brazen, and looking much like her photograph on the Dining Room Wall. Janet's jaboos, scarcely concealed within her crochet Spiderweb halter, sway with massive appeal. Her round jaxy ripples behind her, and her jipijapa of black pussy hair unleashes itself in every direction around and *through* her small Spiderweb Bikini's g-string.

And that's just her physical presence. Elle tries to connect the stories from the Bathroom to this real person.

The second memory stems from the first: seeing in the flesh, and later hearing, Corvette Pledge Ginny. This memory sears them.

Even what Beka and Elle have heard about Ginny doesn't prepare them for what they witness as Janet sweeps them into the Corvette Parlor.

Corvette Pledge Ginny sits stark naked, gluteal hemispheres and heels on the floor, and locked in the Cravat, a medieval bondage device that collars her neck and connects to two rigid angled irons which jut away and secure Ginny's ankles so they are widely spread, and which lock her wrists midway near where her knees are bent.

"Say hello to Ginny. This Whore-For-Life begs penance for her Roommate." Janet gestures to the immobilized, naked Corvette Pledge. "May it please Gamers to plug Ginny's holes or rent them we will. And it will please us."

Beka and Elle know this is understatement, and they don't even see the plug sunk up Ginny's rear gut. Although the newbies are thin on any

Ginny and Lee backstory, they are not thin on Ginny's irons. Both their eyes drift from the secured ankles and wrists up to the iron collar at the top of the Cravat. The collar is inches tall and formed tightly to Ginny neck. *And that's just the easy part.* Attached to the collar is an iron fork, one that frames Ginny's face, and which arcs up the sides of Ginny's head, passing each ear and across overhead to the other side. A third piece of iron also ascends from the collar, only this one at the back of her neck, and following the contour of her head upward until it meets with the two side pieces at the top of her head.

Janet lets Beka and Elle eye the details. "Yes, two pins screw from the bar over her head into Ginny's two ears to ensure she does not turn her head. And also the O-ring gag that holds Ginny's mouth wide open is double secured to the bar. It's all very hygienic, of course."

Maybe Ginny can't turn her head, close her mouth, or move an arm or leg. But Beka and Elle can look into Ginny's eyes. Helplessness there.

"She's helpless," Elle offers the obvious.

"Safety first!" Janet ringmasters her guests. "Ginny's head and arms and legs aren't going anywhere. Nothing much she can do to hurt herself."

Elle finally allows her eyes to settle on Ginny's privates. Everything looks freshly shaven; the only hair is a racing stripe far above the shaven gynecology. Elle startles. Ginny's pussy lips are clamped and tied with cord to her toes... so that her gash stays wide open. Vicious. Brutal.

Janet showboats, "You probably heard about Ginny from Kimju and Molly. They were all Nuggets last Term. The same night that Kimju and Molly ran topless to the Cosmos House at the beginning of this Term, Ginny and Lee Lollydor streaked naked to this Corvette House. They have remained naked ever since their arrival. Here's one of them."

Beka and Elle gulp and take Ginny in. Lee Lollydor might be nowhere to be seen, but neither Cosmos decides it is polite to ask about her.

Janet briefs the newbies about Ginny's fuller backstory. "Maybe you already know this, but, like your Tiffany, Ginny's also a former Whore... from before she Stripped with Kimju and Molly at the Nugget last Term." Janet graces Ginny's cheek inside the head brace. "Apparently Ginny had to confront an Opt Down to Slavesex, and, in desperation, she pleaded to become a Whore-For-Life... and be sexually available no matter what her Caste. So she promoted to the Nugget last turn, where she had not just danced, but, you know, was tricked in the Champagne Room and shot porn in the Inner Sanctuary. Even though strictly speaking she was of Stripper Caste."

Yes, Elle remembers Kimju and Molly telling about this. Molly had elaborated, "Ginny lapdanced naked, just like Kim and I did, except with a rocket in her garage."

Beka and Elle had demanded to know what would happen might Ginny gain clothes and promote this Term.

"She'd be a Monitor but still be a Whore-for-Life," Molly had said. "And MomCap could trick her anytime."

Kimju had focused upon now. "Ginny might cover her body more, but for the time being, as a Corvette Pledge, she is Janet's most valuable asset."

Tiffany had interjected, "Ginny likes being a Whore-For-Life."

Kimju and Molly had protested, "No, she doesn't."

But Tiffany had affirmed, "She likes it. But she's just a Whore. I am a Porn Star!"

Elle confronts the present again. She forgets about decorum. "Maybe Ginny's a Whore-for-Life, but should a Pledge be in bondage?"

Janet chooses to ignore Elle's indiscretion in asking a question. She enjoys the shock in the Cosmos' faces and explains, "Ginny's new Roommate, Trixi Tubes, crossed her legs and requires 'memory training,' so Ginny volunteered to sit in for her and practice learning to hold a position. The Cravat helps Pledge learn. Yes?"

Beka should be more respectful in her address, but she isn't. "Maybe it's not good that one Pledge can sit in for another. Elle spent the night in the Doghouse because I wasn't supposed to open my eyes. When I should have been punished."

Janet knows more about sitting in the Cravat than she chooses to reveal to Beka and Elle. She overlooks Beka's poor form also. "It's so sweet when Roommates share. If I were to strip Trixi Tubes naked and discipline her in the Cravat, all I can do is Cam her and force her to climax. That's sweet for a lucky Pledge. But Ginny?" Janet whistles through her lips. "Ginny secured in the Cravat is a screwable commodity; she's already a Whore-for-Life. A role model of possibilities for Trixi to aspire to: a bondage fuck, sitting in for her." *Not my decision,* Janet admits, *but good practice until you-know-who gets to try it out.*

Ginny drools through her O-ring gag, and the newbies can see it catch on her chin, then surge and swing down toward her milk glands.

Beka freshens. Elle feels an urge to pee.

Janet smiles at the astonished newbies. "So yes, Ginny's in bondage. It's like she's a Slavesex, except she's not; she's a Corvette House discipline special."

Beka tries to be funny. "Ginny must love her Roommate."

Janet smiles. "And Trixi must love Ginny. Trixi say she feels horribly guilty and conflicted. But she's also not volunteered to swap places, which would be a polite thing to do."

Elle tries to be helpful. "Maybe Trixi should give Ginny one of her Tubes."

"Give her both of them!" Beka reacts, "I bet Ginny prays Trixi will remember to never cross her legs again."

Ginny gurgles, and Janet panders to her. "Don't worry, you are going to get fucked. Get fucked again and again. All holes, all sexes. Soon. Just hang in there."

Seeing Ginny locked in the Cravat live, if only a glimpse, help impress Beka and Elle to *never* forget to obey their Monitor.

Janet makes it easy. "I gather if BB wants to sign you newbies to spread your legs wide open so that both of you ready, willing, and able? Even if you have to pullaside, before you pull pink and rub-a-dub? No arguing. No splitting hairs?"

Beka and Elle trade a quick glance and cobble an answer together. "Ma'am, ready, willing, and able, Ma'am."

"Dining Room." Janet points the way through a Living Room. The newbies finally take their eyes off Ginny Cravat as they leave the Parlor.

§ Beka & Elle: Admire Corvette House Baseboard Strippers

The third visual impression relates to a suite of four framed Pictures hanging on the wall of the Corvette Dining Room, similar to those in the Cosmos House, except Beka and Elle haven't visited the Cosmos House Dining Room yet.

Experienced Gamers would immediately recognize two differences. The first is that here at the Corvettes a picture of Janet sits on top, whereas Babs occupies the second tier. Beka and Elle lower their eyes to two naked baseboard Pictures, and Janet appraises them, "That's Penny and Coco, presenting themselves like the Strippers they have become, and which I understand you beg to be. Is that correct, Pledge?"

What? Huh? Beka and Elle stumble but manage to spill out, "Ma'am, yes, Ma'am."

The second difference is that whereas at the Cosmos House all the Pictures are from the front, here at the Corvettes all four Pictures present backsides. Yes, Janet does indeed have a crochet g-string up the middle of her big rounded rump. And in the picture and in the here-and-now Beka and Elle can see that the g-string fits in between two long labial lips that hang out of her jepoot, weighted down by three rings in each side.

"This Dining Room Picture of your own Monitor Babs confirms what you might have suspected," Janet airs breezily, "which is that BB's nombril hung so low that her posterior rugage cracked above her waistline."

The newbies study Babs' substantial butt crack, nod their heads in unison, and carefully trade eyes. Janet reads their minds that they haven't yet had a chance to observe Babs' Dining Room Picture back in the

Cosmos House and observe Babs' folded-down nombril and humiliating hairage from the front side. "BB's got a treat awaiting your eyes," Janet teases. And catches Elle's scandalized stare at her Bikini. "I haven't changed; nothing I could do about it. Look at me. Crochet Spiderweb Bikini. I'm all out." Janet adds a tidbit. "Did BB tell you that both of us lost our tops during the Mudwrestling Contest?"

Beka twitches, and Elle looks down and shuffles her bare feet. *No, Babs did not so inform us. Although Robyn had alluded to something about BB spilling out of her low-cut bra....*

Janet breezes onward and extracts her g-string partly out of her jepoot. "Be sure you share the secret of Babs' rugage when you return back to the Cosmos House," Janet tweaks. "And BB will teach you the pleasures of eating soap."

Beka and Elle squint eyes on this one. They wisely do not ask why Janet still wears the same vulgar string crochet Spiderweb Bikini she wears on the wall.

"Prostrate yourselves," Janet commands. "Elbows and knees, legs spread wide apart, but slide your forearms forward, hands together, and rest your head on your hands!"

Beka and Elle comply awkwardly.

"Lift that bohunkus and naka-nake up in the air," Janet clarifies. "It shall please you to fixate on Penny and Coco's humiliations... and consider them for yourselves."

Beka and Elle admire Penny and Coco together. In the low-hanging, framed Pictures the two former Cosmos also pose on hands and knees. Here at the Corvette House, the Baseboard Strippers dangle boobs and present their asses to the camera, pull their butt cheeks apart so that their rosaries are full up and their sex organs gape. The pictures are so sharp that both Cosmos observe freckles on Penny's inner lips and a little ball of flesh just next to the entrance to Coco's colon.

"Penny's freckle and Coco's keloid," Janet details. "Might you meet them some time, be sure to beg them to show you the real deal."

Beka and Elle study the two faces before them. The shots, taken at the very end of last Term just prior to Penny and Coco's streak to the Nugget, catch the two now-Strippers at their moment of their defeat and dejection. Elle sees a flush in their cheeks and a plaintive look as their eyes, as they look back from in between their spread legs.

"Poot and coot, except that's you two next Term. What shall we call you? Boneroo and Nookie?" Janet nods her head approvingly. "Say put. And no talking!"

Elle can sense Beka trying to get her attention, but she provides stoic attention upon the sphincters and opened vaginas in the photos before her.

Beka wants to tell Elle that now, down on all fours, her shirt hangs away from her body so that her boobies are totally visible inside her armholes. Then Beka wants to tell Elle that she can feel that her miniskirt rises up, and given her current booty-up position her own sphincter, which points straight up, slowly inches into clear view. *My brown star, my bronzo, my borehole. Yikes.*

Elle possesses no illusions about escape, but she remains in denial about the extent of her own exposures. *Yes, my halter hangs away from my noogies, so the entire front of my torso is exposed. But Janet can't see my nipples because she's lording over me and at the wrong angle. And she doesn't seem like the type to get down on her knees to purview me.*

Correct; Janet leaves the room.

It takes a long time, but eventually Elle starts to twitch from the irritation of the inseam of her jeans shorts rubbing against the nether aperture of her GI tract. More twitching only encourages the inseam to irritate her nitro button, attempt to bury itself into her nook, and force more nest aghast to both sides.

Robyn had tossed a line at the newbies as the they had exited the Cosmos House. "Beg a thermoprobe up your asshole." Now, with asses raised up, this thought recycles itself inside Elle's brain.

§ Beka & Elle: Overhear Ginny Throated & Fucked

Beka and Elle hear voices enter the Front Door, footsteps out through the Living Room and into the Parlor, but they keep their eyes on the naked Baseboard Strippers before them. They hear what appears to be unmistakable sounds of Ginny, O-ring gagged and spread in the Cravat, being sexually used, although the two Cosmos cannot be sure what is happening.

Beka projects that someone abusively fucks Ginny in her mouth and deep throats her; Elle does not imagine that the ring gag could accommodate cock and so envisions Ginny pitched back and fucked vaginally, with the moaning noises coming through the ring gag. But neither dare take their eyes off the baseboard sphincters presented for their intimate inspection.

And then Ginny's quiet again, and when Janet reappears she clues them in. "Don't worry about Ginny; she'll keep taking on fresh spunk. She's a Whore-for-Life." Janet fingers her jewels. "Let's worry about you. So has BB taught you how to beg to Strip next Term?"

Babs has, and Beka and Elle chant together, "Please let me Pledge naked and become a Stripper next Term."

The Chant trips Beka, and she squeezes her boneroo in synchronization with reciting the Chant; booty high, bonnie smooth lips arching upward and parting as if inviting a doggy style fuck. Beka starts pumping brodeas in rhythm with the words.

Elle doesn't look, but she can smell Beka's gush. *It will start to hang down soon. I know. There is no way Beka can stop Beka gush.*

Ell hears other footsteps enter the room, see another bare foot and then a knee on the floor, and she knows hands release a Cam nearby. But she keeps her eyes glued on the two spread pussies and assholes in the Pictures before her. Currently Nugget Strippers Penny and Coco, last Term Cosmos Pledge. Elle quiets her shaking and listens to the hovering eyeball dart about, audio-locates it as it sweep near the floor, senses it look into her tight spaces and purview her from untypical angles. *Once again I have just been cammed down my halter. I might as well be topless.*

Patience, please.

Beka feels a toe encourage her croptop to fall forward and down toward her armpits and neck, and as her shirt forwards both boobs come into full view. No looking in through the armholes; full view and any angle the Cam collects.

It is all Beka can do to not look back under her body and confirm what she can feel, which is that her conical berries have become excited and bumpy, with the tips indenting back into her beige areolas. Now that they are more fully exposed, Gamers can see a darker band of pigment around both circumferences.

Beka's nipples have always elicited positive feedback. Beka's nipple indentions into this most sensitive part of her body produce arousal, although Beka remains largely unaware of this vehicle of her self-stimulation. Or that this is but one component among many.

Beka hears the two pairs of footsteps move around behind her raised buttocks and consider her exposed breech and borehole. The breech is totally smooth, with dark brown lips trying to hide an emergent clitoris— Beka's bolus, her bingo-bango-bongo button. Darker skin also surrounds Beka's borehole.

Beka's miniskirt has risen high enough up so that even the narrow landing strip of hair forward of her breech has been brought into easy view.

"Beka Broda," Janet advises her. "That's your new name."

Beka doesn't know what Janet is talking about, but Elle does. *Broda is Italian slang, short for brodeas, the vaginal secretions produced during arousal: valiva. Men lube; females cream. Brodeas before blast-off.*

"Ah," Janet exclaims, "not only is your horny box transuding brodeas, but your brownie wants penetrated too! No secrets for you!"

Beka's face flushes. Her vulva flushes its shaven finest. Raised flesh around her brownie radiates infrared. No secrets indeed.

No secrets except for the secrets Beka and Elle don't know, such as who the camer's feet belong to.

Janet knows; it's Darleen, her sidekick and Roommate.

Beka feels a long, thick, heavy probe penetrate into her vertically-held borehole. Beka squeezes herself tight, but the slippery stainless steel rod quickly accommodates itself and slides into her. Gamers watching via the Cam understand that hands implant Beka with a thermoprobe, a thermometer with advanced sensing and transmission capabilities. Janet and the camer walk away, but as the day progresses, every time Beka relaxes gravity slowly pulls the thermoprobe deeper and deeper into her back bore. Beka hazards a glance along the floor underneath her body; boobies almost touching the floor, boneroo lifted up, and a streamer of broda hanging all the way down to the floor.

Elle, sometimes drawn into competition with a Roommate sometimes overly horny, now imagines that hands pull the hem of her ripped jeans to the side, apply lipstick or grease to her proffered nether aperture, and insert a long and slender suppository into her rectum. *Into my nadir way.* Elle finds the thought repulsive, yet arousing. *The suppository melts inside me and, given my ass-up position, runs up my colon. If it's a purgative I will void my bowels. I won't be able to stop it.*

And what's arousing about it? *Something about loss of possession.* Elle tries to organize her thoughts; she rotates her eyeballs but not her head. *I need to concentrate on holding my position and keeping my eyes on the Baseboard Strippers.*

May it please Gamers to worry Elle. Elle fails to void her bowels, or, to the curiosity of the Gamers, produce any naughty secretions from inside her nookery. Gamers know that if Elle is actually administered a laxative or an enema she actually will void her bowels. Today Gamers, in their infinite wisdom, simply test and study their Pledge to determine what might turn her on.

Janet orders a different Chant: "Hot hot hot. Titters and twat. 98.6 in my anus." They do. Elle finds it demanding to not break pace, and she discovers Beka following her, although one or twice prompting her forward.

They do well and continue to chant when new voices enliven the Dining Room: guests to bear witness, pop flashes and steady Cams. The newbies keep their eyes glued to "poot and coot" and keep chanting. Neither Cosmos knows who collects what.

They lose count of how many cocks and pussies Ginny serves.

And they bless each other to help stay on the path of the Chant. "Hot hot hot. Titters and twat. 98.6 in my anus." Beka relies on Elle for steadfastness, but might Elle falter Beka assists in getting them back into rhythm. The stricture arouses Beka even more, and she squeezes a glop of brodeas so heavy it threatens to break her drop. *I want my picture taken just like Penny and Coco. I'm already tittered and trimmed and vagged. What I need is some cock about now.*

Elle finds the initiation demanding. I can't stand looking at Penny and Coco make pink-wet-and-ready, and I feel like something melted in my nadir way. Beka whispered to me she's bearing a long rod in her borehole. And Ginny's getting thrashed. Another certain thing: Janet is way more harsh than Babs, so I am much better off at the Cosmos House.

Some time or another the Roommates find themselves silent, absent a Chant, and Beka, in a pique of horniness, begs a different beg: "Please let me Pledge naked and become a Stripper next Term." Which she repeats and repeats again with a tone to try to get Elle to dig in, and Elle, realizing it is the wrong Chant but a Chant nevertheless, falls in with her so that they now chant together, "Please let me Pledge naked and become a Stripper next Term."

At the end of the day Janet collects the Pledge into a kneeling position, points to Beka's drip on the floor, and reprimands Elle, "You're not keeping up with your Roommate!"

Elle's eyes dance between getting out-competed and embarrassment for her Roommate.

Janet pats Elle on the cheek. "Don't worry, you'll learn to freshen before the Term ends." Janet pauses, surveys the puddle of brodeas Beka has left behind on the floor, and gives Elle the nod. "But for now you can clean Beka up." Elle hesitates, but obeisance is her only option; Elle lollys. Beka's white brodeas on the floor is tasteless.

"You're Elle Lollydor now." Janet pats Elle's head. "Right now all you got is valiva on your tongue and lips, but if you try hard maybe we'll help you find some boy spill to lick up."

Janet enjoys grinding the Pledge. On their way out the door she hands them each a package. "Here are some photos and vids for BB to share on your Screens. You two on your hands and knees today, and a bunch of shots of Molly and Steph from the Bachelor Party, from before you arrived but which you won't want to miss."

Janet jiggles both jugs in her hands. "And when you see Steph, be sure to tell her I loved her titter and vag at the Bachelor Party. And that I'm looking forward to her visiting me, pulling pink, and masturbating her sloppy slot until she wails in climax. And that the Cravat will free up eventually."

Beka takes the package in hand gladly, but Elle only slowly extends her hand. Janet raises an eyebrow and coaxes, "You should both be proud that you're getting passed around the Prefecture. By now Gamers are even masturbating to you. Boobies and noogies, box and notch, bronzo and nether gate."

Janet turns and torments Elle. "After you two Flip-Flop you can come back and share your upskirt!"

Elle flushes; Elle flusters; Elle knows. *If I were to wear Beka's miniskirt it would be my own nadir gate and nookie opened wide to the Cams, no more hem.*

Protocol requires that Elle pay respect. "Ma'am, thank you, Ma'am, for taking humiliating pictures of us, Ma'am." Elle knows full well that neither she nor Beka shall have any control over their own files.

Beka blurts, "And letting us have a copy to take to the Cosmos House!"

"Bye." Janet close the door, closes her eyes for a moment, and shakes her head.

"We're in a fix," Elle observes to her Roommate as they walk back. "We're in a Game where all the knowledge and information gets tightly controlled for us."

Beka voices less concern. "Hey, we got to visit the Corvette House. No other Cosmos got that. And nothing happened to us."

"Nothing happened?" Elle exclaims. "We barked like dogs. We didn't just titter, we hung out our noogies for hours. I wanted to close my eyes. How long can you stare at pussy? That could be us next Term."

"Jeez, Elle, you shouldn't complain," Beka argues. "I had a long, fat rod in my bowels."

"And you hung broda outta your box. I oughta know. I licked it up," Elle affirms.

"Hey, we got to see Ginny too." Beka values a dubious achievement.

"Maybe I'll cross my legs and we'll see how much you like getting locked in the Cravat," Elle jokes darkly.

"No, Elle, please." Beka places a bare foot carelessly on a stone. "I looked at you by accident. Really. I'm really sorry about the Doghouse."

"At least we got exposed to the real Janet," Elle adds. "She's a Monitor, like Babs."

Beka waves a hand. "Elle, it's really simple. We're both gonna keep our two pieces and promote next Term. Opt up, Opt Monitor, whatever."

Elle bites her lip, hesitates to voice more thoughts, but does not feel she returns from the Corvette House a winner. The encounter with Janet and Ginny, the imprints of Penny and Coco, and strangers camming her noogies and nookie and nates all contribute to a feeling of unease and uncertainty.

Beka tries to help out. "Elle, this is cinch. Topless Kimju and Molly are gonna Opt Stripper. Steph's gonna Opt Up. All we have to do is follow Babs."

Elle grimaces and says, "What if our assumptions are unrealistic or flawed? What if Babs or Janet tries to test our resolve or see if we'll break the Rules? What if we have to shuck our tops? Pull pink and masturbate? What then?"

Beka pooh-poohs her Roommate. "You're such a silly Cosmos! You should talk. I'm the one who got her bronzo sounded and hung broda out."

§ The Cosmos Debrief Beka & Elle: What Did Janet Do?

After they return to the Cosmos House and ring the Bell, Babs ushers Beka and Elle in the Back Door and herds them into the Dining Room. Five Cosmos await them there also. BB asks, "How did it go?"

Elle replies, "Ma'am, it was a most disconcerting experience, Ma'am."

Beka adds, "Janet seems like a much harsher Monitor."

"I will try to rectify that," BB tells them cheerfully. It is not the answer they had hoped to elicit. "Dismissed."

All the other various Cosmos await an opportunity to corner Beka and Elle and drill for any core samples that might be relevant to them.

Tiffany learns little of substance, nor is she able to discern why Babs would relinquish control of her just-arrived newbies to Janet. *I spent a day drenching myself with my own pee after failing to disclose that I climaxed the Double Dong with Janet. Could Janet's similar failure to inform Babs have been forgotten about?*

Or perhaps Janet did a lot of good deeds for Babs last Term and has been forgiven.

Robyn inquires, "So was Janet Jintoe still wearing her spiderweb?"

Beka and Elle look at each other. Elle provides the news. "Janet said next time she sees you you're supposed to remind her to sit youself in a corner, spread your legs, and cam yourself."

Kimju and Molly also demand Beka and Elle tell them what happened.

"So you saw Ginny. I'm so relieved." Molly touches her fingertips to her temples. "They streaked and made it."

"Well, we didn't see any Lee, but Lee's not Ginny's Roommate any more," Elle hastens. "Apparently it's somebody named Trixi Tubes."

"We didn't see her either," Beka augments. "Except she had done something bad."

"Trixi had crossed her legs, that's what she'd done." Elle hasn't forgotten. "And the opposite Roommate got punished. Like Beka sending me to the Doghouse for the night."

"So Ginny was getting sexed in the Cravat," Kimju seeks to clarify.

"That's what it sounded like," Elle recounts. "We didn't dare look. Janet kept a Cam on us all the time."

"We couldn't see around the corner anyway," Beka defends. She expounds, "I think Janet even invited friends over to cam us. And then gave us a copy to bring back to Babs."

Kimju reacts, "Pictures of you two titter and vagflash?"

Elle hedges, "Well, maybe. Titter for sure both of us, but I still have a hem between my legs."

Beka shakes shoulders. "I don't. And they cammed my beaver and slid something long down my brownie."

Elle tries to offer help. "Janet also gave us something featuring you two at a Bachelor Party? And that maybe Tiffany's going to lose her monopoly on the Pee-Cam? What's that all about?"

Molly knows what it's all about.

Steph catches Beka and Elle at a different moment in the Dining Room. "So you got to meet Janet. How'd she treat you?"

"We got to see Ginny Cravat," Beka rushes a first impression.

Steph blinks. "Nobody cares about Ginny Cravat. Tell me what happened with Janet."

Elle elaborates, "We had to get down on our hands and knees and study the Baseboard Strippers."

Beka interrupts, "There's a picture of Babs from behind. Butt crack."

Elle continues, "We stayed like that for like hours."

Beka hurries, "People came in and cammed our boobies. And then my miniskirt rode up, and Janet said some of my brodeas leaked out."

"And what about you?" Steph directs this question to Elle.

"Ma'am, I'm not sure, Ma'am." Elle offers unwarranted respect, but Elle Lollydor neglects to inform Steph that she licked Beka's brodeas up.

"We brought back some files and gave them to Babs," Beka volunteers. "Janet told us to beg to get ourselves screened."

Elle offers a tidbit. "Janet said she also included some vids of you and Molly, something about a Bachelor Party and you splattered with piss."

Beka queries, "Yeah, what's that all about?"

Later. Steph knows what it's all about.

§ Robyn Torments Beka & Elle: Begging vs. Garment Count

Beka and Elle realize that the four Dining Room Pictures provide the opposite of the four Pictures in the Corvette House, and once they get a moment alone they attempt to explore this asset. They are in the midst of examining Babs' hairage, Janet's Spiderweb, and Penny and Coco's naked and spread revelations when Robyn breezes into the Dining Room.

"Oh, look at you two!" Robyn bops. "Prospects conniving on the fastest way to the Strip!" Robyn curls her nose and barkers the Dining Room Pictures. "On the top, the Boss Bitch, who must live with this vulgar and in-her-face reminder of her despicable past. Janet Jintoe underneath." Robyn looks at the two naked Pictures at the bottom. "And I bet you two will do *anything* to be the next Baseboard Strippers!"

Elle takes umbrage. "Hold on, Robyn. Beka and I are going to promote next Term."

Beka supplements, "We both got two pieces."

Robyn straightens her frame. "Don't be stupid. You are both already begging to 'Pledge naked and become Strippers next Term.'" Robyn slants her eyes.

And Beka and Elle look at each other. The both clench arms to their sides and squeeze their thighs together.

Robyn laughs at them and points a toe at the two horizontal Baseboard Strippers, Penny and Coco. "Last Term, Cosmos; this Term, Nuggets. Pulling pink on the baseboard. Kimju and Molly report they got shaven bare and climaxed center Stage the night they arrived at the Nugget. Some debut. I hear they double donged before they left the Cosmos House, but nobody saw them."

Robyn waves her hand, and the Screen on the opposite side of the Dining Room lights up. Beka and Elle recognize Kimju and then Molly stripping naked on a Stage with flashing disco lights. Robyn clarifies, "Last Term's Strippers, this Term's Cosmos."

The scene changes to a solo sequence of Kimju, shot on a bed, playing with her nipples and clit, squeezing her pussy, then pulling pink, and finger-fucking herself to an inevitable climax.

The scene changes and Molly appears, naked on Stage, lying on her side with her legs apart. Robyn narrates and derides, "Hairy Molly Mammoth. This moerskont sticks a procto up her mawk port with one hand and sinks a dildo into her mutton with the other."

Elle watches, mortified, but Beka rises to the challenge. "Double Penetration," Beka defines. "I can match Molly DP any day."

Elle tilts her head down and looks through raised eyebrows. She watches, transfixed, as DPed Molly touches a finger to her maraschino and mambos.

Robyn rudely talks over Molly's ongoing climax. "I'm gonna make sure you get to see Kimju and Molly masturbate in sync with their own videos, so they can cum with themselves." She laughs.

Beka squeezes her boneroo beneath her miniskirt. And Elle figures, *I don't need to be watching what I am seeing now.*

Robyn gestures and changes the feed. This Screen shows a confused Beka and Elle arriving at the Backyard yesterday and Robyn camming titters of the both of them. "This Term's Cosmos; next Term's Strippers!" Robyn twirls and cackles. The image follows Elle as she crawls into the Doghouse.

Beka blurts, "You gonna show us the videos of whoever cammed us at Janet's? From the Corvette House?"

Robyn wrinkles her nose like a foul smell has passed through air. "You wish. Maybe Boss Bitch has already traded them with the Peacock House. So everybody knows and everybody's seen. Except you two, and especially you, Elle Lollydor."

Elle flushes. *If Robyn knows I lollyed Beka Broda then she's seen the video.* Beka squeezes her boneroo once again.

Elle asks, "What do you know about whatever else Janet sent back with us? Something about Molly and Steph at a Bachelor Party?"

Robyn augments, "Perhaps even a Medical Exam. Or some Figure Drawing Class surveillance video. I told BB to save it for later, but she may have shared it with some of us. And besides, at the Bachelor Party," Robyn flaunts, "Steph says Molly pulled a bloody tampon out her meatlocker, spread herself with a speculum, and chewed the tampon to bits in her mouth while she masturbated and pissed and came. So when the time is ripe I will cue Babs, and roll the video. That should pretty much qualify Molly to beg the Pee-Cam. Don't you think?"

Elle accepts that something like this might have happened. *I am only the messenger, bringing the package from Janet to Babs. Sneaker net, were I not barefoot. I did not make this Bachelor Party video, and I was not a Stripper last Term.*

And besides, the way I heard the story, Steph laid the panties on the bar and dared Molly to pee on them. And when Molly did, Steph dared her to pick up the panties with her teeth and stuff them in her mouth. Molly did, and then hi-tailed it out of the joint.

Well, something happened.

Robyn breaks into Elle's reverie. "You're lucky. Already Tiffany and Molly insist they want to Strip next Term, so with you two that fills up four slots and leaves the other four of us to Opt Up next Term. Babs can Hover or Opt Up, and Kimju and Steph and I will Opt Monitor. It's a done deal. First thing is that Steph is gonna take Molly's panties for good, and then everything after that will follow."

Robyn squares her shoulders and fingers her buttonhole. She rotates her finger into her button as she struts to the double door that connects to the Kitchen. "Remember," she says as she turns on her way out, "if you feel the urge to play with yourself on the Cam, then just slip outside the Back Door and practice on the Landing." And she's gone.

Beka wonders out loud, "Jeez, I wonder how Kimju and Molly feel about Robyn playing their videos."

Elle realizes that the Screen has been black for a while now. She advances her own pragmatic concern. "I wonder how *I* feel about Robyn playing my video." Elle pauses. "I'm sorry; *our* video."

§ Beka & Elle: Concerns About Other Cosmos as Threats

Elle looks at the Screen again, and latent images of Kimju and Molly dance before her eyes. She turns to Beka. "As for Kimju and Molly, their indifference to self-exposure conspires to make them dangerous to us. They posses few inhibitions and bring unpredictability to any struggle."

"Robyn's gonna make them rub-a-dub in sync with their cum vids from last Term," Beka recounts. "I want to see that."

Elle does not. She tries again. "I am by no means eager to test them, tangle with them, or seek out Games. We could lose."

"Yeah, well, maybe. But we don't just have to keep a lookout for Kimju and Molly," Beka grumbles. "Robyn keeps suggesting that Babs pit Steph against me in some sort of upskirt contest."

"Right," Elle agrees. "You gotta worry about Steph, even though she's not your Roommate. She still need another piece, and I'm worried that Babs might let her prey on you."

"Jeez, Elle, relax," Beka patters. "It's already decided. Steph's gonna take Molly's panties. I hear she's already tried them on."

Elle retorts, "But she had to give them back. I bet that unnerved her."

The Roommates laugh together uneasily.

Beka asks, "So, what happens next?"

"Well," Elle advances, "winning's not going to be easy for Steph. Molly keeps trying to give Steph her panties, but I think Babs wants to let Steph take a drop."

"Not let her have them?" Beka checks. "Make a Stripper outta her?"

"You watch," Elle affirms. "Babs' gonna give Steph a smaller minidress."

"*Smaller* minidress?" Beka discounts. "Come on, Elle, that's already happening. Steph can't help but titter and vagflash!"

The twosome laugh together again, albeit uneasily. They again consider the four Dining Room Pictures, especially the naked and spread Penny and Coco. Cosmos last Term; Strippers this Term. One looks away, and the other makes wet.

Finally, it is a mistake on the part of the newbies to not also assess the risk Tiffany presents. But because Tiffany's former self is *so* beyond the pale and because she *already* wears two garments, Beka and Elle discount her.

Beka and Elle flip through the pages of Tiffany's Calendar on their way back through the Kitchen. They pause on an image of Tiffany totally covered in mud, facing the camera, and sitting with a cock in her tinderbox. "Porn Star," they agree.

Elle fails to appreciate the degree to which Tiffany actually desires to forfeit her Garments. Elle's own assumptions about promotion make it difficult to understand that Tiffany *likes* tramping around in topless see-through, relishes cracking her tail trough, and enjoys the effect of showcasing hairage or'top her skin-tight, crotch-cameltoed, low-rise stretch slacks.

Elle fails to appreciate that Tiffany angles to stay nude, and not just on the Bathroom Cam. Tiffany's goal remains to permanently abandon both Garments and stay naked. It's the least she can do for her fans.

Upstairs in the Bunkroom, as Beka and Elle settle into their bunks for the night, Elle calculates, *Tiffany has two pieces. Babs has two pieces. Beka and I have two pieces. So the four of us stand to Opt Up and Monitor, and Robyn and Kimju and Molly and Steph will all Opt Down and Strip.*

Elle still worries as she drifts off to sleep. *Something tells me it's not really going to happen like that.*

19 Robyn Works Kimju & Molly: Hand Signs & Climax (D12)

§ Cosmos: Bunkroom Reveille Lineup Faces Mirror

Lineup at Reveille the morning of Day Twelve occurs in the Bunkroom. Robyn and Kimju, Molly and Steph, and Beka and Elle all watch themselves stand spread surrender in the Bunkroom Mirror. Elle inventories six pairs of eyes, armpits, and legs; six navels; and two pairs of nipples atop knockers and mams. Elle notes that Molly's panties remain gathered into her muliebre and moonshadow, and that Steph wears a new minidress: small buttonhole, very short... and strapless! The floppy string straps of the last three days seems to have been exchanged for a management problem of a different kind.

§ Babs & Tiffany: Evaluate Cosmos Politics in Bedroom

Boss Babe retains Tiffany in the Bedroom to groom her and make her beautiful.

The Pledge wait.

Tiffany, still naked from sleeping and yet to dress, encourages the Bikini Babe to resign herself to luxury, and Babs acquiesces. Tiffany works on her hands and knees to first lather, then shave, BB's long legs, then her armpits. She trims her eyebrows and eyelashes, paints her finger and toenails, brushes her hair, and makes up her face.

BB knows Tiffany prefers to makeup Cosmos in the Bathroom, but here in the Bedroom there is no hovering Cam. *Automatron doesn't collect me; Caste has privileges. And besides, Tiffany need to care more about giving me her personal attention, rather than vamping for her fans on the Pee-Cam or trying to convince Pledge they all want to Strip.*

Babs had secretly, and with reluctance, watched clips of Tiffany's piss extravaganza in the Bathroom from five days ago. BB watched Tiffany show her tailpipe tattoo to the Cam, drink copious amounts of water, roll her legs up over her head, part her sex lips, and shoot yellow urine all over her body. Watched her sputter pee; watched the clip of her spending the night lying in her own stink. The Bathroom Cam had registered every intimate detail, and after watching it Babs felt horribly guilty. *I still feel guilty. Yet somehow Tiffany doesn't hold it against me. Okay. I really don't have any reason to obfuscate her desire to Opt Strip, and I'll help her if I can. And besides, Tiffany helps me sometimes.*

Tiffany does practice genuine penance. BB considers, *Tiffany tipped me off to a secret containment strategy to minimize the risk of spilling my babambas outta my bra.* Babs touches her bra straps. *Last Term if I leaned over I had to hold myself into my bra cups.* Or wished she could. This Term BB still presents two globes of cleavage, but besides controlling her posture and movements, an enlightened BB has taken advantage of Caste. *This Term I have secretly glued my breasts to the inside of the bra with gum arabic. Take that, Gamers. No spillage.* However, there remains nothing BB can do to stop the edges of her areolas from flowing out. *Areolage 24x7? Some things have changed; some will change soon.*

"I know of no Rule that forbids gluing," Tiffany had said, then added, "Besides, everybody uses glue. Eyelashes, pasties, even keeping a jewel glued into your navel."

And gum arabic is in the Makeup Case, after all. Caste has privileges.

Tiffany advances BB's face to Cleopatra status. Babs continues, "And now that everyone's arrived my costume choices resolve. Janet was right: once I can cover up, my bling doesn't bother me anymore."

"Good for you," Tiffany grins. "You're making progress."

Babs trusts Tiffany enough to confide to her, "These two newbies, they don't know anything. One of them just wants excitement, and the other doesn't want to make any mistakes."

Tiffany commiserates, "I heard them say that your Dining Room Picture at the Corvette House 'cracks butt.'"

"Posterior rugage. I don't doubt it."

You already got both newbies begging to be Strippers next Term," Tiffany gently teases. "*I'm* the one who needs to be a Stripper next Term. Remember?"

All true, but Babs chooses to elaborate about the newbies. "Listen, Beka and Elle didn't just bring back their own clips from their Corvette House visit; Janet also sent over Molly and Steph's vids from the Bachelor Party. So maybe you no longer have a monopoly on the Pee-Cam."

Tiffany acquiesces, "Molly said she also got a Medical Exam. I'll do that too. You can have Madam Nurse spread my twat wide open with a speculum, put an anoscope up my tailpipe, take my blood type, give me an enema, put me on a cath, and put a feeding tube down my throat. If you insert an endoscope my fans can look inside me and not just at my skin. Inside my tinkle tube, down my throat, up my tailpipe, and all around the inside of my tinderbox. All of that's legal for a Pledge. I've done everything explicit. All holes, all sexes. Anything to please you, Ma'am."

BB mentally rolls her eyes. "Robyn's bugging me to let her train the newbies. She claims I already appointed her to train Steph on Hand Signs and cam her titter and vagflash."

Tiffany steps back to survey Babs' makeup, and again gentles truth. "You already let Robyn make Steph spread her legs on the Library steps, the Kitchen, and the Back Door Landing. It's very convenient for you to let Robyn provide Steph with that special touch of sadistic enforcement. Perhaps Robyn might also enjoy training Kimju and Molly, signing them to hold their hands over their knockers and mams and endlessly breastplay titter." Tiffany advances, "You've always preferred them covered up."

"Stop it!" Babs orders in a friendly fashion. "I've gotten over them stalking around topless. And you too, whether you wear your see-through croptop or run around in just your slacks."

"You know I'll dance naked with a Post in the Backyard. Kimju's not the only one who can make it slick!" Tiffany rises quickly to the draw.

"Double stop it!" BB decries, and the Roommates laugh together.

Babs takes a moment to gather her next thought. She brushes a hand through her long black hair. She makes sure her waistline contains her bushy tuff, then touches her bling. "Roommates Robyn and Kimju are both teasers, but in very different ways," BB advances carefully, inviting discourse.

Tiffany gathers the flows of conversation. "For Robyn, the tease provides a way to garner attention and control the situation. When men are involved Robyn likes to tease mercilessly and then dismiss her admirer. She has total self-confidence in her ability to affect outcomes. Who could be worthy of her? Maybe a White Knight, but somebody at this School?"

Babs watches as Tiffany fingers her vast expanses of bellage and continues her analysis. "Kimju is a more blasé exhibitionist. Like Robyn, she will draw in a Gamer's attention, but Kimju's cooler about it. She knows she gets looks, but she doesn't milk them. She's bolder, but she also has more dynamic range."

Babs considers, "Okay, both Pledge are naturally attractive and accept, even relish, getting looked at. But—"

Tiffany completes, "—for Robyn the looking must be done on her terms, whereas Kimju will let anybody look, even stare at her... dressed or naked. She might sit so that her arms block her knockers, and then move so one can admire her knurled control knobs on top. So instead of being suggestive and pulling back, Kimju will reveal increasingly intimate secrets."

"Just for asking," BB confirms.

"Right," Tiffany agrees, making sure Babs' eyelashes are perfect. "Kimju likes the admiration and takes it like a performer on Stage. Kimju's tease isn't a wink and a wiggle, it's a slow reveal... even if her knockers and kaboose are bare all the time. She knows there always exists an edge to be discovered."

BB holds still so that Tiffany can finish her eyes. Babs frets, "Kimju probably knows more about seduction than I do. And she might be an exhibitionist as you suggest. But I don't think she wants to pink and cream for the Cams. Or return to the Nugget next Term."

"Ah, true." Tiffany fingers her Eraser Heads and shifts gears. "Nor does Steph. But if *you* take Steph's minidress you can cover *your* bling up. You really have no other choice. Kimju and Molly are topless. Beka and Elle won't stop areolage, and Robyn's strapless maillot cutout won't contain you. You've already dismissed my clear vinyl croptop. So Steph's your only choice."

Babs tugs at her bra straps. "At least now I'm in control of my blushing. Well, most of the time, anyway." BB advances, "As for Steph, one piece or zero, as far as I'm concerned she can Opt Strip next Term. She knows I'm letting Robyn haze her. She's not stupid."

"Ah." Tiffany raises a finger. "She believes that Robyn hazes her in ways you haven't authorized. And you turn your head the other way!"

Babs shakes off the accusation. "Well, if Steph thinks Robyn gives her unauthorized orders I don't know why Steph obeys them. Especially given that Robyn contributed to Steph's downfall. I think they need to work some things out."

"The reason Steph obeys Robyn," Tiffany muses as she touches up Boss Babe's eyes, "is because she knows that if she doesn't obey Robyn as your agent and you let her get away with it, then maybe you'll come back later on and ask why *your* orders didn't get followed. She's trapped."

"I'd never do such a thing," Babs decries.

"Fair enough," Tiffany agrees, "but if you don't come down and crush her then some other Gamers will."

"Some other Gamer, like Janet," Babs suggests, then worries, "or even MomCap." Babs considers her torso in the Mirror. Cleopatra! Bling! She exasperates to Tiffany, "Listen, I'm trying to be fair and balanced with Steph. She escorted Molly to the Figure Drawing Class, but didn't have to get naked. She escorted Molly to the Medical Exam but didn't get examined. She escorted Molly to the Bachelor Party, but didn't have to pee. She's in demand," Babs defends. "What can I say? I know her. She's going to get testy."

Tiffany says delicately, "It's very simple." She aligns BB's final eyelash. "Steph must obey you."

Babs ponders, "Steph doesn't appreciate me signing her, directly or indirectly."

"She's not supposed to," Tiffany agrees. "That's why you have to do it."

§ Molly Begs Babs: Second Pee-Camer & Piss Mouth

Babs and Tiffany return to the Bunkroom.

Tiffany attaches herself to the end of the Lineup adjacent to Robyn. She remains naked. Babs walk behind the Lineup of seven Cosmos Pledge and observes their standing spread surrender front sides by looking into the Mirror. She observes a faint smile on Tiffany. Confusion in Robyn's eyes. Kimju's gaze into her own eyes doesn't waver. Molly's eyes dart around, awaiting direction. Steph looks hostile and tries to look out of the edge of her eyes while at the same time appearing to match her own gaze. Beka and Elle have stood spread surrender longer than they care do. They look worn, but they tighten up when Babs passes behind.

Babs addresses her clan. "Congratulations, Pledge. You're making great progress. First, Tiffany begs piss, soap, and Opt Down. Next, Robyn exercises her Roommate Kimju on the Post. Then Roommates Molly and Steph turn in command performances. And finally newbies Beka and Elle can't resist outreach at the Corvette House. May you all collect fans. May Gamers watch you. So which of you want to go begging today?" Babs' question is unexpected.

Molly, selfless, finds it easy to go first; she begs the obvious. "Ma'am, you saw my vids from the Bachelor Party. You know I should no longer be allowed to shower or urinate while the Bathroom Cam sleeps. Everybody at the Party cammed me, so please, Ma'am, it's not like I wasn't a Pee-Camer all last Term. So if Tiffany is allowed to Pee-Cam naked, then so should I, please, Ma'am."

"Very well," BB states solemnly. "You've earned it, and may your clips travel far and wide. So from this now on the Bathroom Cam shall alight when not only Tiffany enters, but you as well." Boss Babe waggles a finger. "But don't get too cocky. I'm sure more Pledge will beg to join your Pee-Cam Obeisance."

Molly rushes, "Please, Ma'am, I'll pee on any Cam. Inside or out. Anywhere, in front of anybody, anytime. Please let me give my panties to Steph. Ma'am, please let me kiss the Mirror stark naked. I'll masturbate and meringue and mambo for you. I'll audition the Nugget."

BB reaches around Molly from behind, grabs both her mammaries in her fists, and shakes them. "You're gonna beg your own Alumni Reprise. Maybe it's your turn to Double Dong the Nugget center Stage. You'd love the Pee-Cam to advertise you to the Nugget."

Molly winces. "Ma'am, I've surrendered all expectations of privacy."

Boss Babe plays hard to convince. "You think that sharing your micturition with Gamers who watch through the Cam increases your odds of returning to the Nugget next Term."

Molly agrees, "Ma'am, yes, please. I peed once a day center Stage last Term. And the toilets there were out in the open, made out of glass, and had Cams inside and out. No secrets for Strippers, you know?"

Babs doesn't quite know what to say.

So Molly explores, "Ma'am, you could let me bring the Bathroom Cam into the Bunkroom and watch me make out with Mirror."

Babs explores, "So you intend to pee while you mambo the Mirror, is that part of your plan?"

Molly lets out her breath. *It isn't. It doesn't matter.* "Ma'am, may it please you, I'll lose control of myself completely."

"You clean up after yourself?" Boss Babe throws a twist.

And can hear the gasp of Molly air. Unanticipated consequences.

BB rescues her Pledge. "Perhaps Tiffany can clean up after you. She's a Piss Mouth."

Molly stumbles, "Ma'am, that wouldn't be right, Ma'am. I can clean up after myself."

"Maybe you and Tiffany need to clean up together," BB suggests.

"Ma'am, may it please you, Ma'am." Molly looks in Mirror at Babs. Babs has let go of Molly and stands behind her.

"Maybe your Roommate should clean up after you," BB says soberly. "She wants to share your panties; maybe she should share your Pee-Cam."

Molly volunteers unthinkingly, "Ma'am, may it please you Steph can share the Pee-Cam with me, share my Piss Mouth, and lick up after me. And she can keep my panties for good."

Steph shuffles in the Lineup, but she is not the only Cosmos disturbed by this remark. Kimju, despite wearing only a tanga, resents Molly's willingness to create expectations for ex-Strippers. *I have no wish to Pee-Cam. I wish obtain a second Garment to cover my knockers. And Opt Up next Term.*

Steph considers her strapless miniskirted self in the Mirror. *I find it particularly irritating that my success in reducing Molly at the Bachelor Party has resulted not only in Molly regaining her panties, but also requires that I can't use the Bathroom any time Molly enters and lights up its Cam.*

BB discharges her Lineup, ordering, "At ease." She heads back to her Bedroom.

Steph turns upon Molly and hisses, "You didn't do any good begging the Pee-Cam. You and Tiffany are both pariahs. Now if either you or Tiffany use the Bathroom no one else can use it."

"That's not true," Tiffany interrupts to defend Molly. "Anyone can still go pee. And it's not like Molly and I are ganging up on you and keeping the Pee-Cam lit. Besides, from what I hear about what happened at the Bachelor Party, you're the one who turned her into a Pee-Camming Piss Mouth in the first place." Tiffany fingers her belly somewhere below her navel. "Be nice. Your Roommate is a Nugget-wannabe. She's like me, and we're both pretty willing to pink, pump, and piss all over to get there."

Steph narrows her eyes at Tiffany. "Fine. You do what you need to do. But I have no need to join your wretched pee Camcast." She turns upon Molly, "I shall not be sharing your Pee-Cam, Roommate."

Molly blanches under the attack. "Jeez, Steph—"

Steph picks up the pace. "Maybe I can't avoid vagflashing, but leave me out of your Pee-Cam enthusiam! No matter how much you want to clean up. You want to be a Piss Mouth? How about I piss in your mouth?"

Tiffany again comes to Molly's defense. "Be nice. Don't your forget that Molly and I always light up the Bathroom Cams, because the two of us can make sure that *you* get to share Pee-Cam fame."

Balance of power. Wide angle or close-up, Cams have consequences.

§ Steph: A Strapless Minidress with a Demanding Buttonhole

Aside from Molly's rambunctiousness, Steph also doesn't quite know how to interpret this morning's new cutout minidress. Unlike the loose-fitting strapped minidress with the too-big cutout she has worn ever since the Bachelor Party, this morning's minidress is a particularly risky, tight-fitting, strapless concoction with a small buttonhole. If Steph tugs the neckline up securely, the buttonhole wants to rides up above her navel, yet if she tugs the hole down into a safe and stable position, she magnifies the risk of popping her smurfs out.

Steph appraises herself in the Mirror. *I don't deserve this.* The tight stretch-fabric rubs and irritates her spouts just enough to remind them to stand at attention. Steph seethes that her nipples erect. But the more Steph tries to "dim her headlights" the more her concentration on them tightens their hardness… and drives her toward releasing splurt from her sweet spot.

Steph scowls. Besides the dangers the elastic strapless neckline presents, Steph knows that were she to sit down—and ensure that her thighs don't touch—*that my short, tight minidress will ride upward, and that ragabash Robyn will sign my legs apart and vagcam my upskirt again. In private, in public; she'd even let the paparazzi collect my sanpan. And if I'm not careful, they'll document me all slippery. She's out of control. I might be her former Monitor, but she denies ever knowing me.*

In fact Robyn has some new Hand Signs to try out.

§ Babs & Tiffany: Advanced Hand Signs for Strippers

Learning Hand Signs is part of the training for all Pledge, and Gamers anticipate that as the Term progresses Babs will advance their practice, especially for the newbies, who know them not at all.

The newbies shall learn that the significance of Hand Signs includes their lack of ambiguity and their ability to communicate in public or private spaces directly and with stealth. It is not necessary that others know why a Pledge chooses to lean over and titter or uncross and open her legs. Only the Pledge needs to interpret the signals... and obey them.

Hand Signs represent a level of commitment. Of learning and practice and patience. Are they like verbal orders, which can have a similar nature? Sure, although the vocabulary of Signs specializes in things like body position, movement, and count.

Monitor Babs is well-versed in all the basic Hand Signs: Hand Signs to flash, Signs to cover or reveal the breasts, bush, or butt. BB knows the Signs to cross and uncross legs, keep legs apart, to open them halfway, and to spread them wide. BB knows how to order Pledge to sit or stand, and how to command them into surrender position, with their legs braced wide and fingers clasped behind their heads. BB knows how to sign a mouth open, control the position of a tongue, or direct eyes forward. There is a Sign to close the eyes, a Sign to stand at attention, and there is a Sign for "at ease."

Babs has confided in Tiffany on this issue. "I mastered all the Hand Signs for basic actions during my Pledgedom last Term. I did a magic fingers demonstration that contributed to my promotion to Monitor. I know the power in fingers." And then she had more carefully said, "I'm sure you know everything I do... more, too."

Tiffany had pondered this thought before acknowledging, "I suspect so. And certainly both ex-Strippers already know how to obey Hand Signs, they've certainly been in School long enough. I suspect they both already know the Signs to play with their nipples, how to pullaside, pull pink, make wet, and stay ready. They know different ways to masturbate, you know: roll their clits, finger fuck, eat their own cream, and so on...." Tiffany dallies, but goes all in. "Cum even. Strippers cum, after all."

Babs had pulled one side of her cheek in tight against her teeth as she had considered this overture.

Tiffany had read her mind. "You don't want to project weakness by asking me to show you these Signs. It's all right. I can show you some of the more advanced signals. No charge."

Babs had put a plan into action. "How about you clue Robyn in so that she can practice on Kimju and Molly, or even Steph, and give them a workout?"

Tiffany had nodded her head. "Ah, the hidden hand at work. No problem. I will pass along a catalog of Signs and put your request into production."

Babs had expressed no qualms about doing this, and Tiffany had teased her, "You're not making it easy for Robyn to win friends!"

And Babs had laughed, "I'm sure Robyn has forgotten everything she ever learned about Hand Signs. But I bet if I assign her to train Kimju and Molly she'll get her memory back."

Tiffany had then advanced the Caste of the Stripper. "Perhaps after Robyn gives Kimju and Molly a workout, you should let her train Beka and Elle. After all, they are the ones begging to Strip."

Babs had frowned at this assertion.

Tiffany had picked up any slack. "Hey, you're the one making them beg. And both newbies deserve every possible opportunity! They'll pick it right up, despite the fact that you will use their new knowledge to humiliate them."

Babs had opened her mouth to counter this assertion, but Tiffany had waved her off. "No problem. It's fine with me that they get reduced. Just as long as you let me be a Stripper first. Please, Ma'am."

BB had chosen not to reply.

§ Robyn Signs Kimju & Molly: Pink Wet Ready… Climax!

And so this afternoon Robyn jumps to the task of signing the ex-Strippers. She recites: *Two fingers together and chattered downward is a signal to downblouse and titter. Crossed fingers, crossed legs; open fingers, open legs.* And so on.

Robyn corners her reluctant Roommate Kimju, then invites Steph to volunteer her Roommate—the hairy, plump, and compliant Molly—to join in Hand Sign practice. Robyn gestures Kimju and Molly into the Bathroom with a hand sweep, closing in on them from behind before Molly can get her panties off. "Stand spread surrender!" Robyn shouts, and both topless buttage obey her.

Steph drifts in behind the others and observes, *Now is not the time to introduce correction that Molly shouldn't be wearing panties here in the Bathroom.* Steph audits the Cam. *Yes, you came alive when Molly came in. Rude of it to cam irrespective of whether she wears panties or not.*

Steph tucks a shoulder up under her neck. It feels good. She attempts to repeat the operation on the symmetrical other half of her body. *Harder.* She rotates her shoulders around. *Careful with my strapless, and especially careful to keep my button hot. Possibly that's all that matters, and besides, I've already given them titter and vag. How much more could they want?*

"Sit spread surrender," Robyn commands Kimju and Molly, pointing to a vertical short wall that is actually the side of a bathtub. A mirrored wall lies ahead, not too far away.

Kimju casts her eyes about the mirror. She shares a disgruntled shrug with Molly's eyes and squares her posture. Knockers vs. mammies. Spread crotch: tanga vs. panties, crossing through and stretched tightly across their pubic hair. Armpits. Navelage 24x7.

Steph rubs the ball of her palm against her hidden nipples and observes Robyn. *Robyn sits Kimju and Molly down just like she and I got sat down the day I arrived. Backs to the tub and our legs spread. Not just open; spread. I spread sanpan for the Cam my very first day. And Boss Bitch has made me vagflash and spread every day since.*

Now there's a claim worthy of audit.

Naked Tiffany herds Beka and Elle into the Bathroom. Robyn stands between the two sitting Pledge and the mirror they face, which is behind her. But the threesomes' eyes shift once again as BB trails in and takes control of the scene. Tiffany has pushed Beka and Elle closest to Robyn and the two ex-Nugget Strippers. Now BB focuses on her two newbies and commands, "Kneel, legs together, hands behind back. Watch and learn how to obey Hand Signs."

The Cam seizes upon this fateful chance to document Babs: bra with widely-spaced shoulder straps and nombril briefs. Navelage, cleavage, and bling! Automatron indexes areolage. Babs knows the Cam collects her. She commands it, casts her eyes around the Bathroom and inventories seven Pledge, ignores Molly's infraction at failing to discard her panties on her way into the Bathroom, bows, and exits. She returns to her Bedroom and leaves seven Cosmos to play. BB can watch on the Desktop, may it please her. Or not watch at all.

Molly takes it in and talks to Kimju via the mirror. "I guess it's my turn to Pee-Cam."

Patience, please.

"Enough with the talk," Robyn sasses, then signs the two topless ex-Strippers to oval their mouths. She escalates and demands they perform tongue and lips actions. "Lick around the inside of your lips like you're a couple of hot sluts," Robyn purrs. "Now lick your lips with your tongue and loll your head around like you're drunken klute and mephitis dancers."

Robyn laughs at Kimju and Molly's hapless antics. She is the only Cosmos to do so. Steph watches with a hand to her mouth, covering a wry smile. Elle and Beka have forgotten to keep their hands crossed behind their backs, and they watch with both hands on their mouths. Tiffany sits off to the side on the bidet, opens her legs, and swabs her insides out. She fails to draw the Cam away from Robyn.

So do the two topless Cosmos really already know an advanced Hand Sign vocabulary? Robyn signs them to roll their nipples erect, and they do. Kimju resents the intrusion, but when Robyn signs Molly to suck her own majonkers Molly doesn't think twice about it.

Robyn pitches a curve ball. "Here's another Sign to try out!" Robyn makes a gesture. "You're supposed to know this one."

Kimju and Molly do know it, of course. Tiffany has shown Robyn a gesture using animated curly fingers to sign a Pledge to pullaside and display her lady parts, so now Kimju and Molly pullaside a thong and panties in front of the whole House... and whoever else might be privileged to watch the Bathroom Cam feed.

Like you, Gamer, Kimju fumes. *I really resent showcasing my kypsey, especially with Robyn in command. I had to pullaside in the Kitchen, but this is my first time on Cam this Term.* Kimju keeps track of her Game. *Gamers joining this Term and lacking access to Automatron finally get to see between my legs.*

Well, intimate details up to a point: a brunette bush that is trimmed short, but not so short one can determine if there is a clithood ring down inside.

Gamers know that Molly's overgrowth of black minge is ragged. Robyn compliments, "Gamers know you turned your clithood ring out at the Bachelor Party." Robyn twitches her nose and upper lip. "Don't worry, Molly Mammoth, you'll get to turn your ring out again. You both will."

Fresh vag for the Prefecture, Kimju scowls to herself. *Didn't I leave enough of this behind last Term? And shouldn't Beka and Elle be doing this, instead of me?* Kimju finds them in the mirror, and they trade looks. Beka pivots her head and torso, keeps her hands on her hips, but stays kneeling. Elle kneels firmly, again hands crossed behind back, and pivots only her eyes.

Robyn asserts control over the two open-legged, pullaside Pledge. "Beg to get fed live to the Nugget," she commands.

Kimju and Molly stumble but do it together. "Ma'am, please feed our Cam live to the Nugget, Ma'am."

"Good girls," Robyn mocks, then teases, "Don't get too excited, because lots of acts want to play there."

Kimju seethes, but she and Molly continue to hold the tanga and panties to one side while the Cam collects them close-up: full topless body, head to toe. Vag, too.

Beka studies the details of Kimju's and Molly's pubic hair and parted crotches. Elle memorizes the Signs by repeating the actions with her own hand, still behind her back. Tiffany, who has returned to stand behind them, observes Elle practice the Signs with both her left and right hands. Tiffany touches a finger to her nose and takes a whiff of herself. She dabs under each nostril, tastes herself, and licks herself clean. *Good!*

Steph watches on high alert. *Once, before Molly gave her panties to me, and here, where she shouldn't have them, presents a perfect moment for me to acquire them.*

Somehow Robyn seems to possess memory. "Now practice this," she vocalizes, and then leans in and makes a Sign with her thumb and two fingers. The former Strippers know this meaning as well. Butterfly: the name comes from the shape made. Molly is quick about it; she keeps her panties pulled aside with her little finger and parts her sex lips with the thumb and fingers of her opposite hands. Kimju pulls her wings apart with reluctance, using the fingers of one hand and retaining her tanga to the side with the other.

Two experienced ex-Strippers demonstrate form. Their clits make the heads of the butterflies, and the pulled wings show the pink body inside. Molly premiered pinking at the Bachelor Party; for Kimju, this is her first open exposure this Term, and she doesn't like it one bit. *Wrong signals. Wrong direction. Not where I want to head.*

Robyn directs the Cam's attention toward her Roommate and lifts her chin. "Tell them your name, you bedizened beat moll wannabe."

Kimju replies carefully, "Ma'am, I'm Kimju, Ma'am."

Robyn gathers saliva and spits on Kimju's foot. Molly almost loses her grip on her panties and parted muliebre, but Kimju never wavers. Robyn proclaims in the voice of a ringmaster, "Fresh koot with a hard karat standing up on top."

Kimju seethes at Robyn's reference to her deeply pigmented inner lips surrounding a rosy pink keyhole and now-erect clit. *This ragabash intends to cream me today!*

Beka and Elle clench their hands to their mouths; for the first time they and the other Cosmos now confirm what some have suspected, that Kimju, like Molly, has a ring in her clithood. It sparkles.

Robyn picks on her Roommate. "Kimju's not just offering to let you look at her kooch," Robyn proclaims to the Cosmos clustered around. "This kooch begs use." Robyn addresses Kimju directly. "I bet you Double Penetrated when you were a Stripper last Term. Yes?"

Once again Kimju feels publicly humiliated. Her face flushes, her nipples erect, and her sex lips rouge with blood. She considers rebellion. *But what if Robyn has Charm?* She glances at Molly, darts eyes in the mirror....

Molly interjects to answer Robyn's question. "Ma'am, Kimju and I both carried DP last Term." Molly adjusts her weight against the surface behind her back. "It's not a secret. You can search out our DP in the Automatron."

Like Kimju, Molly holds her mooe wide open; unlike Kimju, Molly has already secreted a pool full of white muscovado inside her deep brown muliebre. Its scent tingles the nostrils of everyone in the Bathroom.

Robyn trails the scent to its origin. "You both need to be wet," she proclaims and rolls her thumb and finger together. Kimju pines but follows Molly and rolls her clit between her thumb and forefinger while still holding her tanga pullaside and her sex lips butterflied. *Pulling pink and making my kunny get klammy. There is no longer any hope for escape. I know what I have to do; I have done it many times before last Term. But I thought I was done with letting go in front of Gamers.*

Kimju hears Molly breath deeper and realizes she must play with herself harder. *It's not hard when you know where to go. My turn to freshen and add my aroma to the room.* She does. She abandons her self-analysis, moans, and kloops; she can't help herself. She vibrates, and the whiteness pumps out her held-wide lips.

"Pink, wet, and ready!" Robyn decries. And so they are. Steph doesn't know she's wet, but her nipples are hard. Tiffany, shamelessly naked, once again fingers herself. Beka crosses her hands in front of her chest, feeling her bits through her croptop. Elle keeps her wrists crossed.

Kimju and Molly hear Robyn through a fog and loose themselves into a steady masturbation. It's a first for Kimju this Term, but it's hardly a first for either former Stripper. If Kimju could think right now she'd really resent Robyn making her reveal herself in front of everybody. Except Kimju isn't thinking right now; she's getting ready to climax.

"Stop!" Robyn orders and again signs the two ex-Nuggets to butterfly.

Kimju breaks her rhythm, leans forward, leans back, furrows her brow, starts thinking again, and hurls Robyn a question. "So who's teaching you these Hand Signs?"

Robyn seems baffled that Kimju would speak and retorts with a terse, "That's none of your business, you kohlrabi kootch kitty!"

Kimju senses weakness and presses, "It's not Babs! So who?"

"Shut up. I sign. You obey me." Robyn stomps her feet and signs them once again into a clit rub. Molly had never really stopped, only slowed down.

Kimju uses the moments to evaluate. *I know Robyn doesn't have this kind of Sign vocabulary.* And her eyes alight on Tiffany in the mirror. Tiffany watches with a wry smile, a finger across her lips, and the slightest of head tips. Kimju feels trapped. *I didn't sign up to Pledge wet, and I'm not sure I should be masturbating.* Kimju scans the Bathroom. *Babs is not here. So must I keep masturbating until I am directed to stop?* Kimju checks to make sure she holds her pullaside firmly and flies her wings widely. *My keystone rises, and a knittle of kloop dangles down. This is not okay.*

Molly, sitting next to Kimju, just rubs unabashedly. Molly doesn't question. Her eyelids hang low and she secretes even more mung from inside her deep muliebre; it overflows and floods her minge and uplifted inner thighs.

Kimju's eyes seek out Tiffany, but before she can speak Robyn reminds her, "Listen, Kimju Knock, know that if you were not here, you'd be a Whore at Flesh Ranch. You'd be sucking cock and getting your koot and kawazoo filled up."

Robyn spits at her Roommate again and lands spit on her inner thigh. "Masturbate faster, you knockabout koekjedoodle. Catch up with Molly."

Robyn lectures to the cluster of Cosmos who surround her, "You'll get to eat each other out to climax some time, but right now wait until I snap my fingers before you start climaxing!" Robyn betrays Tiffany with a look, but Kimju has ceased to pay attention and shifts into total body sensation mode. She finger-fucks, goes crazy with multiple fingers, and abrades her clithood ring back and forth against her full karat.

Tiffany plays with herself lazily as she watches as Kimju and Molly increase their heartbeats until they are breathing hard, panting in unison, fingers sloppy with cream. "Huh, huh, huh, huh, huh… " Steph becomes aware that she fingers her headlights and slicks her inner thighs. Beka and Elle clench themselves.

Robyn snaps her finger, and both former Strippers release themselves into howling rolling climax. Creamy Cumming Cosmos! Cam feeding the Prefecture.

Just when it seems like they are about to stop climaxing, Molly gasps and breaks into a new rhythm. Hard, hard, soft, hard, hard, soft. Kimju follows, thoughts coming back to her now, when she hears Robyn command through the fog, "Look at yourself in the mirror." She does, seeing herself there, watching her image breathe faster again and into a run and pure vibration, matching eyes, until suddenly the pain of the climax! And then backing off, taking deeper, slower breaths, finding Molly, and synchronizing with her.

Tiffany ensures Robyn lets them down easy. Kimju and Molly come out of the trance to encounter a quivering finger, a Sign they interpret correctly when they bury curled fingers, scoop out fresh valiva, touch their fingers to their mouths, and taste themselves. They scoop out more, wipe their faces, turn toward each other, and kiss. They rest.

Beka and Elle trade a glance, and Elle whispers, "We might have done guys together, but we never witnessed women masturbating themselves."

"Not just women, Elle," Kimju whispers back. "Cosmos Pledge, cumming in tandem."

Robyn frowns at the whispering. "Kimju and Molly climax not just in front of you worthless Cosmos Pledge, but beg to audition in front of the entire Prefecture." Robyn hardens her posture toward Beka and Elle. "I trust you won't forget these Hand Signs," she sasses, "when it comes time for you to practice!" The newbies will not forget; the Signs have been seared into Beka and Elle's brains and are more than they want to know.

Robyn catches Kimju looking up at her from the floor. "You thought just because you're a Cosmos now you don't have to pink cream and climax? That thought is over. You're gonna climax the Double Dong center Stage at the Nugget during your Alumni Reprise. And you can take the newbies with you."

Molly rushes to volunteers. "I'll pink, cream, and climax as much as you want, Robyn. I'm a Pee-Cam Pledge. I'll Double Dong the Nugget and lose my pee during climax."

Robyn waves her off. She reserves her final dart for Steph. "Since the Gamers didn't get to see much of you last Term, they now want more, so besides just flashing your smurfs, scrag, and spheroids, during *The Runup* you're gonna lean how to open up your snapper, squeeze out some slush, and scream-cum for your fans." Robyn gestures to Molly, leaning back casually, hands to her sides, panties bunched, and augments, "See if you're up to your Roommate."

Steph scowls at her, then detects laughter behind her back. Steph decides to snide, "Don't try to play my Game, Pledge. You know, I used to think you were the top dog because you had the smallest buttonhole. But you know something—my buttonhole is as small as yours." Steph rests.

Robyn straightens and rises to the balls of her feet. Babs isn't here, and Robyn doesn't seem to consider that the Cam could be her window in. "I control men with my navelage, and *I* have the smallest buttonhole of all. But that doesn't matter." Robyn focuses on Steph. "I'm not a titter slut; I don't upskirt and vagflash; no cheeky buttage. I'm not showing areolage 24x7. Nada. I've got straps. I am the one in control. Obey me."

§ Babs Requires Elle: Locate Her Old Measurement Nudes

Babs, concerned about Janet usurping her power with the newbies, and Elle, concerned about the unfolding developments at the Cosmos House, find themselves sitting down at the Kitchen table together.

Elle, still wearing her halter and jeans shorts and squeezing her thighs together, volunteers a complaint. "Janet threatened to Flip-Flop Beka and me; she said she was going to make me expose my nookie and nadir way."

Boss Babe tightens a wry smile.

Elle asks, "Can Janet tells us what to do?"

Babs smiles, "Well, at least you're diplomatic enough to not complain that your noogies and nest have become public domain."

Elle blushes. Unlike Beka, who threatens to display her bare box and landing strip upon sitting, Elle's hairage leaks out the sides of her shorts. And she must lean forward to flash noogies down the halter.

Elle hastens, "And Robyn. Can she really sign Beka and I to pullaside and spread our legs apart?"

"And then sign you to butterfly your notch, make your nectar flow, push your nitro button, and climax?" Boss Babe states the rest of the question.

Elle stirs uneasily. "Ma'am, that's pretty extreme, Ma'am. Maybe for Kimju and Molly it's okay, but they were Strippers. Robyn's even shown us some of their clips from the Nugget last Term. But Beka and I, we're newbies. We... I never did anything like that before."

BB listens, waves in the air to make the Kitchen Screen come alive, and shows Elle a picture of herself at a nightclub during her previous self. It depicts Elle wearing a dress with both her noogies swinging free.

BB raises her eyes up.

"Ah, Ma'am, yes, that's er, ah, me, Ma'am." Elle confesses. "Yes, but that was all... a fashion statement. And besides, you know, breasts aren't exactly the same thing as vaginas, and besides—"

BB completes, "—you're already flashing your tits here at the Cosmos House."

Elle seeks the safe harbor provided. "Okay."

Babs pops another image up on the Screen. This one captures Elle getting out of a car at a nightclub, also from before. It's rude, embarrassing, humiliating, and unnecessary. Unnecessary?

"That's you, nizzy. Yes?" BB inquires. It is. One of Elle's feet reaches for the pavement, and the other pushes against the car doorframe. "No panties on that nookie. No hem in that notch."

"Ah, yes, Ma'am. Yes," Elle stammers. "I didn't do that on purpose."

"But you're not exactly a virgin flasher?" BB lifts an eyebrow.

Elle casts her eyes down.

BB advances a statement. "Maybe Janet is right and you do need to swap clothes with your Roommate. Flip-Flop!"

Elle attempts a feeble defense. "Ma'am, Robyn already showed Beka and me the clips of our arrival. Everyone could see our noogies. And we're supposed to beg you to screen whatever Janet shot of us at the Corvette House."

"Beka transuded broda onto the floor and you licked it up," Boss Babe summarizes. "Beka Broda and Elle Lollydor. Yes?"

"Ma'am, please, Ma'am." Elle doesn't know what she begs.

"Yes indeed!" Babs is cavalier. "You should beg me to serve up all your old pictures. Videos too."

Elle blanches as she ponders the magnitude of this suggestion. *Does this mean they will be on the Cosmos House Screens? The other Houses at School? The entire Prefecture?*

Of course it does!

"Ah, Ma'am..." Elle considers how to respond. "Please post pictures of me flashing my nips and my nookie." Elle pauses, then qualifies, "That you have already collected." Elle feels unsure, so augments, "Plus the clips Robyn shot of us in the Backyard... me and Beka both."

"And whatever else you might bring me!" BB progresses. "Besides what you brought from Janet."

Elle quietly considers. *Whatever else? What might Babs mean? Like there might be nudes a former boyfriend took. There could be....*

Boss Babe elaborates, "I hear you sent over shots of yourself holding a tape measure. Three pictures, one for each of your measurements."

Elle deflects but does not deny. "Ah, Ma'am, that would have happened before this Term began. Ma'am."

Babs heartily agrees, "Obviously. They arrived before I became the Cosmos Monitor. They would have arrived with your application. Yes?"

"Ah..." Elle wonders out loud. She remembers the self-shots but had assumed they had been discarded. *Perhaps now is not the time to test that hypothesis.*

"Describe them to us, Pledge," Boss Babe commands into Elle's silence. "Truth becomes you."

Elle takes a deep breath. "I took three head-to-toe images in a mirror, totally nude. In one I hold a measuring tape around my bust; in another I hold it around my waist; and a third around my hips. My Measurement Nudes, and yes, they were part of my application, Ma'am."

"So what did you tape in at?" Babs inquires.

Elle halts, understands. "Oh. 34-24-34. That's me. I'm a 34B, except this halter is looser than that."

"You don't have your Measurement Nudes anymore?" BB asks a trick question.

"No, Ma'am," Elle responds quicker now, expanding, "I don't have anything now except for my two Garments."

Touché.

BB smiles, appreciates, but very much remains in charge. "Very well. You shall locate them, procure copies, and bring them to me so I may examine them."

This is a dubious order. Elle repeats carefully, "I must locate my Measurements Nudes just so you can see me naked?"

Boss Babe swoons. "You make me sound selfish. Why don't we say you must locate them so you may post them so that the entire Prefecture may view your measurements?"

Elle doesn't know about Automatron yet. She protests, "What if whoever has them doesn't want to give them to me?"

BB ducks her chin lower and looks at Elle with eyeballs rotated higher in their sockets.

Elle, not sure of Babs' intentions, protests obliquely, "I'm not sure I signed up for this...."

"Not sure, Pledge?" Boss Babe speaks quickly. "You checked the box that said you'd show your whole body and not hold anything back! And what are you begging of me?"

Elle casts her eyes down. "Ma'am, please let me Pledge naked and become a Stripper next Term."

Babs points toward the Dining Room. "You're dressed enough. Go find them. Study the Baseboard Strippers, Penny and Coco. Pledge last Term; Strippers this Term. They are role models for you to aspire to."

Elle gets ahead of the Game. "Yes, Ma'am. Please let me hunt for my Measurement Nudes." Elle pauses. "And anything else I can find." *Whatever that means.* "So you can show me off, Ma'am." Elle does know what that means. *And I suspect Babs will.*

Well not quite. Babs nods and issues final words. "So you can show yourself off, Pledge."

Elle knows what that means. *And I suspect I will.*

20 Robyn Cams Steph & Beka: Upskirt & Vagflash (D13)

§ Babs Humors Steph: *All* Cosmos Shall Keep Legs Apart

Lineup on the morning of the Day Thirteen occurs around the Dining Room table. It's not exactly a "Lineup" of course: Babs has ordered, "Stand spread surrender, each of you, and face away from the table."

The Cosmos Pledge obey her. Tiffany, at the far end of the table, faces away and is stark naked and made up. Armpits smooth. Tush facing toward the back of the Room and the windows into the Backyard.

Beka and Elle comprise the furtherst pair. One of them faces the wall with the two windows and the Screen between, and one of them faces the four Dining Room Pictures. Open-armhole croptop and miniskirt; button halter and zipper shorts.

Molly and Steph likewise face away from each other. Molly's panties gash her front and backsides, hairage, buttage, no top of course, and hairy underarms, hairy everywhere. Steph still wears the strapless minidress, only today she wears it inside out, and once again it appears that Steph wore nipple makeup a day before. And today her belly button appears decorated.

Robyn appreciates that she need not face Kimju. She faces the four Dining Room Pictures and appraises, *I am much more covered up than either Boss Bitch or Janet Jintoe, and I'm much more secure in my maillot since I told BB to give me my straps. I understand, standing here like this with my armpits, button, and legs extended that I'll do that as part of this act, but it's not real. What's real is BB's areolage and hairage on the wall, Janet's Spiderweb, and the spread punt and cunt on the Baseboard, halfway to Whore.*

Robyn squares her posture. Too bad Boss Bitch hasn't gotten to dance at the Nugget. Janet has. Penny and Coco are. And at least four Cosmos Pledge are already begging to go Strip next Term. This is easy.

Kimju faces the window nearest the rear of the house. She detects the presence of a Cam looking at her through the glass, surrounded by the hedge that grows along the side of the House. She jerks but holds her topless tanga position. Kimju doesn't realize that the Back Door Cam has already surveilled her and all the other Pledge through the two windows looking out onto the Backyard and that it has made a special effort to work around the side of the House and document her full on. Yes, today Kimju wears the tanga gashed so that, like Molly, she too may display full hairage. Unlike Molly's sprawling mange, Kimju displays an inverted triangle of butched kava, and her body is smooth: shaven legs, shaven arms and armpits, shaven belly and back. Kimju feels heat come into her body. *The Gamers collect me, but I can take it. I begged Tiffany to make up my knobs. I begged Robyn to pullaside, pull kleave, kloop, and koekjedoodle! I can take this 'Kimju knockers and kava-kava.' What I need is a second Garment. But if I challenge my Roommate Robyn, she gets to call the Game. And if she has Charm she'll pick a Game I'm sure to lose.*

"Pledge can be toxic sometimes," Babs remembers Janet saying some time ago. "And you're gonna have to watch out for your former Monitor, Steph Sorostitute, because she really will try to break you."

"She was your Monitor too," Babs had protested.

"Yes, and I will help you keep her under control," Janet promised. "But she remains your Pledge after all, not mine. Okay, you're symbolic of you and me both, so I will help you train her. But she will try to force you first; you're nearest. Force you to Pledge again next Term. Like what has happened to her."

"Steph did it to herself," Babs had affirmed. "If anybody had license to bunk on Steph it was any Pledge but Robyn. She got favored treatment. Yet it is she who signs the affidavit Steph covered her buttonhole. Steph gets Opted Down and Robyn gets redacted. And they both end up my Pledge."

"I'll trade for her," Janet had reminded BB. "She's dangerous. She possesses a combination of resentment, vengeance, and privilege, and she never passes up an opportunity for self-advancement... or poisoning a well."

Babs, still very much a Bikini Babe, remembers this conversation as she sweeps into the Dining Room. "At ease, all of you. Sit down. Relax."

And they do, all facing inward now. They turn and look at Bikini Babe, now seated at the head of the table. Bling!

Steph seizes the opportunity to argue to Babs, "No one Pledge should be singled out for training. Your Rule that I have to keep my legs apart isn't fair because I'm the only Pledge flashing her stuff."

The Cosmos all cast her a glance and look to see how Babs will react.

BB drolls, "You're a good vagflasher."

"Vagflashing!" Steph's strapless minidress and parted thighs revel fine blonde hairs, a slit underneath, and a stamen wanting to pop out. Steph advances her case. "You got my thighs apart so I am *always* a visible upskirt."

"So."

"It's not flashing. It's not like Beka, flashing now and then; it's all-the-time."

Boss Babe tosses long black hair back over a shoulder.

Steph continues, "And it's not just the Cosmos who get to look. Paparazzi feed unauthorized Gamers."

"Perverts from the outside!" Tiffany titillates.

"And the entire Prefecture when I let the Cam inside!" Robyn claims history, although frequently the Cam is guided by Automatron or by Gamer hands.

BB takes charge. "Silence, all of you!" She draws her hands up to her forehead, opening her armpits and then closing them again as she draws her arms down the outsides of her face and neck until she rests them under her chin, squeezing her boobs but covering her areolage.

Boss Babe concedes, "Steph, you're right! It is so unfair! To be singled out!" BB scans the room. "So, from now on, each and every Cosmos shall keep their thighs apart all of the time! And I mean no contact ever!"

All together now: "Thank you, Steph! Legs apart 24x7!"

§ Robyn Cams Beka: Back Door Sanpan Open Upskirt

Newbie Pledge Beka appears to be the main benefactor of Boss Babe's more egalitarian legs policy. Beka's pantyless miniskirt enables delightful views of her unobstructed bare beaver, complemented by her trimmed vertical landing strip slightly above where her lips come together and where a clit hides inside, a bolus wanting to ball out.

"You." Robyn rises and points to Beka. "Come with me." And so Beka follows Robyn out to the Back Door Landing, where Robyn sits her leaning back so sun shines up her short miniskirt. The Back Door Cam collects her legs apart, including whatever sunlit intimacies might hide beneath barely apart inner thighs. Knees up, back and hands bracing against the railing. While the Cam shoots, Robyn taunts, "You're gonna beg to more than just legs apart upskirt all-the-time." Robyn drawls as she signals Beka to open wider, "You're gonna beg Tiffany bring the Makeup Case and shave off what's left of your bristly landing strip. You're gonna open your breech up and finger fuck your broom closet. You're gonna make your bolus rise outta its hood. Do you understand me?"

Beka thinks so, and speaks carefully, "Ma'am, yes, Ma'am." She opens her legs to a middle position. Plenty of sunlight.

And Robyn cams brodeas trying to leak out.

Robyn flairs her nose as she looks down at her trainee. "You think hootchy-kootchy Kimju and mumbo-jumbo Molly are the only Roommates who are gonna cum for my Cam? You and Elle Lollydor are already begging to Strip, and you both are gonna cum for me when I say." Robyn piles on a cheap thought. "Next Term, once you are Strippers, you'll be begging to Whore. Once Beka Broda makes Whore you can turn your beaver into a burse!" Robyn cackles. "You can be a Beka Bursar full time."

Robyn leans in to better examine the one-inch wide, two inches long, landing strip Beka presents for inspection, but Cam tilt lower as Beka squeezes her bare breech, and a blob of brodeas runs down toward her asshole. Also sunlit.

"Janet says you call that your borehole, your bronzo, your brownie. Is that true, Pledge?" Robyn queries.

Beka speaks in a frank kind of way. "Ma'am, I can't stop my leaking brodeas running down to my bowel sphincter, Ma'am. Once I get excited it just keeps making béchamel. Trust me, if I stay here a while it will drip down onto the Landing."

"Wouldn't want Elle to have to lick you up out here," Robyn jests as she sees an opportunity to make a scene change. "On your feet," she commands. "I shall not allow you to leave béchamel behind. Follow me." And they both ring the Bell.

§ Robyn Signs Beka: Quad Upskirt 24x7 • Elle Rescues

Enough for the Cosmos House Cams; paparazzi may not have been able to zoom in on Beka's broom closet on the Back Landing, but the route to the Lecture Hall facing the Quad affords no protection. Of course Beka isn't sitting with her legs apart either, until Robyn pulls to a stop and points to a bench in front of the stately brick structure.

"Sit," she commands. "You heard Boss Bitch recite the Rules: 'thighs never touching.'"

Beka breathes in through her nostrils as she adjusts her legs apart in this very public venue. "You've been a vagflasher all your life," Robyn snorts, "but you are no longer a vagflasher." Robyn advances, "You are legs apart 24x7. But you already know that. BB anoints me to train you to obey the signs for legs apart, legs open, and legs spread... and then train you to hold those positions. Sometimes for minutes... sometimes for hours. You'll stay legs apart position and not abandon it unless I sign your legs wider still. Do you understand me, Pledge?"

Beka does. "Ma'am, yes, Ma'am," she responds, becoming bewildered.

"See ya, Beka Broda," Robyn waves goodbye. "Now pump some béchamel outta that bare brim while you keep sitting there with your legs apart." And abandons her.

Beka cringes and again feels her insides get wet.

Beka assesses that passersby appear to ignore her, and she chaffs at her lack of importance. But then she spots a paparazzo across the Quad, the real deal, not shooting from a blind. She spots another to the oblique, and then, as if out of nowhere, a class of photography students descends upon her... and feasts upon her every angle. Beka has no particular position she must keep except sitting lets apart, so she strikes poses with her arms and head, cups her armpits, and smiles. And what's not to love—an acre of belly and back, a narrow vertical navel, berries inside of armholes, and, for the student willing to crawl and shoot up, a shaven mons with a trimmed landing patch above it.

All alone now. Well, sort of. *Maybe my broom closet and bristles were a secret before, but now a gaggle of shooters transcribes this part of my soul. Out here, by myself, yet surrounded.* Beka squeezes, and a line of brodeas pushes its way out from within her sex lips. Beka's sitting position differs from the leaning back in that instead of oozing a blob down toward her asshole, the béchamel collects into a long string that dangles in between her held-apart thighs. Somebody in the photo class takes her with a flash, and Beka parts her legs ever so slightly more and extends the glistening stalactite of brodeas.

Elle rescues her, but not before the broda reaches the bench. Beka pauses after Elle gets her up on her feet, casts her eyes back upon her secretion, and worries to Elle, "Not a secret."

Elle knows what to do. *I might not have to expose myself any more than I do normally, but I do have to do this thing. Lolly. I can't leave Beka traces behind. I know Janet didn't exactly put it that way, but Robyn already knows, so Babs knows also. So I have to 'volunteer.'*

Elle titters a leanover and cleans with one lick, then takes Beka by the hand. "Come on, you're wanted at the Cosmos House to vagcam together with Steph. I think you're supposed to induce her to cream."

Bell and Back Door, then inside. Now Beka must face her own revelations on all the House Screens. She's not sure how she feels about that. "But maybe I like it!" she confides to Elle.

"Maybe you like it too much," Elle responds, and makes sure her own jeans shorts ensure her navel stays in its V-notch.

§ Robyn Cams Steph & Beka: Vagflash Upskirt Together

That afternoon Boss Babe commands Steph and Beka to stand at attention and provides them some cavalier goals. "Will you learn to flash quickly in very public places, even under camera fire? Of course you will. And will you learn to hold a pose for long periods of time? You shall."

BB, still very much the Bikini Babe, evaluates her two Pledge. Steph's strapless cutout minidress hangs on her nipples, but it does oval her navel in its taunt buttonhole. Beka's open-armhole croptop and low-slung miniskirt uncover an expanse of belly from her lower ribs down to where her inguinal arches down her pelvis. And of course both the minidress and low-slung miniskirt barely cover their crotches.

"I am too busy to train you two to match your skills," Boss Babe provides, "so Robyn has volunteered to train the both of you to work as a team. Maybe later Tiffany can add finishing touches beyond your 'Cleopatra's Wannabe Strippers' makeup. But right now dispatch yourselves to the Front Porch steps and await her further instructions. Move."

Steph and Beka move quickly. All hear the Back Door Bell get rung twice as the sanpan Pledge depart the Cosmos House, wind their way past the Porch to the front, and sit themselves side-by-side on the wooden steps up to the Front Porch, legs apart and thighs not touching. Shadows dance, and Gamers argue whether their sanpan scruff and bare beaver might be accessible to the longest telephotos of paparazzi. But they are extremely convenient for the Front Door Cam, which wakes up and shares their upskirt with the Prefecture.

Beka tries to start a conversation, but Steph rejects her. "Shut up. It's bad enough I have to get my spooters and snizz cammed. But it's worse when I have to share the bill with a bimbo like you."

Beka lapses into silence and, when the Cam isn't looking, touches her breech to check for brodeas production. *I had to open and cream for the Back Door Cam this morning, and I creamed with by legs barely apart on the Quad. Elle lollyed me. Steph has spread her legs a lot already, but has not secreted love splurt.* Beka considers the Cam considering her again and gives it a look. *Yes, go ahead and collect me! I'm going to open my legs and drip on the Front steps... and bring Steph along with me.* She cheats her legs open a tiny bit.

In due course Robyn appears, and whatever commiseration Steph and Beka had been sharing gets interrupted.

Robyn stands on ground level, looks up at the two Cosmos sitting on the top step, and zeros in on Beka. "Show us where Boss Bitch marked you," Robyn demands.

Beka hesitates.

"Open you legs, bimbo," Robyn commands, then turns, and signs Steph, "Beka opens; you open too."

There is a moment of awkward silence as the sanpan Pledge open their legs—halfway to spread—and wide enough there are no crinks where the thighs and pubis intersect. The Front Door Cam hovers and collects serious intimate detail.

Beka feels the fresh air upon her bare boner-box and a gentle breeze rustle the vertical broom-shaped patch of butched pussy hair. Beka nervously adjusts her posture and puts her hands to her sides. Beka feels it necessary to offer explanations. "Ma'am," she concedes as she leans back with opened legs, "I'm shaven bare except for a racing strip up above my boneroo."

Steph feels rufescence flush her vulva and labia, and the inside of her thighs feel hotter. *I have wavy hair overtop my slit; Beka presents a bald box. The Cam already collected her titter, and the most Gamers get from me are headlights.* Steph leans back and rests her elbows on the step above. The posture affords support for the strapless minidress. *It helps keeps the hole to the navel. Donating to the vagcam, well, that's unavoidable, but popping a nip or two might not be worth it. Instant rolldown. But if Robyn makes us do jumping jacks, I'm also a pop out.*

Robyn permits herself the advantage and addresses the newbie. "Welcome to the Cosmo House, Beka Broda. You're upskirt without panties. You're not just vaging the Cosmos House; all the Houses share the Cam feeds. In fact, every Gamer in the Prefecture can see your bare box and bristle line."

"Ma'am, yes, Ma'am," Beka accepts, not entirely sure how to interpret this broadcasting of her intimate secrets.

Not sure how to interpret all this attention?

Robyn explains to Beka, "I had you open your legs for the Back Door Cam earlier today, and you creamed. You barely exposed yourself to paparazzi and a camera class in front of the Lecture Hall, so why didn't you offer them some open shots?"

Beka stammers, "Ma'am, you told me—"

"Oh, shut up," Robyn commands. "It doesn't matter; you shall catch up now. I told Boss Bitch to make sure that whenever a Cam collects your open sanpan to be sure it feeds the Prefecture. But listen to me, you browsabella bewer bok. Say hello to whatever House across the street or next door might harbor a paparazzi with a long lens. People walking by on the street. A delivery person. Hover cams."

Beka constricts her pelvis, and once again the brodeas expresses itself as a line of white cream in between her labia. Sunlight highlights legs open.

"Ah, béchamel again!" Robyn praises. "Tell me, bedizen," Robyn demands, "what gets you so excited?"

"Ma'am..." Beka pulls for an answer. "Ma'am, getting looked at makes me wet. Béchamel, brodeas. Elle made me realize that a long time ago. Transude valiva. Cream."

Steph, sitting with her legs equally upskirt, leans into the conversation and advances a warning to Beka. "Be careful about getting excited by Gamers looking at you."

Beka considers this advice. "Maybe one is good, but more is better. Maybe you should be careful about getting excited spreading your snatch in my face."

Robyn smoothes her maillot and rotates on the balls of her feet.

Steph smells Beka freshen, wrinkles her nose, and once again turns and speaks to her. "We might both upskirt, but unlike you, I don't leak slush."

Robyn decides to take charge and hammers Steph. "Maybe you don't get to leak slush... yet. Beka might be begging to Strip, but she possesses two pieces. And all you have is your minidress. So you're gonna beg whether you want to or not. You're begging already."

Robyn especially likes to take liberties, so she shakes her shoulders and rears back. The Front Door Cam now takes on Steph's opened legs. Yes, Steph's tight strapless minidress rides up. Steph's thin hair doesn't completely obscure her slit beneath. And her anger has raised her stamen up.

Robyn beats the drum. "You're a snatch-flasher's dream."

The more Robyn prolongs Steph's exposure the more displeased Steph becomes. *But unlike Beka, I'm not going to secrete sexual discharge.*

Beka want to help. "Ma'am, I'll—"

"Shut up," Robyn commands. "If I have to tell you again, you'll roll your croptop up and hold it in your teeth." Robyn considers them both. "Too bad you two aren't Roommates and can't Game for Garments right now. But you can still Game. The one of you with one minidress and pussy hair sits poised to Strip next Term but doesn't want to; the one of you with a croptop and miniskirt but no hair misdirects you toward a Monitor slot, when in fact you're already begging the Nugget. Seems like you both need to give up something the other's got and get equal."

Neither Cosmos quite accepts this analysis. Steph objects, "It's not right that I have to display my sex alongside a newbie Pledge. Especially one who presents herself as overly excited."

Robyn considers this foray and weighs in to Steph, "I'd say Beka has more Garments than you, but she exposes more skin. More secrets than you."

Steph ignores Robyn and turns tighter in to Beka. "You really are shameless. You keep her thighs wider than necessary, and you let your excitement dominate your Game. Even outside here your brodeas just keeps brimming out."

Beka cringes; she hangs a bead of brodeas down toward the next lower step. "Yeah, okay, so...."

Robyn voices disgust. "You've made a fresh mess of yourself, Beka Broda!" Robyn makes a high-pitched, very Oriental laugh into her fingertips. "No secrets for you anymore, you bocca bourse bimbo!"

Steph evaluates the addition of a second Cosmos vagflasher. *Unfortunately for me it fails to draw attention away from my own opened legs.* Indeed, Beka stimulates a competition between the blonde and the brunette that Steph resists being draw into but seems unable to avoid. *I might not be able to prevent my stamen from standing up; I might be slippery inside; but unlike Beka, my splurt stays under control.*

Robyn curls a lip to Steph. "I'm not going to bother give you signs anymore, you scraggly skeeze skank. I'll give signs to Beka, and whatever she does, you follow."

Robyn watches Steph's lips twist as Steph considers the source of this particular command. Robyn flaunts to her, "May your titter and vagflash collection accumulate. Especially since none of it belongs to you anyway. Not your real-time upskirt feed, or what you're about to make in *The Runup.* You practice making splurt with Beka now, because she's your newest role model." And Robyn departs around the Porch side of the House, toward the Back Door.

The Front Door Cam lingers with Steph and Beka presenting upskirt. Be honest: presenting open leg sanpan crotch, one with hair and a stamen growing out, one bare with a racing stripe. And oozing brodeas. Gamers who hate Robyn still appreciate her presentation of delicacies.

§ Steph & Beka & Elle: Front Porch Vagcam & Visitors

It arouses Beka that Gamers might masturbate to her, and soon her suspended drip pools on the step below. Steph regains confidence. *My presentation of self portrays a fuller individual. Beka is an over-eager newbie who will be swept by forces acting upon her. She's not my Roommate, and I'll get Molly's panties when the timing is right. So competing with her is mostly just sport. Gameplay with ambiguous outcomes.*

A deliveryman approaches up the sidewalk carrying a large box. Upon seeing the two sitting-open Cosmos, he pauses, considers them, alters his grip on the box, turns, and exits back to a delivery van parked on the street.

A young man with short brunette hair and wearing only a jockstrap approaches them. Possibly Steph might have seen him dance in a Club last Term; Beka's never seen him before. He cams their upskirt, broda and stamen side-by-side, then orders them, "Show me your assholes."

The order flusters them both, but the directions require only an incremental movement for both vagflashers, so they draw their fingertips to the insides of their butts, pull their cheeks apart, and reveal this intimate asset. *I had to do this at the Corvette House,* Beka remembers, *except not in public.*

Steph's gaze toward the jockstrap cameraman is one of hatred. He smiles, spins on his heel, bends over, flashes them his own asshole, and exits. His action is too quick for the Front Door Cam, which watches them relax their grips on their butts and return their arms to their sides or behind them while keeping their legs wide open. Beka's drip continues to hang down and pool on a step; Steph's stamen continues to push its way up through her soft wavies.

Soon after, an otherwise naked and shaved Gamer arrives wearing only a sock around his cock and balls. This creature kneels before Beka and commences to wash her feet with his tongue. Beka doesn't quite know how to take it. It tickles. *But I also know it's an honor.*

Steph doesn't quite know how to take it either. She resents Beka getting honored before her; *still, foot worship is a repulsive activity I need not lend a foot to.* The man wearing the cock sock exits without treating Steph, and she finds herself furious. *Boss Bitch desires to torment me. She thinks I was responsible for her foot worship last Term, but it Madam Nurse Beautician who trained her. She volunteered to wash feet with soap in her mouth last Term; nobody forced her. And so she sends this creep over to honor Beka with a foot wash. And ignore me. I should have ensured BB Opted Down last Term, and now she hides and lets Robyn haze me.*

Steph checks her posture to make sure her knees are far enough apart *so you paparazzi with gyro-stabilized telephotos across the street can get a clear view.* Not a long enough minidress to make shadows. *I know.*

And I'm going to do anything I can to assist the both of you to Opt Down. Stripper for you, Robyn Redacted. As for the Boss Bitch? If somehow Tiffany can Double Opt Up, maybe Boss Bitch can Double Opt Down and also be a Stripper next Term. Now that's something worth wanting to see.

Newbie Beka enjoys no worries about Terms past, but back inside the Cosmos House Elle worries about Beka's indifference about who might possess her graven images... and what they might depict. Elle begs Babs to plead for Beka's rescue from the Front Porch steps, and in the course of this conversation she makes a plea-bargain that includes a complication beyond Robyn teaching her to practice Hand Signs.

Now Elle paces around the side of the house, and, like Robyn before her, approaches the front steps and looks up into two vages, one lightly haired with its strophoid elongated outward, and the other hanging brodeas all the way down and puddling on the next step. Elle worries about herself when she sees Beka's open bare crotch. She shifts eyes to Steph and sees an alternate role model. *Short hairs over the snatch. No leaking love cream.*

"Close your legs, dispatch yourselves to the Bell, and await the Back Door," Elle orders.

Steph breaks position and tells Elle, "You're next!" Then she flounces out of the picture.

Beka lingers, looks at her pool of broda on the step, and says, "Sorry, Elle. Be careful about splinters in your tongue."

Elle blinks. Licking up hadn't been a part of any plea-bargain. Elle considers the hovering, expectant Cam. She looks around to see who might be watching. *It doesn't matter.* She kneels and provides the Cam a total down-halter, both noogies handing free and both nipples in clear view. And licks her Roommate up off one wooden stair step. Carefully. The Front Door Cam collects this also, and after Elle stands up and squares her bearings, she gives the Cam a look of humiliation.

"Thanks for rescuing me," Beka says. "I don't mind showing my boneroo, but Steph is really mean to me."

"You're welcome," Elle says. "I want you to know that I had to beg to practice Hand Signs and then Flip-Flop with you."

The twosome walk toward the side of the Porch so they are out of view of the Cam. "Gotta admit, Elle, the Cosmos House is really wild," Beka cheerleads. "It's like we're clubbing again."

Elle counters, "It's not. Before we enrolled and became Pledge we controlled our own titter and vagflash in order to manipulate a situation." Elle adjusts her halter and tucks her fingers into the waistband of her jeans shorts. "Now it is Babs, via Robyn, who controls our titter and vagflash and manipulates the situation. Her dictum that 'legs shall not be touching' remains absolute. Not crossed, not sitting together, not ankles curled over each other. Apart. So Gamers can look in."

Beka squints. "Listen, Elle, my increasing popularity may be a good thing! And besides, face it, after we Flip-Flop, you're next." Beka reaches under her miniskirt. "Okay, all the Pledge keep their legs apart, but only Steph and I have nothing through our crotches. You'll see. Vag-all-the-time. Big difference."

Beka licks her lips. "Hey, Elle, lighten up. Okay, I'm the one who got Cammed mostly, but you did get to lick up after me twice today, on the Quad and the Front Porch. And who knows where I'll cam tomorrow? A bar or restaurant? Anywhere, really. Gamers get the feed live, and they can take their time looking at the replays."

"Right," Elle reminds. "And Gamers who look can see that looking makes you all wet."

§ Babs & Tiffany: Assay Steph & Beka's Upskirt Displays

Later, upstairs in BB's Bedroom, Babs and Tiffany discuss the two skirted beauties entertaining the vaginally curious. Babs reclines on her bunk; Tiffany sits on BB's desk chair (by acquiescence of course) but positioned so she wraps her legs around the back of her chair and points her tail trough, arched above her low-rise slacks, in BB's direction.

Tiffany has taken her shirt off and studies Babs by looking over her shoulder.

Babs speaks first. "I'm in no hurry to see Steph acquire panties again. Every time I see her and Beka together all I can think of is that Steph's snatch needs to be as bare as Beka's beaver."

Tiffany leans forward and stretches her expanse of bare back. "Well, there is a razor in the Makeup Case. Plenty of soap around."

"I know," BB humors, "you're already begging to shave your thicket so it doesn't show off overtop your slacks."

"I'll shave my entire thatch," Tiffany offers. "I'll shave my head bald too. I know you don't make deals, but really, I'll do anything legal for all of my fans."

"You'll do it for me," BB asserts.

"Ma'am, absolutely, Ma'am," Tiffany firms. "I'll mix soap and pee together, use my mouth as a dispenser, and shave myself bare, bald, and naked."

BB rolls her eyes and shakes off this suggestion. She refocuses the agenda toward Steph and suggests a callous deprecation. "The further away I am from Steph, the better off I am. Maybe she should Flip-Flop with her Roommate Molly instead of a Winner-Takes-All? Let them both keep only one Garment and both Opt Down."

Tiffany buttresses the thought. "Molly will still achieve her main goal."

BB nods. "I do like the idea of Steph topless!"

Tiffany hedges, "Ma'am, please remember *I* want to Strip too. I'll suck your babambas. I'll eat your bajingo. I'll lick your butt hole. I'll let you pee in my mouth. I'll—"

"Stop it!" BB commands. "You'll do nothing of the sort." Boss Babe shifts position, folds a leg differently. "Not everyone wants to dance and Strip, you know."

"I know," Tiffany says. "It's okay, I know your type; you want to work in the ticket booth."

BB wags a friendly finger and steers the conversation. "Actually, once *The Runup* begins, I figure Beka and Elle for the first Flip-Flop. This would provide Elle a chance to air her notch out."

"And show her noogies off from a new direction." Tiffany locks into the new rhythm. "Armholes instead of a halter leanover." Tiffany pauses and poses a question, "So do you also intend to let Elle share the upskirt experience with Steph?"

BB runs her hands through her long black hair. "Ah, what a sweet thought. But maybe later. Beka torments Steph naturally; she doesn't need to be trained to transude brodeas."

Tiffany applauds, "Steph clearly finds herself in a Game she does not want to play. Tittering and vagflashing with an eager bare beaver. Newbie Beka Broda!" Tiffany leans forward and rubs her Eraser Heads against the back of the chair. She continues, "Steph controlled her crotch last Term because she was the Monitor; this Term you control it."

BB shifts again. "Beka provides a happy surprise. She drips when she gets excited and already wants to open up."

"She's sweet," Tiffany affirms. "Let her drip for awhile and see what kind of turmoil Kundalini builds up inside her."

"Beka's lack of inhibition scares her Roommate and old friend," BB observes, referring to Elle. "I let Janet get the upper hand on me when she made them admire the Baseboard Strippers at the Corvette House."

"Beka scares Steph too," Tiffany opines. "Maybe you should put Steph and Beka on their hands and knees let them stare at the Baseboard Strippers downstairs."

Babs curls a lip. "Robyn would love to force them to stare at pink puddy and creamy cunt... for hours and hours and hours."

Tiffany sweetens, "Maybe Beka can induce Steph to squeeze some splurt outta her skuddy. Although ultimately these are your machinations, especially when you let Robyn make them upskirt together."

"You give me too much credit," Babs demurs.

"But isn't Robyn your agent?" Tiffany asks cautiously.

BB tightens up. "Robyn does things on her own."

Tiffany grins. "You're making Steph Sorostitute match Beka's eagerness. Like sitting with her legs apart with her starter button poking out."

BB must relent. "And so resenting it!" she humors.

They both rest a moment. Tiffany slides her fingers through the hairage that rides above the low-cut waistline of her skin-tight slacks.

Tiffany sparks a question. "You gonna let 'em lift their skirts and rub their bare asses together? Make 'em ride Double Dong together?"

"Shame on you," Boss Babe teases. "You know there is no Double Dong here at the Cosmos House."

Tiffany turns serious. "Be careful with Steph," she warns the Boss Babe. "You have to handle her carefully. She might not be as dishonest as Robyn, but she is more clever. She resents authority; she's vengeful; she doesn't take responsibility for her actions; and she intimidates. That said, she's extremely shamed every time you screen her images or vids, because they remind her she got broken."

"Yeah. And I make her stay exposed." Babs ponders, "I'm not sure I treat her right."

"Wait a minute." Tiffany slides a finger down into her slacks and organizes her tinderbox. "Steph invited this Term upon herself; don't forget that. So let her have it."

"Whereas newbie Beka just wants exposure," Babs settles.

BB announces a decision she's made. "I need to do things at my own pace. I don't want to rush. I've decided to go slow. I guess we'll all have to learn perseverance."

And Tiffany leaves a spot in her cameltoe.

§ Molly & Steph: Roommates Reaffirmation

Indeed. Steph feels isolated and finds flashing together with newbie Beka so humiliating that she brings herself to complain to her Roommate Molly that night in the Bunkroom. "Beka Broda has no shame. She might be a newbie, but she's way too willing. And Boss Bitch wants me to keep up with that bocaccio! Robyn signs Beka, and I have to follow? That's disgusting."

Molly opens her mouth, but Steph signs her to silence and continues, "First I have to flash my snatch, then I have to keep it exposed all the time, and now I have this horny bimbo out there competing with me. Hanging broda outta her box. Talk about insults."

Plump Molly listens, content to remains topless 24x7, pleased to keep her panties bunched in between her posterior mound and sunk into her muliebre so that her thick minge always spills to both sides. Molly touches Steph's arm and attempts to placate her Roommate. "Look at me, Steph. I have to keep my legs apart thanks to you. I'm showing full hairage. And I've told you I'll give you my panties. But I can't stop Babs from hazin' you."

Steph seethes angrily. "Let's face it. Flashing has an aspect of deniability, but sitting there with one's legs ganged apart while the whole Prefecture surveys your snooch... that's harsh. And then to just keep right on sitting and holding the position while Gamers takes their time with you, however long... why?"

"Because you must practice perseverance," Molly insists. "Perseverance raises the stakes. Strike a pose, but then hold a pose. I know. The Gamers stare so long they finally lose interest or satiate, and eventually they go away. All you can do is hope they return to take you in more, bring a friend, or use a different lens."

"Or forget about you." Steph adds.

"Yeah, that can happen," Molly reluctantly agrees.

Steph scowls, "I know that some of the voyeurs are not Gamers, but I can't even stop them from looking."

"This is what Babs demands of her Cosmos Pledge," Molly shrugs. "No matter how much you resent it."

Steph hedges, "It not fair to get coupled to that bedizen. Beka Broda can't control herself."

"You're not coupled to Beka," Molly insists, grappling with two large mazoomas. "Steph, you are coupled to me. I am your Roommate! Our Roommate Game comes first, and you'll take my panties away in a Winner-Takes-All contest. Please!"

Steph considers her Roommate. *Molly confounds me with a different set of problems than Beka. She's never aggressive toward me—that's not even her nature. The fact that she lights up the Cam is what makes her dangerous. Tiffany's also a Pee-Camer, but Tiffany isn't my Roommate. It's bad enough I can't use the Bathroom when either of them are there, but if Gamers except me to share micturition with my Roommate, that's something I won't do.*

Molly finds Steph's silence disturbing and tries to brighten Steph's mood. "Steph, listen. I know Monitors can hover, but they can also Opt Up and Down. You know? I wasn't here last Term, but I do know that us Pledge *must* either rise or fall, so that you and I will become either a Monitor or Stripper next Term. Yes, I begged to be a Pledge this Term because I didn't want to go Whore, I'll admit it. But listen, Steph, please. I don't want to become a Monitor either. Maybe my actions don't matter that much, but I do know that anything I try to manage always falls to pieces. I could never Monitor. I'd lose a Pledge and become instant Slavesex. I know what I need. I need to end up Stripping again next Term. And you need my panties. Please, Steph."

Steph scowls, "So you can oscillate back and forth? Listen, you Stripper Wannabe, *I* know how Boss Bitch thinks. I had to spend a whole Term managing her. As soon as *The Runup* begins she's gonna Flip-Flop Beka and Elle so that I have to upskirt with Elle too. BB's got it in for me, and she treats me like I've kept secrets from her. After Elle and I vagflash you can challenge me to a Winner-Take-All, and I'll pick a Game you're sure to lose."

"Sure, Steph. Deal," Molly accepts. But she also finds the delay discomforting and speculates, "So maybe, if you get lucky, besides flashing with Elle you can lolly together. Or ride the Double Dong with her and Beka. One at a time, of course. And then you and I could Dong together, center Stage at the Nugget."

Steph hardens her line. "Enough out of you, Pledge. You wanted to be a Cosmos Pledge; I was betrayed, and now paparazzi chase after my bad side as opposed to my glamour. You just better make sure when it comes time to play Winner-Takes-All that I get my panties back!"

"Yeah, sure. They're yours, Steph," Molly affirms. "They're yours for good. They always have been."

21 Steph & Beka: Worship Penny & Coco's Pictures (D14)

§ Tiffany & Molly: Pee-Camers Make up Five Pledge

Morning of Day Fourteen begins. Robyn and Kimju, Steph but not Molly, and Beka and Elle all manage to bathe and do toilet while Tiffany remains sequestered in the Bedroom tending to Babs' needs. Molly, now also committed to enter the Bathroom only while naked and to pee on the Cam, politely remains bunk bound while five Cosmos practice without the benefit of the Cam. Besides, *Steph told me to wait until last.*

Steph, who slept naked overnight, enters the Bathroom naked and escapes naked. She presents herself naked at Babs' Bedroom doorway in front of the Desktop and begs, "Ma'am, please give me my cutout minidress."

Babs purses her lips but says nothing. She affords Steph yesterday's minidress inside out a second time, making the strapless cutout minidress right side out again. Steph pulls it on overhead and adjusts it onto her body so her button center holes and her sprites don't pop out. As for vaging hairage... well, Steph expects she will donate again.

A naked Tiffany emerges from under Babs' bunk, comes up onto her knees, and offers Steph a look at herself in the Makeup Case mirror. Once again Steph witnesses two waxy discs of color centered around her standouts. Steph flushes, and her stalks grow headlights into the stretched, colored disc; the minidress is waxy on both sides now.

Steph play coy. "Thank you for making up my nipples, Tiffany. So I could rub makeup into my dress and everyone would know."

"About yesterday and the day before," Babs says. "Now go fetch Beka, follow Tiffany to the Bathroom, and beg her to put a Wannabe Stripper faces on you. Tell Beka to advance herself to 'legs open' position." Boss Babe gives a little snarl. "And, of course, you follow."

"For the Bathroom Cam, Ma'am?" Step seeks clarification.

"From now on. 24x7. Halfway between ajar and spread as wide as you can." Boss Babe scratches her chin. "Easier that way." Babs snaps her waistband. "Any other requests you should be making?"

Steph knows she is supposed to beg Tiffany for nipple make up; she tests the oblique. "Well, Tiffany can make my nipples up again if she wants," she says.

Tiffany rubs her Eraser Heads with the palms of her hands. "Come. But you should thank your Monitor." Steph turns, but BB shoos her out.

Once in the Bathroom, Beka and Steph sit next to each other on the makeup stools. Steph sits with her legs ajar.

Tiffany clarifies Babs' direction to Beka. "Babs says open-legged from now on, 24x7." Beka adjusts her posture, repeating a clarification of open-leg-ness and total vagcam of her bare box and butched bristly above it. Steph follows, and shares Beka's open-legged upskirt, angered somewhat, of course, that she is demeaned by the politics. *I do know how to open my legs myself, after all! I don't need Beka to guide me.*

The Bathroom Cam has migrated from Beka's bush to her own short and wavies. *It watches Tiffany turns my face into one of Cleopatra's Wannabe Strippers. Boss Bitch insults me. Insults all the Pledge. But me especially.*

Steph comes out of her reverie to discover that the Cam has become distracted after a naked Molly came in to clean herself and divest her body of unnecessary components. With the Cam dwelling on Molly, Gamers don't know if Steph gets nipple makeup or not... or if Beka boils over.

The Bathroom Cam glides with Molly as she joins Tiffany, then the twosome Pee-Cam together, right in from of the two sitting, vaging Cosmos. The Cam actually gets confused about what to look at.

Now the morning session of Tiffany making up Cleopatra's Wannabe Strippers gets into full swing. Steph is sent to order Elle into the Bathroom, and Elle, following Beka's model, also opens her legs and shares full hairage with Cam. "Has Robyn taught you how to pullaside yet?" Tiffany inquires.

Elle flusters, "Ma'am, no. I did see Kimju and Molly pullaside, and I think somebody at the Corvette House pulled my hem to the side and cammed my nether aperture."

Tiffany purses her lips. "Possibly they cammed your nookie as well."

Elle defends, "It felt like a big gelatin pill got shoved into my rectum."

Beka volunteers, "I got a thermoprobe in my borehole. Besides, pullaside for Elle don't matter anymore; Elle's begging Babs to Flip-Flop. So she titters her armholes and upskirts all her nappy, not just leaks it out."

Elle seeks to answer this, but Tiffany orders them both oval mouth, and Molly helps her complete the makeup. After dobbing both buttons with color, Tiffany sends them out to fetch Robyn and Kimju. Robyn sits legs apart on the stool; Kimju takes a cue from Molly and sits with her legs open and her thong tightly gathered into her mooe and moonshadow, so tight that her inner sex lips show out. Kimju gets her face, nipples, navel, and finger and toenails worked up, a streak of color in her hair, and a dusting of color into her hairage.

Robyn collects face and nails, but Tiffany leaves her belly button, framed in the smallest buttonhole possible, in its natural state.

"How come you made up Kimju's navel and not mine?" Robyn demands of Tiffany. "You put marks on Beka and Elle's buttons too."

Tiffany ignores Robyn's question, finishes two Wannabe faces, and addresses both Roommates. "Babs requests you roust your fellow Roommates outta their bunks and assemble yourselves for Reveille around the Dining Room table. Babs' orders, 'Each Pledge shall stand spread surrender behind her chair and face the table. No talking.' I will put the Makeup Case away, inform Monitor Babs that the six of you are underway, and follow and join you. Now move."

§ Babs Orders Steph & Beka: Admire Baseboard Strippers

Tiffany, electing to stay naked, follows into the Dining Room and positions herself at the far end of the Dining Room table. Three pairs of Roommates stand spread surrender across from each other on opposite sides of the table. Beka and Elle face each other and stand closest to Tiffany and the locked door to the Parlor. Molly and Steph face each other in the middle, and Robyn and Kimju stand facing on opposite sides near the end of the table nearest the Kitchen. An end with a slightly bigger, and empty, chair sitting at the head of the table.

Babs arrives. She circumnavigates the table, pausing behind Tiffany to use a Skeleton Key to unlock the door to the Living Room, and returns to sit at the head of the table and survey her seven Pledge. The one at the far end of the table, Tiffany, looks at her with calmness, armpits cupped, Eraser Heads made up, belly tucked, and thin red thatch.

Babs turns her head to consider the three Pledge sitting to her right side of the table: Robyn, Molly, and Beka, with Robyn being closest to her, at the right hand of the Monitor Boss. BB pans her eyes across the wall behind this trio: two windows looking out into the bushes outside, and a Screen in between them with images flashing by, images of the three Pledge who face away from the Screen. These three Pledge, eyes forward and mouths closed, see before them in turn their Roommates, and behind them on the wall, the four Dining Room Pictures.

Babs turns to study the three Pledge who sit to the left side of her table: Kimju, Steph, and Elle, with Kimju being closest to her.

These three Pledge see the montage of images and shots that flows silently on the Screen facing them and behind their Roommates. All quickly assess that this montage features the three Roommates on the other side of the table, who have their backs to the Screen and don't know their Roommates watch bits and pieces of them from earlier this Term: Robyn watching Tiffany pee in the Bathroom; Molly spread naked, pink, wet, and wildly climaxing; Beka full titter and vag. Sometimes snippets repeat, but never in the same order.

Elle rebels at watching the ever-changing montage and looks instead out the window at the hedge outside. Steph, who finds the Screen dead ahead, blocked only by Molly's squat body, smiles at Molly and Beka's humiliations and tries to ignore Robyn's pomp. *One of them thinks she's in charge; one couldn't care less; the third relishes them.* Steph blocks Robyn. The third watcher, Pledge Kimju, makes sure she keeps her face forward but allows her eyes to angle to the Screen to improve the peripheral details. *I'm not fooled,* Kimju asserts to herself. *I know we are all being tested. And we all know it… well, most of us anyway.*

Sometimes the three watchers know they were present during a moment they see on the Screen, but never do they see themselves. Only Robyn and Molly and Beka appear. Kimju ignores the Screen and looks out the side window toward the hedge along the side of the lot. *I don't like that I'm being tested, but I don't need to like it. I just need to pass.* Steph watches the clips, absorbs the misfortunes of her fellow Pledge, and forms headlights in her strapless minidress. And Elle just follows the Rules.

Boss Babe rests her elbows on the table, folds her fingers together, and rests her chin.

Monitor Babs appreciates the "Lineup" positioned around the Dining Room table. She again looks leftward, and this time she looks past the three standing Pledge toward the four Dining Room Pictures behind them. *That's me at the top. Bling then; bling still. Hairage and rugage; not anymore. And most important of all, no more bling blush!*

Babs casts her eyes down to Janet, next down. *The last time I saw Janet she was still wearing that same crochet Spiderweb Bikini. With a halter that juts her nipples out, shows areolage through the web, and adjusts to, but does not contain, her jumboblats.* Babs expects Janet might visit today. *I bet her jipijapa still grows wild around and through her open-mesh triangle g-string and her rippled jaxy hangs out. Okay, so Janet committed to the Spider 24x7 all this Term, and she did promote to Monitor. Well, I guess I committed to navelage 24x7 all this Term, and I promoted too. That's something.*

Babs casts her eyes down to the Baseboard Strippers. *I have not forgotten about Penny and Coco.*

BB suspects wandering eyes in the Room. She tightens. "Look into the eyes of your Roommate across the table. Don't look anywhere else!" She snaps her fingers, and the Screen calms to a medium gray.

Better. Now I can get down to business. She catches a twinkle in Tiffany's eyes but turns her focus to Roommates Beka and Elle. Babs envies their experience under the tutelage of Monitor Janet.

Elle feels BB's gaze upon her, testing her ability to keep her eyes looking into Beka's. Very hard to maintain. Swimming sometimes in the eyes, tearing. Elle figures, *I will have to Flip-Flop Garments with Beka, and I will vagflash, assuming I want to keep two Garments and Opt Up.*

My price to pay to Opt Up. Elle recalls that BB put the still of her getting out of the car at the nightclub on all the Cosmos Screens. *And now that Automatron serves them to the Prefecture I'm supposed to locate my self-shot Measurement Nudes from before I Pledged the Game?*

Yes. *And anything else I can offer up. More price to Opt Up.*

Beka falters gazing into Elle's eyes, glances to see who BB might be watching, and looks square into Babs' eyes. Oops. Beka snaps her gaze back into Elle's pupils and opens her mouth to apologize.

Boss Babe speaks first. "Oval mouth. Maybe later you can masturbate to your vids spilling brodeas for Janet, and then masturbate to Elle's vids licking it up. Right now you get on your hands and knees and position yourself in front of the Baseboard Strippers."

Beka hustles. She did this once before: knees and feet wide apart, elbows and arms forward, head down and resting on hands. Her uplifted bottom up is her greatest height. Poot 'n' Coot lie directly ahead.

With Beka no longer across the table, Elle looks out the window to the outside. She startles. *Do I see a camouflage hood with eyes looking at me? A Cam?* She blinks and refocuses. *I don't see anything now but bushes.*

She looks at Steph out of the corner of her eye and sees that Steph has pantographed Beka and ovaled her mouth. Elle wonders, *What should I do?* Then she decides, and ovals her mouth too.

BB has been waiting for an opportunity for her Pledge to gaze upon the Baseboard Strippers. *Janet teased me since the very first day, and I let her get ahead of me. But if that gives her pleasure, then fine, she took some of my Karma last Term. Now it's my turn.*

Babs considers Cosmos Pledge Beka worshiping the Baseboard Strippers. *Beka has done this before.* Yes, and BB has even watched the video. *Along with her Roommate Elle.* BB scans Elle looking out the window. *But my goal is not to repeat Janet. My goal is to do something different.*

Boss Babe scans the other Roommates. Steph and Molly maintain eyes; Kimju maintains Robyn, but Robyn strays carelessly. Babs trades eyes with Tiffany, standing at the opposite end of the table, and smile and signs her at ease. BB taps a finger. "Sit." Tiffany relaxes her naked frame in the end chair.

Robyn makes the mistake of catching Babs' eye, and BB raises a finger. "Pledge Robyn, I have unlocked the sliding door to the Living Room. Open it, go fetch the Front Door Cam, and return." Robyn looks befuddled, so BB adds, "Now!"

Boss Babe points a finger at Steph, "You, Pledge. Join your sanpan sister on the floor and worship the Baseboard Strippers. Move it. Now. If you have any doubt as to what to do, consult Beka. She's done this before. And whatever she does, you do the same."

Steph scowls and scrambles. It is hard to avoid what she must gaze upon. The Fate of Pledge who fail to acquire a second piece: Baseboard Strippers. *I need a second Garment to avoid this vocation.* She rolls her eyes upward across Janet and Babs' Pictures: both present vertical heads and torsos. She tilts down again upon the Baseboard Strippers leaning back horizontal, naked, shaven, and spread. *One of them pulls her wet hole wide open, and one of them masturbates her clit and oozes thick white curdle,* Steph assesses. *Not for me. I know what you are. I'm higher Caste.*

"You," BB points to Molly, "take her," BB points to Elle, "upstairs with you and introduce her to Minxy Mirror. You two can kiss it together. Now scram."

Molly and Elle scramble out.

Babs considers Tiffany and Kimju, the only two remaining Cosmos Pledge standing spread surrender at the table. "Move the table back," BB orders, then addresses them. "You two go out to the Backyard and masturbate on the Post Henge."

Kimju flusters, "Ma'am, Robyn made me do that before, Ma'am. I had to chant 'I love you, Post, hug 'n' kiss, rub my tits, masturbate.'"

"Kimju, you were great." Boss Babe rises onto tiptoes, then settles. "Gamers certainly wouldn't want you doing something over, would they? So let Tiffany try your thong on for size, and *you* can chant, kiss, rub, and masturbate the Post naked. And this time let it all hang out."

Kimju opens her mouth, then looks at Steph and Beka on elbows and knees. She closes her mouth.

BB instructs, "Last time you rubbed a Post you counted to 1000, but you rubbed the wrong Post. This time get the Post right. It's the one near the end, but not the end, that's reserved for my Roommate, Tiffany. Practice counting twice, then count to 1000, and come inside."

"That's 1 to 3000." Kimju complains.

"So good you know you know to add," BB enjoys.

Robyn returns with the Cam and collects Kimju as she shucks to naked. Tiffany takes the tanga in hand, bats her eyes, and whimpers, "Ma'am, I won't be naked, Ma'am."

"Poor you," BB affirms. "This way you can both get something you don't want. Now get to it. On your way out, tell the Back Door Cam to keep an eye on you. Kimju should climax again, but not you."

Steph and Beka hear Tiffany pull the tanga up her legs to her waist, hear the Back Door open and close, and hear the Bell ring. *Three thousand seconds is almost one hour,* Steph computes. *And that assumes Kimju doesn't lose count.*

Okay.

Babs rises, walks behind Steph and Beka, and commands them from above, "Let's trim up. Keep your legs wide open! Keep you eyes on Poot 'n' Coot! Don't look elsewhere!"

Beka, already practiced in admiring similar Baseboard Pictures with Elle under Janet's tutelage at the Corvette House, accepts the challenge as a playful competition, but Steph glowers that Boss Babe again aligns her with such an obviously inferior Pledge.

"You make perfect observers," BB assesses, "one of you already begs to Strip, and the other of you is dressed for the drop. Janet says you need to get your acts together. So contemplate these two vulgar Strippers through and through, and contemplate this possible Fate for yourself."

Steph grits her teeth at the fact that BB threatens her with an Opt Down. *All Gamers know I still wear only one Garment, my strapless cutout minidress, and that absent a second Garment* I *will be a Baseboard Stripper next Term. No way!*

§ Robyn Cams Steph & Beka: Titter & Upskirt Vagflash

Robyn returns with the Cam moments after Steph and Beka hear BB's footsteps depart to the Kitchen, leaving the two sanpan Pledge to the mercy of Robyn and the Cam once again.

Robyn gets to work. Gamers expect Beka's open-armhole croptop will provide sideboob revelation of her shallow 33A bobbers. It does. Beka senses the Cam as her nipples arouse and indent. The fine hairs on her stretched bare back stand up. And of course her high hemline rises up her fine legs.

Unfortunately for Steph, her hands forward and knees position causes one of her nipple stalks to suddenly pop out of the strapless top of the minidress. The occurs while the Cam looks elsewhere, but after the Cam discovers Steph's spout hanging free, it waits diligently until Steph's second nipple pops out. Patience to acquire the magic moment. Now two totally bare 32A flat sinewaves hang in full view, and there is nothing Steph can do to hide her beige areolas and nipple stalks.

Robyn leans over both of them. "Looks like you two are in for a long day. You already got your boobs and smurfs out, and it appears that your minidress and miniskirt may not be very successful in combating gravity."

This is correct. Steph and Beka keep their butts lifted high, their knees opened, faces floored, eyes on their targets. They feel air between their legs.

Beka discovers she can shift her eyes back and forth between the equally explicit Baseboard Strippers and study the former Cosmos before her. Beka has never met them. But Steph remembers them clearly. *I know you two. You are my former Cosmos Pledge. You are exactly where you deserve to be. Naked and spread, pink and wet, dancing at the Nugget. And as far as I'm concerned, next Term you can both Opt Whore.*

Robyn chirps in, "Like what you see? Enjoy the view, because that's you two next Term. You're gonna leak satchel splurt and breech broda."

Steph chaffs at the Baseboard Strippers. *It's one thing for you two to pump pudding and curdle out outta your poot and coot, but it is extremely inappropriate to Robyn to suggest that I emulate your intimacy.*

Beka feels her beaver get wet.

Robyn knows their exposures will only increase. "Keep your eyes on that poontang and cooch. Keep your own legs apart, and stay put," she declares. "Study every cunt hair, every mole, every freckle, every keloid, every drop of cream. Because right now you're the ones on the Cam." Robyn gathers a ball of saliva into her mouth and lets it drip out onto the bottom of Steph's foot. "Nothing you can do," Robyn taunts, retreating to Babs' chair and letting the Cam rest on the table to watch Steph and Beka continue their Picture study.

Steph chaffs at Robyn. You were careless and stupid and damaged me last Term. I'm here because of your mistakes, your indifference, your betrayal. And certainly not for your Charm, or lack thereof. Steph controls herself, but she cannot control the humiliating upward crawl of her minidress. Indeed both her minidress and Beka's miniskirt slowly inch upward, so that after an hour or two, two completely bare round asses emerge into view. However much tempted, neither Pledge dares reach around and address these revelations.

Steph constricts her vagina and feels her pelvis draw tight as she relishes Penny and Coco's unfortunate Fate. Her exposed nipples tighten like berries folding into themselves, and her fully exposed, beige-colored, sand-dollar shaped areolas crinkle. She listens to the equally upskirted Beka rustle on her hands and knees next to her. *It's bad enough I had to escort Molly to the Figure Drawing Class, Medical Exam, and Bachelor Party. But it's disgraceful to get paired up with this bimbo who can't control her secretions. Beka Broda. Somehow I need to make sure this brazen bimbo understands she really isn't my equal.*

And when no one is looking, I'm going to crucify Robyn.

§ Janet & Darleen Encounter Robyn: Turn Cam On Self

The quiet of the Dining Room is interrupted by the sound of the Front Door and heavy footsteps through the Living Room. Robyn looks up from the table to see Janet and a second woman enter the Dining Room.

Steph and Beka hear the footsteps as well, but use the moment to double check their indiscrete postures and focus on the Baseboard Strippers' opened vaginas before them.

Janet, still wearing her Spiderweb Bikini, scans the Room but gathers her eyes upon Robyn. The woman accompanying her wears a longsleeve pullover top and tight slacks and holds the posture of a superior Caste.

Robyn has met Janet once since her Redaction, when Babs took her to the Corvettes so Janet might probe her mind. Janet had accompanying them back to the Cosmos House when Steph arrived. But she has never met the trim woman wearing the pullover and slacks, a woman who eyes Robyn but speaks to Janet. "I think we got a Pledge asleep on the job."

Robyn opens her mouth, but Janet cuts in, "Shut up." She turns to her trim companion wearing the pullover and slacks. "Don't mind Robyn, she's Redacted." She turns back to Robyn again. "Aren't you supposed to remind me to sit you in a corner, spread your legs, and cam yourself?"

Robyn doesn't argue with Janet's logic. She had heard something to that effect after Beka and Elle came back from the Corvette House, but she hadn't paid much attention... or bothered to remember. However, images of Janet's treatment of Steph the day Steph arrived in the Parlor remain vivid. Robyn glances at the kneeling Steph and Beka, looks to Janet, and replies, "If you say so."

Janet snaps, "It's 'Ma'am' and 'please.'"

Robyn gathers the Cam as she retreats. ""Ma'am, please let me cam myself, Ma'am."

"If you insist!" Janet points to a corner, then augments, "Do not cease camming yourself while Darleen and I are in this Room or we will strip you, stuff your maillot into your mouth, and you will be camming yourself naked and spread. Am I clear?"

Robyn moves to her new role in life. She adjusts herself in the corner, licks her lips, opens her knees to the two adjacent walls, and cams herself. Robyn should feel lucky to have straps and cloth in her crotch. But ambivalence prevails. *I don't like it Janet bosses me, but I'm decent, and she's made me the Cam star of the Cosmos House. Gamers want to see more of me.*

But nothing compels Robyn to look at the Cam that cams her. So she looks around. Steph and Beka continue to stare at Poot 'n' Coot. Robyn examines Janet and Darleen. Janet is the same as her Picture: Spider Bikini. Darleen wears two Garments. This time Robyn's face-value assessment is correct; more precisely, when Darleen stands straight, the bottom of her pullover top and the waistline of her pants meet perfectly, but for all other motions, Darleen flashes bellage.

Robyn watches as Darleen raises and points her Cam at her camming herself. Robyn is about to open her mouth when Darleen puckers her mouth and signals silence. Smiles. But then Darleen turns, her Cam still in her hands, and she commences to collect her main assignment, the two knees-and-face Pledge admiring two naked Strippers. And this produces deeper ire: *I resent that Darleen feeds Beka and Steph out to the Prefecture. This is my House, and I am the Official Cosmos Camer! How dare Darleen make my Cam unnecessary?* Robyn short stops and looks into the eye of the Cam she holds looking at herself. She looks confused. She is confused. Wants it both ways. *Maybe I'm more important.*

§ Janet & Darleen Visit Steph & Beka: And Hear their Pleas

Steph and Beka hear Janet haze Robyn behind them with both delight as well as fear that Robyn's haze is at most a soft pick-up note. Both Pledge recognized Janet's voice immediately and connected it with the heavy, bare-footed steps. Steph had reacted with a full body quiver that wiggled her already topless strapless down her ribs and crept her hemline further up her stern.

Janet, Steph processes, *Another of my Pledge from last Term! And whom I enabled to be the Monitor of the Corvette House. Janet, here in the flesh. So far this Term we've encountered each other only once, when I greeted her in the Parlor the Day I arrived. BB and Robyn were there too, but Janet treated me like she had more Caste.*

Well, doesn't she?

Newbie Beka recognizes Janet's voice and footsteps from her visit to the Corvette House three days ago. *When Elle and I admired a similar but different pair of Poot 'n' Coot Pictures: backsides lifted up, not unlike my pose right now.* Beka feels brodeas steaming to brim. *I wish Elle were here with me now, instead of Steph.*

Janet's voice resonates from behind the two faced-down Pledge. "Nice butts!"

Beka tries to tell if other feet patter adjacently, but she keeps her eyes focused on the naked Nuggets before her.

"Nice pussies!"

Steph, unable to quite connect the voice when it had spoken to Robyn or overhear much of that conversation, now completes a pattern match: *Darleen! One of my fellow Monitors last Term. What are you doing here?*

Beka also recognizes this voice and associates it with being cammed during the newbies' visit to the Corvette House. *Does Darleen still have the Cam?* Beka bends her head to look and sees a pair of bare feet with slacks above calves, but then a sturdy toe from elsewhere hooks against her cheek and guides her eyes back to the naked Baseboard Strippers' spread pussy and cooch.

Darleen touches a toenail to the bottom of Beka's upturned foot. "You're already begging to Strip, so that's you on the wall next Term."

Beka finds herself suddenly possessed by Penny and Coco's haunting eyes. *That's me looking out.*

Beka hears Janet speak to her from above. "If I catch you looking elsewhere again, you will be looking at your own picture."

Beka responds hurriedly, "Ma'am, yes, please Ma'am." But feels béchamel wetten her own insides to the brim.

Steph curls a lip. Darleen acts like she doesn't even know me, even though we both Monitored last Term, albeit at different Houses.

Steph feels the top of a foot jostle a loose-hanging nipple; Steph's chest might be a flat 32A, but she still has sensitive sweet spots. The toes irritate, and painted toenails scratch. Janet speaks. "If I catch *you* looking anywhere else you will be masturbating to your own Picture."

Steph chaffs under her former Pledge's certitude. "I didn't turn my head, and I'm not looking at my own picture. I'm only looking at Penny and Coco here." Steph considers, then adds, "Ma'am."

"So nice to see you again, Steph Sorostitute." Janet says, still towering above Steph's head. Janet moves and runs a big toe inside Steph's thighs, checking that her knees are fully spread. Steph flinches but keeps her chin resting on her forearms on the floor, eyes glued to Penny's visage. Steph checks to make sure her knees and feet are widely spread. They are.

"Admirable of you to beg BB to let all the Cosmos keep their legs apart all the time," Janet praises Steph.

Steph rotates her upheld stern in the air, but doesn't know what to say, so she says, "Ma'am!" Then she augments, "You're a Monitor because of me, you know."

Janet angles her head, then uses a toe to tickle the bottom of Steph's upturned bare foot. "Tell me, oh sassy one, when I arrived as a Pledge last Term, what was I wearing?" Janet moves and rolls the ball of her foot atop Steph's head.

Steph proceeds carefully. "Ma'am, you came in naked after Stripping before. You were BB's Roommate, and BB was a newbie then."

And what am I now?" Janet tests.

"Ma'am, you are a Monitor now." Steph talks fast but keeps her eyes riveted on Poot 'n' Coot. "You wore two pieces the last time I saw you, in the Parlor the day I arrived. Wearing the crochet Spiderweb Bikini." Steph squirms.

"And what Caste did you used to be?" Janet inquires.

"Ma'am, I was a Monitor last Term." Steph constricts her stern tunnel and states the facts.

"And what are you now?" Janet lingers.

"Ma'am, I'm a Pledge this Term," Steph regrets. Her face flushes, her exposed spigots erect, and goose bumps form on her inner thighs. A droplet of pee releases from her bladder but does not migrate far enough down her urethra to appear at the outside end.

Janet admires, "I saw you let one of your snuggle pups loose in the Bachelor Party clips, but I see today you're making sure Gamers get to see your full set."

Steph's chest flushes. It is exposed, after all, all the way below both breasts.

Janet augments, "And I love your crackly stern star and blonde satchel scruff."

Steph must stop her body from shaking and reduces a quiver to a rolling around of her body muscles. Isometrics, ending with isometrics around her sex organ. Kundalini gathers.

"Thank me," Janet commands.

"Thank you?" Steph carefully raises her voice.

"For coming to visit and admiring your Fate." Janet touches her big toe into that negative space where Steph's pelvis meets her inner thigh, and Steph tenses. Janet augments, "Thank me and beg me to punish you for asking a question."

Steph breathes in and out quickly and turns her head just enough to bang into a Cam. She looks back the naked Baseboard Strippers and recites to her former Pledge, "Ma'am, thank you for coming to examine me." Steph finds it hard to catch all her thoughts. "And please punish me for asking a question." Steph pauses. *Did I get it all? Almost.* She adds, "Ma'am." And feels the minidress ride up another inch. *It's gonna squirm all the way up to my waist.*

"You're welcome." Janet offers a suggestion, "And you'd be welcome to come visit me at the Cosmos House. Ask me nicely."

Steph squeezes to make sure pee doesn't leak. She feels the bottom of toes press against her cheek to prod her response. "Ma'am," she says slowly, "please let me come visit you at the Corvette House, Ma'am."

"I shall consider your request." Janet wiggles a toe up under Steph's body in search of her belly button, and the big toe finds it somehow through the hole in the minidress. "It seems fair," Janet delivers. "After all, you let me visit the Corvettes last Term, didn't you?"

The question catches Steph by surprise. "Ah, er, ah, yes, Ma'am."

"You sent me to be put into the Cravat?" Janet rests a foot atop Steph's bare shoulder blades.

Steph catches up gracefully. "Ma'am, that was last Term. And it was your decision. You begged to be punished for Babs' crossing her legs. You could have had let her take the training, but you sat in for her. I haven't told her. Maybe she still doesn't know, Ma'am."

Janet accepts this analysis. "Did Babs show you the video of Ginny getting throated and fucked in the Cravat?"

Steph fails to answer the question. "Beka and Elle said you made Ginny sit in for her Roommate because Ginny's a Whore-for-Life and you could monetize her bondage. And that they brought back media of themselves, along with Molly. But Babs hasn't shown us any video of Ginny in the Cravat."

"Maybe Ginny needs relief," Janet suggests.

"Listen, nobody ever monetized you!" Steph snaps, suddenly defensive, but still keeping her eyes on the pearl ahead of her.

"I was naked and spread and I couldn't move," Janet delineates.

"Listen, you volunteered," Steph reacts, then taunts, "Automatron forever serves your files. By the way, your Bikini Babe Roommate never crossed her legs again," Steph remembers. "Guess I'm pretty effective."

"You made me streak to get there," Janet affirms. "You didn't need to do that."

"You were naked from the Day you arrived," Steph scoffs, still looking forward, wishing she could pull her miniskirt down toward her hips and pull her neckline upward.

"It's one thing to be naked or pinking inside the Cosmos House," Janet brushes off, "but streaking to the Cravat entailed risks that transcended your Monitor power. Streaking is being naked where you aren't supposed to be. You could have given me something to wear. You didn't."

Darleen dangles, "Oooh, some rogue gang gets their hands on you, wrestles you to the ground, and three-hole gang bangs you. They disappear, leave you spunked, and there is nothing you can do about it."

Steph growls, "I made sure Janet never got arrested. Jail could be far worse."

Janet considers her former Monitor and jangles a thought. "Steph, I hear your Roommate Molly is the only Cosmos streaker thus far. Huh? What do you say? Aren't Roommates supposed to be equal?"

Steph anticipates what Janet has in mind. *Except I will not streak over to visit you at the Corvette House!*

Janet dangles, "I mean, you had Molly's panties for a while, but then you gave them back to her. How sweet. Maybe it's worth a streak to get them back again? Risk it all; get it all. You could let Molly wear your minidress. Two pieces, just like you did for her!"

Darleen kicks in, "At least you know that two Garments are the last thing Molly wants."

Steph gulps. More pee gathers in her urethra. She hurls a thought at Janet. "Your Roommate never streaked last Term; you streaked on BB's behalf. So maybe it's Molly who needs to streak more."

Steph finds her view of the naked Baseboard Strippers suddenly blocked by Darleen's slacks and bare foot. Darleen puts the Cam in hover mode, indicates tracking points on Steph's increasingly exposed body, and steps out of her frame. *Darleen doesn't even acknowledge we were fellow Monitors last Term,* Steph simmers. *She knows me, yet she has the audacity to cam my spuds and smoo like I am some kind of newbie bimbo Pledge.*

Well, yes. Steph flushes. *Darleen deliberately annoys me by collecting my slit, trying to make my strophoid come out, and then showing me to everyone in the Corvette House.*

Well, almost; show Steph to everyone in the Prefecture, actually. And as for Steph's strophoid, it already stands out. Once again Steph spasms. This time a trickle of pee makes it to the terminus of her urethra, but instead of spilling onto the floor it turns sideways and runs down her inner thigh. Steph feels it, but neither Janet nor Darleen observe this immodesty.

The Cam points toward a different tracking point on Steph's bare shoulders and chest. Janet speaks down to Steph directly. "Darleen cammed Beka's boobies, borehole, and bourse three days ago. Now it's your turn."

Darleen digs, "You keep sitting spread with Beka, but you've yet to secrete slop out your satchel. You're depriving Elle of something to lolly." The Cam hovers lower and collects Steph's strapless and now topless minidress all the way down to her sternum, always inching downward.

Janet laughs, "Betcha if we put them stalks on a milking machine we'll collect splurt out the seam."

Steph flushes from her face down to her exposed chest. She flushes her sand dollars and spigots also. *How dare Beka let herself leak brodeas! And increase my risk! How dare Darleen treat me like a shake bag; we were peers last Term!* Steph quivers her upraised stern, with her split and sewer star. *Who is Darleen to suggest Elle lolly either of us up? Is she a MomCap? Again a Monitor and peer of Janet? And who is Janet to suggest creaming me on a machine? So I have to take it from not just Monitors Babs and Janet, but also Darleen, whatever Caste she might be?*

Sounds like a plan.

Janet the Jovial lifts, "Sorostitute, the least you can do for Elle is drop a spot for her on the floor. You can do that for us, can't you? I mean, we're not asking you to keep up with newbie Beka Broda and hang a streamer out. But just one spot. Try, please?"

Steph reluctangly agrees, "Ma'am, please let me spot the floor, Ma'am." She feels a little crazy. She feels her skin, where a trickle of pee ran down her inner thigh and has since, thankfully, dried. *I can feel pee inside me. And I know if I lose pee and Darleen catches it on Cam, I'm a Pee-Camer for sure.*

Crazy memories of making Janet Pee-Cam in the Mudpit last Term dance through Steph's head, and she hears herself speak her next thought out loud. "Ma'am, I'll make a pearl of sexual discharge and drop a spot so Elle can lolly up after me." Steph quivers her belly. *I can't control myself completely anymore. Maybe I don't have to keep up with Beka, but I'm gonna seep soon, whether I want to or not.*

"I hear you beg to get your spice rack made up every morning," Darleen advances. "How's that go, Pledge?"

Steph breathes hard air out of her nostrils and lifts her chin up. Wet open pussy ahead, and her own stern upended. "I beg to Tiffany, Ma'am. I say 'Tiffany, please make up my nipples,' and she does or she doesn't." Steph knows her own nipples hang totally free above the floor. Tight spigots.

"Beg me," Darleen commands.

Steph twitches a nostril and lip as her anger builds toward Darleen. She keeps her eyes on Coco's nipples, quivers, and obeys. "Darleen, please make up my nipples."

Janet's voice intercedes, "Maybe there's hope for her after all."

Again Steph quivers, but then she gathers her energy and commences to slowly rotate her upheld bottom. She lets air out of her lungs, puts her stern rotation on autopilot… and finds precious moments to think. *Maybe Darleen hovered and remains a Monitor this Term? That's why she acts like an equal with Janet. Or maybe Darleen got promoted, made MomCap, and is Janet's superior, her big sister now.*

Steph calculates deceptions and misconstructions. *Or it could be an illusion that Darleen is a MomCap or a Monitor; she really is Janet's Roommate and a Corvette Pledge.*

No matter what, it's disgusting that a peer of mine last Term would order me around and vulgarize me. Especially if she's a Pledge like me now. I hope so. I want to watch her beg to cum and be a naked Stripper next Term! Steph smiles.

The hovering Corvette Cam returns around behind and below Steph's risen minidress, examines her raised stern, and sees if her slit brims. The flush on her sex lips is less visible, but the Cam adds an infrared sensor that captures flare. Steph's body quivers, and she constricts her stern tunnel.

How dare Boss Bitch allow Janet and Darleen to mess with me?

Janet takes over. "Don't be confused," she advises Steph. "You're the headliner today, Steph Sorostitute! Gamers watch you worship your destiny for the first time: those Baseboard Strippers dead ahead of you.

You and lowly newbie Beka Broda. Congratulations, you two tits and ass Pledge."

Steph seethes, *Once again my former Pledge attempts to dominate me. I will get back at both Janet and Babs. And Robyn.*

But Steph does not take her eyes off the Baseboard Strippers. *I feel battered. I fear Beka Broda lacks self control. Maybe I have to look out for her, if only to look out for myself? I shouldn't have to take on her haze, but Gaming might become safer that way. And then I will find an opportunity get back at Beka too.*

Janet presents a more immediate challenge, and Steph hears her voice curl downward. "I haven't forgotten you made me streak last Term, and not just to the Corvette House." Janet adds, "You made me streak to the Nugget, dance naked, and climax the Dong with Tiffany. You made me pour shots in front of the Nugget Crowd. Live, in front of all the Nugget Cams."

Nothing in Janet's claim might make Beka think that Steph was there and secretly watched. Steph cannot resist a risky response. "You had no other way to get there. You Pledged naked and stayed naked. Besides, you liked doing the Nugget again." She considers, then decides to add, "Ma'am."

Janet adjusts the string of her necktie. "You're welcome, Pledge. Once *The Runup* gets going you're going to pink, cream, and beg me to climax you out of your body. You'll gonna like it even more that I did."

Steph clenches her teeth; she tightens her hands into fists, her toes curl.

Janet nudges Steph, "So are you gonna streak to get to the Nugget, just like I did?" Janet smiles and sounds curious.

Darleen snides, "If you are begging to Pledge naked and Strip next Term, you'd only have to streak one way."

"Ma'am, no, Ma'am!" Steph startles, and adds a caveat. "Ma'am, that's not true. I'm begging nothing of the sort." She tosses her head. "Beka's the one who has been begging to Strip!"

Beka constricts her vagina as Janet and Darleen's eyes turn upon her.

"Right you are!" Janet expresses, surprised. "How could I forget? Beka's already visited me!" Janet turns and probes Beka's belly with her big toe. "And begging the Strip wasn't your only achievement, was it, Beka Broda?"

Beka acknowledges, "Ma'am, no, Ma'am." Beka shuffles on her elbows and knees, and her croptop slides upward and exposes her under boob.

Janet nudges Beka on the tickle spot to the side of the ribs. "Maybe you and your Roommate belong on the baseboard next Term?" Janet points a foot at Penny and Coco's photos. "BB and I ought to know. We enabled this pair of Strippers. Now you beg for me."

And Beka eagerly begs, "Ma'am, please let me pledge naked and become a Stripper next Term. Elle too. We want to be the ones looking out from the wall." Beka's already shaven breech parts slightly, and béchamel lubricates the divide.

Beka hears Darleen directs her Cam to zoom in for close-ups. The attention excites Beka; her areola pucker up, her berries indent. She constricts her vagina tight, and her brim overflows.

"My, my," Darleen mocks Beka, "what a performance. Broda outta the boneroo and an uplifted radial brown star awaiting a thermoprobe. You'll lead; Steph can follow."

Beka relaxes her muscles, and her freshened and swollen love box oozes a gob of wetness that slowly stretches into a stalactite of béchamel swinging down between her legs.

"Too bad the Cams can't record the scent with the picture!" Janet advances, and she and Darleen laugh at Beka's immodesty.

Beka constricts again at the realization that Darleen's live Cam records her every indiscretion. More béchamel squeezes out of her broom closet, and the stalactite thickens and distends lower. Beka concentrates on the two vaginas pictured before her, both pulling pink, one fingering her clit, and both wet inside. *Hard to look at,* Beka admits, *but hard to avoid. And I can't forget that right now I not only offer up my brownie for plunder, but also drip again. I might not be pulling pink like Poot 'n' Coot, but I'm secreting a lot more cream than either Baseboard Stripper!*

Janet catches the base of Beka's croptop between her toes, and slides it upward, or, to put in more correct physical terms, slides it downward toward Beka's armpits, neck, and the floor. Slides it so that both of Beka's boobs emerge into full view.

Darleen relishes detailing Beka and Steph's every intimate recess absent demanding they butterfly. "Bet you two never quite thought through just how revealing 'full model release' could be when it comes to showing one's stuff, did you?"

The attention and a deeper understanding of the term "everything" excites Beka, and she pumps out more of her evolving long white streamer. Beka quivers, and the stalactite swings in the air between her wide thighs, stretches, and contacts the floor. It vibrates but doesn't break.

Steph shifts the position of her head on her arms and can feel Beka next to her eager to climax.

So can Janet, so she declares higher stakes. "If *either* of you start cumming, then *both* of you will be streaking to the Nugget and be cumming center Stage."

Steph tries to keep her mind blank and let the Baseboard Pictures become a blur. *If Beka goes over the top I'll be dammed if I get forced to follow.* Steph grits and finds it increasingly difficult to hold her pose.

Steph and Beka hear Darleen's laughter and Janet's heavy bare feet step toward the sliding door leading into the Living Room. But then they hear the feet pause, and Janet delivers Steph a parting line. "Right now all you need to do is secrete a liquid sphere of your sweet slippery until it gets heavy, detaches, and falls to the floor."

"Please don't disrespect Elle Lollydor," Darleen pleads.

Janet caps, "Be nice to BB and beg her to let you streak when you pay me a visit. I'll find you a bunk and a chamber pot and you can spend a few days. Afterwards you can streak to the Nugget, combo the Dong... and stay there."

Steph snaps, "Ma'am, you're not *my* Ma'am, Ma'am." But Janet and Darleen really are gone. The pee affixed inside Steph's thigh tickles and irritates her, so she shakes her body and it falls onto the floor.

Robyn has yet to break out of camming herself in the corner.

§ Babs & Janet & Darleen: Parlor Encounter

Babs intercepts Janet and Darleen before they exit the Front Door. She has come from the Kitchen, having used the second Skeleton Key to the door to the Parlor. BB draws her guests toward the chimney and grand stairs in the Parlor, away from the Living Room.

"I like what you did to Robyn," Babs compliments her former Roommate.

"Thank you," Janet replies. "Meet Darleen; she's my Roommate at the Corvette House. Darleen, meet Babs. Boss Babe to her friends, and Monitor of the Cosmos House."

BB and Darleen exchange nods.

"Darleen and Steph are old acquaintances," Janet jockeys. "Both Monitored last Term."

"And now both of us masquerade as Pledge." Darleen utters her first words, and smiles. "And I love your bling."

Bikini Babe stiffens at the reminder. BB accepts her long legs, bare belly, and extreme cleavage, but she must pretend her *crescents d'areolage* don't wax and wane. *I don't care, but they really do require I bend the limits of social space.* BB eyes Darleen. *I don't like being invaded in my own space.*

"Darleen's my guiding light," Janet compliments, "sort of like your Roommate Tiffany." Janet pitches her head in the direction of the Dining Room. "Steph and I caught up on some old business."

"Very kind of you to pay her attention." Babs cocks her head.

"She's begging to pay me a visit," Janet proclaims.

Darleen snickers, "Maybe if Robyn ever stops camming herself you'll direct her to cam Elle licking Beka up. I'm the one who cammed her the last time."

"Your diligence to duty is so appreciated, Darleen," Babs prides. "And did you record any Steph splurt today?"

Darleen brags, "I cammed her spouts and slippery and stern pipe."

"But she still needs help to drip the satchel slop," Janet adds, then grits her jaw. "I like that you make the slut titter and spread her legs. Has she got to meet the Mirror yet?"

"Side-by-by and topless with Molly," Babs nods. "But nothing close to full power; just enough to keep her engaged."

"Make her spread as wide as she can, shave her short and curlies off, and butterfly her slit, and I bet she'll ooze syrup," Darleen sweetens.

"I'll take her over the top, BB," Janet asserts. "Trust me. I'll make it a total transformation."

Babs hesitates.

"I thought you told Janet you'd let Steph come and visit," Darleen prods.

"I did," Boss Babe acknowledges. "But we didn't discuss cumming her."

Janet wrinkles her nose at Darleen. "Babs want to let Robyn make her cum first."

"Wait," Babs protests. "That's not it at all!"

Darleen wiggles in, "If you're gonna let Robyn force cum the slut, then let Janet do it for you."

Janet confirms, "I would do a much better job."

"Stop it, both of you!" BB stomps a foot. "This is my House, my Pledge, and I will do it my way."

Janet and Darleen look at each other.

Babs looks to Janet. "I will consider your offer. I will consider deploying 'my surrogate,' Robyn. And I will consider force-cumming her myself!"

Babs snaps her waistband. "There, it's all decided!"

Janet glances out toward the window that looks over the Front Porch and stairs. She floats an idea. "Maybe you should make Steph lick your soapy feet off. After all, isn't that what she did to you?"

BB sharpens Janet a look. *I cleaned every Cosmos foot with my mouth last Term. Your soapy foot too.*

Janet refreshes Babs, "After you made a mess Steph put you in your bunk with a chamber pot. Too many soapy feet."

"I'm sorry," Babs apologizes. "Steph said that somehow I 'infected' you and we traded places. I'm really sorry about that, Janet. I know she made you stay in your bunk too, because we were Roommates then and Roommates share. You knew I was prepared to surrender, and just as you saved me, Steph vanished."

Janet jutters her heavyset body. "Lucky you. There's a lot of Roommate things I did for you last Term," she reminds.

"I know," Babs nods, "and I'm appreciative. You climaxed in the Mudpit after you arrived. And then again, later in the Term, allegedly on my behalf. I never watched."

"I've done more of your Karma than you know about," Janet advises.

"I know," Babs nods. "But to hear you tell it, you also shot some great videos."

"Come here," Janet orders and gives Babs a kiss.

Babs flusters, and they both laugh.

Darleen, annoyed at being ignored during this banter, interjects an offering to the Boss Babe. "If you don't want to volunteer a soapy foot for Steph to clean off I'm sure that Monitor Janet might assign one of her Pledge to take on the task."

Babs lays her two hands over both breasts, aware as she does so that she covers not only her underwire bra but also her areolage. She scowls to Darleen, "I don't need to discuss Steph licking soapy feet with you at this time. Maybe that's a Game for Steph to play with her Roommate Molly."

Babs takes a turn to ask a leading question. "Janet, do you still have to pee for the Gamers? And how come you still wear the Spider? And did you really give Tiffany the Pee-Cam when you were both Strippers two Terms ago?"

That's three questions, but given that Babs and Janet are equals, it doesn't matter.

Janet identifies, "Tiffany did indeed acquired my Pee-Cam Obeisance, may she be praised; she retains it to this very day." Janet preens, "I'm free to pee whenever and wherever I choose." She smiles, tucks her chin, and waggles a finger. "Listen, Babs, you've got to be careful with Tiffany. If you let her she'll infect your whole House."

Babs fiddles a bra strap. "I know. Molly's already signed on for the Pee-Cam. Maybe even Piss Mouth."

Janet offers, "Molly doesn't matter; the antidote to Tiffany is Steph. Just send me Steph, and Darleen will cam a clip of her peeing."

"It can be her Pee-Cam audition," Darleen interjects.

"And just for kicks Darleen will shoot a clip of me peeing in her mouth," Janet perks.

"Oooh. That's harsh." Babs fiddles with bra straps.

Janet scowls, "That's what she deserves."

"Well, it does make her equal to her Roommate Molly," BB concedes.

Darleen interjects, "And with Tiffany, too."

"Easy with the Roommates thing," Babs backs Darleen off. "I'm Tiffany's Roommate, don't forget, and I'm no Pee-Camer or Piss Mouth."

"So you're not a Porn Star," Janet shrugs. "Tiffany is, and maybe that's Steph's destiny. So for starters, Steph can join the Pee-Camers and Piss Mouth brigade. Maybe time for Roommate sharing."

Babs looks to Janet, and Tiffany augments, "I bet Steph would take Molly's panties, even if they were piss-soaked and worn in her mouth."

Babs suddenly feels sorry for Steph. "Caste matters a lot to her, Janet, and stuffing piss-soaked panties into her mouth seems like a cruel way to give her two pieces. Worse than titter and vagflash. You just want to break her."

"Break her this way, break her that way, break her into a thousand pieces. They you can put her together again in a new way."

"Jeez, Janet, is that what happened to you? You got brainwashed and reassembled?"

"Me?" Janet laughs and opens her hands away from her plump, near-naked body. "No way. Me, I was born this way!"

BB stops herself nervously gracing her cleavage with a fingertip. She finds her inner well and answers, "Janet, I feel I must help my Pledge grow. Become good Pledge. After all, I was a Pledge, once. So I know what they need to go through. I know the regimen."

"Oh, get a head on your shoulders!" Janet decrees. "Please. How about you take care of yourself first."

Darleen worms in, "Or else you won't be taking care of anyone!"

Janet sterns BB, "Do not let your Pledge intmidate you! I make up the Rules, and I can pass judgment as to whether they are followed or not. My Rule is law! You must remain indifferent to the Fates of your Pledge; you must be tough and not sorry." Janet gathers breath. "My Pledge don't dare threaten me!"

Babs retreats into her thoughts. *It is never so simple, is it? Responsibilities versus repression? Covering-up versus exhibitionism? Management versus selling one's labor?*

Janet shrugs, "Caste doesn't matter. It's no better for a Cosmos to become a Monitor and take Pledge under ones wing or to just Opt Strip and dance naked and spread." Babs looks quizzical, so Janet explains, "The Pledge who gains two Garments strengthens her Caste, but also her responsibilities. The Cosmos who sheds loses position, but gets to show her tits off to the world! So who is to say which Cosmos ends up better off?"

Darleen does a little dance and flashes bellage. The Cam, still under her control, hovers to collect a three shot, close-ups of all of them.

Babs brushes her hands back through her long black hair, and the Corvette Cam collects luscious armpits and breast rotation. "You know, Janet, I guess this being my second Term I really can consider myself a Gamer, a Gamer actually in School. I'm not staff or faculty; I don't live in the Village; I'm not part of the Crowd at the Nugget. I don't sign on and have a virtual presence, and I don't just watch or read. I'm right here in the Cosmos House."

"Hard to believe life is real sometimes," Janet points out. "We've got a lot to worry about, and you need to keep a firm grip on seven Cosmos Pledge. Especially the one who dares threaten you: our former Monitor."

Darleen chimes in, "It's not right that you have to handle her all by yourself."

"I appreciate your help," BB bows to Janet, "but it's not just Steph. I don't like it that's Robyn's Redacted."

Janet snorts, "Robyn's a rancorous, raffish ragabash, and that's putting it kindly and in her terms. It doesn't really matter if she's the same Robyn or not."

Darleen snides, "All that matters is fairness."

Janet observes, "We were nice to her in the Dining Room. We should have rolled her maillot down to her waist and yanked it into her rump crack, and she could be camming herself topless tanga."

Darleen curls her nose. "We left that for you to do."

Babs looks at Darleen, then looks at her Cam.

Janet guides, "Surely you're not going to let Robyn have a second Garment?"

Babs waffles, "Well, she did judge the Mudwrestling Contest, and we did come out victorious. What's not to like about that?"

"You know something?" Janet scratches her belly. "I'm glad she's Redacted. She doesn't need to know about what she doesn't need to know about."

"Wait a minute, Janet," Babs intercedes. "She was supposed to redact any Mudwrestling vids that got shot."

"So, too bad she got Redacted and forgot. Too bad if your babambas might end up outted." Janet shrugs and jiggles her own jaboos in her palms. "Gotta play the Game."

"We were Pledge and now we are Monitors," Babs asserts. "We're the same, Janet."

"No, we are not the same," Janet differentiates. "I've been a Stripper before. And I don't know about you, but I'm going to Opt Up and become a House Mom el Capitan, a MomCap, next Term. And that's what I recommend for you, too."

Darleen snides, "Bikini Babe would need to acquire a third Garment by the end of the Term."

Darleen starts to get on Babs' nerves. Babs furrows her brow. *I wish for sure I knew Darleen's Caste.*

Janet advocates, "It's really simple. Yes, it's up to you if I you want to Hover or Opt Up. You know that Pledge costume is yours for the taking; that's why you are BB, the Boss Babe."

"I know, Janet," BB intones. "I know I have two choices: I can Hover or I can Opt Up. But I don't need to rush when it comes to making a decision. I need to see how well I do in my current position, as Monitor Boss. I need to take charge of my body, cover myself more, and draw less attention to myself. Then I'll decide if I want to Hover and stay the same Caste next Term, or Opt Up and advance, like what you want to do."

Janet offers free advice. "Babs, Opting Up to MomCap is the only path to the Castes even higher. Like Madam or Game Mistress."

Darleen interrupts, "I hear you saw Madam Nurse Beautician last Term. You foot trained at the Beauty Salon. Isn't she a role model?"

BB snaps, "I never saw Beautician above the knee."

Darleen taunts, "But Molly and Steph got to meet Nurse face-to-face at the Medical Exam and see her full figure. What makes them special?"

Babs scowls. "Because they were the ones getting examined," she retorts.

Darleen opens possibilities. "But only Molly got examined."

Babs turns to Janet. "Are you allowed to tell her to shut up or might that lie outside your power?"

"Be nice," Janet replies. "She could be a mole from some other Caste."

And so Darleen presses, "I saw that once upon a time you got to kiss the feet of Game Mistress and saw Slavesex China Doll toe-tied." Darleen flairs, "But maybe you prefer soap-foot."

Boss Babe asserts, "Darleen, I'll have you know that Game Mistress was wearing boots. I kissed her boots, not her feet."

Janet dominates. "BB, I still suggest that you Opt Up with me next Term. The higher the Caste the greater the servitude of those beneath you."

Babs lifts her head. "True. However, the increased rewards of power and lifestyle compound one's responsibilities. The rewards have their own risks and complications. Not just here in the Game. Everywhere."

"So you're going to Hover? It's decided?" Janet confirms. "I can't talk you out of it? The higher your Caste, the more you can determine your Fate."

Babs lays a palm over her mouth. "I knew when I enrolled that the Game is risky, and I am just learning there is a lot of risk I didn't anticipate, and much I don't know about yet. It just keeps coming at me. I'm in over my head as it is. The last thing I need to do is promote."

"You can trade Bikinis with Janet," Darleen spins drolly while collecting the reaction.

Babs blushes for the first time in a long time.

"Still two Garments," Darleen dangles, "Bi-kini." Darleen holds the Cam again and collects how the sun tans BB's purple crescents. BB's blush recedes.

Janet teases Babs, "Darleen flashes bellage, but you are bellage 24x7. Belly up and belly down."

"And besides," Darleen sasses Babs, "I've got no navelage requirements at all. I don't show my legs, cleavage, or bling."

Babs narrows her eyes, looks down at her cleavage, and sees that her bling has bubbled up. She straightens, snaps her waistband, and looks Darleen's Cam in the eye. *I am not about to spill my babambas, flash hairage, or sit and crack my butt. Not for you or for any Gamer.* BB turns to Janet and lightens, "Sometimes I think that my bikini is all that I control, except I didn't pick this bikini."

Janet shrugs. "I negotiated for this Spider. It's pretty much however Gamers want it to be, a web no matter how small or attached. And I'm not like you, Babs. I can't trade my Spider for something else. I'm committed for now."

"But you can add a third piece over it," BB observes the obvious.

"And I shall," Janet says.

Darleen revives a thread. "You know, Babs, you don't have to just Hover or Opt Up. Make your life easy. Beg to Opt Down. You would not be the first Monitor to prostrate herself naked and beg admission to a subservient Caste."

Janet teases, "And should you for some reason end up with fewer than two pieces you'll be Pledging for sure."

Babs draws her chest full and stands erect. "I understand that some Gamers just can't get to the bottom fast enough. Godspeed, but I am not one of them!"

The threesome laugh. BB stiffens. "I don't appreciate Gamers who toy with my exposures, and I don't wish to have my exposures managed by Gamers. My goal remains advancement, and becoming the Monitor of the Cosmos House provides a first step."

Janet shuffles like she readies to leave and tells Babs, "Don't get too cocky."

BB agrees. "I know. It's not just Steph, either. I'm afraid of payback from Penny and Coco. Robyn's still a wild card. Even you, Janet, because I owe you so many favors."

Janet accepts, "Well this is my fourth Term, same as Tiffany. But I don't owe Tiffany anything. And visa versa. Tiffany's a great gal. She wants to make fresh porn again."

"I still find her unbelieveable," Babs confesses.

Janet conveys, "Gamers love Porn Stars for their courage, spunk, and selfless abandonment. And Porn Stars love their fans."

"Porn Stars get to climax on cock," Darleen observes. "But you need to train your wannabe Porn Star to climax on Piss Mouth."

Babs finds the suggestion offensive and draws air into her body as she prepares to defend Tiffany.

Janet interrupts, "Easy does it. Slavesex, Whores, and Strippers climax, and your Pledge are allowed to climax also."

Darleen yarns, "Everybody with a Screen watched your Kimju and Molly climax in the Bathroom two days ago."

Babs firms her defense. "Robyn signing Kimju and Molly to masturbate to climax isn't the same as Tiffany climaxing while getting pissed on."

Janet curls, "Do you know that the Double Dong remains at the Nugget?"

Darleen forswears, "Maybe you know that Strippers aren't allowed to share the Dong. But your Pledge are."

Babs huffs and settles her breasts into place.

Janet attempts to persuade. "You could send Kimju and Molly over to the Nugget for an Alumni Reprise and have them bring the Dong back to the Cosmos House."

"Stop it," Babs firms, "both of you. Now. This is my House. And besides," she retracts, "a Dong in the House sounds dangerous."

Janet doesn't stop. "If you take Steph's minidress you can pick one with a big buttonhole so you don't have to worry about accidentally covering your navel."

"And a tight-fitting top," Darleen proposes. "No more bling."

Babs again scowls and touches her bra straps.

Janet queries, "So is it true you sleep with Steph's minidress as a blanket or pillow?"

BB shrugs, "So? Steph sleeps naked. If it pleases me I issue her a minidress in the morning."

Janet escalates, "So nice of you. But still, with just one Garment Steph still holds a ticket to Opt Down. You don't need to wait for her to Opt Strip before she gets naked. You can make her naked right now. Then make her visit me."

"She'd have to streak to you," Babs worries.

"Listen, Steph Sorostitute made me streak to the Nugget and back," Janet argues. "She deserves it."

"I hear you pulled a shot glass outta your jam pot and peed center Stage," BB queries.

"Wait a minute," Janet protests. "I told you that."

"Perhaps, but you didn't tell me Tiffany downed the shots."

"Babs, please," Janet protests, "That would have been rude of me."

"And I suppose it would have been rude for you to tell me the full story about the Alumni Reuinion. Like that you climaxed the Double Dong with Tiffany," Babs settles.

Darleen watches Janet with interest as Janet pulls up a response. "Okay, I understand. Tiffany and Kimju and Molly all witnessed and sooner or later you found out. But I protected you as long as I could."

"It would be nice if I could find out from you first," BB snipits.

"I told you about Steph taking me over. Betcha that's still a secret," Janet mocks.

"Yeah, right, Janet. Not a peep out of her," Babs concedes.

Gotta go." Janet shifts her weight. "And Babs, listen. There's more you don't know about, too."

"I know you protected me, Janet, and I appreciate that," Babs thanks.

"You're welcome." Janet Jintoe bounces on both heavy feet. "So it's agreed then. You'll let me have Steph for a while?"

"Whether she has to streak naked or go visit you in her minidress?" BB asks Janet a question.

"Naked or dressed," Janet agrees. "You got a deal."

Babs feels overextended. A heartbeat or two, then counter play: "Wait a minute. Didn't you tell me before that if I let you have her for a Day that you'd let me break one of yours?"

Darleen fidgets.

Janet confirms, "Any Corvette Pledge you pick shall Opt Nugget next Term! You got a deal. A whole Term in exchange for one Day."

Babs hedges, "I didn't promise you you'd get to climax her first."

Janet agrees, "No problem. But she will cum for me."

The two Monitors kiss goodbye. Darleen smoothes her pullover top tight against her belly, flashes bellage, and follows Janet out the Front Door.

§ Steph & Beka: The Peril of Oval Mouth

Steph and Beka hear the Front Door close and the sound of Babs' footsteps pace back through the door from the Parlor to the Kitchen. Steph, still astute, confirms the sound of one of BB's Skeleton Keys turning the lock. Robyn, still sitting in the corner camming herself, had heard the voices in the Parlor and her name occasionally, but it had been too much work to pay attention. Robyn knew to keep camming herself as long as she heard voices. Right decision. But after a while her arms got tired holding the Cam pointing at herself, so she sat it down on the floor and let it cam her foot. *Toenail to ankle and I'll relax,* Robyn said to herself. *Maybe the Prefecture deserves more of me or maybe it doesn't, but I've decided, and Gamers should be grateful for whatever they get.* Gamers get golden toenails, the best of Tiffany's nail painting.

Now, as silence descends over the Dining Room, Steph and Beka hear Robyn rise up from the corner, pause behind them, exit to the Kitchen, and head upstairs. Steph surmises that Robyn shall cam Molly and Elle making out with Mirror in the Bunkroom. Steph scans her eyes around the wall ahead of her. *At last, I have been left alone. No more Janet and Darleen, no Robyn Cam; just the creaking sounds of the Cosmos House. Only this nitwit next to me.*

Unlike Robyn, Steph had tried to follow the flow of the conversation between Babs and Janet and Tiffany, but the background noise of the House had rarely combined with the air currents to tinny her ear. Steph glances sideways, then ahead again. She and Beka are alone, except for the Baseboard Strippers, who, frozen in time, lean back, spread and pink, look Steph and Beka in the Eye, and present tits, pussies, and assholes. Steph struggles to not look around, fearing Cams, if not motion sensors, that might still monitor her and Beka's every move. The two Pledge keep two exposed asses high in the air, one borehole and one stern pipe totally puckered. That, plus one breech belching brodeas and one slit parted and slippery underneath soft, wavy hairs.

Steph tries to focus on the recent Front Door interaction between Babs and Janet. *It doesn't matter what the conversation was about. It matters that it happened without me.* Anger toward Babs builds. *Boss Bitch thinks she decides if she Hovers or Opts Up next Term? Think again. She's gonna fall, just like I did. In my case, my most pampered Pledge framed me. In Babs' case I am going to get her.*

Steph is correct that Babs fails to consider her own fallibility, that third case, the Opt Down. *That's what I want to see,* Steph almost smiles at the baseboard Strippers before her. *I want to see Monitor Babs sacrifice her Bikini and Pledge all over again.*

No one has forbidden Steph or Beka to talk, and no Cam hovers, so as her hostile outrage boils Steph fumes out loud to Beka, "How dare Boss Bitch let Janet Jintoe make fun of me? Janet, with her jaboos and jipijapa and jaxy all hanging out of her Spiderweb Bikini. Janet juiced and jacked the Double Dong with Tiffany at the Nugget last Term. That juju was *my* Pledge last Term, and *I* made her what she is today. She owes me."

Beka sneaks a glance at the floor between her legs to see how big a broda puddle she's dripped onto the floor.

Steph expands her praise. "That demimonde douchbag Darleen needs to get fucked with a dick in her dungway. And my other former Pledge, that raptatorial ragazze Robyn Redacted, needs turned into a rum doxy."

"A rum doxy?" Beka hesitates to ask what this means and worries about more immediate concerns. "Hey Steph, do you think Babs should Hover or Opt Up?"

Steph stiffens her body. "Listen to me. Last Term I never took her modesty away from her, like what she's doing to me. So as far as I'm concerned Boss Bitch can strip naked and Opt Down. If I'm her Monitor and she's my Pledge again, next time BB will pink, cream, and cum on Day One."

Beka hesitates. "Are you sure it's okay for us to talk like this?"

"Listen, you aspirant beat-moll," Steph snaps. "You can talk unless Boss Bitch tell you to shut up. Or orders you oval mouth."

"Oval mouth?" Beka isn't sure she heard right.

"Yeah, oval mouth. Hold your jaw and lips wide apart. Oval mouth. Try it sometime. Try it now."

And Beka does.

Steph takes a deep breath and inhales Beka's scent into her nostrils. "Lick your lips with your tongue and then hold your mouth open. If you feel your lips getting dry then moisten them with your tongue. Most of all don't talk. It's bad enough I get positioned next to a bocaccio like you, and it's worse if I have to listen to you."

Beka obeys. She finds herself staring deeper into the shaven lips and wet holes framed before her; she empathizes with the helpless eyes looking back. *Pink, wet, and ready, naked Baseboard Strippers! That's me next Term!*

§ Molly & Steph and Beka & Elle: Dining Room Roommates

Upstairs in the Bunkroom, Babs liberates Molly and Elle from making out with the minxy Mirror and orders them downstairs to the Dining Room to check on their Roommates. She places inattentive Robyn body and face forward against the magical reflective surface, lets the Cam fixate upon her as the Mirror clenches her, and retreats to her Bedroom and Desktop. Instead of providing pleasure, as Mirror did to topless Molly and an astounded Elle, Boss Babe had decided that Mirror will provide Robyn with pain... should she elect to detach herself.

Molly and Elle scramble downstairs but carefully tiptoe into the Dining Room. At first neither Pledge on her knees takes their eyes off the Baseboard Strippers, but then Beka sneaks a look and finds Elle's eyes.

"Jeez, Beka," Elle observes with genuine shock. "This is like a repeat of what we had to do for Janet."

Well, perhaps. Beka and Elle certainly adopted a similar posture admiring the Baseboard Strippers at the Corvette House, and Beka's miniskirt has once again ridden so high that her borehole exposes itself. *Only this time the stern passage next to you belongs to Steph, not moi.*

Elle remains frustrated that she has not been afforded an opportunity to discover what was pushed into her nether way. *I don't need to see any clips of myself, thank you,* Elle admits. She glances at the gray Screen on the opposite wall. *But I did see a clip of Beka, and she's right that something long and metallic got sunk into her bowels. And taken out. Something got pushed into me, too, but it never came out. It melted inside me.*

Perhaps it even got absorbed by the intestines.

Elle considers her own costume, one halter and ripped shorts, and worries about her Roommate's up-ended commitment. *Poised for reception, ass up, awaiting a procto... again.* She casts her eyes to Steph. Steph still keeps her eyes fixed on the Baseboard Strippers. *Like, Beka, Steph's minidress rides all the way up her stern, and unlike Beka and me, Steph's stern tunnel hasn't been violated yet. I reckon that's about to change.*

Elle leans over to examine the floor between Beka's legs. *Yes, you are indeed pumping béchamel outta your box.* Elle purses her lips. *And am I going to have to lick it up once again?*

Later. Molly and Elle don't know that Janet has already come and gone.

Beka forgets about oval mouth. "Elle, please help me cum and be a Stripper next Term. Lolly me up please. I'll—"

"Maybe you shouldn't be talking right now," Elle suggests, then switches from concern for Beka to concern for herself. "I mean, you assured me before we pledged that we might get photoed and videoed, and okay, I agreed to that. But we are now getting cammed in uncompromising positions and situations. This isn't like some wild party, an uninhibited after-hours private club, or even an underground fashion show. You've got us into something that is way over the top."

Beka opens her mouth to talk. "Elle—"

Steph interrupts, "Get your eyes on the Strippers, you stupid bimbo." She snorts. "The last thing I need is to get punished for your transgressions."

Beka tries to apologize. "I'm sorry, Steph—"

Steph interrupts, "Shut up." Yet she takes her eyes off the prize and turns her head around to look behind her at Elle. "You shut up too, you nigmenog neophyte. You're gonna Flip-Flop with Beka and be the next Cosmos squeezing nectar outta her upskirted nook!"

Elle takes in a breath, but Molly, silent until now, awkwardly makes her presence known and pleads to Elle, "She's right, Elle. You and Beka are both begging to be Strippers next Term. You two and Tiffany and I, we're all begging to get to the Nugget."

Elle mentally shrugs. *Maybe a Flip-Flop is a fair thing. Beka and I each have to titter and vagflash the same ways, yet we both retain our two Garments, which is, after all, what Opting Up requires.*

Steph, suspicions confirmed that the heavy footsteps accompanying Elle belong to her plump Roommate Molly, returns her gaze to the Baseboard Strippers, and issues brusque direction, "Listen to me, Molly Mammoth. You swing your lazy fat majonkers into action, get down on your hands and knees, and lick my pee up. I know you're a Piss Mouth from the Bachelor Party. So don't shirk on me."

There isn't much pee to lick up; Molly lowers down to her elbows and knees, with her back straight and her breasts hanging down like horseshoes, with the bag at the bottom the widest and the upper sac stretched thin. She lowers her lips to the floor, collects the pee standing there in a single lick, and then runs her tongue up the inside of Steph's thigh, much to Steph's dismay and amazement. Before Steph can stabilize Molly rises back onto her feet, gathers Elle by the hand, and leads the both of them back to the Kitchen.

Molly answers the question she reads in Elle's eyes. "We got outta there before Steph decided to empty even more of her bladder. I might be a Piss Mouth, but that doesn't mean I relish licking up Steph's urine."

How about giving Elle a kiss?

§ William & Rodney Measure Steph & Beka: Hot Assholes

It becomes quiet again in the Dining Room, and once again Steph and Beka acquire sensitivity to the sounds of the House and the noises that percolate from the outside through the windows and walls. It is without difficulty that they hear the Front Door open and close and hear two pairs of footsteps tread through the Living Room until they pause behind them here in the Dining Room. The two gazing Cosmos hear merriment behind and above them, and another compliment erupts. "Nice assholes! One sewer gate. One bowel star."

Steph recognizes this voice immediately: it's William, Monitor of the Peacocks last Term. Steph's body convulses in a visceral reaction to this humiliation. But she keeps her eyes on the clits in the Pictures.

William chortles to Steph, "I just passed Janet Jintoe on her way out. She wonders if you remember that you and I were both Monitors last Term?"

Steph stiffens at this insult to her memory and agrees, "Mister, yes, Mister." She also eludes any indication about their chance meeting on Steph's way to the Bachelor Party earlier this Term.

"I'm still the Peacock House Monitor," William proclaims. "And pray tell, what have you become?"

Steph coughs it out. "Mister, I'm a Cosmos House Pledge." In her mind Steph recalls some last Term seductions. During the chance meeting Steph had felt in control, but now the power balance feels different. *William should not treat me like this!*

"Looks like you're modeling your smurfs and shrubbery this Term," William appraises. "Janet says you need help making the sop transude outta your snatch."

Steph keeps her mouth shut. *Not a question in need of an answer.* Steph might not be a good sport, but she is a serious Gamer and knows not to try to determine what William might be wearing.

Beka, once again careless, bends her neck to look backward and discovers herself looking square-on into a handheld Cam. The face that accompanies it is male and good looking but not the voice above. The young man on his hands and knees gives her a silent "gotcha" look as his Cam collects a clip that captures Beka's face, hanging boobies, and the streamer of broda that hangs from her bare boneroo all the way to its languid pool on the floor.

Beka snaps her eyes back to Penny or Coco's naked Baseboard Pictures and ascertains her male camer wears only a tight Spandex jockstrap. And bulges inside. It is the same man who approached her and Steph sitting on the Front steps yesterday, then also wearing a jockstrap, and who had cammed their spread legs... and yesterday's hanging brodeas. Beka's bolus stands up, and transudes still more béchamel.

A while back Janet had pushed Beka's croptop up above her armpits and around her collar. So now the man cams her fully exposed boobies and indented buds. Should Steph get a look she should also recognize the man from the Front steps, but neither knows that the face belongs to William's Roommate, Rodney.

Beka knows she got caught, but she still jumps when she feels the pressure as a squishy, egg-shaped orb slide into her bowel. The fat shape feels cold, greasy; she pants and tries to resist but it stays, so she relaxes her bowel around the foreign object. But what's a newbie to do? Beka moans, gushes more brodeas, and recites meekly, "I'm hot hot hot. Titters and twat. 98.6 in my anus."

William and Rodney look at each other and smile.

The penetration into Beka's rectum resonates with the first time when Elle comforted her at the Corvette House, three days ago. *First Janet drops a probe into my bore, now these men ream me.* Fear suddenly grips Beka, and she begs out loud for her friend and Roommate. "Please, Elle knows how to beg to Strip together with me. Please let Elle lick me up!

Please let her lick my pussy too. Please let her exchange clothes with me. Flip-Flop. And I'll eat her and lick her up too!"

Steph cringes at newbie Pledge weakness. She feels something cold touch her sphincter, and she squeezes her stern tunnel tight. A finger graces her thigh. She relaxes her stubborn squeeze, and groans as her rectum gets penetrated for what seems like forever. Gravity, and grease on the probe, slowly overcome resistance. Steph fears, *does William think he can give me an enema?*

No, Steph is not so fortunate. The thick thermoprobe in her stern tunnel encourages her stamen to stand up and a bead of sex sauce to form amidst her parting sluice gates.

"Hot hot hot!" William leads, and Steph hears Beka follow, "Titters and twat!" Steph feels a bare foot prod her body, and she completes the Chant, "98.6 in my anus!"

Steph fumes silently at Beka. *I know the "Hot Titter and Twat Chant;" I administered it to my Pledge last Term, but I should not be the subject of its administrations, especially paired with this overeager belladonna who desires to repeat her performance with Elle at Janet's Corvette House.*

Steph grits her teeth, but holds her gaze on the Baseboard Strippers. *I will have to have a talk with William about his behavior.*

William tells Steph, "Be nice to me and my Roommate cameraman, and maybe you can convince us to screen your spigots and sop to the Prefecture. We got great coverage of the look on your face as your probe slid into your sewer pipe."

"Bring your Roommate and come visit us at the Peacock House," Rodney offers. "Tiffany already came over and did a shirt change. Maybe you two can eat each other's pussies out."

Steph doesn't dare look, but she finally recognizes the voice. *So the jockstrap man who cammed my spread leg appearance on the Front steps yesterday is William's Roommate! I had to show him my stern tunnel. Today he also collects my fully exposed spooters and sweet-tips.*

"In the Game stay the Game," Steph hears William recite.

Steph feels the thermoprobe vibrate inside her stern tunnel, and she drops a pearl of sweet splurt onto the floor. Voila! Her first cream donation.

The laughter of success emerges from behind Steph, and she and Beka hear William and Rodney's bare feet lumber out toward the Front Door.

I will not just make Beka pay for this, Steph forswears. *I will make Boss Bitch pay for sure. And William. William's supposed to be my friend. My buddy. And he cams my stern tunnel getting plundered. I'll be damned if I ever fuck him again!*

Well, maybe Boss Babe will pay for Steph's training, or maybe Steph will pay first. Boss Babe returns from the Kitchen, and Steph and Beka hear her turn a Key and secure the sliding door leading to the Living Room and through that, the Front Door.

Steph hears the lock turn. *I know BB holds both Skeleton Keys. And I have checked the locks... or at least all I can get to.*

BB doesn't need Steph silently plotting; she orders that Steph and Beka steady their Chant, "Hot hot hot! Titters and twat! 98.6 in my anus!"

It requires concentration to keep doing this over and over, but it keeps the brain clean.

§ Babs & Tiffany Discuss Babs' Costume Options

Tiffany returns Kimju's tanga when the twosome return inside from the Post Henge, but she stays naked and makes no attempt to retrieve her Garments from the Bedroom upstairs as she huddles with Babs inside the double-door frame between the Kitchen and the Dining Room. It is an unusual, yet sheltered, location, midway between Tiffany's Porn Star Calendar and Babs' areolaged and hairaged Black Bikini atop the four Dining Room Pictures.

Babs considers, *Okay, I still bling, but I'm stepping in the right direction.* She considers her naked Roommate and Tiffany's Calendar. *At least I'm not getting three-hole gangbanged or peeing in my own mouth.*

Four Cosmos Pledge squeeze past them into the Dining Room and observe kneeling and bowed Steph and Beka admire the two naked, pink, wet, and ready Baseboard Strippers framed before them. Steph and Beka chant in unison, "Hot hot hot! Titters and twat! 98.6 in my anus!"

Unlike Penny and Coco, neither kneeling Pledge pinks. Beka continues to hang her bead out her bare box and puddle the floor; Steph seeps a slippery wet line beneath her wavy short hairs but has still managed to contribute only one spot to the floor. Both rotate their uplifted buttocks in slow motion. Beka's shirt bunches around her collar, boobs and berries on full display. Steph's strapless minidress continues to gather around her upper ribs, leaving both breasts totally exposed, two sloping gradients with two intricate sand dollars and erect spouts pointing down toward the floor.

Robyn, the first Cosmos into the Room and still with the Front Door Cam under till, updates the Cosmos House feed to the Prefecture. Both Steph and Beka endure something inserted deep into their rectums: one stern tunnel thermoprobed and one bowel with a squishy, melting egg. Steph and Beka know to not break their own rhythm. "Hot hot hot!

Titters and twat! 98.6 in my anus!" If either gets confused about chanting, then the other, if not a trickle charge from the thermoprobe, will assist them to reestablish rhythm.

"Distributed processing," naked Tiffany nodes toward Steph. "Some of the intelligence up the ass, some of it wirelessly connected to Automatron. I'd say Steph's mind is sufficently incapacitated that she doesn't even wonder if and when her thermoprobe might be removed from her rectum."

"I don't know, either," Babs admits. She finds the chanting, buttplugged pair of Pledge disturbing. "Steph never did anything like that to her Pledge when she was the Monitor last Term."

"Well, not that you know of," Tiffany circumspects. "But so what? You already let Janet thermoprobe Beka."

Babs studies her Roommate. Tiffany's made-up Eraser Heads do not smear the inside of her clear vinyl longsleeve front-button croptop; she isn't wearing it. Her red hairage doesn't erupt upward from skin-tight, hip-hugging, cameltoed slacks; she's not wearing any. Both Garments continue to hang on the back wall of the Bedroom. Robyn drifts nearby, snarls at Tiffany, and collects her naked milk-white skin on the Cam. And Tiffany smiles, pinches her Eraser Herds, ripples bellage, and makes her tapis wave like it's on fire.

Robyn cams Babs too, but BB waves her off.

Tiffany Transparent reads Babs' thoughts and senses BB's emotions as the Roommates scan the Cosmos Pledge observing the kneeling and faces-on-the-floor, butt-plundered Steph and Beka. Tiffany draws Babs into conversation. "Ma'am, I'm sorry Robyn cams you. We all know you want to cover up more, either by adding a third Garment overtop your bra and nombril, or by exchanging your two piece Black Bikini for something more decent."

"More decent?" Boss Babe stands up straighter and rolls both shoulders.

"Ma'am," Tiffany advances, "less daring. Ma'am, of course you are decent no matter what you wear. And you're beautiful, too, Ma'am. Really, I mean that. And your bling is fabulous, Ma'am."

"Thank you," BB acknowledges, then hikes her bra, holding her widely-spaced straps where they meet the top of her deeply-cleaved underwire cup. Three hooks behind. The bling doesn't go away, and BB continues, "I told Janet I still intend to Hover next Term, despite her encouragement to Opt Up. But I plan to obtain a different two pieces. Bling doesn't matter to me anymore, but dressing for power does. Longsleeves and slacks, like Darleen perhaps, except keeping my button out, obviously."

"Navelage 24x7." Tiffany cocks her head. "Nothing stopping you from carrying three Garments for a while. But if you want to cover your bling you really do have limited choices. You've already declined to accept my transparent croptop."

Babs looks across the room toward where it appears Robyn now directs Kimju and Molly to French kiss, unaware Kimju tastes a Piss Mouth. The two ex-Strippers hug and rub their breasts together. "Knock-a-mam," they overhear Robyn decry as she cams.

Tiffany says, "Ma'am, thank you for letting me masturbate the Post with Kimju, Ma'am. I behaved myself. You can check the clips if you didn't watch me live. Kimju desires power, but once Kundalini seizes her it takes her a while to channel. She lost count twice."

"Lucky for her you were there," Babs muses. She looks across the Room and observes Kimju's tanga.

Tiffany says, "Ma'am, I'm the one who slathered it with tapioca, but when Kimju put it on she was already thick with kloop. So was her Post. Both of ours, actually." Tiffany cocks her head. "I don't think Kimju can make a useful donation to you, Ma'am, be her thong creamy or dry." Tiffany advances carefully now. "Although she'd be happy to accept my croptop, may that please you Ma'am. She'd make a good Monitor, Ma'am, and deserves a second Garment. Kimju can live with see-through, and I can live without it."

BB curls, "So you can head for the Nugget wearing just stretch slacks!" Babs casts her eyes up and down Tiffany's lithe body, still naked, and her eyes twinkle. "Maybe I should send you upstairs to put your slacks on so you could practice topless for a while."

"Ma'am, may I please you and wear whatever you assign me, but please let me stay naked. Maybe I'll get an opportunity to pink the Cam."

Babs scratches herself between her eyes and smiles. "You may stay naked and continue to beg to be a Stripper next Term, no matter how much you deserve to be a Porn Star."

"And you, Ma'am, must use your Caste to your best advantage." Tiffany raises her chin toward Molly and reminds Babs, "Molly's panties, like Kimju's tanga, do not help to advance your coverage, nor does Beka's open-armhole croptop, nor Elle's halter. And I doubt Robyn's maillot, even overtop your bra and nombril, would reduce your areolage at all, Ma'am."

BB collects herself. The taming power of quiet.

Tiffany reaches a finger and twirls it down her tail trough. She examines her twat to make sure there is no sand or dust inside and refocuses the conversation upon Babs. "Ma'am, surely you must know your true prospect remains Steph. You control the cutout minidresses, so that you can fit it onto your body however you want. It will cover your bling and reduce your overall exposure."

Babs carefully fingers her belly button. Navelage 24x7.

Tiffany advocates process. "Ma'am, if you don't want to keep three pieces and you really do want to Hover, you always shed your bra or nombril later, or wear something different underneath."

"Like Robyn's maillot," Boss Babe suggests with a twist. "After all, Kimju won't need it if I let you give her your transparent croptop."

Tiffany grins, "Ma'am, I'm yours to command. I'm Tiffany Transparent. Pee-Cam, Piss Mouth, Cosmos Pledge. Hairage, rugage, cameltoe. Please take my shirt, take my slacks, and let me show you my tail trough and tail pipe in blacklight."

"Maybe you'll tell me if you've got third tattoo somewhere?" Babs' phrasing doesn't entirely make this a question.

"Ma'am, I'll reveal myself totally. Every hole, inside and out. I'll shave bare, bald, and naked. I'll cum on cue."

Babs takes a breath.

Tiffany insists, "Ma'am, you should allow Kundalini to stir and see who it pleases you to plunder. Whatever pleases you. Beyond just snatching a minidress."

Babs considers her Roommate. *Tiffany has become an ally, a confidant.* Babs wrinkles her lips. *What does Tiffany want in return?*

Tiffany answers the unspoken question. "Ma'am, I'll do anything to make the Nugget my next stop. I'll do anything Steph and Beka do or have done. I'll sit on the Front steps and open my legs, only I will do it stark naked. I'll pull pink, squeeze tapioca out of my twat, and masturbate to climax. I'll do anything *you've* ever done. I'll soap your feet and lick them clean, and you can put me in my bunk with a chamber pot. I'll lick your buckeye. I'll let you pee in my mouth. I'll eat your buttermilk!"

"Stop it!" Babs calculates. "I get it. You are a wannabe Porn Star who needs to be a Stripper next Term. I think you're the only Cosmos who actually desires to shed Garments."

"Ma'am, maybe Molly also begs naked," Tiffany admits. Now she begs sotto voce, "Ma'am, I'll even take on someone else's Karma if you'd let me Double Opt Down."

"Enough!" BB shakes her shoulders. "You may even take on bad Karma and obtain no benefit, Pledge." BB snaps her waistband. "Tiffany, I shall keep in mind both of your requests. And I am sorry. As your Roommate, that there is nothing I want to Flip-Flop or take from you. I can't use your shirt, and your pants' waistline is way too low, below what I got already."

Tiffany pulls a tuft of pussy hair through her fingers and steers to a different pair of Roommates. "Ma'am, I gather everyone's curious if you're gonna make Beka and Elle Flip-Flop, Ma'am." Tiffany carefully does not frame this as a question.

"You just want Elle vaging her nookie 24x7," Babs lightens, knowing full well the effect of wearing the miniskirt. "And tittering armholes instead of showing off her nips down-halter."

Tiffany parlays, "Ma'am, even after a Flip-Flop, Beka or Elle will still have the two Garments to Opt Up... except you got them both begging to Pledge naked and Opt Strip next Term."

"I'm not sure they believe their own words," BB apologizes.

"Ma'am, please let me give them Stripper lessons," Tiffany pitches. "It matters not that the newbies don't comprehend what they beg. After they Flip-Flop, Robyn can sign Beka to pullaside, and Elle can open up her legs for the Cams. Although I doubt if she's as equally liquid as her Roommate."

"You're bad," BB admonishes Tiffany with a laugh.

"Ma'am, it would be good for them, Ma'am. Help reality to sink in," Tiffany asserts. "They'll learn, and they will love it!"

Beka especially; Elle not so much.

§ Tiffany and Kimju & Molly: Evaluate Robyn & Steph

Kimju and Molly are still hugging each other and French kissing off to the side in the Dining Room when naked Tiffany taps them out of their trance. Kissing is a good thing to do when one needs to occupy time. Robyn abandoned camming them a while ago.

Communications at the Cosmos House remains strictly controlled, and this is rare opportunity for the threesome to compare notes. Gamers know they shared experiences at the Nugget last Term, including watching Janet's Alumni Reunion, with its Pee-Cam Piss Mouth handoff and Double Dong climax.

Kimju cocks her eyebrow and smoothes her tanga; the shadow of hairage still lies just outside her tanga's legline, and her keister remains buttage, 24x7. Molly tugs up her panties and makes sure they are gathered into her mooe and moonshadow.

If Molly doesn't consider what might have happened to Tiffany and Kimju in the Backyard, it's not because she's uncaring or rude; she's just anxious. "Tiffany," she says, "please, help me get naked."

"Hey, me too, except you've already got one piece," Tiffany advances, naked at the moment but with two Garments on the hook upstairs. "What I don't entirely appreciate is you two telling Babs that I performed Piss Mouth. Where did you get that idea?"

"Center Stage at the Nugget," Kimju darts. "You begged your own Piss Mouth last Term to avoid Slavesex. Now it becomes you."

"You knew what you didn't want," Molly interjects. "Besides, Tiffany, you're not the only Piss Mouth here. I had to squeeze pee outta my panties at the Bachelor Party. And lick up Steph earlier today. Maybe you're infectious."

Kimju extends defenses. "Tiffany, you got scratched up before we arrived because you pretended you didn't know Janet. You ate soap because you lied about the Alumni Reunion. And Babs made you Piss Mouth because you failed to tell her what you knew about climaxing the Dong with Janet. Molly and I can't help it that you kept secrets about things everybody knows about. Including Janet."

Molly apologies, "Kimju and I are really sorry about how all that ended up."

"You're forgiven." Naked Tiffany twists in place and lifts a finger. "Provided you don't get in my way of making it to the Nugget next Term!"

Kimju snorts, "Not me. Molly perhaps. She's the one with one piece who wants one piece less."

"Tiffany, I just want to get to the Nugget with you," Molly affirms. "Except Babs keeps holding me back from giving Steph my panties."

"Well, okay," Tiffany acknowledges, "but don't forget that you got to share panties with Steph once already. Steph got to wear panties underneath her cutout minidress and you had to streak naked to the Bachelor Party. Doesn't matter that you're fat; you're still the only Cosmos streaker."

"Maybe it's time for Roommates to share." Kimju gestures toward the two kneeling and chanting Pledge. "Robyn says Darleen cammed Steph begging Janet to streak over to their Corvette House."

"Oooh, sweet." Tiffany expresses amusement. "Perhaps Steph could give Molly here her cutout minidress to wear when she decides to make any such naked departure." Tiffany addresses topless Molly directly. "Over panties, of course. Maybe Roommates get to share after all: costumes, streaking, that kind of stuff."

"Maybe Steph can share your Pee-Cam," Kimju suggests to Molly.

The threesome giggle, but Molly remains silent. *I know that Steph is primed; I know, I licked her pee up. The only thing standing between Steph and the Pee-Cam is the Cam. Because if I start a flow going, Steph won't be able to hold back.*

If indeed Steph represents Molly's upcoming Roommate Game challenge, so does Robyn confront Kimju.

Tiffany tests Kimju. "You don't resent that Robyn already made you and Molly to pull your pink, cream, and climax this Term? Show off your clithood rings? She says that during the Runup you're both going to Pledge naked, cum in synchronization with your own videos, and beg to Opt Strip next Term."

Kimju straddles and pushes an answer forward. "I resent that Robyn forced us to cum, and live, on the Bathroom Cam." Kimju shakes her head. "I'm sorry, but maybe Molly can Pee-Cam, Piss Mouth, streak, and beg naked Stripper next Term. Maybe you too, Tiffany. But I have no intention of letting Robyn sign me for any such Obeisance, even if she is my Roommate."

Molly hefts her mams and interjects, "It was Steph, not Robyn, who turned me into a Piss Mouth. I'll volunteer to bleed my next period into a single sanitary napkin, soak it in piss, and let you stuff Steph Sorostitute's mouth." Molly turns to Kimju. "Robyn remains your Roommate, after all, so you will get to play a Roommate Game with her first."

Kimju stirs and cups her bare knock-knocks in both hands. She surveys her Roommate across the room and considers if it really is possible to acquire Robyn's maillot cutout. *What if Robyn's Charm might be real? What if she takes my tanga? Then it will be me staying naked the rest of this Term... and next Term as well.*

Kimju turns. "Tiffany, there are compromises I will make in order to acquire a second Garment, like wearing your shirt, but begging Robyn to manipulate me with Hand Signs is not right. But what if Robyn really does have Charm?"

Tiffany agrees, "My free advice about Robyn is that instead of a Winner-Takes-All, you might go ahead and call a Flip-Flop with her— you have nothing to lose. Robyn believes she doesn't have to worry about how she will come out on top, and besides, she gets to call a Game, and you can measure her Charm."

"If you win, claim her maillot and turn her into a topless tanga," Molly describes, then jokes, "Maybe BB will want Robyn holding a handbra once her rigamarole comes out."

Tiffany steers again. "If you lose, Robyn will take one look at what you're wearing and decide to keep what she's got. And you'll still be topless tanga. Nothing lost."

Kimju appreciates reasoned advice. Now she enlightens, "And I'll have played my initial Roommate Game, which qualifies me to Game with other Cosmos."

Tiffany smiles. She watches Robyn cam Steph and Beka worship Penny and Coco's Pictures, elbows and knees, asses raised up, with a thick long thermoprobe descended into Steph's stern pipe. Steph and Beka try their best to maintain a soft chant. "Hot hot hot. Titters and twat. 98.6 in my anus."

§ The Cosmos Admire Steph & Beka: Elle Begs to Lolly

Babs and Tiffany, Robyn and Kimju, Molly, and Elle form a semicircle around the two bowed Cosmos who worship the Baseboard Strippers—heads, hands, elbows, knees, and feet on the floor. Robyn directs the hovering cam to showcase Steph and Beka's exposed hanging tits and raised asses. The two hemlines, riding high above one stern tunnel and one borehole, display a satchel partly hidden behind some soft shag and a bare beaver with butched bristles above. The Prefecture may have witnessed much of this terrain in Days gone by, but today, for the first time, Steph offers her stern upwards. Steph clenches her teeth as she focuses. *Penny Poontang and Coco Cunt. I just need to get through this.*

Steph feels the fat rectal thermoprobe deep inside, *penetrating my sewer,* but she cannot see what the Cosmos and Cam see: the gleaming end of the long shiny buttplug sticking out her stern tunnel and wagging in the air.

Beka's borehole appears empty. None of the Cosmos except perhaps Boss Babe saw Rodney's recent Peacock Cam feed. Some assume the passageway has been forgotten about, some assume it will soon be plundered. Elle's experience at the Corvette House makes her suspect Beka's borehole might contain an egg-shaped suppository inside. *Something to melt and enter the body from the exit way.* Elle swallows. *No way to feed Beka and me.*

Steph and Beka continue to softly chant, "Hot hot hot. Titters and twat. 98.6 in my anus." Both gently rotate and quiver their upraised buttocks, and both constrict their rectums. No pushing out.

Beka can barely control her desire, and she breaths deeply. Her boobies sway, her berries crinkle and indent, and her box secretes heavy, thick brodeas that has ozed like a bead of white honey all the way down to puddle on the floor.

Beka's lack of control worries Elle. *It's one thing that Beka's exhibitionism gets her wet, but she's also getting too willing. It's one thing I might have to lolly her up, but I don't need to vagflash or beg to be a Stripper next Term. Some Gamers just watched whatever happened to her, just like some Gamers have watched me at the Corvette House.*

Babs finds herself at a loss for words, but Tiffany seizes the moment; she applauds and emphasizes with Beka's quivering frustration, "Gamers say there is nothing sweeter that a Pledge who wants to climax but isn't allowed to. You can taunt and tease Kundalini, and Kundalini taunts and teases back. Coil muscle, build yet harness energy, and manage release. And be release managed."

Steph rotates her upheld and plundered stern. Steph's smoo might be slick and show more than one line, but Steph struggles that no more secretions seep out. *One drop already is one drop too much.* Automatron wirelessly fine-tunes the thermoprobe and lets Steph stay slippery but not sluice. Babs touches her hand to her mouth.

Robyn, ever the ringmaster, directs the hovering Cam to pan across the four Cosmos Pledge standing about. "Thanks to Steph all of you get to keep your legs apart 24x7. But only Steph and Beka enjoy a monopoly on offering sanpan spread views. Sphincter and slit; borehole and brim." Robyn laughs.

Robyn steps back from the semicircle, and Babs doesn't stop her from letting the Cam try to sneak a moment to record her Black Bikini. Underwire bra and nombril. BB nods and smiles. *Bling! Navelage 24x7.*

Robyn faces the four Pledge, curls her lips, and gestures to indicate the two kneeling Pledge. "One of these Pledge needs to shed one garment, and the other needs to shave off her pussy hair," Robyn snorts. "That way they can both be bare, and trot their one piece to the Nugget next Term." Robyn cackles at the bowed worshipers. Steph grits her teeth; Beka feels the urge of liquid brimstone between her legs.

Robyn taunts the group of standing Pledge, "Actually, during *The Runup,* maybe more of you will shave off your pussy hair!"

Babs watches a ripple of uncertainty pass through the four Cosmos. *Tiffany naked and slowly fingering herself, Kimju and Molly topless and buttage, Elle still wearing her halter and ripped shorts. Plus me in my Bling Bra Bikini.*

Tiffany raises an arm in the air. "Wait a minute, Robyn." She drops her hands and traces the waistline of her stretch slacks, absent at this moment. "I've already offered to shave off the hair that shows *above* my waistline, but I'll stay naked and shave my entire twat!" Tiffany knows at this moment she commands the Cam and seizes an opportunity to pink and finger dip. She adds, "I'll cream and climax for real."

Molly rushes toward opportunity and raises her stakes. Topless Molly's panties remain twisted and pulled into her mooe, and Robyn cams hairage to both sides of the yanked-up fabric. Molly appeals to Babs as Robyn wanders behind her to collect the yanked-up panties revealing two full moons. "Ma'am, if you let me give my panties to Steph," Molly haltingly offers, "I'll shave myself bare, all my mooe. Just like Tiffany. And I'll stay naked, from *The Runup* through the end of the Term. And become a Stripper next Term!"

Robyn leans in and snarls at her, "The only reason you beg is because you're afraid someone will discover you lost the Watering Can!"

Molly glances at Babs but sees that her Monitor directs her gaze elsewhere. Babs worries that the two Baseboard Strippers *lie in wait for*

Janet and me, plotting payback. They might also lie in wait for Steph or Robyn, who refereed the Mudwrestling Contest, but that's not my problem.

Robyn steps forward toward Molly. "You'll do anything Steph tells you to? Ha. Look at your Roommate now. You want to Strip so bad, you mangy mumping moil, maybe you should trade places with her. You want to shave your mooe bare? How about you shave all the fur growing around your mawk hole? You're the Cosmos with the most, I mean, the most, copious body hair. Molly Mammoth, that's what you are. A fat furry overweight slug of a creature."

Molly begs, "Please—"

"Shut up," Robyn commands, then rotates her shoulders and toys, "Molly Mammoth, if you can get a razor through that thick muff of yours, then why not also shave your hairy arms and legs, your mangy armpits, your eyebrows? Even all the hair on your head! That way you can be totally bare, bald, and naked!"

Molly rushes the opportunity. She begs, "Ma'am, please let me shave bare, bald, and naked. Every inch of my body. And become a Stripper next Term."

Robyn rolls her eyes and swings her attention to Elle. "And what about you?" Robyn snarls. "Don't you want to trim your nappy back so it doesn't show outta your jeans crotch?"

Elle finds herself confused and turns to appeal to BB directly, "Ma'am, may it please you, I'll shave so my hairage doesn't show out the sides of my shorts."

Babs smiles and advises her Pledge, "Your Roommate has already volunteered to Flip-Flop with you so that you might share your entire nook with the Prefecture. Help me remember that as soon as we start *The Runup*. Maybe you won't need to beg a trim after all."

Elle understands and quickens. "Ma'am, please, I'll Flip-Flop and shave it all off," she offers, then speaks for her Roommate. "Completely bare. Beka and I both will."

"Remind me to Screen the Videos you brought back from the Corvette House worshiping the Baseboard Strippers," Boss Babe commands.

Elle stumbles. She wonders. *Who might watch? Who has seen already? Will I have to watch myself, either alone or in front of others?* Too much thinking time, so out with it. "Ma'am, please Screen Beka and me with our bottoms up, "Ma'am."

BB pinches both of Elle's cheeks. "Good Pledge. Now, is there anything else you might be begging for!"

"Ma'am." Elle catches her breath. Her head spins, then she recites, "Ma'am, please let me Pledge naked and become a Stripper next Term, Ma'am."

"You won't forget?" BB tilts her head.

"Ma'am, no, Ma'am." Elle adds, "And Beka too. Please. Both of us."

Again Beka shakes, and the long string of thick béchamel breaks, swings to the side, and affixes itself to her inner thigh.

Elle senses Beka losing all control. Her thighs quiver. Her bore and bourse constrict. She pants.

Boss Babe adjusts the dynamics. "Elle, you and Beka may strip naked and shave later." BB points Elle to the spot of Steph sauce on the floor and the puddle of Beka brodeas. "Right now, how about you get on your hands and knees, lolly up after our newest Cosmos creamer, and then lolly up after your Roommate?"

Elle doesn't hesitate. Steph's thermoprobe vibrates and two bare butts rotate in the air, one quite on its own. Elle drops to her hands and knees, face to the floor, tongue out, and starts to lolly the two chanting Cosmos.

"Hot hot hot. Titters and twat. 98.6 in my anus."

22 The Cosmos: What Happens Next? (After D14)

§ The Cosmos: The Arrivals Come to an End

And so *The Arrivals* draw to a close. Eight Cosmos have all arrived. At the moment two of them, Steph and Beka, practice chanting in front of a future Option, a Chant that consumes their attention and makes it very hard for them to think about the other six Cosmos who watch them. "Hot hot hot. Titters and twat. 98.6 in my anus."

Tomorrow *The Runup* begins. Will Steph and Beka still be here in the Dining Room admiring the Baseboard Strippers?

During *The Runup* the Cosmos Roommate Games will commence. Pledge may make moves, and Pledge may get moved upon. Any Cosmos not already serious will need to get real serious real soon. Even Monitor Babs, apparently able to decide if she Options Up or Down or simply Hovers, must remain cognizant of MomCap's presence, the unseen power of Game Mistress, the uncertainty presented by fellow Monitor Janet, misbehavior by her own Pledge, and the possibilities that now-Strippers Penny and Coco may plot revenge.

So do the Cosmos play a Game about sexual power? Indeed, they study and learn the arts of Kundalini, the sex force in Nature. Sex power is one of Nature's dynamics present on Earth, maybe throughout the Universe. Opposites complement: in physics, in electro-mechanics, in animal development. Cosmos must temper their desires amidst Kundalini coils and learn to channel sex power.

And will our Cosmos Pledge master the skills to acquire or keep two Garments, Opt Up, and become Monitors next Term? Gamers know some Cosmos aspire to that goal. And will some Cosmos command the skills to acquire or keep but one Garment—or none at all—and Opt Down and become Strippers next Term? Absolutely!

But can every Pledge get what they want?

Perhaps. Perhaps not.

§ The Cosmos: A Look Ahead to the Rest of the Term

The stories of the Cosmos as they begin their Roommate competitions continue in *The Cosmos: The Runup,* the next and second Book. During *The Runup* imbalances and alleged inequities between and among eight Cosmos and their few associates will attempt to find equilibrium... or not.

As the Term progresses the Cosmos Pledge struggle with each other to determine who shall Opt Up and who shall Opt Down. The Cosmos shall play Games, endure hardships, submit to hazing and humiliations, pass examinations (or not), and outwit one another (or not). Kundalini, Karma, unforeseen circumstances, complications, chaos, and cheating will likely all contribute to determine who wears what pieces at the end of the Term. As will talent, of course.

Physics permits four Cosmos to Opt Up and four to Opt Down next Term. But physics often has fine grain and more than one way to resolve equilibriums. Learning requires observation and patience. Calm. Memory. Steerage. Deals with Gamers can turn out with unforeseen consequences; they can have the potential to turn out a Pledge before a Pledge knows what is happening.

Furthermore, "Opts"—winning and losing—can involve complex Gaming, because they involve not just how many Garments a Cosmos wears, but also what Obeisance might be required to acquire and to hold or divest them. In fact, "winning and losing" are loaded terms, as are "Up" and "Down." Certainly not all Cosmos aspire to the same Fate. Many argue that all Castes are equal before Kundalini, although they are unequal in power.

Some Gamers anticipate that the events which lead to their ultimate Fates at the end of the Term will be resolved in *The Cosmos: The Beach Day,* the third and middle Book of the Term. Actions precipitate the fourth Book, *The Cosmos: The Runout,* however it will require a fifth and final Book, *The Cosmos: The Play Party,* to fully detail and resolve their outcomes.

May Kundalini smile.

§ The Cosmos: Manifests, Diagrams, and Appendices

This section details the various front and end materials that are part of *The Cosmos, The Arrivals.*

Gamers of all ilk are reminded that Diagrams at the front of the book detail floor plans of the Cosmos House lot, including the front and Backyard, the Cosmos House's first and second floors, and a preview of the Nugget, seen only fleetingly in *The Arrivals* but which various Cosmos have experienced... and which some desire to experience again (or not) during *The Runup.*

The Table of Contents includes the Chapters as well as Scene (§) divisions.

Appendices are near at the back of the book, following this last Chapter. They include:

The Frame of the Eight Castes compares each Caste versus its properties (e.g., number of Garments, Hover Options, applicable Rules, etc.).

The List of Hand Signs and Positions suggests a minimum vocabulary every Cosmos should know.

The List of Capital Words and details on words capitalized includes most if not all of the Props, Locations, and Events that are capitalized, as well as other classes of words that are not, including many Obeisances (e.g., 'coitus' or 'lapdancing') and Exposures (e.g., 'areolage' or 'hairage').

The Location List provides a hierarchical list of all Locations with capital letters. All Locations are also found in the Index in the form *Location: GamerName.*

The Props List provides a list of all Props with capital letters, as well as a few objects included in the Index that do not have capital letters. Note: Props starting with capital letters are indexed thus: *Prop: GamerName,* whereas props that are lowercase are indexed *GamerName: prop.*

The Event and Time List provides a list of all Events and time-related words with capital letters. All of these are indexed thus: *Event: GamerName.* Besides Events such as the Bachelor Party, this list also includes the word 'Clock,' which is an important index term that tracks day-by-day action, and the word 'Midnight,' which defines the end of the last day of the Term.

A Summary of Garment Exchanges logs all costume exchanges between the individual costumes during The Arrivals; this is also found in the Appendix.

An Inventory of Chants (lest Gamers need reference for training) is also found in the Appendix.

Two Manifests detail the Cosmos' physical bodies and Garments. The first details their physical features and initial costumes. The second details the ebb and flow of their Garments, Props, Obeisance, and Exposures throughout *The Arrivals.*

A Glossary defines many Capital Words as well as many of the specialized language used throughout. Most of these terms are also found in the Index.

Finally, an Index provides ways for Gamers to search out individual Cosmos, Locations, Props, Obeisance, and Exposures (body parts), as well as other themes central to our Game. Individual plot lines (that is, the back and forth dynamic between Cosmos and other Gamers) may also be found gathered there.

§ The Lady-Part Words

Neither the Glossary nor the index records Lady-Part Words, those terms used by Cosmos to refer to their own as well as each other's body part. These more intimate parts of the body including the breasts, areola and nipples, pubic hair, vulva, clitoris, anus, as well as the valiva (herein called 'cream' generically).

Robyn catalyzes the introduction of many of these terms, but she is by no means the sole source. Even Babs has words for own intimacies.

Gamers recognize that not all Lady-Part Words are always equal. Space and time are elastic. Some Lady-Part Words are self-referential, some are generic and professional, and some intend to debase and vulgarize the referent. Robyn especially favors the insult.

In general Lady-Part Words share the same initial letter or sound as the name of the Lady Cosmos here in the House. Astute Gamers recognize that although both Babs and Beka share "b" that they have different Lady-Part Words (as perhaps they should!). Elle's Words all start with an 'n' and are an exception to this general rule, with a vestige perhaps only Elle knows.

§ Acknowledgments

The Professor wishes to thank a small cadre of readers and editors for their invaluable contributions to this book. These include Louis Peluso, whose insight into character relationships and wordplay has been unrivaled; Thomas LaRossa, whose early readings helped provide focus; Riley MacLeod, whose editorial reviews contributed much to strengthening the plot, lightening the touch, and line editing the writing into shape; and finally the management and staff at All Ivy Writing Services, who have provided consultation and clarity throughout the project.

Thank you also to Stefano Bolognini for one of the images incorporated into the cover and distributed on the Wikimedia Commons, under the Creative Commons Attribution 3.0 Unported license.

§ The Cosmos: Danger Ahead

The School and the Cosmos House is a challenging place. It is a challenging place to read about, a challenging place to go visit, and it is a particularly challenging place for the Cosmos Pledge, who are attracted to the School to study and play the Game for real... and learn how Kundalini manifests in their mind, bodies, and souls. May they attain Nirvana.

The Cosmos House is not necessarily a place to come when you want to practice safe, sane, and consensual BDSM. Like all great books of sexual abandonment, it teters on fantasy. But it is about power trips, power exchanges, and power sex. And arousal and love and friendship and trust. Transformation.

Finally, remember this: although all the Cosmos begged to be here, signed up to play, volunteered... that once they start to play the Game, there really is no way out. "In the Game Stay the Game" is the first Chant.

Some say the Rule applies to all Gamers.

Appendices

The Frame of Eight Castes

Caste	Residence	Proper Address	Garment Count	Tasks, Requirements, Restrictions	Movement Potential
Game Mistress / Master	Castle?	Mistress Master	5	Owns Slavesex, manages Madams	Hover, Opt Slavesex
Madam Pimp	Whorehouse (e.g., Flesh Ranch)	Madam Sir	4	Leases Whores, manages MomCaps	Hover, Opt Up, Opt Down
MomCap DadCap	Strip club (e.g., the Nugget)	House Mom, el Capitan	3	Bosses Strippers, manages Monitors	Hover, Opt Up, Opt Down
Monitor	House (e.g., Cosmos House)	Ma'am Mister	2	Manages Pledge	Hover, Opt Up, Opt Down
Pledge	House (e.g. Cosmos House)	Pledge	0, 1, or 2 (total 8 in House)	Beg pink, cream, climax, solo toys, lesbian acts, share Double Dong	Opt Up, Opt Down
Stripper	Strip Club (e.g., the Nugget)	Stripper	0	Nude dancing, lapdancing, solo toys, pinking, cream, climax, ALL sex acts forbidden, Double Dong forbidden	Opt Up, Opt Down
Whore	Whorehouse (e.g., Flesh Ranch)	Whore	0	All Pledge tasks, all Stripper tasks, all sex acts, Double Dong	Hover, Opt Up, Opt Down
Slavesex	Dungeon	Slave, Slavesex	0	All Pledge, Stripper, and Whore tasks, plus bondage and pain	Hover, Opt Up

Rules of Engagement by Caste

Inner-contact means within a Caste, e.g., Pledge-to-Pledge. Fondling is defined as contact outside of Caste. Sex is defined as lesbian, homosexual, or heterosexual oral-genital or genital-genital contact. Bondage is defined as restraint, possibly coupled with physical punishment.

Pledge: inner-contact allowed, fondling forbidden, sex forbidden, bondage forbidden.
Strippers: inner-contact (including sharing Double Dong) forbidden, fondling allowed, sex forbidden, bondage forbidden.
Whores: inner-contact allowed, fondling allowed, sex allowed, bondage forbidden.
Slavesex: inner-contact allowed, fondling allowed, sex allowed, bondage allowed.

Capital & Lower Case Words

Capital Words are used in the Cosmos to denote a series of proper nouns relevant to the Game. A comprehensive list of them will be found in the following four sections, which detail capital words for Gamers, Locations, Props, and Events. Also detailed are other classes of words that tend to not be capitalized (e.g., individual exposures such as 'areolage' or 'hairage').

Gamer Words List

All names of Gamers
All names of Houses; e.g., Cosmos House

Pledge, Stripper, Whore, Slavesex
Monitor, House Mom el Capitan a.k.a. MomCap
Madam or Pimp, Game Master or Mistress, GM
Roommate, Roommates
Crowd
Revelers
Gamer(s)
Prefecture
Matron
Manifest
Baseboard Strippers
Automatron
Kundalini
Cam

Locations List

Cosmos House
   Downstairs
      Kitchen
         Tiffany Porn Star Calendar
         Screen
      Dining Room
         Dining Room Pictures
         Screen
      Parlor
         Washroom
      Living Room
         Screen
   Upstairs
      Bunkroom
         Mirror / Screen
      Bathroom
      Bedroom
         Desktop Screen
         private bathroom
   Backyard
      Bell
      Doghouse
      Garage
      Mudpit
      Post Henge
   Transition
      Front Door & Porch
      Back Door & Landing
   Cams
      Front Door Cam
      Back Door Cam
      Bathroom, a.k.a. Pee-Cam

School
   Quad
   Library
   Lecture Hall

Laboratory
Gymnasium
Village
Beauty Salon
Figure Drawing Studio
Medical Room
Bachelor Party Place
Nugget
   Camera Lounge
   Champagne Room
   Inner Sanctuary
   Stage
Jail

Not Capitals
   alley
   flagpole
   stocks
   hitching post
   van (capital Van in index)

Props List

See Index. Prop: *PropName* for more complete list. Only Props with upper case are listed here.

Alabaster Flask
Cravat
Dice (two different colors)
Dining Room Pictures
Double Dong
{Double Penetrator, a.k.a., DP}
Makeup Case
Measurement Nudes
Pink Pages
{Shaving Kit (scissors, razor, soap)}
Skeleton Keys (2)
Tiffany Porn Star Calendar
Watering Can

Events & Time Words List

Alumni Reprise
Mudwrestling Contest
Figure Drawing Class
Medical Exam
Bachelor Party
Day
Term
Clock
Midnght

Obeisance, Exposures, Opts List

Option, Options, Opt Up, Opt Down, Opt Strip, Opt Monitor, Double Opt Up, etc.
Garment(s)
Obeisance
Exposure
Redacted
Charm
Fate
Karma

  See Index Obeisance: *ObeisanceName* for full list of Obeisances. Most Obeisances are not capitalized (e.g., pinking, streaking), but two are:

Pee-Cam
Piss Mouth

  A list of Exposures is also found in the Index as Exposures: *ExposureName*. No exposures are capitalized (e.g., hairage, navelage).

Summary of Garment Exchanges

§ Exchange Equations

< indicates single costume trade to the party on the left.
> indicates single costume trade to the party on the right.
<< or >> indicates two pieces

§ The Garment Exchanges

  Molly > Steph. Topless Molly gives Steph her panties, which Steph dons under minidress.
  Steph > Molly. Steph gives naked Molly panties back and wears minidress sanpan.
  Tiffany < > Kimju. Voluntarily nude Tiffany borrows Kimju's tanga during Post Henge; returns afterwards.

List of Hand Signs & Positions

§ Standard Body Postures

Stand
Sit
Kneel
Belly Prone
Back Prone
Hands and Knees (Table)
Hands and Elbows (Worship)

§ Standard Arm Positions

Surrender > Hands behind head
Present > Wrists crossed behind back
Attention > Hands at sides
Horizontal > Held wide away, horizontal
Veed > Hands held away and upward
Handbra > Hands crossing breasts (3 ways)

§ Hand Signs for Legs

Legs Crossed > Cross fingers
Legs Together (Touching) > Close fingers
Legs Apart (No touching) > Two fingers open
Legs Open > Two fingers midway
Legs Spread > Two fingers held wide

§ Commands for Movements

Walk
Crawl
Grovel
Stop
At ease

Oval mouth > Thumb and 2nd finger
Close eyes > Thumb and 2 fingers together
Open eyes > Double snap
Present tongue > Two adjacent fingers extended
Lick tongue around mouth > circle in air w/finger

§ Hand Signs for Arousal

Leanover > Two fingers waving downward
Nipple play > Roll thumb & 2nd finger
Pullaside > Thumb & 2 fingers, sweep
Pull pink (butterfly) > Thumb & 2 fingers apart
Clit play > Roll thumb & finger
Finger Fuck > Wiggle middle finger
Rub Masturbation > Rub thumb atop 1st knuckle

Inventory of Chants

§ Gamer Chants

  In the Game stay the Game.

§ Pledge Chants

  Please let me Pledge naked and cum be a Stripper next Term.
  Hot hot hot. Titters and twat. 98.6 in my anus.

I love you, Post. Hug 'n' kiss. Rub my tits. Masturbate.

Please let me shave bare, bald, and naked.

§ Stripper Chants

Please let me pullaside, pink, and finger my holes.

Please keep me pink wet and ready. I'll cum on cue.

§ Whore Chants

I've done everything explicit, all holes, all sexes!

Inventory of Garments

Garment inventory is not included in these Appendices, however all Garments are indexed at Garments: *garmentName*, and by individual Cosmos, *GamerName*: Garments: *garmentName*.

Infrequently Asked Questions

What is a *culotte* nombril? A bikini bottom with a waistline below the navel yet high enough on the hips to not threaten hairage or rugage. Usually with leglines horizontal to or slightly above the crotch. The lower half of Babs' Black Bikini.

What is navelage? Areolage? Each 'age' corresponds to an exposure of a body part, like cleavage, leggage, bellage, buttage, areolage, hairage. Index directs you to *GamerName: -age,* since their control and abandonment matters across culture and time.

What are the Rules of the Game? There are many of them, some secret. Start your search in the Index under Game Rules.

Where is the School? Cyberspace?

What is the purpose of School? To gain knowledge, to learn about the self, to discover Kundalini, to explore power exchange, to achieve harmony with romance, power, and pain. *See The Cosmos: The Arrivals,* for more details.

Is Kundalini real? Gods are expressions of Forces in Nature. The Forces of Nature give rise to existence, to space and time and momentum, and the structures forced at many Castes of the Universe, from the subatomic through Gamers. So of course Kundalini is real, and if welcomed, will speak.

What are some of the Games? The Roommate Games will be played during The Runup, and they pit pairs of Roommates together against another pair of Roommates (Roommates Together) or they pit Roommates against each other (Roommates Apart). Other Games alluded to include Dice Games, the Mudwrestling Contest, performances such as Tiffany's visit to the Peacock House upon her arrival, and the backstory behind Babs and Janet's Bikinis.

Which Pledge have danced at the Nugget in the past? Tiffany (two Terms ago), Kimju and Molly (last Term), Janet, Monitor of the Corvette House (two Terms ago), and Corvette Pledge Ginny and Lee (last Term).

Which Pledge were Monitors last Term? At the Cosmos House, only Steph. At the Corvette House, both Darleen and Louise were Monitors last Term.

How do Redactions take place? Is it induced by drugs? Brainwashing? Trauma? Self-inflicted?—Sorry, but that's four questions.

What are the sizes of G-strings? Table follows. Assume triangle, A = ½ width x height.

Mini g-string: 2.83 x 2.83 inches = 4 square inches.

Micro g-string: 2 x 2 inches = 2 square inches.

Nano g-string: 1.41 x 1.42 inches = 1 square inch

Pico g-string: .22 x .22 inches = ½ square inch (or, one knot near the anus and two cords up through the vagina up both sides of the clit).

The Manifests

Overview and How to Use

§ Overview

This reference harbors the costume descriptions, exposures, and costume counts of each Cosmo at various points through the story. These manifests are probably more useful after a Gamer is deep into the story and needs to recall the status of one of the Cosmos at a particular point in time.

There are two Manifests:

The Beginning of the Term
The Arrivals (Book I)

There do exist style rules for writing this reference, but they are not detailed herein except that costumes are described outside in, top to bottom. Props, shaving details, and exposures compliment the costume descriptions. Props, obeisance (forfeits), body hair details (especially shaving), and exposures (which part of the body is visible) complement the costume descriptions. These also contain the critical costume count for each Cosmos.

In all Manifests except for the first and the last the Manifest also contains a concise overview of changes and events that occur during that Part. If there is no change in the costume then the costume description will not contain a doff or a don, and Gamers may assume the costume was unchanged during the last part. Otherwise the first costume listed is the costume at the beginning of the period, and the last costume listed is the costume at the end of the period.

The order of the individual Cosmos Gamers (and other Houses) is that of paired Roommates, beginning with the Monitor and her Roommate, followed by two pairs, and ending with the two newbies. This order is consistent through the Manifests, and it does but it doesn't imply an internal hierarchy, if only because multiple internal hierarchies exist.

§ A Note on Codes

Unless otherwise noted all Gamers have hair on their heads, shaven legs and armpits, hair on their pubic region, and bare feet. All Cosmos have their navels bare 24x7. Molly is totally unshaven. Their only costumes are the costumes described. The exposures are the parts of their bodies that are not covered and are coded as follows: T = Top (cleavage), M = Midriff, L = legs, B = breasts, A = ass, P = pelvis, C = male chest. The order is always in sequence, TMLBAP (full nude). TML is the exposure produced by a bikini, or a bra and panties lingerie. The N- code is the inches of waistline below the navel.

Flashing indicates that an exposure is intermittent and is not logged as an exposure code. Cleavage is the partial exposure of breasts, nippage is flashing of nipples, hairage is the exposure of pubic hair, posterior rugage (or just rugage) is the exposure of butt crack, pubage is the exposure of the pubis, and buttage is the exposure of the butt cheeks.

Occasional copy in curly brackets ("{}") is provided for reference only because it includes information not currently visible to Gamers in the Cosmos House. This reference is found in some of the initial physical descriptions of the Cosmos; sometimes it includes actions which are secret; some copy in brackets includes probably changings which are not visible to the Cosmos and are deduced and for the edification of the serious Gamer.

The use of the vertical bar character "|" connotes the end of the definition of an opening position at the beginning of a Book. It is not used in the very first Manifest, but it is included in all the others. Note that the only the very first Manifest contains a full description of each Cosmos' physical description.

Manifest: Beginning of Term

§ The Cosmos: Garments & Props & Obeisance & Exposures

Babs (BB, Bikini Babe, Boss Babe, Boss Bitch): Long black hair, olive skin, black pearl eyes, 5' 11", 140 pounds, 37D-24-36, hourglass figure, full bust, deep maroon areolas with milk glands, cratered remains of a center-knot navel, {full black bush}, full butt, shaven legs and armpits, {deep purple vagina}. No tattoos or bodyart. Arrives wearing bra and *culotte* nombril bikini a.k.a. the Black Bikini; TML; N-4; cleavage, areolage. Was newbie Pledge last Term. Roommate is Tiffany.

Tiffany Transparent: Longhaired redhead, milk-white skin, blue eyes, 5' 10", 105 pounds, 32A-23-33, flat chest, a deep curvy belly, small butt, round carnation-colored areolas and cylindrical nipples, navel is a vertical slit set inside a harder, firmer rim, and with a question-mark dot at the bottom, {thinnish red bush}, shaven legs and armpits, {burgundy-colored vagina}. {Tattoo of words "Porn Star" on inside of lower lip, reversed so can be read in mirror}. Invisible ultraviolet ink tramp stamp tattoo descends to anus and becomes visible and surrounds anus. Ultraviolet ink tattooed nipples. No piercings but Eraser Heads. Pee-Camer. Arrives wearing sleeveless translucent silk croptop and low-rise stretch slacks; M; N-7; headlights; hairage, rugage, cameltoe; M, TMB in see-through. Stripper two Terms ago, Whore last Term, and a Double Opt Up. Roommate is Babs.

Robyn Redacted: Big hair streaked blonde, skin that tans easily, green eyes, 5' 6", 108 pounds, 34C-25-34, curvaceous figure, modest butt, {rose-colored areolas}, outie navel, {trimmed blonde bush}, shaven legs and underarms, {raspberry colored vagina}. No tattoos or bodyart. Arrives wearing Spandex strapless maillot with navel cutout; TML (M is cutout navelage). Was Pledge last Term. Roommate is Kimju.

Kimju (Kim): Not quite shoulder-length brunette hair, polyglot South or Latin American skin (a mixture of Spanish, Asian, African, and indigenous Indian), brown eyes, 5' 8", 117 pounds, 35C-24-35, stacked figure, taut butt, beige silver-dollar sized areolas with puckered details and knob-like nipples with lines in them, vertical oval with a custard swirl inside navel, {trimmed brunette bush}, shaven legs and underarms, {deeply pigmented inner lips surrounding a rosy pink vagina}. 14 gauge clithood ring hidden beneath pubic hair, and astrological sign tattoo (Pallas) secreted in navel. Arrives topless and solid color Spandex tanga; TMLBA; N-1; inguinal. Was Stripper last Term. Roommate is Robyn.

Molly: Long black hair, Irish-Spanish skin, gray eyes, 5' 3", 140 pounds, 38DD-30-37, a square face, a fleshy Rubenesque figure, large splotchy sepia areolas, deeply set navel, {a full black bush}, big butt, unshaven legs or underarms and copulous body hair, {deep brown vagina with purple deep inside}. Hidden 14 gauge clithood ring and small alchemy sign tattoo (phosphorus) hidden on her body. Arrives topless and soiled pale rose cotton panties underwear; TMLB; N-3. Was Stripper last Term. Roommate is Steph.

Steph: Long blonde hair, white skin, blue eyes, thin lips, 5' 7", 105 pounds, 32A-23-32, slender figure, brown nipple stalks on beige areola that burst forth like fruit, small puckered navel with round crater with flesh around the edge and a hard outie bulb in the middle, medium butt, {thin blonde pussy hair}, shaven legs and underarms, {scarlet vagina with distended clitoris}. Arrives wearing hacked cutout minidress; TML (M is cutout navelage); flashing nippage and hairage. Was Monitor last Term. Roommate is Molly.

Beka: Longhaired brunette, half-Asian blood, brown eyes, 5' 7", 105 pounds, 33B-25-33, shallow conical breasts with beige areolas with a dark brown circumference and pigmented dots, and nipples that indent when excited. A flat belly, a long and narrow vertical ovaled navel that suggests a lightning bolt, smallish butt, shaven legs and underarms, trimmed pubic hair, {a vagina with inner lips tinted dark brown and darker pigment around her anus}. Arrives wearing sleeveless cotton open-armhole croptop and miniskirt; TML; N-6; able to flash nippage, titter, upskirt hairage, and vagflash. Newbie; 1st Term in the Game. Roommate is Elle.

Elle: Curly-haired brunette, Middle Eastern skin (Jewish / Lebanese / Palestinian), brown eyes, 5' 10", 115 pounds, 34B-24-34, petite frame, nipples and coffee-colored areolas resemble a weathered volcano, with crevices that run from the tip of the nipple down to the very edge of the pigment; the navel is a horizontal oval with an overhang on the top, buttocks medium proportioned, legs and underarms shaven, however a full growth of bush extends into her inner thighs and is partly visible inside her shorts, {with darker brown vagina and inner lips and a violet vaginal canal}. Arrives wearing front and neck button halter and ripped jeans shorts; TML; N-1; able to flash nippage and titter; hairage, cheekage. Newbie; 1st Term in the Game. Roommate is Beka.

§ Others: Garments & Props & Obeisance & Exposures

From the Corvette House:

Corvette Monitor Janet (Janet Jintoe): Dark hair, beige skin, dark brown eyes, 5' 7", 180 pounds, 40EE-34-46, plump figure, heavy bust, large brown areolas with bubbly milk glands, very full pubic bush, large buttocks, shaven legs and armpits, long sex lip. {One hidden tattoo, the name "Janet Jintoe" on the inside of lower lip, which reads reversed so it can be read in a mirror.} One pierced labia, consisting of three holes on each side worn with whatever stainless Games might let Janet wear, including rings {and a chastity perhaps} currently. Arrives wearing crochet Spiderweb halter and g-string, a.k.a. the Spiderweb Bikini; technically TMLA; N-7; nippage, areolage, cleavage, hairage, buttage; in practice the open-mesh is essentially TMLBAP. Erects nipples into Spiderweb. Was Cosmos Pledge last Term (was Babs' Roommate), Nugget Stripper two Terms ago (and Tiffany's Roommate).

Corvette Pledge Darleen: Sender brunette. 33A-30-32. Pullover shirt and slacks, flashing bellage. Was a Monitor last Term.

Corvette Pledge Ginny: Slender brunette. Nude; TMLBAP; racing stripe. Possibly three hidden tattoos or credits thereto; clithood ring and credits for two more piercings. Was Stripper last Term (and Roommate of Lee Lollydor). Roommate of Trixi Tubes. Whore-for-life.

Corvette Pledge Trixi Tubes: Slender brunette, 34A-26-35. Six Tubes, bands around the body ranging from one inch to 32 inches wide, worn any two at any one time around breasts, torso, hips, and pelvis (1" magenta, 2" orange, 4" green, 8" blue, 16" violet, 32" red); Conservatively TM, with most if not all of the less conservative combinations in play. Roommate of Ginny. Newbie; 1st Term in the Game.

Corvette Pledge Lee Lollydor: Blackhaired Italian with full figure. Nude; TMLBAP; racing stripe. Lollydor. Possibly one tattoo; clithood ring. 36C-24-35. Was Stripper last Term (and Roommate of Ginny). Roommate is Louise.

Corvette Pledge Louise: Curvy blackhaired Portuguese, 36D-28-36. No piercings or tattoos. Bandeau and T-front maillot. Was Monitor last Term. Roommate is Lee Lollydor.

Corvette Pledge Caroline: Petite blonde, 33B-22-34; crimson areolas. Shares Lingerie Kit with Roommate Wendy, and each may wears any two pieces. Newbie; 1st Term in the Game.

Corvette Pledge Wendy: Randy brunette, 34B-24-34; ruddy areolas. Shares Lingerie Kit with Roommate Caroline, and each may wears any two pieces. Newbie; 1st Term in the Game.

From the Peacock House:

Peacock Monitor William: Dark brunette, full but light body hair. 5' 10", 160 pounds. Shirt and slacks. Was Monitor last Term, Hover this Term. Roommate is Rodney.

Peacock Rodney: Blonde, blue-eyed, wiry, 5' 10" 140 pounds. Shaven body, including bare-chested, arms, armpits, legs, buttocks, privates. Wears jockstrap or thong; TMLCA. Was Stripper last Term. Roommate is Monitor William.

Six Other Peacocks: Nude, TMLCAP. Past Terms not detailed. Roommates not detailed.

From the Nugget:

House Mom: Brunette, body details redacted. Front-button front tie shirt and jeans or shorts plus casual shoes. Navelage; M or ML, 24x7.

Nugget Stripper Penny: Full-breasted brunette. Nude; TMLBAP; heart-shaped pubic hair trim, spreads, pinks, anus; cream. Freckles on her inner lip. Scheduled to cream, cum. Scheduled for one piercing and tattoo. Was Pledge last Term, begging to cum (and Roommate then and now of Penny).

Nugget Stripper Coco: Full-breasted brunette. Nude; TMLBAP; heart-shaped pubic hair trim, spreads, pinks, anus; cream. Keloid adjacent to anus. Scheduled to cream, cum. Scheduled for one piercing and tattoo. Was Pledge last Term, begging to cum (and Roommate then and now of Penny).

From the Beauty Salon:

Madam Nurse Beautician: Body details redacted, although believed to be 36C-25-36 figure. Low-cut white nurse minidress over rubber hose and panties, shoes; T; cleavage. History unknown.

From the Dungeon:

Game Mistress (GM): Body details redacted and veiled. History redacted. Owns Slavesex.

Slavesex China Doll: Longhaired blackhaired slender Asian; 5' 8", 100 pounds, 31A-24-32. Nude; TMLBAP; vulva shaven bare. {Assume spreads, pinks, anus; creams, cums, cunnilingus, dildos, dongs and sexes all holes.} Probably pierced and tattooed. Surrender includes all skin and holes, all body functions, all control over eyes, ears, mouth, nostrils, rectum, vagina, pee hole, skin, muscle, and the mind inside. Total control. Mind Body and Soul. Slavesex has been owned by Game Mistress for many Terms.

{It: Male. Nude. TMLCAP. Shaven, caged.}

§ The Cosmos: Garment Counts

Babs: 2.
Tiffany: 2.
Robyn: 1.
Kimju: 1.
Molly: 1.
Steph: 1.
Beka: 2.
Elle: 2.

Total Cosmos: 12. At the beginning of the Arrivals four Cosmos have two Garments and four Cosmos have one Garment.\

§ Others: Garment Counts

Corvette Monitor Janet: 2.
Corvette Ginny: 0.
Corvette Lee: 0.
Five Other Corvettes 2 costumes each: 10

Total Corvettes: 12. At the beginning of the Arrivals six Corvettes have two Garments and two Corvettes are naked.

Nugget House Mom el Capitan (MomCap): 3
Nugget Penny: 0.
Nugget Coco: 0.
Other Nuggets: Unknown.

Madam Nurse Beautician: 4.

Game Mistress: 5.
Slavesex China Doll: 0.
{It: 0.}

Manifest: The Arrivals (Book I)

§ The Cosmos: Garments & Props & Obeisance & Exposures

Babs: Body as above. Bra and *culotte* nombril bikini (Black Bikini); TML; N-4; cleavage, areolage (crescents d'areolage). | No change.

Tiffany: Body as above. Arrives Pee-Camer wearing sleeveless translucent silk croptop and low-rise stretch slacks; M; N-7; headlights: hairage, rugage, cameltoe; M, TMB in see-through. Brings Pee-Cam Obeisance. | Observed naked, spread, sexing on Porn Star Calendar performing Whore Obeisance. Exchanges silk croptop for transparent clear vinyl longsleeve front-button croptop with same low-rise stretch slacks; M; N-7; hairage, rugage, cameltoe; M, TMB in see-through. 1st Cosmos who begs to Pledge naked and cum be a Stripper next Term (Begs Stripper). 1st Cosmos begs Pee-Cam; pees. 1st Cosmos begs Piss Mouth; performs. Topless or nude at House whenever allowed, TMLBA, TMLBAP. Pull down pinking flash, masturbation, cream. Legs apart 24x7 after Steph arrives.

Robyn Redacted: Body as above. Spandex strapless then strapped maillot with navel cutout; TML (M is cutout navelage); crotch. | No change. {Pees.}

Kimju (Kim): Body as above. Topless and solid color Spandex tanga; TMLBA; N-2; inguinal, hairage. 14 gauge clithood ring hidden beneath pubic hair, and astrological sign tattoo (Pallas) secreted in navel. | Tanga occasionally gathered into kypsey with even more hairage. Reveals deeply pigmented inner lips surrounding a rosy pink vagina. Reveals clithood ring but not any hidden tattoos. Spreads, pinks; anus; pullaside, masturbation, creams, 2nd Cosmos to climax. Muddy. Nude once in Backyard, TMLBAP. Legs apart 24x7 after Steph arrives.

Molly: Body as above. Topless and soiled pale rose cotton panties underwear; TMLB; N-3; totally unshaven with leg, arm, and underarm hair. 14 gauge clithood ring, and small alchemy sign (phosphorus) tattoo hidden on her body. | Acquires Watering Can. Panties see-through when wet; TMLBAP. Doffs panties (to Steph) to nude; TMLBAP; full hairy black bush. Loses Watering Can. Streaks, spreads, pinks deep brown vagina, reveals clithood ring; anus; creams; 1st Cosmos to cum. Pees. 2nd Cosmos who begs to Pledge naked and Strip next Term. 2nd Cosmos to beg Pee-Cam. Acquires panties (from Steph) via Piss Mouth to topless and soiled and wet pale pink cotton panties underwear, sometimes yanked into moonshadow as if tanga;

TMLBA; N-3; and/or into mooe forcing hairage. Pullaside, masturbation, creams, climaxes together with Kimju. Legs apart 24x7 after Steph arrives.

Steph: Body as above. Cutout minidress; always TML (M is cutout navelage); flashing nippage, upskirt hairage. | Arrives wearing cutout minidress, hacked (D4). Ordered legs opened and vagcammed. Sleeps nude, TMLBAP. Acquires sleeveless with oversize armholes (D05), a high-collar and sleeveless (D06), a haltered (D07), scoop neck (D08), also with panties that she acquires from Molly, a strapped (D09, with panties then sanpan upon panty's return, D10, then inside out, D11), strapless (D12, always sanpan, inside out to reveal previous nipple makeup, D13, and inside out again, D14). Legs apart, legs open, legs spread, both solo and with Beka, and, except for the time she wears panties, always sanpan. She extends her legs apart 24x7 Obeisance to all Cosmos Pledge. Upskirt, vagflash, holds legs open for vagcam. Reveals thin, blonde, short and wavy pubic hair, occasionally the parting line into her sex cavity; also anus. Practices rectal thermoprobe. Produces one drop cream.

Beka: Body as above. Arrives wearing sleeveless cotton open-armhole croptop and miniskirt; TML; N-6; able to titter and vagflash. | Sits legs apart, legs open, legs spread, both solo and with Steph, always sanpan. Reveals vagina with pronounced inner lips tinted dark brown and darker pigment around her anus; shaven bare on vulva, butched racing stripe above. 4th Cosmos who begs to Pledge naked and Strip next Term. Practices rectal thermoprobe; creams excessively. Legs apart 24x7 thanks to Steph. Chants 98.6 while admiring Baseboard Strippers two locations. Practices rectal suppository, creams excessively. Forbidden masturbation.

Elle: Body as above. Arrives wearing front and neck button halter and ripped jeans shorts; TML; N-1; able to flash nippage and titter; hairage, buttage (cheekage). 3rd Cosmos who begs to Pledge naked and Strip next Term. Lollydors Beka. Legs apart 24x7 thanks to Steph. Lollydors Steph and Beka. Begs Flip-Flop.

§ Others: Garments & Props & Obeisance & Exposures

From the Corvette House:

Corvette Monitor Janet: Body as above. Arrives wearing crochet Spiderweb halter and g-string, a.k.a. the Spiderweb Bikini; technically TMLA; N-7; nippage, areolage, cleavage, hairage, buttage; in practice the open-mesh is essentially TMLBAP. Erects nipples into Spiderweb. Labial rings. | No change. Crusty string. Clit sticking out.

Corvette Pledge Darleen: Body as above. Pullover shirt and slacks, flashing bellage. | No change.

Corvette Pledge Ginny: Body as above. Nude; TMLBAP; racing stripe; clithood ring. Whore-for-Life. | Streaks. Spreads, pinks. Practices Cravat, buttplug; blowjob, coitus, anal. Pees, peed on.

Corvette Pledge Trixi: Body as above. Any two of the Six Tubes; typically, TM, TML | Legs together when they should not have been.

Corvette Pledge Lee: Body as above. Nude; TMLBAP; racing stripe, clithood ring. Lollydor. | No details.

Corvette Pledge Louise: Body as above. Bandeau and T-front maillot. | No details.

Corvette Pledge Caroline: Body as above. Shares Lingerie Kit with Roommate Wendy | No details.

Corvette Pledge Wendy: Body as above. Shares Lingerie Kit with Roommate Caroline. | No details.

From the Peacock House:

Peacock Monitor William: Body as above. Shirt and slacks. | No change.

Peacock Rodney: Bare-chested and jockstrap or thong; TMLCA. | Spots his jockstrap, ejaculates.

Six Peacock Pledge: Body as above. Nude; TMLCAP. | All erections, masturbate, ejaculate.

From the Nugget:

House Mom: Body details redacted. Shirt and jeans or shorts plus casual shoes. Navelage; M or ML, 24x7.

Nugget Stripper Penny: Body as above. Nude; TMLBAP; heart-shaped pubic hair trim, spreads, pinks, anus; cream. Begging to cum. Scheduled for one piercing and tattoo. | Streaks to arrive, spreads, pinks, creams, cums, shaves bare center Stage. {Acquires Double Dong to share (but never together at the same time) with Coco.}

Nugget Stripper Coco: Body as above. Nude; TMLBAP; heart-shaped pubic hair trim, spreads, pinks, anus; cream. Begging to cum. Scheduled for one piercing and tattoo. | Streaks to arrive, spreads, pinks, creams, cums, shaves bare center Stage. {Acquires Double Dong to share (but never together at the same time) with Penny.}

From the Beauty Salon:

Madam Nurse Beautician: Body details redacted. Low-cut white nurse minidress over rubber hose and panties, shoes; T; cleavage. | No change. Appears to have access to large collection of medical Props.

From the Dungeon:

Game Mistress: Unknown. | Boots. Witness reports: Black full or décolletage leather or rubber bodysuit with many zippers and cutout holes around navel and clit. Clithood ring.

Slavesex China Doll: Body as above. Nude; TMLBAP; bare. {Assume spreads, pinks, anus; creams, cums, cunnilingus, dildos, dongs and sexes all holes.} Probably pierced and tattooed. | No details.

It: Nude: TMLCAP. | No details.

§ The Cosmos: Garment Counts

Babs: 2.
Tiffany: 2.
Robyn: 1.
Kimju: 1.
Molly: $1 - 1 + 1 = 1$.
Steph: $1 + 1 - 1 = 1$.
Beka: 2.
Elle: 2.

Total Cosmos: 12. At the end of the Arrivals four Cosmos have two Garments and four Cosmos have one Garment.

§ Others: Garment Counts

Corvette Monitor Janet: 2.
Corvette Ginny: 0.
Corvette Lee: 0.
Five other Corvettes: 10.

Total Corvettes: 12. At the end of the Arrivals six Corvettes have two Garments and two Corvettes are naked. No change.

Peacock Monitor William: 2.
Peacock Rodney: 1.
Six other Peacocks: 0.

Total Peacocks: 3.

Nugget House Mom el Capitan (MomCap): 3
Nugget Penny: 0.
Nugget Coco: 0.

Madam Nurse Beautician: 4.

Game Mistress: 5.
Slavesex China Doll: 0.
{It: 0.}

Glossary

Alabaster Flask – A **Prop** Babs locates in the Bedroom desk drawer. Function unknown.
Alumni Reprise – An **Event** last **Term** involving Tiffany and Janet, also Kimju and Molly, Steph.
anal – An **Obeisance**. Sexual penetration of the anus and rectum by a penis, strapon, dildo, dong.
anus – The rear entrance to the rectum, a.k.a. asshole.
areolage – An **Exposure** or partial exposure of the areola of the breast.
Automatron – A giant Artificial Intelligence data storage system somewhere.
bandeau – A species of *soutien-gorge,* which covers the breasts but lacks straps. Has two edges.
begs, begging – Usually made by a Gamer of a lower Caste to one of a higher rank, requesting
  privileges or punishments.
bellage – An **Exposure** of the belly, not necessarily including the **navel**.
belly-up belly-down – **Bellage** above and below the **navel**.
bikini – A two-piece **Garment** consisting of a *soutien-gorge* and a *culotte*, strictly a **nombril**.
bra, brassiere –A **Garment** and species of *soutien-gorge* that covers the breasts and has two
  shoulder straps. A brassiere has four edges.
blowjob – An **Obeisance**. The gratification of a penis using the mouth and tongue.
boobage – An **Exposure** of one or both entire breasts. It could involve a single-bare-breasted
  maillot, an evening gown uplifting the breasts, or bare down to the waist, as in **topless**; see also
  cleavage, areolage, nippage, titter.
bottomless – A "Garment" which is the absent case of itself. The baring of the body below the waist.
  Presumes **pubage** and full-frontal (bottom-half) nudity. A bottomless could **vagflash** but not
  upskirt. A **topless** plus a **bottomless** equals a **nude**.
breastplay – An **Obeisance**. Arousal of breasts and nipples, especially self-arousal.
bukkake – An **Obeisance**. Multiple discharges of male ejaculate onto a subject's face and body.
buttage – An **Exposure** of the **buttocks**; the entire buttocks, if not a substantial portion. A **g-string**
  or **thong** is always buttage. Compare to **cheekage**. A buttage is not a **bottomless**.
Cam – A still or video camera.
Caste – One of the eight ranks in the **Game**. The Castes are **Game Mistresses or Masters (GMs)**,
  who manage the **Slavesex; Madams or Pimps,** who manage the **Whores; House Mom (or Dad)**
  el Capitans (MomCaps or DadCaps), who manage the **Strippers; Monitors** who manage
  Pledge; Pledge; Strippers; Whores; and **Slavesex**.
Chant – A series of words, sometimes with an accompanying action, designed to train endurance,
  inculcate ideas, or produce arousal.
Charm – Possibly a magical property, which some Gamers think protects them and provides good
  fortune, and which some Gamers don't believe exists.
cheekage – An **Exposure** of the bottom, or cheek of the **buttocks**, where the buttocks meets the leg
  in a crease. The act of hanging butt cheeks out the bottom of briefs or shorts. The opposite of
  rugage.
cleavage – An **Exposure**. The partial exposure of breasts. See **décolletage, downblouse, leanover,
  lift-up**.
climax – An **Obeisance**. A male or female sexual release, possibly accompanied by fluids.
Clock – A timepiece that keeps track of **Days**. In the Index most references include a time in the
  form (Dnn), where nn ranges from 01 to 14.
coitus – An **Obeisance**. The sexual joining of the penis into the **vagina**.
concerns – Anxieties and fears of **Pledge**, be they irrational or the result of careful evaluation.
conflicts – Situations between two **Gamers** that involve clashes of personality, style, or **Option**.
Corvette – One of eight **Houses** at the **School**, as well as a resident thereof.
Cosmos – One of eight **Houses** at the **School**, as well as a resident thereof (singular and plural).
costume – *See* **Garment**.
Cravat – A **Prop**; an iron bondage frame for holding a **Gamer** in a fixed position, sometimes for
  long periods of time.
cream – **Valiva**, the vaginal secretions a female produces during arousal. As a verb, the process of
  transuding secretions.
culotte – A **Costume**; the generic term for a bikini or underwear bottom regardless of its species;
  briefs. Examples include **g-string**, **panties**, **tanga**, shorts, and a *bikini* **nombril**.
Day – The days of the **Term**. During *The Arrivals* Days One through Fourteen pass.
décolletage – An **Exposure** of the **cleavage** of the breasts resulting from wearing a low-cut neckline.
  Also a low-cut neckline that exposes the neck, shoulders, and parts of the breasts.

Dice – A **Prop** located in the desk in the Bedroom, under Babs' control. Dice have Games.

diuretics –Substances that induce a body to void urine.

Double Dong, Dong, DD – A **Prop** with special Rules and powers, and currently believed to reside at the Nugget. For those who are permitted the experience, the Double Dong enables two **Pledge** to share the Dong in their vaginas, rectums, mouths, or any combination thereof. **Pledge** and **Whores** are allowed to Dong; **Strippers** are not.

Double Penetration, Double Penetrators, DP – A **Prop**; two toys that may be used together to penetrate both the **vagina** and **anus**. A single **Pledge** or **Stripper** may enjoy both toys together, or a pair may each enjoy one-half of the DP combo. DPs include the Ben-Wa Balls and the Procto.

downblouse – An exposure of the breasts and/or nipples created by leaning forward.

el Capitan – *See* **Caste.**

Exposure – A part of the body that is uncovered or alluded to. A full list of Exposures is found in the Index. All are lower case words and are indexed subservient to a *GamerName*.

Event – A performance or contest, e.g., the Mudwrestling Contest, the Alumni Reprise.

Fate – Each **Cosmos'** outcome at the end of the **Term** (at **Midnight**).

finger-fucking – An **Obeisance**. The insertion of one or more fingers into the **vagina**, either by one's self or another individual(s).

full-frontal – An **Obeisance**. The baring of the breasts and the pubis (hairy or shaven). Not all **nudes** are full-frontal, and not all full-frontal exposures involve total nudity (e.g., hose and heels).

g-string – A **Garment**; a *culotte* that covers the pubis but not the buttocks, and ties with strings.

gangbang – An **Obeisance**. Sex by many individuals upon a single one; presume all holes taken.

Game – The practice at **School.**

Game Mistress or Master (GM) – the highest Caste in the **Game**; see **Caste.**

Game Rules – The Rules of the **Game**. *See* the Index, Game Rules: *GamerCaste.*

Gamer – One who plays the **Game**, both those who play in the **Cosmos** and those who look in.

Garment – A single costume piece that **Cosmos** might wear.

GM – *See* **Game Mistress or Master.**

gokuraku-ojo – Sexual orgasm resulting in death.

goal – Something a **Cosmos** seeks to achieve. Indexed by *CosmosName:* goal.

hairage – An **Exposure**. The partial exposure of pubic hair; any pubic hair that leaks out, be it above the top or to the sides of a *culotte*, be it an accidental or a deliberate **pullaside**, or, in relaxed usage, pubic hair viewed **upskirt** (via a **vagflash** or an extended spread).

halter – A **Garment** and species of *soutien-gorge* that covers the breasts and has a neck strap and a back strap. A halter has three edges and multiple fastening possibilities.

handbra – A **Garment** and species of *soutien-gorge* that covers the breasts with the hands.

Hand Signs – Commands made with hands and fingers to indicate body positions and actions.

headlights – An **Exposure**. Aroused nipples that form shapes in clothing.

House – One of eight **Locations** where students who attend **School** reside.

House Dad el Capitan – The third highest Caste in the **Game**; see **Caste.**

House Mom el Capitan – The third highest Caste in the **Game**; see **Caste.**

Hover – Game movement where a **Gamer** doesn't change **Caste** at the end of a **Term**. Only available to certain Castes, including **Monitors** and **MomCaps**. Not available for **Pledge** or **Strippers**. Compare to **Opt Up, Opt Down.**

Jail – A place of detention maintained by the **Game** at which **Game Rules** applying to a **Caste** member may be violated. A quick way to Jail is to be apprehended while **streaking.**

Karma – Good and bad will disbursed into the **Game.**

kissing – An **Obeisance**. Mouth upon the body of another individual; sometimes mouth-to-mouth and augmented with the tongue, a variation called French kissing..

Kundalini – The sex force in the Universe.

Lady-Part Words – Words tactical to an individual **Gamer**'s body parts. They are not listed here or in the Index; they include words for breasts, areolas, nipples, pubic hair, **vagina**, **valiva**, **buttocks**, and **anus.**

lapdancing – An **Obeisance**; dances by **Strippers** performed in the laps of Patrons.

laxatives – Substances that induce a body to void bowels.

leanover – A body movement that permits a voyeur to look **downblouse**. The resultant **Exposure.**

lift-up – An action which lifts a shirt, either using the hands or via movement, and reveals breast.

Lineup – The collection of **Cosmos Pledge** into a line, often for morning **Reveille.**

lipage – An **Exposure**. The exposure of the labial lips, often to the sides, opened. See **pink.**

Location – A place where **Events** take place, e.g., the **Cosmos House**, the **Nugget**, the Kitchen.

lollydor – An **Obeisance**. One who licks up semen or **valiva**. Verb is "to lolly."

Madam – The second highest **Caste** in the **Game**, equivalent to a **Pimp**; *detailed at* **Caste**.

Makeup Case – A **Prop**, controlled by the **Monitor**, that contains makeup and beautification products and tools. As an upper case **Prop**, it is a primary **Index** item.

masturbation – An **Obeisance**. Sexually arousing one's self, often by touching one's sex organs.

Measurement Nude – A **Prop**; full-frontal shots provided by newbies showing dimensions.

media – Records of events, sometimes served by **Automatron**, indexed by *GamerName*.

messy – An **Obeisance**. Coverage of the body by substances such as food, mud, paint, cum.

Midnight – The end of the last **Day** of the **Term**.

Mirror – A.k.a. the **Minxy Mirror**. A special mirror, located in the **Bunkroom**, which reflects, can serve as a **Screen**, and function interactively with a participant on its surface.

Monitor – The fourth highest Caste in the **Game**; *see* **Caste**.

Mudwrestling Contest – An **Event** last **Term** which determined the outcomes for Babs, Janet, Penny, and Coco this **Term**.

Mudpit – A **Location** in the Backyard where **Events** take place.

navel – A body landmark. A scar resulting from the detachment of the umbilical cord during birth.

navelage – An **Exposure**. The exposure of the **navel**. Cosmos must be navelage 24x7.

newbie – A **Pledge** attending their first **Term** in **School**; first **Term** in the **Game**.

nombril – A *culotte* with a waistline below the **navel**.

nippage – An **Exposure** of the nipple. A term seldom used during *The Arrivals* because the term **titter** pervades common usage. *See* **titter**. Do not confuse nippage (titter) with **boobage**, an exposure of the entire bare breast, or **topless**, which is a "**Garment**" and absence of top.

nepenthe –An ancient drug to induce forgetfulness.

nude – A "**Garment**" and absence of clothes. **Topless** plus **bottomless** equal **nude**.

Nugget –A **Strip** club near the **Village**. Some current **Pledge** danced at the **Nugget** last **Term**; some last-**Term Cosmos** dance there now; some current **Cosmos** will dance there next **Term**.

Obeisance – A merit gained or a forfeit made; examples include **shaving bare** and/or **bald**, **Pee-Camer**, and/or **Piss Mouth** status. See a full list at this **Index** entry.

Options, Opt Up, Opt Down –Promotion or demotion at the end of the **Term**. *See also* **Hover**.

orders – Commands issued, usually by a **Gamer** of a higher **Caste** to a lower, to be obeyed.

paparazzi –Unauthorized gatherers of images and video outside official **Game** channels.

pee – The discharge of liquid body waste via the urethra. *See also* **Pee-Cam**.

Pee-Cam – An **Obeisance**. A Pee-Camer urinates on camera and in public, in front of anybody.

phlegm – Liquids produced in the back of the mouth, nasal passages, and throat. May be produced by **throating**.

pink, pinking – An **Obeisance**. The inside of the **vagina** or the action of exposing the inside of the **vagina**, often used as a status or command, regardless of the actual color of the inside. An invitation to sexual penetration; an element of **masturbation**, **finger-fucking**. Indexed as *GamerName:* pinking.

Pimp – The second highest **Caste** in the **Game**, equivalent to a **Madam**; *see* **Caste**.

Piss Mouth – An **Obeisance** that involves getting pissed on, possibly in the mouth.

Pledge – The fourth lowest **Caste** in the **Game**; *see* **Caste**. Pledge are both singular and plural. Is not capitalized when used as a verb.

position – An **Obeisance**. A formal body arrangement, e.g., stand spread surrender. See Appendix for lists of and Hand Signs for.

Post Henge – A **Location** in the Backyard where **Events** take place.

posterior rugage – An **Exposure**. *See* **rugage**.

Prefecture – The vast collection of **Gamers** who view the events of the **Cosmos** through **Screens** or who read this book.

Props – An object that may migrate among **Gamers**, especially **Cosmos**. Not to be confused with an **Obeisance**, which each individual **Cosmos** **may** take on.

pubage – An **Exposure**, of the pubis, with or without pubic hair. **Bottomless** presumed; may be achieved with a **pullaside** or **upskirt**.

puke – An **Obeisance**. The offering of stomach contents. Produced by throating, gagging, drugs.

pullaside – An **Obeisance**. The drawing of fabric in the crotch to the side so that the sex organs and/or anus may be observed. One way is to **vagflash**.

redaction – Various processes of removing memories and records of the past.

Reveille – The morning **Lineup** of **Pledge** for inspection by their **Monitor** Boss.

Roommates – Pairs of **Cosmos**, defined by who shares over and under bunks in the Bunkroom and Bedroom. There are four pairs of Roommates in the **Cosmos House**.

Roommate Game –A **Game** played between **Roommates**; the first Game of the **Term**.

rugage – **A.k.a. posterior rugage**. The **Exposure** of the top of the crack of the buttocks. Opposite of **cheekage**.

School – The place where the **Cosmos** study and the **Game** is played.

Screen – An area where images and videos are displayed. Monitor Babs control all Screens inside the Cosmos House.

semen – Male discharge, ejaculate, cum.

shave bald – An **Obeisance**. Removing all the hair from the head.

shave bare – An **Obeisance**. Removing all the hair from the pubic area.

Shaving Kit – A **Prop** alluded to but not yet seen, including scissors, soap, and a razor; it is carried inside the body.

Skeleton Keys – A **Prop**; two keys which control access to a door from the Kitchen to the Parlor and the sliding doors from the Dining Room to the Living Room. Both keys together are needed to open the door from the Kitchen to the side of the Porch.

Slavesex – The lowest Caste in the **Game**; *see* **Caste**.

slitage – An **Exposure** descending from the top of the (usually shaven) **vulva**; see **lipage**.

soutien-gorge – A **Garment** worn to cover the breasts but which leaves the arms and midriff bare. *See* **bandeau, brassiere, halter**.

spit, spits – An **Obeisance**, rather than an **Exposure**, connoting action, rather than body fluid.

streaking – An **Obeisance**. The transport of one's self while naked from one **Location** to another. Always volunteered; capture enables violation of a **Pledge** outside of **Game Rules**.

Strip – A **Location** where **Strippers** work.

Stripper – The third lowest Caste in the **Game**; *see* **Caste**. Prerequisites include undressing, **nudity, shaving, pinking, cream**, dildos, buttplugs, **double penetration, climax**, and **pee**.

Switch– A **Gamer** who vacillates between dominance and submission.

tan lines – **A.k.a. edge lines**. The edges of a **Garment** such that if exposed to ultraviolet light the part of the skin not covered will tan.

tanga – **A.k.a., a thong**. A species of *culotte* and a **Garment** that covers the pubis but not the **buttocks** and which has solid sides. Not to be confused with a **g-string**.

Term – A collection of **Days** that entails a passage of learning at School.

thermoprobe – A **Prop** and variety of buttplug; a long rectal probe that collects temperature and vital statistics. Can vibrate, electrically stimulate, and communicates wirelessly with **Automatron**.

thong – *See* **tanga**.

throating – An **Obeisance**. The insertion of a penis into a throat. Presumes a **blowjob**; the superior throater knows how to relax the gag reflex and allow the penis to pass down into the throat.

Tiffany Porn Star Calendar – A **Prop** in the Kitchen featuring Tiffany photographed when she was a Porn Star and **Whore**, containing explicit images.

titter – An **Exposure**. The flashing of the breasts and nipples. Often accomplished by a **leanover, downblouse**, sideboob, or **lift-up**. The transitory and positional nature of a titter differentiates it from the **boobage** and **topless**.

topless – A "**Garment**" which is the absent case thereof. The baring of the body above the waist. Presumes **boobage**. Not to be confused with a **titter**. A topless plus a **bottomless** equals a nude.

transude – Verb; the process of excreting **valiva**.

upskirt – An **Obeisance**. The purview of the crotch up a skirted **Garment**. If legs are apart, open, or spread, upskirt may reveal undergarments or **pubage**, in which case the upskirt is a **vagflash**.

vagflash – An **Exposure** of the **vulva** (with or without pubic hair), often fleetingly, but sometimes a position held for prolonged periods. Achieved by **upskirt** or **pullaside**. A vagflash does not entail the opening of the sex lips to expose the interior of the **vagina**, which is called **pinking**.

vagina – The interior of the female sex organ. The exposure of the vagina is called **pinking**.

valiva – Female lubrication transuded from the **vagina**; casually, **cream**.

Village – The town where the **School** is located and the **Game** is played.

vulva – The external parts of the female sex organ. *See* **vagflash**.

Whore – The second lowest Caste in the **Game**; *see* **Caste**.

Index

§ Tips on Using the Index

The major topics in this Index, that is, the topics that are listed at the topmost level, include each Cosmos and other Gamers, the Locations, Props, and Events. Body parts (a.k.a. Exposures), Obeisances, and Garments are all indexed beneath the Cosmos or other Gamer they relate to. The following paragraphs will first detail the indexing of the Cosmos and other characters, followed by details about indexing Locations, Props, Events, and other topics.

The Gamers include all the Cosmos, as well as Gamers who reside at the Corvette and Peacock Houses, certain Strippers at the Nugget, a few other players, and sometimes virtual Gamers as well. P.S., any Gamer detailed in the Manifests also appears in the Index.

Each Cosmos is indexed by the exposure of their individual body parts in the format *GamerName:* body: *bodypart* (e.g., Babs: body: areolage) The *bodyparts* include the parts of the body (e.g., face, belly, legs), body marginals (e.g., hair, pee), and exposures (e.g., titter, vagflash)..

All costumes (including 'nude') are indexed as *GamerName:* Garments: *garmentDetails* (e.g., Robyn: Garments: maillot cutout). The body Exposures and Garments details together occupy about 1/3 of each Cosmos index and are the biggest sub-sections therein.

Each individual Cosmos index also identifies Obeisances, which imply some kind of action or commitment and are indexed *GamerName: obeisance* (e.g., Molly: masturbation). Obeisances include blowjobs, breastplay, climax, coitus, masturbation, mirrors, name play, pinking, positions, and streaking. Note that an Obeisance is always subservient to a Gamer and are not indexed directly, although sometimes references are made to individual Cosmos.

The difference between Exposures (body parts) and Obeisances (submissions) is that *GamerName:* body: *bodypart* typically identifies which part of the body is exposed, whereas a *GamerName: obeisance* commits a Pledge to action. All exposures are lower case, and all obeisances except for Pee-Cam and Piss Mouth are lower case.

Each Cosmos index includes, in addition to the aforementioned Gamers, bodyparts, Garments, and Obeisance entries concerning: the Cams each Cosmos appears upon; their Front and Back Door and Bell soundings; and a selection of themes including "assumptions, begs, commitments, compromises, concerns, conflicts, consequences, goals, media, memories, momentum, motivation, name, and orders."

Each Cosmos index includes all interactions with all other Cosmos, and at all Locations. Typically this part of the Index almost always refers to Scenes with two or more Gamers. The basic format is:

GamerName1: GamerName2: Location: See Scene
GamerName1: Location: See Scene
Location: GamerName1: See Scene
GamerName2: GamerName1: Location: See Scene
GamerName2: Location: See Scene
Location: GamerName2: See Scene

All Scenes that involve two or more Gamers are also indexed by the two players and a single location. See now the italics above and note that the three elements each reference each other. Thus using the Index observe that each Cosmos is indexed by all the Locations they appear in, and by all the other Cosmos they interact with. Conversely, each and all Locations are indexed by each and every Gamer—mostly Cosmos obviously—but also others. And of course the second Pledge indexes the first as well as the Location.

Conflicts between pairs of Gamers are indexed bidirectionally. During The Runup these struggles will acquire power points.

There does exist a correlation between Scene names in the Index and the Scene Titles (§) in The Chapters, but the match is not a lock step. Scenes typically change when one or more Gamer(s) enter or exit, or when the Location changes.

Gamers are reminded that the Index follow alphabetical and *not* temporal sequence. Use the Day numbers (e.g., D14) and page numbers to help sequence. Also, the alphabetical order of the Cosmos is not their Lineup order, nor reflective of the Roommate pairings.

However: note that in the names of Scenes (§ Titles), the name always begins with Gamers. And the order of the Cosmos' names always follow their "position in the Lineup" and are not alphabetical. In the Cosmos House, the "position in the Lineup" sequence is: Babs, Tiffany, Robyn, Kimju, Molly, Steph, Beka, and Elle. Roommates are Babs & Tiffany, Robyn & Kimju, Molly & Steph, and Beka & Elle. In other words, a scene with Robyn & Kimju & Elle is always indexed with these three Cosmos listed in this order. And to repeat what one might expect to find in the Index, each of these three Cosmos plus the Location should all index each other.

Janet shares rank with Babs but since the Cosmos is Babs' House, Janet extends Babs the courtesy of going first, so always Babs & Janet. However, Game Mistress, Madam Nurse Beautician, and MomCap precede Babs in a sequenced list.

Each Location identified in the Location List in the Appendix that starts with a capital letter is included in this Index. Locations are often further divided: *Location: GamerName;* this usually consist of a list of Scene references. Locations inside Locations (e.g., the Mirror in the Bunkroom, the Mudpit in the Backyard) are indexed at the top Index level, same as the environment that physically contains them. In many Index references the Location is found inside parentheses at the end of the citation; note that this is the Location where the reference or fact is revealed, not necessarily where the event occurred. For example, Beka and Elle were brunettes before they enrolled in School, so that a reference (to Cosmos House D04) contextualizes when that fact is introduced, not that their hair acquires a new color.

A list of Props found in the Index includes all the Props listed using Capital Letters on the Prop Words List in the Appendix, as well as a number of lower case props. In general a Prop is an object that may be shared among Gamers; a Pledge belong to a Prop, not the other way around. Thus Props are indexed as primary references, *PropName: GamerName: activity.* Upper case Props include the Cravat, Dice, the Dining Room Pictures, the described but never seen Double Dong and Double Penetrators, the Makeup Case, Pink Pages, Skeleton Keys, Tiffany Porn Star Calendar, and Watering Can.

Lower case Props are always indexed by Gamer first, e.g., *GameName: propName: activity.* Many of these are medical equipment.

A series of Events and time-related words are also indexed, and because Events often involve multiple Gamers, they are also a primary index, *EventName: GamerName: details* (e.g., Bachelor Party: Molly: pees in a stein). The Events include the Alumni Reprise and Mudwrestling Contest from the past Term, as well as present Term Events like the Figure Drawing Class, Medical Exam, and Bachelor Party. See the Events and Time List in the Appendix for a full list of Event words. Note: Midnight (at some Day in the future) marks the end of the Term.

For a full chronology of the 14 Days that transpire during *The Arrivals,* see "Clock" in the Index.

§ The Index Proper

The Cosmos: Backstory

Not far away, and possibly someplace you may have passed through unknowingly, there exists a small School, a campus with a Village nearby. This place blends the real and the fantastic, and here it is, now, with you peering into it. Blink twice and you can pop into the Game. Move around: you see trees, buildings, streets, and people in motion.

Here at School, you're a Gamer now.

If you travel on foot, the School appears to be a place of learning, instruction, and knowledge. Old trees, brick buildings. A Library, Lecture Hall, and Laboratory face onto a Quad, complete with a flagpole, stocks, and a hitching post. The Village nearby contains a Beauty Salon and a restaurant. Down the road lies a Strip club, but you must drive to Flesh Ranch. Some people who live nearby never imagine the Game exists.

The School is akin to a school for wayward girls, except it is different than that. The eight rambling boarding Houses might be akin to sorority or fraternity houses, except they are different than that. Some of the Houses are inhabited by gals, some by guys, and some are not segregated by sex or gender preference. But there are always eight Gamers per House, one a Monitor who is in charge, and seven Pledge, who compete for the Options.

Our narrative focuses on the eight gals of the Cosmos House during one Term at School. We meet them during *The Arrivals,* as they enter both one-by-one and in pairs. Some are veterans, some newbies, but all must value the Garments they wear, accumulate Props and Obeisances, and manage their Exposures. Yes, they shall play a power Game.

"In the Game stay the Game," is one of the Chants.

But beware should *you* decide to continue! The School is a most unusual playground, a Game of high-stakes stimulation, where Kundalini, the sexual force, gets teased into awakening. The Game here at School demands deeper commitment than your typical zip fuck, overnight passion, or prolonged dungeon visit. At School, Gamers play for real. Lifestyle 24x7, on the grid. Up and down, back and forth, sideways. Here at School, Gamers study the arts of Kundalini, a creative power manifest in Nature, and learn ways to make love and balance power.

Make no mistake: volunteering to attend School is a non-trivial commitment. The Game combines knowledge, power, and passion. Have the Cosmos been pressed into service? No; they have all competed to be here! Begged to attend! Perhaps as the Term progresses they may be persuaded to reveal their reasons for wanting this challenge. Or not. But remember, for the eight Cosmos, there is no turning back.

Students always need to Game, and Gamers need always be students.

"In the Game stay the Game," is one of the Chants.